the Villain institute

PRISON FOR SUPERNATURAL OFFENDERS BOOK ONE

MEGAN LINSKI & ALICIA RADES

We the authors acknowledge that the United States of America is a country formed on stolen land. We respect and honor the indigenous peoples who have lived here for centuries, and we recognize there is still much work to do to make reparations and heal the damage caused to the many indigenous nations who were first here, both in the past and today.

May we remember the atrocities once committed, create a better world in the present, and look forward together for our future.

This book features characters with the following medical conditions. The information included is meant to educate readers on disabilities featured within the *Prison for Supernatural Offenders* series.

BIPOLAR DISORDER

Bipolar disorder is a mental illness that causes unusual shifts in mood, energy, activity levels, concentration, and the ability to carry out everyday tasks. Moods range from extremely elevated to extremely depressive, and can be intense. Psychosis, anxiety, eating disorders, and other conditions may develop. With proper treatment, people with bipolar disorder can lead full and productive lives.

BLINDNESS AND VISUAL IMPAIRMENT

Blindness is defined by an individual having severely impaired or absolutely no sense of sight. Total blindness is described as being unable to see anything with either eye. Vision loss typically affects an individual's ability to perform functions of daily living.

charlie
ONE

I'd often heard the world was black and white, but I didn't believe the lies. Bad things happened to good people all the time. There were no rules when it came to what was fair and just. We lived, we died, and everything else just *was*. Right, wrong— it didn't matter, as long as you made it to tomorrow.

Right now, two hundred bucks would get me a hell of a long way toward tomorrow. Rent was due, and if I didn't want to end up on the streets again, I had to find a way to come up with the money.

Hustling assholes down at *Flying Phoenix Inn*, a pub on my side of Detroit, was a sure-fire way to make the money. To be honest, I wasn't sure how the owners managed to fit so much ego into one building. The place attracted quite the arrogant crowd.

I entered the pub, and a musty scent covered by beer hit my nose. I stepped in a puddle of something wet and sticky— someone's spilled drink. To be honest, I'd be surprised if the floors were *clean* in this dump. The place was almost deafening with chatter and music, and sports-enthusiasts complained loudly at the game on TV. Someone bumped into me and kept on walking, as if being blind made me invisible.

I didn't like to drink— I had to keep my head clear— but it was part of the con. I had to blend in. I ordered a whiskey and took a seat close to the dart boards, sipping on my drink to make it look like I was busy.

Three sets of footsteps approached, and each fell in a heavy, overly confident beat.

Target acquired.

The tap of beer bottles being set down on a table nearby met my ears.

"Who wants to lose first?" the first man asked while cracking his knuckles. He had a deep, smug voice.

"If you go up against me, you'll be the first to lose, bud," his friend said, clapping him on the back.

"Oh, really?" the deep voice responded. "We'll see about that."

A chair screeched across the floor, and the third guy laughed as he sat. "He's not wrong, you know."

"Shut up," the first guy snapped. "Challenge me to darts any day, and I'll kick your ass."

His friend laughed. "Oh, I'm sure you would... after I won."

"You'll be eating your words once this is over."

The third friend was obviously amused by their trash talk. "How about we let the score speak for itself, huh?"

The guy with the deep voice huffed. "Fair enough."

The men scuffled around, until they retrieved their darts. They went quiet, and heavy footsteps walked up to the starting line. The man took aim, and the dart flew from his fingers. I knew the second it began spinning through the air, because I could feel the flutter of current coming off the fletching.

I didn't know how I could do it, but I could *feel* things in the air that other people couldn't. It was almost like my body was making up for my lost vision by tuning into the smallest shift of air current around me. I could feel every person as they moved through the bar, just by the shifts in the air currents around them. I could feel the air as it moved around items, feel what took up space. You could call it my own personal echolocation, just with air instead of sound. It was how I got around so easily and fooled people into thinking I could see.

The dart landed somewhere near the corner of the dartboard, and the guy groaned. His opponent laughed. "Better luck next time."

"Screw you," he responded.

The game continued like that— nothing but trash talk. Neither guy was any better than the other. It was like watching two losers compare dick size when they both had a micropenis. It was honestly a total bore to listen to... until one comment caught my attention.

"You're so bad, even a blind guy could beat you," one of the friends said to the other.

The man with the deep voice chuckled. "Too bad there's no one around to test that theory."

I smirked and set my whiskey aside. "I'll give it a shot," I offered.

The three men turned to me. The first guy must've been sizing me up, because he scoffed a moment later. "You think your blind ass could beat me at *darts?*"

I shrugged. "I'll bet you a hundred bucks I can hit the bull's eye."

All three of the men laughed, but the man with the deep voice responded. "You don't *look* blind."

It wasn't the first time I heard that one. My foster families had told me that my whole childhood.

"I don't have to look blind for it to be true," I said. "But hey, if you're afraid a blind guy will beat you—"

He huffed. "I'm not afraid of *anything*, hear me?"

I took a step forward. I felt the air currents around his form. He was bigger than me, so much that his breath passed the top of my head. He must've been at least six-five, but I wasn't scared of him. Marty had taught me how to hold my own in a fight.

"Then prove it," I challenged. "If it helps, I'll even close my eyes— not like I need them anyway."

Air moved through his nose quickly, like his nostrils were flared. "Fine," he conceded. "A hundred bucks for the bull's eye."

His friends laughed, and someone placed a dart in my hands. I ran the tip of my shoe along the hardwood floor to feel for the line of tape, then stood behind it. I drew a deep breath and squeezed my eyes shut tightly. I couldn't see the dartboard, but I'd sat in this pub listening to the sounds of darts hitting the wall long enough to know exactly where the board hung.

I thrust the dart forward, and it flew out of my fingertips. Ripples of air rushed past the fletching, and I knew I'd aimed slightly off course.

I didn't know how I could do it, but when I prayed for the air to follow my command, miracles happened. I could feel the air particles shift around the dart, nudging it back on course in mid-air.

A *thud* came, then cries of disbelief. The man I was challenging must've been gaping like a fish, because I could feel the air coming out of his mouth in waves.

"That-that's impossible," he sputtered. "He's *blind!*"

"Oh, come on," one of his buddies encouraged. "Pay up."

"*Told you* a blind man could beat you," the other taunted.

My opponent huffed his disapproval, then reached into his back pocket. "A deal's a deal, I guess."

He sounded more willing than I'd anticipated. I was expecting a double or nothing deal here. I heard the sound of a bill sliding over another, and I held my hand out for payment. He placed a crumpled bill in my hand, and his friends' laughter grew. They tried to hide it, but it was pretty apparent. I knew immediately that I was being swindled.

"We agreed to a hundred," I snapped.

The man scoffed. "We also agreed you couldn't see."

I'd only been guessing about the swindling, but that was all the confirmation I needed.

"I can't, jackass!" I fumed. I really needed that money. "I just happen to know when I'm being taken advantage of."

The man laughed and grabbed his beer off the table. He took a swig before responding. "Oh, go walk off a bridge... if you can find one!"

He and his buddies roared with laughter.

Anger bubbled up inside of me. *No one* used my blindness against me. I curled my hand into a fist, crumpling the bill even further. I brought my fist down onto the table, startling the three men.

"We had a deal!" I growled.

The man stepped closer. I could feel the heat rolling off of him. "It was all just fun and games. Now run along. Don't walk into the door on your way out."

"I want my money, dipshit!" I demanded.

Apparently, that was the wrong thing to say, because the next thing I knew, air rushed toward my face. I was so furious that I caught it too late. The man's fist cracked across my jaw, and I went spiraling toward the table. I grabbed the edge to catch myself, but I couldn't slow my momentum. The table crumbled beneath my weight, and I crashed to the floor. Bottles shattered, and liquid seeped into my jeans. The smell of beer hit my nose, but it barely registered. I was freaking *pissed.*

I took just a moment to process the assault. The whole bar was in an uproar, so much that I could barely hear the music. Chairs screeched across the hardwood, and people started yelling. The main asshole laughed with his buddies. He didn't even realize when I pulled myself to my feet— must've thought a blind guy wouldn't fight back or something. I knew exactly where he was by feeling the air around his form.

I launched myself at him and tackled him to the ground. My fist connected with his face three times, each one as satisfying as the last. Then a hand clamped around my wrist, dragging me backward.

It was one of his friends. He yelled obscenities at me, but my breath had grown so ragged they didn't register. As I was being hauled to my feet, I reached my hands out and swiped the man's wallet from his pocket, then slipped it into my jacket. He threw me backward, but I'd been so smooth about it he didn't notice the wallet missing. I crashed into another table, but this one didn't crumble beneath my weight.

"Get out of here!" the jerk shouted. "We'll beat your ass!"

I was more than happy to oblige. I wiped blood from my lip, then held my hands up in surrender. "No need. I'll show myself out."

One of the men huffed, but at least he didn't come at me. I turned and started toward the door. The bar had quieted, but I could feel the patrons' eyes on me as I left.

Just as I reached the door, I heard, "Where the hell is it? He stole my wallet!"

That's when I knew it was time to get the hell out of there. I took off, sprinting out the door, pumping my arms as fast as I could as I ran down the sidewalk. I sensed the air pressure around me, filling in the cracks between streetlights and cars, which allowed me to create a mental map of the street ahead. I dodged around someone heading my way, and I turned the corner. The sound of heavy footsteps and shouts followed me. They weren't far behind.

Something made me slow. It was like running into a mental wall—something that just told me to dig in my heels and stop right there in the middle of the sidewalk.

I skidded to a halt. Someone coming from the opposite direction bumped into me. I stumbled sideways into an alley. The sound of car horns echoed off the brick buildings squeezing in around me, and the air felt damp and smelled of garbage.

I should've kept on moving, but I remained rooted in place. Call it intuition, but I could sense something ahead. I didn't know what it was, but I knew it wasn't dangerous. It was more like a beacon calling me forward, offering me sanctuary.

That was saying a lot, considering sanctuary was tough to come by in my experience. I could barely make sense of the feeling.

I focused on the alleyway, trying to map it out in my mind using the sounds of the city and the air pressing in around me. The best I could tell, the alley was empty. I must've been imagining things.

"Where'd he go!?" one of the men from the bar shouted, snapping me out of my daze.

My heart leapt. I wished I could say I was in this for the thrill, but these things didn't excite me anymore. Not after what happened to Marty.

"There he is!" someone shouted.

Hell.

I knew I wasn't getting out the way I came without getting my ass kicked, so I turned and hightailed it in the opposite direction. I could make out the sound of cars on the street ahead, coming closer and closer as I ran—

Then something tangled around my legs, and I smashed to the ground. My face hit the asphalt so hard, I couldn't make sense of which way was up and which was down. It took me a moment to realize someone had tackled me. Before I could react, a foot connected with the side of my ribs, and I grunted.

I didn't stay down long. When you grew up the way I did, you learned pretty fast how to defend yourself. I swung my leg out and knocked one of the men on his ass. I jumped to my feet and kicked my elbow back into the second guy's nose. He yelled as he went stumbling backward. I stood my ground, surveying the air for the next attack.

Heavy footsteps approached, and I forced my breathing to slow so I could listen carefully. A threatening laugh bubbled up from the man's throat. It was the guy with the deep voice. Something smacked into his palm, like he was carrying a weapon and was showing it off. A baseball bat, perhaps? *No*, I realized. It was one of the legs of the table I'd broken back at the bar.

"Normally, I wouldn't hurt a blind guy," he said sardonically. "But I'm going to get real pleasure beating you—"

He cut off as a deep growl came out of the shadows. Air rushed past me as a large figure leapt toward the man. I didn't know what it was at first, until my attacker began to scream. Angry barks and the snapping of jaws echoed down the alleyway. It was a *dog*.

I was so dumbstruck at its sudden appearance that I took a few steps back. The other two men scrambled forward, trying to save their friend from the canine attack. The dog snarled, and one of the men screamed like he'd been bitten.

"Get the fuck off of me!" the man with the deep voice yelled.

I heard a loud *smack*, then a whimper from the dog. Best I could tell, the man had used his weapon against the creature. The air knocked out of my lungs, as if he'd just swung the weapon straight into my abdomen, though I hadn't been touched.

My hands curled into tight fists, and my arms shook in rage. I couldn't explain the primal instinct that took over me in that moment. All I knew was I had to protect that creature— or die trying.

I jumped forward. "Leave him alone!" I shouted.

A second *smack* came as the dog slammed into the side of the building. Another whimper escaped the poor creature's throat, and my stomach plummeted to the asphalt.

"Or what?" one of the men threatened.

He took a step forward, and I threw myself in front of the dog. "You don't want to know the answer," I growled. I reached into my pocket for my knife and flicked it open. "Get out of here while you still have the chance."

The man laughed. "Your little switchblade doesn't scare me. Three men against one blind guy and his dog? Who do *you* think is going to win?"

Me, I thought instantly.

The man stepped forward and swung the table leg at me. It connected with my hand before I could pull away, and my knife went flying across the alley. He took another step, but I was so enraged I wasn't willing to let him get any closer.

"Fuck off!" I screamed.

I threw my hands outward. I meant to shove him away from me, but something else happened entirely. A strange power unlike anything I'd ever felt before surged through my body and shot out of my palms. I could feel the shift in the air as the blast sent the men flying a dozen feet away from me. They crashed into the ground next to the dumpsters nearby.

My hands shook. I couldn't even process what had just happened.

The men warily got to their feet, but they didn't advance on me. One of them whispered something to the others, but I couldn't make it out. My pulse pounded in my ears as I tried to understand the power I'd summoned. Had it been *me?* No, that was ridiculous. There had to be some other explanation.

But the way the men huddled together, they seemed terrified of me.

"I said *leave!*" I screamed, raising my hands threateningly.

That was all it took for the men to scramble away with their tails between their legs. Wood clanked to the asphalt, then came the men's retreating footsteps. Whatever had happened had scared them off.

Satisfied they were gone, I turned to the dog behind me. I could hear its labored breathing, but more than that, I could sense its heartbeat as if it were my own. I'd never had a pet before, but the urge to protect this poor animal was so strong I might as well have been tending to my own broken leg.

I stepped toward the creature and held out a cautious hand. I wasn't sure whether it would attack again, but something told me it wouldn't—as if the dog had been protecting me from those men.

"Don't worry, boy," I said. "I'm not going to hurt you."

I lowered myself to my knee and touched the top of the dog's head. The second my fingers sank into his soft, thick coat, the alleyway spun around me so quickly I couldn't make sense of it. The asphalt might as well have dropped out from under my feet. It was as if nothing in this world existed outside of me and the dog. Color blasted across my vision, though I could hardly remember what colors *were* from before I went blind. The air smelled like fresh rain, and the smooth, sweet taste of lemon meringue pie swept over my tongue. The sounds of the city faded and were replaced with the rustling of trees in the breeze and the sound of bird calls. I swear I could even hear the ocean waves in the distance. The feeling of sunlight hit my skin, and I felt as if I was being embraced in a warm hug.

None of it made any sense, and yet... I couldn't bring myself to question it. Something about it felt right. More real than the city ever had.

Soon, the strange sensations settled, and I was pulled back to the present in the alleyway. I couldn't help the smile that spread across my face. There was no explanation, and yet for the first time, I felt like I'd visited a place that was my first true home.

I didn't have extra money for food to feed this guy, but it didn't matter. I already knew I wanted him.

"Did you do that?" I asked the dog aloud, though I knew he wouldn't respond.

I stroked the dog's fur as he got to his feet. He was big and strong. The shape of his ears suggested he was a husky, or a similar breed.

"You're a nice doggy, aren't you?" I said, scratching him behind the ears. I checked his neck for a collar, but didn't find one. "You were protecting me from those bad guys. I think I might just keep you. What's your name?"

Oberi, a voice responded in my mind.

Given the last few minutes, I should've been halfway to a mental institution by now. But something about that voice seemed so familiar... like I'd been listening to it my whole life. Hearing it inside my head didn't seem unusual at all.

"Oberi," I repeated. "It was you calling me down this alley, wasn't it?"

The dog didn't respond with words this time. Instead, he licked my hand, and in that moment, I *knew*. This dog was special. This dog was *mine*.

This dog was my sanctuary.

Days passed, and Oberi never once left my side. I didn't know where he'd come from, and I didn't question it, either. Somehow, I knew he was meant to be mine.

The wallet I stole had enough money to cover rent, plus extra to buy supplies for Oberi. I always avoided credit cards if I could, because I knew that was a good way to get caught. I was the kind of guy who liked to stay *off* the radar. Learned that one the hard way.

Oberi became an asset when it came to making money. Turns out people had a sweet spot for dogs. All I had to do was sit on the sidewalk with a cup at my side and people would drop money in like a slot machine. Oberi was quite the charmer, and I brought back double my usual haul over the next three days.

My grocery run that week was phenomenal. I managed to afford the cheesy chips I loved so much— the definition of pure luxury. The employee helping me shop seemed annoyed by how long I took to decide, but it was hard when I had so many choices in front of me. Oberi followed behind me as I climbed the stairs in my apartment building.

The place was nice— well, as nice as a cheap Detroit apartment got. The rug on the stairs had holes in it that I'd nearly broken my neck on more than once, the creak of the pipes kept me up at night, and there was a constant unidentifiable smell that was less than pleasant. But it was a roof over my head... for now, anyway.

Mrs. Miller, the old lady subletting me the place— illegally, mind you— had been on an extended vacation to visit her daughter in Florida. She never gave me a time frame on when she'd be back, so I knew my stay here was limited. I could be kicked out any moment. But that's how things had always been with me. My life had been uncertain since the day I was born.

I reached my door and stuck the key in the lock, but was surprised when the key turned smoothly and without resistance— as if the door was already unlocked. I twisted the handle, and sure enough, the door swung open with ease.

"Mm..." I mused. "I thought I'd locked it."

I shrugged, and Oberi stepped into the apartment in front of me. I stopped dead in my tracks the second I walked in the door. I didn't know what it was at first, but something was *wrong*. Oberi came to a halt beside me and sniffed the air.

I smelled it, too. I couldn't put my finger on it, but it was something akin to ocean water— totally out of place. Then I heard it, the sound of footsteps in the kitchen.

An intruder!

I held my breath and motioned for Oberi to stay quiet. Slowly, I set my bag of groceries on the ground, careful not to make a sound. I pressed myself to the wall and inched closer to the kitchen.

A man began humming a tune I was sure I'd never heard before, but sounded vaguely familiar. He had a roughness to his voice, and his footsteps moved slowly, like he was old.

I listened for signs of other intruders, but he seemed to be alone. There came the sound of something scratching, then metal hitting the counter. Silverware, perhaps? Was the guy making himself a *freaking sandwich* in my kitchen? What the hell, man?

I reached into my pocket and pulled out my knife. I flicked it open just as I heard the man open the refrigerator. When he turned his back, I lunged out of my hiding spot and into the entrance of the kitchen.

"What the hell are you doing!?" I demanded, holding my knife out threateningly. It was pretty clear I'd use it if I had to. The old man better not test me. I wasn't afraid to use this damn thing.

The man paused a second. It went so quiet I wasn't sure if I'd given him a heart attack or something. "Come now, Charlie," the old man said. "There's no reason to fear me. Put the knife away."

"Put it away?" I balked. "I don't know who the hell you are. How do you know my name?"

"I've known about you for a long time, Charlie," he said.

I racked my brain, trying to place the voice. I knew a lot of people from being shuffled around between foster homes when I was a kid, but surely none of them cared enough to come find me. Not like anyone had a reason.

"You're not a cop, are you?" I accused.

The man chuckled. "No, not a cop at all. Just a hungry old man looking for a sandwich. You hungry?"

He took a bite, then held the sandwich out so close to me I could feel him.

I curled my nose up. "No, thanks. Who are you—?"

Oberi cut me off by giving a happy bark and skirting around me into the kitchen. He went over to the man like he knew him, making gross licking noises with his tongue.

"Oh, this must be your Familiar!" the old man said, like we were two old friends catching up. I was caught off guard, to say the least.

"Familiar?" I questioned. What was he talking about?

The man spoke to Oberi like he hadn't heard me. "You want a sandwich, buddy? Here you go. Just a bite."

"Hey, don't feed my dog that," I objected, but he must've not heard me, because Oberi wolfed the thing down in seconds.

He scratched Oberi behind the ears. "You're a long way from home, aren't you? Yes, you are."

The man seemed harmless, and Oberi appeared to trust him, so I lowered my weapon.

"Will you stop talking to my dog like he's an infant?" I demanded. "What are you doing here?"

The man straightened. "Yes, of course. You must be so confused. Why don't we sit down and talk?"

"I don't want to *sit down*," I growled. "Tell me what the hell's going on."

The man took a deep breath, then tapped his fingers on the counter. "Let me ask you this. Have you noticed anything strange lately?"

"Yeah. There's a weird old dude in my kitchen," I stated flatly.

"I mean since your Familiar arrived," he said.

I furrowed my brow. "My Familiar?"

"Yes. Perhaps you've noticed... powers."

"Powers?" I repeated. "Okay, grandpa. You gotta go."

"But you need to hear this, Charlie!" he protested. "Your father had the power to control Air, which means you can, too!"

I was just about to grab the guy and shove him out the door, but what he said made me pause. I instantly thought of what happened the night I found Oberi, how I'd blasted the three men back with no explanation. Had I been controlling the air around them?

"I don't know what you're talking about," I said.

"Yes, you do," he argued. "I saw it in your eyes just now. You've used your Air magic before, haven't you?"

"I don't believe in magic," I told him, but it felt like coughing up rocks. Something about saying that out loud felt wrong.

"Please listen to me, Charlie," he insisted. "My name is Professor Elliot Baine. I'm an Elementai, like you."

I took a step back. "Elementai?"

The man was talking crazy. And yet... I swore I'd heard the word before.

"Please, if you'd just sit down, I'd like to explain. I want to help," he assured me.

Like hell. The only people who ever said *I want to help* only wanted to help themselves. Another lesson I'd learned the hard way. Marty had been the only person I ever met who meant it. He was a true friend up until the day he died.

But this old man was a stranger. Surely he had ulterior motives.

And yet... he had me intrigued. Something *had* happened the night I met Oberi, and I hadn't been able to explain it. Hell, there was a lot about my life I couldn't explain.

"Let me prove it," he insisted. He walked over to the sink and turned on the faucet while he spoke. "I'm Toaqua, which means I can control Water."

I jumped when something cold touched my arm. I swiped at it, only to realize that it was water. The water droplets washed away, only to return a moment later. They crawled over my skin, then soaked into my shirt. It was freaking eerie, like the water had a mind of its own. A moment later, the water was being sucked out of my shirt, and the fabric went dry again. The water wrapped around my arm like a snake. As it slithered away, I reached out a hand and discovered that it was floating in mid-air.

I stood there, mouth agape, unable to believe what he'd just done. Magic? Could it be true?

"Fine," I agreed. "Tell me everything."

I couldn't believe I was actually welcoming this stranger into my home. Had I gone insane?

The old man— Professor Baine— and I left the kitchen and sat in the living room. Oberi lay at my feet.

"Like I said, I'm an Elementai," Professor Baine started. "We're a group of supernaturals who are able to manipulate the elements— Fire, Water, Earth, Air, and Spirit."

I scoffed. "Spirit— like healing?"

"Exactly."

"If you're offering to heal me, you can go fuck yourself," I snarled. I didn't need to be able to see to have worth in this freaking world. I was blind, but that didn't matter. I still meant something.

"No, no, you misunderstand," he said calmly. "Even if we wanted to, our healing wouldn't help with your... condition. It doesn't work that way. I'm here because you were born in our society, Charlie, and we've been looking for you for a long time."

"I... what?"

"You were taken away and put into foster care when you were only a toddler," he continued. "That was back during the Hawkei Civil War, when your parents were arrested for treason—"

"Hawk-eye *what*? Back up, old man," I insisted. "You'll have to start from the beginning— if I'm even going to entertain what you're saying at all."

Professor Baine took a deep breath. His words came out sounding thoughtful. "The beginning... okay. The Hawkei are a Native American tribe living in Northern California. Long ago, when the colonizers waged war on us, our ancestors granted us magical powers to protect ourselves. We were split into five Houses, named for each of the five elements. Children are born into the House of their parents, as they will inherit the same type of magic. With this blessing also came magical creatures, which we were tasked with protecting and caring for. Some of these magical creatures bond with us. They are our other halves, our soul and the source of our powers. We call them Familiars."

My brow furrowed the more he spoke. It was a fun story, but it couldn't be true. "And Oberi is my... Familiar?" I questioned hesitantly.

"Yes," Professor Baine confirmed. "He is bonded to you now. If one of you dies, you both die."

My heart jumped at the thought. I could be gone tomorrow, and Oberi would perish with me? That didn't seem fair.

"But I'm not Native American," I argued. Truth be told, I didn't know *what* I was. I knew I had darker skin, but people had treated me like dirt my whole life. I didn't think I belonged anywhere.

"Of course you are," Mr. Baine said. "Not all Hawkei look Native American. After we were gifted our powers, we sought to expand our tribe. Men and women from all over the world joined us, and so our culture is very diverse, influenced heavily by both our Hawkei and non-Hawkei ancestors."

"Where's *your* Familiar?" I asked rather harshly. I wanted the proof.

"I'm afraid Thalassa is too big to bring on such a journey," he said, before continuing with his story. "Twenty years ago, the Hawkei underwent many disagreements, one of them being whether couples from separate Houses— or those with different powers— should be allowed to mate. At the time, it was thought that mixed-House children would have diluted powers, and many feared losing our magic. Interhouse relationships were outlawed, and anyone found to break that law was sentenced to prison— or death."

I shuddered.

"I'm afraid your parents were among those sentenced," he said sadly. "Your mother was Nivita— an Earth Elementai— and your father was Yapluma— an Air Elementai. People from those two Houses were not allowed to be together. Or have children."

My hands curled into fists. How dare he try to use my parents against me! I blew a breath and spoke sarcastically. I didn't believe him. "And that's why I was taken away and put into foster care?"

He took a deep breath, like it pained him to admit the truth. "Yes. Unfortunately, the Elders— our government— did not think you worthy of the tribe. But things have changed, and the Hawkei have been trying to get these interhouse children back."

My body went rigid. Holy shit. He was serious.

"Why?" I asked in disgust. "Why would I go back to a society that thought me worthless?"

"We're not like that anymore," he insisted. "But you've been very hard to find, Mr. Wahkin."

"How *did* you find me?" I demanded.

"Remember that break-in you were wanted for last year?" he asked.

I crossed my arms. I couldn't believe he'd bring that up. I didn't do break-ins— not anymore. But since Marty died, I was desperate. I fell into the wrong crowd, and they convinced me to get in on a burglary job. It ended in five arrests, and only three of us got away. It hadn't been pretty— hence why I preferred to stay *off* the radar.

"Yeah, I remember," I bit.

"Well, there's been a warrant out for your arrest ever since," Professor Baine explained. "You were caught on camera in a bar fight a few days ago. It tipped off our officials on your whereabouts."

"Okay, I get that, but seriously, how did you find me *here?*" I asked. "My name's not on the lease."

It was one of the reasons the police hadn't arrested me on that warrant yet. They didn't know where to find me.

"Ah, yes. That was a tricky one," Baine said. "Once I had a general idea of where you were staying, all I had to do was follow the scent of magic."

"Scent of magic?" My eyebrows shot up.

"Well, not literally," he said. "I'm a particularly gifted Elementai. I've mastered techniques many others have not. Among them, I'm able to siphon magic from creatures who are not my own Familiar."

I went rigid, and I instinctively placed a leg in front of Oberi's lounging form.

"Not to worry, Mr. Wahkin," Mr. Baine said. "I have no reason to draw from your Familiar. However, the technique allows me to sense the magic around me. Since Oberi is the only magical creature in the area, I was able to sense her from a great distance."

"Him," I corrected.

Mr. Baine hesitated, like he was confused. "Yes, of course. Sense *him.*"

Silence settled between us for a few moments. I was still trying to absorb everything he'd said. I could feel Mr. Baine's eyes on me.

"You do believe me, don't you, Charlie?" he asked.

I contemplated it. Did I believe him? It was all so crazy... yet seemed to make all the sense in the world.

"I don't know," I admitted. "For the last couple of years, I've been able to... I don't know how to explain it. I can *sense* the world around me through air pressure. It's like my eyes don't work, but I can get an idea in my mind of what a room looks like just by how the air moves."

"That makes perfect sense!" Baine sounded delighted. "You came of age, so your magic started working. Now that you and Oberi have bonded, you will begin learning magic at a rapid rate. Soon, you'll be able to control the Air itself."

I gaped, and he must've noticed.

"What is it?" he asked.

"Well, I-I think I already did that." And it wasn't just that blast in the alleyway, either. I could do it playing darts and things like that, though on a much smaller scale.

Holy shit. This guy wasn't lying. There really was a society of magical people who could control the elements... and I was one of them.

"What do you want from me?" I finally asked.

"Nothing." He sounded genuine. "I only want to help."

"But why me? I'm nothing special."

"You are very wrong about that, Mr. Wahkin," he countered. "You are an Elementai, a member of the Hawkei tribe. You belong in Kinpago with the rest of us. There, we can teach you how to use your element and strengthen your bond with your Familiar. There's a school, Orenda Academy of Magical Creatures—"

"A college?" I balked. "No, I'm too old for college. Besides, I don't even have a high school diploma."

"Precisely why we will give you an education. You can get your GED *and* a college degree. All Hawkei deserve that much."

"Wait... give it to me?" It took a moment for what he was saying to sink in. "Like, a scholarship?"

"All Orenda Academy expenses are paid by the tribe," he explained. "You will have room and board, food, money for supplies—"

"Thanks for the offer, but this all sounds too good to be true," I said bitterly. "What is it you *really* want in return?"

Baine took a long breath. "We want to make amends, Charlie."

I scoffed. "Then the Elders who threw me out can go drop dead."

Baine got really quiet. "They are. The council is new now, full of people who want to restore balance to our tribe, instead of tear it apart like the ones who came before. Reaching out to our outcasted members is one way for the tribe to atone for its many sins."

My blood ran cold. I still didn't want to go. "Why would I go back to a society that executed my parents and made me an orphan? You abandoned me."

"You can't stay here," he pointed out. I opened my mouth to protest, but Baine continued. "Sooner or later, your warrant will catch up to you. We can provide you with a good home and proper education. If you stay here, you'll end up in prison... or worse."

Hell, this old man was right. I was basically holding my breath waiting for an arrest or to bleed out in a gunfight.

Maybe I could use this new place to my advantage. It'd be a new playground for my cons, and I could plot my revenge on the tribe while I was at it.

I wasn't sure I had a choice.

"Okay," I said. "I'm in."

ava-marie

TWO

The day I was born, the world went mad.

And I went mad with it.

The pounding of the hippogriff's hooves beneath me was like a war drum beating a prayer song. I could feel the music that resonated through the earth as it sent power flowing through my blood. The valley ahead of me was green and open, welling with sunlight on a fresh August morning. The hippogriff herd pressed around me as the mountains of Northern California rose in the distance, redwoods like soldiers standing tall against the blue sky.

I could feel everything that was alive, smell the resonance of life as energy ricocheted through the air. I could see the entire universe, spread out like a map that was mine for the taking. I rode upon a euphoric high, feeling more powerful than a god and never wishing to come down as the colors began to bleed together into a watercolor painting.

I dug my hands into the creature's feathers and held on tight, pressing myself to the bird's neck and urging it to go faster. The half-horse, half-eagle creature let out a low whinny, enclosing its wings around my legs. I laughed along, giving a sound that was shrill and ignited the world.

Eventually, the valley came to a close as the mountains grew higher above us. The hippogriff slowed, until it jogged to a stop by the opening of a cave entrance. I slid off and patted the hippogriff's neck as the colors of the world bled away and became normal once again. "Good girl. Thanks for the ride."

The hippogriff snorted, blowing back my hair before taking off into the sky. The herd followed, spreading their wings to follow the lead mare into the clouds.

I looked back. My brother was clinging to the back of the slowest hippogriff, who rounded up the last of the herd. His black hair was wild and stuck up on one side, and his cheeks were bright red.

"Ava-Marie, wait up!" he complained. His hippogriff skidded to an abrupt halt. Ezekiel yelled as he was tossed forward and sent sprawling into the ground, tearing a hole in his jeans.

I put a hand over my mouth and laughed again as Ezekiel spat out dirt. The hippogriff huffed and kicked up its hooves, flying into the sky with the rest of them.

Ezekiel gave me a sour look. "You could wait for me every once in a while."

"You wouldn't fall behind if you were a better rider." I reached out a hand to pull him to his feet. Ez and I often raced hippogriffs, but he rarely beat me. He could never tell which ones would be the fastest. I could.

We turned toward the cave entrance. Ezekiel's mouth fell open as he gazed upward, taking in the sight of the cave— and the various signs around the entrance warning that further venturing would be trespassing on government property. As this cave was outside the Hawkei reservation, whatever was found within it was free for anyone to take— as far as the colonizers were concerned.

"Are you sure we should be doing this?" Ezekiel asked. "It definitely counts as illegal activity."

"Stop being such a baby." I reached into my backpack and took out a headlamp, fastening it before clicking on the light. "It's the weekend. No one's at the worksite."

"If we get caught here, it's a federal crime," Ezekiel said, pointing at the cords roping off the entrance.

I rolled my eyes. "What, like the colonizers committed a crime by *stealing our land?* Those artifacts are Hawkei property, Ez. They belong to the tribe. Now we're going to get them back. Do you really want the colonizers to put our heritage in one of *their* museums? It's not right."

"No, but—"

"Then what's the issue?"

Ezekiel's tone was flat. "I don't feel like going to jail."

"You're such a goody-two-shoes. Let's go."

"Ava-Marie!"

I'd slipped under the ropes before he had a chance to stop me. Ezekiel fastened on his own headlamp and hurried in behind, like I knew he'd always do. The sunlight vanished as we wandered further into the cave.

I got that Ez was nervous, but he needed to chill. This was the *right* thing to do. The supernatural world had suffered enough from humans in the past— the Hawkei being one of their greatest victims.

The Hawkei were an indigenous people who'd lived in California for thousands of years. We'd nearly been exterminated when the colonizers came to our territory and began terrorizing our tribe. We'd pleaded with the ancestors for help, and they'd answered our prayers, and gifted us our powers— the magic of the elements.

We became the Elementai— elementals— and grew strong enough to defend ourselves from the humans. We separated into five Houses for each of the five elements— Koigni, for Fire; Toaqua, for Water; Nivita, for Earth; Yapluma, for Air; and Anichi, for Spirit.

Though we had to keep our magic a secret, I wasn't about to let some colonizers get their filthy hands on what belonged to us. I was doing the right thing. They were trying to steal our culture. Now I was stealing it back.

The headlamps didn't provide enough light, so I lifted my hand. A ball of fire burned within it, illuminating the path ahead with light.

Ezekiel looked on in awe. "I'm so jealous. I can't wait to get my powers."

"You're eighteen. They'll show up soon."

Supernaturals got their abilities when they came of age, but Ez hadn't shown any magic yet. I was over a year older than him, but I'd gotten my Fire magic the day I'd turned eighteen.

Though Ezekiel's powers would be different from mine. Our parents were from separate Houses. My mother was Koigni. My father was Toaqua. Elementai always inherited their powers from their same-sex parent, so Ezekiel would have Water magic instead of Fire like me.

Ezekiel scowled as the walls of the cave began getting narrower. "You could at least tell our parents where we're going. I don't like lying all the time. If he finds out we're here, Dad will be madder than when you got your tongue pierced."

I waggled my piercing at him. "Well, someone's gotta be the rebel."

"Not all the time. Can't we have a *normal* day for once?"

"I do what I want."

I held my arm out as the cave path came to an abrupt halt, leading to the edge of a cliff. I sent the fireball sailing downward. It landed on the cave floor twenty feet below, where it shone light on piles of pick axes, shovels, and wheelbarrows full of dirt. The fireball fizzled out, leaving the area below in darkness.

"There's the excavation site." I slipped off my bag and began pulling out my gear. I pounded an anchor into the floor and strung a rope through the safety clips before slipping on my harness. I was rappelling down the side of the cliff before Ezekiel even had his harness on. I landed on the ground safely and unclipped myself while Ez clumsily— and fucking *slowly*— descended.

Ezekiel got tangled up in his climbing gear a foot above the ground. He struggled with the ropes and glanced at me helplessly as he spun in circles against the rock.

"Um, can you help? This harness is strangling my balls," he whined.

"Ancestors, Ez, you're so clumsy." I got Ez loose, and he staggered against the wall. I had to resist rolling my eyes again.

"Hey, I'm a fat kid. I don't do things like this."

"You're not fat, Ez, you're fluffy."

"Easy for you to say. You can't weigh more than a hundred pounds."

"Shut up."

I called another fireball into my hand as I observed the excavation site. There were footprints in the dirt, and a lot of tools, but I didn't see anything of value.

"They must've not found it yet," I reasoned.

"Do you hear that?" Ezekiel tilted his head. There was a trickling sound. I followed the source of the noise across the area until my boots splashed upon mud and water. The fireball in my hand displayed a river ten feet wide, and probably just as deep.

"It's an underground river," I said. "How fascinating."

I reached into my bag and pulled out a leather guidebook. I scribbled a few things down while Ezekiel groaned. "Ava, can we go? I don't want to get caught down here."

I snapped my guidebook shut. "Look. When you're navigating ruins, you're supposed to document *everything*. Otherwise, you could miss a crucial clue that's important later. I have to practice; otherwise, I'll never be—"

"*A real explorer*," Ezekiel echoed for me, like he'd done a million times. "I get it. Where is this thing, anyway?"

"Grandpa said the artifact would be down here." I followed my instincts and began navigating the river. Ezekiel nearly slipped into it, before I caught him.

"Grandpa's wrong about a lot of things," Ezekiel grumbled, but I ignored him. We moved ahead, leaving the excavation site behind us.

We walked for half a mile in silence. The walls of the cave narrowed. Eventually, the river ended, but not before I noticed a small slit in the cave wall near my feet. I'd fit through it, but not Ez.

I had a feeling there was something lying beyond. Ezekiel frowned when he noticed it. "You can't be serious."

"Where's your sense of adventure?" I asked. I had already dropped to my knees and began squeezing myself through the hole. "I won't be long."

Ezekiel danced nervously by the gap as I pushed myself through the claustrophobic space. For a moment, I did get stuck— momentary panic struck me, but I shoved it aside. Fear was a useless fucking emotion. It wouldn't get me what I wanted.

I finally slipped through. As I did, I was able to stand and light a fireball. I stood in a small circular area, and lying on the floor was exactly what we'd come here for.

I reached out and picked up a small gold sculpture in the shape of a person. It was as big as my hand, and depicted each of the five elements throughout. The face showed half the face of a man, and half of a woman. It was meant to be a carving of one of the Hawkei gods— a piece of the Great Spirit we worshiped alongside our ancestors.

After a quick inspection, I rendered it had to be authentic. A piece like this was invaluable. To the colonizers, such an item would sell for millions at auction, but to our tribe, it was priceless.

I wriggled out from underneath the gap, and Ezekiel sighed in relief. His smile brightened when I showed him the figurine.

"Finally. Let's head out." We turned to go, but as we did, the idol in my hand started to burn. I let out a gasp. Being Koigni, it shouldn't have hurt, but the statue was actually able to singe my skin. Both of our mouths dropped open as we realized the idol was glowing bright red. From the mouth of the idol streamed black smoke, which formed into a transparent man with a malicious grin.

Shit. The idol was a piece of Spirit Art. Grandpa had told me about these things. If a supernatural cared about their creation enough, they could actually seal a piece of their soul inside it, preserving their spirit forever within an item they treasured here on this earth. Usually, people who made Spirit Art were benevolent and kind beings, meant to help others.

But whoever had made this piece of Spirit Art was a fucking asshole, because this spirit was obviously not here to help. Dark magic like whips began gathering at his sides as the entity readied to attack. I saw fire flickering on the spirit's form— this man had been Koigni in his former life.

"Ava, run!" Ezekiel cried. He grabbed my wrist, but the dark entity lashed out, knocking him to the ground. His headlight went out, and I heard glass crack.

The spirit smacked me across the face. My helmet went flying off, and the light broke against the stone.

We were locked in darkness. I threw a fireball in the direction I thought the dark spirit might be. It sailed right through him. I saw with horror that the monster was advancing on Ezekiel, who was scampering backwards trying to get away from it. The evil spirit reached out its dark tendrils, wrapping them around Ezekiel's form and squeezing him tight. He gasped, pulling at the tendrils around his neck as they suffocated him, his feet kicking at the water of the river as he tried to escape.

When I saw that my brother was in danger, I didn't think. I reacted. I flung out my left hand, expecting flames to shoot out my fingers at the entity, though I knew it wouldn't do any good.

That's not what happened. A shiver ran from my core all the way out to the tips of my fingers as I felt my skin turn cold, not hot. I'd never experienced such a chilling feeling before. When I cast Fire, there was anger, passion, exhilaration— nearly on the bounds of being out of control.

This magic was different. It was calming. Cool. And had an ancient power within it that scared me.

The water in the river rose upward. The riverbed drained. Ezekiel gasped. The spirit just had time to look up before the wave crashed into him. The dark entity gave a wicked cry as the water smashed into his body, putting out the flames licking his form. There was a sizzling sound, and the spirit dissolved, leaving the idol silent and immobile on the ground. The water trickled back into the river, and I was left completely dumbfounded.

What did I just do?

Ezekiel shook, but it wasn't because of the entity. "Ava, you— you just used Water magic!"

I clambered to my feet. "No... it isn't possible."

"It has to be." Ezekiel got up, and his feet splashed on the stone. "I saw you do it. You're not just Koigni. You're Toaqua, too."

Denial flashed in my mind. I was a Fire caster, through and through. I had the fiery temperament for it. The ability to call upon Fire was as easy for me as breathing.

And yet... I'd told the river to protect Ezekiel without any effort whatsoever, and it'd obeyed.

I wouldn't accept it. It wasn't real. I couldn't have inherited my father's powers, too. This had to be a fluke.

I wouldn't have one more thing that made me more different than I already was.

"Ez, you can't tell Mama and Daddy about this," I said as he approached. "It has to stay between us."

His face fell. "If you're both Houses, it's important for them to know."

"No! I want to be Koigni— I want to be normal," I pleaded. "I'm already a fucking freak."

Ezekiel's eyes turned sad. "You're not a freak, Ava."

I let out a snort. Yeah, right. I'd been the weird kid at school. And weird was putting it lightly. People were afraid of me.

It was exceptionally rare— nearly unheard of— for an Elementai to have the ability to cast more than one element. Most could only cast the element of the House they were born into. Sure, there were exceptions, like my mother, who could use both Fire and Spirit magic.

But there'd never, in the history of all the Hawkei, been an elemental who could use both Fire and Water. The elements were total opposites. And I didn't want to be the first anything.

I picked up the idol and shoved it into my bag. "Come on. Let's go."

"Ava!"

Ezekiel protested all the way behind me— even as he struggled to climb the wall that led back out of the cave. When we burst out into the sunlight, he grabbed my shoulders to stop me.

"This isn't something we can hide," he said. "Nor should you."

Ezekiel was stubborn. He wouldn't give up.

"Let's just drop the idol off at Grandpa's," I said with a sigh. "Then we'll talk about it."

Or like, never.

Ezekiel's shoulders sagged. "Okay. We can stop by on the way home."

"Like hell! I *need* makeup." I could deal with jeans just fine if I was running around in a cave, but any other time of day, I wanted a dress on. Crawling in the mud was no excuse for not looking fabulous— and I was *not* walking through town with my hair like this.

"Ugh. Fine. I guess I'm hungry, anyway."

"You're always hungry."

The hippogriff herd had returned by this time. They were grazing in the valley beyond. The lead mare lifted her head as I walked toward her. I pulled myself onto her back, and Ezekiel climbed onto the same tawny stallion he'd fallen off of earlier. I nudged my heels into her sides, and the hippogriff spread her wings, taking off into the air.

There was nothing like feeling the wind on your face while you were flying on a hippogriff. I looked down, and as the valley shrank beneath me, I turned my gaze toward the city beyond.

Kinpago was my home, and always would be. I admired the beautiful skyline as the hippogriff tilted in the air, directing us toward an island that sat surrounded by the crystal clear ocean.

The two hippogriffs landed on the sandy beach of the island. Ezekiel and I fed them treats before bidding farewell and walking up the brick pathway to the grand stone mansion beyond.

I loved our house. It was open-concept, decorated in white and blue tones with a crystal chandelier hanging in the main entrance. The kitchen connected to the living room, and the porch doors were open, letting in the breeze from the beach. Some would say it was too big, but I had such a large family, it always felt warm and welcoming to me.

My younger sister sat on the couch, reading, like usual. Her red mane of hair fanned out behind her on the pillows. She looked up as we entered.

"Where've you guys been?" Alana asked. She was only fifteen, but she was fucking sharp— nothing got past her. She got off the couch and threw her book aside as Ezekiel began rummaging through the cupboards to make a sandwich.

I took the idol out of my bag and set it on the counter. "Getting this."

"No way. You found it?" Alana's eyes widened as she took in the statue.

"Yeah. It only took vanquishing an evil spirit out of the statue," Ezekiel said with a mouth full of food.

"Really? How'd you do that?" Alana asked.

I glared at Ezekiel, and he shut up as Alana inspected the idol.

I could hear swear words coming from the garage. I poked my head in.

My eleven-year-old brother, Maverick, was sprawled on the floor, surrounded by tools as he messed around with an old motorbike. The bike was an antique. It had been my grandfather's, passed down to my dad, then passed down to me. I took it to the mainland sometimes to ride it around. Maverick was itching to be old enough to drive it. I'd told him he could tinker with it. He was good with mechanical things. His brown hair was matted with oil as he tightened loose bolts.

"You got it, Mav?" I asked.

Maverick threw a wrench down. "Stupid chains are busted."

"Well, if you need help, ask."

Ez and I took after our dad— Alana and Maverick our mom. Ezekiel and I had tan brown skin, while Alana and Maverick's was lighter. Ez and I looked native, and the other two didn't— even though we had the same Hawkei blood running through our veins.

I returned to the kitchen. "Where are Mom and Dad?" Ezekiel asked Alana before he chugged a glass of milk.

"Dad's at the office," Alana said. "I guess Mom went with him for some reason."

Thank the ancestors that Mama and Daddy weren't home. Ezekiel had a big mouth.

"If they're both there, it must be important," Ezekiel said.

Alana shrugged. "Maybe."

Daddy was the chief of Toaqua, and responsible for everyone in the Water tribe. Mama was on the Koigni Elder Council, working alongside him to maintain peace amongst the Houses. During the Elementai Civil War twenty years ago, there'd been a prophecy about my mother and how she would save the tribe. I'd only been a baby then, but according to my parents, it'd been a terrible time of war and suffering amongst the Houses. As the chosen one, my mother had led the tribe into a new age of peace— but not without a lot of sacrifice.

Because I was her firstborn, I was expected to live up to her incredible story. And I'd thoroughly disappointed everyone.

As if being the daughter of the Water chief wasn't enough publicity. My parents were tribal heroes. Me being able to cast magic from two different Houses would cause more undue attention to our family.

Like I hadn't done that enough already.

While Ezekiel ate, I ran upstairs. I showered, dried and curled my hair before flinging open my closet door— which was packed to the brim with poofy dresses, bedazzled jean jackets, and six-inch pumps.

I stood at the door and tapped a finger against my chin. What was I in the mood for today?

I had this fabulous pink tulle skirt I'd sewn myself that fell around my knees, with a cut-off cream shirt. They'd go perfect with a white pair of heels. I slipped them on, then sat at my vanity and began applying primer and foundation before working on contouring my cheekbones. I tossed lipsticks and eyeliner around my messy room carelessly, looking for the right one.

I was nothing more than thinly organized chaos. Everything in my room was pink— I *loved* pink— though you could barely tell under the piles of clothes I had lying around. My bedroom had a theme; unicorns. I had a unicorn bedspread, unicorn posters, and unicorn lamps.

I collected unicorns. I was fricking obsessed with them. I even wanted a unicorn tattoo one day. It was all so pink and girly, and it made me feel fabulous. Anyone who thought my room looked like a five-year-old's could suck a dick, because I liked it, and that's what mattered.

I had a wardrobe full of makeup products. I didn't need them as much anymore... not since I quit my beauty vlog, but it felt like a sin to throw them out.

Mama and Daddy wanted me to pick it back up again. But I hadn't made a video since Monica died. It felt like a betrayal to make one without her.

Thinking of Monica always made a pang run through my chest. I threaded my fingers over the bracelet she'd woven me, which I never took off. Red and green, for Koigni and Nivita.

It was the last piece I had left of her. Sometimes, I still heard her laugh echoing through the house. The memory of her smile got me through my bad days.

I had a lot of those.

I rummaged through my vanity drawer, looking for the final touch. If Uncle Jonah had taught me one thing, there was never enough glitter. I dusted a tiny bottle of it over my arms and cheeks before I posed in the mirror.

I looked *so hot*. Looks were everything. People judged with their eyes. I loved makeup, because there was nothing you couldn't hide with it.

Ezekiel was messing around with his guitar when I came downstairs. "Finally."

He put his guitar aside. Alana gave a wave as we headed out. We'd asked her to come with us, but she was an introvert and liked her alone time.

We took the motorboat into town. I watched as dolphins and whales swam between hippocampi— half-horse, half-mermaid creatures. Their scales sparkled in the water, making me wish to reach out and brush my fingers over their spiny manes. Everything about my world was magical, and I savored each moment of it.

We docked the boat before walking up the winding path to Kinpago. As we entered the city, another invigorating sense of *home* struck me. I watched from the streets as dragons flew overhead, twirling with griffins and birds with rainbow feathers that were bigger than buildings. The streets were packed with Elementai walking side by side with direwolves, basilisks and three-headed animals like chimeras.

The perytons were always my favorite. The winged deer had such spirits as they bounded through the streets, bobbing their antlered heads.

The Elementai had the most important job in the world— protecting and defending magical creatures. We were their caretakers as designated by the ancestors themselves, and the creatures depended on us for survival. Every magical creature imaginable that existed in the world had a species based here in Kinpago. More often than not, we were the only thing that prevented them from going extinct. As a result, many of them became our Familiars.

A Familiar was an Elementai's soul, the part of their spirit that existed outside of their body. Every Elementai was bonded to one, and you usually met them sometime after you got your powers. Elementai couldn't live without their Familiars, as they were the source of our magic, our life energy. If you died, so did they.

I hadn't gotten my Familiar yet. I'd desperately looked for one the first day I could cast my element, but I hadn't found them. Somewhere, I knew my soul was out there waiting for me, and the longing to join the pieces of myself together was almost like an obsession. What would they be, and what would my Familiar mean to me?

There were so many colors in Kinpago. Streamers hung from buildings, and Hawkei music played as people danced in the streets beneath the skyscrapers and shops. I smelled fry bread, cinnamon, and freshly baked pizza. Vendors on the street sold beads for making jewelry, white sage and woven baskets.

I wanted to stop and look— shopping was my favorite activity— but Ezekiel pulled me along in the direction of my grandfather's house. He knew once I went on a shopping spree, I wouldn't stop until I was flat broke.

In the distance, I saw the spires of a white castle rise into the clouds, and my heart thudded with just a little bit of magic.

Ezekiel nudged me knowingly. "Are you ready? Just a few more days now."

Excitement welled in my chest. I couldn't wait to attend Orenda Academy of Magical Creatures. I'd heard so many stories from my parents about how amazing it was when I was growing up. I wanted to have those incredible experiences, too.

"I'm glad I'm going with you," I told Ez. I'd taken a year off after graduating from high school and postponed my enrollment because... well, Monica.

And something else I didn't want to think about.

But now I was ready. I was sure of it. And Ez would be there, right alongside me in the same grade. I could handle it.

Ezekiel came to an abrupt halt. I nearly slammed into him, but held myself back at the last minute.

An annoying laugh caused a twinge of irritation to pass me by. I saw the bleached blonde mane of hair before anything else. Ezekiel's mouth became thin, though I felt the hints of desperation oozing out from him.

I grabbed Ezekiel's arm and steered him in a different direction. "Just ignore her. She's not worth it."

His eyes remained glued to the back of blondie's head. I took another glance back. When I saw who she was talking to, my mouth ran dry.

I *really* didn't like Rosary, but it was the sight of the person beside her that churned my gut. I took a short look before I set my eyes forward. The small movement was just enough to make a smirk cross John's face.

Fuck him. I *hated* him.

I forced my hand not to shake on Ezekiel's arm, and we took a different path. Even when we were well out of John's sight, I still felt sick to my stomach.

I wouldn't acknowledge it. I'd forgotten. That was that.

Ezekiel hadn't noticed my momentary panic. He was still miserable. "Do you think there's a chance she'll take me back?"

I focused on the conversation with Ezekiel, to redirect my nauseated feelings. "You've gotta let her go, Ez. She's no good for you."

"I know." His shoulders slumped. "Just wish things would've turned out different."

Rosary had completely broken my brother's heart. He'd never been the same after she dumped him.

Good riddance. I thought of wrapping my hands around her neck and squeezing, and a smile crossed my face. "She was abusive. You can do so much better."

Rosary had hit my brother once. I'd made sure she'd never do it again. The burns were so bad she still had a scar on her arm. *Nobody* fucked with my little brother.

"I'm sure things would've worked out." He dropped his head. "If the baby would've survived."

Okay, Ezekiel was a goody-goody until it came to one thing— girls. He thought with what was in his pants instead of in his head. I guess the condom broke one time. Not gonna lie, it was kind of nice when Daddy and Mama found out. They'd grilled Ezekiel's ass instead of mine, for once. He and Rosary were set to become teen parents— until Rosary had lost the pregnancy last year, and dumped him right off the bat.

My brother had taken the miscarriage harder than Rosary had. Ez had such a sweet heart— he'd cried for days. My whole family had just managed to bring him out of it. And as much as I despised her, I felt sorry for Rosary. No one should lose a baby, but the way she'd treated Ez after the fact was just plain cruel.

I felt the tension in the air alter as Ezekiel changed the subject. "Maybe you should try talking to Johnny again. I know you guys had a falling out after Monica died, but you two were really close. It's sad you don't talk anymore."

A pit in my stomach opened up and devoured me. He wasn't Johnny anymore. He was John. And Ezekiel didn't know what happened between us. Nobody did.

Thoughts came rushing back. I tried so hard to push them out of my head, but they kept coming, pouring over me like an endless waterfall. I literally felt the color from my face drain. I let go of Ezekiel's arm, so he could no longer feel my hands quiver.

"Ava, are you okay?" Ezekiel noticed my pale expression. "Did you take your pills this morning?"

"I always take my pills." Not that they helped. I was still three fries short of a Happy Meal.

Ezekiel watched me carefully. "Are you sure you'll make it to Grandpa's? Maybe you should go back home."

"You're probably right. I'm not feeling great," I mumbled. I reached into my purse and gave him the idol. "Take this to Grandpa's. I'll meet you later."

He eyed me up and down. "It might be a good idea to walk you back."

"I'm fine, Ez. I promise."

I was not fine. Yet Ezekiel knew I hated it when people hovered over me, so he stepped back to give me some space. "Okay. You can take the boat back. I'll grab the ferry. See you."

Ezekiel started down the road. I turned the other way, though I didn't go back the way we came.

I needed to take a different path. I had to be alone.

As I wandered down the city streets of Kinpago, I felt a burst of energy fizzle through my brain. It felt like I could run a hundred marathons without breaking a sweat. I wanted to run right now— get all these eyes off of me. Dozens of people were passing me by, and it felt like all of them were staring right through me.

They're spying on you, Ava.

They're following you.

You're not safe.

Run!

"Shut up," I whispered under my breath. I shut my eyes for a few moments to make the voices stop, but they kept coming, so numerous I could no longer make out what they were saying. It was like an entire auditorium was screaming at me all at once, amplifying the volume with every word.

I could taste metal. I could smell blood. It was so overpowering it made me want to vomit. All those eyes were still on me. The buildings were leaning inward and threatening to topple over. I diverged from the main street and began jogging down a deserted alley, trying to escape the ringing in my ears.

"It's just a hallucination. Ignore it," I told myself.

Yet I couldn't. Voices. So many voices echoing in my head. There was no way of escape—

I was thrown off balance as someone slammed into my side. I thought it was another part of the hallucination, until I felt a strong hand on my arm keep me from falling over. I tottered on my heels and my purse slipped off my arm, falling onto the pavement. The voices abruptly stopped as I turned to face the person I'd accidentally run into.

"Easy there, pidge," a cool, smooth voice said. "Don't want to scrape up those pretty little knees."

I caught the flash of a remarkably cocky smile, and for no reason at all, it instantly put me at ease. My eyes roamed up and down the man who'd caught me. He had to be in his early twenties. He was a few inches taller than me, around six foot two. His dark hair fell into his murky eyes. We were so close together I could see the emerald flecks within the hazel tones, which appeared to be honey pools I could dive into. His skin was brown, darker than mine, and his body was corded with muscle. His ripped jeans and tight t-shirt was like something straight out of a magazine.

A bad boy. I liked bad boys. At his side, a gray husky with a star marking on its forehead sat panting in the sun.

I tried to place what ethnicity the guy might be. He had to be Hawkei, like me— he had a Familiar after all— but besides being an indigenous North American tribe, the Hawkei had been intermingling with other races for centuries. I thought I could place him as Latino, but I could see some Middle Eastern features as well, mixed in with African traits.

Hey, I liked multicultural guys, and this dude looked like a world tour. For my vagina.

Then I noticed something— how the man's gaze didn't quite connect with mine. The dog eyed me with a shining expression, one that was confusing to put together.

The man was blind. I felt stupid for not noticing sooner. Should've paid more attention instead of ogling over him like the god he was.

Which is why what came out of my mouth next was just as stupid. "How... how can you tell I'm a girl?" I asked. I didn't know if it was a rude question, but he couldn't see me, right?

The man smirked again. This time, I noticed he wasn't actually looking me in the eye— he stared in my direction, but his gaze went right through me, confirming my theory he was blind. "Most men don't wear perfume, pigeon. Or dresses that make that much noise. Your heels click on the stone."

His hand was still on my arm. The feel of his touch smoldered against my skin. I knew he couldn't see me, but when I looked into his eyes... I don't know. I felt a powerful connection, something that drew me in and absorbed my thoughts, making everything in my universe center upon this one man.

I didn't like being alone with guys, but this was different. I had an immediate knowledge that this stranger wouldn't hurt me. I noticed there was a jar on the ground, filled with a collection of coins and a few dollars. He'd been panhandling.

Sympathy filled my chest. I came from a rich family, so I'd never known what it was like to suffer financially. And however this guy had ended up in his situation, I didn't feel he deserved it.

"You dropped your purse." The guy took my purse from the husky's mouth. The dog must've fetched it, but I hadn't seen.

I took my purse back from him, still fixated on the sight of this guy. What was it about him that drew me in? "Thank you."

"No problem, pidge."

I felt like doing backflips. "Why are you calling me that... pidge?"

"Short for pigeon." He flashed another attractive smile. "Old timey slang for a hot dame."

He thought I was hot? I mean... he couldn't see me, but he had to be attracted to me all the same, to say something like that. Butterflies fluttered in my stomach. I *loved* vintage movies. I'd grown up on black and white films from the 1940s my Grandmother Eleanor loved. I thought the nickname was cute. "You new around here? I've never seen you before."

"Charlie Wahkin, ma'am," he drawled. "And you?"

"Ava-Marie." I knew better than to give him my full name. And yet we were like two magnets, drawn together as if by fate. Charlie. I liked it.

"You might want to be a little more careful next time," he said. "There are worse things in these alleyways than me."

I laughed. "Now why do I doubt that?"

He cocked his head a little. "Just mind what I told you, pidge. The back parts of any town are no place for a lady."

Charlie's smile smoldered, and my eyes went immediately to his lips. I had the thought of pressing mine against his... just to see what he would taste like. Gunpowder and lead came to mind. It would be explosive. I mean, it was insane to think of kissing a homeless guy, even one that was really, really cute. Hot damn, this guy was a full-course meal with dessert on the side. Could I put in an order for delivery? Because I'd totally eat him up.

I brushed off my skirt— it'd gotten some dirt on it when Charlie had grabbed me. "Well, Charlie, I hope I see you again soon."

"Don't count on it, miss. I don't stick around."

He inclined his head. The tiniest movement he made was sexy. I smiled back, though I realized he couldn't see it, so instead I said, "Thanks again, Charlie."

When I was at the end of the alleyway, I dared to turn around. Charlie was gathering the few things he had, stuffing them into a backpack before he and his husky wandered the other way.

Once Charlie was out of my sight, cold deadness settled back into my chest, bringing my heart down with a heavy weight. As I left the man behind me, the hallucination came pouring back into my thoughts. If I hadn't run into Charlie in the alley, and stopped the hallucination, no telling how far I'd fall into it this time.

I suffered from psychosis. Often. It was a symptom of my bipolar disorder. Not all people with bipolar saw and heard things that weren't there, but I did. I'd talked to invisible people long after it was appropriate to have imaginary friends, and described things I could see that other people couldn't. Sometimes, it happened in school and I'd scared my classmates. By the time my doctors had put together a medication regimen that lessened the severity of the hallucinations, my reputation had already been tarnished. Crazy Ava-Marie. That's what people called me.

Growing up, the response to that would always be I *wasn't* crazy, but now I wasn't so sure they were wrong. I'd been in and out of therapy all my life. I wasn't going now, because I'd been crafty enough to convince my parents I didn't need it. The truth was, I'd just given up hope, and didn't see how talking to someone would help me now if it hadn't in the past. The hallucinations had been under control, before Monica died.

Ever since? They were worse than they ever had been.

I got back on the boat so I could head home. I rummaged through my purse to find the boat key. I found it, but not much else. My guts bottomed out when I realized my wallet was missing.

What the hell? How did I lose it? My mind raced. I hadn't touched my wallet once since we'd left the house. I had no idea how it could be missing.

Then I pieced things together. My purse had fallen off my arm when I'd stumbled into Charlie. His Familiar was the one who retrieved it for me. The dog must've snatched the wallet before Charlie had given me back my purse! I'd had over a hundred dollars in there. This was bullshit!

I let out a huff and rolled my eyes. What the fuck ever. I never carried my credit cards with me, anyway, so those were safe. If that guy was lousy enough to steal, he needed the money more than I did.

Geez, what a loser. I thought that guy was hot. I had the shittiest taste in men.

I drove the boat back to the house in a bad mood.

It was a Sunday, so like always, my giant family was here, getting ready to have our afternoon get-together. My Uncle Cade was at the grill, while my Aunt Imogen was doing the hula to tropical music that played on the radio. Her fox Familiar, Sassy, rose up on her hind legs to sway to the beat. Four of their boys, all various ages, were playing football on the beach. Their fifth son— the oldest, same age as my younger sister, was talking to Alana as he swam around the pool. Alana never swam— she was afraid of water. She sat on one of the lounge chairs and screamed as Luis tried to splash her and missed. I kicked off my heels in the boat and walked barefoot to the house.

"Ava, my darling!" A wet kiss was placed on my cheek as I felt arms the size of tree trunks wrap around me and squeeze.

"Can't breathe," I gasped. I fell several feet as my Uncle Jonah let me go. He was a giant of a man, but he had the biggest heart.

"You'd better be taking my dance class this semester," Uncle Jonah said as he waggled his finger at me.

"I've already signed up." Jonah was the Dean of Yapluma at Orenda Academy. He mostly taught Air magic and psychology classes, but his dance class was not to be missed. His Familiar, a hippogriff named Squeaks, trotted up to me and nudged me with her head.

Her offspring were a part of the hippogriff herd I'd gotten a ride from that morning. I scratched her shoulder feathers, and she cooed happily.

"Don't expect to get by so easily because you're my niece. I fully expect you to shake that booty until it falls off," Uncle Jonah teased, and his eyes sparkled.

I laughed. "Yes, Auntie."

Whether we called Jonah auntie or uncle depended on what personality he'd decided to put on that morning. He was fine with either. He crushed the beer can he was holding against his head and ran down the beach, screaming, "Save a touchdown for me, boys!"

His husband, Jake, was tossing the football. Jonah hurtled toward him and tackled him onto the sand, where they wrestled for dominance. Squeaks danced around them awkwardly, until her tail swished and knocked a tray of hot dogs off the picnic bench and onto the ground.

Jonah's daughter, Josee, was messing around with a soccer ball like always. She kicked it to Maverick, who tried to navigate it around her to score a goal. He failed when she snatched it out of the air effortlessly.

Josee was a total tomboy. All she cared about was sports. Not me. I liked looking pretty, thank you very much. She waved me over to join them, but I shook my head no and continued onto the porch.

Mama was there, taking pictures with her professional camera. The cutest little creature sat on her shoulder. It had big eyes, with fluffy brown fur, a poofy tail and long ears like those of a fennec fox. Her name was Buttercup, and she was a kurble— a type of marsupial. Buttercup trilled when I climbed the porch steps, and Mama looked up.

I always thought Mama was one of the prettiest women alive. She had long brunette hair with eyes that were always welcoming and kind, and she held herself in a dignified way I never thought I could imitate, or achieve. My mother radiated power like the sun radiated heat, and people respected her for it.

Mama put the camera down and smiled as I came by.

"Did you and your brother have a nice hike?" she asked.

"Yeah," I lied. "He's still out there. Wanted to stop by Grandpa's for a minute. What did you and the council talk about?"

Mama's smile faltered for a brief moment. "It was nothing important."

Nothing, huh? I wasn't the only one telling tall tales.

Just then, a dragon's roar rang across the wind. I looked up. A ruby red dragon, with scales glistening in the sunlight, spiraled down from the sapphire skies. The dragon was massive, and was almost as large as our house. As the dragon landed, shock waves resonated across the beach, and a man slid off the dragon's back.

"Watch your tail, Julian," Daddy said. "You nearly knocked down the house."

Julian grumbled and curled his tail the other way. It hit Squeaks and sent her flying into the water. The hippogriff made an angry sound, while Julian grumbled an apology.

Daddy was tall, with long black hair and a strong jawline that made him appear proud. The chief of the Water tribe always looked strong, even when he was at his weakest.

I wished I could emulate that kind of confidence. My dad had never been a fish out of water.

Unlike my Mama, Daddy was very sick. I could see it clearest when he was trying to hide how he really felt. Daddy suffered from a rare disease that caused his magic to weaken his bodily systems, his immune system getting the brunt of the illness. It was genetic, but so far, neither me nor my siblings had developed it.

And I hoped none of us ever did. It was tough growing up, watching your dad be in and out of the hospital. A few times, he'd barely pulled through. But I'd never have it any other way, because I really loved my Daddy, and I didn't care if he was sick, so long as he was here.

As he drew closer, I noticed the bags under his eyes, and the way his steps faltered slightly on the sand. He could smile, but I wasn't fooled. He was tired today.

Still, he put out an arm and drew me into a hug. "There's my peanut. I missed you this morning."

My stomach wiggled uncomfortably. I'd left before Daddy had gotten up, to retrieve the idol. "Ez and I wanted to get a head start on the hike."

"See anything interesting?"

I swallowed. Lying to Daddy was always the hardest. "Nah. Nothing out of the ordinary."

Daddy gave me a warm smile. Before he could ask anything else, I said, "You and Mama were gone for a long time. You don't work on weekends. Is something up?"

He frowned slightly. "You know tribal business can happen at any time. It's nothing to be worried about."

I knew exactly when Daddy wasn't telling the truth. He blinked twice.

It was strange Mama and Daddy were being shady about the Elder meeting this morning. Why didn't they want me to know about it?

I decided I didn't care. I trusted Daddy with everything. If he was keeping something from me, it was for my own good. He wouldn't lie to me about something important. He never hid secrets from me that mattered.

Mama bit her lip as she took in my father's appearance. "You look tired, Liam. Come inside."

"Only for a moment." Daddy's eyes crossed to Aunt Imogen and Uncle Jonah, who were shaking their butts on the beach to the music. It was very typical of them. That was my crazy aunt and uncle.

Daddy shuffled slowly up the steps. I walked behind him, to catch him just in case he fell.

"I don't need to be nannied, you know," Daddy said crossly as he sat on a kitchen chair. He sent a surly gaze to me as Mama placed a glass of water on the table.

"What kind of daughter would I be if I didn't?" I asked. I hovered beside him, but not too close. Buttercup perched beside the glass of water and tilted her head before Daddy took a sip.

Mama sat across from Daddy and laid a hand on his chest. As she did, a white glow emitted from her fingertips and spread over Daddy's body. I watched, entranced by the silvery strands that wrapped around Daddy's form.

Mama could treat Daddy's disease with her Spirit magic. She couldn't cure him, but she could heal him partially, and treat his symptoms. Her powers were the only thing that kept him going most days. Watching her use her magic on him was always beautiful. Spirit magic came from love, and I could really tell that Mama loved Daddy.

All at once, the color in Daddy's face brightened, and he sat taller. It was like I could see his illness visibly ebbing away from him as Mama's Spirit powers worked their magic. When she was done, the glow faded and Daddy's voice was stronger.

He turned toward me. "So, what path did you and your brother take today?"

Before I could answer, the door burst open and slammed against the wall. I heard footsteps run into the kitchen as Ezekiel screamed, "Ava's got Water powers!"

Fucking dammit. Couldn't trust Ez to keep a secret to save his life.

Ezekiel skidded to a halt. The color drained from his face as he realized I'd gotten back first. My lips formed into a sneer. Mama and Daddy's mouths dropped open at the same time, looking from me to my brother in surprise.

I pounced. I jumped on Ezekiel's back and locked my arm around his neck. "You little snitch!"

Ezekiel grabbed my arm as he fell to his knees. We struggled violently before he wrenched me off. I went tumbling to the floor. I went to launch myself at him again, but Daddy held me back.

"Ow! You kicked me in the face!" Ez complained, holding his eye.

"Good, you probably look better," I shot back at him.

"Enough," Daddy said firmly. "Ava, what's this about?"

I took a few ragged breaths and refused to answer. But Ezekiel, who went to pieces under any sort of interrogation, blurted, "Ava and I were at the dig site, and—"

"You two went to that excavation?" Daddy leapt up from his chair. "I specifically told you not to mess around in those caves— don't roll your eyes at me, young lady!"

He'd caught me at it, but come on. This was stupid.

"Forget about that," Mama said quickly. "Ezekiel, you said Ava used Water powers."

"Uh-huh." Ezekiel's head bobbed like he was a little boy. "We found the idol, but it turned out to be a malevolent Koigni Spirit Art. It was going to kill me, until Ava commanded the underground river within the caves to attack it. I watched a wave rise up and destroy it."

"Honey, is this true?" Mama's eyes were wide. Buttercup mirrored her expression.

"I mean..." I shrugged. "Yeah, it happened, but it must've been a one-off thing. I don't have Water powers. I'm Koigni!"

"That's not what she asked," Daddy said. I was trying his patience.

"Look, I just did it to protect my brother! I don't know if I could do it again!" I said.

Mama nodded. She'd first discovered her powers doing something similar, defending her sister from an attacking lion years ago.

I fisted a hand in my hair. "Maybe we shouldn't have gone to the caves. But whatever happened this morning, it won't happen again. I've never felt partial to Water. I like Fire. I'm a Koigni through and through, and—"

As I was rambling, Daddy purposefully knocked over the glass of water that was sitting on the table. I gasped and reacted instinctively. My left hand shot out. The water that was about to hit the floor suspended in the air, hovering at my command.

I was so shocked that the spell broke, and water splashed all over the hardwood. Nobody moved to clean it up. Everyone stared at me, like I was some sort of freak animal.

Daddy took in a breath. "Ava, you're incredible." Daddy was fit to boasting. He was proud I'd inherited his side of the magical spectrum. But why were they all so happy about this? I didn't feel like it was anything to celebrate.

There was no denying it. Or hiding it. I did have Toaqua powers. I just didn't understand why.

"How could this have happened?" I asked. "I thought Elementai always inherited the powers of their same-sex parent."

"Ava, you have multiple generations of Fire and Water running through your veins. The same-sex parent rule must be canceled out once your genetics become diluted enough. Fire and Water are both dominant traits in your genes," Mama said, marveling at her own words.

"Does this mean I might get Fire powers, too?" Ezekiel asked in excitement. He was thrilled about becoming a dual-caster, but he didn't get it. It wasn't a gift to be different. It was a curse.

"It depends on what traits are dominant. My traits are from my Spirit and Fire side, but they can co-exist peacefully. But I've never heard of Fire and Water traits being dominant at the same time," Mama said.

"Exactly. It's never happened before." I couldn't keep the bitterness out of my voice. This was just one more thing that would set me apart from everyone else.

"Ava, the ancestors chose to give you this gift," Daddy said. "Why not use it for good?"

"Because I just want to be normal, that's why!" I burst. "People already think I'm crazy. What are they going to say when they find out I'm a dual-caster? The press is going to go nuts!"

As the daughter of the Toaqua chief and the chosen one, I'd been the subject of Hawkei tabloids multiple times. Most of the articles weren't very kind. I couldn't imagine this one would be, either.

Mama's eyebrows scrunched together. "You're not crazy, sweetheart. You have bipolar."

I blew a lock of hair out of my eyes. "Big difference."

Ezekiel came close to me. This time, he looked a little bothered. "Are you okay, Ava? I was worried about you when you left earlier."

"I told you I was fine." Did he really have to bring this up in front of our parents? He could've asked me later.

"I just... I don't know." Ezekiel shrugged. "You had that look in your eyes you used to get when you were hearing things."

Daddy and Mama went rigid. I suppressed a groan. "You're hearing voices again?" Mama's eyes narrowed in concern.

"No," I lied. "I haven't heard anything. I was just tired earlier."

"Ava, you'd better be telling the truth," Daddy warned.

"Not a single sound."

I couldn't let them know the voices were back. They'd give me a kiss and ship me off to the loony bin before I had a chance to pack my designer heels. I'd told them the voices had stopped years ago, to keep them from worrying, when in reality they never had.

Ezekiel gave me *the look*. It was a secret gesture only we understood, and he was telling me I was full of shit.

"Ava, whatever happens, we're here to help you," Mama said gently. She took my hand, like she was good at doing, and squeezed it tight. "If you're hearing voices, or if you don't understand your magic, we can work it out. There's nothing we can't do together as a family."

Tears started to bead at the corners of my eyes, but I pushed them back down. I didn't cry. "You guys don't understand. I'm tired of being different. My magic was one thing that felt safe. And it doesn't feel like that anymore."

I turned away from them and ran. My parents called after me, but I ignored them. Everyone on the beach looked up as I bolted to the shoreline.

I didn't think about what I did. Just like my Fire, my Water magic erupted from me by feeling. I didn't know how I did what I did, but one moment, I was on the sand, and the next, a wave had risen up to catch my feet. I continued running, and the Water crashed upward to support my weight. I fell into the water and surfed across the waves like I would on my surfboard. People gasped when they saw me riding upon the water. I heard more cries, but I pretended like I didn't hear them, keeping my eyes on the horizon.

Soon, the island was long behind me. I collapsed on the shore of the mainland on all fours, breathing heavily. My shoulders shook. My clothes were soaked, but I didn't care.

I felt like I was going to crack. If I didn't maintain control, I *would* crack, and everything I was holding inside would break free. I had to get it together. I forced myself to stand and slicked back my wet hair, eyeing the span of the empty beach.

I was so empty inside. The hollowness just wouldn't go away, and I didn't know how to fill it.

I was Toaqua now. Maybe I could drown it.

As the dark thought crossed my mind, I heard a rustle in the trees coming from the forest beyond the beach. I stood up slowly as a creature emerged.

By the ancestors, she was beautiful. The creature was a tall and slender unicorn, with a coat dark as night and an obsidian horn rising out of the center of her forehead. The mare's eyes were black, and her mane and tail burned with flame, sending embers to the ground as the fire that made up her hair trailed over her neck and withers.

A Fire unicorn. I'd heard of them, but I'd never seen one before. She was looking right at me.

I advanced toward the Fire unicorn. As I drew near, my clothes and hair dried automatically at the presence of her heat. The air around her was hot, but I didn't mind at all. The unicorn was completely still as she faced me head-on. In the middle of her forehead was a singular white mark— a seven-pointed star. She nickered as I dared to reach out a hand. I placed it on her velvety nose.

The moment I touched her, the entire world opened up. I saw so many colors at the edges of my vision, colliding together in a gorgeous rainbow. The purpose of my life entwined together with this creature, sucking me in and holding me in an embrace that was welcoming and home. I felt the fires of her passion burning away at me, taking away anything that was bad and leaving behind only what was right. This wasn't like the visions I experienced during psychosis. This was real, and it was comforting. I smelled sandalwood, the ocean, and the remnants of a burning fire. I heard my brother's laughter and the sound of Monica singing. The song continued, wrapping around me as I felt Daddy's hug and Mama braiding my hair. I imagined sunlight hitting my face, and the glow of a candle in the dark. Images flashed before my eyes, like they would if I was experiencing my last moments before death; but instead of death, this was a new awakening.

The unicorn placed her nose to my chest. When she touched my heart, I felt such a powerful wave of emotion that my knees buckled beneath me and I cried out.

As the music faded and Monica's voice ebbed away, I knew immediately that I had bonded. I didn't need to question it. This unicorn was my Familiar. My soul. Familiars always came to you at your weakest point— and she had known I needed her now.

"Who are you?" I whispered. I was completely enchanted by her.

The mare blinked. She didn't speak to me, but I felt a strong feeling in my heart, and a name popped into my head... *Oberi.*

"Oberi." That was her name. I reached out and wrapped my arms around her neck. The unicorn turned her head inward and nuzzled me, as if hugging me to her chest.

The hollowness inside me went away, and I reveled in the feeling of touching my Familiar for the first time. I had found who I was. I'd discovered myself. Everything in my life tied me to this creature, and I knew then that I wasn't alone.

As I pulled away, the unicorn turned to me, offering me her back. I reached up to take her mane in my hands. Though it was made of Fire, the flames didn't burn me. I pulled myself onto the unicorn, and Oberi gave another knicker. She bounced a few times on her hooves before giving a tiny rear, then bolted forward.

Her feet kicked up sand as she galloped down the beach. My hair was blown backward by the wind, and I gave a cry of joy. This was entirely different than riding the hippogriffs. It was like Oberi and I were one, a singular being with no start and no end. Her flames blew by as I twisted them in my hands. It was like my spirit left my body as I felt her powerful strides pound the earth, creating a song in my heart as we splashed against the waves. As we ran, I saw other unicorns made of Water rise out of the ocean, charging alongside Oberi.

I had done that out of my emotion. My magic. Maybe being Toaqua wasn't such a bad thing after all.

Oberi slowed to a halt, and I took deep breaths to stabilize my shaking form. I slid off her back, still winded. My mind calculated the possibilities as I stroked Oberi's midnight coat.

I'd bonded with a Fire creature. This proved I was Koigni, right?

Maybe I could hide my Toaqua side. Nobody needed to know about it, right? They'd never guess, not with a Fire unicorn at my side.

As I was still taking in the incredible moment, an angry cry rang out across the beach. "Get away from my Familiar!"

I turned around. My stomach bottomed out when I realized who was shouting at me. It was Charlie— the blind man I'd run into earlier. The one who'd taken my wallet. He stomped up the beach, his bag thrown over his back.

Anger rose within me. This guy was a piece of work. What the hell was he doing, bothering me and Oberi? How did he even know where we were? He couldn't see us.

"You're going to get a fireball to the face," I snarled. I conjured one and drew back my hand to throw it.

Before I could, Oberi gave a high-pitched whinny. She ran toward Charlie, tossing her head. The fireball dropped out of my hand and fizzled on the sand as I watched Oberi change. In seconds, she'd morphed from a female Fire unicorn... into the same male husky I'd seen with Charlie earlier.

The husky barked and wagged his tail at Charlie's side. Shock twisted my guts when the husky turned to look at me. I noticed the same seven-pointed star on his forehead that Oberi had.

This was impossible. How could Oberi have two different *genders*? Two different *forms*? I'd never heard of such a Familiar before.

My heart twisted sickly as I watched Charlie pet the husky. Then I knew.

I wasn't just bonded to this creature— to Oberi. I was bonded to *Charlie* as well. His Familiar was also my own.

My spirit was split into two pieces. And the other half belonged to him.

I shared a soul with a complete stranger.

charlie

THREE

I wasn't even here for a freaking *day*, and already I'd run into trouble. *Ava-Marie.* The sound of her voice was irritating. How *dare* she touch my Familiar!

Apparently, first impressions weren't all they were cracked up to be. At first, I felt bad for stealing from her. Now I knew it was karma at its finest.

Ava-Marie stomped her foot into the sand. *Real mature.* "This *can't* be happening."

"What?" I bit. "Getting caught trying to kidnap my Familiar?"

"Kidnap!? As if," she growled. "Oberi and I just bonded."

I went still. "How do you know his name?"

"*Her,*" Ava-Marie countered. "Oberi's a *girl.* And I know because I just bonded, like I told you, jackass!"

No way. Professor Baine said Oberi and I shared the same soul. I wasn't about to give joint custody to this stranger. I wanted to snap back at her, but I hesitated. I didn't know much about this world. I needed answers.

"Does that happen often?" I asked.

"What? Two people bonded to the same creature? Of course not!" she cried. "Is this your first day in Kinpago or what?"

I crossed my arms. "Actually, yes."

"You—" Ava-Marie cut off, like it took her a second to process what I'd said. Her tone softened. "This is seriously your first day?"

"Yeah. Some guy named Professor Baine showed up at my apartment and said I had to come learn my powers," I explained.

"*Professor Baine?*" Ava-Marie huffed, before lowering her voice to a mumble. "What the fuck is Grandpa up to now?"

"Excuse me?" I balked. "Did you just say Professor Baine is your *grandfather?*"

Ava-Marie didn't answer. I heard a subtle vibration, and realized she was punching the screen of her phone. I could practically hear smoke coming out her nose as she spoke. "Hi, *Grandpa.* Care to explain what some guy named Charlie is doing on the beach claiming he's bonded to *my* Familiar?"

Professor Baine's voice came from the other end. "Ancestors, Ava. You've *bonded?*"

Ava's voice was seriously irritated. "Kind of not the main issue here. Can you please get down to the beach and convince this... *impostor* how bonding works? We can't be bonded to the same Familiar. It doesn't work like that!"

"I'll be there right away," Professor Baine said. "Don't go anywhere."

Ava-Marie scoffed. "As if. I'm not going anywhere without my Familiar."

Ava's phone vibrated as she hung up, before she directed her anger back at me. "You have real nerve showing up here thinking you can just bond with whomever you want!"

"You say that like I planned this," I shot back. "Oberi came to *me* first."

"*You're* the one who came to Kinpago," she accused. "You should've stayed in whatever hellhole you crawled out of."

My hands curled into fists. Had no one taught this girl manners?

"That hellhole's better than standing here arguing with you," I snapped. "Besides, Oberi didn't find me in Kinpago. He found me in Detroit."

"Sure she did," Ava-Marie said sarcastically. "Because magical creatures just leave the boundaries of the reservation every fucking day."

"Well, *he* left to find me!" I countered.

She gave an obnoxious noise. "There has to be a way we can figure this out fair and square," Ava-Marie insisted.

"What, like put Oberi between us and see who he runs to?" I replied flatly. "That sounds like a great idea."

"Yeah, it does," Ava-Marie sneered. "Oberi, come."

Oberi stood, but I placed a hand on his neck. "No, Oberi," I commanded. "Stay."

He hesitated. I hadn't heard his voice in my head since the night I met him, but I could feel his emotions ebb and flow through the bond. He was conflicted.

Eventually, Oberi settled and obeyed my command, but Ava-Marie wasn't happy about it. "You're being unfair!" she huffed. "Oberi is *my* Familiar!"

Air began rushing toward me a second later. On instinct, I reached out and caught Ava-Marie's wrists before she could shove me backward. She stumbled forward until we were so close I could feel her heartbeat against my chest.

Warmth swelled throughout my abdomen, though I couldn't explain it. I hated this girl, yet something told me to wrap my arms around her and pull her close. The conflicting instincts were enough to make me want to throw up from nausea. Ava-Marie blew a breath of disbelief.

"I wouldn't do that if I were you, pidge," I warned.

"Oh, yeah?" she challenged. "What are you going to do about it?"

I opened my mouth to answer, but I was cut off by the sound of Professor Baine's voice carrying across the beach.

"Ava!" he called.

She shoved herself away from me. Spite filled her voice. "Oh, good. My *gran-pataa* and Aunt Imogen are here. We can finally get some answers."

Professor Baine approached, along with another pair of footsteps. This must've been Ava's aunt. The woman barely made a sound in the sand, like she was walking barefoot. A four-legged creature followed beside her, though I couldn't tell what it was at first. It came up to sniff my feet, and I bent to pet it. The creature was the size of a small dog, with a short nose and pointed ears— a fox.

"What seems to be the problem?" Professor Baine asked.

"Charlie *stole* my Familiar!" Ava-Marie accused.

"Stole?" I nearly choked on my words. "I bonded to him first!"

"Well, I bonded to her, too!" Ava-Marie shouted.

"Oh, dear," Professor Baine mumbled. "This is quite the conundrum, isn't it?"

Ava-Marie blew a breath. "Understatement of the century. Charlie must be lying."

I gritted my teeth. This girl was really starting to get on my nerves.

"Professor," I begged. "You must know I bonded with Oberi. You said yourself it's how you found me!"

"Yes, yes, of course," Professor Baine said, sounding thoughtful.

"Auntie Imogen." Ava-Marie turned to her. "Tell me this isn't possible."

Her aunt sounded intrigued by the whole ordeal. "I've never seen it, but there's a way to find out the truth."

"There is?" Ava asked, relieved. My chest felt lighter.

"Yes," Imogen said. "Professor Baine knows a ceremony that will reveal the truth of the bond. Let's find somewhere comfortable to sit."

Their footsteps shuffled through the sand ahead of me. Oberi nudged my hand, and I placed it on his back. He led me forward, and I followed the three of them to an outcropping of rock.

"It's not far, Charlie," Professor Baine said. "Just a few more steps."

"Thanks," I mumbled, but I was less than grateful. I didn't need to be treated special just because I was blind. I could navigate my own way through this world. Rock and earth were especially easy to maneuver. It was like I could sense them as an extension of myself. They had a vibration of their own, like the air did.

My hand moved over the rock, and I sat down. I listened as Ava plopped onto the rock beside me, and felt Oberi's fur as he sat in the sand between us. Imogen cleared her throat on the other side of her.

"So, how does this work?" Ava asked impatiently.

"It's an ancient Hawkei ceremony," Professor Baine explained. "I will ask the ancestors to reveal the true nature of this creature's bond. You can both relax."

I let my shoulders fall, but it was difficult *relaxing* beside Ava-Marie.

I worried she might grab Oberi and run off with him. She was the kind of dame that would do that.

But she seemed totally chill beside me— like calling upon the ancestors calmed her. To me, this was uncomfortable. I didn't know what the hell to expect.

Professor Baine began speaking in a language I didn't recognize. After a few moments, Ava gasped.

"What?" I asked breathlessly. "What is it?"

"Oh, it's *beautiful*," Ava practically sang. She leaned toward me slightly and spoke lowly, as to not interrupt her grandpa. "Ancestral light is swirling around Oberi. It has so many colors... like a watercolor painting. I wish you could see it."

I scoffed. Fat chance of that.

Professor Baine continued the strange incantation. The wind picked up around us, and Oberi barked. Goosebumps broke out along my skin, and a shiver traveled down my spine.

"What's happening now?" I asked Ava-Marie.

"The Spirit magic is shifting. It's breaking into two long tendrils and — ah!"

I felt it the same time she gasped. A warm energy shot straight into my chest. I jumped at first, until I noticed a calm wind wash over me. It was like touching Oberi for the first time all over again. I reached my fingers up to my chest, and they passed through a strange energetic current.

"What the hell?" I muttered.

"It's Spirit magic," Ava explained, but she sounded angry. "And it's connecting *both* of us to Oberi!"

"Ancestors!" Imogen breathed. "Professor, do you know what this means?"

"Th-this can't be," Professor Baine stuttered.

"How is this possible?" Ava demanded.

"What?" I asked. "What's going on?"

"You were right," Imogen said. "You're *both* bonded to Oberi."

"Which means you are part of the same soul." Baine sounded like his head was in the clouds. I didn't think he'd ever seen anything like this before. He kicked sand forward onto my shoes as he stumbled and steadied himself on the boulder beside me.

"This makes no sense!" Ava protested.

"It does," Imogen insisted, like she'd just realized something. "Many supernatural races have legends about people sharing the same soul. They call them twin flames. In the Miriamic Coven, identical twins share a soul. In the Hawkei world, you are what's referred to as *minai*."

"But what does that *mean*?" Ava asked. "How could we share a soul?"

Imogen sighed. "The mechanics are unclear. I presume Charlie's older, so when he was born, his soul must've fractured. And you, Ava, are the physical manifestation of what was left of it."

It was too much to wrap my head around. I'd gone speechless. I shared a soul with this strange girl? That couldn't be true.

"What, so I got the shitty half?" she questioned.

Imogen sounded disappointed. "Come on, Ava. It doesn't work that way. You're still your own person, but you and Charlie are connected. Just as your spirit was never complete without your Familiar, you and Charlie are not complete without each other."

I got a sour taste in my mouth. She sounded like she meant it *romantically*.

"So, Ava's like a second Familiar to me?" I asked.

"Don't say it like I'm some sort of *pet*," she growled.

"That's not what I meant," I snapped. God, she knew how to get on my nerves.

"Calm down, children," Professor Baine said. "I believe all Charlie meant was that you two are connected the same as you are connected to Oberi."

"It's not the same thing," Ava insisted.

Professor Baine didn't seem to hear her. "You two must learn to get along, as you will be sharing a Familiar for the rest of your lives."

"I don't want to *share her*," Ava whined.

I'd be damned if I didn't feel the same way. I didn't know Ava. I hadn't had Oberi long, but he meant everything to me. I didn't want to give any of my time with him to this stranger I'd just met.

Ava shifted on her rock, and she leaned down for Oberi. The

moment I heard the rustle of his fur, something changed. I felt it deep down in my belly— like sensing a shift in the air. Oberi's energy suddenly felt less playful and became serious. There was a passion to our connection that felt different from anything I'd ever known.

Imogen and Professor Baine both gasped in unison.

"There's my Oberi I bonded with," Ava-Marie sang in a baby voice. "You're a good girl, aren't you?"

"What happened?" I growled, shooting to my feet. "What'd you do to him?"

"I didn't *do* anything," Ava countered. "Oberi shifted. Come here."

Ava grabbed my hand and yanked me forward so hard, I nearly fell over. She pressed my palm against something warm and soft. Oberi's energy pulsed through my hand, and I splayed my fingers over his form. But he was different. He was taller than I was, and his long husky coat had shrunk to short, velvety fur. I ran my fingers up his snout and felt his ears.

"A-a horse?" I questioned.

"A *unicorn*," Ava corrected. "And she's a girl now."

Curiously, I moved my hand over her forehead, and my fingers curled around a warm, smooth horn. It was enough to nearly knock me off my feet. It felt like some sort of trick, but I knew it was real.

"Oberi's a shifter," Professor Baine said aloud, though it seemed like he said it more for himself than anything.

"Ancestors, this is amazing!" Imogen squealed.

"You've heard of shifting Familiars?" Ava asked, like she'd never heard of one herself. "Does it have to do with sharing a soul? Like she takes one form for Charlie and one for me?"

"No," Imogen said. "I believe Oberi may be a *mutabeecha*."

"A muta-what?" I asked.

"*Mutabeecha*," Imogen repeated. "They're shape-shifting creatures known only to lore. Legend says they can only be found in the spirit realm as a companion to the Great Spirit. I never thought I'd see one with my own eyes."

"Yeah," I deadpanned. "Me, neither."

Ava-Marie was the only one to catch my sarcasm. She scoffed, like it wasn't that funny.

Imogen continued. "*Mutabeecha* take on a single form for every element. The Fire unicorn is obviously for Fire, and the husky must be for Air. She must've appeared to each of you in those forms, because they're your element."

Ava stroked Oberi's nose. "So Oberi has more than *two* forms?"

"If she is, in fact, a *mutabeecha*, she could have as many as five, for each of the five elements," Imogen said.

"*If?*" I asked. "Are there other possibilities?"

"Not that I know of," Imogen admitted. "But it's just so strange to see one. No one's ever encountered one on earth before. They exist only in the afterlife— in spiritual realms."

"The spirit realm?" I asked.

"Don't tell me you've never heard of the Ancestral Lands," Ava said.

What part of *I'm new here* did she not understand?

"Can't say I have," I stated flatly.

Professor Baine was the one to explain. "The Ancestral Lands are our afterlife. It is where the ancestors and the Great Spirit Himself reside."

"So if these... *mutabeecha* only exist in the spirit realm, how does anyone know they exist?" I challenged.

Ava elbowed me lightly in the side. "The ancestors speak to us. We're not totally clueless about the Ancestral Lands."

"Still new to all this, remember?" I sneered.

"Well, you have a lot of catching up to do," Ava-Marie said. It wasn't an insult, but this girl could come across rather harshly.

Professor Baine piped up then. "Which is *precisely* why Ava should show Charlie around."

"*What?*" the two of us yelled at the same time.

Imogen laughed, like we were amusing. I found the whole thing fucking annoying.

"Well, why not?" Professor Baine said, like it was the best idea he'd ever had. "You two share a Familiar. You'll be spending a lot of time together. Ava-Marie can show you around Orenda Academy and get you acquainted with our history."

"More like she'll snatch my Familiar and run off," I accused.

"That's actually not a bad idea," she shot back.

"Ancestors," Imogen groaned. "You sound like your mother, Ava."

"Is that a bad thing?" Ava challenged.

"Unfortunately, you don't have a choice," Professor Baine said. "I may be retired, but as an honorary Head Dean of the academy, I appoint you as Charlie's student guide."

"Student guide!" Ava nearly choked. "That's a pretty hefty demotion from *granddaughter*."

"I don't like this, either," I interjected. "I don't need a guide."

"I'm not doing this to punish either of you," Professor Baine assured us. "But Charlie needs a peer mentor, and you *both* need to learn how to share a Familiar."

"But Grandpa—" Ava started.

"No buts," he said. "My mind is made up. You two will either work together— or compromise the bond with your Familiar. The choice is yours."

👮

SCREW PROFESSOR BAINE. Who the hell did he think he was to make me work with *Ava-Marie?* The girl was insufferable.

We walked along a path toward Orenda Academy— or I assumed that's where we were going. Ava-Marie casually mentioned tar pits in the area. Wouldn't be surprised if she lured me to them and threw me in just so she could have Oberi all to herself.

Then again, the tar pits were probably a lie. Everything else she said sounded like one.

"Grotesque monsters roam the grounds of the school, so you have to be careful which corridors you use," Ava-Marie said. "And don't get caught out at night. That's when the ghosts come out."

I tried to ignore Ava and instead focused on the sound of Oberi's hoofbeats on the path. But her voice was like a mosquito trying to fly into my ear. It wouldn't go away.

"Stop messing with me, pidge," I demanded. "I don't believe in ghosts."

"Why not? You didn't seem to have a problem believing in the ancestors. What's the difference?"

I hesitated. "I don't know. I don't know *what* I believe yet."

"Well, you better believe it, because it's true," she said.

A silent beat passed, and I waited for the confession I knew was coming.

"Okay," she caved. "Maybe I made up the thing about the monsters. And we don't really get ghosts in Kinpago. That's more of a witch thing. But rumor has it the old tower of Orenda Academy is haunted. Most of the castle is new, after it burned down twenty years ago."

"Yeah, okay," I said, still not believing a word she said.

"*Hey,*" Ava-Marie snapped. She stopped ahead of me on the trail. I nearly ran into her, and Oberi stopped at our side. "I may have joked about the monsters, but I do *not* joke about Hawkei war history. My Grandfather Liwanu *died* when the castle burned to the ground. I never even got to meet him. Don't go make me out to be a liar when it comes to shit like this."

My shoulders relaxed, and my tone softened. "Okay, I believe you. What exactly happened in the war?"

Ava huffed and started walking again. "Forget it. It's not like you'll listen to me, anyway."

"That's not true," I countered. "If I'm going to live in this world, I want to know its history and all about the magic."

"Why? So you can challenge me in a magical duel over who gets Oberi?"

I pressed my palm to my face. "Oh, my god. You're impossible. Maybe I *will* battle you if it gets you to shut up."

"How dare you!" she gasped.

Ava seemed less than pleased with me. She quickened her pace and stomped ahead of me on the trail. I stayed close to Oberi, so she could lead me through this unfamiliar terrain.

I got a whole five seconds of reprieve from Ava, before she whirled around and stomped back toward me. "I'm not leaving Oberi."

Neither am I, I thought, though I didn't say anything. The last thing I needed was to fuel this girl's fire. I mean, she literally had Koigni powers. She could fry me in one blow.

We didn't talk again until we made it to the castle. I could tell when we arrived, because the air seemed to expand, giving way to a wide-open courtyard. The sound of students chatting met my ears, and I could sense the air currents of Familiars prowling through the courtyard. Strange animal calls I'd never heard before filled the area. A roar sounded, and I could've sworn it was a lion, but no way were there just *lions* walking around school grounds... right?

There were so many creatures that it was hard to make out all their sounds. I heard the whinny of a horse and the cry of an eagle. Wings flapped overhead, but it was unlike the wings of any bird I'd ever heard. Whatever it was must've had a twenty-foot wingspan.

I reached my senses out wider, and my magic stopped at a tall stone wall a hundred feet ahead of us. Ava hadn't been lying when she called Orenda Academy a castle. It was huge— I could tell by the way the wind currents moved around it.

"Ancestors, I love it here," Ava breathed.

"Is it that great?" I questioned.

"*That great?*" she repeated. "It's the most beautiful building in the world. It's too bad you can't see it."

For once, she actually sounded genuine. It made my insides soften. I caught it immediately, and they went right back to rock solid. I didn't fuck around with emotions. That was a good way to get hurt.

"Can you describe it to me?" I asked, hoping she'd say yes.

"Sure, but you'll have to keep up." Ava spoke as we walked across the courtyard to the castle. "The castle was built long ago by a friend of the Hawkei. The guy was mega-balls rich. After three-quarters of the castle burnt down, they tried to keep the same aesthetic in the rebuild. My parents say they can hardly tell it burnt down. Outside, the walls are made of stone. There are four main towers, and so many beautiful stained-glass windows. I love coming out here around sunset because the dragons like to perch on the spires and watch the ocean."

"Dragons!" I gasped. "There are really dragons here?"

"Well, yeah," she said like it was obvious. "This *is* the Academy of Magical Creatures."

"What other creatures are there?" I asked, intrigued.

Ava stopped just as we started climbing the stairs to what I figured must be the main entrance. She seemed to be taking a calculating survey of the courtyard. "Literally everything. Chimeras, manticores, phoenix, alicorns, griffins— take your pick."

The sound of hooves approached, and warm feathers brushed by my arm.

"Oh, and that was a hippogriff," Ava said.

I couldn't help but gape. I never in a million years would've thought these creatures were real.

Ava-Marie must've noticed the longing in my features, because she whistled and called out to someone she knew. "Hey, Josee!"

A few moments later, sneakers sounded in the grass as someone jogged over. "Hey, Ava. What's up?"

The voice was female— probably a girl around our age.

"I've got a peer mentee," Ava said. "He's blind and has never seen a magical creature before."

Yeah, just go announce it to the world, why don't you? I despised her.

"Could he hold your dracavern?" Ava-Marie asked.

"Yeah, of course," Josee answered, and I heard something preen. "I mean, I don't let just *anyone* hold Cassie, but I can already tell she likes you."

Josee set something warm in my arms. It was barely the size of an infant, but as I ran my fingers over the creature, I realized that it was shaped like a small reptile. It had scales that were cool to the touch, and soft leathery wings that folded over its back. Spines ran along its back and down its tail, but they didn't hurt to touch.

"What's a dracavern?" I asked. "I've never heard of one."

"They're cave dragons," Josee explained. "They're really small, so they can fly through tight caverns."

I stroked Cassie's nose. She sneezed, sending air as cold as ice across my fingers. I jerked my hand away.

"Don't worry. She's harmless," Josee said.

"That was really cold," I said, shivering.

Josee reached out for Cassie and pulled her back into her arms. "Cassie's an ice dracavern."

"I thought dragons would breathe fire," I said.

"Some can," Ava replied. "Depends on the dragon. Come on, Charlie. I'll show you inside the school."

For a second, it was like Ava had forgotten our disagreement. She was too wrapped up in the magnificence of the academy as we said goodbye to Josee and moved on.

"This is the Grand Entryway," Ava-Marie explained. "You might be able to feel it with your Air magic, but the foyer reaches up five stories. There's a balcony on each one. What you may not be able to feel is the *ah-mazing* chandelier above us. It's gold-plated and has real diamonds!"

"Holy shit," I breathed. That chandelier sounded crazy expensive. How did the Hawkei afford it?

"I know, right?" Ava said. "It took the Hawkei ages to rebuild that after this section burnt down. It wasn't cheap."

"No kidding. You aren't lying to me again, are you?"

Ava scoffed. "About Orenda Academy? Fuck, no!"

"How do the Hawkei afford it, though?" I questioned. "This isn't exactly what I pictured when I was told I was coming to a reservation."

I'd never been to a native reservation before, but from what I'd heard, most indigenous nations were deep in poverty. It was common to experience overcrowded and inadequate housing, without luxuries like running water and electricity— along with underfunded healthcare.

"Don't get me started on the living conditions of Native Americans," Ava growled. "It's disgusting the way the government treats us. Luckily for us, the Hawkei have money."

"But how?" I asked. "Casinos, or what?"

Ava-Marie laughed. "No. We make our money on magical exports. It makes for a very comfortable lifestyle for the tribe."

"Magical exports? You don't ship off magical creatures, do you?"

"What? No." Ava sounded offended. "We sell things like unicorn hair and dragon scales to other magical societies. It's harmless, but we're the only suppliers, so we can charge whatever we want. The tribe makes bank off it. Anyway, shall we move on?"

Ava continued leading me through the castle. She spoke fast and skimmed over details, like she expected me to already know them. We turned so many hallways I couldn't make sense of where I was, and I was usually great at mapping out my surroundings. I had to be.

Eventually, Ava led me outside. Floral scents hit my nose, and the air seemed clean. A few people walked around, but their footsteps were quiet and serene. Even Oberi's hoofbeats beside me seemed calmer.

"What is this?" I asked. "A garden?"

"Are you *sure* you're blind?" Ava sounded skeptical.

"There's more to seeing than looking with your eyes," I told her.

"What do you mean?"

"Come here." I reached out for Ava's shoulders and situated her in front of me. Gently, I placed my hand over her eyes, just to make sure she wouldn't cheat. "Stand here and close your eyes."

"Um... okay."

"What can you see?" I asked.

"Not a damn thing," she said flatly.

"What about the bee buzzing near the rose bushes?" I questioned.

Ava shrugged. "A wild guess, perhaps? How do you know those are rose bushes?"

"I can smell them," I told her. "The flap of the bee's wings is unique — unless you have some weird magical insects around here, too."

"No, just bees," she said.

"What else can you see?" I pressed.

Ava quieted. A nice few moments, for once.

"I hear heavy hooves two paths over," she said. "Someone's Familiar... a unicorn, maybe? And there's laughter outside the garden. Two people... a boy and a girl. I think they're flirting."

Ava went quiet again. In the silence, it was actually really nice to be around her. Her shoulder was warm under my hand, and her eyelashes tickled the palm that was covering her face. A light breeze passed by us, and her hair brushed across my cheek. She had a really nice scent— like raspberries.

"I smell all kinds of flowers, but there are too many to make out the varieties," Ava continued. "In the middle of the garden is a fountain. I can hear it trickling, but it's muffled by the bushes around us. There's a bird perched atop the totem pole."

I could hear the bird chirping, but I'd missed the totem pole altogether. "How do you know what it's sitting on?"

Ava shrugged again. "I've visited the gardens before and know the layout. The totem pole is the most important part of the gardens. It was built after the fire as a memorial to those who died."

I listened closer and realized she must be telling the truth. The bird's call was high above us, but wasn't muffled by any branches or leaves.

"And where's the path?" I asked.

Ava swallowed. "Straight ahead."

"How would you know that without seeing it?" I wanted to get her to think. If we were going to be spending time together like Professor Baine said, I needed her to understand how I saw the world.

Ava-Marie thought about it for a few beats. "I can tell where the bushes are because of the way sound travels through the gardens. They absorb it— like you can sense a wall there."

Ava's shoulder moved, and she reached out to the nearest flower bush. "And I can feel the bushes, too. I don't have to see them to know they're there."

I leaned into her without realizing it. My nose was only an inch from her hair. That sweet scent of hers filled my nostrils. I came in so close my front pressed against her backside. Adrenaline surged through my chest and downward.

Holy shit!

I leapt backward, nearly tripping over Oberi's hoof. Ava cleared her throat and broke the spell. All the serenity within the garden seemed to wash away. It didn't seem like a calm place anymore, not the way my heart was racing.

"Get it now?" I asked. "I don't need my vision to see the world around me. You might be surprised at how much I see. Perhaps sometimes more than you, pidge."

Ava stayed far away from me near one of the rose bushes. She snapped a flower off and started picking at the petals. I could feel each one flutter to the ground when she dropped it.

"That was a nice lesson, but I think the tour's over," she said. "It sounds like you can navigate the academy just fine yourself, so we can go our separate ways now."

One semi-nice moment with her, and she was already back to her normal self. *Great.*

Fine. If she didn't want me around, I didn't have to be here.

"Oberi and I will just find our way back to my dorm room, then," I said. "Professor Baine hooked me up with a sweet room this morning."

"No way!" Ava protested, grabbing me by the arm before I could get anywhere. Her hand was scalding, which I mistook as some sort of passion at first— until I remembered she had Fire power. "You're not going anywhere with Oberi."

"Well, I'm not leaving her!" I insisted.

Ava-Marie dropped my arm. "I can't be left alone without her. I just bonded."

"She has to sleep somewhere. She can't stay with us both tonight," I argued.

"You're right." Ava put herself between Oberi and me. "Oberi will stay with me."

"That's not fair! I bonded first."

"Like that makes you special," she spat. "How am I supposed to secure my bond with my Familiar if you're always around?"

"What do you mean, *secure your bond*?" Professor Baine had never mentioned it.

Ava sighed, like she didn't care to explain. She did anyway. "When you bond, you make a magical connection, but the emotional one isn't there immediately. Every Elementai has to go through something diffi-cult— usually traumatic— with their Familiar to make that emotional bond. Only then will your powers reach their full potential. I can't fully bond with Oberi with you in the way."

I raised my eyebrows. "We have to go through something traumatic? Oberi and I should be good after a few days listening to *you* talk."

Ava gasped. "You're an asshole, you know that?"

I leaned in to whisper to her. "And proud of it, pidge. I'd rather be an asshole than spend another minute with you."

"You *jerk!*" Ava shoved me backward, though I barely moved. "We can't share a Familiar. This is never going to work."

Oberi huffed and stomped her hoof, like our fighting was bothering her.

"Great, now you've upset Oberi," I growled. "We obviously don't like listening to you *whine*."

"I do not whine!" she protested.

"You're the definition of a cry baby!" I shot back.

"You're just mean," she snapped. "You've already had plenty of time with Oberi. It's my turn. I need her tonight."

"You're a stranger," I argued. "It will scare Oberi to be without me."

Ava started leading Oberi down the path, but I grabbed her hands to stop her. She shrugged me off. "Oberi is *my* Familiar. We may have just met, but I've known her my whole life!"

"That makes no sense. We need to figure something out."

"Like what?" Ava challenged. "Neither of us wants to leave her. We can't just sleep on the couches in the Commons all semester. She'll sleep in my dorm tonight. It's my turn with Oberi."

I groaned. "*Your turn.* What the hell do you think Oberi is, a toy?"

Oberi whinnied to get our attention, but neither of us responded.

"I'm just trying to protect my Familiar," I insisted.

"Don't forget she's *mine,* too," Ava hissed. "I can do with her whatever I like."

Ava-Marie started walking away again. Oberi seemed indecisive for a moment, then I heard the sound of her hooves beneath her.

"Ava, wait!" I reached out for her arm again.

"Back *off!*" Ava's skin turned red-hot, burning my hand.

I jumped back. That freaking *hurt.*

"Don't touch me, or my Familiar!" Ava shouted.

I heard the crackle of the fireball before it left her hand. Instinctively, I shot my hands up in front of my face. I didn't know how I did it, but the air followed my command. It blasted backward, and the fireball changed direction. It crashed into a bush nearby, and my stomach plummeted. Heat rolled off it in waves as the whole thing lit aflame in seconds.

My nostrils flared. "Pidge, what'd you do?"

"Me?" Ava-Marie sputtered, like she couldn't believe her eyes. "You should've let the fireball hit you!"

"Yeah, because that was the smart idea," I said sarcastically. "Can't you put it out? You have Fire power."

"I'm trying!" she growled through gritted teeth. "I can't work my magic when you're yelling at me. Fuck!"

I knew what was wrong the moment Ava-Marie cursed. The fire was getting hotter and louder. I didn't know how many bushes it'd consumed already, but the magical Fire was spreading quickly, eating away at the garden far faster than any normal flame.

"Oberi's a Fire creature!" I realized. "Oberi, help!"

Oberi whinnied, as if to tell me she was doing her best.

My pulse pounded in my ears. We were in so much fucking trouble.

Polluted air filled my lungs. My eyes burned, and I struggled to breathe. I tried commanding the air around the Fire. Maybe if I could pull the oxygen away, the Fire would die out. But I barely knew how to control my element. My magic did nothing but make it worse.

"Ava, we have to go!" I yanked on her wrist, but she stayed put.

"I can do this!" she promised. "I can put it out!"

"If you could put it out, it'd be out already," I argued. "We have to go get help!"

"*Fuuuck!*" she shouted.

"What now?" I groaned.

"The Fire's heading toward the totem pole!" she screamed. "We have to— ancestors!"

Ava-Marie went totally breathless. I thought she might collapse beside me. I knew by the sound of her voice that the totem pole had caught fire. My stomach plummeted as the sound of Fire crackled. The smell of paint and burning wood filled my nostrils.

"No!" Ava-Marie wailed. It was obvious the totem pole meant a lot to her— to the tribe.

Across the garden, people began to scream. Some were fleeing, while others were calling for help.

"Ava... there's nothing... we can do," I said through coughs.

Just then, the doors to the school burst open. Heels clicked against the stone path. Air billowed around the newcomer, as if she wore a long velvet dress. Two other sets of footsteps followed her.

"Ava-Marie!" the woman sounded worried. "What happened?"

"It was an accident," Ava said. At least she was telling the truth.

I barely sensed the woman flick her wrist, and I felt the heat in the gardens recede as the Fire started to die down. She must've been a very powerful Fire Elementai to control such a large fire, whoever she was.

I drew in a deep breath, happy to be able to breathe again. Being without air was literally one of my worst fears.

"I don't *believe* this," the woman gasped. "The memorial totem pole... it's been destroyed!"

"You don't understand, Grandmother," Ava pleaded.

"Grandmother?" The word slipped out of my mouth.

The woman turned to me and snapped, "That's Head Dean Doya to you, *boy*."

My jaw dropped open. Ava and I had nearly burnt down the entire Orenda Academy gardens, and we'd been caught by the Head Dean? Could this day get any worse?

"I understand more than you know," Head Dean Doya said. She spoke in such a refined and dignified way, it was nearly off-putting. "Your grandfather just stopped by. Care to explain?"

When Ava didn't respond, I realized she wasn't asking her. "Me?" I questioned.

"Yes, you," Doya snapped. "What could possibly possess you to light the school grounds on fire?"

Whoa. This woman seriously thought *I* was to blame?

Of course she did— because her precious granddaughter could do no wrong.

"It wasn't me," I said. "I don't have Fire power."

Head Dean Doya gasped. "Ava-Marie. You *didn't*!"

"Charlie made it worse with his Air magic!" she said, like that helped the argument.

One of the people who'd followed the Head Dean outside stepped forward. "Head Dean, if I may," a man cut in. "Student duels are against school policy outside of class. Precisely for the danger they pose, such as in this instance."

"Come *on*, Bren," a second man with a much deeper voice said. "I'm sure Ava-Marie didn't mean it."

"Uncle Jonah's right," Ava said. "I didn't mean it."

Seriously, was this girl related to half of Kinpago or something? She had connections everywhere.

"You threw a fireball at my head, pidge," I reminded her.

"Ava's only nineteen," Jonah said. "We can't expect her to control her powers at all times. I'm sure it won't happen again."

Head Dean Doya sighed. "Forgive me, Dean Chanee, but I believe Dean Emberly is right. I can't be seen playing favorites as the Head Dean."

Her voice became even more stern. "Accident or not, what happened here must have consequences."

"You can't seriously be punishing me, Grandmother!" Ava said. "I only just got here! Can't I be let off with a warning?"

"Oh, I think you misunderstand me, Ava-Marie," Head Dean Doya said. "*I* will not be punishing you at all. It would be a conflict of interest, and unfortunately, destruction of tribal property— even on school grounds— is within the Elders' jurisdiction. You will have to appeal to them regarding what happened here today."

I smirked and gave Ava a salute. "Nice knowing ya, pidge."

"This isn't fair!" Ava-Marie shouted.

"Ava, I have let you slip up too many times without any consequences," Doya barked. "Do not expect me to keep making allowances for you."

Ava-Marie didn't give any backtalk, for once in her goddamn life. It was clear she respected this woman.

"And *you*," the Head Dean added. "Mr..."

"Wahkin," I told her. "Mr. Wahkin, ma'am."

"Mr. Wahkin," she repeated. "Don't think that you're getting off scot-free. It seems that you had just as much a part in this duel as my granddaughter."

I could hardly believe my ears. I get attacked, and *I'm* the one being blamed for the arson? What kind of messed up society was this?

"You will both appear before the Elder Council," Head Dean Doya said. "You are both responsible, and therefore, whatever the Elders have in store for you, you shall both endure. You better get used to it."

That was all she said before she turned on her heel and started back toward the castle. My body gave a shudder in the silence that stretched between Ava and me.

Something told me Head Dean Doya was referring to far more than this minor infraction. Ava-Marie and I shared a soul— and a Familiar. Whatever happened to one of us happened to us both.

I wasn't eager to find out what sort of trouble Ava-Marie might get us into next.

THREE DAYS PASSED before our hearing, and Ava-Marie was getting on my nerves more than ever. We couldn't agree on how to handle this situation, so Oberi more or less came and went as he pleased. Kind of pissed me off when he disappeared to go find Ava. My first companion, and he was already ditching me on the daily. Made me want to stay here *so* bad.

Professor Baine claimed Kinpago was where I belonged, but I didn't feel like I fit in. I was more comfortable sleeping under a bridge than in the private suite in the Yapluma dorms they'd given me they called a "dorm room." It all felt like some sort of joke— like they were going to come knocking on my door one day and ask for their hundred grand to cover my tuition.

I wasn't used to staying in fancy places. I'd gone from a shitty apartment in Detroit to living in a palace. It was too much too soon.

It felt somewhat appropriate to find myself in a courtroom my first week here. Honestly, being prosecuted felt like the most familiar thing I'd experienced in Kinpago. I'd frequently gotten into trouble with the law before, for minor infractions, so going in front of a judge was something I was used to— so much so that it was nearly comforting.

I hadn't really thought things would go this way, though. Had someone told me a week ago this is where I'd be sitting, I would've thought it'd be for petty theft— not whatever the hell this was.

"Ava's late," Professor Baine grumbled. He sat beside me in the courtroom, tapping his foot impatiently. He was the only person I really knew in Kinpago, so he'd offered to accompany me to the hearing. He never outright said it, but I think he felt bad for me, because he knew this was all Ava's fault.

Oberi sat near my feet, licking his paws. He'd shown up that morning in my dorm room after I'd woken up. I stroked the top of his head to calm myself. There were others in the courtroom, too, but everyone spoke in low whispers. In the row just behind me, a man and a woman sounded worried for Ava. I guessed those to be her parents. Someone fidgeted beside them— a sibling, perhaps?

Not far from them, I recognized her Aunt Imogen and Uncle Jonah's voices. There were two other men with them, but I couldn't tell who they were. I didn't think I'd met them. At the table across from us, a man kept clearing his throat impatiently. I could hear the occasional pound of hooves on the hardwood floor.

"Don't worry," Head Dean Doya said to Ava's parents. "You know the Elders never go too hard on Ava."

"They're too scared of Liam," her mother joked.

"I'm *not* scary," her father argued.

"When it comes to your daughter you are," Ava's mother said.

"This isn't Ava's fault," her father huffed. "It's *that boy's.*"

I whirled around in my chair. "*That boy* is innocent. If your daughter told you otherwise, she's a liar."

"How dare you speak of my daughter like that!" the man boomed.

"Liam," Professor Baine warned. Somehow, he was able to calm the situation.

After a few moments to steady my breath, I turned to Professor Baine. "What should I expect?"

"You and Ava will get a chance to plead your case," Baine explained. "Then the Elders will read you your sentence."

"Who are the Elders, exactly?" I asked.

"In Hawkei society, each House has a chief and four Elders to represent them, for a total of twenty-five members on the Elder Council. This is a minor case, so you'll appeal to a panel of three Elders who will determine your sentencing. The panel has been chosen to avoid any bias, so you won't see any Toaqua behind the judge's table."

"Why not?" I questioned.

"Well, because Ava's the daughter of the Water chief," Professor Baine said simply.

"Seriously?" I gaped. No wonder she had so much privilege.

Professor Baine sounded confused. "I thought she would've told you."

I scoffed. "Believe me, Ava doesn't say much."

"Huh. She's usually quite the chatterbox."

"Oh, hell yeah. She just doesn't say anything that matters."

Just then, the doors to the courtroom burst open dramatically. It got loud as everyone turned and started whispering.

"I hope you haven't started without me," Ava announced loudly, her heels clicking as she walked to the front of the room. God, she sounded like she was the guest of honor, not some criminal about to be read their sentence. How did I get wrapped up with a girl like her?

"I had a minor wardrobe malfunction," Ava said, like that excused her late arrival. "Nothing to worry about. I got it all sorted out."

The whispers quieted down as Ava took a seat beside the man at the other table. "Ava," he hissed. "That outfit is hardly appropriate for the courtroom."

Ava's fingers brushed across the fabric. "What's wrong with pink, Sean?"

"For the last time, I am your lawyer. You may call me Mr. Andre."

Lawyer? I hardly thought she needed one for this.

"With all due respect, *Mr. Andre*, I love pink. I think this power suit is fantastic on me. My ass looks great."

"Ancestors help us," Mr. Andre mumbled.

A voice came from near the judge's table. "All stand in honor of the Elder Council— Koigni Chieftess Vanessa Emberly, Yapluma Elder Riley Brandt, and Nivita Elder Sam Gardner."

I stood with everyone else. Doors at the corner of the room opened, and three Elders came breezing in. Air billowed off their judge's robes, and their footsteps echoed as they climbed the steps to their table.

"You may be seated," the female chieftess said. Once the courtroom quieted, she spoke again. "We are here today to address the case of the Hawkei Tribe versus Ava-Marie Mitoh and Charlie Wahkin. Both are charged with co-perpetrating an underage magical duel, destruction of tribal property, and vandalism."

Ava-Marie shot out of her chair. "Objection, Your Honor!"

Chieftess Vanessa spoke calmly. "Please, Ava. There is no need. You will have a chance to plead your case. First, the Elder Council would like to hear from Mr. Wahkin. Mr. Wahkin, can you tell us exactly what happened regarding the events of August twenty-fourth?"

I leaned over to Professor Baine. "Do I have to go to the witness stand?"

"No, no," he assured me. "Just stand right here and tell your side of the story."

I nodded, then cleared my throat and stood. "Your Honors, the events of August twenty-fourth began as a disagreement between Miss Mitoh and I over my Familiar." I gestured to the husky beside me. "She threw a fireball at my head, and I deflected it with my Air. It was pure instinct."

"See? He *admits* it was his fault!" Ava cried.

I kept my cool. "On the contrary, just the opposite. Miss Mitoh was the one to attack. I was only acting in self-defense."

"I see, Mr. Wahkin," Chieftess Vanessa said. "We will take that into consideration. If I may, what exactly was the disagreement about your Familiar about?"

I cleared my throat, stalling. I waited for Professor Baine to give me some sort of advice, but he remained silent. "Well, you see, Your Honor... Ava and I *both* bonded to Oberi."

Gasps traveled around the courtroom. One of the Elders smacked their gavel at the front of the room.

"Order!" Chieftess Vanessa yelled. "Mr. Wahkin, that's impossible."

"I'm afraid not, Chieftess," Professor Baine piped up. "I performed the identification ceremony myself. Ava-Marie and Charlie do, in fact, share a Familiar."

"O-oh," Chieftess Vanessa stammered. "Well, this is... new. I'm afraid it won't impact the outcome of this hearing, but we will certainly take note of this. Miss Mitoh, is there anything you'd like to add?"

Ava's chair screeched across the floor as she stood. Her lawyer cleared his throat, but Ava stopped him. "I've got this, Sean. I can speak for myself."

Ava's heels clicked against the floor as she stepped out from behind the table. She began pacing in front of the judges. "August twenty-fourth was meant to be the greatest day of my life— the day I bonded. It was a beautiful, brisk day. The ocean waves were rolling across the sand, and the sun was shining its beautiful blessing down upon me, when to my surprise, a magnificent creature stepped onto the beach. The moment I touched her, my whole world titled on its axis. It was as if a Vincent van Gogh painting had come to life, or an original Shakespeare play was happening before my eyes. It was like—"

"Ava, we don't have all day," Chieftess Vanessa said calmly. "Can you just tell us what happened?"

Ava turned on her heel and finally stopped pacing. "Chieftess, do you remember what it was like to bond?"

"Of course I do, but this isn't my hearing," she said flatly.

"Then you must know how special it should be!" Ava-Marie said passionately. "But I was *robbed* of the experience by none other than Charlie Wahkin!"

I leaned over to whisper to Professor Baine. "She's pointing at me, isn't she?"

He chuckled lightly. "Yes."

"Charlie Wahkin *stole* my Familiar, Your Honors," Ava claimed. "He bonded with her first and yanked the most precious experience of my life right out from under me. And that's not the only thing he's taken from me! Your Honors, he *stole my wallet!*"

"Oh my god," I mumbled. Could this girl get any more infuriating?

"Charlie Wahkin is a thief," Ava accused. "If anyone should be sentenced today, it is the man sitting in that chair."

"Still pointing at me, huh?" I asked Professor Baine. I *so* wasn't amused.

"Mr. Wahkin, is that true?" Chieftess Vanessa asked. "Did you really steal Miss Mitoh's wallet?"

I could've strangled this girl. "Your Honor, I found it after she bumped into me. I intended to return it."

It wasn't a total lie. I *had* found it— on her. And I'd gladly give the *wallet* back, but I was keeping the money.

"Then why haven't you?" Ava-Marie demanded. "Stealing my wallet wasn't enough, was it? You had to go steal my Familiar, too. Are you starting a collection of all things *Ava* now? Are you obsessed?"

"God, no," I snapped. "I'd rather I never met you."

A gavel pounded, and Chieftess Vanessa called out, "Order! Miss

Mitoh, please take your seat. If the defendants have nothing else to add to their statements, we can proceed to sentencing."

I couldn't exactly add what I was thinking. *Ava-Marie is a psycho bitch who needs to stay the hell away from me.*

"That's all, Your Honor," Ava said, before taking her seat. "I rest my case."

Chieftess Vanessa shifted in her chair. "Very well. The council will take a brief intermission to consult on this hearing."

The gavel banged again, and the Elders shuffled out of the courtroom to speak quietly. Before they left, I heard one of the male Elders whisper to the other. "Ava-Marie *can't* keep showing up here. We let it slide every time. We can't keep giving any more favors to her parents."

"Agreed," the other replied. "Something's got to happen this time."

That was all I heard before the doors shut behind them. Meanwhile, the courtroom got loud again as people started whispering.

A bit of rage burned in my guts. Ava-Marie was a spoiled little rich girl who had powerful parents and too many friends. I'd never had such favoritism in the court system. The government had never failed to throw the book at me. Why not her, too?

"Oberi," Ava called. "Oberi, come get a treat."

A bag rustled open, and the smell of dog treats wafted over to me. Oberi perked up and padded over to Ava across the aisle.

"Ugh, you have to be kidding me," I groaned. "Oberi doesn't like dog treats, pidge."

"How would *you* know?" she snarled.

"Because I tried feeding him some the other day," I told her.

Oberi's teeth clicked together as he chewed on the treats.

"Well, he likes *my* treats," Ava said proudly. "They're homemade."

I scoffed. "With what? The blood of your enemies?"

Ava laughed, but it wasn't cute or sexy. It sounded evil. "Not a bad idea, Charlie. I'll use your blood next time."

"Ava!" her mother scolded.

I crossed my arms and turned away from Ava-Marie. I'd quickly learned the best way to get her to shut up was to stop talking myself. The girl always had to get the last word in. It wasn't worth it with her.

It wasn't long before the Elder Council returned. They called the court to order again, and everything went quiet.

Chieftess Vanessa cleared her throat. "In the case of the Hawkei Tribe versus Ava-Marie Mitoh and Charlie Wahkin, the defendants have been charged with three misdemeanors and are hereby sentenced to eighty hours of community service and six months of probation."

My shoulders immediately relaxed. I could live with this. It was basically a slap on the wrist.

Ava-Marie, on the other hand, was furious. She slammed her hands down on the table as she shot to her feet. "Community service! *Probation?* I can't have a misdemeanor on my record, let alone three!"

Chieftess Vanessa didn't sound amused. "It's not as bad as it sounds, Miss Mitoh. Be glad we're not sending you to the Darke Institute, because the next time we find you in court, rest assured, you *will* be going there. This is your last warning. If you mess up again, you will leave us no choice."

A shiver ran down my spine at the name. The Darke Institute. Hell yeah, I was glad I wasn't going there. It sounded ominous as hell.

"But I'm the daughter of a chief! You can't do this to me!" Ava burst.

"Ava, peanut," her father said softly as he approached her. "It's only community service. As long as you're on your best behavior, you won't even notice the probation."

"That's not the point, Daddy!" Ava cried. Like literally *cried.* "Charlie stole my Familiar. Now he's stolen the next six months of my life. It's not fair!"

My stomach twisted. Could she really blame me for this?

"Ava..." I stood and reached out for her. I didn't know why— I just felt like I had to comfort her. Maybe I could talk some sense into her. I'd seen so much shit go down in the legal system. This was nothing.

"Get away from me!" Ava-Marie snapped. "I don't want anything to do with you. Thanks for ruining my life!"

Ava-Marie took off running out of the courtroom. I couldn't *stand* this girl, and yet a part of me couldn't help but feel sorry for her. It had to be the whole soul-connection thing, because I sure as hell didn't feel bad about her sentencing. Maybe a little community service would do her some good.

Oberi whined at my side. I sighed. "Yeah, boy. You might as well go after her. She needs you."

Oberi nudged his head into my hand, then ran off behind Ava. I could still hear Ava-Marie's cries echo down the hall.

Dear God. What had I gotten myself into?

FOUR

Fuck Charlie Wahkin. He could go straight to hell.

I had to get up early to attend community service. Oberi wasn't with me— my Familiar spent most of the time with Charlie.

I *hated* him. He'd had more time with Oberi, and as a result, she was closer to him than me. The one thing I'd been looking forward to was having a Familiar, and he'd messed that up. I felt incredibly alone, and it was all his fault.

I made sure to wear something cute— because maybe my probation officer was hot— before I went downstairs. When I got there, Daddy, Mama, and Grandpa Elliot— or as Charlie called him, *Professor Baine*— were all sitting around the table near the kitchen. They weren't eating anything, and like hawks, their eyes fixated on me once I walked into the room.

Oh, great. Another intervention, *again*.

"Guys, can we please save the guilt trip for later? I'm so not in the mood."

"Honey, we need to talk about this," Mama started. "Sit down."

I groaned and made a show of dragging myself into a chair and collapsing into it. Daddy rolled his eyes.

Mama folded her hands and sat forward. "Ava, we're all concerned. I think it's obvious that if your father wasn't who he was, you'd be in hot water right now."

I scoffed. "Please. The Elders won't touch me."

"And that's the problem! You believe you don't need any consequences." Daddy was already irritated. I noticed he had more bags than usual under his eyes. He was exhausted. Had I done that?

"Your father's right," Grandpa Elliot broke in. "This has been going on for too long."

Grandpa pulled out a list. "As of right now, Ava's current list of infractions include arson—"

"That was an accident. I'd just gotten my Fire. I didn't know how to use it," I argued.

"Minor shoplifting—"

"It was just a dare." I hadn't meant to steal the shoes *and* the sweater, just the shoes. It was a harmless freaking game. I was going to bring them back.

"Property Damage—"

"That was a good one."

"Possession of Supernatural Contraband—"

"Like love potions should be illegal."

"Grand theft auto—"

"*Grand theft auto?!*" both of my parents screamed at once.

"Grandpa, you weren't supposed to tell them about that one," I growled. They knew about all the others.

"You stole a *car?*" Daddy yelled. Holy ancestors, he was mad.

"It was just a little joyride. Nothing serious," I said. If looks could kill, I'd be a puddle on the ground right now.

"It took some convincing to get her out of that one, along with a large bribe," Grandpa Elliot said. "Though the record still stands."

"I can't believe you bought her out of a car theft charge and didn't inform us," Mama snapped. "This is out of line."

"Well... look at her. She's so sweet." Grandpa Elliot gave me a warm smile, and I flashed one back.

"That's because she's so innocent looking! She wouldn't have gotten away with half of this crap if she wasn't so damn cute! People give her whatever she wants," Daddy bellowed.

"Like you can talk, Liam." Mama was fuming. My charm wouldn't work on her, and unlike Daddy, she looked *scary*. I was surprised her hair hadn't caught fire.

"None of this stuff should be illegal, anyway. No one's getting hurt. It's all in good fun," I argued.

"You can't think that way," Grandpa Elliot insisted. "You're on probation. That means no trouble of any kind. If you miss community service or reporting to your officer, it's immediate jail time."

I huffed. Like that would ever happen.

"Ava, you've got an addiction for causing trouble. You're always pushing to see how far you can go. It's like you need the adrenaline rush," Daddy said.

"Oh, gee, I wonder where she gets *that* from," Mama said sarcastically.

Daddy narrowed his eyes, and Grandpa Elliot stepped in.

"Look, the bottom line is, Ava's record is far from clean," Grandpa Elliot said firmly. "We can go on about this all day, but even if she wiggles out of this one and attends Orenda Academy, employment will be difficult for her to obtain after graduation. No one will want to hire her with a track record like this."

He sighed. "But there is another option— the Darke Institute. If she attends the Institute, she'll be given a clean slate. Opportunities will be better for her."

Fear wasn't a common emotion for me. I wasn't scared of much. But the Darke Institute was one of those things I *was* afraid of. I didn't know much about it, but I did know it was where the magical world shipped all their bad kids— and that it had been brought up as an option for me several times in court.

"You guys can't be serious about sending me to a prison for supernatural delinquents," I stated flatly.

"It's a reform school!" Grandpa Elliot protested.

"It's a *prison*," I clarified.

Just then, the doors blew open with all the fury of hell. Grandmother Eleanor strode in with her head held high, her dress billowing around her. I always admired how good my grandmother could look while scaring the living daylights out of people. I wanted to have nice hair when I was mowing people over.

Mama's gaze hardened when she looked at her mother. I sensed there was going to be an argument.

"My dear, we weren't expecting you." Grandpa Elliot shrank under her harsh gaze. He lost a foot in height.

Grandmother Eleanor's eyebrows pinched as she raged, and she placed a manicured hand on her elegant hip before jutting it out sharply. "I will bring hell down upon *anyone* who forces my granddaughter to attend an institution for low-life thugs. There won't be a school left standing when I'm done!"

"Grandmother, you were the one who sent me to court in the first place," I mumbled.

"I *am* Head Dean. I have to keep up appearances, and I can't let others see my granddaughter getting special privilege," Grandmother Eleanor argued. "Even if you *do* get it behind closed doors."

Grandpa Elliot always cowered to Grandmother. He said nothing in protest, but Mama stood up. "No. I'm sorry, but this has gone on long enough."

"Sophia, don't be delusional," Grandmother snapped. "Ava-Marie doesn't belong in a prison academy."

"Maybe she does." Mama turned to Daddy. "Liam, we've tried everything to help Ava, and it hasn't worked. The Institute might not be such a bad idea. Maybe this is the help she needs."

"Can you stop talking about me like I'm not even here?" I asked, but Mama didn't even acknowledge me. I hated her saying that I needed *help*. I didn't need *help*. I was fine.

Daddy's look was cold. "Have you forgotten what Maddie told us about the Institute years ago?"

"I am aware," Mama replied. "But we can look into it. Maybe things have changed."

My ears perked up at that. Aunt Maddie was my dad's sister. She wasn't just an elemental— she was a *naderei*, a prophet. She could foresee the future. Had my aunt seen something about the Institute that was a threat?

"What did Aunt Maddie say?" I leaned forward, keen on finding out.

"Never you mind," Daddy said. "The bottom line is, you're not going anywhere near the Darke Institute. That's the end of it."

Mama let out an angry breath, but didn't add anything more. I should've been relieved— I really didn't want to be sentenced to the Institute.

But he *told me no*. And that was always the first way to catch my interest. Why didn't he want me going there?

I decided I needed to find out.

"You're going to be late, Ava," Daddy said with a look at the clock. "Run along."

He still talked to me like I was a little girl. I couldn't decide if I loved it or hated it. I grabbed my purse and left. I was sure the four of them weren't done with this conversation, and were having a talk on what to do with me.

It was ridiculous. Didn't anybody care to ask what I wanted?

My probation officer *was not* hot. He led me to a local park. Charlie and Oberi were already there. My heart started when I saw Oberi, though my mood totally soured when I saw Charlie. He was scanning the ground for garbage using a trash picker and putting it into a bag.

Oberi was in his husky form. He barked, then changed when he saw me, transforming into the unicorn mare.

I rubbed Oberi's head as she came to me. "Hey, girl. How are you?"

Oberi nickered. The probation officer handed me a bag and a trash pick. "You'll be cleaning up the park today. Once this place is spotless, you can go."

Red cups were everywhere. A bunch of kids had a party here last night. I wrinkled my nose, but I knew complaining wasn't going to do me any good, so I got to work.

Oberi stabbed cups with her horn and put them into my bag as we walked. Charlie kept silent. The probation officer watched us carefully as we cleaned up the area. I was already bored. It didn't take long for me to lose interest, and I was thinking of ways to get myself out of this.

"You think if I run he'll catch me?" I asked Charlie under my breath.

I didn't like him, but I needed someone to talk to out here. The silence was deafening.

Charlie's look was incredulous. "Picking up trash too much work for you, princess?"

"No," I shot back. "I just have better things to do."

"Fuck that." His tone was pissed. "I'm not letting you run off and get us into more trouble."

"You wouldn't be able to stop me."

Charlie's features blazed. "Try me."

"Believe me, I'd love to." Running off would be a stupid idea, but at least it'd bring some excitement. This job was *so dull.*

"You're such a brat." Charlie steamed. "Someone should teach you some manners."

"Like you?" I stood in front of Charlie and got so close I could feel his breath on my cheek. His body stiffened. I didn't know if the guy was going to yell at me... or kiss me.

Either would be interesting. Both made my heart race. And if he kissed me, I'd get the excuse to punch him across the mouth... which I *really* wanted to do. Win-win.

"Hey, you two, break it up," the officer called. His voice held a warning.

I stepped away. Charlie smoldered in my direction before he turned his back and went the other way.

Charlie didn't get it. Boredom was always the best way to bring on more psychosis. And I'd do *anything* to stop that from happening— including cause a fight.

I could hear the voices bordering on the edge of my mind, fighting a way to get in. I picked up the pace and cleaned up that park like it was my life's work. Charlie's expression grew confused as he heard me rush from this place to that. My probation officer was obviously impressed when I handed him a full bag in less than an hour.

"You two can go," he said, giving me side-eye. "Just don't get into any more trouble."

I sighed. Finally. As the probation officer left, I turned to Oberi. "Come on, girl. Let's go."

Oberi trotted forward, until Charlie let out a note of protest. "I'm not letting you run off with Oberi."

"You've had her for a full day!" I complained. "It's my turn."

Charlie's jaw tightened. "I don't care. I need Oberi more than you do."

He had no idea. I went to say something back, but Oberi tossed her head, her horn glinting in the sun. She stomped her hoof a few times, pounding it into the dirt.

"Oberi, what's wrong?" I asked. I went to touch her, but she backed away. The Fire unicorn let out a whinny before she whirled around and took off, racing into the woods.

"Oberi!" I called. I took off running after her. What had gotten into my Familiar?

Twigs snapped beneath my feet as I followed Oberi into the woods. I caught sight of her flaming tail, leading me onward.

I hoped I'd left Charlie behind, but no. I could feel gusts of Air move around me as Charlie used his magic to navigate his way through the woods. I felt the bond between us tug, and I realized he was using it as a guide, to feel his way after me.

I couldn't get rid of this guy. He was fighting for Oberi, but he didn't understand. If I had my Familiar, maybe I could make the voices go away. I *had* to have her near.

The forest sloped downward, into a hill. Oberi continued down it, still several paces ahead. Eventually, my feet met sand, and the trees broke as Oberi and I stepped onto the beach.

But this wasn't any ordinary beach. My mouth dropped open as I surveyed the incredible sight around me. Washed up on the beach near an alcove of rock were all kinds of sailing ships. They were wooden, with white sails and tall masts. Strange carvings, in runes I didn't understand, decorated the sides of the ships, while ropes twisted in the wind.

Figureheads spanned the front of the ships. They were carvings of beautiful people— people with pointed ears that had their arms thrown backwards against the wind.

Many of the ships were broken or had holes in them. They looked like they'd been left here for ages— a hundred years or more.

I found myself transfixed by one of the male figureheads, staring into its wooden eyes. For some reason, the figurehead seemed... so familiar.

Charlie took deep breaths as he reached the shore. "What's going on?" He'd noticed I wasn't speaking.

"Ships. Dozens of ships," I said in a mystified voice.

Charlie cocked his head. He put his hand out and felt the ship closest to him. His expression became awed as he moved along the ship's edge, feeling how massive it was.

"Why are these here? Did the Hawkei leave them?" Charlie asked.

"These aren't Elementai ships," I said. "Toaqua are the only Hawkei who sailed, and they used canoes, not schooners or brigs."

"So who brought them here?"

"I don't know. They must've come from another supernatural race— that's what I can tell from the carvings. But whoever left them here, they're long gone now. These ships have been abandoned for at least a few decades."

"Do you think anyone on the reservation knows about them?" he asked.

"I don't think so." I peered into a hole in the belly of one of the ships — it was empty. "My grandpa's an explorer, and if he knew about this place, he definitely would've told me about it. It's been abandoned for years. The alcove must've hid it from everyone."

The explorer in me wanted to look around, document what I found here in my guidebook. But my gut told me I needed to get the hell out of here. Something about this place was off. It was more than eerie— it was haunted, like the spirits of the sailors who'd been shipwrecked here wanted me to leave them alone. I got a sick feeling in my gut just being here— as if the spirits around me were pressing in, suffocating me.

Charlie must've felt it too, because he said, "Let's go."

For once, I didn't argue with him. Oberi walked between us as we trekked uphill through the woods. I didn't speak again until we'd almost gotten back into town.

"Oberi led us there. Why do you think she wanted us to find it?" I asked.

"I'm not sure. But we probably shouldn't go back," Charlie said. "I don't know a lot about magic yet, but I know well enough not to go messing with stuff you shouldn't."

At least we could agree on *something*. As the grass turned to cobblestone beneath our feet, the voices in my head got louder and louder. They hadn't left, but their tones had been a dull buzz when we'd been at the ships. Now, they were roaring in my head.

I clenched my teeth. I put a hand on Oberi's coat, and the voices grew quiet for a few moments. I let out a sigh of relief. Oberi's presence *did* have an effect on the voices, and that was all the information I needed to know she had to stay with me today.

Charlie's head turned in my direction. I couldn't explain how, but Charlie must've felt what I was experiencing through our connection. His face twisted, like he was going to be sick.

I didn't want to share that with him. That kind of information was private. He didn't know I was seeing things, but he could feel my emotions about it... and I didn't like that.

Why couldn't I feel his emotions? If we were connected through Oberi, I should've been able to... but Charlie was a brick wall that I couldn't break through. It wasn't fair he could feel what I went through and it didn't work the other way around. It made our connection unbalanced.

Once we entered into Kinpago, Charlie came to a stop. "You can have Oberi," he said abruptly. "Just bring her back later."

I was so shocked it was hard for me to get any words out. "Uh... thanks?"

"Sure. Whatever."

Charlie turned on his heel and walked away. I watched him as he carefully navigated the streets back to Orenda Academy. I caught myself counting the steps he took.

I had been assigned a dorm, but I was still spending most of my time at home, as classes hadn't started yet and I hadn't moved all my stuff. I went back to my house on the island. Oberi changed into a male husky once I walked into the house, so he could fit better.

My brother was carrying boxes around the living room. Ezekiel had a dorm, too, but he hadn't moved anything. He did everything last-minute.

"How was community service?" he asked.

I threw my bag on the couch. "It sucked. I can't believe the Elders sentenced me like that."

"I mean, can you blame them? The Hawkei court system basically has to pencil you in every month. It's like a recurring thing," Ezekiel said.

"Chieftess Vanessa is practically our aunt! Her son is the same age as us. We grew up together. She should let me off easy," I grumbled.

"She has— a million times," Ez protested. "She can't keep letting it slide. I think she's serious this time, Ava. If you mess up again and violate your probation, the Elders are going to send you to the Institute. You don't have any option but to behave."

"No woman who ever did something great *behaved*."

Ezekiel shook his head. "I'm just saying, you're on thin ice."

"And I've been coasting along just fine. Lay off it." I got a water bottle from the fridge before I flung myself on the couch. As I did so, Oberi lay across my legs.

A thought came to me as I stared up at the ceiling fan. "Do you think Mama and Daddy are hiding something from us?"

Ezekiel put a box down. "Why do you say that?"

"Daddy mentioned something about Aunt Maddie this morning, something she told them about the Institute. He wouldn't tell me what it was. And they've been pretty shady about their council meetings lately," I said. "Usually they're so open. They're acting off."

Ezekiel's face was concerned. "If it was serious, they'd tell us, right?"

"I'm not sure." I reached down to scratch Oberi's tail, and his tongue lolled out. "Where would they keep something they wouldn't want us to find?"

"Probably in the safe." Ezekiel's face fell as he watched a smile spread across my face. "Ava, no. That's private. We shouldn't be poking around in there."

"Why not?" I sat up, and Oberi jumped off my legs. "If we find nothing, I promise I'll drop it."

"We don't even have a combination," Ezekiel whined.

"I don't need a combination. I have Water powers." I began running up the stairs. Ezekiel followed, letting out protests, while Oberi barked in excitement.

Mama and Daddy weren't home, but they would be soon. This was the perfect time to look.

I snuck into my parents' bedroom while my brother trailed behind. In the walk-in closet was a large metal safe. I'd never been inside it— hadn't felt the need to look until now.

But for some reason, it was calling to me. I was undyingly curious. It'd got me into bad situations one too many times before, but this didn't feel like a bad thing— it felt like something good.

I knelt by the safe and uncapped the water bottle. I moved my hand in a circular motion over the bottle, and water rose in a steady stream. I sent droplets into the small crack that lined the safe's door. I could feel the water as it moved into the safe's locking mechanisms, through the pores of the metal. Briskly, I froze it, and I heard the lock audibly break as the water shattered it.

"They're gonna see the lock's broken, you know," Ez said sourly.

"Better to ask forgiveness than permission." I opened the door of the safe. It was heavy. Oberi put his shoulder against it and moved it aside for me.

At first, I was disappointed. There wasn't much— some money, important papers like birth certificates, and a couple family valuables. Nothing stood out.

Then I saw it. A small leather journal, sitting on the topmost shelf. Ezekiel went pale as he saw it.

"Ava, what if it's a diary?" he asked as my hand reached out to grab it. "This is wrong."

"I'll only read the first page. I won't intrude." It was like my fingers were magnetized to the journal. I couldn't describe why... only that the feeling in my gut told me this journal was meant for *me*. Oberi's eager eyes were on me as I took the journal and opened it to the first page. From what I could tell, it'd been written by my Aunt Maddie— and in a hurry. A poem, scribbled tightly across the page.

The balance between the light and the dark
Will be brought together by the light of the new dawn

A discovery of the ancient ones on the island of shadow
Will change the course of our universe

A second war breaches the horizon
Mountains will fall and villains will stand

The heavens will crumble and hell will open wide
Unleashing the demons that fester within

The path she will walk determines our fate
She dances the line both dead and alive

A new world formed from gods of old,
One from ashes or one from light
The choice is hers alone.

As I ended the script, a sickening feeling settled into my organs. This wasn't a poem.

It was a prophecy.

"What the fuck?" Ezekiel whispered as his eyes moved over the words. I shared his exact reaction. As I turned the page, a note fell onto my lap. I turned it over. The note was in Mama's handwriting; *For when Ava turns eighteen.*

Fire burned in my chest so brightly, it felt like it was going to explode out the top of my head.

I'd turned eighteen over a year and a half ago. I'd be twenty in four damn months. And they'd *kept* this from me this long?

Reality set in. This prophecy was about *me.* Aunt Maddie had foreseen my future and written it down for me years ago. I'd always been different, but now I knew just how much. I was a chosen one— just like my mother was.

And my choices were going to determine the future... determine the fate of *everyone.*

I heard the front door close, and a dragon's roar as Julian took off from the beach outside. Ezekiel went to grab me, but I jumped up before he could stop me and ran downstairs. I kept the journal tucked tightly to my side as I flew down the stairs so fast, I nearly got dizzy. Oberi was hot on my heels, nails clicking against the hardwood.

Mama and Daddy were placing groceries on the counter after taking a trip into town. Buttercup was eagerly ruffling through the bags to see what they'd bought. For once, I was glad Alana and Maverick weren't around— they didn't need to hear this.

"You're back early," Mama said as she turned to face me. "Was community service okay?"

I didn't answer. I wasn't about to fuck with that shit when something serious like this was on the line. "What the hell is this?" I shouted. I took the journal out from under my arm and tossed it on the table in front of them.

At the same time, both of their faces went completely white. My suspicions were confirmed. They didn't want me to find this.

Mama was the first to speak. "How did you—?"

"It doesn't matter." I was aware of Ezekiel shifting awkwardly behind me. "Why would you keep something like this from me? A prophecy, really?"

Daddy cleared his throat as he shuffled forward slowly. "We didn't want to hurt you."

I gave a laugh. "Whatever's in this book couldn't be worse than you lying to me."

"It is, Ava." Mama sat at the table. Her hand trembled as she lifted it to her head. "You don't understand what you're getting into."

"Have you read it?" I asked.

"No!" Mama slapped her hand on the table. "It was meant only for you. Maddie made that clear."

"When? Why wouldn't she tell me?" I felt like I was being betrayed by my entire family. My parents, my aunt... who else knew?

"Maddie made the prophecy a few months after you were born," Daddy said. "She told us to give it to you when you came of age."

"I need to talk to Aunt Maddie. I have to understand what this means," I said firmly.

"Maddie is in the Himalayas right now, doing research. You won't be able to get ahold of her for at least another week," Daddy said.

I huffed impatiently. Aunt Maddie was a teacher at a school for seers, but she often took research trips with her husband for her alchemy projects. This was the worst possible time for her to be out of reach.

"I deserved to know. That you kept this from me is unforgivable," I shot at them.

"You have to understand. The prophecy about your mother— it nearly ruined our lives," Daddy said weakly. He put a hand on the counter to steady himself. "We didn't want that for you."

"It wasn't your choice!" I protested.

Mama had gone through horrible things in the Hawkei Civil War— I knew that. But if I had known about my own prophecy years ago, it would've given me more time to prepare. Who knew when my aunt's words would start coming true?

"Ava..." Daddy's tone was strained.

"I can't believe you!" I took a few steps closer. I could feel my Fire burning up and down my skin, dying to get out. "I'm not a little kid anymore. I'm almost twenty! You have to start trusting me to do the right thing!"

It happened in an instant. While I was still shouting at him, Daddy's eyes rolled back in his head, and he collapsed. Ezekiel gasped, and Mama shot up from her chair. Oberi began barking in alarm.

The stupid prophecy was gone from my mind in an instant. I rushed forward to catch Daddy before he hit his head on the counter. He was heavy, and my arms couldn't support him. We crashed to the floor, and I rolled under him so I took most of the blow. My shoulder smacked against the counter, but I refused to let out a cry of pain. I needed to protect him.

"Liam!" Mama fell beside me, while Ezekiel helped pull Daddy off me. He was already coming to, but his eyes were bleary. He looked dazed, like he didn't know where he was. His hands shook, and he appeared so pale.

Tears instantly welled in my eyes, and my lip trembled. This was all *my fault*. I knew Daddy had a medical condition, and I'd pushed him. I shouldn't have questioned what he did. I just wanted him to be okay.

"Help me get him to bed," Mama told Ez. She dragged Daddy to his feet, and my brother helped her. I worried as they carried him up the stairs. Daddy fainting wasn't exactly an unusual occurrence, but I always felt terrible whenever it happened.

Once Daddy was put in bed, Mama fussed around like a mother hen. She fired up the oxygen machine and slipped the nasal tubes over his face before looking for a fresh bag of IV fluid to attach to the surgical pole.

Julian was nosing at the bedroom window. He knew something was wrong. Ezekiel opened it up for him, and the dragon poked his large snout in, sniffing in concern— it was the only part of him that would fit.

"I'm fine, Jules." Daddy raised a weak hand to pat Julian on the nose, and the dragon snorted.

"I *knew* you weren't feeling well this morning." Mama poured water into a mug from the sink, then warmed it up with her Fire magic and slipped in a tea bag before giving it to Daddy. Daddy made a face as she pushed it at him, but he drank it without his usual complaint that it tasted like shit.

I sat on the side of the bed. Guilt bubbled within me so bad, it made me feel like I was drowning. "Daddy, I'm so sorry."

"It's all right, peanut. You didn't mean it," he offered in a weak voice.

Daddy always said that no matter what came out of my mouth. I felt really guilty this time.

I swallowed. "About the prophecy..."

"We'll talk about it later, Ava." Mama's voice had become gentle again. She swept back Daddy's hair, and I took that as an indication he needed to rest. Ezekiel shut the door behind me slowly. By that time, Daddy was already asleep.

Ezekiel gave me a sad look. "It's not your fault, sis. It's bullshit they kept this from you when you had a right to know."

"It *is* my fault. He barely survived the last trip to the hospital." Two tears leaked out and ran down my cheeks before I dashed them away. I wasn't a girl who cried, but for Daddy? I cried buckets.

"He hasn't been admitted in three years. He's doing really well," Ezekiel said. "We just caught him on a bad day."

Ezekiel jerked his head toward the stairs. "You think we should take another look at that?"

The journal came back to mind. I realized that Oberi had gone downstairs and retrieved it for me— it was in his mouth. He nudged me with it, and I took the journal from his jaws.

Mama wouldn't leave Daddy for hours now, which meant Ez and I had time to look at that prophecy alone. I slipped into my room, and the others followed. I lay on my bed with Oberi while my brother sat in the computer chair and twirled in circles. I recited the prophecy aloud three times, but it still didn't make sense.

"Is there anything else in that journal?" Ezekiel asked. "What about a clue?"

I shuffled through the pages. There were drawings and riddles, but they were just as cryptic as the prophecy was. The pages were only half-filled. In the middle of the journal, the writing grew more and more frantic, until the words abruptly stopped altogether. What had my Aunt Maddie been thinking?

This wasn't helping. I read the prophecy again. One line stuck out above all the others.

"*A discovery of the ancient ones on the island of shadow...*" I read aloud. Oberi's ears perked up at the line.

Ezekiel sat forward. "That sure sounds like Darke Island to me."

"It damn well does." Darke Island was where the Institute was— the last place I wanted to go.

Ezekiel caught the look on my face before I could speak. "Ah, no. You're not going to suggest what I *know* you're thinking."

"Excuse me? Have you *heard* this prophecy?" I waved the book around.

Ezekiel frowned. "Only the first five times you read it."

"Yeah, and it's pretty fucking obvious it means business. We don't know what's going to happen, but we do know what's to come *isn't good.*" I flipped the journal shut.

"So what do you want to do about it?" Ezekiel raised an eyebrow.

I took a deep breath. "What else is there *to* do? I have to go to Darke Island."

Ezekiel groaned and rolled his eyes. "That's not what I had in mind."

"Information is critical when you're dealing with prophecies. If I know what the future is before it happens, I have a better chance of changing it," I argued.

"Why don't you just wait until you can call Aunt Maddie? That's the logical choice." Ezekiel crossed his arms.

"That's a whole week! It can't wait that long. We're talking about the fate of all supernatural kind, here. One day could be the difference between life and death for a whole race of people."

It sounded dramatic, but I wasn't over exaggerating. Whenever my mother had talked about her own prophecy— and that was very rare— she always made it clear that the fate of the elementals had been determined by her choices as chosen one, and hers alone. Her decisions had saved... and killed... countless numbers of people in the Hawkei Civil War.

If I was a chosen one, too, I had the same responsibility. Waiting around could cost the people I loved. I wouldn't take that chance; not if it meant being decisive now could save lives.

Ezekiel scowled. "You're being impulsive, Ava."

My temper spiked. "This isn't my bipolar."

"Sure acting like it."

"Do I have a choice? Look, I'll go to Darke Island, investigate the prophecy, and figure out what it means. I'll be back in a few days, before classes at Orenda get too far ahead for me to catch up."

Ez looked pretty damn skeptical, but he knew there was no stopping me, so he sighed in defeat. "So when are you leaving?"

I knew the answer the second I looked into Oberi's eyes. "Tonight."

It was around midnight when I crept out of bed, fully dressed. By moonlight, I walked over to my backpack. It was packed with my exploring gear, my guidebook, the journal, my wallet, and clothes that would be suitable for crawling around in ancestors knew where.

I really wanted to take my designer dresses, but I knew I wouldn't need them. I slipped my phone into my pocket and grabbed a picture off the nightstand. It was one of my entire family, at a big summer party last year. It never left my bedside, and no matter what, I was taking it with me.

As a second thought, I took the unicorn nightlight I had since I was a baby and tossed it in.

So I was afraid of the dark. Big fucking deal.

Oberi watched me as I sat on my bed and laced up my boots. There was nothing left to pack.

"It's just a few days, right?" I asked weakly. "I won't be long."

Just a few days.

Or weeks.

Or... months...

Oberi placed a paw on my knee. By the look in his eyes, I felt deep in my gut that I wasn't coming back home for a very, very long time.

Who knew how long this prophecy would take to figure out? I had to be prepared to not see my family for a while.

That really freaking sucked. It wasn't like I wanted to get away. I was really close with all of them.

Especially Daddy.

I couldn't think about Daddy; otherwise, I wouldn't go. I crept downstairs and left a letter on his desk, just for him, written in Hawkei.

I didn't leave myself any more time to hesitate. I walked out of my house with my head held high, into the cool night.

Ezekiel was waiting outside to say goodbye, as he was the only one who knew about my plan. But he wasn't the only one. Mama was also by the shoreline, watching as the waves came in and out.

Dammit all. Had Ez told her my plan? What a freaking snitch. I sighed and prepared myself to march right back in the house. Everything was ruined now.

When my mother turned around, her eyebrows pinched at the sight of the backpack on my back. Oberi transformed into a unicorn beside me and tilted her head, horn glowing in the moonlight as her embers fizzled into the air.

In Mama's arms was something small and folded. She held it out and pressed it into me. "Here. My sister gave me these jeans, the day I left for Orenda Academy with your father. They're good luck. You'll need them."

Shock ran through my body as I tucked the jeans into my bag. "You're letting me go?"

"I can't stop this, Ava-Marie. I knew from the moment you were born you were destined for great things, and anything I did to prevent you from walking your path would only separate us," Mama said. "You're a chosen one. You're part of a prophecy. Whatever you do from this moment on is your choice alone. I trust that I've raised you well enough to make the right decisions."

Tears welled in my eyes. My parents *never* trusted me. It wasn't like they didn't want to. I'd just messed up so many times that to do so would be foolish. But Mama was trusting me now to make the right call, and that meant everything to me. "What about Daddy?"

"Your father doesn't know. I'll explain to him when you're gone." Mama rubbed her hands up and down my arms. "Liam isn't going to understand, but he will. I know what you're going through. And I want to make it as easy as I can, because trust me, the road ahead won't be. But I know you have the strength to carry on through it."

A shiver raced up and down my spine at her words, and I suppressed a shudder. Mama dropped her hands from my shoulders. After a moment's thought, she reached behind herself and unfastened the clip of a gold chain, taking it off her neck before looping it around mine, fastening the chain at the base of my neck.

"Mama, no. Not your necklace. Daddy gave it to you on your wedding day." I touched the pendant. It was a copper key, aged with green patina. There was a crown sitting at the center of the key's handle, which was formed into a heart. She never took it off.

"You need it more than I do," Mama said. "When you wear this necklace, you carry my heart with you wherever you go."

I flung my arms around her. Mama held me tight. I thought I heard a sniff from her before she pulled away. "May the ancestors be my eyes, watch where you go and guide your path. May the Great Spirit help you achieve wisdom, which you can use when you lose your way. May your spirit guides always keep you safe, until they lead you to a place where we can meet again."

Mama touched my head and ran her fingers through my hair, completing the blessing. When her fingertips left the tendrils of my hair, it felt like my entire body was glowing. It was as if the ancestors themselves had enlightened me for the road ahead.

Ezekiel came forward to give me a hug. "I wish I could come with you."

My heart ached. I didn't want to leave my brother. We hadn't been apart more than a few days before. He was my protector, and I didn't know what I was going to face out there.

"I wish you could, too." I squeezed him tightly and pulled away. Letting him go was like prying what I loved most out of my arms, but I had to do this. To save everyone.

Before I could lose my nerve, I climbed onto Oberi's back. She reared on her hind legs before she started forward. As her hooves reached the ocean, I used my Water powers to support our weight, so she ran over the ocean, ice hardening beneath her at my command as we galloped full speed away from the only home I'd ever known.

I knew it had to be killing Mama to let me go. She lived for her kids. But she knew I could do this. I couldn't let her down.

When Oberi and I got to the mainland, I saw the spires of Orenda Academy shine in the distance, and I thought of Charlie. I'd promised to bring back Oberi to Charlie later... but I was going on a quest. A *dangerous* quest, one where I'd be in terrible peril, and fight monsters, probably, and all that adventurous bullshit.

I needed a Familiar to protect me. Charlie could get by until I came back.

My mind worked on a plan. Darke Island was in the middle of the Pacific Ocean. I needed a boat to get there— a big one.

The strange marooned ships I'd seen earlier came to mind. I could use my Toaqua powers to sail one out to sea. I just had to find one that didn't have any holes in it.

Oberi galloped through the forest, weaving in and out of trees. I held on tightly to her mane and flattened myself against her neck as I heard a wolf howl against the night.

I thought this was only temporary, but as I raced away from Kinpago, I was certain this was the first night of the rest of my life.

We came to the shipwrecks. I slid off Oberi's back, and she nickered as I began looking through the wreckage for a boat that would sail. I found an old schooner that was more intact than the others sitting on the far shore. I climbed onto it, and Oberi transformed back into a husky, padding up to the mast and taking a seat.

I looked out at the ocean. At my command, the waves began churning up the beach, flooding the sands. The ship slowly began to rise. I ordered the water to cradle the ship, and I held on to a banister as the ocean righted the ship in the proper direction. We sailed out to sea. Once we were in deep water, I urged the ocean to rush us forward, and the waves started pushing the ship at top speed, racing along the edges like we were on a speedboat.

Oberi fiddled with the sails, trying to yank one free with his teeth while I took a map out of my backpack. Darke Island was six hundred miles off the coast of California, to the west. Though I was pushing the ship, it would take me a day or two to get there.

I went to the front of the ship and looked out at the wide, open ocean. The shoreline of California was already long behind me. My heart raced as I looked ahead. I *loved* the horizon line. It called to me like nothing else. I always wanted to know what else was out there. Today, I'd finally get the chance to know.

Oberi let out a couple loud barks behind me that sounded excited. I turned around. Rage welled up in my chest as I saw a man crawl out from behind a few crates. Seriously? This guy ruined everything!

"You think you can get away with abducting *my* Familiar?" Charlie's voice had taken on a hard edge. "Nice try, pidge. I'm not that gullible."

My hands clenched into fists. This was ridiculous. Charlie Wahkin had stowed away on *my ship*.

He had seriously picked the wrong day to fuck with me— and I was going to let him know it.

FIVE

The sound of Fire crackled, and heat waves rolled out of Ava-Marie's palm. "Jump ship now, or you're getting a fireball to the face," she growled.

I wasn't scared of her. I took a casual step her way and sat down on a nearby crate. "You wouldn't do that, pidge."

"Try me," she hissed.

I shrugged. "It's your choice. But then you risk this whole ship going up in flames."

Ava-Marie's fireball faltered, and I heard the last of the sparks fizzle away to nothing. But her rage had gone nowhere. "Get off this boat, Charlie, or so help me, I will make you."

"You threatening to drown me, pidge?" I questioned. I didn't think she could do it, even if she wanted to.

"We're not that far from shore. You can swim back."

No, I couldn't. But I wasn't about to admit to her that I couldn't swim.

"We have to be miles off by now!" I cried. "No way am I swimming back. Turn the boat around."

"I'm leaving, and nothing you say will stop me."

I crossed my arms. "You're free to leave, but you're not taking Oberi with you."

"Well, I'm not leaving without him," she snapped. "How'd you know where to find me anyway?"

"Oberi and I have a connection," I reminded her. "He was worried for you— practically begged me to come talk you out of it. I followed the bond to where you were."

"Th-that's not possible," she stammered.

Did I detect a hint of jealousy in her tone? Ava's connection with Oberi must've been weaker than mine.

"You can hear Oberi speak?" she asked, sounding irritated.

I tilted my chin up proudly. "Yes."

It was true, but it wasn't quite what she was asking. Oberi had spoken to me once— to tell me his name. This time, it'd been more or less a feeling, a notion that I had to come stop Ava at whatever cost.

Ava-Marie huffed. "So help me, Charlie Wahkin. You get off this boat *now*, or I'll—"

"You'll what?" I was in front of her in a second. We were so close, I could feel the heat of her skin on mine.

Ava-Marie breathed heavily, but she didn't answer.

"You forget I'm the one with Air magic, pidge." I lifted my hands. At my command, a gust of wind caught the sail, and the boat lurched. Ava stumbled into a stack of crates, and they crashed to the deck. Much to my disappointment, she hadn't fallen on her ass.

"Stop it, Charlie!" Ava-Marie cried, stomping toward me. "How are you doing that? You have no training. You shouldn't be this good."

I spoke coolly as we started turning toward shore. "I've been navigating the world by magic for a long time. I'm a natural."

"Cut it out!" Ava-Marie screamed. She reached for my arms and tried to yank them down at my sides, but I was stronger than she was. I kept them raised. Oberi didn't like to see us fighting. He barked, and it echoed over the ocean toward shore.

"Shh, Oberi," Ava hissed. "We're going to get caught."

"What are you running away for anyway?" I asked. "Did someone hurt your poor little feelings?"

"None of your business." Ava shoved her way past me and headed toward the stern of the ship. The boat rocked, and something fought against my Air power to turn the boat around.

"What are you doing?" I demanded.

"I'm making sure *you* don't mess this up," she shot back.

"You're Fire. You can't control the boat," I claimed. "How are you doing that?"

I could hear the smirk in her tone. "I have something better to help me sail the seas."

"What's that? An oar?" I cracked.

"Water power!" she shot back.

The boat went dead silent. I'd never heard Ava-Marie go so quiet. I might've thought she'd fallen overboard, but I'd never heard a splash. She must've realized she said something she hadn't meant to say.

"How's that possible?" I asked. "Professor Baine said Elementai inherit the powers of their same-sex parent. You can't be Fire *and* Water."

"Well, I'm not going to explain it to *you*," Ava sneered.

My mind raced. If this was possible, maybe I could control more than Air. Professor Baine said my mother was Nivita— an Earth Elementai— which meant that her power traveled through my veins. Could I be two elements— Air and Earth?

I unfortunately didn't have the luxury of pondering it. I had to get this boat turned back toward shore, but Ava-Marie's powers were *strong*. It was impossible to fight against the water currents themselves.

"You can't take me with you," I growled.

"You're right, I can't," she practically sang.

"Finally," I huffed. "We agree on something."

Oberi didn't seem to think so, because he barked in protest again.

"Which is why you need to leave while you still can!" Ava-Marie insisted.

"I told you, I'm not going anywhere without Oberi. So what are you going to do, pidge? Kidnap me?"

"You're the one who got on this boat in the first place," she shot back. "I didn't force you to come."

"No, but you—"

"*Attention!*" a voice boomed over the water, as if projected through a megaphone. The boat rocked beneath us, and the air no longer shifted to my command. It was as if someone had ripped the controls right out of my hand.

"Fuck! How did they find us?" Ava-Marie muttered. She started rushing around the boat, pulling on ropes and who knows what the hell else.

"What's going on?" I tilted my head toward the sound of the voice, but I couldn't hear anything over the churning water beneath us.

"The Toaqua Coast Guard," Ava-Marie growled. "*You* brought them, didn't you!?"

"No, I didn't—"

"We have you surrounded!" the voice called. "You are in violation of coastal code forty-three. You will now be escorted back to shore."

"What the hell does that mean?" I asked her.

She spoke between clenched teeth as she tugged hard on various ropes. "It means we're in possession of an illegal sea craft."

I raked my fingers through my hair. "Hell, you say that like you've violated code forty-three a million times."

Ava-Marie didn't seem bothered. "Once or twice."

The boat continued rocking, and I had to grab the mast to steady myself. "What are you doing, pidge?"

"I'm trying to get this thing moving," she snapped. "The Coast Guard is using Water magic to turn us around. We have to overpower them."

"Overpower them?" I balked. "No way. Not if they're taking us back to shore."

"Charlie, you don't understand," Ava pleaded. "I *have* to leave. The fate of all supernatural societies depends on it."

"Ah, why didn't you say so?" I asked sarcastically. I didn't believe her for a second.

"I don't care what you think," she snapped. "It doesn't matter— ah!"

The boat lurched forward— harder than before. Crates crashed to the deck as Ava-Marie fell into them. I couldn't stay upright, either, and I went spiraling downward. Oberi caught me before I face-planted onto the deck. I must've distracted Ava, because the Coast Guard had over-powered her. The ship sailed full-speed toward shore, and cool wind rushed through my hair. I had to hold on tight to Oberi to steady myself on my knees. Ava made a ruckus trying to stand upright, but she toppled over every time she got to her feet. I chuckled lightly under my breath.

It didn't matter how much Ava tried. She couldn't regain control of the ship. The boat slowed and came to an abrupt halt as it bottomed out at shore.

"Ancestors!" Ava cried, sounding in pain.

"You okay, pidge?" I asked breathlessly. I was glad to be back on shore, but the shakiness of her tone alarmed me.

"No, Charlie, I am not okay," Ava wailed. "I *broke a nail!*"

"Oh my god," I groaned.

"*Ancestors,*" she corrected me with a sneer.

Footsteps pounded across the beach and through the sand. "Ava-Marie Mitoh and Charlie Wahkin," a man said. "You are under arrest for the theft of this seacraft."

I opened my mouth to object, but Ava beat me to it. She started wailing— literally *wailing*. The sound pierced my ears and made me flinch.

"Thank the ancestors you're here!" she cried. "Ch-Charlie abducted my Familiar and t-tried to take her away. I had to stop him!"

"Ancestors," I sighed, for her sake. "You're a compulsive liar."

Several men climbed onto the boat, and their footsteps pounded across the deck.

"*I* was the one trying to stop her," I said. "I didn't steal anything."

Someone grabbed my arm and yanked it behind my back. Metal cuffs clinked and tightened around my wrists. "Your record suggests otherwise," the man stated.

"You can't touch me!" Ava-Marie cried as someone cuffed her. "I'm the daughter of a chief!"

Oberi growled at the men, and Ava screeched, "Get that muzzle off my Familiar!"

Ancestors, I could strangle this girl. We wouldn't be in this mess if it wasn't for her.

"I didn't do anything wrong!" Ava cried as the men started leading us off the boat. "Ask my mother!"

"Ava, I'm just doing my job," the man in charge told her. "You can speak to your mother when you get to the Elders' Quarters."

"That won't be necessary, Jack," a female voice cut across the beach.

My feet sank into the sand, and Oberi's paws padded beside me. Two pairs of footsteps shuffled across the beach toward us. One was quicker and more heavy-footed than the other.

"Let them go," a man boomed. He used a tone of ultimate authority.

"Yes, Chief," the Coast Guard captain stammered. The cuffs on my wrist loosened, and I breathed a sigh of relief.

"Daddy!" Ava-Marie cried. She ran forward, and a *thud* sounded as their bodies collided. "Thank the ancestors."

"Ava," her father said, but she didn't seem to listen. He spoke more firmly. "Ava!"

I sensed Air rush between the two of them as she drew away from the hug. "What is it, Daddy?"

The chief cleared his throat, though his words came out sounding strained. "I'm not here to save you. I'm here to sentence you."

"Sentence me?" Ava balked. "What do you mean, Daddy?"

Ava's mother spoke softly. "He means you're going to the Institute—properly."

Ava went silent for several beats. Her voice came out smaller than I'd ever heard it. "Really?"

The feeling of Ava-Marie's hair in the wind settled as her father smoothed it down. "Your mother told me what you were planning. You stole a boat, peanut. You violated your probation. As your chief, I have no choice but to sentence you to four years at the Darke Institute for Supernatural Offenders."

I expected Ava-Marie to protest, but she didn't say a damn thing. The silence was too weird, and her father's tone too soft. It was like he spoke of her probation to justify the sentencing to everyone else.

But Ava? She almost seemed *glad*.

I wasn't buying the charade. Something was up. I could feel it in my connection to Ava. This didn't make a damn bit of sense. A couple of days ago she was willing to do anything to get out of going to the Institute. Now she was going there willingly?

This girl was up to something. And I needed to find out what it was. Her father was *helping* to get her there somehow. But why?

"Well, if I have no choice..." Ava-Marie said, in a tone that sounded totally fake. Then her voice changed, and became genuine. "I love you, Daddy."

"I love you, too, sweetheart," he replied. "The bus is already en route to the Institute. It will be passing through Kinpago in the morning. The two of you will leave at sunrise."

"*The two of us!*" Ava and I shouted at the same time.

"Of course," her father answered, like it was obvious. "You both violated your probation. You will *both* be attending the Institute."

"I wasn't the one who stole this boat!" I protested.

At the same time, Ava-Marie said, "Charlie's *not* coming with me!"

Her father's tone hardened. "As Toaqua Chief, I have the authority to make this call. Charlie *will* be accompanying you, Ava, and that is final."

I crossed my arms as rage built up inside of me. "Shouldn't the Yapluma Chief be the one to sentence me? I *am* from the Air House."

"Oh, believe me," he snarled, "the Yapluma Chief will agree with me. You're going whether you like it or not."

"But Daddy—" Ava started.

"No buts," he insisted. "Mister Wahkin, may I have a word?"

Not a chance, I thought. But I didn't have a choice. The man was a chief.

My hands curled into fists as he led me down the beach away from Ava-Marie, her mother, and the Toaqua Coast Guard. I feared what he might have to say to me. Probably wanted to wring my neck for getting his daughter into this mess. I suppose he wouldn't believe me if I told him it was all her fault.

"Sir—" I began to say, but he cut me off.

"Look. I'd rather not send you to the Institute if I can help it." His tone was rough. This guy meant business.

Oh? I perked up and listened closer.

"Whether you believe it or not, I'm doing you a favor," he told me.

My eyebrows shot up. "A favor?"

"Yes. I know what it's like to lose a Familiar, and it is not something I wish upon any Elementai— not even my worst enemy. Ava-Marie *must* go to the Institute, and she will need Oberi there with her."

Ava must go? What did that mean? Is that where she'd been trying to run away to? Why in the hell would she do that... run away to a literal prison?

The chief placed a firm hand on my shoulder. I tried shrugging him off, but he didn't move. "I'm sending you with her so you can stay close to your Familiar. In exchange, I'm going to need you to do something for me?"

Oh, sure. Being sentenced to prison is such *a favor. I'd do anything to repay you.*

"I'm not doing anything for you," I snapped. "You're sending me to a prison. This is a death sentence."

"It's only a death sentence if you can't handle it," he growled.

"I can handle anything," I said in a clipped tone.

"Then you'll do this for me," he stated, no question.

"Oh, and what's that?" I asked, with no intention of providing *any* favors. His daughter kept dragging me into her crimes. I didn't deserve this.

He took a deep breath. "I need you to keep an eye on Ava."

I almost snorted. "I'm not sure I could do that, even if I *could* see. Ava's one strong-headed bi— girl."

"I don't like it any more than you do," he assured me. "But if anyone can do it, it's you. I wouldn't be sending her to the Institute if you weren't going with her."

I furrowed my brow. "Why me?"

"Because you two share a connection," he reminded me. "She is part of your soul, and just as you would with your Familiar, you will protect Ava as well."

He wasn't threatening me. He was more or less stating the facts. Whether I wanted to protect her or not, self-preservation would kick in, and I'd do whatever it took to keep her alive— if just to protect my own soul.

All three of us— Oberi, Ava and I— had to stay alive for the rest to keep living. So I was obligated to protect her... if only to save my own ass.

Ava's voice carried across the beach, though I couldn't hear what she was saying. Warmth settled into my bones before I could tell it to fuck off. Damn it. The chief was right. I *had* to go with Ava— not because I wanted to, but because I was being pulled by some unknown force.

Damn magic.

"You *have* to do this, Charlie." The chief wasn't begging me. This time, it *was* a threat. It was obvious he hated my guts and wouldn't hesitate to blame me if anything happened to Ava. "You don't want to know what I'm capable of if Ava-Marie gets hurt."

A lump formed in my throat. "I won't let anything happen to her."

He clapped me on the back. "That's exactly what I like to hear. Now, go get cleaned up. You have a bus to catch."

⛓

"WHAT IS *THAT*?" Ava-Marie sneered as I approached the bus stop the next morning.

Oberi was in husky form at my side. He'd spent the night with Ava, but came to help me at sunrise. I didn't think I'd have found the bus stop without his help.

"This?" I asked, gesturing to myself. "Some people call it a walking chick magnet."

"Not you!" Ava smacked my shoulder. "The garbage bag?"

I shrugged the bag on my shoulder. "It's my luggage."

"Luggage?" Ava balked. She turned away from me, flipping her hair so that it smacked in my face. "Nobody told me I was going with a guy who carries his clothes in a garbage bag."

That really pissed me off. As a foster kid my whole life, I didn't have any other choice. Garbage bags were all we had when we moved. The only other bag I had was a ratty old backpack I'd found in a dumpster a few years ago.

"Sorry I'm not *rich* enough for your taste," I snapped.

"I'm not rich," she protested. "These designer bags were on sale!"

Ancestors, she was bringing designer bags to *prison*? How did she not realize how well-off she'd been her whole life? Her pretty little ass wasn't going to last a day.

"Ava, please," our probation officer said, sounding more than a little irritated. I hadn't even realized he'd been there. I suppose it made sense. Someone had to make sure we made it on the bus.

"What? I was just—" She cut off as the sound of a diesel engine approached. "Oh, look. Our ride is here."

My guts knotted. Oberi must've sensed my unease, because he leaned into me. I stroked the top of his head for comfort.

The brakes squealed as the bus came to a stop in front of us. Ava was quick to rush in front of me, even before the doors squeaked open. She climbed onto the bus, and I followed, using Oberi as my guide. Several footsteps followed behind me, and I realized we weren't the only Elementai being sentenced to the Institute. Our probation officer stopped to talk to the bus driver, but I was already so distracted that I didn't hear what they said.

The second I stepped onto the bus, my senses went into overdrive, trying to pick up every little thing. It was so much that I found it overwhelming. To start with, there was a strange buzz in the air that seemed to suck the energy right out of me. I gripped tight to the railing as I climbed the stairs.

Ava leaned back and whispered. "It's noxite. The bus must be reinforced with it."

"What's noxite?" I asked.

"It's a magical metal," she explained. "It affects your powers. They don't want us to escape."

I swallowed, feeling a heaviness settle in my gut. Without my powers, I'd have one hell of a time navigating the Institute. I'd come to rely on them more than I realized.

"Don't worry," Ava assured me. "I did my research. Most of the Institute is noxite-free. Part of their reform program is teaching us how to use and control our powers. You'll feel better once we get there. Just watch for the noxite tranquilizer guns. Those things will knock your powers out for hours."

"Good to know."

We started down the aisle, and various overwhelming scents assaulted me. It was as if someone had shoved an old leather seat up my nose. I wanted to gag. Underneath that was the scent of sweaty socks and something coppery— like blood.

Then there was the noise. Judging by the voices, there were nearly a dozen kids on the bus with us. They bitched at each other so loudly I couldn't make sense of one conversation over the other.

"You think you're so great because you're a fucking fae? Eat a whale cock."

Whale cock? Where the hell did that expression come from?

"You're mermaid scum," someone shot back. "You're an *animal!*"

"Oh, and your angel friend there isn't? I've never seen a *human* with wings before."

"Would you all shut the fuck up?" a guy groaned. "I'll drain you, I swear it."

"Come at me, vamp," a girl challenged.

Ava-Marie passed by everyone and stopped toward the back of the bus. I sensed a man a few seats back. I could tell by the way the air moved around him he had a strong build. No air moved through his hair, so I assumed he was bald. He kept quiet.

"Is baldy back there dangerous?" I whispered to Ava as she sat in an empty seat. I took the seat across the aisle, since there was plenty of room for us all. Oberi opted to sit by Ava, and my frustration swelled.

Ava chuckled. "It's a guard, Charlie. Considering he's not stopping these degenerates, I think it's safe to say he's harmless."

"Who the fuck are you calling a degenerate?" a girl snapped. She was two seats ahead of Ava. I could practically hear the murderous intent in her tone.

Ava tossed her hair over her shoulder, sending the smell of her perfume in my direction. "Oh, I suppose *you're* innocent. That's why you're on a prison bus."

The girl cracked her knuckles. "Hell no. I killed a warlock with my bare hands. Sucked him dry."

"Oh, so you're a vampire?" Ava sounded less than impressed. "I'm so scared."

"I'm no vampire, kitten," she snapped as the bus began to move. "I'm a succubus. I'm far worse than any vampire."

Ava chuckled. "A succubus, huh? So you're a vampire who fucked a demon."

"Hell yeah," she snarled. "Best lay of my life. I've got powers you couldn't even dream of."

She sounded serious about fucking a demon, but I'd bet anything she was lying about killing a man with her bare hands. If she was a murderer, she'd be cuffed, and certainly wouldn't be on the bus with a couple of minor thieves.

Ava chuckled. The soft sound of her fingers running over Oberi's fur met my ears. "I don't have to dream of power. I've got enough of my own. Don't underestimate an Elementai, or you just might find yourself burned alive."

"You threatening me, bitch?" the succubus snapped. "What are you going to do? Set your little dog on me?"

Oberi growled.

Ava's laughter turned maniacal. "Oberi's not a *little dog*, and he doesn't appreciate being called one, either."

The succubus scoffed. "Doesn't change that you brought your *pet* with you. Poor Elementai needs her emotional support animal?"

"Oberi's my Familiar," Ava snapped. "Elementai are permitted to bring their Familiars with them to the Institute. Say one more thing about him, and I'll pound your face in—"

"Stop!" I shot to my feet and put my hand on the seat in front of Ava, positioning myself in front of Oberi. I lowered my voice and hissed, "You're provoking her, Ava. Quit."

"You Elementai act like you're so—" the succubus started, but I cut her off.

"Leave us alone, or you'll regret it," I snarled.

"What are you going to do?" she challenged. "Sprinkle me with a little water?"

I kept my temper in check. "You underestimate the Elementai."

"They're not worth it, Naya," a girl cut in. "The Institute will eat them alive."

Naya paused a few moments, then laughed. "You're right, Danielle. Might as well let the Institute deal with them. No use getting in trouble on my first day over Elementai scum."

I breathed a sigh of relief when Naya tossed her hair and turned back to the front of the bus. My powers may have been weak right now, but I could still feel the air currents around me. I slumped into the bench next to Ava, squeezing in beside Oberi.

"Why'd you stop me?" Ava demanded. "I could fry that bitch."

I lowered my voice so the others wouldn't hear. "I promised your dad I wouldn't let you get into trouble. Starting fights isn't going to cut it in prison."

The fabric of Ava's shirt rustled as she crossed her arms. "You spoke to Daddy about me?"

"Pidge, you're missing the point. The Elders won't be there to protect you. Your father won't be either. Prison is nothing like Kinpago. You have to be careful."

She scoffed. "You say that like you know."

"I've never been convicted, if that's what you're implying," I snarled. "But I've known plenty of people who have."

Ava considered this for a moment, but it didn't seem to bother her. "Please, Charlie. I can take care of myself."

"Not if you're willingly putting targets on your back!" I hissed. "You don't want attention in prison. We have to keep a low profile and stay out of trouble."

Ava snorted. "Ever met me, Charlie? My brother says *trouble* is my middle name."

"Well, get rid of it," I growled. "Unless you want to end up in actual prison and not just a reform school."

"Big deal. Same thing."

"Not the same thing. These people are criminals, pidge," I reminded her in a low whisper. "You don't know what they've done or what they're *willing* to do. Push the wrong button, and you'll end up raped or beaten to death."

Ava stilled, and Oberi let out a soft whine. My hand was on his back, but he drew away from me to lay his head on Ava's lap.

After a beat of silence, Ava spoke. "You really think something like that could happen?"

I cocked an eyebrow. "In prison? Hell yeah."

Ava got really quiet, so much that I could hear her swallow. "Fine, Charlie. You win. We'll stick close together. But I can't make any promises."

I huffed. "Just try to stay out of trouble, will you?"

"Try," she scoffed, like the idea was ludicrous. "I'll *try*."

The bus began to speed up, and my fingers tightened on the seat in front of us. All around, gasps came from the other passengers. I felt the bus rattle underneath me, like we were driving off-road on rocks and gravel instead of pavement.

"What's going on?" I asked.

"Ancestors," Ava breathed. Her weight lifted from the seat as she stood to get a better look. "We're headed toward a cliff!" There was no fear in her voice. Rather, she sounded thrilled.

"No, we're not," I stated flatly.

"No, seriously. We are!" Ava cried.

I didn't believe her, until the other passengers began crying the same thing.

"What's this moron doing?"

"There's nothing but ocean ahead!"

"We'll drown!"

"Ancestors," I gasped, clutching the seat so tight my knuckles started to hurt. With my other hand, I grabbed Oberi's fur. He was on high alert now, padding his feet on the bench seat. My heart pulsed in my ears. The thought crossed my mind that there was no Institute at all. Officials just loaded up the bad kids and sent them to their deaths by driving off a cliff. "They're going to kill us!"

Ava-Marie didn't seem bothered by the notion at all. She started laughing— a crazy, maniacal laugh that made my skin crawl. Ava was officially a mad woman.

"We're getting closer," she told me, eagerness in her tone.

"Thanks, but I don't need my death narrated!" I cried.

"Closer... closer... aaand... gone!" Ava said gleefully.

My stomach dropped out of my abdomen as the bus went hurdling off the edge of the cliff. Passengers screamed in unison— all but Ava-Marie. The psycho spread her arms wide like she was flying and smacked her wrist into my face, letting out a happy scream like she was on a rollercoaster.

I couldn't stop screaming. My stomach somersaulted, and my heart rattled around in my chest like a rabid dog trying to escape. I'd never felt such terror in my life.

Thwack!

The bus abruptly slowed, and my head snapped forward into the seat in front of me. My head swam, and I rubbed the bruise forming between my eyes.

"We're alive!" Ava cried triumphantly.

"No shit," I growled. "What the hell is going on?"

Ava drew a sharp breath. "Ancestors, it's beautiful."

Oberi shifted between us and climbed halfway onto Ava's lap— like he was looking out the window.

"What is *it*?" I snapped. I was really starting to get pissed. Someone better explain what the hell that was.

"The bus is a submarine!" Ava cried.

I stilled. Though the other passengers were loud and distracting, I managed to focus on the vibrations of the bus. The bus was moving, but it was incredibly smooth— like it was gliding through the ocean. All around me, I heard voices crying out to look at the fish, gasping in amazement at the sea life that was all around us.

"We're underwater?" I asked Ava.

"Yes, and the ocean is so pretty! There are schools of fish every-where. Ancestors, a kelpie just swam by! Charlie, did you see—?"

She cut off before she could finish her sentence.

"Don't worry about it," I said flatly. "I've seen kelpies a million times before."

"Really?" she asked.

I blew a breath. "No, pidge. I'm blind!"

"You can't expect me to know everything," she huffed. "Were you *born* blind?"

"What kind of a question is that?" I snapped. "Were you born with that stick up your ass?"

"Nah, that showed up when I met you," she shot back.

"Unlikely," I stated flatly.

Ava pushed at me. "Go sit over there. You're ruining the view."

"Only if I get Oberi," I insisted.

"No way."

I shrugged and settled deeper into the seat. "Fine by me, pidge."

I closed my eyes and pretended to sleep. Ava groaned under her breath, but she didn't say anything else. I felt her shift in the chair and turn to look out the window again.

I hated her. Not just because she was... well, Ava. But when everything was going to shit, she still found beauty in something extraordinary.

I wondered what that was like. I'd entered into a magical world, but most of the magic in my life was already gone due to the way I'd grown up.

After a few moments, Ava started talking under her breath. "Aw, the sea turtles are so cute. So many different colors— blue, purple, green. Which one is your favorite, Oberi? Oh, look! The eels are *dancing*. Oberi, wave to Thalassa! That's my grandpa's Familiar. She looks so majestic in the ocean— her blue scales twinkling in the sunlight. She's such a pretty sea serpent, isn't she? She must be close to a hundred feet long, I bet."

The more I listened to her, the more I realized how oddly detailed she was getting for Oberi. Unless she wasn't narrating for Oberi's benefit at all, but for *mine*.

Normally, I'd tell her to piss off. I didn't *ask* her to do that. But as much as I wanted to be mad at Ava, the gesture soothed me. For a brief moment, it felt like she actually cared.

At some point, I must've drifted off, because I felt Ava shaking me awake a few hours later.

I startled. "What is it, pidge?"

"Wake up, Charlie," she whispered. "The bus has surfaced. We're here."

ava-marie

SIX

The prison submarine drenched water onto the shore as we rolled upon it. I pressed my nose to the window, watching as the fins retracted into the main hub. There was a loud sound from above, like the starboard fin and periscope were retracting. I felt wheels form beneath us as the submarine transformed completely into a bus, rolling onto the rocky landscape with a jostling motion.

"It must be some kind of enchantment that makes the bus change," I said to Charlie. "Not sure which supernatural race made it, though."

He let out a *humph*, which told me he wasn't interested in finding out. I rolled my eyes. Ancestors, did this guy give a shit about *anything?*

The bus rolled up the rocky beach shore and onto a road that was in poor disrepair. The bus hit a pothole, and Oberi yelped as he was tossed into Charlie's lap. Several people loudly complained.

I continued to observe my surroundings. Darke Island was nothing to write home about. The entire island was covered in a thin layer of fog. Grey clouds above blocked out the sun, and for miles all that could be seen were scraggly dead trees and mossy grass. I didn't see an inkling of life. It was like the plants didn't even want to grow here. We drove past a few swamps and entered into the creepiest looking forest as we went further inland.

Seriously. It was like the trees had eyes here. I couldn't shake the feeling of being watched.

Charlie felt it, too. I noticed he shifted uncomfortably as goosebumps rose over his skin.

Conversation died down completely. Nobody spoke. Everyone had seemingly become very afraid. I wasn't one to admit when I was freaked out, but this forest had something about it that was beyond supernatural. I never wanted to step foot in it again.

When we emerged from the forest, a few buildings caught my attention. They were shabby and in disrepair. I caught names of bars, restaurants, a couple offices. Some buildings were abandoned completely and boarded up, while others had broken windows.

I would've thought the place was a ghost town if it weren't for a few people walking along the streets. One a vampire, the other a witch, maybe. They kept their heads down and their hoods up as they walked against the drizzling rain. I noticed they stayed to opposite sides of the sidewalk as they passed by, like they were wary the other was some sort of killer.

"Now entering Shade Hills," a voice over the bus's intercom announced. This must be the town that surrounded the prison. As the bus took a roundabout, I read off some of the names on the shops. There were stores for necromancy, demonology, and conjuring evil spirits. I bet all those places had loads of magical contraband.

Damn place screamed dark magic. Something that intrigued me, but only for research purposes. As an elemental, I could only wield weather magic. You'd never see these kinds of shops in any other supernatural community. Most of this shit was forbidden.

A shiver crawled across my spine as I realized I was going to a place where plenty of prisoners would have no problem putting a hex or curse on me. Charlie was right when he said I needed to watch my big mouth. There were dangerous people in Shade Hills, and they wouldn't hesitate to kill me.

The bus left Shade Hills, and that's when I saw the fence. Dread crawled up my stomach as I saw miles and miles of iron fencing, the tops edged with curled barbed wire. Four tall guard towers were posed at the corners of the fence line, adorned with spotlights and armed guards.

This was it. We were at the Institute.

We drove down a long, winding road, which led to a large metal gate. Brawny guards in blue uniforms opened the gate, using their magic to pull the two sides open. The bus drove inside, and the last thing I saw of the free world was the sign outside the gate. It read; *Darke Institute for Supernatural Offenders.*

"You okay, pidge?" Charlie asked as I sank lower in my seat. Oberi let out a whine.

"I don't like being put in a cage." My heart was already beating out of my chest. What had I gotten myself into?

"Well, you put us here on purpose, so I hope whatever you're here for is worth it," Charlie grumbled resentfully.

He was right. Somewhere, the answers to the prophecy were on Darke Island, and I needed to find them.

The bus stopped in front of a large stone building, big enough to fit hundreds of people. It was Gothic, with tall, twisting spires and large glass windows— that were fitted with bars. Guards with noxite guns prowled at the doors, preventing any prisoners from getting out.

An insane asylum. They *literally* put us in an abandoned insane asylum.

Beside it, a crumbling cathedral stood tall against the rain, dirty stained glass windows appearing gloomy in the murky atmosphere. The campus... or rather, prison yard... was large and vast, with paths for students to walk on. In the distance was a dark lake. Ancestors only knew what lurked within it.

This place was Halloween all year long— and not the fun kind. This was more of the *serial-killer, get-me-out-of-here* vibe.

The voice came on over the intercom again. "You have arrived at the Institute. Leave your belongings on the bus. They will be delivered to your assigned dormitory."

I *really* didn't want to leave my designer bags, but as Charlie yanked on my wrist, I begrudgingly left them behind. People shoved each other trying to get off. That bitchy succubus girl, Naya, knocked a girl over while swaggering to the front. The girl fell over into the other seat and smacked her head on the window. I flinched as she struggled to sit up.

I stopped and reached over in the seat where the girl had been tossed, holding out a hand. "You okay?"

The girl had blue hair in beachy waves and green eyes that swam like the ocean. She flinched at my extended hand, like she thought I might hit her with it.

She smelled like sea water. She was probably a mermaid. After a moment, the girl cautiously took my hand and got to her feet. "I'm fine," she replied. "I'm Opal."

"Ava-Marie." I gave her a kind smile. Opal seemed very innocent. What the hell was she doing in a place like this?

"Hey, you're holding up the line!" I heard someone shout from the back— a shifter. "Move your ass, prissy bitch!"

"Fuck off, asshole!" I snapped at him. The shifter guy shoved someone aside to get to me, but Charlie blocked his way.

"You might want to back off," Charlie warned. "Don't want to piss off the guards on your first day."

The shifter hesitated as Oberi growled. I moved before the shifter could make up his mind and left the bus. Opal followed me, flanked closely by Charlie and Oberi. As our feet hit gravel, the wind howled, and an eerie chill permeated the air. Loud screeching sounds met my ears. At first, I thought it was someone being tortured, until I realized that the sound was coming from the lake.

"What's that noise?" Charlie asked, cocking his head.

"Sirens," I said in a mystified voice. "They're singing in the lake."

Charlie's mouth opened in wonder as he listened to them. Waiting for us at the gate were six people. A guard shouted at us as we milled about, wondering what to do.

"New arrivals, please go with your student guide, designated by your supernatural race," the guard instructed. "You will be assigned your number and your uniform before you are taken to the Warden for your introductory welcome."

We had to wear *uniforms*? Gross! I totally wasn't here for that.

A crawling feeling crept up my skin as Opal leaned over and asked, "Who's the Warden?"

"I don't know," I whispered. Whoever he was, he didn't sound pleasant.

"Elementals, with me!" a Latina girl shouted. A Mexican gray wolf prowled at her side. It must've been her Familiar. The wolf had red and black mottled fur and keen eyes. The girl herself was curvy, with curly black hair and a scar across her eye that told me not to fuck with her.

I gave a sad wave to Opal as she separated with her guide. It would've been nice to stick with somebody other than *Mister Sensitive-and-Serious* all day. Charlie and I were among the few Elementai. There was one other boy and girl here, neither of whom had bonded with Familiars yet. I didn't know them.

The guide put her hands on her hips. She had to be in her Third Year, and was a bit older than me. "I'm Guadalupe Lopez, but you can call me Lupe for short. My Familiar's name is Rosita. We'll be introducing you to the Institute. Keep up, or we'll leave you behind, and trust me when I say you won't like it when the guards beat your ass for wandering off."

She was a *sweetheart*. Lupe turned on her heel, and the guards opened the big wooden doors that led into the Institute. She gestured us through, while the other groups entered through different entrances.

Above the great doors to the Institute was an insignia, a stone symbol etched into a large coat of arms. A winged snake wrapped in an infinity symbol around a key, which was standing upright. That had to be the Institute's sigil.

When we entered the building, I looked around in astonishment as I took in our surroundings.

"What's it look like?" Charlie asked under his breath. We were at the back of the group, and pressed so close together we could be holding hands.

I nearly wanted to. This place was nuts.

"The outside is an old asylum, with a cathedral attached. It's all fancy inside. There's red rug for the carpet, and the walls have pretty wallpaper. There are statues everywhere of supernatural creatures, and the furniture here is new and well-taken care of. There are portraits everywhere, and the ceiling is so high. It's nearly like a palace," I replied.

"Doesn't sound much like a prison," Charlie said.

"Yet." I wasn't fooled. This might be a pretty cage, but it was still a prison nonetheless. We were trapped here, and there was no way of escape.

My mood flipped instantaneously. I went from good to bad in seconds, and once that spiral started, I couldn't crawl out of it.

"Fuck this place, fuck this place..." I sang under my breath as we walked. The further I got into the school, the more I wanted to run. The absolute finery of the mansion was such a contrast to the barbed wire fencing outside. No matter how much they dressed this asylum up, I had a bad feeling they'd done horrible things to people here. I was going to jump out of my skin with an anxiety attack any second. Oberi put his head under my hand and pressed into me for comfort.

Lupe overheard my words and whirled on me. "Look, you're here, so that means you're guilty. We all are. Just keep your head down and don't get into any trouble, and you might just get out of here in one piece."

Charlie nodded, like he completely agreed with her. I swallowed and didn't argue back. My hands were shaking so badly that it caused my arms to quiver, too. I didn't like this. I didn't like this at all.

Lupe took us down another hallway, one that was sparser and devoid of decoration. She was speaking, but I couldn't decipher her words against the screaming in my head. The voices were getting bad again.

This isn't safe, Ava.

You have to escape, Ava.

The prophecy, Ava!

I let out a whimper. Charlie's head tilted slightly as he noticed. Before I knew it, he'd slipped his fingers between mine and held tight.

Holding his hand should've disgusted me, but it didn't. I squeezed back and pressed into his arm as I tried to ignore the sensation of the walls closing in around me, colors distorting as they suffocated me. Charlie winced as I grasped his hand so hard it hurt, but he didn't let go. Oberi let out a sigh of relief.

I was able to focus on the sensation of Charlie's hand in mine and come back down to reality. As my mind stopped floating and I was firmly back on the ground again, Lupe's voice came back into focus, and overpowered the ones in my head. "Decades ago, the humans attempted to settle Darke Island. They were eventually chased off as they realized the island was a place of heavy supernatural activity. Here, people disappeared without a trace, never to come back. Monsters ran rampant and devoured souls, while ghosts who refused to cross over to the afterlife haunted the woods. Strange things happened here, and while it frightened the humans, the supernatural community saw an opportunity to change the island into a prison."

Lupe tossed her hair as she continued. "The worst of the worst were sent to the cathedral here, which was fashioned into a makeshift prison. The baddest criminals were housed in the cathedral itself, while the rest were sent to building Shade Hills. When the cathedral got too crowded, an asylum was built next to it, to house the most deranged inmates."

One of the other Elementai raised their hand. "Didn't they use to... perform experiments on the inmates here?"

My gut churned as Lupe nodded. "That story's true. They *did* perform terrible experiments on people, years ago. But that's over now. The United Supernatural Union found out about it and shut it down. They changed the asylum into a reform school for supernatural delinquents, which is why all of you are here today."

"Is there any way out?" the other Elementai asked. I could hear an edge of hope in her voice.

Lupe made a *pshing* sound. "Good luck. There's a magical ward around Darke Island. Even if you escape the Institute, the ward will prevent you from leaving the island without permission. There's truly no escape once you end up here. Your only option is to graduate."

I had to spend *four years* here? This was ridiculous. I was starting to think my brother had been right, and this was another one of my impulsive decisions that had screwed me over. Damn my brain.

"Your classes will mostly be centered around reformation," Lupe said. "You'll have one course teaching you the basics of your supernatural race and their magic. The rest of your classes will focus on behavior, substance abuse, and anger management. You'll be expected to attend group therapy every week to chart your progress."

I'd been in and out of therapy all my life and wasn't looking forward to going back. I hated the idea of sharing my deepest thoughts with a bunch of weirdos, who'd probably stab me before they cried with me.

But it would all be worth it, if I could stop the prophecy and save the people I loved. I just had to keep my goal in mind.

Lupe led us down a dark corridor, which stretched into a series of doors. "This is the Elementai section of the prison, where your dormitories are; Cellblock 5. You'll find your name on the door of your cell. Most of the cell blocks are separated by boys and girls, but the Elementai one is not, as it was built in the smallest corridor of the prison."

That was typical, giving the native person the shaft. Lupe stopped at the head of the cellblock. "Change into your uniforms so you can be ready for the Warden's speech."

I searched for Charlie's name before I searched for mine. I caught his last name on the first door in the hallway, before I read my own on the door beside it.

We were right next to each other. I didn't know if I was relieved or annoyed. I pulled him over to his dormitory, then dropped his hand. I didn't want to hold it anymore— touching him felt way too real.

"This is it." I left Charlie at his door before I went to my own. When I opened it, I nearly let out a shriek. *This* was what they were giving us? A metal bed frame was pushed against the wall. On top of the lumpy and stained mattress was a folded, scratchy blanket, with a pillow that looked hard as a rock. The room contained nothing else but a small desk and chair, with a small window that had bars across it.

On the desk was a uniform that made me shudder. These uniforms were a major fashion *faux pas*. There was a long-sleeved white button-up with the Institute sigil on it, along with a black and green tie and a plaid wool skirt that went to the knees. Long white socks and Mary Jane shoes completed the disgusting array.

I put the outfit on with a groan. As I turned the shirt around, I noticed opposite the sigil near the left shoulder was a number: 721.

My prisoner number. My mouth instantly soured. So much for feeling like a student. I was a convict; nothing more, nothing less.

"Do we really have to wear these?" I complained to Lupe when I emerged from my cell.

"During all classes," Lupe said. "You can wear what you like in your free time, as long as it isn't inappropriate."

I bet that meant half my wardrobe. I blew a wayward strand of hair out of my eyes. "Where are the bathrooms?"

"They're down the hall. Communal showers," she replied. "Boys and girls are separate."

I gave another groan. "Do they *really* expect us to live like this?"

"Hey, be lucky that you got your own room," Lupe said. "Most people have to share."

Yuck. Couldn't imagine sharing that closet.

Charlie came out of his dorm with a slight smile on his face. "Seems pretty dry, and it has a nice bed."

This guy must've grown up sleeping on benches if he thought that bed was nice. My back was going to be so sore.

Charlie had put on his uniform, and I had to admit, he looked really cute in a tie. Guy wasn't such a tramp when he cleaned up a little. Oberi barked twice and wagged his tail.

"Yours is better than mine," I complained. His uniform was simple black pants, a black striped tie and a green sweater... which clung tightly to his biceps, by the way. His prisoner number read 137.

"Hey, at least it's not a prison jumpsuit," Charlie said with a shrug.

"Don't joke about that," Lupe snapped. Her wolf let out a growl.

"Um, okay," Charlie started. "Why?"

"The only people who get orange jumpsuits are in Cellblock 9, in the basement of the prison," Lupe said flatly. "Trust me, you don't want to end up down there."

Lupe turned her back on us and walked away. By this point, the other Elementai were dressed and ready to go. Nobody asked about Cellblock 9 as she led us onward.

"Do you think she's trying to scare us?" I whispered to Charlie.

"She seemed pretty serious." Charlie looked concerned. "I wouldn't mess with her, pidge. Asking questions seems like a good way to get hurt around here."

I thought so, too. Still... what was Cellblock 9? And why was it such a bad place to be?

Oberi changed into the Fire unicorn mare as the halls widened. She pressed against me, and I placed a hand against her side, feeling her fiery warmth. I didn't have to worry about getting hurt here. Oberi would protect me, I was sure.

There was a line outside of a classroom near our dorms. Lupe grabbed a box from a desk and began distributing signs. "Everyone at the Institute has to take a booking photograph for identification purposes. You will receive a school ID in a week that you must carry with you at all times."

We were taking *mugshots?* This place couldn't get any more cliché. Lupe handed me my sign, and I looked down.

AVA-MARIE MITOH
RACE: ELEMENTAL - DUAL CASTER (FIRE/WATER)
ID #: 721

Charlie played with his sign. The line moved steadily, until I was in front of a guard with a camera. I smiled sinisterly as he took my photo, making it my every intention that my grin told the Institute to fuck off.

After our mugshots, Lupe led us to what I figured had to be the center of the school, into a hall hundreds of feet long. The ceiling was made of glass, and the floors were marble. A balcony stretched above the main floor, capped by two winding staircases on either side. From the balcony hung black and green flags, the Institute's sigil blazing on it like a warning. The walls were covered in floor-to-ceiling mirrors.

It looked like some kind of ballroom. The people who'd been on the bus with us earlier were here, all dressed in their new uniforms.

"This is the Room of Mirrors. It is where most school events are held, and where the Warden will give his welcome speech," Lupe said. "I've done all I can to get you used to this place. The rest is up to you. Good luck."

Lupe left the Room of Mirrors with Rosita as if her ass was on fire. She certainly didn't want to be stuck with us for longer than she had to. I surveyed the students, looking them over. There was a blonde-haired girl talking to Naya. The girl was muscular and had a stocky build like an athlete. She sneered when I caught her eye.

"Would you mind staring somewhere else?" she snapped. "I'm trying to have a conversation."

As she turned to face me, I caught a glimpse of sparkling butterfly wings. They were dark blue and had glimmering diamonds within them that made the wings appear to be galaxies. They disappeared before I could inspect them further.

Ugh. A fae. They were *so* stuck up.

"I wasn't looking at *you*," I snapped.

"Sure seemed like it." The blonde drew herself up. "You better watch it. I'm Kalina, and I'm going to run this school."

"Says who?" I squared up with her immediately. Naya watched the two of us, an amused expression on her face. She was *loving* this.

"You obviously didn't get the memo. I'm a fae sorceress. We don't associate with those of a *lower class*," Kalina hissed. "Go bother your own kind."

This girl was a bitch. I raised my hand to jam a fireball into her face, but Charlie caught my wrist. "Knock it off," he growled. "You're already looking for trouble."

Naya let out a cruel laugh. "Aw, how cute. She's got a little boyfriend. Come on, Kalina. We have better things to do than fight with a couple of savages."

My. Blood. Boiled. Kalina frowned. Charlie froze, and I added, "You're about to see how much of a *savage* I can be when I choke your ass out."

"I'd like to see you try," Naya threatened.

I was about to jump her and start pulling hair, until all sound in the Room of Mirrors immediately drained out. The lights dimmed as a dark voice from above spoke. "Greetings, new arrivals."

Kalina and I broke off our argument and turned to the balcony above. My heart skipped a beat as I took in the sight of the person above me. The man had deep-set, hooded eyes, and a face that was so taut it looked like a skeleton, skin stretched over high cheekbones. He had a strong build and wide shoulders, and his head was thrown high and proud. His dark hair was cut short in a military style, and his lips pressed tight and thin. He was both beautiful and ugly at the same time. He had great white feathery wings behind him, several feet long in length— an angel.

I knew who he was without having to be told. The Warden.

The Warden beat his wings a few times, and they vanished behind him before he clasped his hands together. "Welcome to the Darke Institute for Supernatural Offenders. I am the Warden of this school, Doctor Ophio Taurus. I'd like to begin by saying you are all very welcome here."

What a lie. This man had a voice that hissed like a snake. He wasn't welcoming at all.

The Warden continued. As he spoke, the sinister smile on his face spread... like he was enjoying the attention. "This will be easier for all of you if we lay down a few simple ground rules. First, forget about your old life. Forget about your family, your friends. You are now the property of the United Supernatural Union, in care of me, your Warden. I have full authority to use whatever means I deem necessary to reform you into a proper member of magical society."

I nearly shook in rage. Forget about my *family*? No fucking way. This dude could go to hell. Charlie put a hand on my shoulder, to tell me to stay put.

"At the Institute, our goal is to succeed by making you succeed," the Warden continued. "The program is simple. You will receive four years of education. If the board considers you reformed, you will graduate, and your criminal record will be wiped clean. You will be allowed to return to your homes as free members of society. We have many employers in Shade Hills who would love to have you."

Yeah, right. Like I'd stick around and get a job on Creepy Island.

The Warden smiled even bigger. "However, if the board determines that you have *not* been reformed, you will be transferred to an adult prison somewhere else on the island. After this, your chances of returning to your homes are lost, and you will be given a life sentence. That is, if you make it that far."

What did he mean by that? There were a couple of uneasy glances, but no one dared to speak.

The Warden spread his arms wide, like he was a benevolent god welcoming us into a heaven that felt more like hell. "Do well in your classes, and you will go far here. Good grades and good behavior will be rewarded with Commissary points and privileges to take trips into Shade Hills. Unruly behavior will result in consequences. If infractions go too far, you will be punished with solitary confinement in Cellblock 9. You have been warned."

So that's what was in Cellblock 9. The worst of the worst were sent down there, and by the sound of it, nobody came out.

"Let's go over a few ground rules. No cell phones are permitted on campus," the Warden boomed. "Students are allowed one phone call a week through the school phones, and as many letters as they can afford to send out. There is a curfew from ten p.m. until six a.m., where you are required to stay in your dorms. All students are expected to contribute to the well-being of the prison by doing chores, which includes cleaning and laundry. There are no cameras, as I assume you all know, technology does not work well with an abundance of magic... however, be very aware that there are enchantments to keep you in. Certain items, such as bobby pins and other items that can be used as weapons, are not permitted. The guards are searching your belongings now, to be sure nothing contraband is on campus."

Great. I wondered what was missing from my stuff. Like I was going to take a bobby pin and stab someone's eye out... though I was sure there were people here that would.

The Warden straightened his tie. "You are allowed to use magic on school grounds. However, if a student has been found to break several severe rules, they will be forced to wear a noxite cuff that will inhibit the power of their magic."

I definitely didn't want one of those cuffs. I resolved that if I broke any rules, I couldn't get caught.

"You will receive your class list and related textbooks in the morning." The Warden tilted his head. "For now, get to know your surroundings. Trust that we are here for you. We care about you. And we are devoted to your future as a contributing member of magical society."

This guy was pure fucking evil. I could feel it coming off him in waves. His words sounded noble, but make no mistake, he was at this job because he loved torturing kids— not because he wanted to help them get better.

I vowed not to let him get to me. No matter what he did.

As the Warden walked through a set of double doors behind the balcony, I turned so I could sink my claws into Kalina. Charlie pulled me away before I could. Oberi began shepherding us back in the direction of the dorms with her horn, throwing nervous glances behind her.

"What are you doing?" I snapped. I yanked my hand out of Charlie's the moment we got in front of our dormitory. "We can't let her talk to us like that!"

"That's the least of our problems," Charlie growled. "For fuck's sake, pidge, can you *try* not to get thrown in Cellblock 9 your first day here?"

"We can't let people walk all over us. They'll take advantage," I protested.

Charlie gave a humorless laugh. "Trust me, pidge, there are times to fight back and times to shut your mouth. You really need to learn the difference."

"At least I'm not going to avoid conflict, like you," I snapped.

Charlie shook his head in disgust. "I'm not going to keep sticking up for you. You need to watch your back."

He fished in his pocket for something. "By the way, tell your old man he can't scare me."

Charlie tossed something, and I caught it last minute. My mouth fell open when I saw it. Daddy's wallet.

I rifled through it quickly. It didn't look like Charlie had taken anything. Everything was still there, including the money. He just wanted to prove a point.

"You're unbelievable," I sneered. "Was that really necessary?"

Charlie shrugged. "You need to learn there are other ways to show people you won't be pushed around."

He turned his back on me and entered his dorm. Oberi let out a soft nicker.

I facepalmed. This guy was really too much. I went inside my dorm. Oberi tried to squeeze in, but she was too big to fit through the door, and she cried out impatiently.

"Hold on," I told her as I pushed her back out. "I'll be there in a sec."

My suitcases had been delivered to my dorm. When I looked at them, sadness flooded my veins.

Did Charlie *really* not have anything to put his clothes in but trash bags? That was so sad.

I sat at the desk. When I opened the drawers, I found paper and a singular pencil. I took them out and began to write.

Dear Daddy,

Everything is fine here at the Institute. I got here safe and well. My dorm is nice, and my uniform is great. I am already making new friends!

I scowled, thinking of Kalina. The letter sounded so fake. Truth was, I was miserable here.

But I didn't want Daddy to worry, so I put as much false cheer into the letter as I could muster, hoping he wouldn't catch on to it.

It looks like Charlie took your wallet. He says he's sorry. Nothing's missing. It's like a game to him, so I hope you'll forgive him. I'll try to mail it back with the letter.

Can you please send along a new suitcase, dark purple in color? I'd like to pay for it— the money's in my account. You know where the card is.

Give Mama, Ez, Alana and Maverick all my love. I'll write as much as I can, and I look forward to your letters.

P.S. Some chocolate would be nice, too. I'm dying for it.

Love, Ava-Marie.

A couple of teardrops fell from my eyes, but I wiped them away before they could fall on the letter. I wanted my parents to think I was happy here, so I'd pretend to be happy. Maybe if I pretended long enough, it would become real.

I wasn't sure where to take the letter, but I'd walk around the school and find a way. I personally didn't feel safe enough to go anywhere alone, but I didn't want to drag Charlie with me, so I left with just Oberi.

I relaxed when I saw Opal standing near a gargoyle, a letter in her hands and looking worried. Her face softened in relief when she saw me. "Hey. Where are you off to?"

"I have to mail a letter to my parents," I said. "Do you want to come with me?"

"Sure." Opal's face beamed. "We can find the mailroom together."

Opal linked her arm in mine. We stayed close as we roamed through the halls. A couple of guys catcalled us, but when Oberi lowered her horn at them, they shut the fuck up.

"Hey, Ava..." Opal said, her voice thoughtful. "What the Warden said. About the people who don't make it far enough to leave the Institute and transfer to the adult prison. Where do you think they go?"

I honestly had no idea. And I wasn't so sure I wanted to find out.

SEVEN

The Darke Institute was nothing like Orenda Academy, but it wasn't the prison I'd been envisioning. Curfew sucked, but at least the food was good. I'd worried we'd be living on stale bread and broth water for the next four years. I was surprised when we were served chicken Alfredo and chocolate pie on our first night there.

"You look like you're enjoying this," Ava-Marie noted in disgust. She clearly thought it was disgusting.

I shrugged. "It's delicious."

Ava leaned across the table to whisper, "Don't let the food fool you. They only serve comfort food so we don't run. It's all an illusion."

"Or they want to feed us... because you know, this is a school," I pointed out.

"A *prison*," Ava snarled.

"A *reform school*," I corrected her.

"Then why is there a fence around the property, locks on our dorm room doors, and bars on our windows?" Ava challenged.

Oberi barked in agreement.

"For people like you who think the rules don't apply to them," I snapped.

"Is that why the kids call this place the *Villain Institute?*" she huffed.

Before I could answer, she continued. "I've heard the whispers in the halls. The Warden thinks we're all criminals— villains."

I snorted. "Well, you're not innocent."

"Neither are you," she shot back.

I blew a breath of annoyance. "I don't even know what I'm doing here. I'm too old for some juvenile reform school."

"Not in the supernatural world," Ava pointed out. "In supernatural societies, we don't get our magic until around age eighteen, which is when we go to college or university to learn how to use it. It isn't until we graduate that we come of age. The Institute is a facility aged between juvenile detention and prison, for people ages eighteen to twenty-two. Some inmates are older, I guess, but only because they were sentenced earlier and have to serve their four years. If we were sentenced to an adult prison before learning our magic, we'd be killed by the other inmates."

A shiver traveled down my spine. I'd be twenty-six before I got out of here. I wasn't sure if me being older than most of the other students was an advantage or a hindrance at this place.

That was the last thing she said to me all night.

In the morning, I woke to the sound of a paper being slid under my door. It must've been six a.m. because the lock used to enforce curfew disengaged with a *click*.

I crawled out of bed and picked up the paper, but it was useless to me. I couldn't read it. Outside my door, I heard the sound of claws scratching. I opened it and bent to pet Oberi.

"Hey, boy," I said, scratching him behind the ears. "I hope things weren't too bad on your first night with Ava. Wish you could've stayed with me, though."

Oberi licked my hand, then nuzzled his head into my arms like he'd missed me. I returned to my room and gathered my things. Oberi helped me find the bathroom, and I showered and dressed.

I returned to my room— and promptly toppled over something that wasn't there before. It'd been sitting right inside my door. Oberi barked as I went tumbling to the ground, then hurried over to help me up.

"What the hell?" I mumbled under my breath.

I reached out and ran my hands over the thing I'd tripped over. It was taller than my knee and about half as wide, shaped like a box and covered in thick canvas. As my fingers ran over the zipper, I realized what it was— a suitcase. Who the hell left their suitcase in my room?

Unless it wasn't a mistake...

Damn it, Ava. I noticed how apprehensive she seemed about my garbage bag. Didn't she realize I didn't want— didn't *need*— handouts? This could only mean she expected something in return.

I wanted to stomp over to her room immediately and return the luggage, but Oberi stepped in my way when I stood. I hesitated, and the thought crossed my mind to keep it. I'd never had anything this nice to hold my things before... and I really wanted it.

Oberi pressed his nose to the luggage, pushing it into my leg. He must've been able to sense Ava's intentions better than I could, because apparently, he really wanted me to have it.

"Fine," I caved. "I'll keep it. But I'm not taking anything else from *her*."

I set the luggage on the bed. Heels clicked in a confident rhythm outside the door.

"Ava, is that you?" I asked.

My door creaked open wider.

"It's me," she said. "Did you get your schedule yet? I thought we could compare."

I gestured to the paper I'd set on the desk. "Is that my schedule?"

The paper rustled as she picked it up. "Sure is. Looks like we have Elementai Magic together."

"Figures." I waited for Ava to say something about the luggage, but she didn't acknowledge it. Instead, I asked, "What are my other classes?"

"Your first is Introduction to Work-Study this morning," she told me. "You've also been enrolled in Juvenile Justice and Substance Abuse."

"Just the classes I wanted," I deadpanned. "I hope they count toward my major."

Ava laughed, but she sounded more uncomfortable than anything. "What are you majoring in? Pissing off the inmates?"

"Just *one* inmate in particular," I teased.

Ava got quiet for a second, before asking, "What *would* you major in, if you could? I wanted to get my degree in Anthropology... before the Institute happened."

She sounded really sad. I quickly answered her question to distract her. "I never really thought about it. I didn't think I'd ever make it to college, considering I never graduated from high school."

"You never *what?*" Ava balked.

I realized I'd said too much, and I snatched my schedule out of her hands. "It's a long story. Anyway, I'm going to need Oberi today to help me get to my classes."

"I need his support, too," she argued.

"You can find your classes on your own," I pointed out. "Until I learn the layout of this school, I need a little guidance."

Ava went silent. "Fine, but I want Oberi to sleep by *me* tonight."

"You had him last night!"

"And?" she challenged. "If you get him all day, I get him at night. We have to play fair."

I snorted. There was no playing fair with Ava-Marie. But at least she agreed to let me take Oberi for the day. That was better than I'd hoped for.

Oberi wasn't a trained guide dog, but he wasn't really a *dog*, either. He was far more intelligent and knew how to navigate the school by instinct. We stopped by the cafeteria for breakfast, then started toward my first class.

As we made our way down the hall, I took note of any major land-marks we passed. Voices bounced off a high ceiling as we walked through the main entrance. Not far from there, I heard the sound of an air hockey table whirring and a puck clicking back and forth.

"Six to nothing," a young voice said.

I realized I was passing a recreation room. Must've been the Villain's Den— it was the nickname for the place where everybody hung out between classes. I made a mental note so I'd remember where it was located.

I counted my steps, and we took twenty more before Oberi turned left down a hall. We slowed and entered a classroom. Voices filled the room as students flooded in. Oberi led me to the back row, and I took a seat at the desk in the corner. He sat dutifully beside me, panting in glee.

At least someone's happy.

"Aww, a *puppy*," a female voice cooed as she took the seat beside me. Oberi let out a low growl.

"Don't pet him." I tried not to sound rude, but it was instinctual. No one touched my Familiar but me... and Ava. "He's on duty."

"Duty...? Dear Goddess, I'm so sorry!" the girl cried. I could hear it in her voice the moment she realized I was blind. "I didn't mean... I'm Alice, by the way. Alice Tucker."

"Charlie," I said. "I've never heard the phrase *Dear Goddess* before. Is that a colloquialism?"

"I'm a witch," she explained. "From the Miriamic Coven."

"Oh," I said like it made sense, but it didn't really. I didn't know that much about other societies yet. I'd only just learned of the Elementai.

"You look confused," she pointed out.

"I'm new," I admitted. "Haven't gotten the whole supernatural run-down yet."

"It's simple," she said, sounding happy to help. "There are six main supernaturals at the Institute. First is the Celestials, like the Warden. They call themselves angels, but they're actually Nephilim, or half-angels. Then you have the Arcanea— fae sorceresses and their shifter mates. Try to stay away from the Midnighters, which are the vampires and succubi. They're forbidden from feeding on any students, but accidents have happened here more than once."

Sure... accidents.

"Then there are witches and warlocks like me, and I'm assuming Elementai like you?"

I nodded.

She sounded pleased as she continued. "And the final race is the Atlanteans, or the mermaids and sirens. We occasionally get Astromancers, but they have their own prison system and don't tend to send people to the Institute."

"Astromancers?" I questioned.

"Wow, you weren't lying. You *are* new." Alice wasn't mean about it. In fact, she sounded really bubbly and nice. "Astromancers are enchanters who get their magic from the stars. Anyway, most supernatural societies are split into their own factions. Elementai, as you know, have a House for every element. In the Miriamic Coven, we're split into Casts. They're—"

"Whoa," I stopped her. "Slow down. I already have five Houses to remember and seven other societies you just mentioned. Give a guy some time to process it."

Alice snickered. "You don't seem like you belong here. You're too nice. What are you in for?"

I groaned. "It's a long story."

Alice lowered her voice and leaned toward me. "Are you innocent, too?"

"I wouldn't exactly say *innocent*," I replied with a coy smirk. "Wait... what do you mean, *too?*"

Alice hesitated a moment. "I shouldn't be here," she admitted. "I was accused of hexing a fae on my trip to Europe, but I would *never*. That's what I get for taking a gap year and traveling. Don't *ever* visit Europe, by the way. Not unless you want to run into the fae. They're horrible."

"Noted," I said.

Alice shifted in her chair and went quiet. She'd been really helpful and nice, but I wasn't sure I believed she was innocent. Like Lupe said when we arrived, no one here was innocent. Even though my crimes in Kinpago weren't exactly worthy of a prison sentence, I was far from innocent. I'd done some seriously shady stuff. I deserved to be here.

The class quieted, and a pair of footsteps marched across the front of the room. "Welcome, students. I'm Professor Cusak, and this is your introduction to your work-study program."

Alice leaned over and whispered, "He's an angel. You'd think you could trust them, but you'd be wrong. I hear this guy is tough on his students."

"Then I guess we better not attract his attention," I replied.

"Your work-study program will begin next semester," Professor Cusak explained. "It is an apprenticeship program to teach you the skills needed to pursue careers outside of the Institute. This semester will prepare you for entering the mines."

"The mines?" I asked Alice in a low whisper.

"There are noxite and crystal mines that run under the island,"

Alice explained quietly. "Students are expected to work in the mines as part of the rehabilitation program. They believe hard work is good for us."

My guts twisted at the idea. Something about it didn't sit right with me. "Do we get paid?"

"A couple dollars a day, I think," Alice answered. "We can cash in at the campus store for clothes, soap, stamps, and things like that."

"What happens to the stuff we mine?"

"I don't know," Alice whispered. "I guess the Institute collects and sells it."

A shiver ran down my spine. I was starting to think maybe Ava was right— this place *was* a prison, and a *for-profit* prison nonetheless.

"That's just—" I started to say.

"Excuse me," Professor Cusak snapped. "You two in the back. Do you have something to share with the class?"

"No," I said the same time Alice answered.

"I w-was only explaining the p-program to Charlie," Alice stammered.

"If you have questions, you may ask me directly," Professor Cusak snapped. "No talking during class, or I'll have you thrown in Cellblock 9."

That seemed a little extreme, based on what I'd heard of Cellblock 9, but I wasn't about to risk it. Alice and I both went quiet.

Professor Cusak continued, ignoring the two of us. "We will start the semester learning the art of transference, as some of you will be assigned to transference for your work-study program."

Professor Cusak began walking around the room. A *clink* came, one after another. I couldn't tell what it was, until he reached my desk and placed something on top of it. I reached out to feel the object. It was cold and smooth in my hand— a rock of some sort.

"As you all know, transference is a very advanced form of magic," Professor Cusak continued. "It involves transferring your magic into crystals so that someone else of your race may draw from it. You are expected to learn transference by the end of your first term at the Darke Institute. You may begin."

My brow furrowed as I tested the weight of the crystal in my hand.

I'd had zero magical instruction before, and I was already expected to perform advanced magic? What kind of a shit school was this?

Apparently, I wasn't the only one who felt totally out of my element, because someone at the front of the room spoke. "Sir, how exactly does transference work? I mean, how do we do it?"

"We will get to that in a later lesson," he replied, sounding less than pleased at the question. "For now, I would like to see if anyone is able to accomplish the task without instruction. Begin."

Nobody spoke, but I could hear the shared frustrations around the room. Someone in front of me hummed in concentration, and a girl across the room kept huffing. Teeth gritted from the row ahead of me, and Alice couldn't stop clicking her tongue.

I had no hope of getting this on my first try, so I didn't even put in the effort. It didn't seem like anyone else knew what they were doing anyway, so why try?

By the end of class, not a single person had managed to transfer their magic into the crystals. Oberi led me out of the room behind everyone else.

"That was a horrible lesson," a boy sneered.

"Agreed," a girl said. "How can he expect us to just *know* these things?"

"He's obviously trying to separate the good students from the great," another boy added. "If anyone got it today, they'd be put into the trans-ference work-study right away."

The girl huffed. "Well, no one did, so the joke's on him."

The voices faded down the hall, until eventually, I couldn't hear the conversation anymore.

"Well, Oberi," I said to my Familiar. "We have some time before our next class. What should we do?"

Oberi barked, and his wagging tail hit my leg repeatedly. He started leading me back the way we came, then stopped at the rec room.

"What is it, boy?" I asked. "You want to go inside?"

Oberi barked and ran away from me, but he came back a few moments later.

I furrowed my brow. "I don't understa—"

Oberi shoved his nose into my hand. I felt something furry and round and grabbed on to it. It fit easily inside my palm. "A tennis ball? You want to play fetch?"

Oberi barked happily.

"Where are we going to play?"

Oberi didn't hesitate. He rounded on me and pressed his head into my leg, pushing me forward. As soon as I started walking, he came back to my side and led me through the rec room. We stopped at a wall, and I reached my hands out to feel my surroundings. My fingers curled around a door handle, and I twisted.

Hot, humid air met my skin, and Oberi and I stepped outside. I could feel the expansiveness of the open air, but my magic seemed to hit a block hundreds of yards away. It felt a lot like when I'd stepped on the bus, though not as strong, since we weren't in confined quarters. I noted the feeling as noxite and assumed that was the fence Ava had mentioned that surrounded the property. Though it was hot out, I couldn't feel the sun on my skin, as if thick clouds covered the sky.

Voices filled the yard— so many that I couldn't make them out. A *twang* sounded each time a basketball connected with the pavement, then came the clink of chains as the ball sank into the basket.

In the distance, someone yelled, "Hut!" Bodies collided together with hard *thuds*.

Ouch. Football sounded like a good way to get beaten inside the prison. I couldn't believe the guards allowed it, to be honest.

"So you've taken me to the prison yard, Oberi?" I asked, stroking his head. I lowered my voice and muttered, "I am *not* looking forward to this."

Oberi whimpered, and I knew I couldn't tell him no. Even magical huskies couldn't be expected to be cooped up inside all day.

"Fine." I sighed. "But only because I care."

I avoided the basketball players and headed to the other end of the prison yard, where the voices were far off. I tossed the ball toward the fence, and Oberi took off running. He yipped happily, then returned a few moments later and dropped the ball into my hand. It was coated in saliva and smelled of dog breath.

"Ew, Oberi," I complained. He barked again and panted. "Hell, why do you have to be such a good boy?"

I drew my arm back and threw the ball farther this time. Oberi went tearing across the yard so fast that dirt flew up from where his paws dug into the grass. Chunks hit me in the leg.

Oberi returned less than a minute later, and I threw the ball again. I heard the football players too late. Someone came sprinting toward us just as I tossed the ball. Cheers followed behind him.

Thwack. The tennis ball hit somebody square on.

"Touchdown!" someone yelled, but it was too far off to be the guy I'd hit.

"What the *fuck?*" a deep voice roared. That was definitely the guy who just took the blow from my tennis ball. *Shit.*

The man stepped toward me. Oberi threw himself in front of me and growled, the tennis ball totally forgotten.

"Who the fuck do you think you are?" he snapped.

I opened my mouth to respond, but I never got a word out. A heavy fist cracked into my jaw, and I was thrown sideways.

"What the hell!?" I growled as I steadied myself. My head spun. I pressed my fingers to my lip, and they came away covered in a warm liquid. "It was an accident."

"Bullshit," the guy growled. "You did that on purpose."

Oberi barked as the man reached out to grab me. His hands landed on my shoulders, and I noticed they were *huge.* "You want to pick a fight with a vamp?" he snarled. His chilling breath crossed the top of my head. The guy must've been a whole head taller than me. "Be my guest, but your sorry ass is going to lose."

Air rushed toward my face, and I ducked his fist. A chorus of *oohs* rang out from behind him. He moved faster than I could react, though, and I didn't have time to dodge the next blow. He swung an uppercut at my jaw, and my feet left the ground as I went flying backward. I slammed to the ground hard, and breath whipped out of my lungs. I gasped. Oberi rushed over and licked my face. I used my magic to force air into my lungs, but it only helped a little. My ears rang, and my sense of balance was shot.

"Go Mad Dog!" someone shouted.

Mad Dog must've been encouraging them, because several others joined in on the cheers, and they only grew louder.

"Get up!" a boy hissed from above me— someone different than the others. His voice was smoother, not quite as rough and angry as the vampire gang. He placed his hands on my shoulders, but they were smaller and softer than Mad Dog's. Whoever it was wasn't gentle, though. He yanked me to my feet. A cat mewed lightly beside him. "You have to fight back!"

"Fight back?" I balked. I was still trying to figure out which way was up and which way was down. That punch had nearly knocked me out. "Who are you?"

"I'm Marcus. I'm the guy who's gonna make sure you don't get killed," he said in a rush.

"I can't fight back," I argued. "He's huge! And a vampire, no less. This isn't a fair fight."

"So he's faster and stronger than you," Marcus said, like it wasn't a big deal. "Use your magic against him."

"What for?" I demanded. Something lurched in my guts. I doubled over, feeling like I might hurl.

Marcus caught me. "You're new here, aren't you? If you want to survive in this prison, you can't let anyone walk over you. You win this fight, you win every fight afterward. This is the only chance you've got. Now get back in there and finish this."

Marcus clapped me on the back, and I stumbled forward toward Mad Dog. I didn't know who my new ally was, but he was right. This wasn't a street fight I could just walk away from afterward. I was locked in here with Mad Dog, and losing this fight meant I'd be marked as an easy target. If I walked away, I was inviting him to come after me again. And not just him, but anyone who was hungry for blood. Winning was the only way to show everyone they couldn't mess with me. I had to do this— not just for myself, but for Oberi. I wouldn't let him become a target, too.

"You throw a good punch," I said, wiping the blood from my lip.

The chorus of cheers died down, and Mad Dog let out a low chuckle. "You must have a death wish."

I shrugged. "Something like that. So, is that all you've got?"

"There's a lot more where that came from," Mad Dog snarled.

I quickly realized Mad Dog liked to fight with his fists, because a punch came rushing toward my face again. I felt it by the change in the air. I ducked out of the way and reacted before he could get another punch in. I thrust my arms outward, and the Air followed my command. I felt the resistance as it slammed into him. The *thud* I expected from his body hitting the ground never came. He barely even stumbled.

Use my magic... not as effective as it sounds.

How the hell was I supposed to fight a vampire? It's not like I could suck the air out of his lungs. He was undead, and didn't need to breathe. It wouldn't affect him... right?

Hell if I knew.

Mad Dog approached me again, but before he reached me, Oberi darted in front of me. He growled and snapped his jaw, but the vampire was faster than he was. Air swirled by me as Mad Dog swung out a foot. Oberi whimpered as it connected with his gut. I heard the *thud* as my Familiar landed in the grass a few feet away.

Pure, unadulterated anger rushed to the surface. I didn't think. I just reacted.

I flung my hands out, and Air magic blasted through them. I felt it streaming around Mad Dog's body, and though he resisted, he couldn't fight the wind gusts enough to get close to me.

"Nobody hurts my Familiar!" I screamed.

My rage came bursting through, and Air magic unlike anything I'd ever used began to circle around Mad Dog. My magic felt like a rope, tightening around the low life and pinning his arms to his sides. I might as well have been summoning a tornado, because that's how strong the winds felt. Dirt swirled through the air, sending particles bouncing off my skin and into my eyes. Trash and other debris could be heard tumbling across the pavement near the basketball courts, and the hoops rattled. Screams filled the prison yard. The guards began yelling to get things under control, but it was nearly inaudible over the winds.

"I'll make you sorry you ever touched my Familiar," I sneered.

I threw my arms upward, and the air followed. The mini cyclone I'd created blasted upward, taking Mad Dog with it. His screams could be heard echoing in the distance as he fell from a great height. I heard a *splash*, but I could barely process it. I just stood there, shaking.

"Holy shit, man," Marcus said as he returned to my side. "Right in the lake! A classic."

I furrowed my brow. "There's a lake?"

"Hell yeah." He sounded pleased. "Mad Dog is siren food. He won't be messing with you again."

"Holy shit. Did I kill him?" My stomach hollowed at the thought. I hadn't meant to take things that far.

"No, he'll be— get down!"

Marcus grabbed me by the neck and shoved me to the ground. We landed side-by-side in the grass as something small whizzed above our heads. I nearly crushed Marcus' cat, but the creature wiggled out from under my arm.

"What the hell—?"

"Noxite darts," he breathed. "The guards will shoot at anyone! Let's get out of here."

I grabbed Oberi's scruff and scurried to my feet. I kicked up another whirlwind around us to throw any noxite tranquilizers off their course. I followed Marcus and Oberi around the side of the building, and we ducked into the school. The entrance was narrow, like a long hallway. I heaved heavy breaths, but it hardly felt like there was enough air in here.

"Holy shit," I gasped as I leaned against the wall.

"Holy shit is right," Marcus agreed. "You beat Mad Dog! Good job, man."

"I'm not talking about Mad Dog!" I cried. "I'm talking about the guards. Did they see us?"

I hoped not. The last thing I needed was to head to Cellblock 9 my first day of class.

"With that whirlwind you created?" Marcus panted. "I couldn't see anything through that. I think you're safe. You've got some crazy skills, though. I've never seen elemental magic like that."

"Mad Dog's gonna want revenge," I stated.

"Nah, you did good," Marcus said. "I got in a fight with one of his buddies my first day here. Won it like a champ, and they haven't bothered me since. Anyway, good luck at the Institute."

"Wait!" I stopped him before he could walk away. "Why'd you help me? Are you an Elementai like me?"

Marcus chuckled. "What, because of my cat? Nah, Rishi's not a Familiar. My tattoo marks me as a warlock. I'm surprised you didn't notice."

I didn't say anything. Marcus hadn't caught on that I was blind, which was a good thing. I didn't want anyone in this prison thinking they could take advantage of me.

I shrugged. "I'm new."

"Well, it was a good thing I was out in the yard when I was," Marcus said. "You have to be careful here, new guy."

I scoffed. "Believe me, I know. Thanks for the help."

Marcus chuckled. "Seeing you kick Mad Dog's ass was worth it."

"This might sound dumb, but..." I wondered how to word the question. "I thought vampires couldn't be outside during the day. Shouldn't Mad Dog and his crew... I don't know, burn up in the prison yard or something? Or is that just a myth?"

"Nah, it's true," Marcus said. "But the cloud cover on Darke Island is so thick vamps don't have to worry about the sun."

Damn. I had so much to learn about this world.

"See you around," Marcus said.

"Yeah," I replied. "See ya."

After Marcus and his cat walked away, I realized that he never told me why he helped me. It was like he'd avoided the question all together — like he was hiding something.

Prison wasn't the place to go poking into people's secrets, but I'd be damned if I didn't want to know what Marcus was hiding.

ava-marie

EIGHT

My brain buzzed with static.

I hated that they woke us up at six a.m. by turning all the lights on and unlocking the doors. I was *not* a morning person.

Today, I doubted if I was even a person.

I hadn't slept but an hour. Since the beginning of the week, I'd been totally wired, and today was worse than ever. My thoughts raced so fast I couldn't comprehend one thought before it surged into another. I was riding so high right now I didn't think I could ever come down.

Oberi whimpered and nosed my feet. He was lying at the edge of the bed in his husky form, and he hadn't been apart from me all night.

I had to do something to get all this energy out of my body. My body was so jittery, it nearly felt like I was on drugs, and I hadn't taken anything.

Maybe a jog around the prison yard would help me calm down. I got dressed in my workout gear and tied my hair back while Oberi let out a whine.

"Go on. Go back to Charlie," I told him as I opened the door. "He needs your help to get around the prison. I'll be fine."

Oberi gave me a look that told me not to go getting into any trouble. No promises.

When Oberi was gone, I walked to the prison yard. I took in the sight of the immense property. There was a basketball court and a small area for lifting weights. In the distance were the sparse woods and the lake that held the sirens. A big track circled the entire yard, which people walked on daily during breaks.

That horrible fence was the worst part. It made me feel boxed in. The yard was still pretty isolated. Two people kicked a soccer ball back and forth on the grass a ways down, but besides that, the place was deserted.

I set a timer on my watch at six fifteen and started running down the track. Within the first few laps, my lungs had already developed a sharp, stabbing feeling, but I didn't allow myself to slow down. Instead, I pushed harder.

It was eight o'clock when my body forced me to stop. I skidded to a halt in front of the double doors that led to the yard and vomited into a trash can. All that came up was stomach acid. A couple people looked at me and edged away, like I was carrying a disease.

I was exhausted, but my mind still whirled like a merry-go-round. I dragged my ass back to the Elementai dorms and washed up in the gross community showers. I turned the water as hot as it could go, to try to drown out the thousands of voices that were already ringing in my ears. No one was in here, thank the ancestors, but I'd seen more ass and boobs in the past seven days than I ever wanted to in my life. Privacy was nonexistent at the Institute... but at least in the girls' showers, I felt safe.

There were locker rooms here for people to get dressed in. I scowled when I opened my locker and saw the same boring uniform I had to wear, day in and day out. It was Friday, so at least I'd get a break from wearing it tomorrow.

Even so. If I had to put on that crime against fashion one more time, I would lose my shit.

I tapped my chin and gave a small smile. This uniform needed a *major* upgrade.

Do it, Ava.

Start something.

Cause trouble.

We weren't allowed to have scissors, for obvious reasons. I took the skirt out of the locker and sawed it on the edge of a bench, until it created a small tear. I ripped the edge of the skirt and threw away the large piece, before I took the white shirt and tore the sleeves off that, too.

I slipped the clothes on. I unbuttoned the bottom of the shirt so it exposed my midriff, then tied it just underneath my boobs. I loosened the top two buttons of my shirt, too, to show off some cleavage. The newly-ripped skirt just ended at my ass.

I looked *so hot*. Very sexy schoolgirl vibe. This would break a million dress codes— and was risky as hell to wear in a place where people were looking for prey.

But right now, I didn't care about the risk. The adrenaline pumping through my blood was so strong, I couldn't avoid the temptation. I walked out of that locker room with my head held high and a big smile on my face.

Students who took medications had to line up to get them from the nurse's station every morning. I had to report; otherwise, they'd come looking for me.

Opal was standing in the medication line outside the infirmary. The mermaid's green eyes widened like saucers when she saw my outfit. "Ava-Marie, what are you *wearing?*"

"I'm still in uniform," I pointed out. All the guys in the hallway were looking at me— some of the girls, too. Nobody made a move, though.

"You're going to get an infraction," she whispered.

"What more can they do to me? I'm already behind bars," I said.

Opal shook her head, but didn't say anything more. When I got to the front of the line, the nurse wrinkled her nose at my outfit, but she said nothing. The nurse handed me lithium and an antipsychotic in a small paper cup. She watched as I took them and made me lift my tongue to show her I wasn't hiding them, to spit them out later.

Ancestors, she reminded me of Mama and Daddy. They'd eventually caught on I was dumping my pills down the drain a few years ago. They'd started watching as I took them. Apparently, this place had the same policy. Nothing got past the staff around this joint.

I wish the pills were helping. Usually, they did.

Not this week.

"You heading to class?" Opal asked as we left the line.

I shook my head. "No. I haven't gotten breakfast yet."

"Better do that. Don't want another violation on your record other than the one you're going to get for your uniform." Opal giggled.

"Sure." We had to report for meals, too. We had to report for *every-thing* around here. Our lives were so structured I felt like I was in kindergarten.

The walk from the infirmary to the cafeteria seemed to take mere moments. I was aware of eyes on me, though any voices that cried out were muddled in the background. If anyone tried to bother me, I didn't notice them. I was too far into my fog.

The cafeteria had to be the most boring place in the school. Long metal benches were placed in big lines everywhere around the room. At the head of the room was the counter, where you could pick up what-ever gross thing the other inmates were serving that day. The area was sparsely decorated, with gray paint, gray carpet, and gray, mushy goo for dinner nearly every night.

My mind started to clear as I walked through the cafeteria line. I didn't feel hungry at all. I was required to take *something,* so I grabbed a breakfast smoothie and an apple. As I turned around to find a place to sit, I smacked into a large, broad chest.

A sharp grin immediately made my insides curl. "Hey, baby. Just where do you think you're going?"

I knew who he was— Mad Dog. He had a reputation around here for being the worst of the worst. He had an ugly pug face, skin so pale it was nearly white. His eyes burned red, and the uniform he wore stretched around his massive frame. For ancestors' sake, he had fangs so large, I didn't know how they fit in his mouth.

"Away from you." I tried to maneuver around him, but Mad Dog blocked my way. His eyes roamed me in a way I didn't like.

"You wouldn't dress like that if you didn't want attention," Mad Dog said. He leaned in closer, and a shiver crawled up my skin. "You smell pretty good. Let's go around back for a quick bite."

A couple of people looked our way, but nobody intervened. No one was brave enough to stand up to Mad Dog.

But I was. He needed to learn he didn't run this school. "Eat shit, dickhead." I walked around him. Mad Dog grabbed my wrist, and that was a mistake. I took the smoothie in my hand and smashed it over his head.

It went everywhere. Mad Dog let me go, and I staggered backward. His grip had been like iron. People weren't kidding when they said vampires were strong.

Mad Dog was still wiping the smoothie out of his eyes. I had to suppress a laugh of glee. The lust in his eyes was gone, though. It'd been replaced with rage.

"You're gonna pay for that, slut," he seethed. "Dress like a whore, you'll get treated like one."

I felt my Fire ignite in my belly. No matter how much time passed or how society changed, there was always some bigot telling a woman what she could and couldn't do with her vagina.

But I *needed* this. I longed to beat the crap out of the first guy who dared to try to hurt me— to get some fucking revenge. I wanted to teach some sick, twisted pervert he couldn't do whatever he wanted to women.

I had magic now, when I didn't before. I had power. All I wanted to do was shove a fireball down this creep's throat, and laugh while imagining it was John. If I couldn't get back at *him*, this was the next best thing. I'd make sure this bastard never did anything to another girl.

But before I could toss a fireball into his face, I heard a growl behind me. Oberi was there, the hair on his back standing upright as he faced off with Mad Dog.

Charlie was right beside him. He swung an arm around my shoulders and said, "Your little swim in the lake didn't teach you much, did it, *Mad Dog?*"

His words were clearly a taunt. Mad Dog paused. His eyes clouded as he looked over Charlie. He was afraid of him.

Mad Dog quickly disguised the fear in his voice. "You know what? You can have her. I'm not interested in used goods."

I felt my face flush. I went to kick Mad Dog in the fucking throat, but Charlie's arms locked around my waist and held me there, hands crossed over my bare stomach.

It didn't bother me when Charlie touched me. Any other guy, it would. But I could sense through our bond that he had good intentions. And right now, his intention was to prevent me from doing something really fucking stupid.

Even I could admit it. Trying to provoke Mad Dog was asking to get my ass beat.

But maybe if it happened, the noise in my brain would stop. The voices were so loud they were nearly shouting now. I could hardly stand it.

Mad Dog left the cafeteria, thank the ancestors. People's eyes turned back to their food, but I could hear the whispers that had started buzzing around us.

"Get off me." I wriggled out of Charlie's grip. "Can't you see I'm trying to fight my own battles?"

"Fight your own— what the hell!" Charlie threw his hands up. "I can't win with you, can I? And what the fuck are you wearing? You barely have any clothes on!"

"Oh, so *you're* feeling me up, too?" I challenged.

He gave an angry noise. "Well, when I've gotta pin you down to stop you from punching a vampire in the face, I'm gonna notice a few things."

"It doesn't matter what a woman's wearing. She shouldn't be attacked, not even if she's walking naked down the street!" I burst.

"I know that, but most men here aren't going to think that way. They're predators," Charlie said. "You have to be careful. Even if guys harassing you isn't your fault."

It felt good to hear someone say it. That it wasn't my fault.

Though Charlie had no idea what he was referencing.

"Well, thanks for the help, but I can handle myself," I told him shortly.

"Can you? Because you act like you have something to prove." He crossed his arms. "Is it really that upsetting I want you to be safe?"

It was the first time he admitted he cared. Warmth spread throughout my core and covered me like a soft, welcoming blanket. It felt so nice.

But his concern was far too close. Intimacy was uncomfortable. So I drove a knife through it by saying, "Just watch your own back, Wahkin, and I'll watch mine."

"Fucking hell. Can you try not to start shit for *one day?*" Charlie hissed. "You are seriously pushing your luck here."

I rolled my eyes. "Look, Charlie, if you're gonna ride my ass, at least pull my hair."

He snorted. "You wish. Come on, let's go."

Charlie grabbed my arm and started hauling me alongside him. Oberi changed into a Fire unicorn and trotted behind us, her head held high. I reached out to her and fed her the apple. She munched on it happily.

"I did what I did because people have to know who's boss around here," I said. "I won't be intimidated."

"I think you did this on purpose, because you wanted to start a fight," Charlie snapped. "Look, you obviously have a bone to pick with someone, and you're looking to take it out on everyone else. I don't know why, but you have to let it go. If you don't, you'll get killed in here."

Rage flared inside me. I could *never* let it go.

"I have you. You'll protect me," I said with a shrug.

"I'm not your personal bodyguard," he grumbled.

"No, but Daddy put you up to making sure I get out of here alive," I said. "Plus, as the other half of your soul, you are obligated to make sure I don't cork off, because if I do, you will, too."

Charlie paused. "You think our bond goes that far?"

"I mean... probably?" I lifted my hands. "Look, if your Familiar dies, so do you. Since we're bonded, I figure if one of us dies, we *all* die. So it's in your benefit to keep me alive."

"Don't you think it'd go the other way around, and you want to keep me out of trouble as well?" he growled.

"Yeah, but I'm not worried about you. I heard what you did to Mad Dog the other day. You can protect yourself," I said with a wave of the hand.

Charlie sighed. "You're unbelievable."

Oberi led us to a corner of the cafeteria, toward a deserted bench. There was a guy sitting there I didn't know. He had wavy dark hair that fell around his shoulders, and five o'clock shadow around his chin. He was muscular and tall, but not so much as Charlie. The sleeves of his sweater were pushed up, exposing the intricate tattoo of a cat on his left arm, winding around symbols like a cauldron and an eye. The tattoo was colorful, done in a graffiti style. There were a few tattoos on his right arm, too, but the sleeve he had on the left was the one that had caught my attention, because it was so beautiful. The guy had a cat sitting on his lap, which was mostly black with brown splotches around the eyes. Dude must be a warlock.

"Marcus, meet Ava-Marie," Charlie said as we slid onto the bench.

Marcus smirked. "The pain-in-the-ass?"

"Excuse me?" I raised an eyebrow.

"Hey, that's just what Charlie calls you," Marcus said. "I'm not involved."

Charlie ate his scrambled eggs and didn't comment. Charlie didn't talk much when there was food around. He inhaled whatever was placed in front of him in seconds.

"Rishi and I saw you provoking the Mad Dog," Marcus teased, and the feline beside him purred. "You have a death wish or something?"

"No. I just like putting jerks in their place." I stroked Oberi's cheek, and she nickered. "What's he in for?"

"Murder," Marcus said, and Rishi meowed. "He killed a couple humans a few years back. Nearly exposed the supernatural world. He's already blown his chances to get out of here. Once he graduates, he's getting transferred to the adult penitentiary."

"Which means he has nothing to lose," Charlie said. He'd paused long enough to lecture me. "Don't mess with him again."

I scoffed, but didn't object. "If Mad Dog is so horrible, why isn't he in Cellblock 9?"

"Because he's not even *that* bad," Marcus countered. "You can't imagine the type of people they drag down there. And once you're in, you don't come back out."

He shrugged. "Not to mention Mad Dog's got guard friends who look the other way..."

Marcus started drawing on his arm with a black marker. He made little designs on the bare parts that weren't covered in tattoos. I noticed he had paint on his hands and uniform. He had to be an artist.

"Did you hear about one of the new arrivals?" Marcus asked as he drew. "There was one shifter that came on the bus with you guys, and he's already dead."

My jaw dropped open. Was he talking about the kid who yelled at me? "He's dead?"

"Yeah," Marcus said. "Got a hex to the face yesterday. Guards couldn't save him."

"Don't shifters heal really fast?" I asked.

"I guess the person who cursed him got him good." Marcus took a bite of his eggs, like this was an everyday conversation here at the Institute.

A chill ran over my skin. Charlie poked me. "See what I mean? People die in here. You need to keep your head down."

I didn't say another word, just messed around with my plate. I guess Charlie was right and I should listen to him.

Wouldn't give him the satisfaction of admitting it, though.

"By the way," Charlie said, "Our first group therapy session is in a half-hour. It's four people, two girls and two boys. Marcus is with us."

Marcus didn't seem too terrible. But I didn't know who the other girl would be, and I was worried about it. I didn't like opening up to strangers. It gave them too much ammunition to use against you later.

"We might as well go together," Marcus suggested. "I haven't been to one yet, so I don't know what to expect."

Neither did I. As we were walking to our group therapy session, I heard a sharp voice cry out, "Miss Mitoh!"

I groaned and turned around. Professor Hemlock stood straight by the entrance to her classroom. Her hair was in a tight bun, and square glasses sat on her pointed nose. Not an inch of her green robe was out of place. She was an elderly fae who taught my Alchemy class. She wasn't *bad*, but damn, she was strict. The woman must've run a convent before she came here.

Her pinched look as she observed my uniform was nearly funny. "I do not think that is an appropriate outfit."

"I mean, I get what you're saying, but if I agreed we'd both be wrong," I said.

Her eyes narrowed. "I am giving you an infraction, for the dress code violation and for your impertinence toward a teacher." Her eyes went to the boys. "And just what do you think you're doing, gawking about? Hurry along!"

Charlie and Marcus rushed off. Professor Hemlock personally escorted me back to the Elementai dorms, where she made me change into a plain uniform and confiscated the one I'd modified. It made me late for my group therapy session.

Just as well. I didn't want to go anyway.

I followed the map I'd gotten from my student packet to the counseling room. It wasn't what I expected. I had to follow a long, winding tower upward. When I opened the door, I saw that the ceiling was a glass dome that let the sunlight in. The room itself was swathed in tones of blue and gold. Star charts and zodiac posters hung all over the walls, and there was a big mahogany desk before a picture window that showed the entire prison grounds. A red-crested crane stood on a perch behind the desk, observing me with intelligence. When it flapped its white wings, bits of starlight fluttered off its feathers and onto the floor.

Charlie and Marcus were sitting in wooden chairs, which had been placed in a circle. Oberi lay beside Charlie as a unicorn and nickered when I entered. In another chair sat an old man. He had a weathered face, with short black hair and glasses that made him appear very studious. His dark eyes were friendly and welcoming. By his appearance, I figured him to be Japanese. He inclined his head to me, and my shoulders loosened. I actually thought this wasn't going to be that bad, until I caught sight of the blonde sitting in the chair across from Marcus.

You had to be kidding me. *Kalina* was in this group? No way was I opening up in front of her. She gave me a scathing look that told me she felt the same.

The old man cleared his throat. He reached out to a side table next to him, where he'd placed a clipboard and a cup of tea. "I'm happy you're joining us, Ava-Marie. I am Professor Takahashi," he said kindly. "I am the head social worker here at the Institute. I will be your counselor for all your group therapy sessions."

"Are you an Elementai?" I asked, gesturing to the beautiful bird.

Takahashi laughed. "No. I am an Astromancer. Aiko is my animal companion, not my Familiar."

That was interesting. As far as I knew, there weren't many Astromancers at this prison. Why had he chosen to leave his own society in order to teach here?

"We were going around the circle, speaking about why we're here," Takahashi said as I took a seat next to Charlie. "Kalina was going first."

"What's there to go over?" Kalina challenged. "I tried to kill the fae king, I got caught, now I'm here."

So she was an assassin. That fit her venomous personality.

Marcus' mouth dropped open. "You tried to kill the *king*? Like, the king of all Malovia."

"Yeah. You wanna be next?" Kalina raised a fist, and Marcus shrunk back.

"Are you comfortable speaking on why you attempted to take the king's life?" Takahashi asked.

"I'm just trying to do my time so I can get out of here," Kalina said. "There's nothing else to it."

Yeah, right. I bet she had a history. We all did.

"Charlie, would you like to go next?" Takahashi began. His tone was so soothing. He was probably the nicest person I'd met at this prison. I warmed up to him immediately.

Didn't mean I wanted to sit here and talk about my feelings, though.

We all waited. Charlie didn't say anything. It was like he was scared to talk. I spoke for him. "We got in an argument," I said. "It got out of hand, and we nearly burnt down a building."

"*You* nearly burnt down a building," Charlie growled.

I ignored him. "We were on probation, until we stole a ship."

Kalina laughed. "A *boat*? That's it?"

"I have a bigger criminal record than that, if you want to sit here all day," I mumbled.

"I think that's enough, Ava," Takahashi said. "Marcus, how about you?"

Marcus puffed out his chest. "I... uh... I killed twelve people. In *cold blood*."

Kalina rolled her eyes, but my own widened. Marcus had done that? I didn't believe it.

"Yeah. That's right." Marcus drew himself up. "I *forced* my Goddess to give me my magic early, because she was scared of me. One time, I got bit by a vampire, and I slaughtered it on my own. With one hand tied behind my back!"

"Oh, *really*," Takahashi said, writing something down on his clipboard. "What else?"

Marcus blabbed on forever. It was like he was trying to fill the silence. Most of the session was taken up by his ridiculous claims. Marcus said he'd beaten up a mermaid, choked out an angel and wrestled with a wolf shifter all in one day, but when Takahashi asked for details, he failed to clarify.

By the end of his speech, I didn't know what was true and what wasn't. What I did know, though, was nobody in this room was fooled by his tales.

Takahashi seemed amused at the conclusion of the rant. "That is a very interesting story, Marcus."

"Bull! He's so full of shit his eyes are brown," Kalina said, pointing at Marcus. "Do you really expect any of us to believe him?"

Marcus cringed, and Takahashi held up a hand. "We don't judge in this room, Kalina. What is spoken here remains within the safety of our circle. I expect all of you to be vulnerable, but more than that, I expect all of you to be confidants of each other. You will be in this group for four years, until you graduate. I hope that by the end of that time, the four of you will regard each other to be friends, if not at least trusted companions."

Kalina scowled. She wasn't looking forward to being my therapy buddy for four years any more than I was.

"Ava-Marie, I understand you've been in therapy before," Takahashi said, turning the room's attention to me. "Would you like to talk about it?"

I swallowed as Charlie sat up, and Oberi's ears perked forward. Talk about my disorder? No, I really didn't want to. But these people were going to find out anyway, so I really didn't have a choice.

"I have bipolar disorder," I said. "I was diagnosed when I was a little girl."

"Bipolar I or II?" Takahashi asked.

"It's unspecified."

"And what do you think is the greatest challenge of being bipolar?" Professor Takahashi asked.

I took a moment to think over the question. "I hate... that people hear my diagnosis and expect me to act a certain way. Mental illness affects everyone differently. We all have different triggers, different symptoms. And people think I'm a bad person when I'm reacting to my illness in a way that's different than what they expect."

Takahashi nodded. "You don't want to be perceived in a way that's inauthentic to who you are."

"Yeah. People think I'm just acting out because I want to. I don't know how many times I've told someone I see something, or hear things, or feel a certain way, and they just throw it out as invalid. *Oh, bipolar disorder doesn't affect people in that way.* My bipolar does. And I need people to support my experience, instead of just telling me what I'm going through is wrong."

Marcus nodded introspectively. Charlie's expression was passive. I couldn't read what he was thinking, or feeling.

Kalina sniffed. "Well *I* don't like people who use being sick as an excuse to be assholes."

"And what's that supposed to mean?" I jumped up so fast my chair fell over. Kalina got to her feet, too. Marcus looked nervously between us, while Charlie tensed.

"It means feeling like crap isn't an excuse to treat people like shit," Kalina growled.

"So says the girl who tried to murder her king!" I shouted back. "Didn't put much thought into how he'd *feel* about dying, did you?"

"Girls, this is a safe environment," Takahashi reminded us.

Neither of us heard him. Kalina struck first. She lashed out with a powerful fae illusion. Her purple magic ricocheted across the room in a thin bolt. I dodged it, and it slammed into the wall, knocking a painting askew. I immediately conjured a fireball and flung it at her, but Kalina spun her arm in a circle, and it manifested a purple shield that immediately caused my fireball to fizzle out when it hit. She sent spells back at me while I tossed fireballs at her. Charlie and Marcus both dove to the floor. Takahashi sat calmly in his chair, observing the situation as magic flew around him. Oberi flattened herself to the rug, while Rishi yowled, hair standing up on his back.

"You think your little fireballs can hurt me? Bring it!" Kalina screamed.

This girl had major anger issues, and ancestors, I was *bringing it*. We abandoned magic and just started swinging hands. Kalina's fist collided with my right eye just as I grabbed on to her hair. I yanked on it as my free hand smashed into her lip, making it bleed. I barely felt Kalina's punches when she hit me, because honestly, it felt good just to have someone who could take it— and she'd give it right back.

"I think that is enough." Kalina and I were pulled to opposite sides of the room as an invisible force yanked us apart. Takahashi remained in his chair, while Marcus and Charlie scrambled back to their seats.

I wasn't sure how astromancy magic worked, but it was enough to get Kalina and I to separate. Takahashi drank his tea in peaceful tranquility while the crane looked on.

How could he be so calm while Kalina and I were wailing on each other? It was eerie. Takahashi gave me a bottle of water from under the table, which I froze with my Water magic to use as an ice pack. I put it against my swollen eye as Takahashi handed Kalina a handkerchief to clean up the blood.

"As we were saying," Takahashi began. "Marcus, would you like to give your thoughts on the situation?"

Marcus gulped, then launched into a story about his mom that was totally unrelated. I shot dagger eyes at Kalina, but she didn't send them back. She held the handkerchief to her mouth, appearing to be deep in thought.

We were dismissed shortly after that. I took off as soon as possible down the staircase, but once I was on the main floor, I felt a hand on my shoulder. "Hey."

It was Kalina. Ugh. What did she want now, to give me another black eye? Marcus and Charlie stood at my sides, expecting another brawl. Oberi tapped her hooves and waited.

"Did you come back for round two?" I asked. "Because I'll fight all day."

"I'm sorry," she started, and I nearly fell over backwards in shock. "I've been mean to you."

"Just a little." I shrugged her hand off my shoulder. Why was she apologizing? This had to be a trap.

"I just wanted to see what you were made of," Kalina said. "I can respect a girl who can take a punch. There aren't a lot of supernaturals who can keep up with me. And around here, you have to command respect, or you don't get any."

I frowned. "That might be true, but it's not the best way to make friends. Maybe try being kind."

Kalina looked down. "I'm uh... not very good at that."

"Then work on it."

"Ava," Charlie warned. He was telling me to get along.

Marcus was dying of embarrassment as Rishi curled around Kalina's legs. She tried to shake him off, but Rishi rubbed his head on her calf, and eventually, she gave up.

I struggled to hold my tongue as Kalina took a deep breath. "I've heard about you. You're the only Elementai who can use both Fire and Water. You feel like an outcast here. So do I," she admitted. "I haven't told anyone this, but... I'm the only sorceress amongst my kind who's a shifter as well. The males of our race are the only ones who can change into animals... except me. I'm the only female fae who has the power to become a wolf, and no one knows why. So you aren't the only one who's different."

That got my attention. Though I didn't like it, a connection immediately formed between Kalina and me. I was a freak, but she was, too.

"It doesn't help you're racist. We know what you think about Elementai," I said scathingly.

"It's not like that." Kalina frowned. "I'm sorry Naya called you guys savages. It wasn't okay. I didn't agree with it. I should've spoken up."

"Then why didn't you?"

Kalina's shoulders dropped. "Look. We might've gotten off on the wrong foot. I'm not so sure I want friends, but I *need* allies. Everyone at the Institute does. And since we're in the same counseling group, the four of us should try to get along. The shifter that was murdered yesterday was a loner. And loners don't last long here."

Marcus scowled. "I've been a loner for a bit. People have left *me* alone."

"It won't work for long. You have to stay in a group if you want to survive," Kalina spat at him, and Marcus recoiled before she turned back to me. "So what do you say? You want to be in mine?"

I wasn't fooled by the nice act. Kalina wanted me around her because I had power, and she sensed that. She wanted to use my magic as a shield, to protect her when shit went down.

I almost wanted to tell her no. But Oberi nuzzled my shoulder, and I said, "Yeah. I guess that's okay."

Charlie relaxed behind me.

Kalina gave a phantom of a smile. "Thanks. I think this will work out for the both of us. A hell of a lot better than trusting Naya, anyway."

"If you don't like Naya, why do you talk to her?" I asked.

"I felt obligated," Kalina said. "Vampires are high on the supernatural hierarchy. As a fae, I'm *supposed* to hang out with them. We're in a similar social class."

"You don't have to hang with anyone you don't want to." Marcus spoke up. His cheeks turned pink as Kalina turned back to him.

Kalina stared at him for a moment before she said, "Yeah, well. Pickings are slim around here."

"Let's just agree to work together," Charlie said. "We might not like each other, but getting along is going to benefit all of us."

"Should we make a blood pact?" Marcus asked nervously. "Something to seal the deal?"

Kalina rolled her eyes. "Matching prison tattoos would be better. Gods, Marcus, you're so lame."

"A verbal pact is fine for now," Charlie cut in, to avoid starting another argument. "So we're all in agreement? I've got your back, you've got mine. For now, at least."

Kalina and Marcus nodded, and realization struck me at the bargain we'd made. None of us *wanted* to stick together, we just didn't have any other choice.

Oh, great. I was in a prison gang. A very *lame* gang at that, with the weirdest people in the school.

But it was a hell of a lot better than going at it alone. And if we stuck together, we just might make it out of here.

∘∞∘

Saturday was my designated day to get my one free phone call a week. I was standing by the phones before anyone else was that morning. No shit, the school literally had *rotary telephones* you had to spin the numbers to dial. It took forever.

These things were like a hundred years old. But they were my only connection to the outside world, and so, I treasured them. Everyone else had handed their cell phone over when we got here, but I'd hid mine under my mattress in my dorm. It didn't get service here in Shade Hills, but I kept it just in case I needed it for something later... whatever it might be.

I really wanted to use my one phone call to contact my parents. I missed them like crazy. But I had to talk to my Aunt Maddie, and I couldn't wait for it to be in person. This prophecy was more important than anything else. I dialed her number on the rotary phone and waited for her to pick up. Each ring sounded like an eternity.

"Ava," Maddie said in a bright way. "I'm glad to finally hear from you. How's the Institute?"

"Why didn't you tell me about the prophecy?"

There was a long, drawn-out silence. "That was your parents' responsibility."

"But you made it." My back hit the wall as I pressed the phone to my ear. "You must've had visions of me. Can you tell me what they mean, so I can fulfill what the prophecy says and avoid all the bad stuff?"

"Everything I have is in that journal," Maddie said firmly. "I haven't had a vision of you in nearly twenty years. What I do remember, I don't understand."

"You *forgot* what you saw?" My voice was incredulous.

"Yes. I'm sorry. I did the best I could, but no matter what I tried, I couldn't comprehend what my visions foretold. I sought help from other seers, but they couldn't decipher it, either. You're the biggest mystery the prophets have, Ava."

Of course I was. It couldn't be easy. "Whatever you could give me at this point would be helpful. Even if it's the tiniest thing," I pleaded.

"After I created the prophecy, the ancestors wiped my memory of anything that might be useful to you," Maddie said. "Every note and clue is in that journal. While I was attempting to translate it, it became clear that you have to be the one to decipher my visions, because the message was meant for *only you*. I was merely the messenger."

"But why would the ancestors do that?" I smacked the wall in frustration. "Why would they take away the only help I have in figuring this thing out?"

Silence infiltrated the space between us, until Maddie said, "I'm going to speak of this only once, and you're never to ask about it again."

"I'm listening."

Maddie took a deep breath. "You will be the cornerstone. The deciding factor in a war between gods."

"Gods?" I squeaked. I began sliding down the wall. When I hit the floor, the line on the phone tugged.

"You know there's another war coming. You'll have the power to shape the outcome," Maddie explained. "The Elementai worship the Great Spirit, but he's at risk, Ava. All the gods of the magical world are. You're the person that will decide what will happen to them, depending on the path you follow— the darkness or the light. You will choose what the fate of the supernatural world will be, if magic will continue to exist or if it will die out. That is all I know."

My mouth went extremely dry. I was so nauseous the room spun. "Do I have to do this? Is there no other way?"

"Prophecies cannot be avoided; they can only be shaped by the chosen one's choices. Which is why it is imperative you make the right decisions," Maddie pleaded. "As your prophet, I am here to support you in any way you need me to. But I can't take the path for you. That journey is yours alone."

I heard my uncle's voice in the background, and Maddie said, "I have to go. But I love you, Ava. Trust that wherever the ancestors are leading you, the destination will end where you're meant to be."

The phone clicked. I let the phone hang there as I stared off into space, comprehending the vastness of what she'd just told me.

This prophecy was no joke. My aunt was telling me that the god my people followed was in danger— as were all the others. How could I possibly wield such power? What was so special about me that I would determine the fate of all supernatural kind?

One thing I did know— if the world was relying on me to make the right choices, we were totally screwed.

charlie

NINE

Any confidence I had in the Institute when I arrived slowly began to unravel over the following week. The facilities were fine, and though Ava gagged at every meal, I liked the food. It was the people who fucking sucked.

"Leave me alone," a male voice spat.

I was on my way to Juvenile Justice when I heard it. The hall was quiet, apart from soft footsteps padding on the carpet.

A female let out a chilling laugh. "You think you can resist me, Carson? I'm a succubus. I'll have you in bed before noon."

"My mother was a siren," Carson growled. "Your powers won't work on me."

She chuckled. "Oh, you think I need powers to seduce you? By the time I'm done with you, you'll be begging for it."

Carson's voice came through gritted teeth. "Naya, I swear to the gods, if you come one step closer, I'll—"

"You'll what?" she asked, amused. "Scream?"

He scoffed. "You'd be surprised at what an Atlantean's scream can do."

"Then show me. I like it when my bedmates scream." She paused for a moment, then added, "I admit, I don't usually go for Atlanteans, but what kind of girl would I be if I resisted *you.*"

I heard a snap, then something flew through the air and hit me in the face as I was passing by. I bent down to pick it up and realized it was the button from our uniform slacks. I just kind of stood there, dumbstruck. Oberi growled under his breath.

"Naya, what the fuck?" Carson cried. He sounded truly scared this time.

"Ooh," Naya sang. "We're starting on the dirty talk early. Say it again, Carson."

"Nay—AAA!" Carson's voice got really high-pitched. It was the cry of a guy who'd just been groped.

Aw, hell. I'd hoped I could sneak by the argument without making a scene. But I'd quickly learned that keeping to yourself was a sure-fire way to become a target at this school. Kalina had been right. We had to stick together around here.

I was done standing around. I reached for Naya's shoulder and yanked her away from Carson. His underwear snapped as her hand came out of them.

"I believe he told you to *back off*," I growled.

"*You* can back the fuck off," Naya shot back. "What are you, an Elementai? I'm a succubus. I can kick your ass any day."

"Oh, really?" I challenged. "With what powers?"

I didn't actually know what a succubus could do. I knew they were some sort of vampire, but I'd already beaten Mad Dog in a fight. I could handle her.

Naya got up in my face, her breath passing over my jaw. She whispered, like she was trying to seduce me. "I can compel you to do whatever I want."

Carson zipped his pants. "How's that working with that noxite bracelet?"

Naya drew away from me and huffed. "So they don't want the succubi compelling the guards. Big deal. I'll find a way to destroy it."

My lips tightened. "Well, until then, you can find another way to get off, because he isn't sleeping with you."

Naya hesitated a moment, then said, "Whatever. He's an Atlantean. Probably tastes like seaweed and saltwater anyway. I don't know why I wasted my time."

Air whipped past me as Naya turned and tossed her hair over her shoulder. Her heels clicked on the thin carpet as she walked away.

Oberi yipped happily. I handed the torn button back to Carson.

He breathed a sigh of relief. "Thanks for sticking up for me, man. The chicks in this place will really eat a guy alive."

I shrugged. "It's no problem."

"Hey, I saw you in my Juvenile Justice class earlier this week, right?" he asked.

"I guess so."

"You headed there now? We can walk together." Carson seemed strangely nice for an inmate. Though maybe he just didn't want to run into Naya again.

A few moments of silence passed.

"So, you're a merman…" I stated awkwardly as we headed to class. "What kind of crimes gets an Atlantean thrown in here?"

"Same as everyone else," Carson said. "Theft. Assault. Arson."

"Arson?" I cocked an eyebrow. "I thought you lived in the ocean. How's that possible?"

"We come onto land," he pointed out. "Don't be surprised if you meet some Atlanteans in for grand theft auto. Living under the surface most of your life gives some of these guys a real fascination with cars. Very expensive sports cars, to be exact."

"So is that what you're in for?" I asked.

"If you read my record, it would be," he admitted. "But it was my buddy who stole the car and crashed it. Well, he *was* my buddy. Not since he pinned it on me, though."

"Wow. One car crash and they toss you in here. How many people got hurt?"

"None," Carson said. "The car belonged to an Atlantean Senator. It was worth over half a million."

My jaw dropped at the number. I couldn't imagine that kind of money. It could feed me and Oberi for life.

"That's… wild." I didn't know what else to say.

Carson scoffed. "Tell me about it."

Oberi turned, and I followed him into the classroom. Carson and I must've been the last ones there, because the room buzzed with chatter.

"Ah, look," he said. "Two spots up front just for us."

This kid was mental if he thought the front row was a coveted seating area. No one wanted to sit in the front at this school.

My eyes didn't follow his, because I had no idea where to look. He must've noticed, because he lowered his voice. "You can't see them, can you?"

I shrugged. "Nope. Kinda totally blind."

"You are a *master* at hiding it," he said. "You could've totally fooled me. I won't tell anyone."

"Thanks," I mumbled.

Oberi led me to the seat in the front row and curled up beneath me. The class quieted soon after.

Heels clicked across the floor in a quick staccato. "What are you all doing just sitting there?" our professor snapped. "Get out your notebooks and a pencil."

Oh, joy. I'd almost forgotten how *lovely* Professor Mazur was. I hadn't picked up on her supernatural race in our first class, but today, I felt the air breeze off feathery wings. She was an angel for sure. It explained the same snippy tone and *above-you-all* attitude. I could tell by the way the air moved around her that Professor Mazur was tall and lean, and she moved with the energy of a younger woman.

"As we learned earlier this week, the function of this class is to teach you the roles of the supernatural justice system, so that you may uphold the laws set forth by the United Supernatural Union upon your rehabilitation," she started. "You are all here because you broke the law. For some of you—"

Professor Mazur stopped her lecture dead. "Excuse me, Mr..."

Carson cleared his throat from beside me, and Oberi pawed at my foot. It occurred to me she must be looking at me.

"Me?" I asked. "Wahkin, Professor. Charlie Wahkin."

"Mr. Wahkin, why are you not taking notes?" she demanded.

I hesitated. "I'm, um, an auditory learner."

"I don't care," she snapped. "I asked you to take notes. You are to do so, or you will fail this class. Do you understand?"

I swore I could feel every eye in the room on me. "I can't," I admitted.

"You can't what?" she pressed.

"Take notes. Miss, I can't read. I'm blind."

She let out a sinister laugh. "That's a new one."

Her voice quickly became serious again. "But I don't take excuses in my class, Mr. Wahkin."

This bitch was *harsh*. I wanted to sink into my seat and disappear.

"It's hardly an excuse when it's true," I said. "There must be something else I can do for credit."

"And how's a blind man supposed to take notes?" she mocked. "What alternative do you suggest?"

My blood began to boil. "If I was provided a laptop, I could take notes, with a text-to-speech program installed to read them back to me. Or you could give me a recording device, so I could play back the lecture later."

"How would such technology be *fair* to your classmates?" she asked, like I'd just requested the moon.

She walked away, then came to stand in front of my desk moments later. Something slapped down onto the desk, and she tossed a long, skinny object into my lap. I reached out to feel both and realized they were a notebook and pencil.

She leaned so close to me, I could feel her angry breath on my cheek. "You will take notes like everyone else in the class. If you interrupt my class again, I'll send you straight to the Warden. Do you understand?"

A lump so large I couldn't breathe grew in my throat. I suddenly had flashbacks of high school. There was a reason I'd never graduated. No one wanted to help a blind guy learn. The school wrote me off as stupid and wanted me to repeat all the classes I'd failed. But it was *their* failure for denying me accommodations.

I knew at that moment the Institute would be worse. I'd never make it through the reform program if my grades were shot. I'd be lucky if I ever made it out of here at *all*.

Professor Mazur turned from me and returned to the front of the room.

"That was bullshit, man," Carson whispered under his breath.

Bullshit didn't even cut it. I was fuming. I squeezed the pencil so tight that it cracked. I wanted nothing more than to storm out of the room, but I knew it wouldn't do me any good. It'd only get me sent to the Warden or thrown in Cellblock 9. I had no power here, and the professors really knew how to rub that shit in.

Professor Mazur continued her lesson like nothing had happened. I opened the notebook and pressed the pencil to the paper, but I more or less just doodled nonsense to make it look like I was taking notes. This class was useless already.

"As you all know, each supernatural society has their own justice system," Professor Mazur said. "It is up to them what to do with their own citizens. Sometimes, the crimes are punished in-house. Other times, they are handled by the United Supernatural Union. This often occurs in situations where rehabilitation is an option— hence, why you were all sent here. Other times, the Union steps in on more serious crimes in which a society does not have the resources to prosecute the accused. Most notably, the Union *always* has authority over intersociety crimes. For example, if a witch attacks a fae, neither the Miriamic Imperium Council nor the Arcanea Alliance reserve jurisdiction to prosecute. That responsibility lies solely with the United Supernatural Union."

Professor Mazur began scribbling something on the board. "I say this to warn you. Any crime committed against someone outside your own race will result in far harsher consequences than what punishments your own government may impose. The United Supernatural Union is unforgiving of intersociety crimes, as even the smallest infractions may lead to war."

There was something dark in her tone. She was trying to scare us— to get us to comply in the Institute. She wanted us to know that if we started fights in here, we'd be answering to a much higher power than the ones who sent us here.

"The United Supernatural Union is very good at their jobs," Professor Mazur continued. "If you think you can hide from them, you'd be wrong. No one gets away from a supernatural bounty hunter."

I'd only been half listening up to this point, but when she said *supernatural bounty hunter*, my curiosity piqued. I stopped doodling and raised my hand.

"Yes, Mr. Wahkin," she called on me, sounding annoyed.

"How does someone become a supernatural bounty hunter?"

"Well, they need a clean record, for starters." She sounded amused, like she never saw me getting out of here and getting a real job. "And they must show incredible supernatural powers. You know, like the power of *sight*."

She accented the last word, and laughter traveled around the room. Oberi stood, but I placed a hand on his back to calm him.

"I don't need my eyesight, Professor." I smirked. "My magic works just fine without it."

She laughed. I didn't need my eyesight or my magic to spot a raging bitch.

"I'd advise you from getting too confident, Mr. Wahkin," she said. "The United Supernatural Union doesn't take well to people who abuse their power. Tread carefully, or you just might end up with the death penalty."

That was a threat if I'd ever heard one. I was so angry, I couldn't hold my words back. "I'm sure the electric chair would be better than this class."

I was horrified with myself for a second, until she began to laugh in a condescending way.

"Oh, child. You think the Union would sentence you to the electric chair?" she asked. "No, your death would be *far* worse. The death penalty is only given when one has committed a crime against all supernatural races, and as such, every race partakes in the sentence. The death penalty starts with the bite of a siren, followed by elemental torture from the Elementai. They'll burn your skin off, starting at your toes. The witches will curse you with nightmares, and the vampires will suck you dry. Angels will draw out your life force, making you age in a matter of minutes. And finally, the fae will open a portal to the afterlife, where any type of monster can escape to eat you whole— or drag you straight into the fiery inferno."

My bones chilled when she started, but by the time she finished, I was unamused. I didn't believe a word she said. She was speaking in half-truths, at best.

"Sounds awful," I said dryly.

"It is," she snapped. "And that's why you *all* best take your rehabilitation seriously."

She returned to the lesson, but I was so pissed at her I barely heard a word she said. I had a teacher who hated me, and what was worse, she wasn't allowing me to learn in the only way I could. This place did everything it could to make sure you failed.

After class, I started back toward the dorms, but Oberi went in the other direction.

"Oberi," I growled. "Where are you going?"

He barked, and I had no choice but to follow.

"I'm not in the mood," I grumbled. "I just want to go back to my dorm and—"

"There you are, Oberi!" Ava-Marie cried cheerfully.

Oh, fun. I got to deal with *her* now.

Oberi's energy changed, and I sensed him shift into a Fire unicorn. She took up a lot more room now, and her heat rolled off her in waves. I placed my hand on Oberi's side, because I was lost and agitated. I had a hard time reading my surroundings.

"Where are we?" I asked Ava.

"Study area," she said. Her voice came from below me, like she was sitting on a chair. She shuffled a few papers, then zipped up her bag.

"What are you working on?" I questioned as Oberi took a few steps forward. I reached out and felt an empty chair, then sat beside Ava.

She sighed, like she was exhausted. "Just studying a formula for my Alchemy class. You?"

I curled my hands around the arms of the chair, and my nostrils flared. "Raging. Professor Mazur's a bitch."

Ava drew a sharp breath. "The tall angel professor? Yeah, I've heard the worst. I don't have her, but if she's bothering you, I'd love to give her a piece of my—"

"Don't bother." I sank deeper into my chair. "It's not like it's going to help. Kicking her ass won't teach me how to take notes."

"Notes?" Ava's voice rose a few pitches.

I tossed her the notebook I'd been doodling on all class period. Ava began flipping through the pages.

"She says they're graded," I growled. "Even for a blind guy."

Ava shot to her feet. "Charlie, this is unfair!"

I scoffed. "You think I don't know that? I have enough problems with inmates already. I don't need to get on a professor's hit list."

"We have to go to the Warden," she insisted. "He *has* to provide you with accommodations."

I cocked an eyebrow. "Does he? I don't think the ADA applies here, Ava. We're under supernatural jurisdiction."

"Those are some big words for a guy who's only taken *one* Juvenile Justice class," she said pointedly.

"Well, I'm not wrong, am I?" I challenged. "Do I have to remind you this is a prison? Inmates don't get a voice. And if you try, they threaten you with the death penalty."

Ava gasped. "She did *not*."

I crossed my arms. "They don't *really* burn you to death and steal your life force, do they?"

Ava sighed and sat back down. "Depends on the society. The Elementai did away with the death penalty years ago, but back then, you were tortured with your opposite element. Toaqua were burned to death, and Koigni were drowned. Yapluma were crushed with rocks, and Nivita were suffocated."

My stomach twisted into all sorts of knots. "That's horrible."

"Which is exactly why they stopped," she said. "But if the crime's bad enough, the United Supernatural Union will still go through with the death penalty. They mostly use monsters— grotesque animal-like creatures created by demons. They want to make an example out of you, so other people are deterred from committing crimes."

"That sounds like bullshit," I said. "The system needs fixing."

Ava scoffed. "Don't get me started on *the system*."

After a few beats, I asked, "What are the monsters like?"

"Anything and everything," she replied. "You never know what you're going to get. It could be an evil spirit possessing the skeleton of a dragon, or a fifty-foot serpent with wings. There are so many. You want a list?"

I knew she was being facetious, but I answered anyway. "No, thanks. It's not like I'll be around long enough to see one."

"What do you mean?" Ava asked.

I shrugged. "Isn't it obvious? We're never getting out of here. This program isn't going to work for me. I'm going to die in here."

"Charlie," Ava sighed. "Don't say that."

"Why not?" I seethed. "It's true."

Ava got really quiet, but Oberi gave a nicker, like I was making her uncomfortable.

"You can't die," she finally said. "Because that would mean Oberi and I—"

"It's not like I have a choice, Ava!" I burst. "*Something's* going to get me in here, whether it's a monster, a professor, or another inmate. And if it's not in here, it'll be wherever I'm transferred to. The system doesn't work for people like me. At some point, you're going to have to accept that."

Ava gave an obnoxious noise. "It's too early to give up, Charlie."

I shot to my feet. "No! I was a goner the second I stepped through those gates."

"Stop being ridiculous," Ava demanded. "We're going to get through this program, and we're going to get out of here together!"

"You think I can last in here for four years?" I scoffed. "Then you're kidding yourself."

"At least promise me you'll try!" she cried.

I gritted my teeth. "I can't make any promises, Ava. The best I can do is survive as long as possible."

But I had to survive— because Ava and Oberi were counting on me.

I wasn't looking forward to the day I let them down.

ava-marie

TEN

"Miss Mitoh, may I remind you that this is the *third* dress code violation you've had this week?" Professor Hemlock tapped her heeled boot against the floor as she stared at my shoes.

I was wearing all the parts of the Institute uniform, unmodified—but for ancestors' sakes, I couldn't go another damn day in those deplorable Mary Janes. They hurt my feet. I was wearing moccasins that had been made by my Aunt Imogen. They were white leather, and had blue beads sewn on to them, and had fringes on the top, and were *so* comfy, and—

"Miss Mitoh, are you listening?" Professor Hemlock snapped her fingers, and I straightened in my seat. "We're all waiting to hear your explanation."

Everyone in the Alchemy lab stared at me. No one dared to speak when Professor Hemlock was lecturing someone.

I cleared my throat and slowly rose from my seat. "If you'll pardon me, madame, but when you interrupt a young woman's school day by forcing her to change her attire, society is saying that it's more important for her to hide her body than to receive an education. By dictating what a female student can and cannot wear, the institution of learning of where she is at, by default, is admitting a boy's education is more valuable than hers. Therefore, for the sake of my own instruction, I implore you to allow me to wear these moccasins— which are extremely cute, by the way. I rest my case!"

Opal squirmed in her seat next to me. She would've jumped out of her seat and applauded, if Hemlock wasn't running the show.

"That is all very well and good, and you've made the debate convincing enough I agree with you." Hemlock scowled. "*However,* this is a reform school, and boys *as well as girls* have to adhere to the standards the Warden sets, for their safety and comfort as much as the school's. I cannot be shown playing favorites. Do I have to send another personal letter to your family about your misbehavior?"

Ugh, no fucking thanks. Daddy had nearly reached through the phone and strangled me when he'd learned about that stunt I'd pulled with the skirt a few weeks ago. I didn't feel like getting chewed out again.

I started to whine. "Come *on.* They're moccasins. I'm a Hawkei. Can't you look the other way just this once?"

Her eye twitched. She gave a long, drawn out sigh. "I will not take away your class time and disrupt your learning for some shoes. But once you are dismissed, I expect you to return to your dormitory and change into proper footwear *immediately.* And sit down, please. For the gods' sakes, this isn't a courtroom."

Score. I loved winning arguments with teachers. Hemlock tapped the blackboard, where she'd written down a potion recipe. "Today we'll be brewing a potion with ingredients that can commonly be found on Darke Island. If made correctly, this potion is an excellent combatant against negative energy. No dark spirits or entities can withstand the effects of this potion— save for some demonic forces, which can be exceptionally powerful and negate the effects of the potion. However, this combination of ingredients is incredibly strong, and is able to banish all but the strongest of negative forces. You will find the necessary ingredients on your desk— get to work."

There was the scraping of chairs as people stood over their cauldrons. Opal and I shared a desk and a small cast-iron cauldron. The mermaid girl chewed her lip nervously as she looked down at the ingredients on the table. There were cloves, thyme, a magical plant called star weed, and a special kind of sage that only grew here.

I narrowed my eyes as I read the chalkboard. "That's wrong."

"What?" Opal tied her blue hair back. "How?"

"Hemlock wants us to add thyme, but that's going to weaken the effects of the cloves," I said. "We need to add bay leaves instead."

"But she said—"

"Don't listen to Hemlock," I said as I started combining ingredients. "Just trust me."

Opal made a face. "Okay. I'm shit at potions, so I'll follow you."

I fell into a stupor as the bustle of the classroom buzzed around me. The Alchemy classroom was cozy and dark, formed by stone walls and stone floors. Candles lit the area, providing light that the tiny windows failed to. Hemlock always kept a hearthfire going at the front of the room, breaking the early October chill. There was a slight drizzle hitting the glass panes, and the smell of sage burning throughout the room immediately put me at ease. Opal filled the cauldron with water and lit a flame underneath it while I began chopping up the star weed. Hemlock wanted us to cut up the other ingredients, but I put them in whole. Opal's nervous expression grew even more worrisome.

"So how's Atlantis?" I asked Opal, to get her to stop fretting. "I've heard it's amazing down there under the ocean. As a Toaqua, I'd love to see it."

"I'm not really from Atlantis," Opal confessed. "Mermaids have colonies stationed all over the world, in places like Sydney, Venice and the Bahamas. I'm from a colony in Honolulu. My mermaid pod mated with the native tribe there many years ago and decided to stay."

"So you've never been to Atlantis?"

"No. But I hope to go, someday."

I stirred the cauldron counter-clockwise, instead of clockwise like Hemlock asked. The potion began bubbling. Our conversation fell flat as Hemlock stomped over, probably to lecture me. "Miss Mitoh, what exactly are you doing? The instructions were clear."

"I understand, but this is the correct way," I insisted. "Taste it and see."

A couple of people laughed under their breath, expecting me to get another lecture from Hemlock. She pursed out her lip and picked up a ladle, pouring my potion into a wooden cup and lifting it to her mouth.

When Hemlock tasted the potion, her expression became amazed. She quickly disguised it. "Yes. I wouldn't have thought to add bay leaves. Very good, Miss Mitoh. You and your partner shall receive full credit for the day."

Opal brightened, but several people around me cursed under their breath. Hemlock re-wrote the recipe on the board. I got a lot of dirty looks from people who'd already added their thyme.

Someone tapped me on the shoulder, and I turned around. A girl I didn't know stood there. She twisted her hands nervously, and was comparable to a lost sheep. She had to be a vampire. Her eyes were red.

"I'm Despona. You seem to know what you're doing, and I'm totally lost," she confessed. "Will you help me?"

She didn't have a partner. "Sure." I walked over to her table. Her ingredients were a hopeless, chopped mess. I began separating them out and slowly added them to the cauldron as Despona watched.

"You had the right idea, but next time, don't mix them all together," I said. "It weakens the potency. Add them one by one next time."

"Thanks," Despona said. "I'm new to all this. I just arrived at the Institute a week ago. I'm one of the few succubi here."

"You... slept with a demon?" It was an awkward thing to ask, but that was the only way a vampire could increase their powers.

"Yeah." She sighed. "First love. I was young and stupid, and thought he cared about me. Big mistake, by the way. Never sleep with a demon—all they care about is themselves."

"So what are you in for?" It was always the first question you asked someone at the Institute, because it was the quickest way to know if who you were dealing with was dangerous. I knew a lot of people's stories by now—except Opal's, because she seemed too upset to tell, and I didn't want to pry.

"I killed someone who was trying to kidnap me," she said offhandedly. "He hired me for a job at his company, but it turned out to be fake in the end. It was just a ploy to get me there, so he could do what he wanted with me. I tried to use my mind control on him, but he was too powerful and it didn't work. I did what I had to, in order to escape. But the judge who sentenced me didn't see it that way."

I felt goosebumps rise on my skin. She'd been defending herself, and the legal system had branded her a murderer. It was so wrong. "I'm sorry. That's awful."

"He deserved it." Despona sighed. "I just wish I hadn't ended up here."

"There are worse places," I offered. "Though not very many."

"Thanks. Better here than in the clutches of that guy, anyway." She shivered.

I said nothing, just handed Despona the spoon. As she stirred, I noticed some jerk inching toward Opal from behind. He had a slimy worm in his hand from the alchemy cupboard. In one quick move, he slipped the worm down the back of her sweater.

Opal jumped into the air and screamed— but it wasn't a normal scream. It was high-pitched and eerie, a sound only magic could create. People covered their ears, and my eardrums throbbed as Opal's yell continued to pulse around the room. I could visibly see the shockwaves as they emitted from her mouth. The glass vials around the room shattered, and the cauldrons tipped over, spilling liquid onto the floor. I ducked under the desk to try to shield myself from the scream, which was nearly strong enough to knock me over.

Once Opal's scream ended, the worm dropped out the bottom of her sweater and inched along the stone floor. Glass was everywhere. Nobody had gotten hurt, but the floor was slick with the remnants of our potions.

Damn. I knew mermaids had powerful voices, but I'd never imagined anything like that.

"I'm sorry. I didn't mean to!" Opal apologized as Hemlock stepped amongst the broken glass. A couple people rubbed their ears. The guy who'd put the worm down her dress— Digger, I think his name was— had blood coming from his own ears, and he winced in pain.

Hemlock sighed. She waved her hands, and her illusion magic dissolved the shattered vials into sand, which sucked up the spilled puddles of potion around the room. "Since Miss Kealoha has shattered our available vials, we will have to pivot and take this week's exam early."

Everyone groaned. Opal reddened. I was busy flipping off the asshole who'd put the worm in her clothes. Digger gave me a look that said he'd love to fight later, but I'd like to see him try.

I returned to my desk. Hemlock flicked her wrist, and a stack of paper that had been lying on her desk began distributing itself around the room. I looked at the sheet in front of me and got out my pencil.

"I expect this test will take all of you the rest of the hour to complete," Hemlock spoke. "You have forty minutes remaining. Begin."

Several others had already begun the test in order to get a head start. Noises of frustration and upset mingled in the room, along with the scratching of paper. Opal had obviously gotten stuck on the first question, and stared at the paper in sheer horror.

I glanced down at the test and nearly rolled my eyes. This was easy. My pencil flew across the paper as I answered every question like it was child's play. Opal took a glance at me in surprise, clearly shocked I was moving through it, but I didn't understand what the big deal was. This test was a piece of cake.

The end of the exam required written formulas. Alchemy was pretty straightforward in most cases, but the most advanced potions needed a lot of math. The last few questions required trigonometry. I used the entire paper to write out my formula, putting numbers down as quickly as I thought of them. I didn't use my calculator. I didn't need it.

I completed the test in ten minutes. Students glanced up in astonishment as I walked to the front of the classroom and placed my exam on Hemlock's desk. "I'm finished."

Hemlock gave me a cold stare. "Miss Mitoh, I will not permit you to fail this exam merely so you can get out of class early."

"I double-checked my answers. Promise."

Hemlock took the paper as she shook her head. As her red pen scanned my answers, her eyes narrowed. She breezed through my answers, looking for a mistake and finding none.

When she'd gotten to the end of the test, she laid down her red pen and took off her glasses. "Very well. You may go, Miss Mitoh."

I got my bag and left. Opal stared open-mouthed after me, while several others clearly desired my demise.

I headed to the cafeteria for an early lunch. I hadn't been eating much of anything this week, but my appetite, little as it was, had finally returned, so I planned to binge as much as I possibly could before another manic period hit and I refused to eat for another three days.

What followed me was an elevated sense of relief. Things were good today. No psychosis. No voices. Didn't know how long it would last, but I wanted to take advantage of it.

I recognized a slender figure shuffling a deck of cards by the cafeteria entrance. He was thin and tall, with feathery wings that were peppered with gray. He smiled as I came near. "Got an offer for you, Mitoh."

"Not interested, Chancey," I said, but it was kind of a lie. There was mischief in his gaze I just couldn't turn away from.

Chancey was an angel who'd gotten sentenced for running an illegal gambling ring. I didn't know his real name, but it hardly mattered. Practically everyone had a nickname here at the Institute. Apparently, he hadn't learned his lesson, because he still bet on anything and everything. There was a rumor going around that he ran the wagers at an underground fight club here at the prison, but so far, I hadn't seen anything to back that up.

"A pretty lady like you should know when the odds are in your favor," he teased, giving me a wink.

I tried not to scoff. Chancey *also* had a major crush on me. He was harmless, so I let him have his fun, but I totally wasn't interested. Angels, even the bad ones, were far too attached to their rules for my taste.

Chancey shuffled the deck in his hands. I watched, pretending to be bored. Chancey always had a deck on him. It's how he got money out of people. He knew how to count cards.

"What are you betting on today?" I asked. He wouldn't be talking to me if he wasn't trying to hustle— and out of everyone at this prison, he knew I was one of the few people who came from money.

"You know Ghost? He tried to break out of the Institute," Chancey said, eyes sparking with excitement. "He actually got past the fence. They're still chasing him around out there."

"What?" My eyes widened. That was unheard of.

"Yeah. Chances are fifty-fifty he'll escape the guards now that he's outside the fence. You wanna take that bet?" Chancey gave a sly smile.

"Aren't angels supposed to be virtuous?" I asked with a sigh.

"I ain't from no heaven, sweetheart." Chancey put the deck in his pocket. "So are you in, or what?"

"Put me down for twenty." I slipped him a note. Gambling was another violation on your personal record if you got caught, but I participated out of boredom. It was practically the only entertainment we got here at the Institute.

I followed Chancey out to the prison yard. Hundreds of students milled about out here at the fence line. I made a beeline for Charlie, Kalina and Marcus, who were standing at the edge by the gate. All of them were pressed against the fence line. Oberi was in his husky form, wagging his tail as I stooped down to give him a pet. Rishi was on Oberi's back, his paws on the fence as he tried to get a closer look.

Less than a quarter mile beyond the fence line, we saw a warlock high-tailing it for the trees. He was followed by a mess of guards. Even from here, I could see the panic on Ghost's face. There was a shifter guard who'd changed into his animal form that was running as fast as he could to catch up. Ghost gave a cry, but he couldn't outrun the wolf.

Everyone moaned in disappointment when the wolf tackled Ghost to the ground. A bunch of other guards piled on top of him, shouting and cursing. They put Ghost in cuffs, then started hauling him back this way. The crowd began to disperse.

"Dammit." Another twenty to Chancey, lost. I had a weakness for betting on the underdog.

Kalina shrugged. "That's on him for being stupid enough to try to break out in broad daylight. If he'd escaped at night, he would've made it."

"Nuh-uh," Marcus said. "*We* tried to break out last night, and it didn't work."

"You tried to break out?" My jaw dropped open, while Kalina gave Marcus the nastiest look she could. He instantly shut up.

"Okay, I've got to hear about this," Charlie said. "What did you guys do?"

Kalina gave an eyeroll, then leaned in. "*I* tried to break out. Marcus decided to tag along."

"Yeah, and you left *me* to be eaten by sirens!" Marcus yelped.

"You're fine." Kalina played with the edges of her ponytail. "Anyway, long story short, Marcus and I tried to escape by swimming through the siren lake and getting close enough to the woods to climb the fence, but we got caught long before we were even close."

"How'd you guys get out of your rooms? We're locked in during the night," Charlie whispered.

"I know how to pick locks, and apparently, the guard who locks Marcus' dorm is a total idiot, and never does it right," Kalina said. "I could teach you how if you wanted to."

Learning how to pick locks would be a useful skill here at the Institute. But I was more interested in breaking out. "Do you think we could all try again, and succeed this time?"

If I could get out of the Institute, I could start surveying Darke Island for what I was really here for— learning about the prophecy.

But Kalina shook her head. "No one has ever broken out of the Institute. I thought I could, but after last night, I'm convinced it's impossible. I was able to get past fae security when I committed my crime against the crown, but these guards are even tougher than that. They're professionals at keeping us stuck here."

My heart fell. So there really was no way out. Even if I tried to break out, I'd probably be unsuccessful. The only way to leave would be to serve my time.

Marcus' voice was gloating. "It wasn't a complete loss. Now you owe me a favor."

Kalina's face reddened, and Charlie asked, "Favor?"

"I owe Marcus a life debt. He saved me from being eaten by a siren." Kalina frowned. "Fae take life debts *very seriously*, so unfortunately, I'm bound to him until I fulfill it somehow."

"And how sweet it is," Marcus sang.

"I'm sure it won't take more than a week," Kalina shot back at him.

"This little debate is cute, but it's not going to help us get out of here," Charlie said. "Let's just stop talking about it. It's pointless to get our hopes up. We're never leaving."

My emotions curdled like sour milk, and they tasted just as bitter to digest.

Kalina shook out her ponytail. "Whatever. I'm hungry. See you guys in an hour."

Kalina hurried off. We had another one of our group therapy sessions soon, but it was clear she didn't want to be seen eating with us.

She was so stuck-up. But my instincts twisted in my gut, telling me something about her seemed... I don't know, off. Like she was pretending to be tougher than she was.

"I already ate," Marcus said flatly. "I just need to be alone."

Marcus turned and left us. He sat on one of the benches in the yard with his sketchbook and started drawing. Rishi perched on his shoulder and observed.

A spark of annoyance crossed through my gut. We had agreed to come together to protect each other, but our little "group" was anything but united. Kalina didn't wish to be bothered with the riff-raff, and Marcus was still too much of a loner to be comfortable in a group.

Which left me with Charlie. Woo-hoo.

I sensed the tension as Charlie and I walked to the cafeteria. Oberi changed into a unicorn and walked between us to give us some distance, but it hardly helped. For some reason, I felt closer to him now than ever before... and I hated it. I could feel the two parts of our bond colliding, and it was uncomfortable. It wasn't like the seamless connection I had with Oberi, that flowed like water and felt comforting. I didn't know how to relate to this guy, or how to incorporate him in my life, and it really showed.

I didn't think he knew what to do with me, either. It felt like a rejection, which only made the resentment grow.

Charlie coughed, and I gave an irritated huff.

His eyebrows immediately furrowed. "I'm sorry, am I annoying you?"

"Only when you're breathing."

"You're acting pissed. Something I said must've bothered you." Charlie's face soured. "What did I do this time?"

"What you said back there, about it being pointless to get our hopes up," I snapped. "Last week you were going on about how we're destined to die in here, and now you're insistent we'll never leave the grounds. I'm sorry if I don't want to be buried on this property like you."

"I'm not saying that, but look at the facts," Charlie snarled. "Kalina and Marcus tried to get out, and they failed. Our chances of surviving four long years at the Institute are slim."

"Look, buddy, I know you think *you're* going to have an early demise, but I'm not putting up with that crap," I shot at him. "I would very much like to live, so it'd be nice if you could be a little positive every once in a while."

Charlie scowled. "I've been around and I've seen things. People I know who ended up in prison rarely got out."

"That's too bad, but we're not them. We have a chance."

"I'm just trying to be realistic. Having faith is setting us up for disappointment."

I didn't like that. I didn't like that at all. I couldn't give up, because if I did, I'd fall to pieces. Charlie *had* to believe we'd get out of here. I couldn't do this all alone.

And I didn't want Charlie to die. He hadn't done anything to deserve it. Was it so bad to admit that I cared about him, even if I really couldn't stand the guy?

So what came out of my mouth next was more out of discouragement than anything else. "You know, I could try to see things from your perspective, but it'd be too difficult to get my head that far up my own ass."

Charlie rubbed his face. "Hell, you are the *most frustrating* person. I'd tell you to take today off from being a jerk, since you're putting in so much overtime."

"And I'd tell *you* to go fuck yourself, but that'd be cruel and unusual punishment."

"You are such a—" Charlie took a deep breath. "I'm not going to sit here and banter with you. You wanna be delusional, fine. But don't try to drag me along on your little road of sunshine and rainbows, because there's no such thing as happy endings, *princess*. Not here."

Charlie pivoted and went the other way. Oberi stuck with me. We'd been here a month, and Charlie had mapped out the school well enough he knew where he was going without her. Apparently I'd ruined his appetite.

I scratched Oberi's chin. "I just keep putting my foot in my mouth, huh, girl?"

She nickered.

I ate lunch alone. I had a salad, but I fed most of it to Oberi. I couldn't stomach more than a few bites.

I had to take a different route to Professor Takahashi's office than I typically did, because there'd been a stabbing in the hallway with a sharpened toothbrush and the guards were trying to clean it up. An unfortunate result of a gang fight, I assumed. Chills ran up and down my spine as I heard the whispered bits of gossip that permeated the hallways, how the student who'd been stabbed might not make it.

Maybe Charlie was right. Scary shit happened at the Institute every day. I might not get a chance to fulfill the prophecy and save the world. Some deranged inmate might kill me first.

But I couldn't think that way. I'd go down a dark path devoid of any hope, and hope was the only thing that would get me out of here.

As was usual, I was the last one to show up to our group therapy session. Charlie's arms were crossed when I sat beside him. He was still pissed at me.

The last few sessions hadn't been very helpful. Most of the time was taken up by Professor Takahashi's speeches on emotional management. None of us had confessed anything personal while we were here. It still felt too raw.

Professor Takahashi observed us with a bright smile. "I'm so happy to see you all have made it. I have a special opportunity I'd like to introduce to you today."

"What is it?" Kalina asked.

Professor Takahashi crossed his legs. "Every year, the Warden offers a scholarship program exclusively for students at the Institute. A competition, if you will, made up of teams of students that compete for the grand prize."

Charlie huffed skeptically. "What, do the guards throw us all into an arena and see who comes out alive?"

"You don't understand, Mister Wahkin. This is no average competition," Takahashi explained. "These are the Darke Games, and the winners receive the chance of a lifetime— the opportunity to have your sentence erased, and release from the Institute as free members of magical society."

A lump grew in my throat. Marcus' face paled, and Kalina gave a strangled gasp.

Charlie had gone so still it was almost unnatural to see. "There's a catch," Charlie objected. "There always is."

Takahashi's smile fell, but only slightly. "It is a... dangerous competition. One that not all survive."

"Of course it is," Charlie said, but Kalina cut him off.

"I don't care," she said quickly. "I didn't know a sentence could be erased."

Takahashi inclined his head. "It can be, but only by participation in the Darke Games— and only by winning the competition with your team. Teams of volunteers are sent out on Darke Island to win points. The team with the most points at the end of the competition wins. However, accumulation of these points can be a bit... deadly."

The question of how teams gathered points was barely a factor to me. My heart pounded so harshly against my ribcage that I longed to rip it out. There *was* a way out of the Institute— it just depended on me putting my life on the line.

If I won these Darke Games, I would be free to pursue the prophecy on my own... and be that much closer to stopping the chaos it was bound to bring.

I had to get a team, and win these games at whatever cost. The supernatural world depended on it.

I leaned forward. "Tell us more."

charlie

ELEVEN

I was skeptical as hell. The Warden wouldn't sanction the Darke Games without a reason. It was more than just a scholarship program— that much was obvious.

An edge to Ava-Marie's tone confirmed she knew it as well, but that didn't matter to her. She'd do whatever she had to in order to get out of here. Which was saying something, considering it was her fault we were here in the first place.

I slumped in my chair. "Yes, Professor Takahashi," I stated flatly. "*Do* tell us more. What's the purpose of these *games*?"

"As you all know, Darke Island is a hub for supernatural activity, due to its location along a dark magic ley line," Professor Takahashi explained. "Once a year, this magical ley line causes a collection of portals to open, unleashing evil spirits and hellish monsters onto the island from the evil afterlife— the Underworld, hell, whatever you wish to call it. The Darke Games were developed to protect the island from these monsters— to eliminate them before they can hurt the residents of Shade Hills."

There it was. They were *using* us, like they did with the noxite mines.

"So the pardon is a bribe," I accused. Only someone who'd lost everything— like the kids at the Institute— would be stupid enough to go up against monsters from hell.

Professor Takahashi sounded offended by the accusation. "The Darke Games are a chance to prove yourself. It's an opportunity to show that you are willing to put your life on the line for your community and for others— to prove that you've truly been reformed, as is the goal within the Institute."

"So shouldn't all volunteers get pardoned, then?" Marcus asked hesitantly.

"Not all have what it takes to make it through to the end," Takahashi explained. "Only those who are mentally stable enough to leave the Institute make it through."

I snorted. Mentally stable, my ass. This wasn't a competition of mental stability. It was all about who was most desperate for freedom.

"I fail to see what you find funny about this, Mister Wahkin," Takahashi said calmly. "Don't you want a chance to win your freedom?"

When I didn't answer, he continued. "The winners don't just get their record wiped clean. They are promised jobs and many other opportunities when they are released. Their futures are set for life."

It sounded like the opportunity of a lifetime. So why did my stomach twist into such ugly knots when I thought of the Games?

"The winners are chosen based on the team that makes the most points," Takahashi explained. "The judges will evaluate your progress as you're filmed fighting the monsters that free roam around the island. Points are earned each time a monster or dark spirit is killed. Make more points than any other team, and you will be released from the Institute."

"Why don't the fae just shut down the portals?" Kalina cracked her knuckles. She sounded willing to go in single-handedly to shut the portals down herself.

"The portals cannot be controlled, I'm afraid," Professor Takahashi said. "It is the way with the island. Since Shade Hills is on a ley line, if you close one portal, another one opens up. They can, however, be predicted, which gives you all time to prepare for the Darke Games."

"When?" Ava asked desperately, like the fate of the world hung on these deadly games.

"The end of December," Takahashi announced. "Each team is made up of four students. I suggest those who would like to compete begin forming their team now, so you have time to train. Sign-up sheets are located outside the Warden's office."

Takahashi excused us, and my classmates shuffled quickly toward the door. Kalina hurried down the stairs in a rush, though her footsteps were light— as was the way with the fae. She seemed to dance down the staircase, though it was less like ballet and more like tap-dancing. Her movements were hurried. Oberi's hoofsteps were light as we wound downward.

"We have to enter, Charlie," Ava whispered lowly from beside me.

"Enter a deadly tournament?" I asked skeptically. "We're better off waiting to serve our time. At least then we have a chance of survival. The Darke Games are a death sentence."

Ava stopped at the bottom of the stairs and grabbed my arm. Her grip was freaking strong. I tried to shrug her off, but she kept a tight hold on me. Kalina and Marcus continued on ahead.

"One second you're sure you're going to die in here. Now it's your only chance of survival?" she snapped. "You make no sense. Charlie, we *have* to do this. The Darke Games are my one chance at getting out early, and I can't go in without Oberi. And Oberi's not going without you."

I finally managed to yank my arm out of her grasp. "You're right— Oberi's not going anywhere. I'm not letting her get in the way of danger like that!"

I reached out to stroke Oberi's velvety nose. "Tell her, girl."

Oberi huffed a breath, though I wasn't sure what she meant by it.

"See? She wants to," Ava objected.

"The answer is no, pidge," I said through gritted teeth. "We're not entering the Darke Games."

"Yes we are."

It wasn't Ava's stern voice that answered, but Kalina's. I hadn't heard her turn around to approach us. I must've been too wrapped up in arguing with Ava, because now I could easily make out Marcus' loud footsteps as the two of them returned.

"You want to be on our team?" Ava asked Kalina, sounding surprised.

"We agreed to stick together, didn't we?" Kalina pressed.

"Yeah, so we didn't get pummeled by some prison gang," I pointed out. "Not so we could attend each other's funerals."

"Look," Kalina said. "I'm not staying in here a second longer than I have to. If there's a chance to get out, I'm taking it."

"At what cost?" I demanded. No one seemed to resonate with the word *deadly* like I did. "This place isn't bad enough to risk your life for."

"If you have plans once you get out of here, it is," Kalina rebutted.

That struck a chord with me, and I quieted. I'd never really had plans for the future. I didn't know what it felt like to risk your life for them. It sounded stupid to me. Wouldn't you rather survive at any cost?

"I'm entering the Darke Games, no question," Kalina said. "But if I'm going to win this thing, I need a damn good team."

"And you want us?" Ava asked skeptically.

"The only way I'm winning this is if I diversify," Kalina pointed out. "I can't team up with fae. They all have the same powers as me, and I'm better than all of them anyway." She didn't sound smug about it. She was simply stating what she believed to be fact. "I need Elementai on my team— someone who can kill monsters with Fire and whip up a storm with Air. And since the two of you seem to be attached at the hip—"

"We are *not* attached at the hip," I protested.

"—Then I'm going to have to take you both," she concluded without missing a beat. "Plus, Charlie beat Mad Dog's ass. I could use a guy like him on my team."

Ava's shoulder brushed up against mine as she shifted, crossing her arms. "And what is it you can offer us?"

Kalina lowered her voice. "You know my secret— that I'm a sorceress *and* a shifter. My illusion magic is strong, so strong I can turn illusions into reality. Try finding another fae in this hellhole who can do that with ease. You need me."

Ava paused for a few moments, like she was actually considering this. "Who do you have in mind for a fourth member?"

"I'm not sure yet," Kalina admitted. "I say we get an angel or vampire on board. We'll need their strength."

"Hey!" Marcus protested. "What about me?"

Kalina's skirt rustled the air around her as she whirled toward him. "First of all, I didn't realize you were standing there."

How could she not? He was the loudest mouth-breather in this place.

"And second, you're just a warlock," Kalina said.

"Just a warlock!" Marcus sputtered. "I'll have you know, the Miriamic Coven is strong."

"*Together*," Kalina emphasized. "Individually, none of you can pull off anything impressive. What are you going to do? Read a crystal ball for us?"

Marcus huffed. "And why wouldn't that be helpful? I could keep you out of danger. Besides, I'm not just *any ordinary* warlock."

"Oh yeah?" Kalina asked skeptically. "What's your specialty?"

"See this?" A thread on Marcus' uniform popped as he yanked up his sleeve. "Every witch or warlock receives a tattoo from our goddess, marking us for our powers. Everyone gets a single symbol— either a cauldron, a tree, an eye, a skull, or a crescent moon. I'm the first to receive *all five*. I have magic from every Cast. My powers are unlimited."

Kalina didn't sound like she was buying it. "Tattoos can be faked."

"Not mine," Marcus promised. "The Goddess wanted me to have my powers so badly, she granted them to me early. I can see the future and raise the dead. I can brew potions and read minds."

"Why haven't I seen you do any of this then?" Kalina challenged.

"I don't like to show off," Marcus admitted. "It's a good way to get my ass kicked around here, being different."

"Prove it to me," Kalina stated. "What am I thinking right now?"

Amusement entered Marcus' voice. "There are other things you'd like to do to my pretty little ass."

Kalina huffed, while Ava and I both tried to stifle giggles. Wow. I guess Marcus really could read minds.

"I-I didn't mean it," she stammered. "It was only a test."

"A test I passed," Marcus said proudly.

"Fine," Kalina caved. "You can be on our team. I guess it will help if we have someone who can predict what's coming."

"Perfect," Marcus said brightly. "Shall we sign up?"

"No!" I protested. "Is anyone listening to me? Takahashi said this thing was voluntary. Well, I'm not volunteering."

"What if Oberi volunteers to go?" Ava challenged.

My teeth ground together. "That's out of the question. I won't let her."

"Oh yeah?" Ava turned to the Fire unicorn. "Familiars are meant to run, to be *free*. You want to leave here as much as I do, don't you, Oberi?"

I reached out to stroke my Familiar. "Ava's wrong. You wouldn't let either of us run into danger."

Oberi ducked her head, and my stomach sank. She drew away from me, and her hooves padded on the carpet as she rounded Ava.

My jaw dropped at the betrayal. "Oberi! How could you?"

Oberi's fur bristled as Ava stroked it. "Because Oberi knows how crucial it is that we win this thing and get out of here. She's with me no matter what. The question is... are you?"

My hands curled into fists, and my nostrils flared. How *dare* Ava use my Familiar against me. Her father did the same thing to get me to this island, and now she was using Oberi to get me to risk my life for... for what?

The problem was, it didn't matter if the outcome was worth it. The risks of leaving Oberi alone were far greater. I wouldn't let Oberi go into that tournament without me, and I knew Ava. One way or another, she'd get Oberi to go with her, like she had the night she tried to run away on the boat. If something bad happened to them in the tournament, I would perish along with them. It was how the bond worked. And so I had to go to protect Oberi... to protect Ava.

"Damn you, Ava-Marie," I growled.

She laughed evilly. She knew she had me.

I stomped down the hall, only to realize I had no idea where I was going. "Where's the damned Warden's office?"

Ava snickered. "Glad to see you so... enthusiastic."

I frowned. "Don't mistake this pretty face for enthusiasm, sweetheart. I'm royally pissed."

"Ooh, *royally*," Kalina teased.

Ava took my arm. "Come on, *pretty face*. It's this way."

"You realize the school is just using us because we're expendable," I pointed out on our way to the Warden's office. "They don't want to deal with these monsters themselves."

"Of course they are," Kalina said. "But why wouldn't we take advantage of it?"

I shrugged Ava off me, because I was mad. Instead, I placed a hand on Oberi's back to lead me through the halls. I spoke to take my mind off how pissed I was. "So, what *are* your plans if we win?"

Kalina spoke from in front of me without turning back. "For one, to get *my* throne back, of course."

"Your throne?" Marcus questioned.

Kalina stammered. "Yeah. Every twenty years or so, the King's Contest in Malovia is held. It's a competition among the fae to choose the next monarch. I lost the crown to the current king's jackass son."

"I'm guessing he's the one you tried to kill?" Ava questioned.

Kalina scoffed. "Yeah. He's lucky my blade missed. He won the Contest by manipulation, not by any talent. He's going to make a shit king. I've been working my entire life to take over as queen. I'm not going to give up due to a little attempted murder charge."

I gave a sarcastic noise. She was nearly as bad as Ava.

Kalina continued. "And the other reason I want to get out... well, let's save that for the therapy session. What are *you* going to do, Charlie?"

Ava was quick to answer for me. "Mope around, probably."

"Yeah, because you'll all be dead," I growled.

Ava skipped on ahead toward Kalina, and they continued talking about what they'd do if they made it out of here early. Ava apparently had plans to start her own designer fashion brand. Typical.

Marcus' footsteps slowed. Rishi walked with light steps beside him. I didn't care to speed up, because I didn't want to catch up with the girls.

"So, what would you *really* do?" he asked me. "If we won."

I shrugged. "Take that job offer, I guess. Save up some money to get myself a decent place. Go back to school in Kinpago to learn my magic."

Marcus considered my words for a few moments. "Is that really all you'd do? Don't you have any dreams?"

I shrugged. "You're the one who can read minds. You tell me."

Marcus lowered his voice and leaned closer to me. "It's only the dirty thoughts I can read. Shh... don't tell Kalina."

I laughed lightly, which was a miracle considering we were marching to sign our own death certificates. "That doesn't sound that useful in the Darke Games."

"No," Marcus admitted, "but I had to say *something* to get on your team. If anyone has a chance of winning, it's you guys."

I furrowed my brow. "Why do you say that? Have you seen the Games in action?"

"Well, uh." Marcus scratched the side of his face. "My premonitions don't work quite like that, but you could say I have a feeling about it."

"Well, that's... encouraging," I mumbled.

We'd turned down so many halls by now I couldn't tell where we were. It was a part of the school I'd never been before. Ava and Kalina's footsteps slowed ahead of us, and we stopped when we reached them.

"Well, are you guys ready for this?" Kalina asked.

"Hell yeah," Ava said, taking a step forward. Though the hall was quiet, the scratch of the pen on paper sounded like painful wails to my ears. It was less like she was signing up for a competition and more like she was signing away her soul— in blood. Too damn bad she was signing mine along with it.

Ava took a step back. "That wasn't scary at all. The Darke Games will be easy."

"Will they, now?" a male voice said from behind us.

I didn't recognize the voice, until Marcus sputtered. "D-Doctor Taurus."

The Warden.

"I like your confidence," he said as he came toward us. "You must believe you'll win."

"That's the idea," Ava replied, though she sounded bitter when she spoke to the Warden.

I didn't think she liked him much, and I couldn't blame her. He'd said all the right things during his welcome speech, but they'd felt ingenuine. I didn't believe he cared about the students here, and the Darke Games were proof of that.

"I can't wait to see what you four have to offer during the Darke

Games," the Warden said. He meant to come off as encouraging, I was sure, but there were dark undertones to his words.

"I'll bet," Ava said.

The Warden sounded confused. "Whatever do you mean by that?"

"I'm entering this thing for one reason, and one reason only— to get out of here," Ava stated. "Don't think for a second it means any of us care about what you're doing here. Your for-profit prison system is unethical, for one, and the Darke Games are simply—"

"Pidge," I warned, but she ignored me.

"— An excuse to throw unskilled laborers to the lions so that you can continue mining—"

"Ava!" I cried. She was launching into one of her courtroom arguments. Normally, I'd let her finish, but this was the freaking *Warden*. He could throw her in Cellblock 9 for sneezing in his direction. I hated to see what would happen to Ava if she seriously pissed him off.

Ava paused for a moment, long enough for the Warden to cut in. "You misunderstand, Miss..."

"Mitoh," Ava stated confidently. "Ava-Marie Mitoh, and don't you forget it."

"No," the Warden said with a smirk in his tone. "I don't think I will. I'm not sure where you got your idea of a for-profit prison, but this is a reform school. The Darke Games offer you an opportunity to prove your reformation and leave the school early. You seem very passionate. If your magic measures up to your temper, perhaps I may award the prize to you."

"There's no question about it," Ava said. "We're going to win this thing."

"Very good," the Warden said, though it sounded more like he was praising a puppy than congratulating her. "I'll be sure to keep my eye on you, Miss Mitoh."

That was all he said before he continued down the hall and his footsteps faded up a flight of stairs to his office.

"Pidge," I complained. "Insulting people around here is a good way to make enemies."

"On the contrary, I think I impressed him," she said proudly. "I did us a favor. The closer he and the other judges watch us during the Darke Games, the better chance we have of racking up points."

I gritted my teeth again. It was starting to hurt my jaw. "I wouldn't be so sure about that."

"It doesn't matter," Kalina cut in. "Just stay out of trouble until the Games, and we'll win."

Kalina approached the sign-up sheet next. The pen moved over the paper smoothly. "Your turn, Marcus."

He hesitated.

"Make up your mind! I can't have a pussy on my team," Kalina snapped.

Rishi hissed at her, like he didn't care for her choice of words.

"Just take the pen," she pressed. "I thought you wanted to win this thing."

"I do," he replied. The pen clinked to the ground as Marcus dropped it. He scribbled down his name, then turned and handed the pen to me.

"I, um," I stammered.

Ava was at my side in a moment. "I already wrote down your name. They just need your signature."

She led me forward and guided my hand to the line where I was supposed to sign my name. My stomach became hollow, and my throat felt like sandpaper.

"Are you sure about this, pidge?" I asked. "Once we sign up for this thing, there's no turning back."

"I'm sure," she stated confidently.

"It's not just your life you're messing with," I growled under my breath. "Every choice you make affects me and Oberi."

"Every choice I make affects *everyone*," she hissed, though she didn't explain what she meant. "Don't treat me like I haven't thought this through, Charlie. I *have* to do this."

"Why?" I demanded. Kalina and Marcus were bickering amongst themselves, but I kept my voice low for only Ava to hear. "Your designer brand isn't going to change the world. I know you think it is, but—"

"This isn't about that," Ava snapped.

"Then why do you want out early?" I asked harshly. "Your own father sent you here. You *wanted* to come, didn't you? That's why you stole that boat."

Ava's breath brushed across my skin. "I wouldn't expect you to understand."

"Then help me," I insisted. "If I'm going to sign my name on this thing, I need to know why."

Ava's head swiveled, and her long hair brushed against my arm. She shot several glances toward Marcus and Kalina before speaking. "I can't tell you here. I just need you to trust me."

I had no reason to trust her. She'd turned her back on me more than once already. But there was something in her voice— a desperation I'd never heard her use before. It wasn't fake, like the act she put on for other people. It was genuine, and that frightened me far more than entering the Darke Games.

I couldn't explain what possessed me to scribble my signature on that line. Maybe it was the bond between the two of us. Maybe it was because I actually *did* want to win this thing— to have a future like Professor Takahashi promised. Whatever the reason, I found myself signing up for the Darke Games.

I just hoped I hadn't made a terrible mistake.

TWELVE

"That was beautiful, Opal. Do it again."

I sat at the edge of the student pool in my bikini as Opal leapt out of the water. She jumped and twisted in the air like a dolphin, her mermaid tail sparkling in the fluorescent light. I cheered, and she twisted to perform a beautiful dive as she fell back into the deep end of the pool.

Each magical race at the Institute had their own personal room with which to experiment. The sirens and the mermaids had an Atlantean bathhouse in the basement. Greek marble pillars lined the bathhouse, and statues of mermaids twisted beside stone archways and fountains. There was an Olympic-size pool in the middle of the room, surrounded by smaller pools of varying temperatures, and even a few jacuzzi tubs. There were even pools for mud baths, and pools that had seaweed in them that connected to the lake outside the Institute. Long reclining chairs and large hot stones that mermaids could lie on lined the room. I could hear the eerie croons of the sirens beneath the murky lighting that set the relaxing tone of the bathhouse, like a song known only to sailors lost to the sea. A mirror covered the entire length of the ceiling, so you could watch yourself swim as you looked up.

I continued to nibble on the chocolate my parents had sent me and watched Opal do laps. She swam around the pool at lightning speed. I was Toaqua, but even with my Water powers, I couldn't catch up with her when we'd raced in the water.

Opal's mermaid tail was beautiful. Her scales were a mottled turquoise and sapphire that glistened like gems in the water, her fin feathery and long like that of a betta fish. She wore a bikini top that was the same color as her green eyes.

Opal came up beside me. "Don't you think it's a little weird this room is so nice? I mean, there are hot tubs in here."

"It's just an excuse the staff can use to pretend they care about us," I said. "They have to keep us happy somehow, and we can't say they're treating us cruelly if we have *some* nice things."

"Guess so." Opal dove and took off like a rocket. She swam around a vampire in the shallow end, who sent her a dirty look. The pool was mostly meant for mermaids and sirens to use, but other students swam here as well.

I was practicing my Water magic. My right hand held the chocolate bar as my left hand twisted above the pool. I made a tiny humpback whale out of the ripples in the pool, and swam it around before transforming it into a salmon, and then a sea serpent.

Toaqua magic was as easy for me as casting a flame. I didn't even have to think about it. I was lucky to be talented in elemental magic, because the class they had here for Elementai was a fucking joke.

The doors to the pool opened. Charlie and Marcus walked in. Marcus was only wearing swim trunks, but Charlie had on a shirt over his thin shorts. Oberi followed Charlie as a husky, his tongue lolling out of his mouth.

I'd talked to Daddy last night. He'd finally gotten his wallet back, and lectured me to be careful around Charlie because, "*That boy is up to no good.*"

My nose wrinkled in distaste as I watched Charlie walk around the pool. Daddy was right. Charlie Wahkin was low-life trash, and Ava-Marie Mitoh wasn't known for getting her nails dirty. He might be bonded to me, and we might be competing in the Darke Games together, but that didn't mean I trusted him.

Marcus jumped into the pool with a *whoop*. It was then Charlie pulled off his shirt. My eyes widened as I took in his washboard abs and chiseled shoulders. Damn, the guy was toned. And tan. And built.

Charlie's swim trunks were almost too big for him. They sagged on his hips and showed off the V that dipped below his stomach. My eyes couldn't help but navigate down his happy trail to the bulge in his shorts. He looked pretty gifted.

Strike that. If Charlie Wahkin was trash, I was a raccoon, and I *loved* garbage.

Charlie slid into the pool. Marcus splashed him, and the two started goofing off. Oberi barked and jumped into the pool. He swam around, his head bobbing as his tail wagged in the water. Charlie grabbed him and spun him around. Oberi let out a few more loud barks that echoed around the pool.

I finished my chocolate and tossed the wrapper away into a bin nearby. Opal pulled herself out of the water and sat beside me. As she did, her mermaid tail transformed back into two legs. "You know, Charlie's single. He's on the market."

I gave a laugh. "Please. There are plenty of hot dickheads around here. Charlie being one of them. I can look and not touch."

"But you *want* to touch," she teased. I summoned a wave to rise up, and Opal yelped as it grabbed her and dragged her back into the pool.

Opal waved her tail fin at me while I continued to watch Charlie wrestle with Marcus. There were perks to Charlie being blind. He couldn't catch me checking him out.

Charlie won and flung Marcus off of him. Oberi saw me and came swimming over. I reached down to pet his head. "Hey, good boy. How are you doing today?"

Oberi barked. Charlie must've heard me speak, because he waded near. It wasn't very graceful... could Charlie not swim? Opal coyly paddled off with a gloating look.

"This is my second time running into you today," Charlie said as he came close.

"Second?" I hadn't seen him all day.

"Yeah. The first was in your dreams."

"Ugh!" I pushed his face away. He sank under the water for a moment, before he reached up and yanked me into the water by my ankle. I screamed before I went under.

What. An. Ass. Charlie smirked. I sent out a jet of water from my left hand. My Toaqua magic socked his stomach and carried him all the way to the other side of the pool.

I dragged myself out of the pool and dried off using my powers. Charlie came up for air, rubbing his gut. "Was that really necessary?"

"Yes. You ruined my hair, jackass." I smoothed down my newly-dried hair and tied it back into a fishtail braid. I helped Oberi onto the concrete as he scrambled out of the pool.

Charlie ducked to avoid being hit by water droplets. "Yeah, your perfect hair. How are you going to manage playing the Darke Games without your precious straightener? You'll probably use a hair dryer to finish off a monster."

"I can be *very* violent with a hair dryer. It's heavy."

Charlie huffed. "Sure."

"You need to stop worrying about me and focus on yourself," I snapped. "Maybe practice a little, so we don't get killed out there, and you can do whatever you want once we're set free. Steal a few more wallets, maybe."

"In my opinion, we either win or we don't." He shrugged. "I'll figure out my plans after it's a sure thing we're getting out of here."

I sighed. "Charlie, you *have* to have some reason for escaping other than just wanting to survive the Institute," I insisted. "Being passive isn't going to help us win the Games."

"Sorry if I don't have anything as grand as a clothing company," he replied scathingly.

I scowled. I'd made up some bullshit about starting a designer label to the others, because I didn't want them to know why I really needed to get out of here. Once I won the Darke Games, I'd be free to explore Darke Island at will, and figure out the prophecy, as well as how to stop it.

Unfortunately, I needed Oberi to help me, and Charlie wasn't going anywhere without her. But I'd figure out how to get rid of him once I won the Games. I'd promised to tell him later the true motives for my escape, but how could I make him understand if he didn't have his own reasons for getting out of here?

"Why don't you ask your spirit guides for help?" I suggested. "They might have some tips."

"What are spirit guides?" Charlie raised his eyebrows.

I gave a noise of frustration. "Ancestors, you're so ignorant. How could you not know this? It's like, the basics of Hawkei lore."

Charlie's tone grew rough. "I don't get what's so hard for you to understand, but I'm an orphan. The tribe threw me out because I was a mixed-House baby, and I was raised outside Hawkei culture. I literally don't know anything about where I came from, so don't blame me."

Sorrow welled within me, making shame creep over my skin. I'd spoken too harshly and too soon, again. As much as I despised Charlie, I didn't want to hurt him. He'd been through enough without my bossy ass telling him off.

"I'm sorry," I offered. "You're right, I'm being a bitch."

Charlie pulled back in surprise. "I'm shocked you admit it."

"I'm wrong about a lot of things." I stroked Oberi's ears. "But you have to know your heritage before we go into the Games. You can't know what you want out of the future if you don't know your past, right?"

"I guess... what are you saying?"

I stood up. "Meet me by the cafeteria after dinner. We need to go somewhere private."

"There aren't a lot of places without guards in the prison," Charlie said skeptically.

"There are more than you think. You just have to be smart enough to notice them."

I walked off then. Oberi watched me, his eyes appreciative and warm.

Charlie had to know where he came from. Survival wasn't enough at the Institute. You had to have something to fight for, something waiting for you at the end. Hope was what would sustain the reward, and if Charlie wasn't willing to put himself on the line for a dream he'd die for, he'd run off once it got tough during the Games. Perhaps learning about who he was as a Hawkei would inspire him.

I also needed to do this before I physically *couldn't*. I was experiencing a rare time when I wasn't in an extremely low or extremely high period of my mood. This was important; I didn't want to get it wrong. Charlie needed to know this stuff, and I didn't want my bipolar getting in the way.

Here's to hoping I could hold myself together during the Darke Games.

Charlie met me outside the cafeteria around seven, as promised. I had a purse around my shoulder, which held some of the things we'd need. It was already dark outside. Oberi sat by him dutifully and wagged his tail. "So where are we going?"

"You'll see." I walked ahead. Oberi changed into a unicorn. Charlie put his hand on her back, to guide him along as we left the doors of the Institute.

I led Charlie into the forest that was still securely locked inside the fence line. We wandered through a collection of pine trees, and Charlie said, "You sure we won't get in trouble out here?"

"We're still inside the prison yard. As long as we make it back before curfew, they won't bother us."

I lit a flame in my hand, to give myself some light. We walked for five more minutes, until Charlie asked, "Where are you going, exactly?"

"I was just going to find an open spot in the trees."

Oberi nudged him, and Charlie shook his head. "I have a feeling. Follow me."

Charlie walked on. Oberi went ahead of him, and I threw my arms up. Charlie took us through a particularly dense part of the woods. Oberi used her horn to clear the way for Charlie, but she forgot all about me as I snagged my uniform on branches and thorns, being careful not to light the woods on fire with my magic.

"Ow. Charlie, do you know where the hell you're going?"

He didn't answer. We finally stepped out of the brush, and my mouth fell open as I looked up.

There was a gigantic stone in the middle of the woods. It was massive. It looked like someone had carved out a cliff side and just dropped it in the forest. If I had to guess, the rock was over a hundred feet tall, and nearly as long.

There were carvings in the rock that looked like doorways, wide enough for large animals to fit through. Oberi walked forward. My fire-light shone off the walls of the stone as we looked inside. Charlie entered and trailed his hand over the stone, as if he could feel what the structure was thinking.

We wound through a twisted hallway until we came to a large room in the center of the rock. It was big enough to hold a hundred people. I expanded the flame in my hand as I looked toward the ceiling.

"Whoa. Charlie, how did you find this?" I marveled.

"I don't know," he mused. "Oberi sort of... gave me the idea. I can't explain it, but I've always had ease whenever I needed to navigate rocks and earth, or plants. It's like I can feel where they are, or sense them, energetically."

"Well, you are half-Nivita." It wasn't that odd. Charlie's father might have been an Air elemental, but his mother had been Earth, and he'd clearly inherited some of her talents.

"A Nivita must've carved it," Charlie said. "I don't know who else could make a room out of rock like this."

"Probably a prisoner at the Institute." Whoever they were, they were long gone now. This place had been abandoned for ages. There were no footprints in the dirt beneath our feet, and massive cobwebs were growing in some corners.

There was a crack as I stepped on something. A wooden bow lay beside my feet, but it didn't look Hawkei. I picked it up, and my brow furrowed.

"What is it?" Charlie asked, noticing my silence.

"A bow, but it's not from our tribe," I said. "The symbols on it... they're the same runes that were on the abandoned boats we found in the shipyard weeks ago."

"That's freaky."

"Just a bit." Why did we keep running into these runes, and what did they mean?

I tossed the bow to the other side of the room and tried not to shiver. "This is perfect. We won't be disturbed."

I sat on the ground in the middle of the room and began rifling through my purse. Charlie sat across from me, while Oberi lay down between us, her flaming mane giving off a warm glow.

"So what are we here for?" Charlie asked.

"You know the basics of Hawkei lore, but you don't know the important things. Since no one else will teach you, I will," I began. I set a bundle of sage and a leather pouch full of incense before me. I slipped bells onto my wrist and set a leather drum into my lap.

I didn't have my smudging wand, but this would have to do. It'd been a pain in the ass to sneak in the few Hawkei things I had. I placed the fireball on the ground, and it burned by itself of its own accord, sustained by my magic.

"What you have to know about the Hawkei is we're survivors," I began. "You already know that Native Americans got the short end of the stick."

"I don't know much, but I have heard that millions of natives died while Europeans were colonizing the United States," Charlie said.

"Yes. The Hawkei were a part of that genocide. That's why we call them colonizers, not settlers. The land was already settled by indigenous people before Europeans ever arrived in America. We had no need to be ruled by their governments until we were forced to do so. What the Hawkei went through was horrible. Our people nearly starved to death. We were driven to the brink of extinction by disease and war with the colonizers. The only reason we survived was because the ancestors bestowed upon us our elemental powers, and gave us the ability to bond with our Familiars. Without that, our people would've been wiped out."

Charlie gave a thoughtful look. "Kinpago seemed very diverse, from what I gathered while I was there."

"The Hawkei didn't remain within their own borders. The people in our tribe went all over the world, to befriend others and to even start families with them. That's why there's so much variation within Hawkei culture, because we've integrated our lives and had children with many other societies while keeping our traditions alive."

I frowned. "Even with our magic, it still wasn't easy. The United States government did whatever they could to stomp us out. We were the only people in the country who could only be considered native if we had enough of a *blood quotient* to qualify— like some kind of animal. Natives weren't even allowed to vote in every state until 1962. My great-great-grandmother was taken from her home as a child and sent to a rehabilitation boarding school, to try to force her to assimilate. They cut her hair, beat her, and forbid her to practice her religion. When she finally escaped, she didn't come back the same."

"That's horrible." Charlie frowned. "Except... I can't help but feel bitter that the Elementai did the same thing to me, by sending me into the foster care system and executing my parents before I could even remember them. Why should I want to be part of a tribe that would do that to me?"

"I know you were sent away because you were a mixed-House child. You weren't lucky enough to stay secret until the laws changed," I said in sympathy. "Your parents didn't deserve to die because they loved each other. It was wrong."

I drew myself up. "But I'm mixed-House, too. My parents are from different Houses, and eventually, the tribe accepted their relationship. I think our people have changed for the better."

Charlie scowled. "I wish I could believe that."

"I understand your skepticism, but you have to give your tribe a chance. The Hawkei have to stick together. It's the only way we've survived this long."

"Have there been other threats to our tribe?" he asked.

I nodded. "Yes. A hundred years ago, during the 1940s, there was a conflict called the Great Supernatural War. It was the biggest war of our time. Nobody had ever seen anything like it before. The fae, the angels, and the vampires joined together against the witches, the mermaids, and the Astromancers."

"What did the fae want to do?" Charlie asked.

"They wanted to expose magic to the humans, and enslave them, along with any other supernatural races they deemed inferior," I said. "It was a huge deal."

"What side did the Hawkei take?" Charlie asked.

"The Elementai tried to stay out of it, but eventually, we had no choice. We had to side with the witches, and stop the other side from destroying the supernatural world. We won, but millions of supernaturals died to keep magic a secret. The Elves went extinct as a result of it."

"The Elves?" Charlie asked.

"Yes. There was a genocide committed against them. There's none left now, because the Great Supernatural War took place. The Elven Union was wiped out. The fae, the vampires and the angels made it a point to exterminate them, and unfortunately, they succeeded before we could stop them."

I shifted uneasily. "Even now, the peace between supernatural races is very uneasy. The wrong thing could tip the balance and send the world back into chaos. Some people even say the Great Supernatural War could happen again, during our time."

Charlie frowned. "Let's hope it never does."

"Maybe." I was worried. If the students at the Institute were any indication of cooperation between magical races, we were bound to go to war again any day.

Charlie took a breath. "Okay. Tell me more about the Hawkei religion— what we worship."

"The Hawkei believe that everything on our planet has a spirit, from the smallest rock to the tallest tree, to the fastest fish to the stillest deer. Everything has an energy they can use to influence the world around them, and a name they can call their own."

Charlie nodded. "I can understand that. I can feel the spirits of the earth when I use my magic to navigate the world. I can even feel the spirit of the rock we're sitting in."

"Exactly. This is why the Elementai respect our earth. We give thanks whenever we plant a seed to grow, or take the life of a creature so we can feed our families. Everything is alive and deserves to be treated with reverence. This is how the Great Spirit intended us to live."

"Who's the Great Spirit?"

"Many indigenous tribes worship their own variation of the Great Spirit. To the Hawkei, he— or she, as I view her— is the Creator of the entire world," I spread my arms wide, and the shadows the fire cast flickered off the wall. "The Great Spirit breathed life into all, and takes life away. He has no end or beginning, merely always was. At the beginning of the world, the Great Spirit separated into hundreds, even thousands of gods. Some pieces became the moon, and the sun. Others became gods like Coyote Spirit, the deity of the Koigni tribe, or Whale Spirit, the deity of Toaqua. The Great Spirit is beyond understanding and manifests in all things. There is a part of him living in all beings, including you and me."

Charlie's look was introspective as Oberi nuzzled his hair. "I always felt like there was *something* out there. Didn't know what, though."

"Most magical races are in agreement there's a divine force at work in the world, though many can't agree which philosophy is right. Hawkei are accepting and inclusive in all religions. We don't dispute that the Goddess of the Miriamic Coven, or the Seven Gods the fae worship, or any other gods in the magical world, are wrong, because in our eyes, they're all just different pieces and variations of the same deity. All gods are the Great Spirit to us."

"That makes sense." Charlie leaned forward, his head in his hand. "What about the afterlife?"

"Our hell is *Aiya Nocshun*— the Mighty Darkness. You don't go there unless the ancestors banish you," I explained. "Most Hawkei go to the Ancestral Lands. You merge with your Familiar and your element, and your soul is united in harmony with the ancestors for eternity afterward."

Charlie's lip curled in disgust. "So... when I get to the Ancestral Lands, I have to share Oberi's body with you for the rest of my freaking existence?"

"Trust me, I'm not thrilled about it either," I shot back at him.

"Why do the ancestors get to decide everything?" Charlie asked. "It seems like they have a lot of power."

"Because that's what the Great Spirit has called upon them to do. We ask them for guidance, and for help on our journey. Some ancestors volunteer to become our spirit guides. They are chosen when we are born, and guide us along our life path."

I picked up the drum. "Firstborns of chieftains can summon the ancestors on any given day. Firstborns inherit the tribe they originate from, and keep our traditions alive and safe," I explained. "I'm going to summon your ancestors and your spirit guides for you, so you can meet them."

"Meet them?" Charlie lunged back.

"Yes. Sit back and shut up."

Charlie scowled. "Just what should I be expecting, here?"

I bit my lip as I began to concentrate. "When my dad summons the ancestors, it's always a big show, you know. Lots of colors, a huge tunnel full of Hawkei spirits that have passed on. My magic's a little quieter. You'll see."

I played the drum and began to sing in Hawkei. When my voice rang out, Charlie stiffened. His expression became complicated as my voice lifted and fell on the different notes, blending with the sounds of the bells and the drum.

Other voices began to join in... that of our ancestors. It created a heavenly harmony of thousands of songs, forging together to create a unanimous chorus. The anthem blended with the sound of a flute upon the air. I stopped playing the drum and removed the wristlet, but the sound of the drum kept pounding, and the bells continued to quiver and shake. Charlie didn't question where the music came from. He relaxed into the song, enjoying the beautiful melody the ancestors were creating.

I lit the sage, then threw dirt into the bowl and called water up from the ground beneath me. Droplets hovered through the air and splattered into the bowl moments before my Fire magic ignited the incense, burning it and the leather bag to smoldering embers.

Once the incense had burned to ash, I grabbed the embers and scattered them throughout the air. The embers hovered there for a moment before the cave exploded with colors.

Beams of blue, green, purple and orange flickered around the cave, like the Aurora Borealis lighting up the skies. The lights danced off the walls of the stone room, and from within them, shadows emerged. Like cave paintings our ancestors had created so long ago, images of animals began forming against the stone. There were dragons, winged deer, serpents and hippogriffs. A whale swam upon the air, while a tiger roared beside it. There were kelpies, krakens, and every other kind of animal imaginable twirling around us in the cave. Some were even extinct, long forgotten by the Hawkei but never by the ancestors.

The creatures ran along the stone wall, until they pulled themselves free and began taking on wispy spiritual forms. The cave became packed with dozens of ancestors. A group of salmon swam by, twirling around me and lifting my hair. I laughed as a thunderbird flew overhead, dancing with an eagle and a flaming firebird while a black wolf kept up beneath them.

Charlie couldn't see the spectacular show around him, but he could feel it. He stood slowly and put out a shaking hand. The ancestors began passing through his fingers. He shivered when he felt the cold skin of the whale, and the feathery torso of the thunderbird as they passed by. Charlie gasped as an enfield— a fox-bird hybrid— passed straight through his chest, as if taking his spirit with him. I could feel the chilly connection the ancestor made through our bond, and shivers ran across my skin.

Oberi whinnied in joy, dancing her hooves upon the stone floor as a Pegasus reared beside her. The creatures came down to the ground of the cave, and as they did so, transformed into people. So many faces appeared in the cave, all of them Hawkei, all of them gone on. They began to dance in time with the music, turning around us as their feet stomped into the earth.

Charlie could feel the vibrations the ancestors made as they danced, hear their song and experience the electrical currents of magical energy they emitted. He turned in place, as if his magic was going haywire trying to keep up with it all.

Five ancestors landed beside me. I waved as I recognized their familiar faces, as I'd summoned them and met them before. A snow leopard transformed into a gorgeous woman with long black hair that trailed upon the ground. A jackalope hopped by my feet and changed into a tall man with a smirking gaze. A three-headed dragon, covered in white feathers, became a tiny girl who'd died young. Beside her danced a hippocampus, a horse with a mermaid tail, who changed into a strong man with clear eyes.

Their clothing was from different time periods, Hawkei that had lived and died while scattered amongst history. The only spirit guide I could name was the grizzly bear beside me, which transformed into a tall, broad-shouldered man who looked so much like my father. He was my Grandpa Liwanu, and he'd died in the Hawkei Civil War. He was one of my spirit guides, and I'd seen him many times. My ancestors bowed to me, and I bowed back before they retreated to join the dance.

Charlie's ancestors came down before him, too. A lynx with horns became a Hawkei brave, his head shaved and arms decorated with indigenous tattoos. A manticore roared, twitching its scorpion tail before he transformed into a pixie-like woman who was thin and mischievous. A tiny deer with wings on its ankles jumped from this place to that, before taking shape into an old woman with a wizened face and a wise grin. A snowy owl became a woman with white hair. She had strange markings on her face that looked like warrior tattoos, but I couldn't place from what tribe. Lastly, the enfield changed into a man with blonde hair, standing before Charlie with a kind and welcoming smile.

Charlie's ancestors looked strong. Instead of bowing to him, they reached out to brush against his hand. Charlie nearly lunged backward, as if in shock, but I was proud to say he kept his feet in place. His mouth dropped open in awe as he observed his spirit guides in his own special way.

Eventually, the ancestors' song grew too loud for us to bear, and their dancing made the stone walls shake so violently, I was afraid the stone room would collapse with their power. I called water from the air, and as a puddle formed in my hand, I knelt to pour the droplets over the last remaining bits of incense that was still burning, bringing the ceremony to an end.

The dance ceased, and the ancestors vanished, taking the music with them and causing the room to go absolutely silent. The lights went with them, casting us into darkness again. Our presence was lit only by the small flame of my fireball, which was still burning on the floor.

There was nothing between Charlie and me but silence, and the sound of Oberi's huffing as she blew wind through her nose. "Well?" I asked. "Was that cool, or what?"

"That was way better than cool. It was *amazing*." Charlie's voice was mystified. "I can't believe I really met my ancestors."

"Yeah." I frowned. "I'm sorry you couldn't see them."

"It's hard to explain, but... I *can* see them, in my head," Charlie said. "When they connect with me, I know what they look like. I saw them once they touched me."

"That's awesome." I'd never heard of that happening before. "Now that you've met them, maybe you can try connecting with them on your own."

"How can I do that?" Charlie asked.

"You can meditate. Sometimes they'll send messages. Other times, if you ask for help, they'll send signs," I explained. "But the only way you can see them in person is to have a firstborn or a chieftain summon them, or contact them on Ancestors' Day. It's a special Hawkei holiday in May."

Oberi grew impatient. She tossed her head and tapped one of her hooves on the stone, letting out a couple of snorts.

"I think she's trying to say it's getting late," I said. "We've been here a while. We should get back, before the guards start creeping around."

"Yeah. Let's go."

I gathered my things, and we left the stone room. The sight of the broken bow in the corner was still on my mind, even long after we'd abandoned it for the darkness of the forest.

Charlie's tone was cautious. "So... since you're firstborn, and first-borns inherit the tribe, are you going to become the Toaqua chieftess someday?"

My soul filled with dread. "I don't think I'm my father's first choice to lead the Toaqua tribe anymore."

"Why not? If you're firstborn, isn't it your obligation?"

"I've got a lot of criminal charges on my record," I pointed out.

"Which will be wiped away if we win the Darke Games, or if you graduate from the Institute," Charlie objected. "Your past won't get in the way of you leading the Water tribe."

I sighed. "I know that Daddy *wants* me to be chieftess. But that's not me. I want to explore the world. I don't desire to stay in any place long enough to get comfortable. Traveling is my passion. I always have to be in a new location. Being a leader would bore me. I have no interest in becoming a chieftess."

I tucked a strand of hair behind my ear. "Besides... there's never *been* a Toaqua chieftess before. The leaders of the Water tribe have all been male. I don't want to be the first. There's too much expectation on me to be perfect, so I can leave the door open for other female leaders in the future. If I screw it up, who's to say they'll let another woman have power in the Toaqua tribe again?"

"What about your brother?"

I nearly laughed. "Ezekiel would make an awful chief. He can't make tough decisions, and he's a follower, not a leader. He does whatever I tell him to... not to mention he's too easily influenced."

"Well, someone has to lead the Water tribe."

"I know." My voice was very disheartened. "I don't want it to be me, but I'll probably have no choice, in the end."

"At least you have a future," Charlie replied dully. "I know where I come from now, but I still don't know who I am, or what I want."

"You'll figure it out, Charlie." I really wanted him to. He deserved to have a future.

But I wanted him to be able to choose his *own* future, for himself. It was the one luxury he was afforded that I was not. No matter what I did, I could never escape my birthright, the prophecy... or my fate as the chosen one.

My future was already chosen for me. I had no choice but to follow it.

THIRTEEN

I never pictured anything incredible would take place at the Institute, but meeting my ancestors was one of the most amazing things that had ever happened to me.

I'd never been very religious. I'd tried to learn Christianity in one of my foster homes— but that ended quickly when my foster dad claimed I was blind because I was a sinner. At twelve years old, I was more or less looking for answers no god could give me.

I never really connected with anything until that moment in the cave. Everything Ava said— about our ancestors, about the Great Spirit — it all made sense. And there was no denying the ancestors now, not after I'd witnessed them for myself. For the first time in a long time, I felt like I actually had answers.

I was still riding the high a week later on my way to my Substance Abuse class. I'd taken the class seriously the first couple of weeks, until I overheard two of my classmates making a drug deal in the middle of class— literally. I didn't know how anyone managed to sneak drugs into the school, but I wouldn't be surprised if there was enough magic in this place to brew it yourself. As soon as I realized how many drugs were being passed around inside the Institute, I gave up on the class. The staff was too clueless to notice. I didn't trust them to properly teach the subject.

Besides, I didn't need to be told to stay away from drugs. I'd had enough bad experiences to run at the first sight of them.

Oberi led me into the classroom, though I'd become accustomed to my normal route now. I didn't need to hang on to him anymore. We didn't have assigned seats in here, and every couple of classes, Mad Dog and his jerk friends would sit in a new spot, just to get a rise out of someone. The rest of the class had quickly picked up on their tactics and stopped falling for it. I could hear them across the room, blabbing loudly like they owned the place. It was obvious they craved attention.

Oberi guided me to an empty chair, and I sat. I listened in as the guy in front of me twisted around.

"Five bucks says Mad Dog initiates a fist-fight before the end of class," he offered.

For a second, I wasn't sure he was talking to me. "Oh, uh. I don't have the cash."

"Right." He sounded disappointed. "Then how about a bar of soap?"

Everything was hard to come by at the Institute, even simple toiletries. People fought over them all the time. "That sounds fair," I agreed. "Though I'm not sure I'd want to bet against that. He's got one hell of a temper."

The guy in front of me snorted. "You could say that again."

"*But,*" I added, "I suppose I could use another bar of soap. I'll take my chances."

I held out my hand, and he shook it. His hand was warm, so I figured I wasn't dealing with a vampire.

"Wesley," he introduced. "You're Charlie, right?"

I furrowed my brow. "How'd you know?"

"There's only one blind kid in this school with a guide dog," he said sheepishly.

"Ah, so I'm a hot piece of gossip? I thought that would've died down by now."

"Don't worry about it," he promised. "It's only people like Mad Dog who give you shit. Everyone else figures you must be innocent."

I reared back a little in my chair. "They do?"

"Sure," he said nonchalantly. "What kind of trouble could a blind kid get into?"

I frowned. "Well, that's stereotypical, but you're half right. I *did* get roped into coming here. What are you in for?"

He paused a moment before answering. "Battery."

My eyebrows shot up. "Oh, wow. It must've been bad to end up here."

"It was pretty bad," Wesley admitted. "Almost killed the guy."

"Wow, what'd he do to deserve that?" It wasn't an unusual question to ask at the Institute. Most people were pretty open about why they were here— either to claim innocence or to show how tough they were.

"Some low-life vamp passing through Malovia tried to drag my sister off the street," he said.

Malovia. Wesley must've been a shifter of some sort— a male Arcanea descended from the fae.

"I'm sorry," I said honestly. "I hope she's okay."

"Oh, she made it out just fine," he said proudly. "Can't say the same for the other guy. Sent him straight to the ICU."

"Good for you," I said. It sounded like the asshole had deserved it. Wesley on the other hand, didn't deserve to be here. He was only protecting his sister.

"And impressive," I added. I didn't know much about Arcanean shifters, but if they could kick a vampire's ass, they were a lot stronger than I initially thought.

"Thanks," he said proudly. He inhaled another breath to say something, but a scuffle on the other side of the room cut him off.

"You want a piece of this!?" a man shouted. I couldn't pick most voices out of the crowd— not unless I knew the person well, like Ava— but Mad Dog's deep voice was hard to miss. "Come at me!"

A *thud* sounded, and gasps traveled around the room.

"What was that about?" I asked Wesley.

"Looks like Jeffrey Johnson tried to challenge Mad Dog to his seat. He lost, obviously."

My shoulders slumped. "Guess I owe you that bar of soap, huh?"

"Nah," Wesley said. "Keep it. I have enough already."

Wesley's offer only confirmed for me he didn't belong here. Other students in the Institute would never pass up resources of any kind.

"What is the meaning of this!?" our professor boomed as he came through the door. He walked in so swiftly I felt the air brush off his feathery wings. Obviously he'd just witnessed the aftermath of the fist fight. It was hard to tell what was going on across the room, but judging by how quickly things had quieted, I'd have to guess Jeffrey had been knocked out in a single punch.

"Guy fell asleep," Mad Dog said nonchalantly. "Must have narcolepsy or something."

"Guards!" our professor shouted down the hall. The shuffle of three pairs of footsteps arrived within moments. "Handle this, will you? I have a class to teach."

The guards dragged Jeffrey, Mad Dog, and a few of his friends out of the room, and the class quieted.

Professor Gael began his lecture immediately. This kind of thing happened so frequently at the Institute, no one batted an eye. It was always the newbies who were most sensitive to it.

"Substance abuse comes in many forms," Professor Gael began. "We have talked about many drugs and their side effects in this class. What we haven't talked about is how to recognize the symptoms of substance abuse in others. Should you notice any of the following symptoms in your fellow classmates, you should report it immediately— so that your friends may be cared for properly."

It sounded like he'd tacked on that ending as an afterthought, to placate us. I got the sense that the Institute was more interested in punishing drug addicts than helping them.

"An individual suffering from substance abuse may show less interest in school or hobbies," Professor Gael continued. "They might refuse to sit with you in the dining hall, or stop hanging out with you in the recreation room. You may notice they stop eating and start losing weight. Their physical appearance might change, such as showering less, or neglecting to wear a clean uniform."

He went on and on with this, but I already knew it all. I'd been around drug use first-hand one too many times. And to be honest, he was hard to take seriously. Professor Gael spoke like he was a saint. He was an angel, so there was no surprise there, but I'd bet he never touched a drug in his life. This guy didn't seem to know shit what it was *actually* like to take drugs— only what he'd read out of a textbook.

I was relieved when class got out. The first thing I noticed when I left the classroom was Oberi stiffening at my side. Then I heard the sound of Ava-Marie's voice down the hall.

"I will not!" she shouted. "Who do you think you are?"

"Uh, oh," Wesley muttered under his breath. My stomach sank.

"I'm campus security," a man sneered. "And you'll do as you're told, or you'll answer to the Warden. Empty your pockets."

Oberi took off running, and I followed quickly behind. My Familiar stopped next to Ava, growling lowly at the guard.

"This is a violation of my privacy," Ava argued.

"Pidge, what's going on?" I asked.

The guard ignored me. "You want to know what noxite cuffs feel like?" he threatened Ava. "Because I can slap them on *real* fast."

I reached out for her hand to find that they were clenched into fists. Her whole body shook. "We don't want any trouble—"

"Step back, or you'll be next!" the guard thundered.

I was suddenly aware of how quiet the hall had become. I sensed a crowd forming, but they barely moved.

"What's going on?" a girl hissed to someone.

Wesley was close by and answered her in a low whisper. "Hey, Alice. Looks like a drug bust or something."

The guard waited another moment, but Ava didn't move. The sound of clinking chains met my ears, and I knew he'd pulled out his noxite cuffs.

Oberi's growl intensified, and I grabbed Ava by the shoulders. "Pidge, you have to do as you're told."

"I'm not doing anything I don't want to do," she snapped. Heat flashed through her arms, and I yanked my hands away like I'd touched a hot stove. The guard must've reached for her, because he yelled, too. The cuffs clinked to the ground.

"Filthy savage!" the guard yelled.

He was on her in flash— so fast it wasn't humanly possible. I could only guess he was a vampire. His elbow shoved me aside with the strength of a boulder, and the wind knocked out of my chest. I gasped for breath, and I heard Ava do the same.

"You want to know what Cellblock 9 looks like?" the guard threatened. "Because you've just earned yourself a one-way ticket for attacking a guard."

"Ah— ow!" Ava cried. "I didn't attack you! I was defending myself. Let me go!"

It took me a few moments to catch my breath and understand what was going on. By the strained sound in Ava's voice, I'd say the guard had pinned her up against the wall. His cuffs clinked again as he retrieved them from the ground. Oberi shifted into a Fire unicorn, and I could feel the anger— the intense urge to protect— rolling off her in waves. She was about to attack.

I wanted to, too. An intense fury bubbled up in my gut. Had he not been a vampire, I could suck the air right out of his lungs, but it wouldn't even faze him, I was sure. They didn't need air to breathe.

You can't attack a guard, Charlie, my rational mind reminded me. I barely heard it, but it was enough to make me switch tactics a split-second before I was about to whip up a wind storm. I had to make this better, not worse.

"Stop!" I threw myself in front of Oberi, next to the guard. "This is absurd. Sir, she's not even worth the paperwork."

"Charlie," Ava gaped. "How could you—?"

"She didn't mean to attack you," I drawled smoothly. "She's only just come into her powers, and doesn't know how to use them well. Pidge, please, just do as he asked."

"Her skill level means nothing," the guard sneered. "She's got drugs on her. I can smell it."

"I don't— ow!" Ava cried. She was in pain, as if the guard had yanked on her arm to shut her up. Oberi reared on her hind legs, but I lifted a hand to calm her.

"Ava's not doing drugs," I assured the guard.

"Oh, you want to bet on that?" he snapped.

I crossed my arms. "Actually, yeah, I do. If you search her and find anything, you can take us *both* to Cellblock 9. If you find nothing, you let her go."

The guard hesitated, obviously intrigued by my offer. We weren't supposed to make deals with the guards, but the opportunity to punish us both must've been tempting enough. I would bet he got some sort of commission off booking us both. And he seemed pretty certain Ava was hiding something.

"I suppose if she's not carrying anything, there's no reason to book her," the guard said, but I heard the darkness in his tone. He was saying it for the benefit of the onlookers— to make it look like he wasn't participating in any sort of off-limits bet. But there was enough edge to his tone that I heard the truth. He was taking me on, and he sounded certain he would win.

The guard stepped away from Ava, and she took a deep breath. "Fucking finally," she gasped.

"Pidge," I encouraged.

"Charlie—" she started to protest.

I leaned in and whispered lowly, cutting her off. "I'm trying to protect you. It's this or Cellblock 9. Just do as you're told, and we can get out of here."

Ava sucked in ragged breaths. Something about her was different today. She was more irritable than normal. I mean, the girl was *always* irritated about something, but this was different. There was no snark, no pep. Just pure fury.

"Charlie Wahkin, you owe me for this," she growled under her breath. Then she turned to the guard. "You want to see my pockets? Fine."

Fabric rustled as she turned her pockets inside out, though I didn't hear anything fall out of them.

"And for good measure, why don't you check my shoes?" she asked as she started taking them off. "And inside my socks."

She yanked her socks off and tossed them at me. I just barely caught them.

"What else do you want?" Ava demanded. "Want to check the folds of my tie?"

She tugged that off next and shoved it in my arms. "Or maybe you want to check my panties?"

Hell, she'd taken this too far. I knew she'd strip those off too under her skirt if anyone let her get that far. I grabbed her hand to stop her. "Pidge, I think that's enough."

Her arm was hot, and her voice cracked. "I *told* him I didn't have anything, and he wanted to invade my personal space anyway! And you of all people, Charlie, encouraged it. So what the hell else do you want me to do? Check my bra? I could be hiding drugs in there, couldn't I? Well, *couldn't I?*"

Ava was raging now. It wasn't in her social-justice speech kind of way, either. She was angry and hurt. I hated to think I had anything to do with that.

"That won't be necessary," the guard said, sounding slightly disgusted. He must've realized Ava wasn't kidding around, and I was sure his job would be on the line if he was caught strip-searching a student in the middle of the hall. He obviously didn't want to deal with Ava, because he let it drop. "You're clearly not hiding anything. Put your clothes back on, and get out of here."

"Oh, joy," Ava said flatly, snatching her socks and tie from my arms. "You're *so* generous."

She blew a breath and began marching away, her shoes clicking together as they dangled from her fingers.

I rushed to keep up with her, and Oberi followed behind. The hall broke into chatter then, and Ava and I disappeared into the sea of students.

"Pidge, what the hell was that?" I demanded.

She didn't slow, just kept on walking like she was determined to get somewhere— anywhere but here. "I don't fucking know, Charlie. I wasn't the one who started it."

"Then tell me your side of the story," I insisted.

"Why?" she growled. "You'll just blame me, anyway."

"No, I won't," I promised. "Please, tell me what's going on."

"It's not like it affects you."

I didn't think Ava knew where she was going, other than wherever her feet took her. She stomped into a large room. Even the quiet pad of her footsteps seemed to echo off the massive ceiling. I only knew one room in the whole Institute that was this large— the chapel. It was left over from the old cathedral, and no one used it anymore.

"But it *does* affect me," I argued. I stepped around her and planted myself in front of her. She stopped in her tracks. "Like it or not, we share the same soul, and when you get pissed off, so do I. So I deserve a damn good reason why I want to rip that guard's head off."

Ava bent over, and her shoulder brushed my leg. Her socks snapped against her skin as she yanked them back on. She grabbed my shoulder for support and slipped on her shoes. She didn't say anything the whole time, as if stalling.

Finally, she said, "I don't want to talk about this here."

"Then we'll go someplace private," I insisted. "I want answers."

Ava huffed, then grabbed me by the tie. "Fine. Follow me."

She dragged me behind herself down the chapel aisle— nearly choking me— until we exited the room into a narrow hallway. She hesitated a moment, then twisted a doorknob. The door creaked open, and she pushed me inside. "In here."

It was hard to tell where we were, until I stumbled forward and caught myself on a flight of stairs. The sound of Oberi's fiery hair wisping with flames died as she shifted into husky form to fit in the narrow stairwell. I rubbed my neck and scowled.

"Well, go on," Ava said. "Up the stairs we go."

"Where does this lead?" I asked curiously.

"Don't know. But it's as good of place as any, isn't it?"

The stairwell smelled musty, like no one had been up here in a long time. The stairs twisted in a circular pattern, like we were climbing a tower. My hand ran along the wall to guide me as we went up.

Finally, the air expanded, and we entered a larger room— I could only guess it was a balcony of sorts. It was completely silent, and I knew we were alone.

Ava whirled toward me, her hair nearly brushing my face. "You want to know what happened? I don't like being told what to do, especially when it comes to my clothes and body. You should know that by now."

I knew Ava was a rebel. It was what landed her here in the first place. But there was something else she wasn't saying. I wasn't sure if it was something I sensed in her tone, or something that came through our bond, but there was real pain there— pain beyond anything I could imagine. I could only make assumptions about what it meant, and it wasn't fair of me to ask.

My anger immediately washed away, replaced by a gaping hole in my stomach. I thought it belonged to me, but then I sensed our bond, and I realized that hole inside was within *Ava*, carving her from the inside out.

"Pidge, I'm sorry," I whispered. It was all I could say.

Without thinking about it, I reached for her and drew her into a hug. It should've felt weird, but it was as natural as crawling into bed at night. Ava was warm and soft. She was wearing a perfume that smelled like pears, raspberries and sandalwood. The scent drove me completely nuts, and I couldn't explain why.

But something was different about her, too. She felt incredibly tiny in my arms... hard like stone but intensely fragile. Instinctively, I knew she was too thin.

Ava didn't shove me away like I expected. Instead, her shoulders slumped, and she melted into me. Oberi leaned into the hug, wrapping his body around us. Ava sniffled, though I could tell she was trying to hide it.

"Don't cry, pidge," I said. I didn't know how to deal with crying girls. "You'll smudge your makeup."

Ava chuckled lightly, but it was only to break the tense mood. It sounded forced. "I'm not wearing any today."

That was odd. Usually, Ava was all fashion, hair, and makeup. I didn't care, since I wouldn't know the difference either way, but I knew it mattered to her. Something was obviously really bothering her, and it set me on edge.

"Ava..." I started cautiously. "You *aren't* doing drugs, are you?"

Hell, that was the wrong thing to say, and I knew it the second it came out of my mouth.

"What? *No!*" She instantly pushed me away. "How could you say that, Charlie? And all those other things you said— that I'm not even worth the paperwork, and I'm not talented. Do you really hate me that much?"

"Absolutely not," I promised. "I lied so he'd go easy on you."

She quieted. "Oh," she said. "You lied?"

"Of course. You didn't actually think I thought those things, did you?" I raked my fingers through my hair. "Pidge, that guard would be *damn* lucky to run your paperwork. And you're the most talented Elementai I know."

It didn't mean much, since I barely knew any Elementai, but Ava seemed to soften at the compliment.

"How did you know I didn't have any drugs on me?" she asked in an even tone.

"I didn't," I admitted. "I only had to trust that I knew you, and apparently, I do. Why'd the guard suspect you, anyway?"

"I don't know. I was just coming from taking my meds when he started accusing me of stuff and threatening to search me. He's a vamp, so I guess he smelled my medication and jumped to conclusions. I refused to be searched, and you saw the rest."

"Pidge..." I blew a breath. I wanted to tell her that she had to follow the rules around here, but how could I say that when I agreed with her? No one had a right to touch her without her consent. And yet pushing back would get you in trouble. It wasn't fair.

I didn't know how to put it all into words, so instead, I asked, "Where are we?"

Ava turned, and her heels clicked across the room. "Some sort of music room above the chapel."

Something screeched across the wooden floor, and Ava mumbled something about *so much dust*. Then came the sound of a music note filling the room— middle C, I realized immediately, from an organ. I half expected the sound of the organ to fill the whole chapel outside our private sanctuary, but it was quiet... meant only for us.

I walked over to join her. "Mind if I sit?"

The fabric of her skirt rustled as she slid down the bench to make room for me. "Go ahead."

There was enough room on the bench for both of us, though we were close enough that our elbows touched. Something strange happened in my chest when her skin brushed mine. It was so foreign, like my heart had turned to light, airy clouds.

Ava had gone really quiet. I didn't know what else to do but reach out and begin moving my fingers over the keys. I tinkered the tune to *Fur Elise* with one hand.

"I didn't know you played," Ava said lightly.

I shrugged. "I know a song or two."

A few beats passed, then Ava started snickering.

"What?" I asked, hovering my hand above the keys.

"Don't stop," she said. "Oberi was dancing. Well, more or less sway-ing. I think he likes it."

"Oh, well, I've got you covered, boy." I ran my fingers over the keys and found middle C again. My fingers moved on what felt like their own accord as I transitioned to an upbeat tune. I hadn't played in years, but my memory didn't fail me. It was like riding a bike.

Oberi's paws padded on the hardwood, and he yipped in excitement.

"Ancestors, he's adorable," Ava snickered. I was just glad to be cheering her up. "What song is that? *Piano Man?*"

"Yeah. An oldie, but a goodie."

"So, are you like, a child prodigy?" she asked, sounding serious.

I frowned. "Way to go stereotyping the blind guy."

"I thought being blind made your other senses better," she said, obvi-ously meaning no offense. "Aren't blind people supposed to be good at music?"

"As good or bad as anyone else," I replied, never missing a beat. "I can only play because of all the practice I had as a kid."

"Oh," she said flatly, like she didn't know what else to say. Another totally non-Ava mood. Usually she had more than enough to say. "Char-lie, can I ask you something?"

"Sure."

"Why did you run away from the guard?"

I stopped playing. Oberi whined lightly, and the organ echoed a few moments before the room fell completely silent.

"I wasn't *running*, pidge. I was..."

"You were running," she finished before I could find a better phrase for it.

"There are certain things you have to do in here to survive," I told her. "Like *not* getting thrown in Cellblock 9."

"You keep talking like that, and it's driving me nuts," she complained.

"Talking like what?"

"You use that word all the time. *Survive.* Ugh, I hate it."

I was starting to get a little irritated with her again. "Doesn't everyone want to survive?"

"Not like you," she said matter-of-factly.

I furrowed my brow. "What's that supposed to mean?"

"You want to *survive*, not *live*."

"What's the difference?"

She blew a breath, obviously exasperated with me. "You don't get the difference, do you? You'd rather dig your own grave and take your time doing it than anything else. I'd rather die young than live a life that's not worth living."

"That's the problem, pidge," I practically growled. "I don't want you to die in here."

"Don't you get it, Charlie!?" Her voice rose several pitches. "I wouldn't have cared if that guard took me down to Cellblock 9 for sucker-punching his ass. I'd die there, but at least I'd go out punching a vampire. That's more than you can say. What have you ever done?"

My nostrils flared. I thought Ava and I at least had a clue about each other by now. Turns out, she didn't know a damn thing about me. "I'm not the one who doesn't get it, pidge. *You* obviously haven't been pushed hard enough into survival mode that it's your only option left."

"Oh, I've been pushed," she argued.

"Yeah, and you're still pushing back," I growled. "I've reached the point where I can't push back anymore. Because I know what happens to people who do."

The thought of Ava pushing to her limits terrified me, because I knew it was a real possibility. I couldn't lose her.

You know... because she was part of my soul or whatever.

I winced as the possibilities flipped through my mind. She'd piss a guard off and be sentenced for life, or get in a fight with a siren and be eaten alive. There were a million ways for her to die in here, each one more gruesome than the last.

I did the only thing I knew to get rid of the thoughts. I started playing the organ. It was a soft, slow melody in a minor key, one I knew she wouldn't recognize. I was half surprised I remembered it after all these years. Then again, how could I forget? I was the one who wrote it.

"I didn't always think like this," I explained as I continued playing the tune. "I guess that's what happens when life beats you down."

Ava didn't say anything. Usually, she couldn't seem to control her big mouth. Today, I was grateful for the silence. I wasn't sure I could tell her the truth if she interrupted me.

"Until Professor Baine found me, I didn't know what happened to my parents," I continued. "All I knew was I was put into the foster care system long before I could remember anything else. I spent my entire life hopping from home to home— if I can even call it that. I've never really had a *home*."

I wasn't sure if it was conscious or not, but Ava leaned closer to me. Her arm brushed against mine, sending tingles across my skin.

The confessions continued to pour out of me. "As I aged out of the foster care system, I moved to Detroit and went on the search for a job— a real job so I could take care of myself. At this point, it was easy to convince everyone else I wasn't blind, but I couldn't convince employers. No way could I work construction without being able to see the blueprints, or work a cash register without knowing which dollar bills a customer handed me."

I paused for a moment, wondering how far I would take the confessions. Ava hadn't said a word, though, and her warm arm was comforting on mine. I actually felt like I could talk to her— *trust* her, even— which was something I hadn't found in a long time.

I continued. "One day, I was down on my luck and just had another job rejection in a long string of denials. I had a single dollar in my pocket and was starving, so I bought the largest thing I could get at the convenience store for a dollar— a slushie. When I finished it, I slumped to the ground on the edge of the sidewalk and placed my cup beside me. I thought I'd abandon it. To my surprise, I heard the sound of a coin clink into the cup. Then another, and another. That was the first time I realized that I didn't need a *job* to make money. Hell, I was *blind!* People would just hand it to me if they felt sorry enough."

I reached the end of the song and started playing it from the beginning again. "The first day, I made enough to get myself off the streets and into a hostel for the night. It was there I met Marty. He soon became my closest friend. He assured me panhandling would only get me so far, and that the only way to make real money was by running cons and a hell of a lot of other illegal shit— drug dealing and illegal gambling, to name a few. If it was criminal and made us money, we probably did it."

I started to choke up at the thought of Marty. My hands slowed over the keys, until I was playing long notes that didn't seem to suit any melody. But I couldn't take the silence, so I let the organ play.

"Marty was shot three years later," I choked out. "He couldn't pay his debt to his drug dealer, and they got to him. The man taught me everything I know— including to stay the hell away from drugs. Never touched any after that. But hell, I survived."

But Marty hadn't, and that shook me to my core.

"We were just walking down the street..." I shuddered as I worked up the courage to revisit that night. "A car drove by, and six shots rang out. I didn't even realize what had happened before the car drove away. Marty collapsed and... never got back up."

Ava reached out and placed her hand over mine. I stopped playing, and the room fell eerily silent. But there was warmth in the air, too. It wasn't so unbearable when she was next to me.

"My best friend died, too," she whispered.

My spine straightened. How was it that we had that in common? It didn't seem fair to either of us. "Really? How?"

"It's hard to talk about," she said, before redirecting the conversation. "That's why you focus on just surviving. Because you don't want to get hurt like your friend did."

I ducked my head. Hell if she saw me cry. I didn't do shit like that. "I'm one hell of a con man, pidge, but I can't outtalk a bullet. That's why I try not to stay in one place too long, because I don't want to draw attention to myself."

"I think I get it now, Charlie," she said softly.

"What do you mean?"

"I get why you don't want to go through with the Darke Games, and why you're so passive with the guards," she said. "You *have* to focus on survival, because you've never known anything else. I never had to worry about where my next meal was coming from, or if I'd be sleeping in a warm bed at night."

"Yeah," I scoffed, feeling kind of jealous of her. "If I can make it to the night with food in my belly and a roof over my head, I'm golden."

"So you almost *want* to stay, don't you?" Ava asked.

I shrugged. I'd never thought of it *that* way, but she had a point. At least in here I knew I wasn't going to starve.

"I'm sorry, Charlie," Ava whispered.

"For what? None of it is your fault."

"I'm sorry you've never had the chance to live."

That struck a chord with me, and the room went really quiet. Oberi padded over to me and rested his head on my knee. I wondered what it was like to live by Ava's definition. She seemed carefree at times, like she actually had something to stand up for besides herself. Her social justice speeches weren't just for her benefit, I realized. She wanted things to change for everyone, for life to give us all an equal shot at greatness.

I hadn't noticed before now how vastly differently we approached things. I always knew I had it rough, but I assumed people like Ava didn't have anything to worry about. I'd thought her behavior was over-the-top and irrational, because she didn't know what it was like to truly struggle. Now that she pointed out we were experiencing things from a different perspective, I realized she worried as much as I did— just about different things.

I didn't want to have to keep worrying about myself. It was damn exhausting. I wished I could be like Ava. She didn't seem to care what happened to her... only what happened to other people.

Ava took her hand off mine, and I began tinkering on the organ again. "So, how did you learn the piano?" she asked.

I sighed as the memories came back to me. "I was forced to learn by one of my foster moms. She thought it'd be good for me because I was blind. She wanted to give me something to do. Turns out, she was using the piano to babysit me and keep me out of the way of her in-house brothel."

"Ew," Ava said. "I can't believe you lived in places like that."

I shrugged. "It was normal. I can't believe you grew up next door to a castle. To be honest, it wasn't the worst place I've been."

"What do you mean by that?" she asked curiously.

I swallowed the lump in my throat. "I lived on the streets. I had to do what I could to survive, and winters can be harsh in Detroit. There were times I had to go home with someone just to stay warm."

Ava stiffened beside me. "Wait. You mean… people took advantage of you?"

"Yes… and no," I hesitated. "We both took advantage of each other. The woman would use my body, and I would sleep in a warm bed and get something to eat. Sometimes, I'd take things before I left, then sell them off on the streets. It'd hold me over for a while."

"That doesn't make what those women did right," Ava said in disgust.

"It was necessary," I replied. It was all consensual— even if I didn't care for the physical part. But it was better than freezing to death on a park bench.

"I'm sorry you had to do that," Ava whispered. After a few beats, she spoke again. "Charlie, can I ask you something?"

"Sure," I said. I'd already made it through the hard stuff. I had nothing to hide from her. If I didn't tell her now, she'd figure it out eventually. She was part of my own soul, for the ancestors' sake.

"How did you go blind?" she asked in a small voice.

I stiffened at first, but I relaxed a little the more I played. "I went blind when I was three, and don't remember much before that. I don't remember how it happened, and nobody ever told me. It was a medical fluke, they said. It's actually unusual to be totally blind, to see absolutely nothing like I do. Most blind people can see *something*— shadows or colors, maybe even just blurry images. It's not like that for me, which made it extra strange."

"You hide it so well," she remarked. "Is that because of your magic?"

I shrugged. "Partially, maybe. I don't have cataracts, so people can't tell at first-glance. Honestly, I just try not to bring attention to it."

"Why not?" She sounded confused. "It's part of who you are. Shouldn't you embrace that?"

She almost spoke like there was beauty to my blindness.

"I didn't want to be treated differently," I admitted, though I rushed to clarify. "I wasn't always treated differently for my blindness. But when I was, people would go to one extreme or the other. Like, foster moms would coddle me extra hard, or kids would bully me. It wasn't uncommon for other foster children to steal my belongings or take food off my plate— straight from under my nose."

I took a deep breath. "When I was fourteen, a group of boys from school cornered me and beat me up before stealing my cane. I was forced to navigate the urban streets without it and find my way back to my foster home alone. My foster parents agreed to buy me a new one, but I was moved to another home shortly afterward, before I ever received a new cane. I was shocked at how well people treated me when I didn't have it. At first, I thought they just felt sorry for me. But the more I began to navigate the world without my cane, the more I realized that without it, people couldn't tell I was blind. Finally, no one stole my food when they thought I had my eyes on my plate. My belongings were safe. Of course, I had multiple run-ins with bullies after that, but it was always for something else— never because I was blind. I learned from then on to act as if I could see. If I did, no one took advantage of me."

"How did you manage without a cane?" Ava leaned closer, sounding intrigued.

"I used my other senses and learned tricks to navigate my world," I told her. "I'd fold bills in certain ways so I knew which ones I was grabbing to pay for things. I had my own way of navigating the world without sight. If I focused hard enough, I could create images in my mind of the world around me just by concentrating on the air pressure. I learned to hone the skill, until I had perfected it by the age of eighteen."

"So, you're like *Daredevil?*" Ava asked. "You're not *really* blind because your magic helps you."

Ava didn't sound like she meant anything by it, but the question rubbed me the wrong way. I'd been compared to the comic book character one too many times. I hated it.

"It's not the same thing," I assured her, trying to keep an even tone. "My powers don't negate my blindness. I'm the same as I was before I got them. I'm just better at hiding it. My powers simply *became* my cane, a tool to help me navigate my environment. I still experience the world as a blind person. Yeah, maybe my magic gives me an advantage, but there's still a lot I miss out on and times I need to ask for help."

"I didn't mean to offend you," she said softly, and I realized how harsh my tone had grown. "I just meant sometimes it seems like you *can* see things."

"I don't, though. I just experience the world in a different way," I explained. "Like I know when someone is walking toward me, because I can hear their footsteps, or I can hear when they turn away from me by the sound of their voice."

Ava's elbow bumped against mine as she knotted her hands in her lap. "I guess I rely too much on sight."

"You use the tools at your disposal," I said, like it was nothing. And it wasn't. "You shouldn't feel guilty about that."

Ava processed my words for a few moments, then spoke again. "How else are things different for you? Do you have to read braille to do school assignments or something?"

"No. I can't read braille," I said. "It's not something every blind person knows. I learned enough to read public signage, like numbers on the elevator. But it's a complicated language and takes years to learn. I'd like to learn, but I never had anyone to teach me. As far as school assignments go, I need accommodations, which unfortunately in my experience many teachers aren't willing to provide."

"What kind of accommodations?"

"I can't read textbooks, but I can learn through audiobooks or videos," I explained. "I can't write with a pen and paper, but I can use dictation software."

"Oh," Ava said, like the thought made her sad. "Has the Institute given you any of that?"

"No," I replied sourly. "There's the whole thing with technology working shitty around magic, right?"

"Sometimes," she said. "Depends on how much magic is being used. At the Institute, I doubt something like that would work— except maybe the ancient computers in the library. There's so much noxite here, and that's a type of magic itself. I'm sorry the school can't do better for you."

I snorted. "Don't worry about it. I'm used to it. It's why I never graduated from high school. The school wouldn't provide adequate accommodations, so they thought I was just dumb and wanted to hold me back. Couldn't keep going to school without a foster home, though, because I needed money just to live. I left as soon as I turned eighteen."

Ava seemed magnetized toward me, because her body brushed up against mine. Warm tingles spread through me, though I didn't think she meant anything by it. This bench just wasn't big enough to keep our distance.

Ava quickly dove into her next question. "What about color? Does it make any sense to you?"

"I get the concept," I told her. "And I sort of remember color from before I was blind, but it's been so long, I could be remembering it wrong. I make associations differently than you."

"What do you mean?" Ava asked. "Blue is blue. Red is red. How can you associate that with anything else?"

I smirked playfully. "They taste different."

Ava chuckled under her breath. It was good to hear her laugh, because she hadn't sounded like herself all day. "Colors don't have a *taste*, Charlie."

"Sure they do," I said. "Red tastes like strawberry candy. Blue feels like water running over your hands, or blueberries. Green is the smell of grass, and yellow is warm, like sunlight on your face."

Ava laughed and shoved me. I faltered on the notes I was playing. "You can't just make up rules."

"Sure I can." I stopped playing and shoved her back. "Rule number one: stop invading my personal space."

I poked her, and she giggled. I couldn't say it with a straight face, because the truth was, I didn't *want* Ava to respect my personal space. I wanted her next to me— to touch me.

I tossed the thought out of my mind the second I thought it. What the hell was I thinking? I *hated* Ava-Marie. And yet when she was next to me, I felt... I don't know. The closest to home I'd ever felt before.

"What was that?" she teased. "Keep invading your personal space?"

She pushed her hips and shoulder into mine on the bench. Oberi jumped back, shaking his fur and barking. I lost my balance and wrapped my arms around Ava to stay upright, but gravity had other plans. I went tumbling off the bench, dragging Ava with me. The organ keys let out noise as we smashed into them on the way down.

Ava crashed on top of me, her hips pressed into mine. She breathed rapidly, the sweet scent of her breath rushing across my cheeks. For a moment, neither of us moved. We simply lay there, my hands on her waist and her breasts heaving with each breath against my chest.

Something stirred deep within my belly. I couldn't explain it, but it must've had something to do with our bond, because I'd never felt it with anyone else before. Or maybe I was just nervous about what she thought of me now— now that I'd let myself become vulnerable with her.

My uniform slacks suddenly began to tighten. Oberi licked my face, and I came back to reality. I was suddenly aware of the very sexual position Ava and I were in. I practically shoved her off of me, and she started laughing again.

"It's not a good rule if you're not going to enforce it," she joked as she reached down to take my hand and help me up.

"It'd be a fine rule, if you didn't insist on breaking it," I shot back playfully. "But that is the Ava-Marie way. If a rule is made, she's bound to break it."

And hell, I *wanted* her to break this one.

"Damn straight," she said proudly. She still didn't quite sound like her normal self, but she seemed better than before— more relaxed, perhaps.

I cleared my throat in the following silence. "Uh, thanks, Ava."

"For what?" she asked, like she hadn't done anything.

"For listening," I said simply.

She didn't know how much I meant it. The way she sat quietly to hear my story meant a lot to me. She cared, and she was one of the first people in my life to do so.

"Oh, well, don't mention it," she said, but there was something in her tone that didn't match her words. It was soft and delicate— like the conversation had meant something to her, too.

"We should probably get back downstairs," she suggested quickly. "Someone might start wondering where we went."

"Yeah." I cleared my throat. "Probably best."

Except I didn't want to leave here. As Ava turned and Oberi followed dutifully down the stairs, I couldn't help but stand there and simply take in the room— the smell of the dust that seemed sweet now, and the sound of Ava's footsteps echoing up the twisted staircase.

This was our little hidden corner of the Institute. I'd shared things with her here that I'd never spoken about to anyone before. The confessions seemed to permeate the walls, to sink into the keys on the organ, and would remain there permanently in this place.

Our place.

"Ancestors' cock," I cursed under my breath as the sunlight illuminated the pages of the journal. I wiped the sleep from my eyes and read the prophecy over again, but like the million times I had before, it didn't make any sense.

I slammed my head into my pillow. I'd been up all night, deciphering the journal, and it was just as confusing as it had been the first day I got it. This was getting me nowhere. I tossed the journal against the other side of my dorm, where it slid against the wall and propped open against the ground.

I'd been studying the journal every day for weeks, and I hadn't made any progress with the prophecy. It was the only thing I could do, seeing as how I was still trapped within these walls. I figured there had to be *something* in the journal that would give me a clue on where to start investigating the prophecy once I got the hell out of here.

There was nothing. I'd read the journal a million times, and though I'd memorized countless wordings, drawings, and hints, none of it made any sense. I'd spoken to Mama about it, but she insisted the prophecy would unfold itself when I was ready, and not before.

I didn't have time. I wanted to stop this *now*, before people got hurt. I was tired of being an instrument of fate.

Your destiny is uncontrollable.

Everyone's after you.

Hide, Ava!

I had to get up. I had class in fifteen minutes. I forced myself out of bed and picked the same uniform I'd worn yesterday off the floor. It was wrinkled and dirty, but I didn't give a shit. I couldn't be bothered to care what I looked like. I slipped it on and tied back my hair without brushing out the tangles that had formed within. I was breaking out along my nose, and yet, I didn't reach for any concealer. On a different day, a single blemish was enough to send me spiraling into a breakdown.

Today? Fuck it all.

My reflection was haunted and gaunt. I looked like a freaking mess. The depression had pulled me so low, I had bags under my eyes. But I'd rolled out of bed, so that was a plus for me. On days like today, breathing felt like a curse.

I was in a low period. A very low period. I missed my family. I'd give anything to talk face-to-face with Daddy, or have a plate of some of my mother's famous Italian. I really wanted to write a song with Ez, go shopping with Alana, or work on the bike with Maverick in the garage. I'd never been away from them this long before, and it was eating me up from the inside out.

The only thing that seemed to help was having Oberi around... and Charlie. There was something different between us— I sensed it now. The way he'd opened up to me the other night felt raw and special. I didn't think he'd ever told someone his story before.

I couldn't imagine what Charlie had been through. To be forced to prostitute yourself for a safe place to stay the night...

I shivered. Our lives were so different, but even though I couldn't understand what he went through, I could still empathize. The only reason I'd had everything I wanted growing up was because I was privileged enough to have rich parents with a lot of power and influence. As a mixed-House child, if the Hawkei Civil War had been lost, I could've easily ended up like Charlie... shuffled from foster home to foster home and desperate to survive.

If Charlie kept fighting, I had to, too. I opened the door and found Oberi outside, waiting for me in the hallway in her unicorn form. She stomped up to me and pushed me over. I went falling back into the wall.

"Ow, Oberi, what the hell?" I complained.

She huffed and shook her head, three times in a row. Her fiery mane went everywhere, and she bumped me again, tossing her head in a circle.

She wanted her mane braided today. I laughed and grabbed a couple of hair ties from my pocket before I started in on her mane. I felt tingles go up and down my fingers as they touched the flames, braiding the tendrils of fire together so they made a beautiful array. My Koigni magic made it so I didn't feel the heat or experience any burns. As I worked, Oberi's eyes closed in relaxation.

"You like being pampered, huh, girl?" I asked.

She nickered as I finished my work. When we passed a mirror in the hallway, Oberi stopped and admired her reflection before pursing out her lips, exposing her teeth and waving her mouth in the air.

Ancestors, she was an attention hog. I giggled and patted her shoulder. "You're gorgeous, Oberi. The prettiest unicorn there ever was."

Smoke emitted from her nostrils as she snorted, as if to say, *I better be.*

Supernatural Behavioral Science was a class about intermagical cooperation. It was held in a dark classroom at the end of the Institute that was damp and musty. When I walked in, I felt a chill wash over me. It was always freezing in here. I heard strange moans, like that ghosts made, and it caused the hair to stand up on the back of my neck. The classroom was decorated with skeletons of supernatural creatures, as well as a skull I was sure was from a vampire, due to the fangs. Fairy wings were held up by pins in glass cases on the walls, and the fin of a mermaid was placed in a case on the teacher's desk in front of the room.

A dragon skeleton hung suspended from the ceiling. I was certain our teacher had killed it herself. Professor McCauley was an Air Elementai who seriously took no shit. She appeared like a corpse, taunt yellow skin and beady eyes, held together by minuscule pieces of flesh and bone. She had to be half-vampire, because she'd taught my dad at Orenda Academy, and she'd been ancient back then. Immortality was the only explanation for why she was still creeping around. I don't know why she'd transferred to teach at the Institute, but it was always good to have another Elementai around, I supposed.

Her Familiar, Bram, remained in a corner of the room and watched us with beady eyes. He was a wendigo, an animal you didn't want to cross. Bram's body was the skeleton of a horse, with a long dragon's tail and paws like that of a wolf's for feet. A deer's skull with violent antlers served as Bram's head, and within it, there were no eyes— only sockets. The taunt black skin that stretched over his form only made him more terrifying.

Wendigos were dangerous creatures. You didn't fuck with them unless you wanted to die.

Kalina was in this class with me. She looked up as I took my spot at a desk, but didn't say anything, just kept her eyes forward.

McCauley counted the number of students in her classroom, making sure all were here before she launched into a lecture.

"Magical cooperation is very important for the survival of our world," McCauley said. "Humans are a threat to us all. They outnumber us, and for the first time, their technology poses a risk. Which is why it is critical all supernatural races work together in order to ensure the continuation of magic."

Bram began moving around the room, his skeletal form clicking together as he patrolled, making sure we all paid attention. McCauley's was the one class in the entire school where no one dared to pull anything. We were all too afraid of Bram to try back talking her.

"There is a type of magic that allows different magical races to combine their powers into one fluent method of power," McCauley said. "This magic is called *simultension*. Simultension allows a mermaid to combine their voice magic with a shifter's telepathy, for example, or an angel's light magic with a witch's necromancy. The possibilities are endless. Only together can certain types of magic be created, through the efforts of two or more supernatural species. Miss Lopez, Miss Demauley. A demonstration, if you please."

Lupe headed to the front of the room. I hadn't seen her much since she'd been our tour guide at the start of the semester, but she worked in this class as a teacher's aide. Despona also rose from her seat. The Elementai and the succubi faced each other, waiting for McCauley's instruction.

"Miss Lopez, use your Koigni magic and merge it with Miss

Demauley's mind control," McCauley said. "Focus your powers on working together, instead of against each other."

Despona appeared a little worried, but Lupe's face was calm. She emitted a stream of fire from her hands, which wrapped slowly around Despona like a ribbon. It didn't burn the vampire, or hurt her.

Despona took a deep breath. As she exhaled, the Fire magic dispersed around her, and Lupe directed it toward Bram. The Fire created shackles around the wendigo's feet. Despona's eyes flashed red, and she lifted her hand, moving it like a puppeteer. Bram began to dance, but clearly not of his own accord— the Fire shackles around his feet appeared to work like strings, moving Bram's feet from one spot to another.

"Excellent work," McCauley said, and the Fire shackles faded as Bram was set free. "As you can see, creativity is the hallmark of using simultension. Everyone, partner up with someone that is not of your own magical race, and get to work. If you create a spell I haven't seen before, you will get an A for the day."

That had to be impossible. McCauley was so old, she must've seen everything. I looked around for a partner, but most people had already been taken.

McCauley assigned one for me. "Ava-Marie, you'll work with Kalina," McCauley said. "Get to it. No use in lazing about."

I frowned. I didn't want to be with Kalina, but she was already moving her things to my desk.

She sat across from me and fiddled with her pencil. "So, what should we make?"

"I don't know. Isn't fae magic limitless?" I asked.

"In a way. Fae have illusion magic. We can create and manifest any illusion we like into reality, as long as we believe it's real. That's the hard part," Kalina said. "If I don't believe I can do it, it won't happen."

"So let's do something easy," I suggested. "What's the simplest illusion for you to create?"

"Weapons," Kalina responded instantly. "I can make a blade appear out of thin air without breaking a sweat."

"What if you try to make a weapon out of my elemental magic?" I suggested. "An Elementai's magic is pretty powerful, but it doesn't last very long. In most cases, weather magic fades pretty quickly once it's been cast. Maybe we should try making it stick."

"Sounds good to me. Give me what you've got," Kalina suggested.

I nodded. I raised my right hand, and a fireball appeared before us, floating in mid-air. I lifted my left hand and uncapped the water bottle next to me. The water began rising out of the bottle, until it became a ball right next to the glaring fire, rippling with tiny waves as the firelight reflected off of it harshly.

"You might want to move fast," I suggested. "It won't last long."

Kalina stared at the fireball so intensely, I thought it might fizzle out at her gaze. But that wasn't what happened. Metal began to take shape around the fireball. My jaw dropped as I watched a sword forge right before my eyes and become solid out of thin air. Within the blade of the sword, fire danced, as if there was a window within the weapon that displayed the flames raging inside.

Kalina created a second sword around the water ball, and it flowed outwardly within the middle of the blade just as the fire did. I froze the water inside the sword, and it became a weapon of ice, the still water gleaming inside the blade.

I could feel Kalina's magic as it merged with mine. It felt a lot like the bond between Charlie and me, but it was farther away. I surveyed the feeling of illusion magic with interest. It felt whimsical, and unbound.

"Badass," Kalina said in approval as she observed the floating swords. "Want to try these out?"

"Sure," I said. We moved the desk aside to make room. I grabbed the Water sword, and Kalina took the Fire one. We squared off. Kalina struck first, and as she swung the blade toward me, I brought up my own to block her. Sparks flew everywhere, and I felt my elemental magic quiver when the blades touched.

To my surprise, the swords held. I thought for certain that they'd fall apart once we struck them together, but as long as my magic was intertwined with Kalina's, the swords remained intact. Kalina struck again. I blocked her a second time, and we sparred lightly, testing the strength of our weapons. Sparks continued to fly, along with water droplets, as the swords clashed again and again.

Kalina swung her sword upward in an arc, and I batted it away. The Fire sword left small remnants of flame trailing through the air. As an experiment, I pointed my sword at her, and an icicle emitted from the tip and flew outward. Kalina ducked to avoid it. When the icicle hit a desk nearby, it immediately froze it.

People stopped what they were doing to watch us spar. Kalina and I put all our might into it and really hammered on each other's weapons, but no matter how hard we struck, our magic didn't break.

"Well done, both of you," McCauley said approvingly. "Full points for the day."

Kalina drew back, panting. I was out of breath, too. I could feel Kalina's illusion magic ebbing away as she attempted to take back the power that was hers. I pulled my magic back from Kalina's. The swords instantly dissolved, as if they were never there at all. The fire faded into smoke, and the water became vapor upon the air.

"It looks like we both have to sustain the spell in order to keep it going," Kalina said. She plopped into her seat to take a break.

"Yeah. I guess simultension doesn't work without cooperation." I took a chair beside her. I wish I hadn't used all the water from my bottle, because I was thirsty now.

Kalina gave a roguish smile. "Have you ever sparred before? You're really good."

"No. That was my first time," I admitted.

"You must be a natural." She leaned back in her seat. "My dad taught me. He's the best swordsman that ever was."

"I guess if I can keep up with you, I'm not that bad, Kalina," I joked.

Kalina's smile faltered, and I felt like I struck a nerve. "Did I say something wrong?"

"It's just... I don't really want to be called that anymore," Kalina said. "*Kalina* is a high-born fae name, and I want to separate myself from that life as much as possible."

"Why?" I loved my name, and couldn't imagine being called anything else, but maybe she had a good reason.

"I was exiled. My people and my country abandoned me. I want to get my throne back, but at the same time, I don't know if I ever can go back to that life," Kalina said. "My name is just a reminder of what I lost. I need to become someone different if I'm going to be happy."

"So... what do you want me to call you?" I asked.

She gave an introspective look toward the ceiling. "I was thinking... Kallie."

"Okay, Kallie," I said. "If that's what you want to be called, then that's who you are to me."

"Thanks. I really appreciate it," she said in relief. "I just need to reinvent myself. Start over, once we win the Darke Games."

I got it. So many people at the Institute wanted to forget their pasts. It was the only way to move on once you'd been thrown in jail.

I giggled. "You know, I'm all for reinventing yourself, but if you want to change your sense of fashion, you'll probably have to wait until we get out of the Institute."

Kallie moaned. "I know, right? The uniforms at Arcanea University are *so* much better. The fae have better taste. I feel so matronly in this skirt."

"Same," I agreed. "I'd do anything to go to the mall."

Kallie cocked her head. "Aren't you the girl who got in trouble for modifying the uniform and making it sexy?"

"That's me," I said proudly.

"I like rebels who don't follow the rules," Kallie said in approval. "If you can't tell, I have a problem with authority."

I snickered. "Girl, I feel you. What good are rules if they're not meant to be broken?"

Kallie nodded. "You're a badass bitch. I could get used to hanging around a girl like you."

"You're not so bad yourself," I said.

Kallie was actually kind of cool. Maybe I hadn't given her a chance. Trusting people was never my strong suit... but even if I didn't trust Kallie, perhaps she could still be a friend, and that was good enough for me.

When I peeked out my door on Wednesday morning, my eyes widened. I saw an array of students walk by, dressed in various costumes like scarecrows, ringmasters, pirates and movie characters. It was so different from the dull uniforms we were forced to wear every day.

Crap. It was freaking Halloween. And I'd totally forgotten.

Oberi wasn't around. She had gone back to Charlie yesterday, and the man got up so damn early ancestors only knew where the hell he was.

My eyes scanned the hall until I saw Opal. She was dressed as a ladybug, waiting for me so we could walk together to the nurse's station to take our pills. I ran over and grabbed her shoulder. "We're allowed to dress up?" I didn't think the Institute approved anything *fun*.

"It's Halloween," Opal said. "It's the one day of the year we don't have to wear those stupid uniforms. They actually let us wear whatever we want, as long as it isn't violent. Most people get their parents to send something, or order costumes from the shop in Shade Hills to be delivered to the Institute."

Fuck. I loved Halloween, but I'd been so wrapped up in my own thoughts lately, I hadn't even paid attention. I didn't have a costume, but I was sure I could find *something*. "Wait here."

I ran back into my dorm and began throwing clothes around. I didn't want to be the only loser without a costume.

I found a pink knee-length wool skirt with the design of a white poodle on the edge. It was a poodle skirt I'd bought a few years ago, but I'd never found the right opportunity to wear it. I'd packed it in a hurry when I was throwing things into my suitcase for the Institute. I put it on, then pulled my hair back into a ponytail and slipped on a plain white button-up. They matched my white tights and black shoes from my uniform. I wrapped a polka-dotted scarf around my hair to use as a headband, and called it a day.

Opal's smile widened as she saw me. "You're a 1950s sock hop girl," she gushed. "Very cute."

"You think so?" I smoothed down my shirt. "I'm really into vintage stuff."

"It totally fits your personality," Opal said. "I couldn't put something together like that last-minute."

As we waited in line to take our pills, I observed all the different costumes people had on. It looked like Mad Dog had decided to fuck the rules, because he'd chosen to dress up as a serial killer, bloody shirt and all. I wasn't so sure the blood was fake, either. He walked around school with a hockey mask, following kids around until they started running out of fear.

Halloween wasn't fun for people like Mad Dog. It was an excuse to terrify people. I rolled my eyes and turned away. I wouldn't let that loser ruin my holiday.

After we took our pills, Opal and I began on our walk to the cafeteria. In the hallway, I saw Naya heckling with a couple of her cronies. Naya had on a really revealing devil costume that looked more like lingerie than an actual outfit. The horns and pitchfork fit her black heart *perfectly.*

"What the fuck are you wearing?" Naya asked a girl who passed by. The girl had on a very large gown, with a big lace collar around her neck. It was a beautiful, intricate costume that had obviously taken a lot of work to make.

The girl skidded to a halt. Her face went pale. "It's... a renaissance period costume," she whispered. "I worked all month on making it in Arts and Crafts."

"Well, it's freaking stupid," Naya snapped. "Try a sexier costume next year, and maybe guys will stop thinking you're such a prude."

The girl blushed and blinked tears away before she sniffed and ran off. I went to give Naya a good piece of my mind— meaning, my fist in her face— but Opal put an arm out to stop me.

"Leave her be," Opal whispered. "You don't want to be next."

The guards were stationed around the area, looking for people who wanted to start a fight. Opal was right. I'd already gotten into one altercation with a guard last week. I was pushing my luck as it was.

My temper steamed as Opal forced me to walk away. I didn't really care that Naya was wearing a skimpy costume. Monica and I had been Playboy bunnies one year, *without* Daddy knowing about it, of course. But Naya was using her outfit to act like she was hotter than everyone else, and shame other girls. It was gross.

Opal had class, so she grabbed something quick from the take-out line and ran off. I stood in line alone to pick up food. I was planning to get the sludge-like oatmeal, so I could use its grossness as an excuse to throw it out without taking a bite.

I yelped as I felt a pair of arms wrap around me from behind. It was Charlie. I knew immediately by the way he smelled— like leather, bergamot, and warm spices that were woodsy and earthy. He picked me up a few feet off the ground and let me hang there. Oberi wagged his tail and barked, running circles around us as Charlie swung me around.

"Charlie, what are you doing?" I asked with a laugh.

"Trying to scare you. Happy Halloween." He didn't make a move to let me down. I didn't mind it like I thought I would.

"You don't have to try because it's a holiday. You scare me every day of the year," I countered.

"Stop." Charlie paused. "You've lost weight, pidge."

He let me go. I slid out of his arms and took a step away. He felt too close. "I've been working out."

Charlie was still in his uniform. I didn't think he had a costume, which made me sad. I went to open my mouth to say something about it, before Charlie cut me off. "So, what are you having for breakfast?"

"What does it matter?" I asked. "I'll just grab something."

His face was slightly puzzled. Or perhaps concerned. "We can share a plate."

Was he trying to outsmart me? It might be working. I said nothing as Charlie loaded eggs and bacon onto a large plate. Oberi was drooling so badly that he made a puddle on the floor.

We sat down on a bench. Oberi shoved his head between us and set it there, staring at the bacon with huge eyes.

Charlie started in, but I didn't touch anything. He couldn't see me. It's not like he could notice if I wasn't—

"You're not eating, pidge."

How could he tell? It was wholly aggravating. "I'm just not hungry today."

"It's more than that. You never eat."

Charlie refused to fill the silence. I sighed. This guy wouldn't take anything less than the truth for an explanation. "When I get in really high manic periods, or really low, I don't eat. I can't explain it, but food makes me anxious. I try to make up for it when I come back down to a somewhat normal state. I'll binge eat until I puke it back up."

"Ava, that's really bad for you," Charlie scolded. "When was the last time you had an actual meal?"

My voice was small. "Yesterday morning."

Charlie frowned. "That's not okay."

"Why do you care? It's not your stomach," I snapped.

Charlie's voice was flustered. "You need to keep your strength up for the Darke Games. You know, so we can win and get out of here."

I let out a *pshing* sound.

"If you're not eating, I'm not eating," Charlie said. He put his fork down and set his elbows on the table.

Ancestors damn him. Nobody had ever managed to get me to eat when I really didn't want to— not even my parents. But I couldn't let Charlie and Oberi starve, and Charlie could hold on to his hunger strike. He had experience with going hungry.

So I had to eat something. Just to keep him happy. He'd notice how much food was left as he ate. I might as well start in.

I ate a few bites of egg and nibbled on a piece of bacon. It felt like a feast, but as I continued to eat, the aching in my middle ebbed, and energy rushed back into my body.

"So... where's your costume?" I asked. I gave an extra egg to Oberi, and he swallowed it greedily, licking the yolk off his large nose with loud laps.

"It's not like I could afford to buy one," Charlie said. "It's not a big deal. Just let it be."

I didn't want Charlie to be left out. When we finished our meal, I jumped up and tugged on his arm. "Come on. Let's go back to your dorm."

Charlie raised an eyebrow. "I didn't realize we had that kind of relationship."

"Ew! Not that, you idiot. You need a costume."

I dragged on his arm and wouldn't take no for an answer. Charlie hemmed and hawed all the way back to the Elementai cellblock while Oberi jumped from spot to spot on the hallway ahead of us, playing his own game of *The Floor is Lava*.

"You aren't going to find anything. I have nothing," Charlie complained as we entered his room.

"You aren't being creative enough." I shuffled through the dresser, but he wasn't kidding— beside his uniforms, Charlie only had a handful of clothes, barely enough to fit in a grocery bag.

But I was Ava-Marie Mitoh, and I'd never been backed into a corner when it came to fashion.

I grabbed a pair of ripped jeans, a white t-shirt, and his leather jacket out of the closet. I threw them at Charlie, and he caught them clumsily.

"Put these on. We'll match," I offered. "We can be Sandy and Danny from *Grease*."

"That movie is so ancient," Charlie complained.

"But still a good one. Stay here." I went to my dorm and came back with a small bottle of hair gel. Amazingly, he'd done as I asked and changed into the clothes I'd picked out for him.

I forced Charlie to sit down in the desk chair and began styling. I coated all of Charlie's hair before I combed the gel through and parted it back, so his hair looked slick and wavy. In minutes, he was a total shoe-in for Danny Zuko.

"You look really cute," I gushed. Nothing was more fun than making Charlie my personal dress-up doll.

"You think so?" He couldn't see it, but he tilted his head from side to side, and reached up a hand to run his fingers through his gelled hair. He seemed... hesitant, but also a little excited. Geez, when was the last time this kid had dressed up for Halloween?

Probably never. His foster mom had been too busy running a brothel to buy him a costume, I bet.

Oberi was barking loudly, spinning in circles. He wanted a costume, too. I reached into my dress shirt pocket and yanked out a pink handkerchief. I tied it around Oberi's neck, and he panted in glee.

"We all match. We've totally won Halloween," I said.

"If you say so." Charlie stood up. "We've got some time before Elementai Magic. Let's go hang out in the Villain's Den. You can tell me what everyone's wearing."

People called the rec room the Villain's Den. Teachers didn't approve of the name, which is what had made it stick. Students hung out there whenever they didn't have class, as it was one of the few places on campus you couldn't be yelled at by the guards for loitering.

The Villain's Den was dark, decorated with purple Gothic wallpaper and dark carpet. Inside were a couple of tables and chairs, along with a rickety foosball table. There was a cart with basketballs and other sports items you could take into the prison yard— save for baseball bats, and anything else that you could bludgeon people with. Old school arcade games, like *Pac-Man* and *Space Invader*, sat in the corner. In the middle of the room was a fireplace surrounded by ratty, holey couches. Above the fireplace was a TV that had a crack in the screen. Usually, the local news was playing, but you could watch an Institute-approved movie as well. None of the other channels worked. There were no computers— the only laptops you could access were in the library, and you had to get permission for those.

It was nothing elaborate, but at least you wouldn't be harassed. The Villain's Den had been decorated for Halloween. Black and orange streamers hung from the ceiling, and decorations had been taped to the walls. A tray of doughnuts and apple cider had been set out for people to grab on their way to class.

It was busier than usual, and creepy music played from the old stereo near the foosball table. Marcus was in here, drawing in his sketchbook at a table by a barred window.

Marcus had painted himself to look like Van Gogh. Colors ran across his skin in thin lines, like oil paint spread carefully across a canvas. He wore a tan suit, though he'd painted over that as well, blending colors together so he appeared to be a moving painting.

At his side, Rishi meowed loudly. Rishi was dressed as a pumpkin. The outfit was hilarious. It made Rishi look like a giant orange ball, a tiny green hat fitted to the cat's head.

Marcus' costume was very creative, but I don't think the idiots around here got it. A guy playing one of the arcade games stopped to look at Marcus in confusion. "Dude, what are you supposed to be?"

Marcus' mouth dropped open in indignation. "I'm a depiction of the self-portrait of Van Gogh that currently resides at the *Musée d'Orsay* in Paris, *obviously*."

"Uh, cool," the guy said, still looking totally lost. Charlie and I slid into the seats next to Marcus.

"Everyone here is so uncultured," Marcus bitched. "Is it really that hard to know the name of a famous—"

Marcus stopped speaking as someone got his attention. Kallie waltzed into the room wearing a superhero costume. A long cape draped behind her, and the pleather skirt she'd chosen to wear rose up on her thighs.

Marcus blushed and put his eyes back on his work. His pencil moved quicker, but the lines were sloppy. Kallie took a seat next to me.

"You teased me for wearing a short skirt. That outfit definitely toes the line," I said.

"This is the first time I've worn a Halloween costume," she explained. "I wanted to go all-out."

"Really?" My eyebrows shot up.

"In Malovia we celebrate a different holiday," she said. "But I'm here now, so when in Rome."

Kallie looked between Charlie and me. "Are you two going steady?" she teased.

"Stop it. This isn't 1954." I laughed, but Charlie scowled.

"You sure act like it," Kallie said as she wiggled her eyebrows.

Oberi had decided to torment Rishi. He picked Rishi up in his mouth by the fluffy pumpkin part of his costume, and tossed him in the air over and over. Rishi yowled in displeasure each time he went up and down.

Eventually, Rishi landed far enough away he could crawl off. Oberi chased after him, but Rishi scampered up the couch and launched himself on top of the fireplace to get away from Oberi. Oberi paced and whined, wondering how to get to Rishi from here. Rishi began knocking things off the fireplace, aiming them at Oberi. My Familiar jumped to the side, but he hadn't been fast enough, and a tissue box had hit him on the head. He growled in annoyance. They were only playing around, but it was funny. I laughed.

Kallie leaned forward. "So guess what I found out. I was passing by Contraband when I went to pick up my costume, and I heard one of the teachers say that it would be unguarded from ten to eleven o'clock."

I checked my watch. "That's fifteen minutes from now."

"Exactly! Let's bust in. I bet there's some good shit in there," she exclaimed.

"How do we know this isn't a trap?" Charlie asked skeptically. "It sounds weird to leave a room like that unguarded."

"The Institute's understaffed at the moment. All that's blocking us from getting in is a lock enchantment, and I know I can break it," Kallie whispered.

"Where are we gonna put it? The guards are gonna notice us walking around with an armful of stuff," Charlie protested.

"Witches and warlocks can subconjure and conjure items," Marcus whispered. "It's like a file on a computer. We can save something and then bring it up again later. It's personal storage for our kind."

"Aren't those searched?" I asked.

"Every week by the warlock guards, but mine won't be searched again until tomorrow," Marcus said. "If we break in now, I can get the stuff and hide it somewhere else, before they look."

"Then let's go," Kallie urged. "Maybe there's something in there that'll help us win the Darke Games."

Marcus gave a wary look to me, but fuck that. This sounded cool. "I'm in."

"Ava, we need to be careful. We shouldn't do this," Charlie said, an edge of warning to his tone.

"Charlie, *please*," I begged. "It'll be fun. I really need to let loose for a change."

His face twisted. "Well... all right. An empty room sounds like child's play. Let's do it."

Oberi and Rishi followed as the four of us took the winding halls down to Contraband. It was near the mailroom, so students were allowed down here, but as we came closer, the halls got sparser and sparser. As we faced the big metal doors to Contraband, a chill came over my body. I don't know why, but something about this didn't feel right— and not in a moral way. Like, a *this-is-going-to-come-back-to-fuck-us* way.

That didn't stop Kallie. She walked up to the doors and placed her hands on the metal. She closed her eyes to concentrate. As she did so, the doors began glowing with a deep purple magic.

I heard a heavy tumbler *click*, and the door unlocked. Kallie pushed it open. I ignited fire in my hand for light, and we went inside.

Contraband was a plain room, filled with metal shelves that were piled with all kinds of different items. Most of it was drugs, but there were other curious things— illegal potions, magical knives, and books that were banned from the library.

"Be careful when touching things. Some of this stuff might be cursed," Marcus said.

Kallie didn't bother. She started throwing things around carelessly, like this was her room. So much for not leaving any traces behind.

Marcus glared at her. She shrugged. "What? They're going to notice stuff is missing, anyway. Doesn't mean they have to know it's us."

At first glance, it didn't look like there was anything here that would help us win the Darke Games. The majority of this stuff was petty weaponry. We avoided the drugs and started looking through the rest of the junk.

"Wow," Marcus said as he lifted a black quill off a counter. "This is amazing."

"What is it?" I asked.

"A tattoo quill. It can give you permanent magical tattoos. They're pretty rare."

Marcus waved his hand, and the quill vanished as he subconjured it into his magical storage space.

Kallie immediately went for the booze lining the shelves. "Score! We can have a party!"

She began handing bottles off to Marcus, who subconjured them as quickly as they came into his grasp.

"Anything good, pidge?" Charlie asked me. He was standing by the door to alert us if anyone walked by. Weird to put a blind guy on watch, but his Air magic would sense if anyone was coming.

"Ooh, diamonds," I said as I spotted a giant ring. "I love diamonds."

I gave it to Marcus, then grabbed a few more things— a supernatural makeup kit, and a pair of earphones I wanted to give to Charlie. If he could get to one of the school computers, he could use them.

Oberi was stubbornly pushing a dog toy against Marcus' leg. Marcus subconjured it. Rishi found a bag of catnip. He placed it on Marcus' shoe and basically screamed.

"No way. You have an addiction," Marcus snapped.

Rishi hissed and swiped at Marcus' shoe. He sighed and subconjured the catnip.

"By the gods, look at all this *porn!*" Kallie cried, holding up a box of magazines. Marcus facepalmed. I laughed.

"If I get searched, I'm not going down because the guards think I'm a pervert," Marcus snapped. "Put it back."

Kallie laughed. "Well, I thought it was funny."

I didn't find anything else of worth, until I came to the end of the aisleway. There was a shimmering green stone sitting on the edge of a shelf, the outside decorated with tiny blue crystals.

I picked it up. On closer inspection, I realized the stone had to be an egg, though I couldn't identify what kind of creature it had come from. I tapped on it. The egg was as hard as stone.

The egg was probably fossilized. Whatever was inside was long since dead, but it looked really cool. I gave it to Marcus. "I want this back later."

"Guys, let's go," Charlie hissed. "We've been in here for ten minutes."

"Relax. We have an hour," Kallie said lazily.

"I never take my time on a job," Charlie said. "We go, and we go now."

Fine by me. There was nothing else in here I wanted. Marcus subconjured the last of the contraband, and we hurried out of the room. Kallie locked it again before we left the area.

"I can't believe we got away with that," Kallie nearly sang. "We made off with so much stuff!"

"Don't brag about it," Charlie said. "Unless you want to get caught."

We heard noise up ahead. It sounded like a fight— typical for the Institute— except the shouts coming didn't sound like that of a student.

Marcus froze. "That sounds like Professor Warbright. He's my teacher for my warlock classes."

Noises of pain rang down the hallway, the sounds of a grown man in trouble. Someone was definitely beating him up.

"He's a teacher. Can't he defend himself?" Kallie asked.

"He's shit at magic. Even I know more than he does." Marcus' face paled with every yell that emitted from Professor Warbright.

"Should we help?" Charlie asked. His voice was nervous.

"We can't. Marcus has contraband," Kallie protested, but her face twisted as she said the words.

"We owe him, Kallie," Marcus insisted. "He got us off when we tried to break out."

Kallie paused, then said, "Okay. Let's go."

We darted down the hallway. At the end, we saw two prisoners— a fae and a vampire— cornering Professor Warbright against the wall. Professor Warbright was on his hands and knees. Blood ran down his face, and his arms shook as he struggled to get up. He was a short, stumpy man in his mid-fifties, and looked about as inept at magic as Marcus said. He went to cast a spell, but the fae raised a magical shield, and the spell bounced back uselessly.

"Hey, dickheads," Marcus called, and the two looked up. "Why don't you pick on someone who can actually fight back?"

The fae laughed. "Quit ruining our fun." He kicked Professor Warbright in the stomach. He groaned, curling into a ball on the floor.

Marcus' tone was deadly. "You better back off."

"Or what?" the vampire spat, and he made a disgusted sound.

"Or I'll make you wish you'd never been born." Marcus looked ready to make good on his threat. He took a wide stance, and Rishi yowled.

The vampire snorted. "You sure act like a peacock, strutting around here like you know it all. Do you really think anyone believes your tough guy bullshit? It's all an act."

"Yeah. Peacock's the perfect name for you. All show," the fae added.

The bullies laughed. Marcus' face flushed, but he didn't speak up.

Kallie did it for him. "Leave Marcus alone," she snapped. "At least he's got a reputation, unlike you losers. Nobody even knows your name."

The fae's eyes flashed. "No one asked for your opinion, *traitor*. You've really sunk low, if you're hanging out with a filthy witch and a couple of savages."

Kallie conjured a purple orb and flung it at the fae's face. The fae took a step aside and snarled. Immediately, he shifted into an alicorn— a unicorn with wings. The shifter charged at Kallie with his horn down, but in seconds, she had changed into a large, silver wolf. She launched herself at the alicorn, and the two began dueling fiercely.

Oberi gave a growl and went to help Kallie. He ran toward the alicorn and jumped onto his back, dealing sharp bites to his wings. The alicorn screamed and went to buck Oberi off, though my Familiar held on tight.

Marcus faced off with the vampire. The vampire charged, his form becoming a blur as he launched himself at Marcus. Then Marcus flung his hands out, and the vampire sank to the floor, screaming out in pain as Marcus assaulted him with battle magic.

Shit. Maybe Marcus wasn't all kidding when he bragged about what he could do.

Charlie and I ran to Professor Warbright. We knelt by his side. "Are you okay?" I asked.

Professor Warbright wavered, then touched the blood on his face. He immediately slumped to the floor.

Great. He'd fainted. I shook him, to wake him back up. "Professor? Professor!"

He didn't rise. I jumped to my feet. The fae had changed back into a man and was flinging out shields to keep Kallie and Oberi back. I summoned a fireball and stomped toward him, ready to shove it down his throat.

"What is the meaning of this?" the Warden's deep voice boomed down the hall, and my stomach fell as I saw him approach, flanked by a whole group of guards.

The fight immediately ended as everyone pulled back their magic, Professor Warbright still on the floor.

The fae pointed at Marcus. "This guy was trying to hurt Professor Warbright!"

"He's lying!" Kallie shouted back. "We found *them* beating him up!"

The Warden raised his eyebrows. "If no one is willing to tell the truth, we'll have to perform an investigation to see who's the most honest. I hope none of you are carrying anything that would be incriminating."

Marcus couldn't get searched. If he was, we were in deep shit.

So I did the only thing I could think of to cause a distraction. I kicked the fae right in the balls.

He went down. The fae gave a groan and curled into a ball on the floor. The guards went to grab me, but the Warden held up an arm and shook his head no.

It gave us enough time for Professor Warbright to come around. He groaned as he ventured back into consciousness, sitting up slowly and holding his head.

The Warden didn't bother to see if his staff member was all right. He got right to business. "Professor Warbright, can you tell me who *exactly* did this to you?"

Professor Warbright trembled at the Warden's appearance. His eyes flickered to the fae and the vampire.

It was enough for the Warden. "Guards, take these two into custody," the Warden said, nodding to the fae and the vampire. "The rest of you may take Professor Warbright to the infirmary. I am going to have a private conversation with Miss Mitoh."

"What?" Charlie snarled. "She didn't do anything!"

"We were all in that fight together. We should all be punished," Kallie snapped.

"Be that as it may, Miss Mitoh was the instigator after I arrived," the Warden said coolly. "I advise that she come with me."

The rest of them went to say more, but I waved them off. "It's fine, guys," I said. "Just take care of Professor Warbright."

"You aren't the one giving the orders around here," the Warden reminded me. "Come."

The Warden turned his back on me, and I had no choice but to follow. Oberi gave a whimper as I left him behind. Charlie's expression was desperate, but I knew when I was walking on thin ice, so I forced myself to walk away.

Out of everyone at the Institute, the Warden was the one person who scared me the most. He was an angel I didn't want to cross. I really hoped he didn't throw me in Cellblock 9 for my actions.

I followed the Warden throughout the school. Everyone's eyes looked at me in fear as they realized I was going to the Warden's office, but I refused to be afraid. *Fear is a useless emotion*, I reminded myself. It wouldn't help me here.

We wound up a tower until we came to a large iron door. The Warden opened the door for me, and I stepped inside.

The Warden's office was huge. The ceiling was a huge glass dome, revealing the cloudy weather outside. It was certainly the most glamorous room in the prison. Supernatural artifacts were placed in glass cases around the room, beside cabinets full of expensive potions. Books lined the shelves next to globes and maps of supernatural cities. In several places around the room, there were gold cages, like those for birds... but they were empty. The largest cage, big enough for a person, was suspended overhead on thick chains. That one was empty, too.

A giant mahogany desk sat in the center of the office, in front of a large, imposing chair. I took a seat on the other side of the desk and tried not to squirm.

"You have an interesting record, Miss Mitoh," the Warden said. He began rifling through a large filing cabinet next to his desk. "Your teachers have reported your behavior to me these past few weeks, and I can say I am... concerned."

"I'm nothing special," I countered. Why had I been singled out? This guy was wasting my time.

The Warden kept thumbing through files. "You can fool your teachers, but you certainly can't fool me. You are not my average criminal."

The Warden slapped a file on the desk and sat across from me in that big, overbearing chair. "You speak four languages. You became an exceptional pianist at a very young age, and a talented vocalist. The laurels hardly end there. You were a championship ballroom dancer, the Captain of your high school cheerleading team, and even earned a Cosmetology certificate through a trade program before you finished your Junior year of high school. Unlike most of your peers at the Institute, you seem to be a prodigy at whatever you do."

"So I pick things up quickly, big fucking deal," I muttered under my breath. Was this a lecture, or an interrogation?

The Warden continued. "You have an outstanding IQ score, and you passed all your standardized tests with flying colors. In fact, you were set to become the valedictorian of your graduating class... until your unusual choice to withdraw from school, and finish your studies at home in your senior year, where you earned an unimpressive C average."

The Warden learned forward, eyes narrowed. "Now why would such a talented student throw all that away?"

Fuck. How did this guy get his hands on my records? He was a dirty bastard. That he'd investigated me so thoroughly was downright concerning. It was like he'd waited for the moment I'd mess up, so he could get me in here for a private conversation.

I crossed my arms. "Seems like you know all the answers. Why don't you conjure up a solution to your last question?"

The Warden smiled, and by the ancestors, it made goosebumps trail over my skin. "I think you're hiding something. People don't end up here by accident. Make no mistake, your attendance here is for a reason. I just haven't figured it out yet."

I gave a skeptical sound. "You act like this was my first-choice college. I hardly figure employers are going to be interested in hiring someone with a degree from the Darke Institute of Supernatural Offenders."

"Of course they will. Employers know that any graduate of the Institute is a reliable, upstanding member of society."

I huffed and crossed my ankles. "Whatever label you slap on me, I'm never going to be a changed woman."

"I don't think we're clear, Miss Mitoh. Rehabilitation is not optional here at the Institute. It's a requirement. If you want your degree, you'll come to learn how things work around here. If we have to, we'll take whatever measures necessary to make sure you become a non-violent individual. If it proves to be an impossible feat to ensure your compliance, well... no one has ever graduated from the Institute without becoming an obedient individual of magical society. It's simply not done. And I will not put the Institute's perfect record for reforming supernatural delinquents at risk for anyone."

A shiver ran up my spine at his words, and I realized his meaning. People were forcibly rehabilitated by the Institute. You either got in line, or got taken care of.

If I wasn't a brainwashed indoctrinate of the Institute by the time I walked out of here... I wasn't walking out of here at all.

Ever.

No wonder the graduation rate was so low. Kids really did die in here. It hit me how crucial it was to play along with the Warden's games. His reputation for reforming magical criminals was on the line, and he would kill people to keep that reputation untarnished.

"I am very good at my job," the Warden went on. "The magical world hangs in a delicate balance. One false move, and it could be destroyed forever. I am here to either reform— or destroy— those that threaten to upset that balance. It is my duty to keep the supernatural world safe from the next criminal mastermind."

I let out a harsh laugh. "And you think that's me."

"I have absolutely no doubt it could be you, Miss Mitoh. You are too smart to have landed yourself in here by accident, and if I'm not mistaken, I believe you *wanted* to be here. Deep down, you know this is the only place where the world can be safe from you."

"Bull," I spat, but a tiny bit of guilt festered within me at his words. He thought I was a criminal genius, just biding my time for the right opportunity.

I couldn't say he was wrong.

The Warden smiled again. He knew he caught me in a lie. "Regardless, your bad attitude will not continue to be tolerated. Consider this a warning. You might want to work harder in your group therapy sessions. Before I have to consider more *permanent* options for you."

The Warden bent over his paperwork, as if the conversation didn't happen at all. It was clear our discussion was done. I rose slowly from my seat. Paranoia crept over my skin like spiders as I turned my back on him to leave. The Warden was someone you should never turn your back on, ever. He'd put a knife in it the first chance he got. The feeling of being watched followed me even as I left the Warden's office far behind.

I had to win the Darke Games. I wouldn't survive four years of schooling. Not here.

The pressure was on, and the Warden would make good on his threats. He wasn't kidding around.

But neither was I. If the Warden thought his will was strong, he hadn't met mine yet.

charlie

FIFTEEN

Ava-Marie was avoiding me.

Not in a physical sense, but she hardly spoke a word to me over the following week. It was driving me crazy, because the sound of her voice was the only thing keeping me sane at the Institute. I'd tried to ask what the Warden had said to her, but she refused to spill the beans. She had a million reasons to keep quiet— she didn't want to talk about the Warden, didn't want to hear me lecture her on healthy eating, and was all around going through a low episode.

It was really starting to worry me. Oberi wouldn't stop nudging my hand during mealtimes, trying to get me to talk to her, but I finally resolved to let her come at her own pace.

I wanted to ask her to take me back to the rock formation we'd found in the woods, to summon the ancestors for me again. When we'd gone there, it was like I could forget we were at the Institute at all. I wanted to go back. Whether it was for my own spiritual journey, or to feel close to her again, I didn't know. But Ava didn't seem ready, so I didn't ask her.

I was roaming the border of the prison yard after class one day when I decided to hell with it. Ava or not, I was going back.

Oberi wasn't with me. It was Ava's turn. But surely I could navigate the forest on my own... right?

I couldn't remember where we'd entered last time, so I didn't really know where to go. But this forest was enclosed by a fence. It couldn't be *that* big.

I was wrong.

I figured the forest couldn't be more than ten acres or so, but it turned out ten acres was freaking easy to get lost in when you didn't know where to go. Loose brush tangled around my ankles, and low-hanging tree branches grabbed at my face and shoulders. Surely I'd feel that pull I had before— that ethereal nudge guiding me to our hidden cave. I *had* to find it.

An hour must've passed, then two. I'd fallen down a few times and could feel the grains of dirt embedded in my fingernails. Blood trickled down my cheek from where a tree branch had bit me. The top few buttons of my shirt were undone to let in the gradually cooling air. Though it was the beginning of November, the air was warm. The Island didn't experience the harsh temperature swings I was used to in Michigan. I was sweating buckets.

It must've been twilight by now. I thought about turning around and heading back so I wouldn't miss curfew— it'd take me that long to get out of here— but I'd gotten so turned around I didn't know which way *out* was. I was determined to find that hidden cave again. It was my one sanctuary outside of the Institute.

I pushed through another clump of trees and stumbled into a clearing. My throat felt like sandpaper, as I hadn't thought to bring water. I didn't plan on being out here this long. My mind raced with thoughts of Ava and regrets on coming here alone. I was so unfocused I almost didn't notice the rock.

My Air magic resisted up ahead, bouncing off a large natural formation in the middle of the woods. I breathed a sigh of relief, and the life of the forest seemed to seep into my bones as I relaxed. The rock was easy to feel now, and I honestly didn't know how I'd missed it.

"I made it," I gasped to the empty forest.

I stumbled forward and caught myself on the edge of the giant rock. Though I had Air magic, I couldn't seem to suck in enough for comfort. I leaned my head against the cool stone and gave myself a few moments to catch my breath. When I finally felt like I could breathe, I inched my way along the stone, until my Air magic sensed the opening in the rock up ahead. I slipped through the narrow slit and walked until I felt the small space open to a large cavern.

The magic Ava had conjured the last time we were here was gone, but there was something that lingered. It wasn't magic, but it was close— a sense of peace nestled deep into a recent memory.

I dropped to my knees. "Ancestors," I breathed.

Though my voice was soft, it echoed through the chamber. My ragged breaths filled the silence. It wasn't until several minutes later, when my breathing finally returned to normal, that I realized how eerily quiet it was in here. There were no sounds of flutes floating through the air, no drum beats pounding to the beat of my heart, no fire crackling in the corner. It was empty... lonely.

The loneliness did something to me. I was used to being alone, but it'd been months since I'd experienced true solitude. I thought prison was supposed to isolate you, but it'd done anything but. Even in the privacy of my dorm room, I could hear the other students through the walls. Out here in the woods, in this cavern, I was completely alone. It didn't feel right without Ava or Oberi.

"Ancestors," I spoke again. I didn't know why. Surely, they couldn't hear me if I didn't summon them. And I couldn't— not without Ava. But I had to try. "Ancestors... why? Why am I here? What is any of this for? Ava says I'm just surviving, and she's right. But what is life without purpose? What am I surviving *for*?"

Tears pricked at my eyes, but I choked them back. "There has to be a reason! Why did you send me away from the tribe? What kind of lessons were you trying to teach me? Why did you take away my sight!?"

My voice echoed off the walls of the cave, and a shiver traveled down my spine. I was met with nothing but silence.

I didn't know why I'd brought up my blindness. It wasn't something I was bitter about... just curious. It was a question no one had ever been able to give me an answer to. The ancestors must be able to tell me what happened.

And yet they couldn't... because they wouldn't speak to me.

"Answer me!" I yelled, slamming my fist into the dirt.

My hands shook. I was tired, thirsty, and freaking frustrated. If my ancestors were here to guide me, why weren't they answering? Why had they left me without guidance my whole life?

Why? Why? Why?

The word echoed through my mind. I wasn't even looking for a solution. All I wanted was an explanation.

All I got was silence.

Damn it!

I pounded my fists into the dirt again, until my knuckles felt raw. Sinking to the ground, defeat overcame me. I buried my face into my dry, aching hands.

I wasn't the kind of guy who did this. I didn't get vulnerable, not even in solitude. Vulnerability is what got you killed on the streets. But ever since I'd opened up to Ava, something had broken within me. I felt different.

I *felt...* felt things I'd never felt before, things I couldn't explain or come close to understanding.

It hurt. Everything hurt.

I didn't want to feel this way— down, broken, hopeless. And yet I never wanted to go back to feeling nothing at all. I hadn't realized how detached I'd let myself become, how numb I'd been for so long.

I didn't even know who I was anymore. I wasn't sure I ever knew. And my damn ancestors weren't here to guide me.

Lucky bastards.

I bet it was nice in the Ancestral Lands. I bet they had all the food they could ever want and slept on beds made from clouds. I bet they were surrounded by loved ones and didn't have to question every feeling that tugged at something in their guts.

I wanted that. For me. For Ava. For Oberi. But the ancestors wouldn't take me until I was ready.

I had to make sure that when the time came, I was ready for them. Yet for the life of me, I couldn't understand why I was still here.

GETTING out of the forest was easier than getting in, since I'd finally found my bearings at the cave. I'd snuck past my dorm room and to the showers before Ava could spot me. She hadn't seen what a mess I'd looked like, and yet she seemed to sense something in our Elementai Magic class the following day.

"Is something bothering you, Charlie?" Ava asked while Professor Summers lectured at the front of the class.

"Why would you think that?" I whispered back, avoiding her question.

"You look distant today, like you're thinking about something."

I was deep in thought, but I wasn't about to tell her that— not when my train of thought had revolved solely around her. And it wasn't in a desperate, sexual way, either. I was trying to decipher what the ancestors wanted from me, and everything seemed to come back to Ava. After all, she *was* a part of my soul. Of course my purpose in life intertwined with hers in some way. But... how?

"Don't go worrying your pretty little mind, pidge," I told her. "I'll be fine."

"Mister Wahkin," Professor Summers called from the front of the class. "Something you'd like to share with the class?"

Professor Summers was an elderly woman who could go from *caring grandmother* to *ultimate authority* in point-five seconds. Ava had told me that was the way with Koigni women. They were made of fire— of passion— and that tender fire could shift into an inferno at any moment. It didn't quite help my confidence around Ava knowing that, but Professor Summers was different. I didn't appreciate her inferno the way I did Ava's.

I cleared my throat. "No, Professor Summers."

Her Familiar snorted at me. It was a pig of some sort, though I'd never gotten close enough to really inspect its uniqueness. All I'd felt was its miniature stature when it roamed up and down the rows on occasion. Ava-Marie had described the creature as a red river hog, a type of swine with long red fur and tufts growing off its black ears.

"Well, then," Professor Summers said. "Shall we take this lesson outside?"

Chairs squeaked across the floor as the other Elementai in the class stood to follow her. Almost everyone in here had a Familiar, except for the few unlucky souls who hadn't bonded yet. They probably wouldn't until they got out of this place and back to Kinpago. There were at least two Toaqua students who were bonded but couldn't take their Familiars to class, on account of them being completely water-bound creatures who lived in the pools below the school.

Hoofbeats of equestrian Familiars sounded on the floor, along with the scratch of talons from various birds. I knew at least one guy in the class was bonded to a griffin. The flap of feathery wings sounded above me, and heat traveled over the top of my head— a phoenix. Ahead of us, a young basilisk hissed and slithered on ahead.

Oberi strutted in unicorn form between Ava and me. I leaned into her so Ava could hear me better. "I totally zoned out. What's the lesson on today?"

Ava blew an exasperated breath. "I *knew* something was bothering you. We're supposed to team up today and try to sense the power of another Elementai."

"You think we can do that? Sense an element that isn't ours?"

"I don't know," Ava admitted. "But I'm sure as hell going to try. I need to be able to sense if there's an enemy nearby."

I furrowed my brow. "How could another Elementai be your enemy?"

Ava practically snorted. "I grew up making enemies in Kinpago. It was practically a hobby. If one of them wants to drive a rock through my skull, I need to know they're coming. Besides, every society has their disputes. My parents fought in the Hawkei Civil War, remember?"

"Yeah," I muttered. "I remember."

I just didn't know how anyone could turn against their own people. If I found a place I belonged, people to call my own, I'd never turn on them. Did loyalty mean nothing to anyone?

It was quiet in the prison yard, which felt strange. Everyone was in class, so the sound of basketballs pounding on the pavement and football players slamming into each other was nonexistent. Instead, the noises of Familiars squawking and nickering filled the yard. I could almost imagine I was at Orenda Academy.

"Everyone, pair up with someone who is not of your element," Professor Summers announced. "I will come around with blindfolds. One team member will wear the blindfold, while the other manipulates their element. You must be able to correctly guess *when* the element is conjured *and* the approximate spell cast. You may begin."

The yard filled with chatter as Nivita teamed up with Anichi and Yapluma partnered with Koigni. There were so many different combinations between the five elements.

"I guess that means we're partners, huh?" Ava asked.

When she said the word *partners*, my heart gave a jolt.

I cleared my throat. "Uh, yeah. Partners."

Professor Summers approached us. "A blindfold for you, Miss Mitoh. I'm assuming you don't need one, Mister Wahkin."

I chuckled lightly. "I think I'm good."

She breathed a sigh of relief, like she was worried to ask, then hurried on to the next student.

"What does she think?" Ava snapped. "That this is a joke?"

"Relax, pidge," I said. "I'm used to it."

Before she could say anything else, I grabbed her by the shoulders and spun her around. "Go stand over there and conjure some Fire."

She shrugged me off. "You don't have to tell me what to do, Charlie. I'm a big girl."

"Okay, then I'll give you a choice. Do you want to go first, or me?"

She hesitated a moment, as if surprised I was letting her choose. "I'll conjure first," she decided.

Ava walked off, far enough away that I wouldn't feel the heat of her Fire coming off her. Oberi followed at her side.

I waited, concentrating on the sound of her footsteps through the grass, and feeling the subtle wave of her hair in the cool breeze. The air seemed to dance around her when she moved, in a way it didn't with everyone else. It didn't obey her like it did me. It *honored* her.

I was so concentrated on Ava that my Air sensed every one of her movements. She turned to face me. Several beats passed and nothing happened. Then, something ignited in my chest. It was subtle at first, but it brought warmth to the yard.

"You've conjured a fireball," I announced confidently.

"What?" Ava sounded surprised. "How can you tell?"

I shrugged. "I can feel the heat."

"Oh," she said in realization. "Through your Air power."

"Yeah, sure. Let's go with that."

Truth was, it went deeper than that, but it wasn't something I could put into words. I felt it in my chest, blooming through me. It didn't come from *within* me, but rather felt like whispers of flames brushing over my skin.

Ava didn't say anything, but her magic shifted. Her power grew so large I could sense it in the air. Her Fire ate at the surrounding oxygen, creating a chemical reaction that immediately alerted my magical senses.

"Your spell is stronger," I said, "but I can't distinguish the specifics. It's complicated for sure, like you're creating an image within the Fire."

Ava drew back on her magic, and it fizzled out. "I created a Fire unicorn," she admitted. "How did you know?"

"I used my Air," I explained. "All elements are interconnected, right? When you conjure Fire, you borrow oxygen from the air. The larger the spell, the more oxygen you need to sustain it."

Ava sounded skeptical. "Okay, Charlie Wahkin. Let's try this again. No cheating."

She strolled across the grass toward me, and I felt fabric on my face.

"What are you doing?" I demanded.

"I'm blindfolding you," she said simply. "It's only fair."

I gaped. "You don't believe I'm blind, pidge?"

"Just covering my bases," she said.

I stilled as her fingers brushed over my face to smooth out the blindfold. I couldn't even protest, as I'd turned to a statue. Ava's fingers moved through my hair as she tied the blindfold back.

"Oh, I see," I teased to hide the tension. "This was just an excuse to get close to me."

Ava finished tying the blindfold, and she smacked my chest. "You wish. Let's try this again."

Ava returned to Oberi's side. The seconds ticked by, and nothing happened. She was testing me, waiting for me to guess her spell when she hadn't cast anything at all. A full minute must've passed, and then I felt it.

It was like ice crawling over my skin, but it wasn't unpleasant. I sensed the air around Ava becoming dry, and I knew instantly what she'd done.

"You're conjuring a water ball from the air," I said.

"How are you doing this?" She didn't sound frustrated, but more or less intrigued.

"Please, pidge," I scoffed. "You're making this easy. You want to make this hard on me? Stop drawing from my own element to create yours."

"But I *need* air," she argued. "I need—"

Ava-Marie cut off so abruptly I knew she'd come up with an idea. But she wasn't as clever as she thought she was. I heard the wave coming and the water sloshing above her head as she showed off her powers.

"You're manipulating water from the lake," I told her simply. "The spell is huge, at least ten feet across."

Ava huffed, and the giant water ball she'd created went splashing back into the lake. She was obviously frustrated I was picking up on this so fast. "Let me try."

Ava stomped toward me and pulled the blindfold off my eyes. She tied it around herself so fast a few threads snapped. She clapped her hands, sounding ready for anything. "Okay, Charlie. Show me what you've got."

I took several steps away so she wouldn't feel my Air power. When I was confident I was far enough away, I summoned a stream of Air above me, twisting it toward the ground and back up again. The air blew my hair back, but it didn't touch Ava.

"Oh," she said in surprise. "*Oh.*"

"What is it?" I asked.

Ava paused a few beats, as if she wasn't sure how to describe it. "I feel something, but it's different from Fire or Water. It's like your magic gives off this frequency that touches the surface of my skin— whereas Fire comes from my chest and I summon Water from my stomach. But Air... it's like... like..."

The blindfold fabric rustled as Ava pulled it off. Only when she'd gone quiet did I realize that the students around us had quieted, too.

"What's going on, pidge?" I asked.

"Um... everyone's staring at us."

It couldn't have been *everyone* in class, because I could still hear voices throughout the yard and feel the air moving in unnatural currents from other Yapluma. But as Ava said it, there must've been at least a dozen footsteps shuffling through the grass, closing in on us.

"What do you want?" Ava practically snapped at our classmates.

A timid girl spoke up first. "Can you teach us how to do that?"

"Sure," I offered, before Ava could tell them to go to hell.

Ava approached me. "What are you doing, Charlie?" she hissed.

I shrugged. "What does it hurt to help out? Besides, these people look up to you. I thought you loved being the center of attention."

"Well... when you put it that way..." Ava turned toward the other students. "Everyone, listen up, because this is going to be on the test."

Ava was being sarcastic, milking every second of it. I laughed under my breath. Oberi shook her mane, like she couldn't bear to watch.

"You all know how to sense your own element," Ava began. "When I cast Fire, every Koigni in this clearing will feel it, because their magic is attuned to the element."

A fireball crackled in her hand as she demonstrated.

"Same with Water," she continued. "Every Toaqua should feel me pulling the water molecules from the air, or sense the shift in currents of the lake. You'd know if I were about to make it rain. Easy, right?"

A few students mumbled in agreement.

"Sensing another element is the same, but in a much more subtle way," she said. "You'll feel it in different ways. The first is in how it affects your own element. As Charlie mentioned earlier, when I conjure Fire, I'm borrowing oxygen from the air, and he can sense that through his own powers. Same with drawing water molecules out of the air. But what if Charlie wasn't Yapluma? What if he were, say, Nivita?"

A male student responded. "You'd have to touch his element for him to feel it— like burning the grass."

"Wrong," she stated bluntly. "You *feel* the magic vibrations, like you feel your Familiar, or the magic coming from someone else's Familiar. You tap into it like intrafusion."

"What's intrafusion?" someone asked.

"You've never heard of intrafusion?" Ava sounded a little annoyed, but she explained anyway. "It's an advanced technique of pulling magic from sources that aren't your own Familiar— usually another magical creature. You see, we're all interconnected. Every element affects the others. And so even though we can't *manipulate* all the elements, we can *sense* them, like Toaqua can sense the moon, and Koigni can sense the sun. You have to get outside of your own element and realize there's more out there than just you and your own Familiar."

Ava was really getting into it now, obviously at ease with being the class know-it-all. I didn't mind. It was good that she knew her stuff.

"All it takes is focus," Ava said. "If you're focused enough, you'll be able to feel another element from a hundred yards away..."

I could sense the disturbance in the air with ease now. Ava summoned water from the lake, forming it into a giant ball bigger than the last one, before letting it fall back down into the water and splash ashore.

"Or if you're a mere inch away..." Ava finished.

She came to my side, so close I felt heat radiating off of her. Then something shifted. Ava held her hand above my arm, sending drops of water hovering just inches above my skin. I sensed their coolness, even though they never touched me. The hairs on my arm stood up, and I shivered under her contactless caress.

The chill continued up my arm, over my shoulder, and across my face. I didn't move an inch, afraid that if I allowed the water to touch me, this would be over. There was something serene about it... something oddly intimate about having her magic so close, and yet so far away. It was as if the water droplets held a promise— a promise I wasn't sure they would keep.

Ava was so close to me, her hand hovering just inches from my face as she controlled the water droplets between us. I could reach out and touch her, wrap my arms around her waist and pull her close. My heart began pitter-pattering against my chest.

Ava continued her lesson, but her voice came out soft, almost a whisper. "And when you can sense that kind of magic, anything is possible."

There was something in her tone I couldn't quite place. She wasn't talking to the rest of the class, and I didn't think she was talking about elemental magic, either. Something else was happening between us— like our magic was intertwining together, and that was why I could sense her water droplets like they were my own.

I could lean over and kiss her right now, I caught myself thinking.

For the first time, I moved, and I began leaning toward Ava.

Almost instantly, she drew back. "Charlie, the bond!" she cried.

I snapped out of my daze. "W-what?"

"What if we feel each other's magic this way because of the bond?" she asked.

"Oh," I said flatly. I'd thought for a second perhaps it was something else— a *different* type of bond. I pushed the thought from my mind as soon as I realized what I was thinking. "You might be right. Why don't we try other partners?"

Ava cleared her throat. "Yeah... probably best."

She jumped straight into leader mode and shoved some poor helpless Nivita kid in my direction. He seemed younger than most students at the institute, judging by the youthfulness of his voice.

"Charlie Wahkin," I introduced, shaking his hand.

"Thaddeus Blake," he said, sounding a little intimidated. A creature squawked from his shoulder, some sort of bird— probably a hawk.

"Ready whenever you are," I told him.

A few moments passed as Thaddeus got in position. Then I felt it. The spell was simple, but it was easier to feel than Ava's magic. It was almost as if I was casting the spell myself. Several yards off, Thaddeus was making the grass grow around him. Long blades of grass grew up from the ground, and a couple of clovers sprouted flowers.

"How many buds is that, Thaddeus?" I asked, showing off just a little. "Four? Five?"

"I-it's..." Thaddeus sputtered.

"*Charlieee!*" Ava cried, drawing out my name.

"What?" I asked innocently.

"How are you doing that?" she demanded. "I'm paired with a Nivita, too, and I don't feel a damn thing. And she lifted three rocks the size of my fist! No offense, Thaddeus, but your spell is child's play."

I shrugged. "Nivita magic is easy. It travels through the ground and up through your feet. You have to ground yourself and focus on the magic buzzing through the plants and the dirt."

Ava took a few seconds to mull it over, then spoke slowly. "Charlie, do you think you could recreate Thaddeus' spell?"

"What?" I was taken aback. "Of course not. I'm not Nivita."

"You have Nivita ancestry," she pointed out. "You *have* to be more connected to Nivita magic than we know. Otherwise, how did you guess the clovers?"

"I don't know," I admitted. "It's like walking over the terrain. You can always tell where the grass ends and the sand begins, or when you're about to step on a pile of rocks."

"Yeah, I can," Ava said. "*Because I can see it.* I don't *feel* it like you can, Charlie. This is different."

I furrowed my brow. I *had* always been particularly sensitive to the earth, but I couldn't *control* it like I could with air.

"Try the spell, Charlie," Ava encouraged.

"It's not going to work, pidge."

"Then prove me wrong," she challenged.

I sighed and aimed my hands at the ground. Sure, I could probably sense earth because my mother was Nivita, but Ava was crazy if she thought—

"Charlie!" Ava belted out. Oberi nickered proudly.

The entire yard must've quieted then. The hair on the back of my neck tingled, and I sensed dozens of eyes on me.

"Charlie, you did it!" Ava cried.

I nearly reeled over in shock. At first, I thought Ava must've been lying or pulling some sort of prank. But when I reached my hands out, my fingers brushed over long blades of grass that went up to my waist.

"Another Nivita must've done this," I whispered. Even *I* knew dual-powers were unusual. Ava's case was special, because *she* was special. Things like this didn't happen to me.

I wasn't special... was I?

"That was all you, Charlie," Ava said softly.

As if to reaffirm what she said, Oberi nuzzled her nose into my hair. I shrugged her off, because she was getting snot everywhere.

"I really did that?" I asked in disbelief.

Ava reached out to take my hand, and my heart swelled. She ran her fingers over my palm, as if it might've left traces of magic behind. "You did," she replied in wonder.

"Okay, that's enough for today!" Professor Summers announced. "Class dismissed."

I didn't know why she'd dismissed the class early, until people began dispersing and Professor Summers approached Ava and me.

"Miss Mitoh, Mister Wahkin," she said in her gentle, grandmotherly tone. "What you two have is very special."

Ava was still holding my hand, which I found comforting. Even more so when Professor Summers called us special.

"Dual-casters are very unique in Hawkei society," she continued. "Most mixed children only inherit one power from their parents. Add that to your... *unique* bond. I suspect the two of you may be capable of extraordinary things together."

For how *extraordinary* Professor Summers seemed to think Ava and I were together, she didn't sound afraid. She sounded intrigued.

"Your prospects for employment once you graduate will be great," Professor Summers said. "I am very interested to see where your powers might take you as you continue through my class."

At that, Professor Summers turned and headed back toward the school, her hog Familiar grunting as it hurried to catch up with her.

Once Professor Summers was gone, Ava flung her arms around my neck. I was so shocked, I didn't know what to do at first. Her floral scent filled my nose, and my hands settled on her back as I relaxed into the embrace.

"Charlie, this is wonderful!" she exclaimed.

"What do you mean?" I drew away from her.

"You're a dual-caster, like me! I'm *so* relieved I'm not the only one."

"But it made you special," I argued. I hadn't realized I was running my hands down her arms until they stopped at her hands. Instinctually, I entwined my fingers with hers, but she didn't pull away.

"I don't *want* to be *special*." Ava practically spat the word. "I want to be normal."

Just then, a gust of wind breezed past us, and Ava's hair tickled my face. I reached up to push the strands behind her ear. "Ava-Marie Mitoh, you will never be *normal*. You're too exceptional for that."

Ava froze under my touch, and I realized what I'd said. "You think I'm extraordinary?" she whispered.

I hesitated. Truth was, the girl drew me in for reasons I couldn't explain. I thought it was the bond at first, but as I held her hand in mine,

I felt magnetized to her by some other force. It was a force that wanted her outside of the bond. Something had changed all those weeks ago when she'd summoned my ancestors. It was only amplified in the room above the chapel when I'd opened up to her. Ava was different than I expected, and softer than she let anyone else know. She had so much life inside of her, an energy that put most people off, but drew me in. An energy I wanted to learn from and share with her. I'd never met anyone quite like her.

"You're intriguing for sure," I told her.

"Well, I can live with intriguing, I guess," she teased.

Ava took a deep breath. We were so close now that the rise of her chest caused her breasts to touch me, though only slightly. My fingers were still frozen against her hair. All I had to do was shift my hand slightly to wrap it around the back of her neck... to draw her in and press my lips to hers. It would be effortless. It could be perfect...

Or it could ruin everything.

I drew away from her before I caved to the temptation.

I had one rule about sex— apart from always using protection. Rule number one: *You don't fuck your friends.*

Friends were hard to find in this world, but easy as hell to lose. One white lie, one hurt feeling, one night of bliss...

It could all end in disaster.

And so I could only get so close to Ava. If I let myself fall for her and ruined it, it would level my whole fucking heart. Ava wasn't just a friend. This bond we shared connected us for life, and I knew if something bad happened, I would never recover.

I had to protect us both from that.

And yet there was only so far I could stay away. Ava called to me like a beacon in the middle of a raging storm. She might be annoying as all hell, but she'd become my sanctuary.

Ava had said I was forced into survival mode because I'd never known anything else. And she was right. But I wanted to know something else. I wanted to know *Ava*. She was worth it.

I made a decision I never had before. In the Darke Games and beyond, I wanted to fight for *her*.

SIXTEEN

My dorm room door opened. I scurried to hide what I'd been looking at. The journal was open in front of me. I snapped it shut and shoved it under my pillow, hurriedly gathering the notes I'd been writing.

"Just a sec!" Who'd be so fucking rude as to not knock before entering? This was *my* room, after all.

It was only Charlie. I sighed in relief and gathered the papers more slowly. He couldn't see what I was reading, so I didn't have to rush to hide. Oberi walked forward and began throwing the papers off the bed with his paw. They scattered to the floor. "Oberi, you asshole."

He wagged his tail. Charlie heard the rustling of papers and asked, "Homework?"

"Yeah," I lied as I picked the mess off the floor. "What's that you got?"

"Food." He held up two takeout boxes and placed one in front of me. "I signed for you so you won't get caught skipping dinner. Here. Brought you something."

I flipped open the lid. It was a burger. They were seriously one of the few good things the Institute served. "This is perfect. I'm actually kind of hungry."

I shoved the journal and the notes into my desk drawer, then rummaged through a box by my bed that my parents had sent, and took out a couple of jars. "Do you need anything?"

"I'm good." Charlie had gotten a load of onions, tomatoes and cheese on his burger, smothered in mustard. There was a second burger in his takeout box, with only ketchup. Oberi drooled as he watched him take a bite.

We were only allowed utensils in the lunchroom, save for an ugly brown spoon that was made of a weird material that couldn't be melted down or sharpened. I took the spoon and dipped it into one of the jars my parents had sent. I dumped a huge glob of crunchy peanut butter and strawberry jelly all over the bun, then smashed it together on top of the burger. I took a bite and chewed happily.

"Do I smell... peanut butter and jelly?" Charlie asked.

"Yes," I gushed. "It's amazing on burgers. It's the only way I'll eat it."

"Let me try it," he said curiously. I tore off a piece and handed it to him. Charlie chewed thoughtfully. "It's not the *best*, but I'd still eat it if I was hungry."

"Really? Everyone else thinks it's gross," I said.

"I'll literally eat almost anything," he said. "But even I have limits."

"I used to put all kinds of weird stuff on my food," I said. "My mom came up with the idea. It was the only way she could get me to eat. She'd put mayonnaise on barbeque chicken pizza, or dip my grilled cheese in applesauce. It nearly made my dad puke. He's a really picky eater."

"If you put mayonnaise on pizza, our bond is over," Charlie teased. He took the second burger and tossed it to Oberi. He snatched it out of the air and gobbled it down, smearing ketchup all over his jowls.

There was another knock, then Kallie poked her head in. She slipped inside my room and closed the door behind her. "Are you guys ready for this?" she whispered. "Tonight's the night!"

"For what?" Charlie asked.

"Marcus and I are throwing that party we talked about when we stole the booze from Contraband," Kallie whispered. "We've asked a handful of people. I paid off a couple guards, so they'll look the other way."

"Where?" I asked.

"The chapel." Kallie's eyes gleamed in excitement. "No one will hear us in there."

"What about curfew?" We were locked in at ten o'clock at night, every night.

"Apparently there's a big fight tonight in the illegal brawling ring the guards run. The dorms are left open. It's the perfect time," Kallie insisted. "We don't even have to worry about bed check."

Charlie appeared hesitant.

"We should go," I said. "Let loose a little before the Darke Games."

"I don't know..." he said, and Oberi huffed. "If we get caught, we'll be in big trouble."

I rolled my eyes. "Come *on*, Charlie. You need to start living."

A smile twisted his expression. "Well... I always did like parties."

"That's the Yapluma in you," I said. "The Air House is always the party House, and since you're half-Yapluma, I'm expecting you to have a good time."

"Perfect," Kallie said. "I'll get everything ready. Be there at nine."

We entered the chapel late— because I was never on time. As the doors to the chapel opened, I was overtaken with awe once again. This was the most gorgeous place in the entire Institute, even though it'd been abandoned. The dusty broken pews and the dirty marble floors held a particular beauty against the colorful stained-glass windows. Some of them were shattered, but that didn't interrupt the intricacy of the pictures they portrayed— a person from every supernatural race.

The Elementai window was my favorite. It was near the back of the chapel and portrayed a beautiful Hawkei woman, dressed in regalia with an eagle on her shoulder, feathers woven into her dark hair. A bare-chested Hawkei man stood behind her, his hand around her waist. The other windows were just as glorious in their depictions of mermaids, vampires, angels and others. I felt sad that no one had bothered to repair them in so many years.

But their loss was our gain. About fifteen people had shown up for the party. Most were gathered around a couple of speakers by the wall, which were totally blown and playing pop music. I spotted a few familiar faces in the crowd. Chancey was gambling, as usual, playing a poker game with a couple of shifters. Opal had shown up, to my surprise, and was sipping on a wine cooler while she chatted with Despona in a nearby pew. Opal laughed as Despona shook up a beer can, then sprayed it all over her.

Marcus was sitting at a table in the corner with his tattoo quill, giving people new tattoos. He was currently working on a full spread of roses on an angel's back, eyes knitted as he worked on the intricacies of the petals. Rishi played with a shot glass at his feet. Kallie was beside a pew that was loaded with all the booze we stole, making deals with other prisoners.

"So we're in agreement. One fifth of vodka for a week's worth of cleaning," Kallie asked.

"Agreed," the vampire said, taking the bottle. "I'll clean your room for a week."

Kallie smiled widely, and I gave a laugh under my breath. These poor souls had no idea what they were getting into, making a deal with a fae. They'd live to regret it. Kallie was roping them into more than just cleaning her room, I was sure.

I went to walk forward, but Charlie grabbed my arm. "Hold on." He turned toward the potted trees that were on either side of the doors and waved his hands. Charlie grew the trees, until their branches wound through the handles, bolting them shut.

"There. If the guards come by, it'll give us time to run," he said.

"You've been working on your Nivita magic," I said, impressed.

"Every day," Charlie replied. "Earth is even easier than Air. I can just think about it, and plants and rocks do whatever I tell them to. I can't believe I hadn't noticed before."

"You are a dual-caster, which means you're already a talented supernatural," I said. "It's not surprising you're good."

We approached the bar Kallie was running. She faced us with a smile as she put out a punch bowl on a nearby table, a cocktail brew freshly made. "You guys want a drink? My current offer is one full bottle for one week's worth of homework."

"I don't think so. I'm not going to make a shady deal with a fae just to get wasted," I told her. "You can lay off the tricks."

Kallie waggled her eyebrows. "Should've known you'd catch on."

"You didn't get thrown in here for being a good girl," I pointed out. "What did you make that vampire agree to?"

Kallie leaned in. "He didn't listen to my wording. I said a week's worth of *cleaning*. He doesn't know I just got detention, and was told to clean out the Alchemy classroom all next week by Professor Hemlock. The magic will make him do it for me."

"Tricky fae," I teased. "What'd you get detention for?"

Kallie cackled. "I cut Naya a deal. Two days' worth of Commissary points to use at the school store for an answer key on her exam. Sorry to say, I don't know shit about Vampire Theory and she failed. Once she figured out she'd been fooled, she ran and told a teacher."

"Ooh." Charlie winced. "You don't snitch at the Institute, no matter how bad."

You didn't. We might be prisoners, but we had a code around here, and telling on people was a good way to get a black eye, or worse. It was always better to get revenge on your own.

"I'll get her back eventually." Kallie grabbed a bottle of swirling pink liquid. "This is the strongest stuff I've got, and since you're too smart to fall for my tricks, it's on the house. Enjoy, guys."

Kallie handed me the bottle. Charlie and I walked off near the speakers. I uncapped it and took a swig.

Okay, this drink had to be *magical*. Once I took a sip, a glow settled over my body, and pink butterflies manifested in my vision, kissing my cheeks and nesting in my hair. I giggled and put my hand out to touch them. Oberi could see them, too. He barked and ran in circles, attempting to chase the butterflies around the chapel.

This was some fae illusion shit. Maybe Kallie had enchanted it before the party began. It was strong, too. A few more sips, and I could already feel myself getting intoxicated. I handed the bottle to Charlie. When he touched it, the drink turned purple, and violet butterflies appeared when he started drinking.

He handed me back the bottle with a grimace. "That's some girly shit."

"It's sweet! It tastes like mangoes." I tilted back the bottle and began to chug. More butterflies appeared, bursting around me in a swirling vortex.

I *loved* getting drunk. You couldn't feel anything, and the voices inside my head were muddled with the effects of the alcohol.

The party went on. I danced with Opal in front of the speakers, and Chancey and I played a game of poker. I won, and he challenged me to a drinking game. I won that, too. Chancey scowled as he placed a hundred dollar bill in my hand, and I walked off swooning.

Charlie stood behind me like a shadow as I continued to take drink after drink. I threw back so many shots from the fae vodka, I lost count of how many I'd taken.

When a song came on he didn't like, Oberi climbed on a speaker and knocked it down. Charlie stood it back up, but even then, didn't go too far.

"What's the matter with you?" I complained. "It's a college party. Loosen up. Get wasted."

Charlie was tailing me like a puppy. And I already had one. He was drinking out of the punch bowl.

"I *am* drunk," he said. Charlie took a couple of sips here and there, working himself up to a buzz. He whistled for Oberi, who drew away from the punch bowl and staggered our way.

Was Charlie's voice slurred, or were my ears ringing? Couldn't tell.

The party had been fun in the beginning, but I was starting to get bored. I wanted to do something reckless. My eyes fell on Marcus in the corner, who was tattooing the shoulder of a mermaid nearby.

I got an idea. An awful idea, but one that sounded incredible nonetheless. "Charlie!" I laughed and stumbled toward him. "Charlie, let's get matching tattoos!"

His reaction was curious. "Uh, okay. What should we get?"

"Each other's names," I suggested. "Yours on my wrist, mine on yours."

Charlie's eyes sparked. "That sounds like an *amazing* idea."

Oberi barked in cheerful agreement. We laughed as we staggered toward Marcus, arm in arm. The mermaid walked off, the fresh tattoo of a seashell on her shoulder.

"Marcus!" I cried. "Charlie and I want to get each other's names. Can you do it?"

"Name tattoos?" Marcus raised an eyebrow. "Those are always terrible. Are you sure—?"

"Lighten *up!*" I smacked him on the arm. "Charlie and I are just *friends.*"

"You two are drunk." Marcus scowled. "It's against my policy to tattoo people who—"

"Do you have to be such a limp dick?" Charlie complained. "Just do it, man."

Marcus narrowed his eyes. "Fine. Sit the fuck down."

Charlie sat across from Marcus. He laid his right arm down on the table. Marcus bent over Charlie's wrist and began writing *Ava-Marie* in a pretty script font. I watched as the ink spanned over Charlie's skin, like it would across paper. Marcus took his time, detailing the tattoo and making sure each line was perfect. I bounced impatiently as I waited. The design took a flowing shape, and Marcus finished the *e* in an infinity symbol.

"There. Your turn," Marcus said.

I shoved Charlie out of his seat. He went sprawling out of it, and I plopped down.

I put my left arm on the table— because, like, when we held hands the tattoos would touch, and that would be *so cute.*

"Are you *sure* about this?" Marcus asked again.

I waved a hand in the air. "You really are a limp dick, Marcus. Just go with the flow."

He shook his head and put the quill to my skin. A cool sensation spread across my arm as the ink in the quill began forming letters. It didn't hurt, like a tattoo machine would. It felt more like a massage as the quill's point made Charlie's name take shape. Like the other tattoo, Marcus put an infinity symbol on the *e* at the end of Charlie's name.

"There," Marcus said as he finished. "You won't need to let it heal— the quill took care of that. It's as ready to go as it would be six months from now."

Marcus eyeballed us. "And just as permanent."

Oh. My. Gosh. They looked *so good.* I jumped up, squealed and yanked on Charlie's arm. I already had another idea. "Charlie, play me a song on the organ!" I pleaded.

"I can't play when I'm wasted," he protested.

"Yes you can, come *on*." I dragged on his arm and pulled him up the stairs to the chapel's loft. We tripped and fell several times while going up.

Finally, we emerged onto the loft above the chapel. There was a large balcony that looked down upon the pews below. We were so high up, we could barely hear the music playing from the speakers below. The organ was huge. The pipes reached all the way up to the ceiling. In the loft were a collection of old instruments that hadn't been used in what looked like decades. Violins, drums and clarinets lay discarded everywhere, coated in a thick layer of dust. It was like the Institute had abandoned the chapel long ago and just didn't care to renovate it.

The loft was just beneath the chapel's vast ceiling. A circular stained-glass window with dozens of colors gleamed behind the giant organ. The Institute's sigil— a winged snake wrapped around a key— was depicted in the window's glass. I grabbed the key around my neck Mama had given me the night I left. I held it as I took in the sight of the magnificent window once again, completely awed by it while I was up close.

The chapel was my favorite place in the entire school. It was so peaceful and beautiful up here.

Or at least, it was. Oberi scampered to the old drums in the corner and began banging on them with his tail, being as loud as possible.

"Oberi," I scolded. "Play nice, or you'll break them."

Oberi looked at me, then changed into a unicorn and kicked one of the drums over the balcony. It fell to the first floor with a giant *crash*, smashed to pieces.

"Ugh. You're a jerk."

Oberi whinnied in response. She went to kick another drum over the side, but I pointed at her sharply. She ducked her head, acting like she hadn't seen me and looking in the other direction.

Charlie sat down on the organ's bench and began playing a song. The notes were beautiful and bright. It was a song I wasn't familiar with.

I sat beside him on the bench. "What are you playing?"

"I made it up," Charlie said.

"On the spot?" I was surprised. That was the mark of a spectacular musician.

"Yeah, just now," he said.

"Keep playing, Charlie." I leaned closer to watch his hands, memorizing the placement of the keys and creating a score in my head. The song seemed to hold everything Charlie couldn't manage to say.

"Is it a love song?" I asked. I didn't understand what he was trying to tell me.

"I don't know what love feels like," Charlie said. "No one's ever given a shit about me."

My head fell on his shoulder, and Charlie increased the tempo. "It's for you," he said.

For me? Couldn't be. This song must be for someone else.

The notes swelled around me, and my eyes began to drift closed as the lullaby lulled me into a stupor. Charlie was lying. He thought nobody cared.

But I did.

⌢⌢

I woke up on the floor of the pitch-black chapel loft, resting against Oberi's side. She was still asleep, her fiery mane providing the only light, save for the full moon gleaming through the windows.

It had to be around three in the morning. Charlie was sleeping next to me, on the other side of Oberi. I looked over Oberi's back and glanced through the bars of the balcony, but no one was down there. I didn't know where Marcus and Kallie had run off to, or where the rest of the party had gone.

My buzz had worn off, so I could see clearly now. Fae vodka, for as strong as it was, didn't last very long. The effects were powerful but short-lived.

Charlie's chest rose and fell softly. I studied him carefully. The feeling that came over me was protective and warm. He might be a huge pain in my ass, but Charlie was sweet. Instead of the tight anxiety that usually plagued his features, his face was relaxed, and he shifted closer to Oberi as if he needed her.

It was the first time I'd ever seen him look at peace.

The next thing I saw was Charlie's name on my wrist. I observed the cursive letters across my skin and felt hollow.

Oh, *shit*. What did we *do*? Getting Charlie's name inked permanently onto my skin had *definitely* been a spur-of-the-moment bipolar decision.

Charlie stirred, and his eyes fluttered open. He didn't make a sound as he slowly sat up.

"I don't remember how we got down here on the floor," he said.

I didn't either. We'd been messing with the organ for a few hours, from what I could recall. "I think we just laid down. A nap sounded good."

"Sure. What are we going to do about these?" Charlie waved his wrist in the air, and I caught a glimpse of my name in the moonlight.

I shrugged. "It shouldn't bother you. You can't see it."

"But I *know* it's there," Charlie objected. "And soon, everyone else will, too."

"Psh. Who cares. Everyone's got a tattoo at the Institute."

"People are going to think we're a thing."

"Would you relax? It was just a drunk tattoo. Not like it means anything."

Charlie frowned.

I laid my arm against Oberi. "So how are we getting out of here?"

"We can't go back now," Charlie whispered. "We walk the halls this late, we'll for sure get caught. Let's hope they think they locked us in our dorms and didn't check."

"So, what? We just stay in here until sunrise?"

"Probably our only option."

I groaned and looked at the ceiling. "Three hours seems like forever."

"It's not that long. At least we can be alone."

I think we both blushed then. He was talking about the guards being up our asses twenty-four-seven, but it came out like we actually wanted to be alone together. Like we needed privacy to just be... ourselves? Certainly not a couple.

Yet Charlie and I were a unit. We'd only known each other for a few months, but we were both bonded to Oberi. We shared the same soul. We came as a package deal now, and it had only taken a few weeks to make it confusing to me where he ended and I began. Every day that passed melded us closer together. Would there come a day when we'd be a singular person, one mind and one dream instead of just one spirit?

I couldn't handle that. I loved my independence. I wouldn't get lost in someone else. It was the quickest way to get hurt.

"You seem better than you were last week," Charlie confessed. "I was worried about you. You weren't acting like... Ava."

His concern was sweet, but I wished he wouldn't. Too many people worried about me. "I am, for now. But it's not going to last long."

"Why not?"

Oberi continued sleeping beside us, but Charlie's attention was only on me. Everything was vulnerable at this time, on this night. It was like the things I whispered wouldn't leave this chapel.

"You know I have bipolar. The way my personal condition works, my mood varies week after week," I explained. "I could be up at the start of the month and be down by the end. My medicine stabilizes me, so sometimes I'm just flatline, and that's really nice. But if I have a lot of triggers, the medicine might as well be candy, for all the good it does."

"What kind of triggers?" He actually seemed interested.

"Stress. The past. I really miss my family," I confessed. "Being apart from them this long is really getting to me."

"You have me and Oberi," Charlie offered. "That's got to count for something."

I put my arms around my knees. "I know. But maybe it's a good thing I'm far away from home. I can't hurt anybody."

"You would never hurt anyone you loved on purpose," he said.

"But I do it by accident," I pointed out. "It's a productive day for me if I don't hurt someone's feelings. My emotions are like a live wire. They're destructive. Some days I can't even minimize the damage. I try to remain in control, but it's like taming a wild animal. I only have so much power to restrain this... monster within me."

"You're not a monster. You just have problems. We've all got 'em."

"These are more than problems," I insisted. "This constant rollercoaster of up and down makes me sick. And as much as I hate to admit it, I'd rather ride the high than endure the lows."

I sat back against Oberi. "Depression gets so *boring*, Charlie. The worst part about being sad is that it's incredibly uninteresting. I pick up on things so easily that I get tired of them just as quickly. And I will do absolutely anything on earth to prevent myself from being bored. Even if there's consequences."

I began playing with my hair. "That's why I like things like fashion. It's always changing, and it's so open to interpretation you can't nail it down to perfection. It keeps my attention."

"You were down for a while, but you're not now," Charlie pointed out. "From what I could tell, it lasted a few weeks, but at least you're better today."

"Yeah, well, it's getting worse. I have such a short tolerance when I get in a low period now, because I know it's not going to last. Just a few weeks, or maybe a month, and I can stop feeling like I want to die again. So I get impatient. I just want it to hurry up so the joy can come back. Because that's where I excel. At least if I'm in a manic period I'm out there doing things, not wasting away in some room watching the hours tick by."

"All that can land you in hot water."

"Maybe I tempt the fire because I like the way it burns."

"Is that supposed to be a metaphor for something?" Charlie's voice was on edge.

"No. A lot of people with bipolar self-harm, but I never did. I didn't see the point in destroying myself when I could destroy something else. I liked breaking things— particularly the law. I got a high off the trouble. I guess that makes me fucked up."

"Everyone's fucked up at the Institute. I'm not innocent either," Charlie said. "I've stolen and scammed thousands of dollars out of people."

"You did it to survive. I committed crimes because... you know... why not?" I turned toward him. "Sometimes it was my illness. And sometimes I just wanted the thrill. There were days I was so depressed that I got into trouble because I was worried about being alone."

I scoffed. "And I hardly ever was. I felt so guilty growing up. I had a great family. I had awesome parents. And I put them through absolute hell. The way I act, you'd think I grew up in an abusive home or something, but it was never like that. I was just crazy for no reason."

Charlie shook his head. "People are never crazy for no reason. I'm sure you had your own. People just didn't understand."

His words were so reassuring. It was nearly like he understood. Charlie went on. "I did a lot of fucked up shit in high school. People didn't think I had a reason to be that way. But I was blind with no resources. I was just acting out in my environment. I'm sure you had to do the same."

"Ancestors. High school was absolute hell." I rolled my eyes. "I'd be at the Institute any day before I'd go back to those years. It was just crisis after crisis."

"It couldn't have been that bad," Charlie argued.

"It was," I insisted. "I'm not even being dramatic. I'd just turned sixteen when my dad got sick... I mean really, really sick."

"He has a chronic illness, doesn't he?"

"Yeah. Combined Magical Suppression Syndrome, it's called. Basically, his magic drains energy from his organs and body. My mom heals him with her Anichi magic, but it can't cure him completely. He's been sick long before I was born."

"That must've been rough."

"Honestly? It wasn't *too* awful." I tilted my head as I thought. "He was always tired. He couldn't always play with me as much as I wanted. But no matter how bad he was feeling, he always made time for me. I don't feel like I missed out on anything because he was sick. He was a really great dad, and the best chieftain that ever was."

I made a disgusted noise. "People gave him shit for it, though. Said he shouldn't be chief if he couldn't handle the job. He's done more for the Toaqua tribe than any chieftain in existence. But since he has to take more days off than others, some don't see it that way."

"What happened when you were sixteen?" Charlie asked.

"Daddy had been in and out of the hospital my entire life. The nurses knew our family by our first names up there. Me and my siblings grew up playing in the hallways. It wasn't unusual for him to stay a few days here and there, but this was different. A couple days after Christmas... his lungs collapsed."

Charlie's eyebrows knitted together. Tears burned at the corners of my eyes, but I pushed them back and said, "He was in the hospital for over a month. It was a bad respiratory illness. He'd had a million before, but this one was worse than the others. A bad bout of pneumonia when he was in his twenties had already scarred the tissue in his lungs, so we knew he didn't have a great shot. A couple weeks passed and he slipped into a coma. They had to put a breathing tube in... nothing they tried worked. We had the best Anichi try to heal him, but Spirit magic only goes so far, and their powers couldn't make his lungs work again. There was no chance of recovery."

I dashed tears away with the heel of my hand. "Mama was falling apart. She couldn't function. I had to be the strong one. I had to make sure my siblings ate and rested. I kept everyone together when no one else was fit to stand. I did it because I knew Daddy needed me to."

I played with a strand of hair as I recalled the memories. "I just remember standing outside the hospital room... I'd gone to get Mama some coffee, because she'd been up all night. I heard her crying. She kept saying, *you're not leaving me alone to raise these kids.* She begged Daddy to get up, but by now, he was already half gone."

I let out a sigh. "I knew it was over when Mama told Daddy it was okay to let go. He really deteriorated after that... we had medicine men come in, to give him final rites and prepare his spirit for the Ancestral Lands."

"But your dad's still here, so he had to have made a turnaround," Charlie objected.

"He did. It was a miracle." I scooted closer. "I was with him that last night. The doctors figured he'd be dead in the morning. Mama and the rest of them had gone home to get some sleep, because there was nothing more we could do, but I insisted I had to stay. I sat by his bedside and slept through the night with my head beside his chest. I could hear his breathing... it was really rattled."

My voice cleared. "Then something happened. I remember a bright white light, hovering above the bed. I saw a pair of large blue eyes, like those of a creature, shining in the light, though I couldn't make out the rest of the animal's features. The eyes blinked at me, and— I really can't explain this— I felt the urge to lay my hands on Daddy's chest. The light got bigger, until it was so blinding I had to look away. When I opened my eyes again, the light and the creature were gone. But Daddy's vitals were strong again. They removed the breathing tube the next morning, and shortly after, he woke up. His lungs were absolutely clear. All the scarred tissue was gone. It was like they'd been completely replaced."

I couldn't help the victory that rang out in my voice. "And ever since, his disease has still been there, but it's not as bad as it was before. I didn't tell anyone what happened... didn't think they'd believe me. I knew that creature had to have *some* part in that healing, though I don't know where it came from, or how it showed up."

"Do you think you healed your dad?" Charlie asked.

I bit my lip. "I don't know what happened. I don't have Anichi powers... I think," I said slowly. "And if I do, why haven't they shown up again?"

"Maybe they only come out when you need them the most," Charlie suggested. "Your dad just didn't heal on his own."

I shrugged. "I don't know. Maybe the ancestors did it. Whatever happened, he's alive, and I thank the ancestors for it every day. I couldn't live without Daddy."

"But what about you?" Charlie's voice was anxious. "Did you inherit his illness?"

"I'm already clear. Symptoms would've shown up in me by now, and I have a clean bill of health, save for my bipolar diagnosis. I got lucky. The condition passed me over."

"Do you think your other siblings might've inherited it?"

My voice was guarded. "Maverick and Alana are pretty healthy."

"What about Ezekiel?"

I swallowed a lump in my throat. "When I was five or so, I walked into Ezekiel's room. He was still in his crib. He'd gone pale white and cold. He wouldn't move. I called for Mama. When she saw him, she just screamed and tried to heal him over and over. It worked and brought him around, but he still had to go to the hospital. Ez needed a blood transplant, and I was the only match. The doctor took my blood, and I asked him how long it would be before I died."

I laughed out loud. "It's funny now, but back then, it wasn't. I thought I had to give up myself to save him, and I was totally okay with it. He's better than me. I wanted him to live."

Charlie mused that over. "Do you think your brother has your father's disease?"

My heart twisted and grew black, like a dying old tree. "If he does, he's not going to admit it. Not until he has no other choice."

Ez had been sick on and off for a long time. Nothing quite severe, and he'd never gone to the hospital again after that one time, but there were enough clues to make me wonder. I'd fought with Ez a million times about getting tested, or getting a genetic workup so we had the proof.

Or tried, anyway. He ran away every time I brought it up. After a lifetime of seeing our dad in and out of the hospital, he didn't want to accept what could be his own reality.

"Your mother might have an idea, if she can heal," Charlie suggested.

"I don't know if she does. If my brother's illness feels different from my dad's, or if it's still dormant, my mom might not be able to pick up on it."

"That's rough." Charlie frowned.

"Yeah, I know. And it's not fair that it has to be him. He's the best person. He doesn't deserve it."

"You don't deserve your bipolar, either," Charlie said softly.

I scoffed. "I deserve what I get. Probably why I'm serving my penance."

"Hey, you're here because I pissed you off, nothing more." Charlie laughed.

"I'm not talking about the Institute." He was going to think I was totally nuts. "I hear voices."

"Huh?" Charlie slid back in surprise.

"It's called psychosis. It's a part of my condition. There are voices in my head, telling me to do things. I've always heard them, ever since I was a little girl."

"And... do you listen?" He hoped everything bad I'd done was a result of me obeying the voices inside my mind.

Too bad for him. It was all me, and my own decisions.

I laughed darkly. "I'm kinda shit at doing what I'm told, even if it's my own brain. I mostly ignore them... though sometimes, the voices get out of control."

"Has that happened lately?"

"Not in a long time. They're always talking to me. Even right now."

Charlie leaned forward. "Do they have anything to say about me?"

"The voices get... quiet when they're around you," I said. "I don't know why. Maybe it's our bond. Magic is the only solution I can think of."

Charlie's expression sorrowed. "I wish I'd been around sooner, then."

"I wish you had too. Maybe things would've turned out different." My voice was despondent and aching.

Charlie moved closer. "Like?"

"You know my best friend died," I said. "I feel responsible for that."

Charlie said nothing, and I took a breath. "Monica and I met at a pageant when we were really little. You know, one of those competitions for little kids, with the big dresses and songs and whatnot. I begged my mom to let me compete. I drove her so nuts she finally let me sign up. I practiced for weeks and weeks, because I wanted to win. My Aunt Imogen made me a really sparkly dress, and my Uncle Jonah choreographed this awesome dance for me.

"Then the day of the pageant came. There was a girl there with a homemade costume. Her mom was yelling at her in the dressing room. I could tell she really wanted that trophy. At the end of the competition, they announced my name. I was so shocked. I couldn't believe I'd won! But then I saw the look on Monica's face, and I just couldn't take the crown. I whispered to the announcer I wanted to give my win to her, and they put the crown on her head instead of mine."

A huge grin spread across my face. I couldn't suppress it... didn't want to. "That was the best moment ever. She just lit up. Ever since, we became best friends. She wanted to be a Film Studies major. We made all kinds of videos of me doing makeup tutorials, and wrote songs together. They're still up on my old vlogging channel. We made so many, she hardly ever left my house. She didn't want to."

Charlie gave a thoughtful sound. "I take it her home life wasn't the best."

"Her parents were just garbage," I snarled. "There was a reason she practically lived at my place. When we were seventeen, she got tired of it. She wanted to run away. I agreed, because it sounded like an adventure, and I wanted Monica to be happy. She was never happy when she was around them."

I continued on, voice moving quickly... like I was a murderer attempting to explain my sentence away. "I didn't think we'd *really* run away for good. I figured Monica would have her fill after a few days, and go back home. I thought I'd get grounded for making everyone worry, and she'd hear it from her parents, and that would be the end of it. And it was fun, for a while. We found an old car and drove it all around California. We were free."

My head fell against Oberi, and I stroked her coat for comfort. Her nostrils blew warm air on my shoelaces as she slumbered. "After a couple of days of stealing food from the gas station and washing our hair in bathroom sinks, I'd had enough. I wanted to go home, and told Monica so. But she didn't. She insisted living like this was better than dealing with her parents. We had a big argument. But she won, in the end. She wasn't going back home, and I refused to leave without her."

"That's honorable," Charlie said quietly. "I was homeless for a while. That you stuck with her through it shows you're loyal. I don't think I could live that way again. Not for anyone."

"I don't know how you survived it." My voice wavered on the edge of freefall. "But then, some people don't. Monica was one of them. We were walking out of a rest stop one night when these two guys started following us. I was scared. Neither of us had our magic yet, so we couldn't defend ourselves. They cornered us. One of them grabbed me and tried to shove me into a van. Monica freaked out. She went to protect me, but the other guy pulled a knife..."

I was so choked up, I could hardly speak. I couldn't verbalize what I'd seen. The images replayed so quickly in my mind all I saw was red. I still recalled the shocked look in Monica's eyes, like it'd been only yesterday.

I squeezed the next words out of my throat. "I heard my Grandmother Eleanor. She and my mom had been looking for me for days, and ancestors know there's no rock on earth I could hide under that my grandmother won't turn over to find me. When Mama saw those guys trying to stuff me in the van— fuck, she lost it. She didn't even have to move. Her Fire magic turned both of those guys to dust in an instant. They didn't even burn. There were no flames. They just combusted into a pile of ashes. I'd never seen that kind of power from her before. And then I knew exactly why she was a chosen one, and why she'd brought the Hawkei Civil War to an end. She was, and still is, the most terrifying person I know."

Charlie didn't speak, but his expression was shocked. But the worst part of the story was still to come, so I went on.

"Mama tried to use her healing powers to save Monica, but by then, it was already too late. Her Anichi magic couldn't bring back the dead, and Monica had almost bled out by the time they'd shown up. I fell to the ground and held Monica just before she passed. Her last words were my name. She died in my arms."

My voice was quivering so badly, and I hated myself for it. "Her parents didn't even let me come to the funeral. They said it was *my* fault she died. And every shitty lie they'd ever told me didn't matter, because what they said then was the truth. I should've brought her home... should've forced her. And because I didn't, she's gone."

Charlie remained silent, and I forged a way through my memories, because the only way through them was out. "I just remember them turning me away at the door... there was so much hate. I looked up at Mama, and these tears were just pouring out of my eyes. I couldn't stop them. We rushed home and had our own private ceremony on the beach for Monica. It was the only way I could say goodbye."

I sniffed and wiped my face with my sleeve. "So now you now. Monica's dead because of me."

"She's not," Charlie insisted, softness in his voice. "You went with her because you wanted to protect her. You couldn't have saved Monica any more than I could've saved Marty. They both made bad decisions. We had no choice but to stand there and watch."

I didn't acknowledge whether he was right or wrong. It wouldn't make any difference anyway. Either resulted in Monica being gone.

I cleared my voice and began to speak normally again... finally... achingly. "After Monica died, I just deteriorated. I spiraled into the worst manic period of my life. I couldn't make videos or music again—that was our thing, and to do it without her felt like a betrayal. One day, my psychosis got out of control. I thought I was in the circus... like I was some kind of acrobat. I climbed from the stairs onto the chandelier we have in the living room."

My mouth went dry. "I started swinging from it upside down by my legs. I tried to do a backflip off of it. I would've broken my neck if Ezekiel hadn't caught me. The chandelier fell, and Alana had to jump out of the way. She cut up her hands and knees on the glass, but it could've been worse. The chandelier almost crushed her. She had to be rushed to the hospital so she didn't bleed out. When I finally came down, I couldn't remember anything. The only way I recalled what I did was when my brother told me what I'd been mumbling while I was up there."

Charlie's silence filled the aching space. He didn't rush to explanations or comfort like most people did. He just let me say what I had to say.

"Alana didn't blame me for what happened. Ez didn't, either. Or anyone else. But that my siblings had seen me fall apart and be vulnerable like that gave me so much guilt, I felt bad for merely existing. I almost killed myself and my sister in one go. Just like I killed Monica."

"What happened to Monica wasn't your doing," Charlie said. "And it wasn't her fault that she got killed. Monica didn't want to die. This falls on the person who wanted to end her life."

"She was my friend. People who get close to me get hurt. I destroy everything in my path, and she was collateral damage. And that's what you'll be, if you continue to hang around me."

"I'm pretty good about shielding myself from destructive people. I've done it all my life. And no matter what you think, what happened to Monica wasn't your fault." Charlie grabbed my arm and gave a squeeze, as if he wanted me to believe him.

"There are a lot of things that were my fault." I dropped my voice, terrified someone would overhear us even though we were alone up here. My biggest secret felt so dark, I was afraid of even the ancestors finding out.

Charlie came so close, our bodies were touching. Instinctively, he opened his arms and wrapped them around me. I didn't resist. Instead, I fell into his arms and against his chest. I held his forearms as he squeezed me, and he put his chin on top of my head. I could hear his heartbeat as it thudded on steadily behind me, like the sound of a Hawkei drum.

Cuddling. We were fucking *cuddling*. It'd be freaking adorable if I wasn't spilling my guts right now. Oberi sighed, as if she could sense our barriers falling away and was finally resting in that peace.

As he held me close, Charlie asked, "What happened?"

He implied that he knew there was more, or maybe had guessed. It was useless trying to hide something this vital from someone you had a soul bond with. He could feel my pain. And he knew how broken I was.

I could use the alcohol as an excuse tomorrow morning, but I didn't think either one of us would buy it. We weren't drunk anymore.

But Charlie would go along with the lie, for my sake. Because what I was about to tell him next, I'd never told anyone.

"A couple weeks after Monica died, some people in my class invited me to a party," I said. "Monica and I were never really close with anyone, just relied on each other, but these girls felt sorry for me. I figured I had to get out and try to distract myself, so I went."

My voice was emotionless this time. There weren't any tears, or feelings. I just couldn't muster up any for this situation. I'd put it away, compartmentalized it deep within myself in a place not even my spirit could reach. "There was a guy there. John. He was in mine and Monica's friend group, though she never liked him. I thought he was cool. We talked a lot and I'd known him since I was a freshman. He wanted to go for a walk in the woods, talk about Monica. Nobody ever mentioned her anymore, so off I went."

Charlie's body went rigid as I spoke. "He got me far enough into the woods that nobody heard me scream. I tried to fight him off, but he was stronger. He pushed me face down and climbed on top of me. You can guess what happened after that."

I could still remember what the leaves smelled like, and what the dirt felt like all over my face. I remembered it was so cold that night that

I could see John's breath. Didn't remember much else except how badly I wanted to escape.

Charlie pressed his lips to my hair and rocked me. He wasn't much of a talker. But he always said what he needed to. The movement gave me strength to go on.

"John finished inside of me and just let me lay there... like some kind of object. I was still in the woods long after the party was over. Eventually, I got up off the ground and forced myself to walk into town... because I knew I couldn't go missing again. It would worry my family."

I was rattling off random facts now, snippets of what I remembered. "There's a woman's shelter in Kinpago. The lady at the front counter—her name was Mia— she patched me up, gave me a morning-after pill... asked me to do a rape kit. I did it, because she said it was a good idea, but it never went farther than that. I begged her not to tell anyone, and she said she wouldn't. Then I washed my face and went back home, and haven't talked about it since. Nobody knows but you."

Charlie stiffened a little in shock, but he quickly relaxed. "I never told anyone about Marty, either. I'm glad we can trust each other like that."

Trust. It was such a strange word to me. I couldn't comprehend what it was like to trust again. Outside of my family, I'd never trusted anyone but Monica.

So I launched into another explanation, to avoid the vulnerability. "My mania got worse afterward. I was out of control. I went on a spree and just blew all my savings. Thousands of dollars, gone in a few hours. That's why my parents have access to all my credit cards, and my bank account. I want them to monitor me in case it happens again. So I don't lose everything twice."

"Do you think there's a risk for that?" Charlie murmured.

"I don't know. I can't imagine being in a worse place emotionally than I was at that moment. I took everything out on Daddy. I treated him so terribly after the whole thing, but I knew that I could say or do anything to him, and he'd never hold it against me. I just used him like a punching bag for everything I was feeling, and he just... took it. It was so wrong, and I feel so bad about it. I want to say I'm sorry, but it's not like I can tell him the reason why. It'd break his heart."

I leaned my head into Charlie's shirt. Leather and bergamot… the scent I loved. "Things got so awful between me and Daddy that I told Mama I wanted to move out for a while. I stayed with my Uncle Jonah and Uncle Jake. They're both big guys, you know? I figured no one would be able to hurt me again, not with them around. Josee and I shared a room. I think she suspected something, but she never asked."

I finally relaxed against Charlie's hold and sighed, because the hard part was over, and at last, I felt like my wings had grown back after being clipped— like the chains holding me down for years no longer had any bearing on me. "There isn't much more to tell. I went back home, eventually. I told Mama I couldn't go back to high school— because I couldn't bear sitting in class with my rapist— and made up some excuse. I studied at home and barely got by. Once I graduated, I committed crime after crime… until I ended up here."

I cleared my throat. "The day I got my magic was *the best*. I never felt more powerful than when I conjured a fireball for the first time. I knew if John tried anything again… if anyone did… I'd burn them to ash, like my mother did. And I'd never have to be helpless. I could rescue myself."

Charlie's voice was astonished. "You kept silent about it for almost three years."

"I thought about telling people. But I'm the daughter of the Toaqua chief and the chosen one. It can't get out that I was raped," I told Charlie. "So many people already scrutinize Daddy because he has a disease. They'd say he wasn't capable of protecting his own daughter. They might even ask him to step down."

"Your dad can handle the scrutiny," Charlie said. "Your family's not going to be ashamed of you."

"But I'm ashamed of myself," I insisted. "I was too scared to fight back, so I just took it. After that night, I promised myself I'd *always* fight back, no matter what. I vowed I'd never let anyone violate me like that again. I'd die first."

Charlie's grip tightened around me. "Ava, I want you to listen to me. You could've done *nothing* to stop him. If you had fought back at all, he might've killed you. Keeping yourself alive is nothing to be ashamed of."

His words grew firmer, with a greater conviction. "I didn't *want* those women to use my body. I hated every moment of it. But I let them do it, because staying alive to see the next morning was more important. And no matter how you feel about yourself, you should be damn glad you're still here. I know for certain I am. I would've been missing a piece of my soul forever if you were gone. No matter what's happened to me so far, I think it was worth it just to get to you. You're a fighter. And I'm proud of you for that."

He was proud of me? But how could he be? Wasn't I a monster?

"I'm really tired," I whispered. Telling Charlie all that had worn me out.

"We still have a few hours until sunrise. Might as well catch up on some sleep," he suggested.

"I've barely slept in days, Charlie."

"I know, pidge."

My head fell back against his chest, which was soft and warm. I was closer this time. His heartbeat was louder, and I came to a scary realization.

Charlie made me feel something. The first something in a long time.

I wasn't used to feeling. I didn't like it. I wanted to be numb.

But I needed to feel in order to be free.

"Sleep softly, princess," he said quietly. "I'll ward off your nightmares."

I liked that. I liked that a lot. I let my eyes close and allowed myself to slip back into oblivion, finally safe.

Once the sun rose, we'd go back to hating each other. It was the only way we knew how.

But in the darkness, we didn't have to pretend.

SEVENTEEN

I hadn't been to a party in ages. I'd gotten drunk enough as a teenager to know that alcohol only got you into trouble. But with Ava-Marie, it was different. She was carefree and reckless, and as much as that scared me, I also wanted to be a part of it.

Ava didn't seem to remember much after the fae wine, but while she was downing shots like they were candy, I was drinking in *her*. Someone had to protect her if things got out of hand, after all. I didn't get the tattoo because I was drunk. I got it because... well, I *wanted* it— though I could barely admit the fact to myself. Ava and I were bonded. Whether anything else happened between us, that was never going to change. I only had to pretend it wasn't a big deal, because I knew Ava didn't feel the same way.

But the party, the tattoos, the fun... it couldn't compare to that morning in the loft when Ava opened her heart to me and entrusted me with her deepest secrets. I held her close, inhaling her scent and tearing up when she told me about what happened to her. I didn't think she saw me cry, and I didn't want her to. She'd make a speech about how everyone had been trying to protect her her whole life, and how she could take care of herself. She didn't want me to feel sorry for her.

But I did. Ancestors, I felt the pain sink into every pore of my body, eating at me until my stomach became hollow and my limbs lost all feeling. Ava-Marie didn't deserve what happened to her. I didn't blame her for the way she acted after the fact. Ava may not have realized what she was doing, but I recognized a cry for help when I saw one.

And I wanted with every fiber of my being to be the one to answer that call.

I burned to drive a knife through the men who had killed her best friend. I craved the chance to pummel the face of the rapist who hurt her. I prayed for everyone who had ever left a mere scratch on my poor pidge's heart to suffer the consequences.

Forget the fiery inferno she could rain down upon them. I'd steal the air from their lungs and force dirt down their throats, then crush them with boulders over and over, never giving them a moment to beg for mercy, but not giving them the freedom of death, either.

Those assholes deserved a lifetime of torture for hurting Ava. I'd savor every moment of it.

I would never hurt her, not in this life or the next. I would always be at her side to support her, and to protect her when she couldn't manage on her own.

But Ava would never know. She was a strong, dual-casting Elementai with incredible power. It would be an insult if she knew I was lurking... watching and waiting for anyone who dare touch my pidge.

Ava was back to her normal self in the morning, as if she'd forgotten our conversation altogether. But I knew it was an act. Her tone was hesitant, and I could feel the emotions coming off of Oberi, like she too smelled a hint of Ava's bullshit.

I didn't blame her, though. She didn't want to talk about it, so I wouldn't bring it up. But damn it all if it didn't keep me up at night. I barely slept over the following week, like this was some type of problem I was meant to solve and had no answer to. Not here at the Institute, at least.

I tried telling myself it had happened a long time ago— that I couldn't bring Monica back from the dead any more than I could revive Marty. I couldn't go back in time and change what John had done.

And yet I felt there was something more I could do— something I *had* to do. It hit me one morning. I'd been having a dream... a really good dream, though the details began to drift from my mind as soon as I woke.

I struggled to hang on to the memory. I'd been sitting in a crowd some-where, stroking Oberi's fur. A beautiful voice had filled the room, warming my heart...

It had been Ava's voice.

Not the Ava I knew, but the girl she was before she met me— before all that crap had turned her life upside down.

I wanted to know who Ava used to be, and I wanted to help her find that girl again.

I didn't know how to do it, but an idea struck after I got out of the shower. Oberi was waiting for me in my dorm. He was in husky form, and he shoved something into my hands. I ran my fingers over it and felt soft bristles.

"You telling me I need to groom myself or something?" I teased.

Oberi barked.

"Ah, you want to be brushed," I said with a sigh. "Roll over."

Oberi followed my command, and I started brushing his fur while I tickled his belly. He rubbed his head across the floor in pleasure.

"Five more minutes," I warned. "I've got stuff to do today."

Oberi wasn't satisfied after five minutes of grooming, but I set the brush aside anyway. I really *did* have stuff to do before class. I leaned down and felt behind my dresser, where I'd stashed the few things Marcus had snuck out of Contraband for me. My fingers curled around the headphones, and I tucked them into my jacket.

"You coming?" I asked Oberi, and he yipped happily.

Oberi and I stopped by the dining hall and ate quickly before making our way to the library. The computers here were kind of shit, and not just because they didn't work well around magic. Tons of websites were blocked, and they didn't have any software installed to help navigate while blind. Luckily, Oberi had learned how to help me find the icons I needed, as I'd started coming in here to work on schoolwork.

"Fire up the Internet, bud," I told him.

Oberi pressed his nose against the touchscreen, while I fumbled around looking for the headphone jack. I finally found it on the side of the computer and plugged it in. I wasn't supposed to have these head-phones, but it was early enough in the day that the library was pretty secluded. I didn't think anyone would notice me, as long as I didn't take too long.

It took forever for the page to load. Oberi nudged me once it did. I typed in what I was looking for. Oberi got so excited his tongue lolled out of his mouth and he slobbered all over my arm.

I turned my nose up and wiped the slobber off. "Ew, Oberi. I guess that means we found it."

Oberi leaned forward to press his nose to the screen, and his wagging tail smacked me in the arm.

I was about to complain, until the sound of a beautiful voice filled the speakers. I went as still as a statue.

"Hello, magical creatures," the girl in the video said. "It's Ava-Marie and Monica back with another video. This song was written at two a.m. while we were high on gummy bears and caffeine, so we hope you like it. It's called *Until the Sun Rises*."

It was Ava's old vlog... the one where she and Monica wrote songs and did makeup tutorials.

The sound of a soft piano filled my ears, followed shortly by an acoustic guitar accompanying the slow melody. Ava began to sing, and I swore I nearly fell out of my chair. It was so much more beautiful than anything I could've ever dreamt. The sound of her voice sent a shiver down my spine. I'd heard her sing once— when she'd summoned the ancestors in the cave— but she was more incredible than I remembered.

The stars above won't leave me alone
But they're all just dim disguises.
I won't escape from the dark of night
Until the sun rises.

The whole song was a metaphor that talked about a girl who was being chased by so many guys, but none of them could satisfy her. She was holding out for the one who could pull her from the darkness and brighten up her days. She was waiting for her *sun*.

Could I be the one Ava had been waiting for?

I pushed the thought away quickly. Ava and I were bonded, and that was it. It wasn't like we were dating, or like we ever would. That was a sure-fire way to damn our bond to hell and ruin every good thing we might possibly ever have.

Oberi clicked on another video, and Ava's voice filled my headphones once again. It was really nice to hear her sing at first, but the more I listened, the sadder I got. She was *so* incredible, and she'd let it all go. She didn't think it was fair to Monica to continue without her, but Ava was throwing her talent away. She could use her music for so much good— to reconnect with Monica's memory and help make sense of what happened. Eventually, she could use her music to inspire others to overcome similar turmoil. Instead, she'd turned to raising hell and getting herself into trouble.

It was sad, really. I wished she would play again.

"Hey, man."

Someone placed a heavy hand on my shoulder, and I jumped. I quickly pulled the headphones off and hid them in my lap, but I'd already been caught.

"What?" I asked.

"It's me, Marcus," he announced.

Marcus was nice like that. Most people expected me to know who they were by the sound of their voice or their scent— like I was a dog or something— but it wasn't that easy. Ava's was really the only voice I could pick out of a crowd.

"Since when do you come to the library in the morning?" he asked as he slid into the chair next to me. The computer in front of him made a slight *whirring* noise as it turned on. "I never see you here."

I pressed the power button on the computer so he wouldn't see what I was up to. "I, uh, just had some stuff to catch up on."

"Don't you have class right now?"

Shit. I hadn't realized how long I'd been sitting there listening to Ava's vlog. How many videos had I listened to? A dozen?

"What time is it?" I asked.

"Almost ten."

"Crap." I shoved my headphones in my bag and stood. "I gotta get to class."

"Oh, Charlie?" Marcus stopped me. "Kallie's trying to get everyone together after class to do some training for the Darke Games. You in?"

"Training?" I asked skeptically. I barely knew what we'd be up against during the Darke Games, let alone how to train for it.

"Yeah, we want to win, don't we?" Marcus asked. "We're meeting at the Villain's Den after dinner. You in?"

"Yeah, sure," I mumbled, though my heart swelled. As long as the rest of us were there, Ava would be, too. "I'll catch you later."

I DIDN'T SEE Ava the rest of the day, which was strange because we usually ate together during meals. I was starting to worry when I arrived at the Villain's Den after dinner.

All I had to do was follow the sound of arguing.

"Come on, Kalina. What's in the box?"

"That's Kallie to you, *Marcus*," she said sternly. "And I told you— it's a surprise."

"Can't you give me a *hint*?" he begged.

"Sure," she said brightly. "If you volunteer to be the one who opens it."

Marcus hesitated. "Okay..."

Kalina sounded proud. "Your hint is you'll be sorry you volunteered."

Marcus groaned. "Not fair."

Oberi padded along at my side, but he didn't get excited, which told me Ava hadn't arrived yet.

"Where's Ava?" I asked as I sat down beside them.

"She should be here any minute," Kalina— sorry, *Kallie*— said. She'd insisted she was trying to make a turnaround with her life, so I needed to respect that by calling her by her chosen name.

It was mere moments later when Ava walked in the room. I didn't know how I sensed her, because I was sitting a good ten feet from the door. But her scent hit me immediately, and the whole room warmed when she entered.

"Late, as usual," Kallie teased.

"I'm not late," Ava argued as she approached us. "You're all early...

ancestors, Oberi. Did someone skimp on your grooming this morning? Your fur is a mess!"

Something like glass clinked as Ava set it on the table. She plopped down beside me and started running her fingers through Oberi's fur. The husky barked in pleasure. I swear he'd be purring if he could.

"Where have you been?" I asked. "You missed lunch and dinner."

"Did I?" Ava asked, like she hadn't realized what time it was. "I got held up in the Alchemy room. We're working on a healing potion, but it's hardly effective. There *has* to be a more potent mixture than the recipe in the book. I simply *must* figure it out... hey, Marcus. Maybe you can help. The recipe originated from the Miriamic Coven."

Ava's voice grew strained as she spoke, then a *pop* like a cork sounded. "Here, smell it."

Marcus snorted. "Don't ask *me* about healing salves."

"I thought you could perform *any* warlock magic," she pointed out. "Isn't that what your tattoos mean?"

"I *can*," Marcus emphasized. "I just... haven't taken the class yet."

"Here, Charlie." Ava shoved something into my hands, and I took it. It was a small glass vial and heavy enough to be filled to the brim. "Doesn't this smell off?"

I lifted the potion to my nose and sniffed it. It smelled of citrus, but more on the *tart* side than the *sweet*. "It doesn't smell *bad*, but I haven't taken Alchemy. I don't know what it *should* smell like."

"No matter," Kallie said, taking charge. "We're not here to talk about classes. We're here to train for the Darke Games."

"Where are we training?" I asked as I handed the potion back to Ava. Kalina stood. "Follow me."

The three of us, along with Rishi and Oberi, followed behind Kallie.

"Does anyone know what exactly we're training for?" I asked. "I mean, we know monsters are going to be coming through the portals, but what kind?"

"It could be anything," Kallie answered.

A thought struck. "Just how many possibilities are there?"

"You're wondering how many monsters there are in hell?" Kallie asked, sounding slightly amused. "Thousands of species... millions, maybe. Which is why we have to be prepared for *anything*. Ah, yes. This will do."

I didn't realize where we were going until we stepped into the room. The air was warmer and humid. My Air magic expanded, but it met resistance high above our heads against the ceiling. The room was almost as big as the chapel, but not as tall. The smell of dirt and flowers hit my nose, and my Earth magic immediately sensed plant species of all kinds filling the room. Oberi's footsteps beside mine turned from soft padding on the carpet to scratches, like he was walking over stone. Birds chirped from the rafters, and a small waterfall trickled off in the distance.

"Where are we?" I asked.

"This is the school's greenhouse, sometimes called the Arboretum," Kallie explained. "I'm surprised you haven't been in here before. This room was specifically designed for Elementai."

Ava had been silent, like she was taking it all in, but when Kallie explained the nature of the room, Ava huffed. "Well, no one mentioned it to *us*. Jerks."

Kallie didn't seem to hear her. "Anyway, I thought this would be a good place to train. There's plenty of room, but unlike the prison yard, it's not crawling with people."

Oberi seemed thrilled. Oberi shifted into a Fire unicorn and took off running down the stone path, hooves beating against the ground. Rishi meowed and ran after her.

"Don't go too far," I called.

"Relax," Ava said, like we were parenting a child together. "Let her have fun. She doesn't get many chances to be free."

For a moment, it didn't sound like she was talking about Oberi.

"First things first," Kallie said. "Marcus, hold this."

"Can I open it yet?" he asked.

"Not yet," Kallie instructed. "I think we should start with some sparring. I want to see what you guys are capable of."

Ava cracked her knuckles. "Are you doubting me?"

Kallie scoffed. "You? No. But I need to know what your limits are. Ava, you'll be on Marcus' team. Charlie, you're with me."

Ava huffed. "Who says *you're* in charge? I want to be on Charlie's team."

"I didn't see *you* stepping up to be team Captain," Kallie shot back. "I *am* the one who planned this training session."

"I say we vote on team captain," Ava insisted. "I'd like to nominate myself."

"You can't nominate yourself!" Kallie cried.

I sighed. Ancestors, we hadn't even started training yet and already we were fighting. "Maybe we should draw straws," I suggested.

"No way!" Ava protested. "With our luck, *Marcus* will be named team captain."

"Hey!" Marcus objected.

"Well, this is just a great way to start off our *team training session*," I groaned. "Why can't you two be co-captains?"

"Co-captains?" they balked in unison.

"Excuse me," Ava said. "There were no *co*-captains on my cheerleading squad—"

"And there are no co-captains to the crown," Kallie added before Ava could finish.

"Our team needs one leader," Ava insisted.

"And a cool name," Marcus added.

"How about *you all shut up and listen*," I growled. "You guys want me on your team for the Darke Games? Then you're going to have to get your shit together. There's no way we're fighting monsters if we can't get through *one* training session without arguing over team Captain. So either come to a mutual agreement, or there *will* be no team to captain."

Marcus piped up immediately. "I vote for Charlie."

"Yeah," Ava agreed quickly. "Charlie can be captain."

I groaned. That was *so* not what I meant.

"Fine," Kalina conceded. It was obvious she wasn't going to get what she wanted. "Tell me, Captain, where shall we start?"

I hesitated. I longed to tell them I wasn't Captain material, but that was a good way to stir up another fight. If I had to be Captain to keep the peace, then so be it. "Let's start with some sparring, like you suggested. Ava and me against Kallie and Marcus."

"Okay," Kallie agreed. "Let's find somewhere with more space —ah!"

Kallie's shriek echoed off the windows of the greenhouse. Ava and

Marcus both started laughing so hard that neither of them could hardly breathe.

I was about to ask what just happened when Kallie shouted, "I'm soaked! What the hell, Ava?"

Ava must've summoned water from the greenhouse fountain and splashed it all over Kalina.

"I thought we were sparring," Ava defended between laughs. "You have to be ready for anything, right?"

"Yeah, like my battle orb up your ass," Kalina shot back, though she laughed like she was only joking.

Except the battle orb was no joke. Magic crackled through the air, and Ava gasped. Immediately, I heard the *whoosh* of a fireball and felt the heat cross my skin as Ava threw it past me. The two must've collided, because an explosion sounded between us. Kallie immediately threw another orb, and Ava grabbed me by the shirt to drag me down another path.

"Hell, you two turned this place into a battle zone in less than two seconds," I hissed as we ducked down behind foliage.

Ava chuckled, like she was having fun. Was this normal in the magical community, like laser tag or paintball back in Detroit?

"That's kind of the point, isn't it?" Ava said. Her clothes brushed against me as she stood quickly to throw another fireball. She ducked down just as fast.

"Shit," she muttered under her breath.

"What? Is someone hurt?" I asked in alarm.

"No," she said, like that was the least of her worries. "Kallie's got shield magic."

"Isn't that good news?"

"We'll lose!" Ava cried.

"But she's on our side in the Darke Games," I pointed out.

Ava scoffed. "Yeah, but she's about to murder us in the meantime. Come on."

Ava grabbed me again, and we went sprinting down another trail. Ava stopped in her tracks, and I came to a halt beside her. Something had changed, though I couldn't describe what. The scent of flowers around me vanished, though I could still sense their presence through my Earth magic. The ground below me squished, though I knew I was still on the path. A horrid smell like a rotting carcass filled my nose.

"What's going on?" I demanded.

Ava's voice turned sour. "It's Kallie. Some sort of an illusion. All I see ahead is a dark swamp. I don't know where the path went."

"How do we break the illusion? There has to be a way!"

Ava sounded calm and collected, but I was freaking out. I couldn't navigate my world if I was being tricked by my own senses.

"Kallie's strong, but it's only an illusion," Ava explained. "My Aunt Imogen taught me about fae magic as a kid. It's all in your head, so all you have to do is override the illusion and convince yourself what you're seeing isn't real."

"But it *feels* so real," I argued. My feet sank deeper into the mud, and the stench grew stronger.

"Focus on what you *know* to be true," Ava encouraged.

"I know we're in the greenhouse," I said, my voice calming. "I can feel the plants around us. And the air meets resistance at the ceiling. It's not wide-open like a swamp."

"Exactly," Ava said, though it sounded like she was still trying to fight the illusion herself.

"The rock beneath me speaks to me," I observed. "The mud isn't real."

As I said it, the sinking sensation vanished, and I found myself standing on solid ground again. The illusion wasn't totally over, though. I still smelled the stench of death permeating through the air.

"I know the greenhouse shouldn't smell like this," I continued. "It should smell green and like flowers. There was the scent of dirt when we walked in, too, and some sort of cleaner in the water."

Slowly, the horrid scent faded, and the smells and sounds of the greenhouse returned.

"We're back!" Ava cried, before taking my hand. "Come on. Kallie's illusion slowed us down. Let's get out of here before she finds us."

We took off running again. Oberi's hooves sounded ahead, but she stopped dead when she saw us coming.

"Up you go." I grabbed Ava around the waist and shoved her onto Oberi's back, then climbed on myself. I wrapped my arms around Ava and held her close. She either didn't notice or didn't seem bothered by it. "Let's get to the fountain. You'll need a source of water."

"It's not a fountain," Ava said. "It's a pool. I can feel it."

Oberi took off running, and we made it to the other side of the greenhouse. Marcus was nearby, which was obvious in his heavy footsteps, but Kalina either wasn't moving or was sneaking along soundlessly. We slid off Oberi, and Ava planted herself in front of me.

"Come and get me," she called. "I dare you!"

A growl erupted from behind a large tree, and the brush rustled as a creature lunged from behind it. Instinct took over, and I thrust my Air magic outward. A gust of wind rushed by, snatching the creature from the air. It was large— almost as big as Oberi. It tumbled through the air and landed hard on one of the pathways. A whimper came, but it morphed into the sound of Kalina's groans.

I realized then that the creature *had* been Kalina, though she'd been in her wolf form when she attacked.

"Ow!" she breathed. "That was one hell of a blow, Charlie."

"I'm sorry," I said quickly. "I didn't know it was you."

"Sorry?" she balked. "We can totally use magic like that in the Darke Games. Don't hold back on my account."

"She's right," Ava agreed. "Give it all you've got. Kallie can take it."

And now they were back on the same page. I'd never understand girls.

"Dear Goddess!" Marcus cried as he finally wound his way through the path over to us. "Kallie, are you okay— whoa!"

Marcus must've tripped, because the next thing I knew, the box in his hands had clattered to the ground. Rishi let out a high-pitched shriek, and Marcus grunted a few times before a huge *splash* sounded and water soaked the front of my pants.

Ava cackled from beside me, and Oberi whinnied. Marcus sputtered water and continued splashing it everywhere.

"Do we need to go in and save him?" I asked.

"Relax," Ava laughed. "It's less than three feet deep. Marcus, stop flailing! Your ass is touching the bottom."

"Gods," Kalina sighed. "Marcus, stop fooling around. I could use your help out here."

Marcus must've found his bearings, because he stopped sputtering and splashing. Water dripped onto the path as he dragged himself out of the water. "I-I'm fine," he gasped.

"You better be," Kalina said. "If you drowned in a koi pond, we're going to have problems during the Games."

"You know I don't swim well," Marcus growled.

"Learn," Kallie snapped.

"Hey," I cut in before another fight broke out. I quickly changed the subject. "I think we've all proved to each other we can handle ourselves in combat. But that illusion magic was something else, Kallie. Any chance we'll be up against something like that in the Games?"

"It's possible," she replied. "Honestly, I'm surprised you managed to break through it so fast."

"Your illusion was strong," Ava admitted, "but you put all the details in the scenery. Charlie could break through the rest with ease."

"Mm..." Kallie mused. "I'll have to work on that."

To be honest, Kallie's illusion was enough to convince me. The dead tell was how quickly the scene had shifted. Had she knocked me out beforehand, I never would've known.

"Let's try something else," I suggested. "What's the box for?"

"Oh, this is a good one," Kallie said brightly. She walked over to retrieve the box from where Marcus had dropped it. "Marcus, if you'd do the honors."

Marcus stepped forward, his clothes making *dripping* sounds on the ground.

"Hold up," Ava sighed. "Marcus, let me dry you off."

Ava used her Toaqua magic to draw the water out of Marcus' clothes. It must've been a lot, because it made a *splash* when she dropped it back into the pond.

"Thanks," Marcus said sheepishly, before addressing Kalina. "Are you going to tell me what's in the box?"

"Just open it," she said impatiently.

Marcus hesitated, then a hinge squeaked.

"Ancestors!" Ava cried in a high-pitched voice, as if she was looking down at a newborn baby. "It's adorable. What is it?"

"Ugh, it's ugly!" Marcus sounded repulsed. "What's with all the glitter?"

"Glitter is *fabulous*," Ava argued.

Meanwhile, Kalina just laughed without explaining. It was like she was waiting for something.

"What is it?" I asked.

Ava turned to me, gushing. "It's the most beautiful glowing fairy! She's sitting at the bottom of the box, staring up at us with the most gorgeous ruby eyes. I just want to take her home and—"

Whiz!

It sounded like wings flapping a thousand beats per minute, but it was gone as soon as it came. Marcus coughed, choking on something, and the box clattered to the ground again.

"Ancestors!" Ava cried.

She grabbed for Marcus, but he fell backward into both of us. I helped stand him upright, but he seemed to have lost control of his limbs.

"That thing flew up his nose!" Ava cried. Her awe had vanished. "What is it, Kallie?"

Kallie's laugh was muffled. "It's a minor demon known as an *allure*. It possesses you and makes you want to have sex all the time."

"Kallie!" I roared, still trying to hold Marcus upright. "How could you!?"

"He volunteered!" she defended.

"He didn't know what he was volunteering for!" I shot back.

Suddenly, Marcus went silent. Rishi must've noticed something was off about him, because he hissed.

"Well, hellooo there," Marcus drawled in a seductive tone toward Ava. It was pretty obvious he was possessed, because the real Marcus had the charm of a limp dick. "What's your name, beautiful?"

He went to drape an arm around Ava's shoulder and nearly punched me in the nose in the process. I reeled back a step, but Ava knew how to handle her own.

"Not happening," Ava snapped. She must've had Marcus' hand in a painful hold, because he sucked air between his teeth.

"Feisty," Marcus— or rather, the allure— said in amusement. "You and I could have lots of fun."

"Hell no." Ava shoved him away. "Even if you're possessed, I'm not falling for that. Try it on someone else."

"My, my." Marcus' voice came directly in front of me, so I could only guess he was speaking to me. He drew in a deep, hungry breath. "Aren't you a tall glass of water? And let me tell you, boy. I. Am. Thirsty."

Marcus ran a finger down my chest, and my guts twisted. I grabbed him by the wrists to stop him.

"Kallie, what exactly is the point of this exercise?" I demanded.

"Demon possession," she said like it was obvious. "Do I have to remind you we'll be up against demons from hell? There's a chance we'll have to exorcise one."

I blew a breath. "Are you freaking kidding me?"

Ava burst at the same time. "And you decided to possess our *warlock* — the one race that can actually perform exorcisms correctly?"

"We needed a challenge!" Kallie insisted. "Besides, this demon is harmless. It's just horny."

"Harmless my ass," I scoffed. She was standing there looking pretty while I was trying to keep Marcus at a distance. My hand was shoved into his face, getting slobber all over while he tried to make out with me.

"You think *I'm* sexy?" I challenged the demon. "Check out Kallie!"

I grabbed Marcus by the shoulders and spun him around. He stopped dead.

"Oh," he said breathlessly. "Yes... how could I not have seen you before? You glow like a radiant goddess. I must have you, my queen!"

"Hey!" Kallie protested. "I didn't ask for this."

"It was your idea," I said with a shrug.

Marcus stepped away from me, thank the ancestors. Meanwhile, Ava turned my way, sounding irritated. "You think *Kallie's* sexy?"

I scoffed. "I haven't even seen the girl— literally. I just said that to get him off our back while we come up with a solution."

"Oh." Ava sounded pleased. "Well, I don't know much about exorcisms. I know the Miriamic Coven has rituals to cast out demons, but we're SOL there."

"No, Marcus!" Kallie shouted. "I will *not* sleep with you! Go away!"

I cocked an eyebrow at Ava. "You think he's really possessed?"

"Hard to tell," Ava chuckled. "But if you saw the look in his eyes, then the answer is yes. He looks weirdly starstruck."

"Okay, so a ritual is out of the question," I said thoughtfully. "How do demons survive in a host?"

"I don't know," Ava mused. "Most demon possessions are spiritual, but this one... it was like her body entered his. She's grabbed the controls to his brain and is turning it into a mush of hormones."

"So the allure is like a parasite. What happens if we make the host body uninhabitable?" I asked.

"Uninhabitable how?"

"I don't know," I admitted. "Could we give him some sort of antidote, or maybe something that'll make him sick? If his immune system isn't up to snuff, it could flush the demon out."

"So we want him to run a fever?" Ava asked thoughtfully.

"It's just a theory—" I started, but she cut me off.

"No, it's a good one," Ava said. "I think I know how to do it. Marcus! Come here. I'll have sex with you!"

"Pidge!" I cried. Oberi shook her head like she hadn't heard her right.

"Relax," Ava whispered under her breath. "I just wanted to get the demon's attention."

Marcus strolled up to Ava. "I knew it. My charm works every time."

"Yeah, yeah," Ava said flatly. "Just kiss me, will you?"

My blood ran cold.

"Gladly." Marcus sounded a little too enthused if you asked me, but I had to remind myself it was the demon, and not him.

Marcus slurped on Ava's lips like she was a slushie. I couldn't stand to listen. I had to steady myself against Oberi, because I thought I might puke. Had she *really* just asked Marcus to kiss her? It felt like a knife had embedded itself in my guts. I knew it was a ploy, but still, it felt like a betrayal.

"It's not working!" Ava said.

"What are you doing?" Kallie demanded.

"I'm using my Fire to heat Marcus' internal organs," she explained.

"He's got to have a fever of a hundred-and-four already. If I go any further, I might kill him."

"You've *got* to be kidding me," Kallie sighed. "This is a sex demon, remember? Heat is kind of their thing."

I wanted to get in on the conversation, to throw out solutions so I didn't have to keep listening to the two of them suck face, but I couldn't find my bearings. The whole thing made me sick.

"I've got it!" Ava cried, but Marcus silenced her with another gross kiss.

Kallie gasped. "Gods, Ava, what are you doing?"

Ava drew away from Marcus to speak. "Toaqua can create ice. I'm using my powers to *lower* his body temperature. That should draw the demon—"

Marcus sputtered before Ava could finish her sentence.

"It's working!" Kallie exclaimed. "Keep going, Ava."

Marcus continued coughing, and his hands slapped to the pavement.

Oh, shit. Now we were killing him. That was just great.

"Pidge, no!" I cried. "We'll find another way. We'll get a professor to help."

Kallie scoffed. "So I can get locked in Cellblock 9 for sneaking this demon out of class? No, thank you."

"He's obviously in pain," I pointed out.

"Trust me, Charlie," Ava insisted. "This is working."

Damn it, I wanted to trust her, but I couldn't stand here listening to Marcus cough like that. He was going to lose a lung.

"Pidge," I pressed.

"It's almost out," she promised. "I can feel it. Just a little more..."

Marcus hacked so loud it echoed off the windows of the greenhouse. The demon let out a scream as it tumbled out of his body. Relief flooded through me.

"You did it!" Kallie cried. She shuffled forward, presumably to capture the demon and place it back in the box.

I finally found my legs and rushed over to Marcus. He lay on the ground, wheezing. Rishi raced under my feet. I nearly tripped over him as I knelt beside Marcus.

"You okay?" I asked, slapping him a little to get him to wake. "Marcus!"

"Fuuuck..." he breathed, his teeth clattering together. "It's cold in here. What the hell happened?"

I frowned. "The girls happened."

"Hey, it was a good training exercise!" Kallie protested. "And we did it— without your help, mind you."

"Actually, it was Charlie's idea," Ava said. "Marcus, I'm going to use my Fire to warm you up, okay?"

"O...kay," he whispered, shivering.

I placed my hands on Marcus to calm him. He was ice cold. It was pretty obvious when Ava started funneling heat into his body, because his skin returned to a normal temperature.

"Are you okay?" Ava asked.

"I kind of feel like I'm going to puke," he admitted.

"Here, take this," Ava said.

"What's that?" I asked as I heard a cork pop off a bottle.

"It's the healing potion I made in Alchemy," Ava said. "It should help with the nausea— or not..."

Kallie snapped the top of the box closed, then inhaled a sharp breath when she turned to us. "Gods, Marcus! You're turning blue!"

Marcus had already taken a big gulp of potion, and it apparently wasn't working the way it was supposed to.

"I thought you knew how to brew a potion, pidge!" I growled.

"I do!" Ava cried. "This was an experiment."

Marcus groaned. "You could've warned me. I look like a fucking Smurf!"

"How do you feel?" Ava asked breathlessly.

"How does he *feel*?" I balked. "He's blue!"

His temperature had stabilized, though, so that was a good thing.

"I feel fine, actually," Marcus said. "But, um... am I going to be blue forever?"

"Um..." Ava hesitated. "No, no. That should wear off."

"Pidge," I warned.

"He says he feels fine!"

I sighed and helped Marcus to his feet. "Okay, that's it. As team

Captain, I am banning everyone from putting our teammates in any further danger. I think Marcus has been picked on enough for the day. Marcus, why don't you sit out?"

"I actually feel okay—" He cut off abruptly. "Actually, you know what? You're probably right. I should take it easy. I *am* blue, after all."

"And you'll tell me the second any other symptoms arise," I stated sternly. I wasn't giving him a choice.

"Sure thing, Captain." Marcus walked away to go sit by Oberi, and Rishi followed.

"So, what?" Kallie sounded annoyed. "Our training session is over?"

"No," I snapped. "Clearly, we need to go over a few things— like how *not* to put your teammate in danger."

"I don't know why you're so mad," Kallie sighed. "The exercise worked. We learned something new."

"You went about it in the wrong way," I argued, running my hand over my face. "Let's just forget about it. It's over, and we're not going to try it again."

"Yes, sir," Kallie said sarcastically.

I began pacing. "Look, if we're going to make it through the Darke Games, we have to work together. So let's play up our strengths. What kind of things are we all best at?"

"You've already seen my illusions," Kallie said.

"And she can create weapons out of thin air," Ava added. "I saw it in class."

I furrowed my brow. "You can do that?"

"If I believe in the illusion enough, I can make it real," Kallie explained. "What's your strength, Air boy?"

I hesitated. I had Air and Earth power, but I was still learning what I could do with it. I didn't know exactly how it would help us against monsters.

Marcus piped up from several feet away. "He tossed Mad Dog nearly a hundred yards into the lake. He's gotta be able to levitate."

"Levitation...?" I was skeptical.

"Marcus is right," Ava said. "Yapluma back home can use Air magic to make things fly through the air, including themselves. It could help us escape a bad situation during the games."

"You're telling me I can *fly*?" I gaped.

"Well, yeah," Ava said, like it was obvious. "I mean, probably not over the prison gates, because as soon as you get close enough the noxite will screw with your magic. But outside the Institute? For sure."

"And in here?" I asked.

"Well, this *is* the Elementai room," Ava mused. "These rooms are meant for us to explore our magic. I hardly feel any noxite. I think you should give it a try."

"Any chance you could offer me a theory lesson?" I asked.

Ava didn't sound amused. "I'm not Yapluma. You just... I don't know... manipulate the air currents around you."

"Let's start with something small," Kallie suggested. "Here, try this."

"Hey!" Marcus protested.

Rishi let out a high-pitched shriek, and Kallie swore under her breath. "Jerk," she growled at the cat.

"Yeah, frighten the cat to death," I deadpanned. "That's the way to do it."

"What about this leaf?" Ava asked as she snapped something off a nearby plant.

I cocked an eyebrow at her. "Is that a joke? Of course I can make a leaf fly!"

I swiped my hand through the air, and my magic swept up the leaf and took off with it.

"Perfect," Ava said. "If you can do that, you can levitate yourself."

I gestured to myself. "I'm not exactly a weightless leaf, pidge."

She sighed in frustration. "Just try it, Charlie. It should come naturally."

"Fine," I conceded through gritted teeth.

I walked to a part of the path that was more open, so I wouldn't hurt anybody. I took a few moments to take in my surroundings— the sound of the waterfall trickling into the pool, the birds chirping high above me, and the air buzzing at its magical frequency. I focused on the air and drew it closer to me, pressing the air particles together and creating a small whirlwind around myself. Air swept under my shoes, and my feet became unstable for a moment, though I didn't fall. I settled the air currents to maintain my balance, then tried again.

Air swirled beneath my feet, lifting my shoes from the pavement. I gasped as I went floating several inches into the air. I started to wobble, but I pulled more air particles toward me to keep me from tipping one way or the other.

I stabilized and let out a shocked laugh. "Ancestors, I'm doing it."

Ava clapped, and Oberi nickered. "Keep going, Charlie."

I willed myself to move higher, then shifted the air in another direction. I hovered forward at least three feet off the ground. It was amazing how free and weightless I felt. I figured I had what it took to push further, so I levitated myself higher.

Kallie's teasing voice came from far below me. "Don't hurt yourself up there!"

I teetered for show and plastered a look of terror on my face. Let's see how *she* liked being messed with. "Uh oh!"

I fell forward, tumbling quickly toward the ground. I sensed the plants and dirt approaching, and knew I had plenty of time to save myself.

Kallie and Ava screamed in unison, their voices echoing throughout the room. Just as I was about to plummet into the shallow pool, I caught myself with another air current. I shot back into the air, laughing.

"Charlie, you ass!" Kallie screamed from below.

"Get back down here," Ava insisted. "You're grounded until you learn to behave yourself!"

"Can't," I called back. I looped several times, always trusting my magic to catch me. Then I shot straight upward, arms held straight out at my sides. "I'm off to Neverland!"

I went zooming around the room, feeling totally and completely free. Ironic, considering I was locked in a prison, but for the first time in years, I felt like a kid again. It was like a dream.

Finally, after Ava and Kallie had their fill of yelling at me, I flew to the ground and landed.

"I'm impressed," Ava said.

I tilted my head at her. "I thought you said it was natural for Air elementals."

"Yeah, sure," she admitted. "But the flips and shit usually take some practice. I wonder if you have enough power to levitate one of us."

I shrugged. I was feeling pretty confident. "Might as well try."

"I volunteer!" Kallie offered immediately. "That looked mega fun."

"Don't you have wings?" Marcus asked her.

"In fae form," she admitted, though she sounded irritated.

"Shouldn't you have them in wolven form, too?" Marcus' question was innocent, but it set Kallie off.

"Yes, *asshole*," she growled. "I don't know why I got my fae wings and not my shifter wings. Maybe it's the fact that I'm a *girl* and I'm not supposed to be able to shift at all. It's whatever. If you know what's best for you, you don't ask a fae if they've earned their wings. It's insulting."

"Sorry," Marcus dragged out the word. "I didn't know."

"Anyway, this is different," Kallie said. "I want to see how Charlie's magic feels."

"I can't make any promises," I told her.

"Well, let's see what you *can* do."

Kallie stood ready, and my Air swirled around her. I could feel her stance by the way my magic resisted against her form. I repeated what I'd done with myself and sent air particles swirling beneath her feet. A small space formed between her shoes and the floor.

"Whoa!" she cried. Kallie wobbled, and I tried to stabilize her with my magic, but I couldn't anticipate her movements. I overcorrected, and she went flying straight into a tree. I winced as I heard her smash into it.

"Fuck the gods!" she screamed as she slumped to the ground.

"Kallie, hell..." I rushed over to her, but she shrugged me off. "I'm sorry."

"Ugh, forget about it," she said. "I'll fly myself around."

A *whoosh* sounded, then came the fluttering of her insect-like wings. Kallie jumped and took off, flying so close to me the air blew my hair back.

I turned to Ava, gaping. "Should I say something to her?"

Ava sighed. "Nah. Let her cool down. I think you hurt her pride more than anything. You can try me next."

"No," I declined immediately. I hated the thought of possibly hurting her. "I don't think I can do it. With myself, it's easy, but I couldn't track Kallie's movements. I don't want anyone getting hurt."

"Let's move on, then," Ava suggested. "We already know I'm a badass with Fire and Water. Marcus, what can you do?"

Marcus groaned from where he sat by Oberi. "I'm, uh... not feeling so great right now."

"Do you need a medic?" I asked.

"No," Marcus insisted. "I think it'll pass. Why don't you give Oberi a shot?"

At the sound of her name, Oberi perked up and shook out her mane. The sound of fire crackled.

I stroked her velvety nose as she came up to me. "Okay, Oberi. Show us what you've got."

Oberi blew a breath through her mouth, making her lips buzz together. Her hooves clicked on the path as she readied herself.

"Anytime now," I pressed.

Oberi swung her hips out so her giant ass slammed into my side. I fell on my face away from her, and I swore I heard her *laugh*— as much as a unicorn could, at least.

"She gets offended easily," Ava reminded me, amusement in her tone.

I rubbed my arm. "Yeah, I see that. Is she doing anything yet?"

"She's taking aim at a tree," Ava narrated. "And— ancestors!"

I felt it the moment Ava cursed. Heat exploded through the air, as if Oberi had turned into a fireball herself. A hot ball of fire whizzed through the air and made impact with the tree up ahead. My Earth magic sensed it go up in flame, but I didn't need magic to feel it. The tree blazed so hot I could feel the heat on my skin. My ears rang. I slapped my hands over them, but it didn't dull the ache pulsing through my head. It was excruciating.

"Put it out!" I cried to Ava. "The tree is in pain! Put it out!"

Ava quickly complied, and the room returned to a normal temperature. She stepped toward me and placed a gentle hand on my arm. "Charlie, are you okay?"

My hands shook as I dropped them from my ears. "The tree was screaming," I said breathlessly.

"That's the Nivita in you," Ava said. "I should've realized. But

Charlie, you should've seen it! Flames covered Oberi's whole body, and the fireball came out of her horn. It was beautiful."

"Yeah, well, it would've been prettier if she hadn't destroyed that tree," I argued.

Oberi heard me and sighed, almost like she agreed. The heat coming off her mane disappeared, and I felt a shift in her energy as she shrank to husky form.

"What's he doing?" I asked Ava.

Oberi's paws padded on the stone as he made his way over to the tree.

"He's placing his paws on the tree like he..." Ava trailed off.

I felt it through my magic. The twisting sensation in my gut eased, and I smelled the green scent of fresh leaves. Oberi was using *Earth magic* to heal the wounds on the tree. In the process, new leaves sprouted, and the tree must've grown another three feet.

I gaped as the magic consumed me. "I-I thought Oberi was Air, like me."

Ava seemed equally surprised. "You're a dual-caster, so I guess he has your Nivita side. We know he's a *mutabeecha* and can shift between genders and bodies. My aunt theorized he has a different form for each of the five Houses. I guess his husky form is Earth."

I barely had a moment to process this incredible information before Kallie landed and strolled up to us.

"Well, it looks like your Familiar has earned a spot on the team for the Darke Games." Kallie turned away from us and spoke to Marcus. "What can Rishi do?"

"What?" Marcus sounded clueless. "Nothing. He's just a cat."

Kallie blew a breath. "Lame. So, when do we get to practice simultension?"

"Simultension?" I repeated.

"Ava and I learned about it in class," Kallie explained.

"Yes, we should definitely try with everyone," Ava agreed. "Kallie and I melded our powers together and created elemental weapons. For a while, at least, as long as the illusion lasted."

Marcus finally got to his feet, apparently feeling better. "How's that possible?"

Ava was the one to answer. "Professor McCauley said it's a type of magic where different races can combine their powers."

"Sounds useful," I said thoughtfully. "What can our powers do together?"

"I don't know," Ava admitted. "Anything, I guess. McCauley said the possibilities were endless. We just have to get creative."

I shrugged. "Let's try it."

Ava tapped her foot and mumbled under her breath. "Mm... what can we do? Oh, I have an idea! Marcus can read minds, and Kallie can cast illusions. What if we combined those and cast whatever the person *wanted* to see!"

"That might help mask the illusion," Kallie said thoughtfully. "So they can't break it. Ava, you're a test subject."

"What? Me?" Ava balked.

"Yeah, it was your idea."

I remembered what Marcus had told me about his mind reading. I wasn't so sure this was a good plan.

"Maybe we should start with something else," Marcus suggested.

"You're well enough to read minds, aren't you?" Ava asked.

Kallie quickly added, "We haven't seen you do anything all day. Your turn to shine, Marcus."

Marcus sighed. "How does this simultension work, exactly?"

Kallie was the one to explain. "We'll intertwine our magic, so that it works as a unit. We should probably hold hands."

Marcus hesitated.

"Godsdammit, it's not like I have cooties," Kallie snapped.

"Okay." He sighed in defeat. "I'll *try* it."

"Ready whenever you are," Ava announced.

We stood there in silence for at least a whole minute, but nothing happened.

"You're resisting me, Marcus," Kallie told him. "Stop trying to project your magic on Ava, and focus on melding it with *mine*. This should be easy."

"It's not like I've ever done it," Marcus snapped.

Kallie huffed. "Just work with me here, okay?"

Another several beats passed. Oberi stood at my side dutifully, waiting patiently. I was starting to think this wasn't going to work.

"Something's happening," Ava said. "My vision is changing and—oh, for the love of all the ancestors, *turn it off!*"

"What'd you see?" Kallie asked in interest.

Ava sounded less than pleased. "Like you don't know. That is *not* what I pictured!"

"Actually, I *don't* know," Kallie insisted. "Marcus was the one pulling it from your mind. All I did was project what you wanted to see."

Ava cleared her throat. "Well, it wasn't... I, um... how about I spare you the details? I wouldn't want to corrupt your innocent minds."

Kallie legit cackled. "Oh, princess. You think I'm *innocent?* How sweet."

"Whatever," Ava snapped. "Let's move on."

Marcus came up beside me and elbowed me in the side. "She had eyes on you the whole time, bro."

My jaw dropped. "So she saw..."

I could only imagine what she'd seen, since Marcus could only read *dirty* thoughts— which Ava and Kallie didn't know about yet. My pulse picked up double time, but I quickly told it to calm down.

Ava had been right. That wasn't something she wanted to see.

"I'm sure it was a mistake," I muttered to Marcus. My stomach twisted, and I wanted nothing more than to move on. I raised my voice so the girls could hear. "What can we try next?"

"Charlie hasn't had a chance to try simultension," Ava said thoughtfully. "But what can we fuse with Air or Earth?"

"Your Fire?" I suggested.

Kallie sounded thoughtful. "I don't think simultension works with people of the same magical race."

"It has to," Ava argued. "Maybe you just have to be strong enough to do it."

"And you think we are?" I asked.

"Charlie," she sighed. "You just flew around the room no problem on your first try. I think we can handle it."

I shrugged. "I guess it's worth a shot. What's the objective?"

Ava thought about it a moment. "We can't exactly light the air on fire, so we'll have to work with Earth."

I groaned. "Another tree?"

"It won't hurt it if we do it right," Ava promised. "That's how simul-tension works. We combine our powers to become one."

I felt like I could do it, with Ava at least, but I didn't know where to start. Ava took the lead for me. She approached and took my hand, then led me forward.

"We'll try it on this tree," she offered. She guided my hand to the trunk of the tree, and I ran my fingers up and down the bark. It was smooth, unlike any tree I'd felt before. I might not have realized it was a plant if I didn't feel the life of it pulsing against my Earth magic.

"What kind of tree is this?" I asked.

"It's a magical tree that grows only on Darke Island," she told me. "We learned about it in my Alchemy class. The buds are used for different potions."

"What should I do?" I asked.

"Focus on strengthening the tree," Ava suggested. "I'll work my Fire power on it, but we have to make sure it's strong enough to take it. Are you ready?"

I nodded. "I think so."

Ava and I locked hands again, and her fingers began to warm in mine. I kept my other hand pressed to the tree. I worked my magic into it, feeding it with nourishment from the ground. I could feel it growing beneath my touch.

Ava's hand heated even more, but it wasn't so hot that I couldn't take it. Her magic swelled and seemed to move through me until—

I jumped back as flames ignited across the tree bark. It had singed the hair on my arm, but I was apparently the only one who couldn't handle it. This tree didn't scream like the other one had. It seemed perfectly content with the fire consuming its base and crackling off its leaves.

Ava and I had done it. We'd made our magic become one.

"Wow, Charlie," she breathed beside me. "The tree is on fire, but it's not burning. It's like it created a Fire shield around it and is protecting it. It's— look out!"

Ava grabbed my shoulder and yanked me downward. We barely had time to flatten ourselves to the ground before something *whooshed* by over our heads. A wave of heat traveled over us.

"Was that—?" I started to say, but Marcus cut me off.

"The tree is alive!" he cried.

"Fuck!" Ava screamed, scrambling to her feet. "That's *not* supposed to happen."

"Your magic must've done something to it," Kalina said through heavy breaths.

"Done what?" Ava asked. "Made it grow a conscience?"

"I don't know but— oh, gods!"

Kallie's cry alerted me to another incoming attack. Only this time, the tree didn't aim its branches at us. The ground beneath us began to shake, and the surrounding trees seemed to groan in pain as the sentient one tugged at their roots.

Snap!

Dirt flew everywhere, splattering into my face. The tree was uprooting itself!

"Charlie, get back!" Ava cried.

She shoved me backward, but like hell was I letting her put herself in the line of fire.

"I'm Earth," I argued. "I'll handle this."

"I have to put the fire out," she insisted. "Charlie, if you don't run—"

"Ahhh!" Marcus' scream of terror tore through the greenhouse.

"The tree's got Marcus!" Kallie screamed.

His scream traveled through the air as the tree launched Marcus forward. I caught him with my Air power, but heat seared my magic. Marcus' clothes were on fire! I quickly set him down into the pool, and the fire hissed out. Meanwhile, Kalina threw battle orbs at the tree, but all they did was explode against its trunk with minor *bang*s.

"What are we going to do?" Kallie shouted.

"Hang on!" Ava called back. "I just have to— ancestors!"

Roots slapped against the path, and twigs snapped as the tree took off running through the greenhouse. Oberi barked loudly, but it did nothing to slow it down.

"We have to do something before it escapes!" I yelled. I took off running after it, but for a tree, it was pretty dang fast. You know, since they weren't supposed to move *at all*. We couldn't have picked a worse tree in the whole greenhouse. I should've protested the second Ava said it was magical. Of course this was going to blow up in our faces.

I summoned Air and drew it away from the area surrounding the tree. If I could suffocate the fire, maybe the tree would stop.

Ava's footsteps sounded from a distant path, then rounded back in my direction. "Keep going, Charlie! We've got it cornered."

I willed the tree to stop moving, but I only slowed it down. I couldn't concentrate on Earth magic while trying to use my Air magic to suffocate the fire.

The heat in the air seemed to cool, and I knew Ava and I were making progress. I twisted my hands, pushing my magic harder, until we finally broke through. The temperature returned to normal.

"Charlie, the tree!" Ava cried.

Branches cracked, and the trunk groaned. We'd put the fire out and stopped the tree, but it was uprooted. It had no leg to stand on.

"Timber!" Marcus shouted.

"It's going down!" Kallie yelled at the same time.

I tried to work quickly, to force its roots back into the ground, but it wasn't fast enough. The tree toppled. I heard the glass shatter first, then came the *boom* of the tree slamming into the ground. The greenhouse floor shook beneath my feet, and cool air rushed in through the broken window.

"Fuck!" Ava cried. "Vandalism will get us all thrown in Cellblock 9!"

"Shit," Marcus muttered. "I can't be searched right now. I've still got Contraband in my stash."

"You idiot," Kallie growled. "You were supposed to get rid of that!"

"I did... for a while."

"We can use magic to repair it, right?" I asked desperately. The last thing I wanted was for us to get into trouble. "Kallie can turn illusions into reality, so we just have to clean this up and fix the window—"

"Hey!" a deep voice boomed from the opposite side of the greenhouse. "Who's in here!?"

"Too late," Ava breathed. "The guards already found us."

"Calm down, everyone," Marcus insisted. "I know what to do."

"What?" I growled. He sure was taking his sweet time to explain.

"Run!" Marcus screamed.

Nobody questioned it. We all rushed toward the broken window in unison, because coming back the way we came was obviously not an option. We'd run into guards on the way there for sure.

"Quickly," I hissed.

Judging from the huge breeze coming in, the hole in the window had to be huge, since the entire side of the greenhouse was made of glass. I helped Ava through first, and then Kallie. Marcus, Rishi, and Oberi quickly followed. I ducked out behind them and raced across the prison yard.

"Into the trees," Ava huffed.

"I'm casting a cloaking illusion!" Kallie said. "So they won't see us run."

"Good idea," I said through labored breaths. "Let's get to cover as quickly as we can, just in case."

The team closed in on me on all sides. We ran faster, and I felt the trees up ahead. *Almost there...*

My Air magic felt everything that happened next. Rishi must've not been looking where he was going, because as soon as we reached the trees, he shifted course and darted in front of Marcus. Marcus screamed, and Rishi let out a howl. He tumbled to the ground, and Kallie quickly followed. Ava yelped as she tripped over the two of them, and I was only a split-second behind. I nearly crushed Ava as I fell, but I barely had a chance to process it before Oberi was on top of me.

He shook his head, getting slobber everywhere. After a moment, he started jumping on us, like this was some sort of a game.

"Oberi!" I gasped as his paw sank into my groin. "Oberi, get off!"

The husky jumped off of me, but I could hardly move after the blow I'd just taken to the crotch. I rolled off Ava so I wouldn't hurt her, and lay on the forest floor, panting.

Nobody else moved, either. We lay there in silence, as if waiting for the sound of guards to follow. But it was quiet, all except for the wind rustling the trees above us.

Finally, Kallie broke the silence. "That cat is going to kill us, Marcus."

"Rishi's harmless," he argued.

I waited for Ava to say something, but instead, she broke into a fit of laughter. It was quiet at first, but it soon became too much that she clutched her stomach and rolled over so she was pressed into my side. "Ancestors!" she laughed. "That was..."

She trailed off, unable to finish her sentence. After a few moments, Oberi started laughing, too, though he more or less sounded like a hyena. Marcus couldn't help but giggle, and Kallie's laughter soon followed.

It was infectious. Soon, even I was laughing at the absurdity of it all.

"We're failures," Ava laughed. I wasn't sure if she actually found it funny, or if it was just so sad you either had to laugh or cry. "We're utter failures."

"But we had fun," I said, unable to believe the words were actually coming from my mouth. "That's what counts, right?"

Ava's laughter settled. "Yeah, Charlie. That's what counts."

"Okay, I agree, watching Marcus roll into the pool and possessing him with a sex demon was hilarious," Kallie agreed. "But none of this is going to help us win the Games."

"Hey, we were doing perfectly fine before the sex demon," Marcus teased.

"Ugh," I groaned. "What are we doing, guys?"

"I believe it's called *training*," Marcus joked.

The laughter continued for another few moments, but it quickly died. Ava curled up beside me, and I instinctually ran my fingers through her hair. I stopped the moment I realized what I was doing.

The atmosphere between the group suddenly changed, like we all realized at once how serious this was. The Darke Games were a death sentence if we didn't know what we were doing.

I just hoped we got our shit together in time.

EIGHTEEN

"**A**va-Marie, if your mother and I get another notice of a dress-code violation, I'm going to lose it."

"It's *fine*, Daddy."

I twirled the phone cord around my finger, on the receiving end of another lecture. I looked out the window to see the lightest snowfall. It'd be gone in a few hours, as Darke Island didn't really get that cold, but it was nice to have snow on December first.

Daddy impatiently sighed at the other end of the line. "Why in the world would you think that socks that said *fuck you* are an appropriate addition to your uniform?"

"Well, I thought that everyone should know."

Daddy groaned. "The Hawkei Civil War was a warm-up for raising you."

I couldn't help but let out a mischievous smile. "Just wait until everyone sees me kick butt in the Darke Games."

Daddy let out a couple swear words. "Ava, I don't agree with this."

"You don't have to agree! Just support me." I rubbed my eyes. Daddy and I had been going back and forth about the Games ever since he found out that I signed up, and so far, his attempts to talk me out of it were nothing short of annoying.

"It's dangerous. One of the reasons your mother and I fought in the war is so you and your siblings wouldn't have to partake in deadly competitions. The Darke Games sound like an even worse version of the Elemental Cup."

"I have to do this, Daddy. You don't understand."

"Peanut, I sentenced you to the Institute because I wanted you to *stay there*," Daddy said sternly. "When your mother was looking for answers to her own prophecy, all the clues we needed were right there at Orenda Academy. The Institute could provide the same answers to your own prophecy. The school might be hiding secrets. What sense does it make to end your own sentence, then stay on Darke Island looking for clues that might be in the wrong place?"

"Daddy, I get your motives, but we don't have any proof that my own prophecy is connected to the Institute in any way," I insisted. "The Institute is a distraction. I'm not backing out of the Darke Games now."

"Just think about what I said, all right?" Daddy paused. "Your mother wants to talk to you. I have to go. I'm late for a meeting. Love you, peanut."

Mama came on the line. "Hi, sweetheart. How are things?"

"They're okay," I said, thinking of our disastrous practice for the Games the other day. It'd been fun, but my team had totally bombed. No matter what I said to Daddy, I was worried about how this whole thing was going to go.

"Just okay? Hm."

I rolled my eyes. "Don't be like that. I'm competing in the Games, and that's final."

"And if that's what you want to do, I'll back you up," Mama said. "I'm always here for whatever you need."

I gave a skeptical noise. "Yeah, well, Daddy could do the same, but he's not."

"Never mind your father. You know he complains, but he's behind you all the way."

I kept quiet, and Mama filled the silence. "Ezekiel got his powers. A little late, but now he's casting Water like a natural."

"That's so great!" I'd been worried about him— a semester at Orenda Academy without any magic had to be uncomfortable.

"And we received the school paper," Mama went on. "You and Charlie look adorable."

The Institute sent out a monthly review to all the parents who still gave a damn. Mine and Charlie's Halloween costumes had made the front page.

Mama brought up Charlie all the time. It was so different from Daddy, who liked to pretend he didn't exist.

I chewed on my lip as I pondered what to say. I wanted to talk to Mama about how I felt, but how would she react? Nobody wanted their daughter with a convict— even if she was one herself.

I decided to let it fly. "Mama, I think I'm in love with a criminal."

"Hmm. Are you now?"

Her answer was so cryptic, I couldn't tell what she thought. "Maybe. It's hard to sort out my feelings."

"It wouldn't happen to be Charlie, would it?"

Ancestors, Mama was good with shit like this. It was like she had a fucking radar. "How did you know?"

"You talk about him quite a bit. He seems like a nice young man."

Yeah, and I'm sure everyone else back home talked about Charlie and me a lot, too. I bet Auntie Imogen and Uncle Jonah gossiped constantly about it. "He's really sweet, Mama. But I don't know if he feels the same. Also, I kind of hate him at the same time I like him. Is that weird?"

"I don't think it's odd," Mama mused. "If he likes you, you'll know."

"You don't know Charlie." Guy was secretive as all hell. Reading his feelings was like trying to read a brick wall.

"But I know you two share a bond, and he's probably just as lonely as you are," Mama said. "Give it some time."

The old phone crackled. "Sweetheart, are you *sure* that the Darke Games are what you want to do?"

"Yes, Mama. I'm not backing out."

"Okay. That's all I wanted to know." I heard Maverick yell from inside the garage, and Mama said, "Oh, damn. Your brother set the bike on fire again. I have to go. See you soon, Ava."

The line went dead, and I sighed as I hung the phone back up. At least I knew Mama liked Charlie, but what would Daddy say if he knew about my true feelings? He made it clear he hated Charlie with a passion.

It was hard to think that what Daddy felt didn't matter. I really— *really*— liked Charlie, but I don't know if I could be with someone my father didn't approve of. His blessing meant everything to me.

I started back to my dorm, feeling grumpy as fuck. None of this mattered anyway. Charlie didn't like me. If he did, he would've shown some interest by now, and nothing had happened. I wasn't the kind of girl who chased after guys. Guys chased me, and I didn't want to embarrass myself falling all over someone who clearly hated my guts.

Speak of the devil. I was hanging up Christmas decorations in my room when Charlie came walking in. I couldn't hang any of my decorations that I'd used at home— they were *dangerous weapons* or something stupid the Institute had decided— so I'd made a bunch of my own. Paper snowflakes and red and green paper garlands hung from the ceiling and on every open patch of wall.

Charlie was so tall he walked right into a garland. It wrapped around his neck and nearly knocked him backward. He made a choking sound as he wrenched it off.

"Ancestors, would you get a hold of yourself?" I asked. "How do you expect to win the Darke Games if you get taken out by a fucking Christmas decoration?"

Charlie reached up and felt all the snowflakes I had hanging from the ceiling. "Holy hell, it's like Christmas Town in here!"

"I'm Christmas crazy," I said. "My birthday is on December twenty-fifth, which means all of December is about *me*, and also, Jesus."

"Uh, my birthday's on the twenty-first, so your logic's way off on that one," Charlie replied.

We shared the same birthday month, too? Charlie practically mirrored me in every way.

Oberi strolled behind Charlie in his husky form. He had a big red bow around his neck that I'd tied on earlier, and was parading it around like he was a king with a new crown. He wasn't looking where he was going and bumped into my desk. He growled, rubbing his head with his paw.

"How'd your talk with your parents go?" Charlie knew I always spoke with my family on Saturdays.

"Daddy wanted to nag at me, *again*," I told him. "He went on and on about how the Darke Games were just like the Elemental Cup, and he didn't want me to compete."

"What's the Elemental Cup?" Charlie asked.

"It's a coming-of-age competition that seals the bond between you and your Familiar. Every Elementai has to participate," I explained. "Back when my parents were kids, it used to be a deadly competition. You'd go out into the wilderness, and the Elders would pit magic against you. A lot of people died. My parents barely made it out alive. They fought in the war so no more kids had to die."

I shrugged. "The Elemental Cup still happens, and it's hard, but nobody dies anymore. I thought I'd get my chance to compete this year with Oberi, but since we're at the Institute, guess not."

"Well, maybe the Darke Games can be our way to seal the bond with Oberi," Charlie suggested.

Maybe... but when he said that, I immediately recoiled. Sealing the bond with Oberi would only bring me closer to Charlie, and if he didn't feel the same way about me, it would only hurt. I kinda wanted to keep my distance.

Charlie leaned against the wall. "Marcus and I are going down to the Villain's Den to people watch. We take bets on what they're gonna do. Wanna come?"

"That's okay. I'm just gonna chill out here," I said.

"Oh." Did he sound disappointed? No. Had to be just my imagination.

Charlie turned toward the door. "Well, I'll leave Oberi with you. It's your day to have him."

"Thanks." I felt relief when Charlie finally left my presence. Oberi whined and put his paw on my thigh, and I stroked his ears back. "Guess it's just you and me, huh puppy?"

Oberi sneezed snot all over my hand. *Gross.*

I was still decorating my room that afternoon when Kallie ran inside. "Girl, I've been looking for you all day. Why are you in here being socially awkward?"

"Uh, I just had stuff to do," I lied. "What's up?"

"I thought we could go get dresses! You know, for the Darke Ball?" Kallie asked. "Everyone around here calls it the Villain's Ball. It's a dance the school hosts after the Darke Games are over."

That got my attention. I *loved* dressing up, and there was nothing better than a big, poofy gown. Prom had practically been the highlight of my life— and I'd only gotten one, seeing as how I'd been homeschooled my senior year. A ball sounded fucking amazing— and a Villain's Ball, with an evil, creepy theme, sounded even better.

"How are we supposed to get dresses? Students can't leave campus unless it's on supervised field trips," I said.

"The school has a temporary consignment shop set up in one of the classrooms. People in Shade Hills donate their old dresses and suits for students to use for free," Kallie said. "I figure we should go through them before all the good ones are taken."

"Ooh, let's go."

When we got to the classroom, I saw that it was filled with racks upon racks of beautiful, dresses just waiting to be tried on in the makeshift dressing rooms the school had set up. There was a rack of suits for guys, too, but there were a lot more girls in here than boys. Gushing sounds of women rang throughout the shop as everyone found their perfect dress.

Opal was working the front counter. She waved us over. "Hey, guys," she said. "Here to find a dress?"

"Yeah. What are you wearing to the ball?" I asked.

Opal blushed. "Um... I don't think I'm going. No one's asked me."

"Come with us! You don't need a date," Kallie insisted.

"I really don't think so," Opal said. "It's probably best if I sit out."

I frowned. I really wanted Opal to be there, but I couldn't make her attend the ball if she didn't want to.

"What kind of dress are you looking for?" Kallie asked as we rummaged through the options available. Oberi stuck his head out between a bunch of tulle skirts, and I laughed.

"Um, well, I like pastels, pink especially," I said. "And florals. Lots of rhinestones and glitter. And it's gotta be a big skirt. Like, five feet across minimum."

"Don't know if you're gonna find that here." Kallie tilted her head. "I've literally been to a million royal balls in my life. I'm tired of wearing big, fancy dresses. I want to wear something naughty."

"Like this?" I held up a slinky red dress with a plunging neckline that went all the way down to the waist.

Kallie's eyes sparked. "Exactly." She ran into the dressing room to try it on. When she came out, my eyes widened in appreciation.

"Damn, girl. You've got some nice boobs," I said.

"You think so?" Kallie turned as she looked in the mirror. "Do you think Marcus will like it?"

Why did that matter? "Your goods are on full display, so I'd say so." I giggled.

Out of the corner of my eye, I noticed Naya eyeing the dress with jealousy. She hated how good Kallie looked.

"Then I'm totally getting it." Kallie looked at the bundle of dresses in my arms. "Think you've got enough to try on?"

"Not nearly." I headed into a dressing room. I tried on a white dress with a black bow, and a purple dress with a flared skirt, but neither of them fit right. I slipped on dress after dress, and yet nothing felt good.

I came out in a silver dress that totally washed me out. Kallie shook her head no. There was a rustling sound in the corner as Oberi went through a bunch of cardboard boxes full of fancy hats. He clenched his teeth and waved a wide-brimmed sun hat in the air, making a whining sound at Kallie.

"Apparently he loves hats." I laughed. Kallie went to help Oberi, switching the hats out for him. He made faces in the mirror as Kallie switched from a fascinator to a fedora, fluttering his eyelashes like a model.

Oberi kept changing back and forth between his unicorn form and husky form, trying on the hats and seeing which ones looked best in which form. Finally, Oberi changed into a unicorn. Kallie put a long black veil on her head, decorated with fake black roses that congregated around her horn. She gave a nicker and stomped her hoof. Apparently, that was her Villain Ball look.

"You're too cute, Oberi." I headed back inside the dressing room and continued my endless dress raid. I found I was too skinny for most of the dresses. They fell right off me. I guess Charlie was right and I had lost a lot of weight this semester. I'd barely noticed.

When I came out wearing a neon green dress, Kallie scrunched her nose. "It's pretty, but it's not you."

"I know." I sighed. This was impossible. I really wanted the perfect look for the ball, but none of these even came close to what I had in my head.

Kallie had her dress hanging on one arm. Just at that moment, Naya walked by. She saw the dress on Kallie's arm, then reached out and snatched it for herself.

"Hey!" Kallie shouted. "That was mine!"

"I saw it first," Naya sneered as she bundled the dress in her arms. "I tried it on earlier, and was thinking about getting it before *you* took it from me."

"It was hanging on the rack. No one wanted it," Kallie snapped back.

"Well, I do, so keep your filthy hands off of it," Naya threatened. "That is, if you know what's good for you."

I could see an illusion spell sparking at Kallie's fingers. I stepped in, before she could hurt Naya and get us both into trouble. "It's okay, Kallie. We'll find you a *better* dress," I said, with a nasty look at Naya.

Naya wore this disgusting sneer of victory. She walked away to join Danielle.

Kallie raged, "Why does she get away with everything? I really wanted that dress."

"It had a snag in it. I noticed when you tried it on," I said. "We can do better."

Kallie scowled. "But I'm helping *you* find a dress. You can't go to the ball without one."

"It's fine. I don't think I'm going to find anything I like here, anyway." I changed again, and Kallie and I began looking through the racks once more. We'd searched through the whole shop, and my heart had nearly fallen as I realized there was nothing else Kallie could wear that fit her dream look.

"What about this?" Kallie pulled out a black dress, and my interest piqued as I looked at it. It had all kinds of geometrical shapes cut out of the bodice and a slit going up the skirt.

"Daring," I commented. "Try it on."

When Kallie came out of the dressing room again, my jaw *dropped.* The black dress was way more revealing than the red one. The geometrical slits all over the bodice exposed her midriff and back, covering only her breasts. The slit in the skirt barely stopped just before her panties. I wasn't sure if that dress was actually a dress or just lingerie, but she looked *amazing* in it.

"Do I look okay?" Kallie turned nervously as she looked in the mirror.

"Okay? It's phenomenal!" I exclaimed. "If Marcus was going to be drooling when he saw you in the first dress, he's going to pass out at the sight of you in this one, because it is totally *hawt.*"

That seemed to make up her mind. "I think this is perfect. Let's go, before Naya steals this one off me, too."

Kallie carried out her new dress in a paper bag, while I left empty-handed— save for Oberi's veil. I wasn't sure what I was going to wear to the ball. I could have Mama send me a dress I had at home... but at the same time, I didn't want to wear something I'd already worn. I wanted something new.

"Do you want to get coffee down at Commissary?" Kallie asked. "I seriously need a boost."

"Sure." Oberi whinnied at my response. She *loved* coffee.

Commissary was set up like a student shop near the lunch room. It was almost like a mini-grocery store. There was a small coffee shop inside, along with a couple of coolers for drinks and a few rows of snacks. Commissary was bought with points. You either earned them as a reward in class, or your parents put money on your ID card. Everything you bought in Commissary was purchased with your ID. Students weren't allowed to carry cash money at the Institute, but most of us hid a few dollars under our mattresses and such in spite of the rules.

Despona was behind the coffee counter, grinding coffee beans. I scanned the menu. There were blood drinks for vampires, specialty drinks for angels, and other magical concoctions in every flavor you could think of. I mostly stuck to the basics— magical properties added to my drinks fucked pretty bad with my bipolar meds.

"I think I'll take a white chocolate latte," I told Despona. "Extra whipped cream. And an iced caramel macchiato for Oberi."

"I'll have a vanilla hazelnut frappe," Kallie added.

"Coming right up." Despona made our coffees, then handed them to us with a fanged smile. "So, you guys ready for the Darke Games? My team and I have been working non-stop to win."

"You're participating in the Darke Games too?" I asked in surprise.

"Yeah. I've made a team with Alice, Carson, and Wesley," Despona said.

"Well, good luck," I said. If we didn't win, I hoped Despona and her team did. They deserved to get out of here.

Though, if I was honest, they were kind of the underdog team. No one on that team was particularly powerful. I worried they didn't stand a chance of staying alive, let alone winning the competition.

We swiped our ID cards for our coffees, then sat down at a table inside Commissary. "Aren't the four of them all innocent?" Kallie asked me.

"Yeah," I said. "None of them deserve to be here."

"Isn't it a little weird that most of their stories involve an attempted abduction of some sort?" Kallie asked. "It's like there's something going on."

My stomach tumbled, thinking of the time those two guys had nearly pulled Monica and I into that van. "There might be, but it's not exactly uncommon to get kidnapped. I mean, not with the people around here, right?"

"I guess so."

Oberi lapped at his mug, getting whipped cream all over his face.

"I thought dogs couldn't have coffee," Kallie commented as she watched Oberi.

"Familiars are a bit different," I said. "And Oberi is a *mutabeecha*, a changeling creature. I haven't seen him eat anything that makes him sick yet."

"Fae have changelings in our culture, too, though they're not as cute as Oberi." Kallie patted Oberi, and he burped. "It's crazy that you have such a rare Familiar. I've never heard of *mutabeecha* before."

I shrugged. "I don't think it's odd I got a unique Familiar. Weird stuff happens around me."

"Like what?" Kallie raised her eyebrows.

"Like..." I took a breath. "I haven't really thought about this since I was a kid. But... when I was five or so, I remember this strange voice, calling out to me in the woods. I live on an island, but once I heard the voice, I blinked, and I was on the mainland. I didn't recall how I got there, either."

"Wow." Kallie's expression widened. "That's insane."

"I know, right?" I paused as I mused on that night. The voice I'd heard hadn't been part of my psychosis— at least, I didn't think it was. It didn't explain how I'd gotten from my island to the mainland, or why I couldn't remember.

"What happened after that?" Kallie asked.

"I'm... not sure." I scratched my head. "The memory is fuzzy, but I remember walking through the woods in my pajamas. I wasn't sure where I was going. Then this... *thing* came out of the trees."

I shuddered. "I don't recall exactly what it looked like, but it was literally so scary. It was big, and dark... gnashing teeth and red eyes. I pissed myself, I remember that. I was so terrified, I cried and screamed. I thought for sure it was going to eat me alive. Then..."

I glanced at Oberi. He looked up with a wagging tail. "Something came from behind to protect me. It growled, and tackled the black shape. Some sort of brown blur. I didn't stick around to see what it was. I ran for it. By this time, my parents had half of Kinpago looking for me. I was so terrified I didn't speak for three days. My mom couldn't convince me to go outside for a month. Everyone thought that I must've run into a dragon or something, though they couldn't figure out how I got to the mainland on my own."

"Do you think it *was* a dragon?" Kallie asked.

I shook my head. "No. I was never afraid of dragons, or any other magical creature. This thing was sinister. Like it was straight out of hell."

The strange pair of blue eyes I saw when my dad was healed... the monster I saw in the woods, and the big creature that had fought it off... why had I seen such strange creatures as a child, and why did they seem attracted to me?

"You know... this is gonna sound crazy, but weird stuff happens around me, too," Kallie confessed. "When I was really little, I was playing with my brother in the parlor room. It was early morning, just after breakfast."

Kallie blinked. "Then all of a sudden... it was nighttime. We're talking pitch black midnight. I was completely alone. Then this sorceress appeared. She was beautiful— silver hair with blue wings. I'd never seen her before. She smiled at me, and once she did, it went back to daytime again. My brother was there and everything... as if nothing had happened at all."

"Damn," I said. "That's really intense."

"Isn't it?" Kallie blushed. "My mom's a really powerful sorceress, so I know I must've inherited some of her talent. But some of the stuff that happens around me is just plain odd. I've never told anyone about it, because I'm worried people will think I'm crazy."

"Do you think you had a vision?" I asked.

Kallie made a skeptical sound. "I don't know. It seemed so real... but I couldn't explain it."

"At least we can be weird together," I offered. "It's better than going at it alone."

"I'll drink to that." Kallie clinked her coffee cup against mine. The doors to Commissary opened. Marcus and Charlie walked in, Rishi balancing on Marcus' shoulder. Marcus tugged on Charlie's arm, and they wandered our way.

"Hey girls," Marcus said. "You know, Kallie, there's this dance thing, and—"

"Marcus, you're my date to the ball," Kallie said, without any sort of greeting.

Marcus' eyes popped out. "What?"

"I don't have a date, and I'm not going alone," Kallie said. "You're a slightly less embarrassing option than everyone else, so make sure you wear something suitable. You have to make me look good."

Marcus blushed, but he didn't object further. I resisted rolling my eyes. Kallie made it sound like Marcus was her last option as a date, but I wasn't fooled. He was for sure her first choice.

"Charlie, are you going to the Villain's Ball?" I asked.

He shrugged. "I don't have anything to wear."

"Go to the consignment shop. Suits are free," I suggested.

He paused, as if considering it. "I don't have anyone to go with."

"Well, neither do I," I said, a twinge of irritation working into my tone.

"Maybe you'll find someone," he said.

Ugh. This guy couldn't take a hint. This was a huge signal that he *for sure* didn't like me. Otherwise, why wouldn't he ask to be my date?

"You know, we shouldn't split Oberi up," I suggested. "He has an outfit for the ball and everything. It wouldn't be fair to make him go back and forth between us all night."

Charlie's jaw worked. "Do you... want to go together?"

Fucking finally. "Yeah. I guess that's cool."

"Don't act too excited," Charlie mumbled under his breath.

"Geez, I said it was cool! Don't take it that way."

Charlie blew out a breath. "Come on, Marcus. I need to get a suit."

"Something tailored, please!" I called out. Charlie flipped me off as he left, Marcus scuttling behind.

Kallie sipped at her coffee and eyed me. "You hoping for something to happen on ball night?"

"Psh. Please," I scoffed. Charlie wasn't interested. He was going with me out of obligation.

But then... if that was true, why had he been smiling on his way out?

CHARLIE WAS in a bad mood the next day. I thought it was because of me, but as we were studying together in my dorm that afternoon, I realized the stress of our upcoming exams was getting to him. I was reading some keywords from his textbook out to him, so he memorized it before his big test. Oberi sat at our feet and chewed on the dog toy we'd stolen from Contraband.

"This is useless. I'm not going to pass," Charlie said. "The exam is a written one, and my teacher's not letting me use a computer to type up an essay. She wants them *handwritten*."

"What if you can convince her to make an exception?" I asked.

He scoffed. "Yeah, right. I'm failing Juvenile Justice. My teacher's such a dick. She doesn't provide me with any accommodation."

I frowned. "Don't give up. You'll pass."

"Sure." Charlie sighed. "Or I'll just flunk out of the Institute like I flunked out of high school."

"I'm not going to let that happen. We're walking across that graduation stage together."

Charlie didn't say anything. I reached under my mattress and pulled out my phone. I scrolled through it, then pressed *play* on one of my playlists. The first one that came on was one of Charlie's favorites. I jumped up from my bed and began dancing around the room. Oberi barked and followed me, rising on his hind paws to hop behind.

"What the hell are you doing?" Charlie asked as I gave another hip thrust.

"I have to take short dance breaks while studying," I said. "You wouldn't get it."

I grabbed his hand and tugged. "Come on! Join me!"

"I... don't dance," Charlie said with a shaky laugh. "I can't exactly see what I'm doing. I'm afraid I'll look stupid."

"You *have* to dance at the ball," I begged. "I'll teach you."

Charlie hesitated. "Maybe later."

My heart fell. Charlie was so concerned with what others thought of him. It stopped him from having fun.

Charlie stood up. "We should get something to eat. It's almost dinnertime, anyway."

"Yeah, I suppose." I turned my phone off and hid it again. I wasn't giving up on this dancing thing. Charlie was going to learn how to shake his ass, or my name wasn't Ava-Marie Mitoh.

We walked to the cafeteria. "So, do you know what you're wearing to the ball?" Charlie asked.

I huffed. "No. I looked, but I couldn't find a dress I liked. I'm not sure what I'm going to wear."

"I suppose it's a good thing we showed up."

I knew that voice. I could hardly believe my ears. Tears came to my eyes as I realized that Mama and Daddy were standing right there, in the flesh. They wore lanyards with tags, certifying they'd gone through security and had a visitors' pass. Mama was carrying a big duffel bag, which she had slung over her shoulder.

"Ancestors!" I screamed and jumped on both of them. I hugged them so tightly I thought my arms would break. I missed them *so much.* After all this time, I could finally see them again.

Daddy laughed. "Hello, peanut."

All the bad stuff that happened over the last semester didn't matter. I was in Daddy's arms, and that made everything okay. Oberi barked and ran around us in a circle, going nuts.

As I pulled away, Mama brushed back my hair. "We thought we'd surprise you."

"Hello, Mister and Mrs. Mitoh," Charlie said in a dull tone. He wasn't exactly thrilled they'd arrived.

"Hello, Charlie," Mama said kindly. "I hope you've had a nice semester."

Charlie shrugged and mirrored my dad by not saying anything. The two of them acted so cold toward one another it was awkward.

"What are you doing here?" I asked. I couldn't believe they were right before my eyes. This had to be some kind of dream.

"We're staying in town. We came to watch you in the Darke Games," Mama said. "Your siblings couldn't come, per Institute rules, but they wish you luck."

"*And* we came to supervise the dance, as the school asked for chaperones," Daddy added, with a side glance at Charlie. Good thing he couldn't see it, because Daddy's stare was absolutely glowering.

Ancestors, Daddy, I'm not going to sex Charlie up on the dance floor, I thought. He was sure acting like it.

I grabbed both of their hands and pulled them along. "Come on! I need to show you *everything* about my school!"

I walked along the hallways, pointing at everything and anything that I could. "That's the Alchemy classroom. Professor Hemlock is my *favorite* teacher. She's okay if I brew poisons so long as I dump them out later. And there's the Villain's De— I mean— the *rec room.* It's really nice in there if you don't mind the spiders and rats. Oh, and don't go down that way. The astronomy hallway is really isolated, so it's the best place to get stabbed. Like, three people have died down there this semester."

"Uh... sounds wonderful, peanut," Daddy said. He gave a look to Mama, who shook her head.

As we rounded back to the cafeteria, Charlie asked, "Are either of you hungry? We could have dinner together."

He was just trying to be polite, but Mama said, "I think that'd be nice."

Tonight's dinner was spaghetti and meatballs. Daddy looked grossed out by the soggy noodles. Charlie piled a plate high for the both of us. As we sat down and both Charlie and I began eating, Daddy asked, "You two... share a plate?"

"Oh, it's just this thing we do," I explained. I didn't want to tell them that we'd fallen into this habit because it was the only way Charlie could make sure I was eating. That felt too personal— some things were just for Charlie and me.

Daddy huffed. "Sounds like a good way to share germs."

"It's fine, Liam," Mama scolded. Mama hardly cared that I was sharing a plate with Charlie. She was just happy I was eating.

Oberi had his own plate of spaghetti and meatballs. He wolfed it down, then set his saucy mouth on Daddy's leg, staining his pants with marinara. Daddy sighed but didn't object.

After we were finished with dinner, Mama leaned in. "Sweetheart, can we talk to you privately? There are some things we should discuss as a family."

My insides flip-flopped. Was something wrong? "Sure. See you later, Charlie."

"See you." Charlie walked off with Oberi, clearly happy to be excused.

I got up from the table and led my parents to the prison yard. There were a lot of people out here, but I found a bench by an isolated spot and sat down. Mama sat across from me, while Daddy stood with crossed arms, like he was going to beat up anyone who got within a few feet of my presence.

I rolled my eyes. "Daddy, you're not my bodyguard. I've been here for months and nothing has happened."

"These are dangerous prisoners," he rebutted. "I'm just keeping watch."

"*I'm* a dangerous prisoner! I'm here, aren't I?" I asked. He was being ridiculous.

Daddy huffed. Mama rushed to say something before we could argue. "Ava, the truth is, the Games aren't the only reason we came," she confessed. "We thought we'd spend the next few weeks searching Darke Island for clues on your prophecy."

My eyes widened. "Really?"

"Yes. We thought our experience with my own prophecy might help you unveil your own. That is, if we have your permission to research it," Mama said.

"Of course you do," I replied. "I need all the help I can get."

"If we find anything, we'll tell you straight away," Daddy said. "Your mother and I are planning to turn this island upside down."

He was hoping they'd find something in time to talk me out of the Darke Games. Not gonna happen.

I looked at the big bag Mama carried. "What's that you got there?"

Mama smiled and unzipped the bag. "I heard there was a ball after the Games. I thought you needed something to wear."

Mama pulled a ballgown out of the bag, and I gasped. An A-line dress with a big tulle skirt flooded my vision. It was sky-blue, and had the cutest cap sleeves, with lace petals above the waistline. It was so timeless.

"I wore this to the Elemental Ball my freshman year. Your father was my date." Fond memories flickered across my mother's eyes as she looked at the dress, and Daddy smiled. "I thought I'd pass it on to you."

"Mama, it's so beautiful." My hand ran over the fabric in awe. I'd never seen this dress before. It was gorgeous.

Mama tilted her head. "I know that look. You have an idea."

I bit my lip. "It's... *almost* perfect," I said. "But it needs some updates. Could you go into town and get me some fabric? There are sewing machines in the Arts and Crafts room."

"I'm surprised they let the students around needles." Mama's eyebrows shot up.

"Only with supervision. The Arts and Crafts room is monitored at all times. Can you help me?" I asked.

"I'm not as good at sewing as your grandmother or Aunt Imogen, but I know enough," Mama said with a gleam in her eye. "Let's make your perfect dress."

NINETEEN

Exams were a two-week ordeal at the Institute, and I was *freaking out*. Each exam stretched hours, and classes were split into blocks. We'd take half our exams this week, and half next week, right up until the Darke Games began. So much for training for the Darke Games when studying for exams took up every hour of the day.

These weren't the pesky little exams I remembered from high school. They were *college* exams, complete with written portions and physical assessments. I wasn't worried about the physical part. I could conjure Air and Earth like it was nothing, and I was certain to pass Elementai Magic. It was the written exams I was sure to fail.

I should've been worried about the Darke Games, but exams seemed to be a death sentence just the same. If we *did* survive the Games and didn't win, we'd be right back at the Institute next semester. And if I didn't pass, I'd be repeating classes until my sentence was up. If the Warden saw my grades and thought I hadn't learned enough by graduation to be "rehabilitated," I was going to a *real* supernatural prison, full of convicts with powers I couldn't even imagine.

All for what…? Stowing away on a boat I didn't even steal? No way was I being transferred.

And so I had to pass my exams.

My first exam was Juvenile Justice. Might as well get the hell over to begin with. I'd be back here next semester anyway— assuming a monster didn't rip my head off during the Games. At this point, it might be preferable if I never had to listen to Professor Mazur speak again.

My heart hammered, and my palms began to sweat as I took my seat at the back of the room. Oberi panted and rested his chin on my leg, but even that didn't help soothe me. I was screwed.

"Half the exam will be multiple choice, and the other half will consist of essay questions," Professor Mazur announced. She marched down the rows with a quick staccato to her step. Papers rustled as she handed them out. "Professor Gael will be assisting me in proctoring the exam, so don't even *think* about cheating. If you so much as move your eyes from your own paper, you will be caught, and you will be punished accordingly."

Professor Mazur strolled by my desk, but she completely ignored me, as if I were invisible. I was given no exam, no pencil... not so much as an explanation.

My pulse quickened. Hell, I hated taking tests. Worst part of prison, for sure.

I cleared my throat. "Um, Professor? I didn't receive an exam."

Her heels clicked against the floor as she turned toward me. "Mister Wahkin, what are you doing here?"

I furrowed my brow. "Um... I've been enrolled in this class all semester."

"No, I mean what are you doing *here*? Didn't I tell you Professor Takahashi was proctoring your exam?"

Her tone was harsh, and I wasn't sure how to respond. No, she hadn't told me a damn thing.

"Well...?" she pressed. "What are you waiting for? You're late! Professor Takahashi is surely waiting for you in his office. Hurry along."

I barely had a moment to process the sudden change in schedule, but I hurried out of the classroom as fast as I could. Oberi followed at my side.

I was skeptical as I made my way to Professor Takahashi's office. Professor Mazur hadn't provided me with one accommodation all semester. What had made her change her mind now?

By the time I arrived at Takahashi's office, my pulse had slowed to normal anxiety levels. I knocked on the door, and his voice came from behind it.

"Come in," he called. "Ah, Charlie. I've been waiting for you. Are you ready for your exam?"

Oberi led me to a chair opposite Takahashi, and I sighed as I plopped into it. "Ready as I'll ever be."

Honestly, even if I aced the exam, I wasn't sure I'd pass the class.

"How will this work?" I asked.

"I'll read the questions aloud and record your answer on the exam sheet. Essay questions will be given verbally and graded immediately," he explained. "I am unable to say anything during the exam, apart from reading the questions. Do you understand?"

My hands weren't shaking quite as much anymore, so that was good news. "Ready whenever you are."

Professor Takahashi began reading the multiple-choice questions. I was surprised when I knew the answer to the first three. A couple of the questions stumped me, but overall I was pretty confident in the multiple-choice questions. Takahashi didn't say anything when I gave him my essay answers. All I heard was a slight scribble on the page, though I didn't know if it was good or bad.

I was relieved by the time the exam was over. It felt like I'd been sitting there for hours. A huge weight had just been lifted from my shoulders. Whether I passed the class or not, at least I didn't have to worry about it again for the next few weeks.

Paper slid over paper, like Takahashi was putting my test into an envelope. "You should be proud of yourself, Charlie."

"Does that mean I passed?" I asked hopefully.

He laughed lightly. "I unfortunately can't give you details of your grade yet. I have to return this to Professor Mazur personally. You should stick around, though, seeing as your counseling session begins in..."

He paused, like he was checking the time. "Less than twenty minutes."

"Professor," I stopped him before he could get to the door.

"Yes, Charlie?"

"Thanks for proctoring my exam."

"My pleasure," he said, before leaving the room.

Oberi nudged me, forcing me to pet his head. "One exam down." I sighed. "Maybe I'll survive."

The sound of footsteps came just outside the door. At first, I thought Takahashi had returned, like he forgot something, but the footsteps were lighter. Oberi perked up and started barking. That's when I knew it was Ava.

"You're early," I remarked.

"Hardly," she said. "I came by an hour ago, but the door was closed. It sounded like he was in a meeting."

"Takahashi was proctoring my Juvenile Justice exam," I explained.

Ava didn't sit, but rather paced around the room. "Oh. Mazur let you take it?"

"Yeah, I'm as surprised as you are."

"Well, money talks," Ava muttered. I wasn't sure if I heard her right.

I stiffened. "What's that supposed to mean?"

I think I already knew. It was a miracle Mazur gave me a proctor, to be honest. I should've known something was up.

"Oh, it's just a phrase," Ava said as innocently as a convict.

"Pidge, I didn't need your help," I snapped. I knew Ava's family had money, but using it to bribe the professors sounded like a good way to get in trouble around here.

"I don't know what you're talking about," Ava replied, but I could hear it in her tone. She knew *exactly* what I meant.

I crossed my arms. "If I'm caught cheating—"

"It's not *cheating* to receive accommodations, Charlie," she said harshly. "Just be grateful you got the test out of the way, and let's not talk about it again, all right?"

I hesitated. I really was going to fail the class without taking that exam. It was worth a huge part of my grade. I guess I owed Ava for whatever she'd said to Mazur— or bribed her with— to secure my accommodations. No one had ever cared enough to do something like that for me. I stood to make my way over to Ava, a *thank you* present on my tongue.

But then I realized what I was doing, and I sank back into my chair.

"I don't owe you anything," I finally said.

"Of course not," she replied, still playing stupid. "Because I didn't do anything."

Ava's footsteps continued around the room, like she couldn't just sit still.

"Something on your mind, pidge?" I asked.

She sighed heavily, as if half glad and half annoyed I'd asked. "I think I bombed my Supernatural Behavioral Science exam."

"But you studied so hard!"

"I know, but I rushed it. That's why I was here so early."

"Why rush? You had all that time."

Ava didn't speak for a few beats, just continued pacing around the room. My hand rested on Oberi's head, and he bobbed it back and forth, watching her.

"I can't stop thinking about my parents," she admitted.

"What about them?" I asked. "They're okay, right? I mean, the island is safe... until the Games, at least."

"Yeah, but they're not really here for the Games. They're here for—" She cut off abruptly.

It felt like she was trying to tell me something, but I didn't know what it was. "They're here for what?"

Ava's breath wavered. "I can't sit still. Can we go for a walk?"

I shrugged. We still had twenty minutes until our counseling session. "Sure."

Ava and I strolled down the hall side-by-side, with Oberi beside her. We were so close our hands kept brushing one another. It brought me comfort, though Ava didn't seem to notice. I waited for her to say something, but she didn't speak until we'd climbed a flight of stairs and she opened a door. Cool air rushed through, and we stepped out in the open. Oberi immediately left our side, sniffing around for whatever he could find.

"I didn't know students were allowed on the roof," I remarked. I tried to read the area with my Air power, but it was hard when it was all so open. I couldn't quite tell where the edge was, and I didn't want to get too close.

"This isn't the roof," Ava said. "That's up another level. It's a balcony. I found this place over the weekend. It's a good place to come and relax. I don't think many students know about it, because no one's interrupted me yet."

Ava noticed my hesitation and took my hand. "Don't be afraid. You won't fall off."

She led me forward and placed my hand on a thick stone railing that lined the balcony. I felt around to see that it was made of stone pillars, each one carved into an intricate arch.

"The view is really nice from up here," Ava said as she leaned against the banister. "You can see over the fence— almost all the way to Shade Hills."

"Well, *you* can." I chuckled.

She barely responded, and I could tell something was bothering her.

"What is it, pidge? You said your parents weren't here for the Games."

"No. They want to help me."

"With what?" They weren't going to help her escape, were they? Not after her father had sentenced her here in the first place, right? Unless he was suffering some kind of guilt for it now.

Ava took a few breaths. "Charlie... do you remember that I promised you I'd tell you why I was entering the Darke Games?"

"Yeah," I said, a little bitterly. "You never did."

"Well, I meant to. I just didn't know how to tell you. It's all so confusing. And honestly, I didn't know if I could trust you with the truth at the time."

It took a moment before her words hit me. She *didn't know at the time...*

Did that mean she trusted me now?

"It would help a lot to know," I told her gently. "But if you need more time..."

"No," she said quickly. "I need you to know before we go into the Darke Games, because if anything happens... well, then you know why I have to do *anything* to win."

She was starting to scare me. I knew Ava was intense and competitive, but this seemed to go far beyond that. It almost sounded like it was something she didn't *want* to do, but *had* to do— like she was bound by duty.

I reached out and took her hand, rubbing the back of it with my fingers. "You can tell me anything, pidge."

Ava took a long time to respond, like she was mulling it over in her mind. She didn't pull away from me, but she didn't engage, either. I had no idea what she was thinking, and Oberi wasn't being any help. He was over in a corner sniffing all the new smells.

Finally, Ava spoke. "The truth is, I came here because I've been chosen."

"Chosen...?" I prodded. I wasn't sure I understood what she meant.

"Chosen by the ancestors," she said, sounding completely serious. As soon as the confession came, she couldn't seem to stop herself. "My aunt Maddie is a *naderei*, or a prophet. When I was born, she made a prophecy about how I was to save the supernatural world from some gigantic catastrophe. I can't really explain it, because I don't know what it means yet, and my aunt's visions were never very specific. She wrote it down in a journal, but it's difficult to make sense of. What I *do* know is that the answers to the prophecy lie somewhere on Darke Island. Daddy sentenced me here so I could investigate. But the Institute has been a bust. The answers have to be out *there*, on the rest of the island."

Hell, this was a lot to take in. I would've accused her of bluffing if she didn't sound so scared. My heart broke for her.

"Now that I'm here, my sentence is in the hands of the Warden. Daddy can't get me out of it anymore," she continued. "So you see why I have to win the Games and earn that pardon. I have to explore the rest of the Island for answers— or the entire supernatural world may be in jeopardy."

A shiver ran down my spine. I could hardly wrap my head around what she was saying. Her words felt so heavy. How could my pidge be caught in the middle of this?

"Say something, Charlie," she pleaded.

"It all sounds... unreal," I breathed.

"Well, it *is* real," she said bitterly, finally pulling her hand away from me. She turned to the balcony to look out over the landscape. Her voice turned to a whisper. "It's not something I would choose for myself, but Mama was a chosen one, too. She had to do it during the Hawkei Civil War, and now it's my turn. My parents are here looking for clues, but I'm worried about them. They aren't as young as they once were, and I don't want them anywhere near the island when those portals open and monsters come flooding into our world."

"I bet they don't want you anywhere near those monsters, either," I said reassuringly. "Your parents care about you just as much as you care about them."

"Yeah, but *I* signed up to fight the monsters, to protect the people of Darke Island," she said. "I shouldn't have to protect my parents, too. But Daddy insists, and you don't argue with the chief."

She sighed. "Those monsters are only half the battle, Charlie. I have to find out what this island can tell me about the prophecy."

I could hear the fear in her tone. I didn't mean to do it, but I found myself reaching out for her. I wrapped her in my arms. She stiffened for a moment, before melting into me and embracing me back. A breeze passed by us, rustling her hair. Her scent was intoxicating. I couldn't help it when I leaned in to press my lips to her forehead.

"We'll find the answers, pidge," I assured her.

"We?" she asked in a whisper.

"Yeah," I confirmed, the promise already searing itself into my heart. "We'll win the Darke Games, leave the Institute, and figure out what the ancestors want from you. I'll be by your side every step of the way."

She leaned her head against my chest. "But it could be dangerous, Charlie."

"Which is exactly why you can't do it alone," I reminded her. "I can't exactly let you run off with Oberi, now can I?"

She seemed to understand that and relaxed into me deeper. "No, I guess not. I just hope the answers are actually here. I would hate for this all to be for nothing."

I smoothed down her hair. "It won't be, pidge."

What I didn't say was that it *wasn't*— present tense. Coming to Darke Island, being sentenced to the Institute... it wasn't all for nothing.

Because it brought us together. Prophecy or not, wherever she went, I'd follow.

"Can we just stay up here all night?" Ava asked. "It'd be nice to forget about everything."

"Not if you don't want to disappoint Kallie and Marcus," I reminded her. "Or get another strike on your record. We've got a mandatory counseling session scheduled. We don't want to be late."

She sighed in disappointment and drew away from me. "I guess that means I *have* to go."

I frowned. I didn't want to leave, either. This balcony was quiet and felt safe, though it might have been the company I kept.

"I guess so," I replied reluctantly.

Ava turned toward the door and took my hand to lead me behind her. She patted her leg to get Oberi's attention. "Come on, boy! It's time to go back inside."

Oberi whined. He loved the outdoors, especially when he could feel the air through his fur. After a few more tries, he followed us inside.

We made our way back to Professor Takahashi's office. We could hear Marcus and Kallie talking to him inside the room.

"Ah, there you are," Takahashi said brightly. "I was going to give you two a few more minutes before launching a search party."

"Are we late?" I asked.

"Nothing to worry about," Professor Takahashi said. "Ava, would you close the door, so we can get started?"

The chairs were lined in a circle like normal. I took my usual chair between Marcus and Ava.

"We've reached the end of the semester, and I'm sure emotions are running high over exams," Takahashi began. "However, I'm concerned that we've missed some important points in our counseling sessions. Usually by this point, most groups I work with are a little more... open with each other."

I didn't know what he was getting at. I'd opened up to Ava more than I had with anyone before.

"Today, I suggest we start with an exercise in which we tell our fellow classmates one thing no one else in the room knows about us," Takahashi suggested.

I knew what he was doing. He was trying to make us each vulnerable— like we might spill our deepest, darkest secrets right in front of him. But there were things you didn't tell your counselor— only your closest friends.

"Marcus, would you like to start?" Takahashi asked.

Marcus cleared his throat, but he didn't speak right away. It was like this every counseling session. None of us ever really said much, just mostly listened to Takahashi fill the time with life lessons he thought would help, but rarely applied to us. If he wanted us to get vulnerable and speak to each other, it'd be down in the Villain's Den or out in the prison yard— not in this circle that reeked of obligation.

"When I was, uh, twelve," Marcus began, "I got a really bad sliver in my hand. Hurt too much to pull out, so I let it fester for a week. I nearly went into septic shock."

Kallie snickered.

"What's so funny?" Marcus asked, sounding confused.

Kallie's tone was sarcastic. "Your war story is a *sliver*? In Malovia, you can be impaled by a lance, and fae are expected to yank that sucker right out and keep on fighting."

Marcus blew a breath and mumbled, "It was a bad sliver."

Kallie started to say something else, but Takahashi cut her off. "Let's not argue over who had it worse. This is a judgement-free zone. Marcus, while that story was... interesting... I was hoping you might start with talking about your *feelings*."

Oh, great. Here we go.

"I guess there is one thing," Marcus admitted.

"Whenever you're ready," Takahashi encouraged.

Marcus paused a few beats, and Rishi purred in his lap. Finally, he spoke. "I left someone behind when I came to the Institute. Kellen... he was like a younger brother to me. He was the kind of kid who got suspended a lot. The teachers thought he was trouble, but I knew he was just misunderstood. I took him under my wing and taught him how to draw and paint. Things started getting better, and then... well, then I was sentenced to the Institute, and I never got a chance to explain. That's why I'm entering the Games— so I can get out and make amends."

Everyone was totally silent during Marcus' confession, even Oberi. It was the first time Marcus had ever spoken about his life before the Institute. Kind of broke my heart, to be honest.

After a few moments, Kallie scoffed. "You call that a sob story?"

"Yeah," Marcus snapped. "I do."

"Please," Takahashi pressed. "Let's not go comparing our suffering."

Marcus barely let him finish before challenging Kallie. "Let's hear yours, then."

"You want to hear a *real* sob story?" Kallie asked, obviously up for the challenge. "How about the one where I lost the *fae crown?* I deserved it, too! I won the King's Contest."

"What's the King's Contest again?" I asked. She'd mentioned it before, but hadn't fully explained it.

"It's a competition in Malovia designed to seek out those most worthy of the crown. Winner becomes king— or queen, in my case," Kallie explained. "Before entering, you have to choose a mate, because a king or queen is stronger with their mate at their side."

She didn't quite sound like she believed it, but rather wrote it off as tradition.

"I declared a mate, but I didn't really love him, and I didn't bond with him, either," she continued, her voice intense. "He was obsessed with me. I knew he'd agree to compete if I asked, so that's why I chose him. Anyway, that's a story for another day. But in the Contest, I fought my brother for the crown in the final duel."

"Your own brother?" Marcus asked.

"*Twin* brother," Kallie clarified. "I had to. We were both competing. One of us had to win."

"So he won and sent you here?" Ava guessed.

Kallie blew a breath. "I wish it were that simple. No. I defeated my brother and won the King's Contest. But the Circle— that's like our parliament back home, those sexist pigs— voted that a woman couldn't inherit the country— a woman who could *unnaturally shift*, as they put it. I'm of high fae blood, for the gods' sake! But that wasn't good enough for them, nor was my chosen mate."

She said the words as if they weren't her own.

"So what does the Circle do?" she continued rhetorically. "They give the crown to my brother, the runner up, all because he was born with a set of balls! The king tried to stop the vote, but the Circle forced it."

"What did you do?" Ava asked, sounding invested in the story.

"The only thing I could!" Kallie's voice grew harsher. "I had to get my crown back, so I made an assassination attempt on the future king."

"But that was your own brother!" Marcus balked.

I'd gone totally speechless. I knew Kallie was in here for a good reason, but I didn't know what she was truly capable of.

"A brother who stole my crown!" Kallie shot back. "I was wronged. I worked my ass off and earned my right to the throne, and it was taken away because I'm a *woman*— an outcast considered a freak because I can shift."

Kallie took heavy breaths. "I didn't even get the job done, thanks to the queen. I was caught and almost executed. If my mom hadn't fought for my banishment over execution, I'd be dead right now— executed for treason. My one consolation prize is that going to the Institute gave me a chance to publicly reject my creepy stalker, and I didn't have to mate with him."

Kallie's breaths turned into sobs. It caught me completely off guard, because I'd never seen her cry before. "I *earned* that crown! I worked toward it my entire life! And without it I... I don't even know who I am."

Her voice cracked, and she sniffled. "It feels like I have to find the pieces of myself that shattered after losing the throne, but that I'll never be able to put myself back together. This was all I ever wanted, and now I have to learn who I am without it. Now, I'm nothing but a fake! So forgive me if you got a sliver and lost your friend, but it's *nothing* compared to what I lost. My family, the crown... even myself."

The room went dead silent, apart from Kallie's intermittent sniffling. I was so shocked, I couldn't offer any comforting words even if I wanted to.

Professor Takahashi finally spoke. "Thank you very much for sharing your story, Kalina. I hope you feel better now that you've gotten it off your chest."

"Right now I feel like shit." Kallie hiccupped. "It's someone else's turn."

"I'll go," Ava offered. The atmosphere in the room seemed to shift instantly as attention turned to her. I thought it was kind of her to offer to go next. It gave Kallie an opportunity to compose herself.

"I'm not sure what I can say that no one else in the room already knows," Ava started slowly.

I understood her meaning immediately. All the hard stuff— the kind of stuff Kallie had just admitted to, and the horrors Ava had gone through a few years ago— she'd already told to me. It was a loophole to Professor Takahashi's request, a way to get out of telling Marcus and Kallie the worst of it.

"But there is one thing I've never admitted to anyone," Ava continued. "Everyone says I'm good at arguing and that I should've become a lawyer, and I used to want to be one. I thought about defending people who couldn't defend themselves. Abused kids, maybe rape victims."

A shiver traveled down my spine. To think of what Ava had been through made my whole body turn to stone. I didn't move— didn't breathe.

"My mom talked me out of it. She didn't think I could handle losing cases, and she was right. I'd fall to pieces if a child had to go back to their abusive family, or if a rapist walked free. Besides, my heart was in exploring. I like studying people more like I like fighting over them."

Ava paused for a long breath. "This is going to sound weird, but... I never quite felt like I was part of a group of people. I always felt like I was... different— a freak. That's why I love anthropology and wanted to major in it. I can study people instead of pretending to be a part of them. It's the only way I understand how to communicate with others."

Ava quieted, then reached over to stroke Oberi's head. Her fingers grazed against mine, and I wasn't sure if it was intentional or not.

"You're not a freak," I blurted. It was instinctual. I had to comfort her, even if everyone else watched.

"But I *am* different," Ava argued. "I have to try harder than everyone else to control myself. It's... exhausting sometimes."

She was quick to clarify. "I mean, I know bipolar isn't an excuse for the way I act. It's not like everyone else with bipolar is sentenced to a reform school. I chose the life I did for myself, but that has to make me different, because who else would choose this?"

An uncomfortable silence settled over the room, and I reached out to squeeze Ava's hand. I swallowed the lump in my throat. "We all did, pidge. I chose a life of crime, too."

Ava scoffed. "You did what you had to do to survive."

Oh, pidge, I thought. *We have so much more in common than you think.*

I shook my head. "You don't get it. Want to know *my* secret? I *like* the trouble."

"You what?" Ava asked breathlessly. She seemed so shocked. It was in that moment that I realized how deep I had buried this confession. I hadn't even admitted it to myself.

"Do you think I'd still be stealing and conning if it was merely a survival tactic?" I asked Ava. "If I really didn't like it, or had severe moral objections, don't you think I would've given up by now? I do it because it feels *good* to be in control. There's a high that comes with the scam, and doing bad things is the only way I can get that. It's all I know. Things have been falling apart my whole life. Even if there were better options, how could I stop when those options would fall away from me, too?"

Ava didn't say anything. I wished I could read her expression right now, because it was killing me to not know what she was thinking. Hell, I could barely make sense of it myself.

I crossed my arms and slumped in my chair. "I always had a reason for what I'd done before, but here in the Institute, where I have a warm meal three times a day and a bed to sleep in at night, the cravings haven't gone away. I'm sick of sitting around just waiting to pass my classes. I want to fight somebody or steal something and get away with it. And I can't, because I'll get caught here. I guess that's the true test of a villain, huh? What do they do when they don't have a reason... when they're no longer desperate?"

The question was rhetorical, but I knew the answer. I was a bad guy — a villain. And I didn't even know it until just now. I committed crimes because they *felt good*, and just used survival as a reason to cover it up.

I kept speaking, because I feared someone might interrupt and accuse me of what I'd just realized myself. "When I came to the Institute, there were two choices. I could either keep up the cons, or survive.

I thought I'd been conning people for survival all along, but that was only one piece of it. I'm good at conning and thieving. But not here... without it, it's like I'm just going through the motions. But I don't know how long I can keep up this act, because I don't know how to be anything but bad."

I wanted to say more, just to kill time so I would never have to hear their reactions. But there was nothing more to say. I was bad— it was that simple. And it wasn't because I didn't have any other choice. It was because I didn't *want* another choice.

"Charlie," Ava whispered, like something about my speech had touched her. Screw that. I wasn't here to *inspire* anyone.

Professor Takahashi cleared his throat. "Thank you for sharing, Charlie, but you're not a bad person. Each and every one of you have made mistakes, yes, but you are here at the Institute to correct them."

Ah, here came another lecture. A useless one, I was sure. Takahashi meant well, but I didn't think he understood a damn thing I'd said.

But everyone else had. I felt the tension in the air and the understanding in their silence. They knew exactly what it felt like to crave trouble.

Takahashi spoke the rest of the counseling session. I didn't think he'd expected us to reveal so much, and I bet he felt like he had to fill the silence for our benefit. He let us out early.

Kallie clapped me on the back on our way down the stairs. "I appreciate what you said in there, Charlie."

"Why?" I grumbled. "You should just forget about it. It was dumb."

"It was the *truth*," Ava argued. "I know if I'm not causing trouble, I get bored. It's fun to take risks."

"Exactly," Kallie agreed. "I was expected to be perfect my whole life, and look how far that got me. My own country rejected me. If I'm not good enough to be their queen, I'm damn well good enough to be their villain."

I chuckled lightly, my mood lifting.

"You're good enough to be anything you want, Kallie," Marcus praised. "I was always a disappointment back home. No one took notice of me until I was sentenced to the Institute. The straight and narrow is dull. It's better to be a felon than to be nothing at all."

Their words should've bothered me. I mean, what kind of psycho group of kids preferred this kind of shit to a normal life?

Instead, it only brought me comfort, because I was part of a team that shared in this strange, twisted way of thinking.

The monsters unleashed during the Darke Games wouldn't know what was coming— because they'd never seen a group of villains like us before.

ava-marie

TWENTY

The Darke Games had arrived, and I had never been more ready to kick some ass.

I stood in the prison yard on December nineteenth, before the large gates that led to the outside world with the other competitors. I jogged in place and did a couple of air-punches to warm up, burning off some nervous energy. Above us, drones hovered, recording our every move. It was just before noon, the time when the Games were scheduled to begin.

The Darke Games were televised. The judges would watch our performance and award us points from inside the safety of the Institute while we fought monsters. The students were gathered in the stands in front of a big jumbo screen in the prison yard, where the broadcast of the Games would go on all day and into the night. The school had made this into a big deal. There were booths outside selling popcorn and drinks, and for one night only, the cells would remain completely unlocked so students could go in and out in order to watch the Games.

My parents were in the stands. They'd failed to find anything on Darke Island regarding the prophecy. It made my mission even more crucial. My gut instinct was right. I was the only one who was able to find the true meaning of the prophecy, and to do it, I had to get out there.

My teammates stood around me. Marcus was pale. He kept pacing and muttering things under his breath I couldn't hear. Kallie cracked her knuckles and stretched like this was a sports game. She'd been through similar things in the King's Contest, and to her, this was like any other event.

Charlie was... calm. I thought he'd be freaking out, but he waited patiently for the Games to start like it was the first chance he'd finally be let out of his cage. Beside him, Oberi stood in her unicorn form, staring out at the beyond.

"Why aren't our school uniforms this badass?" Kallie asked. She observed her clothes with pride, and I had to agree. The school had given everyone the same outfit for the Games; a black bodysuit, with elements of leather and breathable mesh, and sleek black boots. The suits were tailored and fitted to our bodies to give us ample room to move. Purple and green piping was sewn on to the legs and arms.

"We look like we're secret agents," Marcus complained. Rishi had already scratched Marcus' uniform.

"Or supervillains," Charlie added, feeling the arms of the outfit.

Supervillains was right. I felt like I was gonna fight Batman in this getup.

"I can't believe they're going to make us fight monsters right after exams. Hell week was hard enough," Marcus complained.

"It wasn't that bad," Charlie said, and I had to smile.

Charlie had passed all his exams. I'd asked Daddy for help, and though he didn't like Charlie, he had a disability himself, and knew what it was like not to receive accommodation. He'd paid off all of Charlie's teachers, who promised they'd give Charlie whatever accommodations he needed in the future to pass.

But we wouldn't need them, because we were getting out of here today. Professors had confirmed that multiple portals to hell had opened up on Darke Island, and monsters were flooding out of them at this very moment.

Even from here, I could hear the moans of monsters and demons as they lurked in the woods beyond. There were some big fuckers out there. Their roars shook the ground, and I watched as tiny pebbles moved over the gravel beneath our feet.

Marcus quivered in his boots. "Tell me again why I can't subconjure weapons and supplies. I'd be a lot happier out there with a sword."

Kallie laughed. "If you could handle one."

Marcus blushed. I doubted he'd ever touched a sword in his life. Marcus' magical stash had been searched this morning, to make sure he wasn't sneaking anything into the Games.

"It's unfair to the other teams," I reminded him. "It'd give us too much of an advantage."

"But why do the judges *care?*" Marcus argued. "Shouldn't they give us every opportunity to kill those monsters? Isn't that the point of the Games?"

"Not to the inmates," Kallie pointed out. "Everyone here is trying to win that pardon. I bet the angels and vampires bitched about witch magic long enough to ban your conjuring abilities."

"Well, it's unfair," Marcus complained. "Might as well ban angel wings and vampire strength. I don't have that!"

"It doesn't matter," Charlie said. "If we want to win, we have to play by the rules— no matter how twisted."

"Agreed," I added. "We'll kick ass no matter what comes our way."

Mama waved to me from her seat in the stands. I gave a huge smile and waved back. Mama's look was confident, but beside her, Daddy looked ready to pass out. He *did not* want me going out there, and had spent up until the last minute trying to convince me to withdraw.

But Mama had taken me by the shoulders and said, "We're Koigni women. We don't back down. Go out there and show them that Fire runs in your veins."

And Water, too, I thought excitedly. Oberi bucked beside me, as if she could hear my thoughts.

"Are anyone else's parents here?" Charlie asked.

"I didn't tell my family I was doing this. I didn't want them to freak out," Marcus said.

Kallie scoffed. "Pretty sure I was disowned when I tried to kill my brother. I haven't talked to my parents since I was banished."

Ouch. So I was the only one here with any outside support. That sucked.

I didn't think that many parents had shown up for the other teams, either. It looked like there were about forty-eight contestants in total, about twelve teams. I thought the number would be higher, but apparently, not even prisoners at the Institute were brave enough to risk death for a chance at a clean record.

Despona, Alice, Carson, and Wesley were strategizing only a few feet away. If we didn't win, I hoped they did. Unlike the rest of us, they were all innocent and deserved to get out of here.

Across the way, Mad Dog barked orders at his team. He'd picked Naya and a couple of his other vampire goons. Naya fawned over him while Mad Dog pushed his teammates around, trying to get them hyped up.

I hoped to the ancestors they didn't win. Mad Dog and Naya were the kind of people who needed to be in jail. Society wasn't safe with those assholes on the streets— and that was coming from me.

The Warden's face came on the jumbotron, and the prison yard went silent. A chill ran up and down my spine as his cold face looked out blankly at the world. "Good afternoon, and welcome to the Darke Games!"

There were a couple of claps, but it was mostly quiet. People were even afraid to cheer when the Warden was amping them up.

The Warden gave a grim smile. "I speak directly to the participants of these games. Outside the fence, monsters lurk. Each monster is given a set of points, which you will gain if you destroy it. You have from now until the end of the Games to gather points. The Games do not end until each monster is vanquished. Once all monsters are killed, the Games are over and the winners will be announced."

My heart stuttered nervously as the Warden straightened his shoulders. "From the moment you step outside these gates, the doors to the Institute are closed. You will not be let back in until the portals to the other world have been shut and all monsters are slain. The portals will remain open for the next twenty-four hours. From this point on, you will receive no outside help— even if you are in dire need, no one will come to your aid. You are on your own. Stay vigilant. Stay alive."

The Institute gates opened. Even as I stepped into danger, the first gust of fresh wind gave me a breath of freedom. I never wanted to set foot inside the Institute again. I'd risk my neck if it meant never going back.

The gates closed behind us, and an alarm sounded as they locked shut. The crowd cheered. I was very aware that the people I loved were behind that fence, and I was now outside it, quite literally walking into the jaws of hell.

We followed the rest of the participants. All the competitors walked down the long road leading to the Institute and into the forest, the drones above us capturing the footage.

When we entered those eerie woods again, I immediately felt something was off. My teammates felt it, too. Charlie bristled beside me, and Oberi let out a nervous breath. People around us began to mutter as we came across trees that had been ripped out of the ground or shattered to splinters. Something big was out here.

A tree toppled. Charlie reached out to drag me out of the way. He pulled me aside just before the tree could smack me in the head, using his Air magic to push it in the other direction. It fell, and I looked up. Several people screamed as our gaze fell upon the first official monster of the Games.

The best way I could describe it was a giant eyeball with tentacles. The monster hovered ten feet above ground, its piercing eye searching as its nasty, slimy tentacles reached out for victims, ripping out trees by their roots. I had no idea what culture it was from, or what kind of magical society could've created it. I'd never heard of something like it before. All I knew is that it was definitely a creature from hell, and that I didn't want to end up smushed.

"What the hell is it?" Charlie asked. He couldn't see it, but knew we'd run into something bad.

"Uh, imagine a giant floating octopus, except that octopus is an eyeball and it literally wants to kill us," I told him. Fear quaked through my guts as the eyeball's red gaze landed on me and narrowed, pinning me to the spot.

Kallie and Marcus dove out of the way of another falling tree. Meanwhile, other competitors launched themselves at the eyeball, trying to attack it. Spells whizzed through the air, but they bounced off the eyeball like they couldn't affect it. One battle spell ricocheted off the eyeball and hit a shifter in the chest. He went down, expression shocked as he felt the giant hole that was in his torso. He slumped to the ground, and I knew immediately... he was dead.

I stared in shock at the shifter's body. To witness his death in such a violent way... it brought back memories of Monica. Her death replayed in my mind as the carnage continued around me. It felt like my feet were stuck to the ground. I was so frozen I couldn't move.

"Pidge, come on!" Charlie grabbed me again and threw me on Oberi's back.

He hauled himself onto her behind me and called for Kallie and Marcus. They were backing off as the multitudes of people tried to fight off the giant eyeball. Mad Dog ran at it with his vampire speed and launched himself into the air, clinging to the eyeball and punching it over and over. The monster screeched and began flinging its tentacles around, trying to get Mad Dog off. One of the tentacles wrapped around a teammate of Mad Dog's. He screamed in pain, then his head slumped lifelessly as the monster crushed his insides and tore his body in two. It wasn't easy to kill a vampire, and this monster had done it no problem.

My jaw dropped open. Two people were gone already. This couldn't be real.

Oberi left us no time to watch. She galloped away, dodging trees as she ran through the forest. Behind us, Kallie changed into a wolf. Marcus climbed onto her back, and he hung on to Rishi, who screeched as Kallie ran to keep up with Oberi.

Oberi didn't stop until we were at least a mile into the woods. Kallie skidded to a halt beside her. Marcus slid off and smoothed down Rishi's fur. It was stuck up every which way, and the cat yowled in displeasure. Rishi was merely a cat— not a Familiar like Oberi— but Marcus had insisted on bringing him along. He never left his side.

Charlie slid off of Oberi, and I copied him, turning around to face him. "Charlie, what are you doing? We could've killed it!"

"We need to play this smart," Charlie said. "Everyone is going to go after that thing. It makes more sense for us to look for our own target, so we can get the points."

I paused. Charlie was right. There was no use trying to kill a monster that almost fifty people were after. We had to find our own.

"Maybe this was a mistake," Marcus said nervously. "The Games have only been going on for five minutes, and two people are already dead."

Kallie shifted back to human form. "It's too late to back out now. Gates are closed. We need to make the most of it and hunt some monsters."

I put my arms around myself and shivered. Charlie laid a hand on my shoulder. "Pidge, you okay?"

The deaths of the shifter and the vampire were mingling before my eyes, along with Monica. I couldn't separate them. The scenes replayed in my mind as the voices in my head grew louder.

Look, they're dead.

So dead.

Dead just like Monica.

You'll be dead, too.

Death will come for you all.

I'd made a massive miscalculation. I wanted this to be an adventure, but I hadn't taken it seriously when I was told people died during this competition. They were called the Darke Games, but there was nothing fun about them.

"I'm fine," I said. "I just... wasn't expecting that."

Charlie frowned. "You have to be ready for anything out here. If you don't put that mask on and separate yourself from the chaos, you'll be dragged right into it. Steel yourself, pidge. It's gonna get a whole lot worse from this point out."

Charlie had become someone totally different. I didn't recognize this part of him. I now saw that this was the piece of him he dragged out when he had to. He had experience fighting to survive. Even with monsters and magic, this was what he was used to— what he'd fought so hard to get out of.

And I'd dragged him right back into it, because I didn't know what I was dealing with. I felt like an ass.

One drone had followed us to capture our participation. I tried to ignore it and said, "Where do you think the next monster is?"

Kallie's head turned. "I can smell it," she said. "My shifter senses are telling me it's not far off."

Marcus looked at the ground, then tilted his head. He knelt by a strange patch in the mud, which might've been a footprint, but I couldn't really tell.

After a moment of observation, Marcus stood. "It went this way." He pointed to the south.

"How can you tell?" I asked.

"My mom's a detective. She taught me how to read tracks and things like that." Marcus shrugged.

"Your mom's a fucking *cop*?" Kallie asked scathingly.

"Yeah. Doesn't make sense for her to have a felon for a son, does it?" Marcus said.

"Lead the way," Charlie said, and Marcus went ahead. Charlie kept his hand on Oberi's back, and she guided him through the trees.

As Kallie and Marcus went on ahead, I whispered to Charlie, "How do you deal with it so well?"

"I have a lot of experience with people dying in front of me," Charlie said. "Marty wasn't the only one."

"What happened?"

"Bad drug deals. Cons gone wrong. People getting shot when you're trying to rob them." Charlie shrugged. "You just learn to deal with it."

I don't ever think I could learn to deal with people dying in front of me. But maybe I could. Kallie and Marcus seemed largely unaffected as well— or at least, they were trying not to show it. Kallie had seen people die in the King's Contest. She'd told me. But Marcus? When that shifter died, he'd barely even flinched. What the hell had happened to him to make him so used to death?

We walked until we came to a wide river. Here, the mud sloped off into the water, like some massive creature had slid from the bank into the river's depths.

"It's here," Marcus said. "Tracks are fresh."

I knelt by the water. I reached my left hand into the stream and used my Toaqua magic to feel around. My magic came to a halt at the bottom of the river, where I felt a giant creature lurking in the depths.

The moment my magic touched it, the creature moved. It swam up to the surface and broke free, screeching its rage to the world. It was some sort of reptile, a cross between a sea-serpent and a dragon. It had black scales peppered with an emerald sheen, webbed feet with long claws, and a spiky tail that would crush you if you were unlucky enough to get smacked by it.

The most terrifying thing about it was it had three heads. Each of the heads had a long snout that reminded me of a crocodile's. Sharp teeth poked out of the mouths. Each head was big enough to swallow Oberi whole.

"Ava, what are we looking at?" Charlie screamed as the creature continued to roar.

"Uh— big water monster, twenty feet long, three heads," I blurted.

"It's a *balur*! Move!" Kallie cried.

She changed into a wolf and shoved Marcus out of the way before one of the giant heads could bite him in two. The balur reached out and snapped its jaws on thin air. Oberi darted out of the way before she turned, pawing at the ground. She lowered her horn and charged, but the balur lunged out of the way before she could stab it in the eye. Oberi fought with the balur, the fire on her mane raging to become an inferno. The balur stayed away, fearful it would burn itself on Oberi, though its eyes raged in anger.

I was an Elementai. I could deal with a magical creature, right? It's what we were born to do.

But apparently not, because when I raised a hand back to throw a fireball, one of the balur's massive webbed paws reached out and smacked me to the side. I flew six feet before I slammed against a tree. I cried out in pain.

"Pidge, you okay?" Charlie shouted.

"Get down!" The balur had noticed Charlie was blind and had taken him for a target. The three heads lunged forward, but Charlie flattened himself against the ground at the last second. The heads collided against each other, smacking together. The balur groaned and retreated a few feet, shaking its head.

Kallie growled and launched herself at the balur. She attempted to rip one of the throats out, but the balur shook her off. Though she'd gotten a chunk of scales in her mouth, the monster was unharmed.

Kallie changed back and shook her head. "I can't bite through its skin. It's too thick!"

Marcus threw balls of battle magic at the creature, but they sizzled against its scales uselessly. It was like the creature's skin was its armor. The balur snapped at Marcus, and he fell backward with a yell. He kicked the creature's middle head to get away, scrambling for cover. Rishi ran up a tree and cowered in the branches.

I summoned the water from the river. I wrapped it around the balur's legs and froze it to ice, to keep the creature contained. But the balur ripped free of my ice like it was nothing. Charlie commanded roots to spring up from underneath the balur. He had the same idea I did, and wrapped them around the balur's legs. Yet the balur reached down and tore the branches in half with his teeth, tossing the roots aside like mere twigs.

Great. All that, and we'd just made it mad. The balur drew a breath, and from all three heads he shot out red-hot flames. I jumped in front of the group and threw out my hands at the last second. The fire misdirected at my command, shooting toward the sky. Even so, it was hot. Sweat ran down my forehead as I kept the balur's breath at bay. I turned it around, so that the balur's own flames enveloped him.

It didn't do anything. His scales heated to a molten-like color and stayed that way. The balur's entire form glowed, sizzling hot. Oberi backed away, tossing her horn and snorting out smoke as she observed the balur's brand-new flaming coat.

"That's cool, just make it more dangerous than it already is!" Marcus called out.

"I'm trying, okay!" I backed away and called up more water from the riverbed to cool off the balur's scales. It landed on the balur's back and instantly evaporated into hot steam. It was so intense it made the area grow unbearably hot.

Charlie yanked me behind a nearby boulder, where the rest of us were taking shelter. Oberi panted, trying to regain her stamina from chasing the balur around. Marcus clenched at his hair anxiously, while Kallie shook.

Nothing we were trying was working. It wasn't that surprising. This creature had spent time in literal hell, for crying out loud. At most, we were annoying it.

"We're gonna be dinner if we don't figure out something in the next five seconds!" Marcus replied. The balur was taking another breath, to blow fire once again.

"Charlie, you're Captain! What do we do?" Kallie shouted.

I could see Charlie's mind work. "We have to combine our magic," he said.

It clicked. "Yes! Kallie, like we did in class!"

Her eyes brightened. "I need whatever you can give me."

Charlie, Marcus and I focused on merging our powers with Kallie's. Three swords appeared in mid-air; one infused with my Fire magic, one mixed with Charlie's Air magic, and one with Marcus' battle magic. We each took our own weapons. I grasped mine tightly, feeling a bit more confident now that I had something to use.

"How is this supposed to help?" Marcus asked as he held up his sword.

"A regular sword won't cut through its skin, but a sword infused with magic might," Kallie said. "They'll break on impact with a monster like that, so you only get one shot. My suggestion is to aim for the neck."

"Okay, so we have to get close enough to cut its heads off," Marcus said warily. "How are we going to do that without being killed?"

"Kallie, can you put an illusion on it?" Charlie asked. He held up his sword, and I had to admit it was pretty cool. There was a little tornado swirling inside the blade that looked badass.

"I can try, but with something that strong, it won't hold for long. You guys are gonna need to move fast," she said quickly.

We didn't have time to come up with another plan, because the balur unleashed his flames once again. Our whole group launched ourselves out of the way as the flames enveloped the boulder. The flames melted the entire stone to molten lava, making a hot puddle on the ground.

Oberi guided Charlie to the left, while Marcus dodged to the right. I remained in the middle and charged. Kallie threw her arms out, and the balur's flames stopped. Its eyes glazed over, and it looked around in confusion as Kallie's illusion spell overtook its mind. The balur took his giant webbed claws and batted at its faces, attempting to end the illusion that had claimed its vision. The monster spun in a circle, and all three of us had to jump over its tail, so we wouldn't get hit. I cried out, to let Charlie know it was time to jump, and the three of us leapt together.

Well, Charlie and I jumped. Marcus more or less tripped. He fell forward and almost smashed his dick on one of the balur's spikes before he twisted to the side and just avoided being shish-kabobbed. He crawled back upward sloppily. As the balur turned back around, I raised my sword, so ready to cut this bitch's head off.

Kallie gave a scream behind me. I glanced back, and I saw that she'd fallen to her knees in pain. Tears ran down her cheeks as she dug her fingers into the earth.

"Run!" she cried. "It broke my spell!"

And apparently the effort had weakened her, because Kallie struggled to get up. The balur saw an opportunity and ran forward with jaws extended to swallow Kallie whole.

"Kallie!" Marcus abandoned the plan and ran back to save her. He planted himself in front of her and swung back the sword. When the balur lunged forward, Marcus swung the sword like a baseball bat. The tip of it almost hit the balur, but the monster jumped back, hissing.

Of course, Marcus let the sword go after he swung. It went flying backward and embedded itself right into a tree. Kallie groaned just as Marcus started to panic.

Rishi launched himself from a tree branch with a yell. He landed on the balur's middle head and began clawing at its eyes. The balur reared up on his hind legs and threw its head back. Rishi went soaring backward and crashed in the river. His yowls could be heard over the battle as the water carried him downstream.

"Rishi!" Marcus screamed as he helped Kallie to her feet, but the cat was already out of sight. Tears dotted Marcus' eyes, yet he stayed by Kallie's side.

I thought we were dead for sure. Then a great wind came in from the west, and the balur was picked up off its feet. The wind smashed the balur back into the ground again. The gust was gone as quickly as it came.

Charlie had pointed his sword at the creature, and his Air magic had come spiraling out of it. He gasped. It took a lot of energy for him to use the sword to knock the monster over. Charlie fell to one knee, and Oberi ran over to him. She put her neck underneath him and lifted him upward. I felt her energy flow from her body into Charlie's as she helped him stand, sustaining him through our bond.

The balur hissed in displeasure as he rolled, stubby legs flailing. Charlie's magic had knocked it down, but it wouldn't stay that way for long.

Kallie hobbled over to the tree that had Marcus' sword embedded in it. She ripped it out with one arm and growled, "Trust a warlock to be shit with a sword. Just get me near the damn thing."

"How?" Marcus yelped.

The balur's flames unleashed once again. I flung out my right hand, redirecting the flames back toward the clouds. As I did so, I tried to stop the flames from coming out of the balur's throats. The flames halted at my command, and although they didn't cause the balur to explode like I hoped, the monster choked and coughed, like it was trying and failing to breathe.

Holding back the balur's flames was really hard. My arm shook, and I felt my knees begin to buckle. I gripped the sword in my left hand for an anchor, until I felt the hilt cut into my palm. I was holding back the strength of dynamite with nothing more than sheer will, and ancestors, it hurt.

I couldn't hold it any longer. I let go, and the flames lunged out of the balur's mouth— directly toward me.

I screamed, but Oberi charged in front of me. The three streams of fire combined into one huge plume, enveloping Oberi like a powerful explosion. Her form vanished completely as the flames consumed her whole.

"Oberi, *no!*" I shouted. My heart broke, and time ceased to move. Terror ran through me as I realized that my Familiar had sacrificed herself for *me*. I would never see her again... she was gone.

But when the flames stopped, I saw with amazement Oberi was still standing, not a scratch on her. Oberi hadn't been killed by the balur's flames. She had *powered up*. The energy of the flames had gone directly to her horn. The horn blazed powerfully, and Oberi reared up. From the tip of her horn burst a huge column of flame, socking the balur right in the chest.

The creature screamed and backed up. Oberi's flames were able to hurt it— little by little, the flame column ate away at the monster's scales, injuring it and leaving us an opening.

Charlie, Kallie and I all ran forward at once. Kallie swung first. She gave a wild yell as she sliced through the neck of the right head, severing it completely. As the head dropped, Kallie's sword disappeared. The balur's other heads gave a scream, but the left head was silenced when Charlie cut through its neck, the Air sword dissolving into vapor.

The only head left was the middle one, and I was coming for it. The balur rose up, ready to attack me with its claws. But I felt a gust of wind rush me upward, and I swung back, not giving myself time to think as I severed the middle head completely off. Blood splattered my outfit, and the sword in my hands vanished. The head came down with a *thud*, and the air carrying me stopped. I fell to the side and landed on my hip next to the balur's nasty skull.

The balur's body fell to the side. It twitched a few times before going still. The monster's body dissolved into ash, floating away on the wind. I watched as the particles dissolved on the breeze, and the three severed heads collapsed into dust on the ground.

I took a few quick breaths, hardly able to believe it. We'd done it. We'd beaten our first monster!

Only a million more to go.

"You okay, pidge?" Charlie was at my side. He reached out a hand, and I took it to get to my feet.

"I'm good. See, you picked me up there," I told Charlie. "Maybe you *can* fly other people around."

"I also dropped you," Charlie pointed out. "We can't try that again. You could've gotten hurt."

I rolled my eyes. He was being overdramatic. Everything was fine.

"Good girl," I told Oberi as I stroked her forehead. She nickered and pushed her nose against me. "I wasn't expecting that from you."

"She's more powerful than I realized," Charlie said.

"That's an understatement. She saved our asses," Kallie said. She wiped off blood on her pants, like it was no big deal.

"What else are you hiding, girl?" I asked. Oberi bobbed her head and stuck out her tongue. I giggled.

"Rishi!" Marcus ran downriver. He hurtled by as fast as he could. The rest of us hurried to keep up with him, and anxiety made my insides whirl. Was Rishi okay? I didn't think Marcus could handle it if his cat was dead.

There was a yowl from nearby, and I sighed in relief. Rishi was clinging to a branch that was hanging into the river for dear life, calling out for Marcus.

Marcus went barreling into the water. He fell down— again— getting soaked. He grabbed Rishi and slipped on the river bank. Kallie sighed and reached out to pull him up.

Rishi shivered in Marcus' arms. I reached out with my left hand. "Here, let me dry you off."

The water seeped out of Marcus' clothes and Rishi's fur as I commanded it to go back into the river. They were fully dry, but Rishi was obviously displeased. The grumpy cat gave a very pissed-off look as the rest of us drew near.

"Good plan, guys," Kallie praised. "We got our first few points."

"Oh yeah, great plan," Marcus bitched. "Typical fae solution. Something bothering you? Just cut its head off!"

"It worked, didn't it?" Kallie asked.

"Guys, that's enough." Charlie crossed his arms. "We need to get along out here. We don't get points if we kill each other."

"If only," Marcus grumbled. Kallie gave him the finger.

The drone that was following us came out of the sky. It hovered at eye-level. From the top of the drone emerged a small screen. One of the judges for the Institute came on— it was Professor Warbright.

"Congratulations on claiming your first kill," Warbright said. "Each monster has a different score value, based on the difficulty of the kill. For slaying the balur, your team has gained four points, putting you in third place."

The screen flashed a quick review of the scoreboard. I ran through the numbers. Three teams had been eliminated already— all of their teammates were dead. The rest of the teams under us had either zero or two points. The second-place team had five points, killing a monster that was only slightly above the difficulty of the balur.

I noticed with spite that Mad Dog and Naya's team was at the top of the leaderboard with seven points. Looked like they'd claimed the kill of the first monster we'd met, and had already found another one.

Warbright came back on screen. "There are still more monsters out there, and plenty of time to claim the prize. Stay vigilant. Stay alive."

The screen went blank and folded back inside the drone. The drone hovered above us again, ready to follow.

"We've gotta move," I said in near despair. "We can't let Naya and Mad Dog win."

"We don't need to be worried about them. We should think about ourselves," Charlie said firmly. "Comparison only leads to distraction."

I knew he was right. And yet, I couldn't help but feel doubt. There was more at stake than just the competition. The world was depending on me to get free, so I could figure out the prophecy.

But if the rest of these monsters were just as bad as the balur, I might not have a chance to fulfill it, because the Darke Games would kill me anyway.

Fuck. What had I gotten us into?

charlie
TWENTY-ONE

Stay vigilant. Stay alive.

That would be a hell of a lot easier if we'd just stayed at the Institute. I never thought I was safe behind those gates, but hell, that was the place to be right now.

But Ava needed me. She had to win, to get out of the Institute and learn about the prophecy. I was done sticking my tail between my legs. I was done playing it safe. Ava was right— survival was fucking boring without adventure.

I'd never felt so alive as when I was fighting that balur. I was hungry for another fight, yearning to slay another monster. At least out here in the Games, I was doing something worthwhile. I was protecting Shade Hills from monsters, not hiding under my bed waiting for them to go away like I'd done when I was a kid. Maybe dying out here wouldn't be so bad, as long as I died with honor.

We forged ahead, staying alert for another fight that would earn us points. The air seemed to expand as we made it out of the trees. My feet met solid earth, and Oberi's hooves clacked loudly. The sound echoed off the nearby buildings, but the street was otherwise eerily silent.

"Where are we?" I whispered.

"Outskirts of Shade Hills," Ava-Marie whispered back. She took slow, calculated footsteps, and her voice came from several directions as she swiveled her head back and forth. "We've reached a residential neighborhood."

Kallie cracked her knuckles. "There has to be a monster nearby. Most of them feed off supernaturals— either literally or energetically. They're attracted to us."

"How do you know so much about monsters?" I asked.

"It's kind of a thing in Malovia," she explained. "We should keep moving."

Ava quickened her footsteps, until she was practically running.

"What is it, pidge?" I demanded.

"I see a checkpoint up ahead," she called back. "Let's get to it before someone else does."

Checkpoints were part of the Games, but the Warden had warned us they were limited. They were boxes filled with supplies like food, first-aid kits, and weapons. If the monsters didn't kill you out here, another team might— just to get their hands on those supplies.

Ava came to a screeching halt and cursed under her breath. "Dammit. Someone else got to it first. Everything is gone."

"We'll find another one," I assured her. It'd taken a lot of our energy to fight the balur, but we were good to go for another fight or two. If we didn't find another checkpoint, there were other ways to get food.

"I hope to the ancestors we do," Ava said. "In the meantime, everyone needs a drink of water."

Ava drew water out of the air and trickled it into our mouths to keep us all hydrated. I wiped my chin clean with the back of my hand.

"Um... guys," Marcus said nervously. "I think we have an audience."

"What do you mean?" I asked.

"I just saw those curtains move," he replied. "People are watching us."

Ava chuckled lightly. "They've been watching over the drones the whole time. I say we give them a good show."

"If we can find a monster," I stated. "The street sounds pretty quiet—"

Meow.

A small mew came from several paces up ahead. At first, I thought it was Rishi, then I heard him hiss from Marcus' shoulders.

"Aww," Ava swooned.

The cat hissed at her, and she jumped back against me.

"Everybody get back!" Marcus shouted. He flung his arm out, catching me in the chest. My heart leapt at his urgency, and I grabbed Ava to drag her away. Oberi stomped several times.

"What's the big deal?" Ava asked. "It's just a cat."

"It has like, a million teeth! And they're *bloody*!" Kallie shouted.

"But it's *sooo* cute!" Ava crooned.

"It's not a regular cat!" Marcus insisted. "It's a *malumuto*— or an evil shifter. It's a creature of Miriamic lore. They can shapeshift into different animals. First, it gains your trust in one form. As soon as you're close enough, it changes and rips your heart out."

"I've never heard of it," Ava said, as if Marcus had no idea what he was talking about.

"I'm serious!" Marcus shouted, pushing us further back on the street. "Those two markings above its eyes are where its horns go in its real form. It can hide them when it shifts, but the markings never go away."

Kallie took another step back, as if she wasn't willing to risk it. The cat meowed.

"This should be easy, then," I stated, swirling my arms around to create a gust of air.

Marcus grabbed my hand. "It's not that easy. Malumuto are creatures of spirit. They can't be killed by traditional means."

Ava had already conjured a fireball next to me, and it crackled loudly. "Then it hasn't felt one of my fireballs yet."

"Pidge," I warned. "While I appreciate your confidence, it's a recipe for trouble. Listen to Marcus. How do we get rid of this thing?"

Marcus didn't answer right away. The cat's footsteps approached, and Rishi hissed again. The four of us, along with Oberi, took another step back, careful not to trigger the cat to shift.

"Marcus!" Kallie cried. "What do we do?"

"I'm thinking!" he shot back. "Just give me a second... there's a spell to vanquish it to the Abyss— or hell. An incantation."

"So say it," I pressed.

Marcus hesitated.

"It's coming closer!" Kallie cried. "Now would be a good time to remember that incantation."

"Yeah, Marcus. Do your thing!" Ava encouraged.

Marcus' arm finally left my chest, and he held his hands out toward the malumuto. *"By candle flame and moonlight's kiss—"*

Marcus was cut off by the sound of the creature screeching. The cat's cry came closer, flying through the air and poised for attack. The thing moved faster than a normal animal, and I barely had a second to respond.

Before I could counterattack, the creature landed on Marcus' chest. He reeled backward, cursing as the monster clawed at him. Rishi yowled and fought back, knocking the monster off of Marcus. Rishi's paws hit the pavement, and he chased the creature around in circles.

Ava, Kallie, and I attacked immediately. Ava's Fire crackled as it whizzed through the air, and Kallie's battle orb exploded like a bomb on the pavement. I thrust my Air upward, carrying the creature high into the sky. Its high-pitched shriek echoed through Shade Hills as it fell from an incredible distance. I heard the *thud* as it landed, but there was no crunch of bones. I wasn't sure that the fall had slowed it down. The three of us kept attacking, while Marcus sucked in deep breaths. A stream of Fire erupted from Oberi's horn, just passing by my face.

"Marcus!" Ava shouted. "Our powers aren't doing shit. This creature is immortal or something!"

"I-I..." Marcus stammered.

"Yeah, you're bleeding," Kallie snapped. "Big whoop. We'll clean you up in a minute. Say the incantation!"

Marcus' breath grew ragged. *"By candle flame and moonlight's kiss, I vanquish you to the Abyss!"*

I expected something fantastic to happen, like for the air pressure to shift. But nothing changed. The cats continued to yowl at one another, and the girls and I kept throwing magic to slow the damn thing down.

"It didn't work!" Kallie cried, stating the obvious.

"Try again," I insisted.

"I-I can't!" Marcus wailed.

"Well, we need to do something," Ava snapped.

I switched from using Air magic and turned to my Earth magic.

Roots snaked out from trees next to the road. If I could trap the monster, then perhaps we had a chance. But every time I came close, the creature slipped out from my grasp.

Oberi pulled back on her Fire and lowered her head, poking my arm with her horn. I stepped aside to give her room. She scuffed her hooves on the pavement and blew a breath out her nose.

I grabbed Ava and dragged her back. "I think Oberi has a plan."

Ava stopped shooting fireballs to watch. Oberi charged, and Rishi shrieked as he jumped out of the way. The malumuto's yowls turned into roars as it shifted into another form.

"Ancestors, Charlie!" Ava struggled beneath my hold, but I tightened my arms around her. Ancestors knew she'd get herself killed if she intervened. "It's shifted into a lion with horns. Oberi's going to get hurt!"

No sooner did Ava say it did I hear the sound of Oberi's hoof smack the lion's head. It growled, then took off running. Oberi followed, chasing it out of range. Sticks snapped, and garbage cans were knocked over as the creature made its escape. Ava struggled to go after it, but I wouldn't let her.

"I think Oberi has it covered," I said, impressed.

Oberi came trotting back, her footsteps sounding proud and happier than ever. The sound of the lion's claws on the pavement faded, but I heard another collection of footsteps approaching.

They weren't monsters, though. They sounded familiar, like sneakers on the street. Something jingled as they moved.

I leaned over to Ava. "What's that tinkling sound?"

Her tone was harsh. "Carabiners on their backpacks. I guess we know who got to the checkpoint first."

"Where did it go!?" Mad Dog's deep voice thundered. He stomped up to me and grabbed me by the shoulders, shaking me. I didn't even flinch. "Tell me where it went!"

"Where did *what* go?" Kallie demanded.

"The monster!" Mad Dog sneered. "Don't play stupid with me, because we heard it."

"And *we're* going to get the points for killing it," Naya snapped.

"Be our guest," I said casually.

"Charlie, no!" Ava objected. "You can't let them get our points."

I turned to her, my voice raging. "That thing attacked Marcus! I'm not going to put my team in mortal danger for a half dozen points. We'll find another monster to kill."

"A half dozen?" Mad Dog sounded impressed. I could practically hear him panting in thirst for the fight.

"Seriously," I said. "Be careful. This one is worse than anything we've seen so far."

Mad Dog's breathing rate increased, obviously growing more intrigued as I spoke.

"It went that way." I pointed to our right.

"Come on," Mad Dog called to his team. "We're in the lead. Let's make sure we stay there."

His team took off running.

It wasn't until they were long gone that Ava turned to me. "The monster didn't go that way."

I shrugged. "So I lied to mislead them. We need a chance to get more points and get ahead."

"Good thinking," Ava replied.

Kallie had nothing to say about that. Instead, she whirled on Marcus. "What *was* that!?" she shouted. "I thought you were a strong warlock! Incantations should be simple for you."

Rishi purred in Marcus' arms while he got to his feet. "I'm sorry to disappoint, but they're not."

Marcus started to walk away, but Kallie kept up with him. "What about all the stories? I thought you were some badass warlock. You must be good at *something*!"

Marcus snapped. "The only thing I'm good at is lying!"

I stifled a laugh. Marcus talked a big talk, but he was the furthest thing from a good liar, and Kallie knew it. She'd been trying to get him to crack.

I wasn't expecting what came next. Marcus broke out in *sobs*— full on hiccupping and everything. "I'm a fraud!" he wailed. "The stories were all fake. I can't do anything."

We all just stood there for a second, stunned. Marcus had never crumbled like this before, or ever admitted he couldn't do magic well.

Finally, Ava spoke. "Then why did you enter the Games?"

"I don't know," Marcus sobbed. "I thought I'd figure it out by now. I-I..."

He trailed off, obviously distracted.

"It's just blood," Kallie said gently— it was odd to hear her speak that way. Marcus' breakdown must've had an effect on her. "Come here."

Kallie led Marcus across the street and to a bench that squeaked when they sat down. The tear of fabric met my ears, and I realized Kallie was ripping up her uniform to tie around Marcus' wounds.

"Have you ever done *anything* with your powers?" Ava asked.

Marcus sniffled. "Once."

"Oh, so you *do* have magic?" Ava snapped, obviously irritated by this fight.

"Lighten up," I snapped at her. I knew what it was like to feel like you couldn't do things everyone else could. Marcus needed someone on his side right now— even if we were in the middle of a deadly tournament.

"My tattoo is real," Marcus said. "I *do* have powers from all five witch Casts. It's just... limited."

"Limited how?" Kallie asked curiously.

"Like, I *can* read minds, but only dirty thoughts." Marcus spoke so quietly I barely heard him.

"Gods, ew!" Kallie cried. "You've been reading my dirty thoughts this whole time!?"

"No," Marcus said quickly. "I-I try not to. It can get disturbing some-times, and I don't want to invade people's privacy. As for my other powers... I don't want to hurt anyone."

"You wouldn't do that," I assured him.

"Wouldn't I?" he challenged. "You don't know why I was sentenced to the Institute."

The street went quiet as we all considered what he said. It was Ava who spoke up, though she chose her words carefully. "Why *were* you sentenced to the Institute?"

"The real story this time," Kallie clarified. "I don't want some bogus lie about a mass murder."

Marcus' breath wavered. "That's just the thing. That one wasn't a lie."

"What?" I nearly choked. I couldn't imagine Marcus hurting anyone — let alone being a serial killer.

"It happened right when my powers awakened," Marcus admitted. "My girlfriend and I got in an argument in the middle of town. She thought I should hide my powers, and I wanted to use them. She figured people would be afraid of me... and I guess she was right. *She* should've been afraid of me. I lost my temper, and I couldn't control my magic. It exploded out of me, and..."

Marcus' voice wavered. "She died... along with ten other innocent people standing nearby."

The three of us drew a breath in unison. Marcus seemed like the kind of guy sentenced to the Institute for stealing a loaf of bread, not killing nearly a dozen people. What he'd gone through horrified me.

"The coven wanted to hang me," Marcus admitted solemnly. "But my mom must've persuaded the Imperium Council, because the priestesses sentenced me to the Institute instead."

Marcus' face came out muffled as he said, "My girlfriend... I blew her to pieces. It was an accident, but it didn't matter. I saw it all."

"Marcus," Kallie breathed. "I had no idea."

I heard the brush of fabric and Marcus' stifled breathing as she pulled him into a tight hug.

"So you can see why magic is difficult for me," Marcus continued when she drew away. "I don't want to lose control. I killed my girlfriend, and so many others. I destroyed so many families, so many lives. I don't want to hurt anyone like that again."

"You won't," I promised, though I had no way to be sure. "You'll learn how to control it."

"Charlie's right," Ava said gently. For a moment, we all seemed to forget we were in the middle of the Games as Marcus' pain permeated deep into each of us, opening our own wounds.

"I just... I..." Marcus didn't seem to know what to say. He seemed like he wanted to say more, but didn't know how to talk in front of all of us.

"Could you guys give us a moment?" I asked.

"Sure," Kallie said, rising from the bench. She and Ava walked off, though close enough that I could still hear their hushed whispers. Oberi followed Ava. I took a seat beside Marcus. He shivered, and Rishi continued purring.

I swallowed the lump in my throat. "I can't say I know what it was like for you, but I was there when my best friend died, too."

"You were?" Marcus sounded surprised.

I wanted to tell him Ava had a similar experience, so he would know he was far from alone, but her story wasn't my secret to tell.

"His name was Marty," I said, because I could tell he needed the distraction from his own confession. "He was my mentor. I still remember the sound of the gunshots, the way his blood felt on my hands when I went to his side. He died in my arms."

"I'm sorry you had to go through that," Marcus said.

"Same," I told him. "But it's not your fault, Marcus. What happened with your magic was an accident. You can't blame yourself."

"I don't blame myself," he countered, but I heard the lie in his tone.

"I know what it's like to be afraid," I told him. "I know what it feels like to replay the scenario over and over, telling yourself you could've done something to prevent it."

Marcus paused for a few beats, absorbing my words. "I might know what that feels like. I'm scared to love another girl, because what if I hurt her like I hurt Anya? And if I get close to anyone, I'll disappoint them, like I did when I left her little brother behind. That's the kid I told you about, who I was teaching art to."

The confession shocked me, because I swore I was getting major love-sick vibes between him and Kallie. "Isn't there *anyone* you're interested in at the Institute?" I asked, hoping to draw an explanation out of him.

"Sure, I guess," he admitted. "But it's not like I've gotten over Anya. To be honest, I'm not sure I ever will. I thought the way to survive in prison was to keep everyone at a distance. That way, I couldn't hurt anyone. But when you guys took me in, I thought maybe things would be different. I wanted to start new, to try to overcome all that baggage. And I knew I couldn't just walk away from you guys because..." He trailed off.

"Because of what?" I asked.

He sighed. "Because the day I met you, I had my first real vision."

I sat up straighter. "What do you mean?"

"One of my powers is the power of a Seer, which can involve things like seeing the past, present or future, depending on your specialty," Marcus explained. "For me, my visions always came through taste, which I gotta tell you is fucking hard to interpret. I never know what they mean. But the day I met you, I *foresaw* Mad Dog beating your ass. I knew I had to step in to prevent it."

I didn't know what to say. "Thanks again for that."

"I didn't know why I did it at the time," Marcus said. "I like to think that maybe stepping in gave you a chance to enter the Darke Games. You, Kallie, and Ava can win this thing for sure. You can get out of here."

"What are you talking about?" I demanded. "You're part of this team, too. If we win this thing, we *all* go free."

Marcus turned away from me. "Come on, man. Don't say that. I've made it through fighting one monster. I'm not going to last another. I couldn't even get through a simple incantation."

Okay, clearly trying to connect with him wasn't working. It was time for some tough love.

I placed a heavy hand on his shoulder and smacked Marcus in the chest. "Listen to me, Marcus," I said firmly. "You possess the mark of every Cast within your coven. You're a strong warlock, and your council knows it. That's why they sent you here. Not because you committed a crime. That was an accident. It's because they were scared of you, because they know how powerful you'll become."

"How can I be comfortable with a power that scares everyone else?" he asked. "Shouldn't I be just as afraid, if not more?"

I shook my head. "You can't be afraid of yourself, because you get to *choose* how to use that power. Good and evil isn't about who has more power— it's about how they use it. And right now, Marcus, you have the chance to do some real good, by protecting Shade Hills from these monsters."

"I never thought of it that way," he admitted. "I just thought my powers were destructive."

"They don't have to be," I said. "Take my Air magic, for instance. Air gives us life— it's literally what we breathe. Without oxygen, there would be no fire, which means no heat in the winter. But tornadoes can level entire cities. I get to choose how I'm going to use that power— by giving life, or taking it away. Warlock magic can't be any different."

I actually didn't know for sure. I hadn't taken any classes on the topic and only knew what I'd picked up from the Institute. But something I said must've resonated with Marcus, because his voice seemed brighter when he spoke.

"You're right," he said. "I've been hiding from it for too long. I'll never figure out the good I can do if I'm not willing to face the bad. I have to do my part and defeat these monsters with the rest of the team."

I clapped him on the back. "That's more like it!"

Marcus cleared his throat and stood. "I think I've wasted enough time. We're losing points as we speak. Let's go find a monster to kill."

"Finally," Ava sighed, her footsteps approaching. "I'm ready for another slaying."

"Agreed," I said. "But before we go... anyone want to explain to me what this is?"

I drew out what I could only describe as a *stick* from where I'd tucked it in my uniform. At first, I'd thought it was a knife or some type of weapon, but it was thinner and smooth on all sides.

Kallie gasped, but her voice turned sour. "Where did you get that?"

I shrugged. "Swiped it off Mad Dog when he came through. Is it useful?"

Marcus yanked it out of my hands and spoke breathlessly. "Are you kidding me? This is a *wand!*"

"Oh." I hadn't realized wands were even *real*, but the answer seemed obvious now. "So it *is* useful."

"If you want to practice dark magic," Kallie sneered.

"This isn't dark magic," Marcus protested.

She scoffed. "Depends on your definition."

"Well, in my coven, wands are perfectly fine," Marcus shot back.

"It's cheating!" Kallie cried. "Your magic should come straight from you, and your power should be measured on your own merit."

Marcus sounded offended. "Even if that were true, which it's not, I'm surprised you of all people would object to dark magic."

"If you're suggesting I used dark magic to win the King's Contest—"

"Not at all," Marcus insisted. "I just meant we want to win this thing, don't we? And wands aren't against the rules in the Darke Games."

Kallie hesitated. "I guess not."

"I say we let Marcus use it," Ava voted.

"If it helps, I agree," I added. "How does it work?"

"Well, it doesn't contain magic of its own," Marcus explained. "Though this one seems to have some magical influence. It was maybe made with... unicorn hair?"

Oberi sniffed the wand and blew a breath, like she agreed.

"How can you tell?" I asked.

"I'm part Curse Breaker," Marcus reminded me. "It's one of the classifications of the Miriamic Coven. A Curse Breaker's magic is a lot more complex than the name suggests, though. They can sense magic and move it from one place to another, even change its intention."

"You can *move* magic?" Kallie balked. "So we could siphon it out of one of the monsters?"

"In theory..." Marcus said thoughtfully. "But I've never done it. The best I can do is sense how powerful they are."

"That's still useful," I encouraged. "Who should get the wand?"

"Marcus, of course," Ava said. "Wands are kind of a witch thing."

"Oh," I said lamely. I didn't know. "Have you ever used one?"

"No," Marcus admitted. "But it might help. Wands are meant to focus your powers."

Which was exactly what Marcus needed. I was glad I'd swiped the wand when I could've gone for the water bottle on the outside of Mad Dog's pack. Marcus needed to focus so we didn't all end up splattered on the pavement.

"Okay, the wand is Marcus'," I said. "Let's head further into town. Kallie said monsters like to hunt supernaturals, so that's our best bet to gather points."

"Agreed—" Ava started to say, but the sound of screams cut her off.

Several pairs of footsteps pounded on the pavement, though as I listened closely, it sounded like the team was several people short.

Ava grabbed my arm. "It's Mad Dog and Naya. They're covered in blood. They must've found the malumuto. It looks like they lost another teammate."

Mad Dog and Naya never even noticed us. They crossed the street and kept on running, the sound of their screams echoing off the houses.

"It was their mistake for not diversifying their team," I pointed out. "I say we find that malumuto and finish it off. You can do it, can't you, Marcus?"

He hesitated.

"Marcus, we don't have time," I pressed. "Are you in or out?"

Marcus' voice became firm. "I'm in."

I smirked. "Then let's go slay a demon."

It didn't take long to find the creature. All we had to do was follow the sounds of destruction. We turned down two streets before coming to a long road. The sound of wood planks— like fences being destroyed— clattered across the pavement. Trash cans clanked, and aluminum cans tumbled down the road.

I reached my Air magic out to get a sense of how far the monster was from us. This was no cat, though. This creature was much bigger, at least my size, but my Air touched something else— wings, perhaps?

Ava breathed raggedly from beside me. Her footsteps stopped, as if she needed a moment to take in the monster.

"A quick description would be helpful," I told her. "Is it the malumuto?"

Marcus was the one to answer. "It's the malumuto all right— in its true demon form."

Ava spoke quickly as she described the creature to me. "It's humanoid, but barely a man. He's shirtless, and his skin is dry and crusty, like rock. His eyes are red. Black, curved horns grow out of his forehead, and his wings are massive and leathery— like a bat's. His hands are... not even hands. He has long, black claws for fingers."

"I'm glad you can't see this, Charlie," Kallie whispered. "It's terrifying."

"What's the plan?" Marcus asked.

"I'm assuming it hasn't seen us yet?" I questioned. Judging by the ongoing sounds of destruction, it was my best guess.

"No," Marcus confirmed.

"Then Marcus is going to swing around the block and come up from behind," I decided. The best way was to make sure the demon never knew he was there. "Ava, Kallie, and I will distract it the best we can, giving Marcus the chance to speak the incantation."

"That's not going to work," Ava protested. "We should go at it from all different angles. It's our best chance to disorient it and take it out. If we all go at it head-on, we create a single target."

"That's what we want," I told her. "We want it focused on us so it never notices Marcus."

"Charlie, we have to overwhelm it," Ava insisted. "It's the only way to weaken it."

"It's not our job to kill it," I reminded her. "We're here to back up Marcus, and that's it."

"Charlie!" Ava stomped her foot.

Not a good idea. I knew the second the malumuto noticed us, because the sound of approaching destruction stopped instantly. I could practically feel its eyes narrowed on us, and dark energy seemed to roll off it in waves.

"Go, Marcus!" I cried, shoving him.

The monster's leathery wings flapped as it charged toward us. Instinctively, I thrust out a blast of Air magic, and it slammed into the demon with enough force to knock him onto the pavement. He must've not felt a thing, because his footsteps began approaching again moments later.

"*Who unleashed me?*" he growled in a voice that sounded anything but human. It was deep and distorted, sending a shiver down my spine. I always knew monsters were real, but I believed they lurked among us. This was a whole new meaning of the word *monster*.

"*Answer me!*" the demon cried in his horrifying voice. "*Who unleashed—?*"

He was cut off by the sound of gurgling, as if he was choking on water.

"Nice shot!" Kallie cried.

"What'd you do?" I demanded of Ava.

She laughed maniacally. "Just funneled some water down his throat and into his lungs."

I fumed. The dirtier we played, the more blood this demon would seek. "We want to distract it, not piss it off!"

"Too late," Ava said innocently.

My whole body shook. You know what, fuck it. This was a demon who freaking ate hearts. It was going to suffer before we sent it back where it belonged.

I blasted my Air magic outward in thin sheets. I expected the Air to slice through the demon's torso, but Ava had been right when she said his skin was like rock. My Air bounced off of it, and no amount could penetrate its shell.

Ava and Kallie weren't having any luck, either. Even Kallie's battle orbs didn't explode upon impact, but went shooting off in different directions. I heard them explode like bombs on either side of us. Ava threw a few fireballs, but abandoned those when she realized they were no use. She continued attacking with water, though the demon seemed to get over the initial shock and couldn't care less, because his footsteps were approaching. Oberi shot Fire out of her horn, and huffed in frustration beside me when that didn't work.

Something flew through the air, though I barely sensed it with my magic before the object made impact. Something sharp tore through my uniform and into the flesh on my leg. I sucked a sharp breath and cursed. Kallie cried out, and Ava grunted like she was trying to hide how much it fucking hurt. I'd been in enough knife fights to know what one felt like, and this was not it. This was something different— perhaps even magical.

"What the fuck?" I growled. Warm blood trickled down my leg.

I hadn't expected an answer, but Ava offered one anyway. "They're like... thorns!"

There came a sickening sound, like Ava ripping one of the thorns from her shoulder.

"Not thorns," Kallie gasped. "*Claws.* He's shooting his claws at us— and they're growing back!"

"Damn it, we have to slow him down!" I said to no one in particular. I hoped Marcus was close by now.

"We are," Kallie replied. "But we have to do better!"

"I'm telling you we go at all angles," Ava insisted. "He won't know who to target."

"Or he'll target one of us and that person will be SOL," I snapped. "Stick to the plan, Ava."

Another set of claws whipped through the air, but this time, I was prepared for them. I sent a gust of wind whipping sideways, and the claws went flying away from us. I tried to do the same to the demon, but he remained rooted in place. My Air magic had slowed the demon down to begin with, but something must've happened to his wings— like he'd shifted them away or something— because my Air moved around him now with ease. I couldn't get to him.

I turned to using Earth magic. Trees on the side of the road fell at my command. I aimed for him, hoping to pin him down, but he sensed them coming. The best it did was slow him down a few paces as we backed away. His rocky skin scraped the tree bark as he climbed over the fallen trees and advanced.

"Oberi, if we use the tree branches, we can hold him down—" I cut off when I realized Oberi was no longer at my side. "Oberi!?"

The unicorn nickered from at least fifteen yards away. Her hooves slapped against the pavement as she trotted in place. What was she —? *Ava!*

I heard her running now. She must've taken off when I was falling trees, so I hadn't heard her. Oberi had followed and now didn't know whose side to take.

Damn her! I gritted my teeth.

The demon moved quicker, so much that Kallie and I started running to stay away— all while throwing magic over our shoulder to slow him down.

"Pidge!" I screamed. I was too fucking angry to say anything else. She was going to get an earful later— if we made it out of this.

I heard the sound of Ava's Fire crackling, but it was more than just a mere fireball. She was whipping up a whole freaking firestorm!

"Hey!" Ava shouted to the demon. "How do you like *this*?"

I sensed the heat of the fire moving through the air, blasting toward the demon long enough to stop him in his tracks. Ava's move had pissed me off, but I couldn't stand here trying to change it. My only choice was to work with it now.

"Kallie," I snapped. "Simultension."

Kallie understood immediately. I summoned Air and quickly felt her illusion magic entangling with it. A huge weapon that hadn't been there moments ago materialized.

"It's an Air cannon," Kallie said quickly. "Use it!"

Before I could, another claw shot through the air and sliced across my shoulder. I screamed out as pain pulsed up and down my arm.

"Oh, no you don't," Ava growled loud enough for me to hear her down the street. I didn't know what she'd done, because I was dealing with my own shit over here, but it was enough to distract the demon. He turned on her, and Ava screamed.

I fucking lost it. I'd never used a weapon like Kallie's before, but I was in no position to stop and learn. I let my intuition guide me and funneled more magic into the cannon. Pressure built up until— *boom!*

An explosion went off, and Air magic so strong it could knock over a building blasted out of the cannon. I felt my magic slam into the demon before he could get to Ava. He tumbled over and over again, but like everything else we tried, he didn't seem fazed.

"*I'll have your heart for that,*" he snarled.

"You won't touch him!" Ava screamed.

Her Fire magic cut through the air like water coming out of a fire hose. Air spun around the demon as he whirled on her.

"Fuck," Kallie muttered. "Marcus is so close. Your girlfriend's going to get him— *Marcus!*"

Her words came out as a petrifying screech. Though Ava's magic continued to blast down the street, I swear my heart stopped as I heard Marcus' body hit pavement. He groaned out in pain.

Kallie took off running. My stomach hollowed out, and I raced alongside her, hoping that it wasn't as I suspected. I could only picture one of those thorn-like claws embedded in Marcus' chest.

Kallie skidded to halt at his side and bent next to him. "Marcus," she cried. "I thought he..."

Marcus sucked a breath. "It's just my arm. But we can finish this. We can—"

The demon's claws sliced through the air like paper as he swiped his arm over us. Something that felt like a bag of bricks slammed into my chest, launching me yards away from Marcus. It was the demon's rock-hard arm. I gasped for breath that didn't come as I lay there immobile. Even my magic wouldn't help me suck air into my lungs.

I'd made a horrible mistake. The thought of Marcus lying on the ground and bleeding out had distracted me more than I realized. The demon had abandoned Ava and Oberi and had come for us. I'd never seen his attack coming.

A loud *thud* came, and Kallie gasped as she too was launched in the opposite direction. Her body slammed into the grass nearby. The demon's wings flapped as it followed her, landing in front of her so her breath seemed muffled from where I lay.

"You *have unleashed me*," the demon growled in that unearthly voice. "*I will carve your hearts out one by one.*"

"Charlie!" Ava cried as she raced over to me. She knelt at my side and helped me sit up.

I shoved her off. "Forget about me. Help Kallie."

The sound of Kallie's uniform tearing sent my whole body quaking. I barely had a moment to take it all in. He was ripping through her clothes. Next, it would be her chest! Kallie screamed as she fought against the demon that was trying to take her heart.

"Leave her alone!" Marcus shouted. Something whizzed out of his palm, but it did nothing except explode against the demon's skin like all of Kallie's battle orbs had. That's when I realized it was the same thing—a battle orb, though not nearly as powerful as Kallie's.

Before Ava or I could react, Marcus ran up to us. He dropped his wand next to me. "I need your magic!" he cried.

Marcus grabbed both Ava and I by the shoulder, and an odd sensation came over me. My whole body chilled, and I felt weak as Marcus drew my magic out of me with his Curse Breaker powers. I went still as a statue, unable to control it.

Kallie screamed again, and I knew we'd reached the point of no return. The demon would take her heart, and soon, we would all die.

"Not today, motherfucker," Marcus mumbled under his breath as he shot to his feet.

This time when he created a battle orb, it was unlike anything I'd ever experienced before. It crackled above my head like electricity. It hurt my ears, and the energy tingled across my whole body. Whatever he'd created was a hell of a lot bigger than the little balls Kallie had conjured. This must've been bigger than Marcus himself.

The battle orb set free and shot through the air, tumbling over and over. It made impact with the demon, thrusting him off of Kalina. He must've flown nearly fifty yards down the street before finally landing. The battle orb exploded so loud my ears rang. Dirt and debris rained down on us.

I barely had a chance to take a breath. Marcus ducked beside me and snatched up the wand he'd dropped. His voice came out stronger than I'd ever heard it before. *"By candle flame and moonlight's kiss, I vanquish you to the Abyss!"*

Magic sizzled over my head as it shot out of the wand. The magic struck the demon, and he shrieked as it overwhelmed him. The cry grew in intensity, piercing my ears and rocking the earth—

Then, silence. Nothing but silence that seemed to weigh a thousand pounds.

"Is... is it over?" I gasped.

Marcus didn't answer me. He raced to Kallie, and I heard him swear as he stumbled over the curb to reach her.

"It's over. He's gone." Ava heaved heavy breaths, matching Oberi's beside her. "The wand, too. I guess it was a one-time use."

"Marcus did it," I remarked, partially surprised but mostly relieved.

"I wasn't sure he could," Ava admitted.

"He has the power," I said, more to myself than to her. "All the wand did was give him the confidence to use it."

The drone buzzed as it came down from the sky. "Congratulations on your second kill," a male voice came. "For slaying the malumuto, your team has gained six points, putting you in second place."

"Damn it," Kallie muttered. "Another team already got a second kill, too. We have to keep up."

"Monsters continue to roam the streets," the announcer said. "Do not underestimate their power. Stay vigilant. Stay alive."

The drone flew away, and Ava turned to me. "Look, Charlie. I'm sorry I—"

"I don't want to hear it," I snapped, cutting her off. "Kallie almost had her heart ripped out. Let's deal with that first."

To be honest, I was so pissed, I couldn't deal with Ava's apology right now. If it hadn't been for her, the demon wouldn't have noticed Marcus. It never would've gotten that close to Kallie.

We all almost died because Ava went off-script. If she pulled that again, we'd be dead by the end of the night.

I'd had enough of Ava's disobedience. I was going to make sure she didn't get us all killed.

ava-marie
TWENTY-TWO

We had to get these wounds patched up. We couldn't continue to fight monsters like this. Kallie was bleeding heavily from her chest. The demon's large claws had ripped her skin to shreds, and Marcus was sporting several cuts and bruises all over his body.

Charlie, Oberi and I were mostly fine. We'd taken hits from the claws and were bleeding, but they weren't bad injuries like Kallie and Marcus' were.

I felt guilty. Their wounds were my fault. I hadn't listened... I'd only been trying to help.

"There has to be another checkpoint somewhere," Charlie said. His voice had a tone of authority— like he wouldn't tolerate anyone defying him this time. "Let's search the area."

Kallie slowly started forward, clutching her tattered jacket to her chest. Marcus helped her walk as Charlie and I went on ahead.

Charlie was smoldering. I could feel his anger radiating at me as it pulsed through our bond. Ancestors, he was pissed. I decided it was best not to say anything and just kept my eyes ahead.

Night was falling by this time. Twilight settled over the horizon, and the sun vanished behind the thick clouds to give way to stars quicker than I anticipated. Rishi let out a yowl from up ahead. I saw with relief we'd discovered a checkpoint that no one had found yet. A small first aid kit was all that was inside.

Marcus strode forward and grabbed the first aid-kit, turning to Kallie. "Don't worry, I'll help you," he said.

Kallie winced as she shrugged off her jacket. Underneath she wore a thin white camisole that was stained with blood. Marcus began putting antibiotic cream on her wounds, and wrapped her chest slowly. Kallie's eyes were wet with pain, but she didn't even so much as hiss in discomfort.

Charlie grabbed my arm roughly and pulled me aside, far enough away so Kallie and Marcus wouldn't hear. Oberi followed us cautiously, keeping her ears up for whatever may be hiding in the woods.

"What are you doing?" I tried to wrench my arm out of his grip, but he held tight.

"Asking you what the hell you're doing out here," Charlie snarled. "That stunt you pulled was completely uncalled-for. It nearly got Kallie killed!"

My cheeks burned. "I'm sorry! I didn't want anyone to get hurt. I just thought it'd be better if—"

"Who's the Captain here, me or you?"

The drone hovered nearby, filming our performance. No doubt the screen back at the Institute was showing every moment of Charlie scolding me. I felt like a little kid who was being punished.

I scuffed my toe against the ground. "You."

"Then *listen to me*," Charlie growled. "I don't understand why it's so hard for you to do as you're told."

"I'm just trying to prove myself!" I flung my arms out wide. "I know my parents are watching. *Everyone's* watching! I want the world to see I'm not just a massive screw-up, that I can actually do something right!"

"You don't have an obligation to your parents out there. You have a responsibility to your team," Charlie said forcefully. "Fuck everyone else. If you want to stay alive, we need to be a unit. That means you need to do as I say, and not whatever you fucking feel like. We won't get through the Games if we're not together out here."

Tears beaded the corners of my eyes, and my throat got tight. He was right. I was so busy trying to impress people by doing my own thing that I put the group in danger. If Kallie, or any of the others, got killed out here because of me, I'd never forgive myself.

Oberi let out a breath that ruffled Charlie's hair, telling him to be gentler. Charlie's body went rigid as he let out a sigh. "Please, just trust me," he pleaded. "You can't keep relying on only yourself. It hurts you, Ava. Let us in and let us help you."

My throat burned even hotter, because that was the hardest thing of all. I trusted Charlie— to a point. Then my walls went up and it was hard to let him in. To be honest, I hadn't just run off because I wanted to display my powers. I was worried his plan wouldn't work, and after a lifetime of disappointments, I couldn't take one more person letting me down... especially not Charlie.

Anyone but Charlie.

But my feelings didn't matter out here. If Charlie was supposed to be my leader, I had to follow him, if only for Kallie and Marcus' sake. "Okay."

Charlie took my hand, tenderly this time. He led me back to the group, where Marcus was finishing bandaging his arm. "You guys good?"

"We'll be fine," Kallie said as she stood. She seemed a little better already. "My shifter powers will heal me quickly, and Marcus was just banged up."

"Here." Marcus handed Charlie and me a few bandages for our wounds.

"Thanks," I said as I peeled off the wrapper and helped Charlie with his leg. He did the same for my shoulder. Soon, we were all patched up.

"We should keep this kit on us," Marcus said as he clutched it to his chest. "We might need it later."

No sooner had he said that than I heard a crackle in the bushes. All four of us whipped around. Four people staggered out of the trees. One of them was clutching his stomach and wincing. The others stood tall. The rival Captain had his eyes on the first aid kit in Marcus' hands.

I didn't know his name, but I knew he was one of the leaders of one of the biggest gangs at the school. The leader sneered and said, "If you know what's good for you, you'll hand that over."

Marcus clutched the kit tighter, and Charlie said, "You can have some supplies to heal your teammate, but you can't have all of it. We'll give you what you need and go."

"Fuck that," the leader snarled. "Attack!"

Everything erupted in seconds. The gang leader had to be a warlock, because he sent a stunning spell straight at Marcus. Marcus jumped out of the way, and Kallie transformed into a wolf. She snarled and charged at the warlock. They danced around each other, Kallie lashing out with her fangs and the warlock shooting off more spells.

Charlie and Oberi took on the other guy, who had to be a shifter. Charlie shot off air funnels at the fae, who dodged him to respond with battle orbs of his own.

I summoned a fireball and flung it at the nearest enemy, which was a merman only a few feet away. He dodged my fireballs and screamed. His sonic voice knocked me off my feet, and I cried out as I went slamming into a tree.

I threw another fireball from my place on the ground, but the merman was super fast. He lunged out and dragged me upward by my hair. I yelled in terror as the merman latched his arms around me. I tried to summon a spell, but it fizzled out at my fingers as he squeezed tight.

I didn't realize how strong merpeople were. This guy was going to turn my insides to fucking jelly. I knew merpeople had water running through their veins, more so than most supernaturals. Maybe if I could summon it, and rush it to his heart, I could kill him.

But the merman was squeezing so tightly, I couldn't breathe. There was no way to command my magic when I felt this lightheaded. He was literally crushing me.

"Charlie," I whimpered helplessly, using my last breath to call out his name.

When Charlie heard me cry out for him, he immediately abandoned the fight with the shifter. Oberi charged at the shifter and chased him off with her horn, leaving Charlie able to come to my aid. He ran to me as quickly as possible. He flung out his hand, and I blacked out for a second as the merman dropped me. I collapsed on the ground, gasping for precious air.

But I wasn't the only one. The merman clutched at his own throat, face turning purple as Charlie used his Air magic to suffocate him.

Blood vessels burst in his eyes, and a horrible noise emitted from his throat as he pleaded for mercy.

The fight stopped. Kallie and Marcus observed in horror, and the teammates of the merman began backing away in fear.

Charlie was going to kill him. I knew he was. I could feel his murderous intent as it rushed through our bond. And as much as the merman might've deserved it for trying to kill me... I wouldn't allow Charlie to have blood on his hands.

I dragged myself up Charlie's body, forcing myself to my feet. "Charlie, stop! This isn't who you are!"

Charlie didn't listen. The deadliness in his face made my body turn cold. The merman slumped to the side, giving a few pathetic gasps.

"Charlie!" I put both hands on the side of his face and forced his forehead to connect with mine. "Just breathe."

Charlie seemed to realize what he was doing. He dropped the spell, and the merman took in a huge gulp of air as he fell to the side. Bruises had accumulated all over his neck.

I stared at the merman, hardly able to believe it. *Charlie* had done that. *For me.*

The gang leader had taken the momentary shock to grab the first aid kit out of Marcus' hands. He wrenched it away and began running. The other teammates followed— even the merman, though he had to stagger to get away.

"Hey!" Marcus cried out.

"Marcus, let them have it," Charlie said roughly. I watched as the other team fled into the woods, until they disappeared entirely.

Kallie scowled. "Great. Now we gave away our only supplies."

"We'll find more. It's not worth dying over." Charlie grasped my arms tightly. "You okay, pidge?"

There were still stars dancing in front of my eyes. "Yeah. I'm okay."

There was a bit of silence. Then Marcus spoke. "Dude, what did you *do* to that guy?"

"Almost crushed his windpipe," Charlie answered casually.

"Gods, Charlie!" Kallie cried.

"He'll live. For now," Charlie said darkly. He moved to put his arm around me and drew me close. I felt my shoulders relax, and Oberi let out a nicker.

Charlie was a totally different person out here. That side of him that ruled on the streets had come out during the Darke Games. I was scared of him.

But I respected him, too. And even more, I was proud to be bonded to him, because it made me feel safe. No one would fuck with me... not when Charlie was around.

I rubbed my temple. I had a headache.

"We should move on," Charlie suggested. "If there are other teams around the area, it puts us at risk."

Fine by me. We started walking deeper into the forest. Charlie's grip remained on my shoulders as we continued onward. Eventually, I got my breath back, and there was only an aching in my body to remind me of what I'd just endured.

We walked in silence for ten minutes before Charlie whispered, "You gonna be okay to get through the rest of the Games?"

"I don't have a choice, do I?" I asked. "The prophecy has to come first."

Charlie opened his mouth to say something more, but didn't. A weird feeling came over me as we stepped into this part of the woods. It was near the same road that led to the Institute, that creepy area where it felt like the very trees had eyes. I had a very bad notion we'd gone the wrong way.

Then I smelled it— a sulfur-like scent. Black pits of pitch black water spanned all around us. They weren't very big— five feet or so across— but they seemed bottomless. They weren't tar... I wasn't quite sure what kind of substance they were. I tried summoning the black water within the pits, but it didn't move to my command.

That scared me. Water had always listened to me before. That these waters didn't was simply unnatural.

Marcus knelt by one of the pools. He put his hand out to touch the water, but Kallie stopped him. "Don't," she whispered.

Marcus stood. We began weaving around the pools, taking care not to touch the water. I pressed closer to Charlie. I felt these frightening pools were one of the most evil things about Darke Island.

Kallie froze. She halted so abruptly that Marcus ran into her. He went to say something, but she waved her hand to shut him up. All of us paused, waiting for her assessment.

Kallie sniffed the air. Then her eyes contracted, and her face paled of all color just as a wicked laugh echoed through the woods.

That laugh made a shiver creep into my bones. It was the most menacing thing I'd ever heard... some sort of sound straight out of hell. Instinct told me whatever happened, we needed to get as far away from that sound as possible.

The laugh echoed again, closer this time. That's when Kallie sprang into action. "Run!" she screamed. She changed into a wolf. Marcus jumped onto her back before she started running away at top speed. He barely had time to grab Rishi.

We didn't ask any questions. Charlie and I clambered onto Oberi's back and held on tight as she galloped after Kallie. The laugh echoed behind us. My heart sped up and beat on in fear as we ran away from a faceless terror.

Kallie ran so fast, she outpaced us. We were losing her. Not even Oberi could keep up, and she let out a whinny, telling Kallie to wait for us. Oberi had to dart between all the black pools lying before us, jumping over some and nearly spinning out in her race to avoid the others.

"Kallie, slow down!" Charlie cried out. She was so terrified trying to get away from whatever was chasing us, she didn't hear, and only increased her strides.

Oberi tripped. Charlie's hands entangled in her mane, and he stayed on, but I lost my balance and fell off. I went tumbling downward, straight into one of the black pits we'd been so desperately trying to avoid.

I sank into the water. Immediately, everything went dark as my head and the rest of my body went under. The black water was slimy. I cast a spell so my Water magic would push me up, but like before, nothing happened. I attempted to swim, but the water was so thick, every movement of my arms and legs was like moving in concrete. I only sank deeper into the pool as the voices inside my mind began screaming louder than ever before.

You killed your best friend.

You didn't mean enough to her to make her stay.

If you were a better person she wouldn't have died.

My heart clenched and began to wither. It *was* my fault Monica was dead. I deserved this.

Your family is glad you're gone.

They love you out of obligation.

How could anyone want a daughter, a sister, like you?

I was such a terrible person that my parents were ashamed of me, too. My whole family was.

Charlie will get tired of you.

You're too much to handle.

It won't take long for him to abandon you.

If I could cry underwater, I'd be sobbing buckets. Charlie couldn't love me. No one could.

It's useless, Ava.

Let go.

Nothing lasts forever.

The voices were right. Eventually, everyone would leave, and I'd be alone in the world.

The darkness vanished as I returned to the day Monica died. Her death replayed in front of my eyes, over and over. The scene switched to John, and that forsaken night he'd forced himself on me. I kept reliving both, unable to escape this awful, cruel fate. My lungs tightened as I began to drown. I welcomed the end, just to make the flashbacks stop.

I wanted to give up. Dying was better than feeling this pain.

"Pidge!" I heard Charlie scream. "*Pigeon!*"

I hated that nickname, but ancestors, I wanted to hear it now. I needed to hear Charlie's voice. It was the only thing keeping me alive.

I struggled not to go under, but it was a useless endeavor. The voices were pulling me to the abyss.

I knew then. I was going to die down here.

Then I felt a hand around my arm. Someone pulled me up. I knew by the feeling of his body against mine that it had to be Charlie. He'd jumped in after me.

Despair grew in my heart. I'd condemned us both. If I was to die, so be it, but I didn't want Charlie to die along with me.

I loved him too much.

Charlie held me tightly to his form. A root wrapped around our middle and began to pull us up. Another root latched around our legs, and our arms. Charlie used the roots to pull us up, and the voices shattered my eardrums. Our heads broke the surface, and my eyes opened as I took a giant gulp of air.

Oberi had changed into his husky form. He grabbed my jacket with his teeth and pulled me out as Charlie used the roots to burst himself out of the pit. We both crawled to a nearby tree, covered in the black muck that was the pit's residue. Charlie opened his arms to me, and I fell into them.

I couldn't help but stutter. "Wh-what... w-was... t-hat?"

Charlie's voice was even, but still held an edge of fright. "Professor Cusak talked about them in class... they're called the Pits of Despair. They're living entities that feed off supernaturals. They make you relive the worst parts of your life, until you give up, and the pit consumes you whole."

My stomach bottomed out, and my voice steadied. "You knew what they were, and you still jumped in after me?"

Charlie nodded. My body gave a shudder as I asked, "What did you hear?"

"Marty. Over and over. He kept telling me to turn back and leave you," Charlie responded, haunted.

"You didn't."

"I couldn't."

Charlie and I held each other for long moments as the wind whipped through the trees. Oberi laid across our legs, to keep us warm.

The padding of paws made me look up. Kallie and Marcus had come back for us. Marcus slid off of Kallie's back with Rishi in his arms.

Kallie changed back. "I'm so sorry. I didn't mean to leave you guys like that— I panicked. I didn't turn around until Marcus said you two had fallen in."

"You came back. That's what matters," Charlie responded. We

listened again for the wicked laugh, but it was nowhere to be heard. What was chasing us must've gotten bored and run off.

Marcus turned toward Kallie. "What exactly were we running from?" he asked.

Kallie's face was still pale. "Don't ask. Just know it's something we can't fight. But I don't smell it anymore. We got away."

As Charlie and I stood, I wavered. I nearly passed out, but he caught me before I fell against the ground.

The black pit had drained me. I'd been inside longer than Charlie had, and as a result, it'd sapped all my strength.

"Guys, we're tired," Charlie said. "We need a break."

"We can't stop," Kallie insisted. "The more downtime we have, the more chances it gives the other team to earn points. We can keep going."

I wasn't sure. All of us were dead on our feet after everything that had gone on earlier. We needed some time to recover.

"A few hours' sleep is better than nothing. We'll be in a better position to fight if we rest now, rather than the teams who've been at it all night," Charlie said. "We should preserve our strength."

Kallie's eyes flickered to me, and my shaking appearance must've made her change her mind. "All right. Hold on. I'll whip something up."

We walked until we were out of the pits. I wanted nothing to do with them, and I was sure Charlie felt the same.

We came to a small clearing, and Kallie stopped. She waved her hands, and before our very eyes, a small cabin appeared. It wasn't huge— four-hundred square feet or less— but it was something. As we stepped inside, I saw that there was only a fireplace, a pot, a couch, and an armchair, along with a room that had a small double bed in the back. Her illusion magic was strong enough to make the cabin real. I pressed a hand against the wall and found it was solid.

Marcus eyed Kallie at the sight of the bare house, and she said, "Look, I'm not very good at big illusions yet. This is the best you're gonna get."

Marcus rubbed his stomach. "Man, I'm so hungry. I wish we had something to eat."

Kallie conjured up a sandwich on a plate and gave it to Marcus. He inhaled it in seconds, frowning as he finished. "I still feel hungry."

"Yeah, because food conjured by a fae illusion doesn't do anything to actually nourish you. It's basically for enjoyment only," Kallie said. "If you're hungry, we need to find something out here."

Oberi trotted out the door, wagging his tail. Rishi followed him in interest.

"Where are they going?" I asked.

"Oberi wants to investigate the area, just to be safe," Charlie said. "They'll come back in a bit. Let's get a fire started."

I was a bit jealous Oberi was communicating with Charlie over me, but I was too tired to argue. I was freezing. Charlie and Marcus went out to grab firewood, and I sat on the floor by the fireplace. I was too exhausted to move much further.

Kallie sat beside me. "Are you okay? Those pits look like they did a number on you."

"I'm fine," I lied. "I just need a nap."

"Same. It's probably for the best we stopped," she said.

She bounced nervously next to me, and I asked, "What's wrong? You seem really tense."

"Well... um, I'm a bit paranoid," Kallie confessed. "It's really awkward now with Marcus."

"Why?"

"He admitted he can only read *dirty thoughts*," Kallie hushed. "And, well... I've been having a lot of them. About... him."

"*Kallie!*" I playfully smacked her shoulder. "Are you telling me you're having daydreams about Marcus sexing you up?"

Her cheeks turned red. "No! Yes. Maybe."

She sat back. "To tell you the truth, we might've kissed when we were trying to break out forever ago. He was giving me CPR after we fought the sirens in the lake, but it turned into... more."

"No shit." I beamed, a smile spreading across my face. "You totally have the hots for Marcus!"

Kallie let out a breath. "It doesn't matter. He's a warlock. I'm a fae. Our races are constantly at war. They hate each other. We can't be together."

"Fuck that. You guys already broke the law. You're both in prison. What's stopping you?" I asked.

Kallie looked down. "I don't know. I've already disgraced my family by messing up so badly. If I mated with a warlock... I'm not sure if I could ever go back home again. Even though I'm banished, I have some hope that maybe one day, they'll take me back. And I don't want to screw that up."

"If your family doesn't approve of who you love, they're not worth it anyway," I insisted. "If you want to be with Marcus, be with him. I'm sure he likes you, too."

Kallie scowled. "If he does, he doesn't act like it. After all, I'm pretty sure he's already seen my thoughts of him screwing me over a table in the Alchemy classroom, and he hasn't acted on any of it."

"Damn, girl, that's so naughty!" I giggled. "Don't get too worried. Marcus is just shy. I'm sure he's got a hard-on for you."

Kallie didn't answer, because just then, Marcus and Charlie came back with a bundle of sticks and fallen branches. Marcus' face was red, like he knew what we'd been talking about. I guess he really *did* only see the dirty thoughts.

Charlie gave me the branches. I arranged them in the fireplace and lit them aflame. Just as I got the fire started, Oberi and Rishi returned. They were carrying small packages in their mouths. When I gave a closer look, I saw that they were bags of freeze-dried food.

"They must've found another checkpoint," I said. "Good boy, Oberi."

He panted and licked my hand. I summoned water from the air to put into the pot. We boiled the food, then ate what was inside quickly—chicken and rice. It wasn't very good, but it made the hunger pangs in my stomach fade, and some of my energy returned.

"You guys have Oberi, so you can take the bed. I'll sleep on the armchair. Marcus and Rishi can sleep on the couch," Kallie suggested.

Charlie took my hand. "Come on, pidge."

I dragged my feet to the bedroom. Charlie closed the door behind us as I drew the shades.

At least the damn drone hadn't followed us inside the cottage. We could get some privacy. We took off our boots, which were caked with mud, and threw them to the side.

Oberi hopped onto the bed just as Charlie and I lay down on it. The husky spread across our feet to warm them, and sighed as he slipped off to sleep. The dirt from the black pit spread over the sheets from our clothes, but I didn't care. It'd all disappear anyway when we left in a few hours.

"Pidge," Charlie whispered, and my eyes fluttered open. I could barely see his face by the moonlight peeking around the curtains.

"Yeah?" He'd better make this quick, because I was two seconds away from passing out.

He moved closer to me. "I'm sorry if I was too harsh on you earlier. I freaked out."

"No, Charlie. Don't apologize. You did the right thing," I said. "I needed a wake-up call."

His voice broke as he said, "You nearly died twice."

"But I didn't. You saved me. That's what counts."

I entwined my fingers with his. "What you said earlier... about listening to you. I think I'm ready to do that now. I can do it right this time. I can be obedient."

His eyebrows crinkled. "I don't want you to obey me because you think I want control."

"It's not like that. You proved you're willing to kill to protect me. I think that kind of devotion warrants my respect."

Charlie rubbed his thumbs on the backs of my hands. "I just want you to make it through this. If something happened..."

"I will make it, because I have you. I respect you so much for what you did out there. I can let you take the lead, because I know you'll make the right call."

He cleared his throat. "I, uh... appreciate all that, pidge."

My opinion from earlier had changed drastically. I thought I couldn't trust Charlie with everything, and then he'd shown me just how far he was willing to go to make sure I got through this competition safe and well. That had earned my submission.

I wanted to prove to Charlie how much I trusted him. I didn't know how, but by the end of the competition, I'd prove how much he meant to me.

"Let's get some sleep," he said. "We've still got plenty to face tonight."

Yeah, we did. I moved closer to him, just because he was warm, and it felt good to have his body conform around mine. I flipped onto my side and pressed my back against his front. He put his arm around me, and the cottage fell silent.

Damn, this was paradise. Charlie molded to me like we were two pieces of a puzzle that'd been glued together. A warm sensation grew in my chest when I felt his heartbeat against my back again... my favorite feeling. His tense muscles loosened as he held me, and I scooted back, just to be that much closer to him.

My ass hit something. *Holy ancestors almighty*, he had a hard-on. Like, the legendary kind girls gossip about, but I wasn't actually sure was real. Proof of the rare perfect dick's existence was pressed up against me, and it was still in his pants, for crying out loud. I think I was obsessed.

Charlie's breaths rose and fell evenly behind me. I think he was already asleep. Did he not notice?

The feel of him against me should've made me freak out, but... I was totally okay with it. It felt natural. I didn't feel the need to do anything with it, either. It just felt good to have him there.

My eyes closed. I counted his breaths, and it didn't take me but a few moments afterward to completely pass into peaceful oblivion.

Charlie and I awoke at the sound of a shrill scream in the night.

We bolted upright, breathing raggedly. It was still dark. We couldn't have slept for more than a few hours.

The door to our bedroom was open, and Oberi was gone. Without a word, we both clambered out of bed, put our boots back on and crept to the living room.

The cabin had gone so deathly cold there was frost on the windows. I could see my breath. Marcus sat on the edge of the couch, hands shaking. Oberi, Rishi, and Kallie were all facing the door, Kallie in her wolf form. The hair on their backs stood up, and their ears pricked. Kallie was still as a statue. Oberi let out a low growl, and Rishi followed it up with a hiss.

"*Something's moving out there*," Kallie said. She used her magic to project her thoughts outward, so she could speak in her wolf form. She put a paw forward, waiting to attack.

There was a sound on the side of the cottage like nails on a chalkboard. Something was dragging their claws over the wood. Goosebumps quivered over my skin, and my eyes grew wide as I realized thick ice was spreading all over the wall. I lashed out a hand to stop it, but as I stopped the growth of one ice patch, another took its place.

"We need to leave. Now." Kallie nudged the door open with her head and began hurrying as silently as she could into the woods. The rest of us followed. Oberi guided Charlie so he could keep up. As I looked behind, the cottage vanished as the illusion faded.

Except there was nothing waiting in its stead to hunt us down. That had to be the scariest thing of all.

There was a crackle in the bushes. Kallie froze. She changed back, clinging to Marcus' arm. Oberi began to whine.

"Shit." Kallie started freaking out. "Shit, shit, shit! He found us."

"I'm guessing you're talking about the monster we fled from earlier?" Marcus asked hoarsely.

"Yes. I thought he'd abandoned the hunt, but apparently..." Kallie swallowed and shook her head, like she was spooked.

"How close is he?" I remained at the ready to light a fireball.

"Close. Maybe we can lose him again." Kallie hurried on ahead.

The forest was so dark I could barely see a thing, even with the moonlight. Then Marcus let out a yell, and my shoe met something soft and squishy at the same time.

I couldn't help it. Instinctually, I lit a fireball for light. I wished I hadn't. My firelight illuminated the forest, showing four bodies... one of the other teams. They'd been ripped open. There was so much blood that the area was coated red. Organs were spewed all over the place. I'd stepped on an intestine while walking onto the scene.

Marcus threw up. I barely held it in myself. I told myself those weren't people. Just animals, deer, like I'd hunted with my dad. I forced myself to look into the trees instead of at the bodies.

I was grateful Charlie couldn't see this, but he could still smell it. He covered his nose to muffle the metallic smell of blood and rotting corpses.

Kallie's voice was hollow. "He made them fight each other, then when he got bored, he eviscerated them. It's how these kind of monsters hunt."

"What is it?" Charlie's tone steeled, preparing himself.

"It's a lichen," Kallie said breathlessly. "It's a sorcerer that's sold his soul to dark forces to literally become demonic."

"He did that to them?" Marcus asked weakly as he wiped his mouth.

"Yes. And that's what we'll be if we don't get out of—"

Kallie didn't finish her sentence, because she was blasted off her feet by a ray of red light. All of us called for her. She sailed through the air and landed on her hip, crying out in pain as she looked at what attacked her.

A sorcerer made of bone stood across from us. A bloody red robe hung around his skeletal form, skull still dripping with rotted flesh. The lichen held a twisted staff forged from dark wood, a red ruby on top that looked like an eye. His bones clicked together as he raised a hand to point at us, and from his rotting fingertips erupted yet another spell. The red ray shot out of his hand and collided with a tree. It began falling over, and Marcus leapt out of the way with a scream.

Rishi didn't stick around. He ran into the trees with a yowl, vanishing into the night as he fled to ancestors only knew where.

"Fuck! We're dead, we're dead!" Kallie screamed.

Kallie's reaction told me everything I needed to know. We'd found the wrong monster, and now, the lichen was going to make us his bitch.

We began an all-out attack just to survive. Every single one of us lashed out with a spell. Charlie flung out his Air magic, I created two tunnels of both Fire and Water, Kallie flung her battle orbs, and Marcus conjured the biggest stunning spell he could muster. Oberi changed into a unicorn and blasted fire out of her horn.

Magic came at the lichen from all sides, but he merely threw a hand up, and a red shield expanded in front of him. Our magic immediately died once it hit the shield.

My mouth dropped open. If I had thought the balur was out of our league, the lichen was practically a god. Nothing we had in our arsenal could handle this.

The lichen pointed his staff at each of the bodies littering the area.

Like twitching spiders, they began to rise. More organs slopped out of their bodies as they walked forward, controlled by the lichen's necromancy magic, blankness in their eyes. Kallie screamed as one of the zombies grabbed her. She kicked it away, though they continued to stalk toward us at the lichen's command.

A surge of protectiveness came over me, and I blasted the biggest Fire column I could possibly muster. I screamed as the Fire column enveloped the zombies, turning them to ash. They flailed against my flames, as if trying to put them out, before they fell to the ground again and dissolved into ash.

The lichen was unbothered. The black holes in his skull glittered... like he thought this was a game.

"Use simultension!" Charlie cried out.

Kallie conjured the swords for us again. I infused my weapon with my Fire, and yelled as I charged at the lichen. He reached out and grabbed the blade, then squeezed. It melted away at his touch, and my chest grew cold. The lichen pounded his staff into the ground, and the swords that the others held melted away, too. Charlie gasped as the molten liquid burned his hand, though he dropped the hilt before any real damage could be done.

The lichen let out that deceptive, mocking laugh, and ancestors, it nearly made me want to vomit. He waved his staff, and before my very eyes, the lichen began to duplicate. He became three different bone sorcerers, facing Kallie, Marcus, and Charlie in turn.

I didn't have time to react. The sorcerers changed into balls of light, and went zooming into my friends' bodies. Each of them cried out as the light settled into their bodies... then went utterly still as their eyes glowed red.

Kallie, Marcus, and Charlie all turned at the exact same time. Oberi gave a nervous noise, and I realized... the lichen had possessed them. I was the only one left still in control of my body.

Charlie raised a hand, and I had to duck as an Air column cut a tree in half behind me. Kallie and Marcus both began firing off battle orbs. They exploded all around me, and I screamed once again. *This* is what the lichen had done to the other team— made them fight each other until they were all dead.

I flung Water magic out at them. Maybe I could freeze the demon out, like I tried in practice. But as Kallie, Marcus, and Charlie halted in place, ice creeping across their skin, I realized my efforts were all but pointless. Their skin was turning blue, and I was certain I was hurting them more than the lichen. I drew away the freezing spell, acknowledging that it had no effect.

If I wanted to survive, I only had one option— I had to *kill my friends*.

I couldn't think, but Oberi had more sense than I did. She used her neck to swing me onto her back, and she turned to gallop away.

"Oberi, we can't leave them!" I protested.

She didn't listen. Oberi fled the area, mane flying backward as her hooves pounded into the earth. I glanced behind. I didn't see the lichen, but his terrible laughter crawled across my skin as he chased me through the dark forest, looming closer and closer.

Ancestors, Great Spirit, anyone! I pleaded in my head. *Save us!*

The lichen's laugh was growing so loud, it rang in my ears. Then all of a sudden... it stopped. I could feel the lichen's presence leave me abruptly, like it turned back somehow. I don't know why it would, but I was so grateful to be free of him that I cried tears of relief.

Then tears of sorrow, because the team I loved was still back there in his grasp.

Oberi slowed to a standstill in a clearing in the middle of the woods. Here, the trees were less thick, and a strong ray of moonlight illuminated the area.

I slid off of Oberi's back and faced her. "How could you do that?" I yelled. "Charlie is still back there!"

Oberi nickered. She bobbed her head, like she wanted me to turn around.

"Why did you even bring me here?" I threw my hands up as I spun on my heel. My frustration with my Familiar fell flat as I saw there was someone else with me in the clearing.

It wasn't a monster. I knew that much. This was something different. The creature in front of me was a coyote, but it wasn't like any animal I'd ever seen before. The coyote's fur was orange, with red lines running through his fur and over his amber eyes. Hawkei runes, like the ones chieftains used to write their edicts, were written over the red lines in a soft blue. The entire coyote gleamed like a candle against the night. His tail was nothing but a flame that fanned out behind him.

The animal gave a toothy grin. *Well, this is nice,* the coyote spoke in my mind. *Usually when I meet supernaturals, they bow before me, professing how great I am. You are a divergence from the typical.*

I tilted my head. I couldn't believe who was standing in front of me... but from all the Hawkei tales I'd heard from my father, I knew this could only be but one deity. "You're Coyote Spirit. The Fire god. You're one of the pieces of the Great Spirit."

I am the Koigni god, yes, Coyote replied. *How coy of you to notice.*

His voice dripped with sarcasm. My heartbeat picked up speed. "Wh— why are you here?"

You called me, remember? Coyote replied. *You asked for help, and here I am.*

I had asked for help... but I'd never had a god show up before me when I prayed before. I threw a nervous glance over my shoulder, and Coyote said, *You need not fear. The lichen will not follow you if I am around. It is afraid of me.*

By all respects, I should've been afraid of Coyote, too. I mean, I was talking to a god, here. And not just any god— a trickster god, one of the most famous to play pranks on supernaturals for his own entertainment.

But I didn't feel any fear when I looked at Coyote. Merely reassurance.

"You want to help me? I didn't think I was that special."

I have been following you for a long time, Coyote said, and he gave a delighted cackle. *I tricked your father to fall in love with your mother, and you are the fantastic result... one of my greatest creations.*

"You made me?" I asked.

Coyote gave a casual shrug. *With the help of others. Many years ago.*

I scowled when I thought of how Coyote said he'd tricked my father. He might've thought bringing a Koigni and a Toaqua together was funny, but my parents truly loved one another. They weren't pawns for him to play with.

But what if he saw me in the same way... as a toy? "How do I know you haven't tricked me, and this isn't a trap?"

Coyote gave a scathing sound. *As if I need to trick you to get you to make the wrong decision.*

Coyote cast his head around, like he was indicating my participation in the Darke Games. Then he paused and said, *Or is it the right one?*

This god was a major douchebag. And part of the Great Spirit or not, I really didn't feel like putting up with his sass.

"Are you here to torment me, or are you actually going to give me a message?" I crossed my arms. "Because I seriously don't have time to be dicking around."

Coyote blinked. Then he shifted, transforming into a man. His skin still had that orange hue, red lines and blue runes running over his form. His clothes were made of animal bones, leather, and furs. His eyes remained animalistic. "*Do you want my guidance, or not? There are other supernaturals who'd be more grateful for my help.*"

I tapped my chin. "Well... can you like, go back there and kick that lichen's butt for me? Because that would be really awesome."

Coyote shook his head. "*I cannot do that. Your participation in these Games is a test by the gods, and you must pass this test to move on to the next one. There will be many more.*"

"Excuse me?"

"*Your prophecy speaks of a war of gods. Here I am, one of the first to appear. There will be others, if you survive.*"

"One of the first?"

"*Different gods have come to you before.*"

Memories popped out at me. Ending up alone in the forest as a child, facing that mysterious creature in the forest. The blue eyes I'd seen the night my father was healed.

"*You might want to get a move on,*" Coyote purred. "*The public is waiting.*"

Coyote pointed upward. The drone hovered above. I hadn't realized it was still following me.

I raised an eyebrow. "Um... aren't you afraid of being caught on film?"

"*You're the only one who can see me. Right now, the audience thinks you've gone insane and are talking to yourself.*"

"That's perfect," I grumbled.

"It's not like you have a spotless reputation," Coyote said.

"So what do I do? My friends are possessed, and aside from my Familiar, I'm all alone," I said in despair.

"You have everything you need to save your friends. Look all around you. The Great Spirit does not lead one into a situation without providing a way to get out," Coyote replied.

"How? The lichen is so powerful!" I objected.

"I didn't say it'd be pleasant or easy," Coyote drawled. *"You've received the lessons you need. All you must do is apply them."*

Coyote began to fade away. His maniacal snickers rang in my ears as he vanished before my eyes. Oberi snorted, and we were once again alone in the clearing... though I felt like Coyote's eyes were on me, watching me.

I wasn't sure if that was one of my psychotic visions or if I'd actually seen a god, but it didn't matter, did it? Coyote was right. I couldn't just give up. There had to be *something* I could do to save my team.

Professor Hemlock's lecture came back to me. The potion we'd brewed in class. She said it was effective for exorcising evil spirits— and all the ingredients were on Darke Island. I was good at potions. I knew I could handle this.

I immediately began scouring the forest. Oberi followed, changing into a husky and putting his nose to the ground to sniff out what we needed.

I remembered the ingredients of the potion exactly. *Bay leaves, cloves, star weed, and sage.* Oberi and I looked everywhere. Dawn began rising over the horizon, igniting the forest in color. As I found the star weed— the last ingredient— I felt a bit of victory, though the next step made me pause.

I had the ingredients, but I didn't have a way to brew them. I needed a cauldron, and a vial. Kallie could generate them if she was here... but she wasn't. I had to find them on my own.

I was just about to give up when I smelled something on the air. Soup... someone was cooking something. It might be one of the other teams.

I could steal their pot away... it might give me a shot. I followed the smell. Oberi pressed close to me as I peered out from the trees.

It was Alice and her team of innocents. They were gathered around a fire, eating some kind of stew from the pot I needed. The pot had been pulled off the fire and looked cool. Beside it sat a few empty food jars that would be perfect for containing my potion.

They must've gotten those items from another checkpoint. I paused. Could I really take from Alice and the others?

If it was to save my friends? Yes. I moved forward, preparing to attack from behind.

My shoe broke a twig, and I cursed. Alice, Despona, Carson and Wesley all jumped. Their eyes met mine, and I gave up. I came out of the bushes, giving a sigh.

"Ava," Despona said. "What are you doing here? Where's the rest of your team?"

"They've been possessed," I admitted. "I'm the only one left."

I raised a hand to show them the ingredients in my hand. "I can brew a potion to save them, but I need a pot, and..."

My head dropped. "You know what, you guys can just kill me. I know you want to win, and my team's pretty much done for, anyway. It would help your rankings if you got rid of us. So, go on. Just make it quick."

Despona stared at me. Then she reached out and grabbed the pot and a vial from the ground. She held them out to me. "Here. Take them."

I blinked. "Huh?"

"We're done eating. You can have them," she said.

"But... you guys might need them to brew your own potion later," I said.

"It doesn't matter. You need them more now." Despona pushed.

I felt so honored by her offer. They didn't need to help me. It'd be in their benefit if they didn't. Yet they didn't just care about themselves out here.

I took the pot and the jar. "Thank you so much. You're literally saving my ass."

"Hey, we all gotta look out for each other out here," Carson said. "Don't mention it."

I gave them a nod, then ran off before they could change their minds. I stopped by a stream that I found in the forest, then washed out the pot and the jar before I filled the pot with water. I lit a fire, then began adding ingredients, using stones as knives to cut up what I needed. I felt a beading of sweat along my brow as I worked faster than ever before. I hoped to the ancestors my friends were still alive, and that the lichen hadn't killed them.

Finally, I poured the finished mixture into the jar. I was certain I had it right, but there'd be only one way to tell.

I had the potion. If I got it down my teammate's throats, I could make it so they were no longer possessed. But that would only go so far. We still didn't have a way to kill the lichen.

A bout of inspiration struck me. I was two Houses— Toaqua and Koigni. What if I could use simultension on *myself?*

Fusing my Fire and Water together seemed impossible. They were total opposites. But it was worth a shot, right? I didn't have any other ideas.

I conjured Fire in my right hand and Water in my left. I began bringing the two sides together slowly, focusing my intention on melding the two.

I thought it would be hard. But it was as easy as breathing. The water ball and the fire combined, and they swirled in my palm until the result was a burning blue flame, suspended at the tips of my fingers. In awe, I felt the edge of the blue fire. It was cool to the touch, like ice. But when I pushed my hand in further to the fire's core, my skin was met with a blazing inferno. I pulled back, marveling at the magic in my hands.

Clever girl, Coyote purred. I looked around, but didn't see him.

I wasn't sure if my blue fire would kill the lichen, but it was the best chance I had. I stood with the potion in one hand and my blue fire in the other.

Marcus seemed like the easiest target. I'd go after him first. "Find Marcus, boy," I told Oberi. He barked and put his nose against the ground, searching out for Marcus' scent.

We walked for half a mile before I saw him. He was walking around, looking for me. His eyes still burned red as the lichen used his body to navigate.

Oberi pressed to the ground as I snuck up on Marcus from behind. When I was close enough, I jumped. But the lichen must've sensed me coming, because Marcus spun around, malice on his face.

I immediately felt a telekinetic burst that erupted out of Marcus' mind. It grabbed me and threw me backward, knocking the wind out of me.

Okay, Marcus apparently wouldn't be as easy as I thought. Shit.

I clenched at my gut and rolled out of the way as Marcus began levitating logs using his mind, tossing them at me at high speed. I'd only just managed to jump to my feet before Marcus used his telekinesis powers to wrench a huge tree out of the ground. He tossed it my way, and Oberi yelped. I dodged the massive trunk of the uprooted tree as it slammed into the ground.

Okay, Marcus was either holding back on his powers, or he didn't believe in himself, because the lichen was using his body like a fucking master warlock. Marcus went to levitate the tree again, to use as a hammer to smack me into the earth. Before he could, Oberi growled and launched himself on Marcus. He pinned Marcus to the ground, and as the tree dropped to the forest floor again, I scrambled for the potion. I unscrewed the cap and forced Marcus' jaw open. I poured it down his throat, and Marcus wretched for a moment, giving a gasp as a red blur shot out of his throat.

One of the manifestations of the lichen appeared. The skeleton clacked its teeth and moved in, stretching his arms toward me. Marcus screamed, but I reached my hand back and flung my blue fireball.

The lichen put up a shield, but the blue fireball sailed right through it. It connected with the skeleton's head and made it explode in a flash of blue light.

I didn't realize I'd been holding my breath until my lungs began to ache. The rest of the lichen's body dissolved into dust upon the wind. Marcus' eyes bulged out of his head.

My blue Fire could kill the lichen. We still had a chance!

"Di-did you kill it?" he asked.

"There are still two parts of the lichen in Kallie and Charlie," I said as I helped him to his feet. "If we can kill both, we'll be safe."

Rishi came out of the woods. He hadn't gone far from Marcus, and was only hiding. Oberi licked his ears as Rishi greeted him.

"Where do you think Kallie is?" Marcus whispered.

"She can't be far from here. Oberi will show the way," I said.

Oberi wagged his tail, then trotted forward. Marcus and I stayed close as he led us to a part of the forest that was far less dense, with fewer trees to hide behind.

I saw a flash of silver fur. Kallie was in her wolf form, eyes shining bright red. She snarled and growled, though there was no enemy in her sight. We were upwind, so she couldn't smell us... not until the wind changed, at least, and I didn't know how long that would be.

Kallie had killed a deer. Her fur was stained red as she tore at it, eating the heart whole. My nose wrinkled. The lichen had to be hungry.

I really didn't want to fight Kallie, especially not in her wolf form. She was a brutal fighter, and she'd rip us to shreds.

"How do you plan on getting that potion past her massive jaws without being bitten in half?" Marcus hissed.

"We can't fight her, that's for sure. We need to trick her," I whispered.

Marcus nodded. "I have an idea. Follow my lead."

He slipped off with Rishi. I waited for a few moments, until suddenly, the dead deer shot upright, blank eyes shooting wide open.

Kallie leapt backward, giving a yelp of surprise. The dead deer bounded off, and I realized Marcus was using his necromancy powers to make it run. The deer's insides and blood slicked out of its body as it ran to get away from Kallie.

Kallie growled and chased after her prey, the lichen's magic driving her on. I remained behind a tree and prayed this would work.

The dead deer ran past. Kallie zoomed by a second later. By then, Oberi and I were waiting for her. Oberi tackled Kallie to the ground with a snarl. Though he was only a third the size of her, he was strong, and he held her down. Kallie's jaws snapped and snarled, but Oberi didn't let her up.

My hand almost slipped on the jar as I danced around Kallie's violent fangs, attempting to spill the potion inside. A few drops fell past her lips. Her eyes widened, and a red blaze erupted from her mouth.

The lichen materialized a few feet away. He flew forward like some cursed ghost, pointing his staff at me, but I had a blue fireball waiting. I smashed it into his face, and the lichen howled before that part of him burst into ash.

Kallie changed back into a woman. There was still blood on her face from her recent kill. The dead deer slumped to the side as Marcus let go of the necromancy spell.

"How the fuck did you kill that thing?" Kallie asked.

"I've been experimenting," I told her, showing her the blue fireball. "And I'm not done yet. We still have to save Charlie."

"Kallie!" Marcus lunged forward and hugged her so tightly, he lifted her feet off the ground. Kallie closed her eyes and hugged Marcus back, body slumping in relief.

"How'd you do that, Marcus?" I asked. "I've never seen you pull off magic like you've been doing in the Games."

"Honestly, I didn't really know I *could* do all that stuff," he admitted. "I just... realized I had to, in the moment."

Oberi barked, insistent we get a move on. Anxiety bloomed in my stomach. Charlie was the last person we had to save, but he was also the most powerful. If we got into a fight, I might have to hurt him to save the others.

I didn't know if I could do that. Hurting Charlie would be like hurting myself. Worse, even.

Though I might have to make a choice to save my friends.

Charlie wasn't far from where the others had been. He waited in the trees, being ever still as he listened for any sound of life. The warmness in his brown eyes was gone, replaced with red.

We had a slight advantage. Charlie was blind, and the lichen controlling his body didn't know how to navigate without sight. He wouldn't see us coming, but he would hear us. We had to be quiet.

All of us remained silent. Kallie brought out her fae wings. She began fluttering in a circle around Charlie, planning to creep up on him from behind. Marcus conjured a stunning spell and went in from the side.

I faced Charlie head-on, a blue fireball in my hands. Oberi was beside me. Marcus drew back his spell. I nodded, and Kallie flew forward.

Charlie must've heard the beat of her wings, because he turned on his heel and waved his arm. A tree limb shot out and punched her backward. Kallie gave a sound of pain as she was slapped against a tree trunk. She slumped against it, unconscious.

Marcus let out a cry when he saw Kallie pass out. He flung out his stunning spell, but Charlie emitted such a powerful gust of wind that it caught Marcus' ball of electricity and sent it spiraling back at him. Marcus' own spell smacked him in the chest, and his eyes rolled backward as he knocked himself out.

Fucking great. Both my allies were down. A wave of terror ran through me, and that's when Charlie turned back around in my direction.

I hadn't made any noise, and he couldn't see me... how could he realize I was right there?

Then I felt a nauseating expression of bloodthirst radiate from Charlie, and I realized... our bond. Charlie had felt my fear. He knew I was right in front of him.

Charlie cut through the air with his palm, and I flattened myself against the ground. A shockwave of Air so powerful blasted over my head, knocking over the trees behind me. Charlie used his Earth power to make the uprooted trees move, their spindly branches reaching for me like fingers.

If those trees got their branches around me, they'd rip me to shreds. I swung my arm outward. Blue fire ignited the branches, and the trees withdrew as their wood burned to ash. I forced myself to my feet before Charlie could make another move.

"I'm just as bullheaded as you, you stubborn bastard," I growled. "And I am *not* letting this monster use you like this."

Charlie sent out another gust of wind, but I rolled out of the way. Oberi came in from the other side and knocked him down. Just as Charlie lost his balance and fell onto his back, I opened the jar and forced the rest of the potion into his mouth.

Charlie coughed and sputtered. The red beam flung past his lips like a beacon, and the last piece of the lichen materialized in front of me. The lichen raised his staff, and red magic pulsed through the air, a crackling noise resonating that threatened to do to us what had been done to the other team.

"Oh, no you don't," I snapped. I shoved my palm outward, and a column of blue fire smashed into the lichen's chest. The lichen dropped his staff, throwing his head back and emitting an inhumane screech.

Sweat ran down my skin as I infused my blue Fire into the lichen's bones, making it spread all throughout his body. The demon's entire form began to glow blue, until the lichen gave one final infernal scream, and I forced my magic outward.

The lichen blew up. Pieces of bone scattered everywhere, pinging off trees, until all that was in the lichen's stead was a dismembered skeleton.

I gave a couple of gasps to recover my breath. Charlie sat up slowly, like he wasn't sure what had just happened.

"Pidge," he said, as if worried the lichen was still here.

"It's over. I got him." I sat back against a tree trunk and allowed myself a five-second break. Damn, that fucker had been hard to beat. But at least we were still alive.

Kallie and Marcus crawled over to us. They'd come around, but moved slowly, as if they were still recovering.

"That was some powerful magic, girl," Kallie said as she leaned on Marcus.

"Don't thank me. Thank Alice and her team," I said. "They gave me the cauldron to brew that potion. Without them, we'd probably all be dead."

"Pidge," Charlie said again. It was like that was all he could say. He leaned forward, and I put my head against his. He was still trembling.

Ancestors, I was so fucking glad he was alive. We'd gotten lucky this time.

Oberi gave a whine, and Charlie reached out a hand to pet him. Rishi sat at our feet and lashed his tail, playing with one of the pieces of the lichen's bones.

I heard the sound of the drone again, coming down from the sky. Marcus, Kallie and I looked up as the screen emerged from the drone, and Professor Hemlock's visage appeared before us.

"Well done," she praised. "For defeating the lichen, your team has earned ten points, tying you up with two other rivals."

The rankings flashed on screen, and my blood ran cold. There were only four teams left— ours, Mad Dog's, the gang leader's, and Alice's group of innocents.

The rest hadn't made it through the night.

With another glance at the points, I realized we were tied up with Mad Dog and Alice. The gang leader's team had fallen so far behind, there was no way for him to catch up.

Professor Hemlock's face appeared on screen again. "There is but one monster left to defeat. Stay vigilant. Stay alive."

The screen shut off, and the drone hovered away. A chill wracked my body as I realized our only option.

We were tied with two other teams. There was only one monster left... one way to gain more points. If we wanted to earn our pardon, and win the Games, we had to find the final monster, and kill it before anyone else.

It was our last shot at getting out of here.

charlie
TWENTY-THREE

y shoulders sagged. Only one monster left. That was good news. But it also meant one more battle with my teammates, and I didn't know how much more we could handle. We'd barely slept, and our meal last night was hardly a meal. Each of my teammates had been in mortal danger more than once. I couldn't handle losing even one of them. I just couldn't.

Get it together, Charlie. The voice in my head was my own, but the feeling had come from Oberi. She was in unicorn form, ready to take on the final monster. She nudged me with her velvet nose, nuzzling into my shoulder. The energy she emitted was calming and sure.

I stroked her nose. She was right. I had to get it together and lead my team through our final battle. All we had to do was kill one more monster, and we'd be free of the Institute. Ava-Marie and I would be free to pursue information about the prophecy. Marcus could go home and resume teaching his mentee. Kallie would have a chance to see her family again and make amends. It didn't seem to matter what shape we were in. The rewards were far too great. We'd do anything to win those points.

"Which way, Captain?" Marcus asked as Ava and I got to our feet.

I sighed and titled my head to the side, listening to the sounds of Shade Hills. The morning sun touched my skin, but it felt dull and cold, like there was a thick layer of clouds in front of it. The island was eerily quiet. I was so used to the bustle of the city. Even in the Institute, mornings were filled with slamming doors and the thump of footsteps as students hurried to class. Out here at the edge of the forest, there was nothing... not even the chirp of birds. It was as if the wildlife was terrified of what hid in the woods.

"I don't know," I admitted. "The monster could be anywhere on the island."

"I told you before," Kallie said, "monsters seek out prey. We have to go back to Shade Hills."

"Are you sure that's *all* monsters?" Ava asked. "If it's terrorizing the town, where are the screams? Where's the sound of destruction?"

Kallie thought about it for a moment. "Maybe it's waiting for its victims, so it can catch them off-guard."

"Either way, that means we have to head back toward town," I decided.

"I agree with the Captain," Marcus said. "We only have one chance to get to this thing first and win those points. We have to give it our best shot."

"Then let's move." I placed my hand on Oberi's back, and she navigated us toward the main road. The air expanded, and the drone above hummed. I paid close attention to the sounds around us, focused solely on spotting any signs of the monster.

"It would've been helpful if they told us what type of monster we were up against—" Marcus said, but I held up a hand to cut him off.

"Shh... I heard something," I hissed.

We all froze and listened intently, but we were only met with silence.

"What did you hear?" Ava breathed.

"Something like a stick breaking," I answered. "It's at least twenty yards off, but close—"

A figure leapt from out of the trees. I could tell by the way it moved through the air that it was about my size— a little bigger. It growled like a human. If I was supposed to be scared, I wasn't.

Marcus yelped, and Rishi hissed.

"Don't move!" a deep voice warned. That's when I realized this wasn't the monster at all. It was Mad Dog.

Another figure stepped out of the trees, though her footsteps were lighter. "Take another step, and you're dead," Naya threatened. "That monster is ours."

Ava took a confident step forward. "Oh, yeah? And you two are going to stop the four of us?"

Naya's teeth ground together. "Turn around, and go back to the Institute."

To my surprise, Marcus followed her instructions. His boots clunked loudly on the road as he walked away from us. I was quick to grab him. "We're not going anywhere! Marcus, don't quit on me now."

"He's not quitting on you," Kallie seethed. "Naya's compelling him!"

The blood drained from my face. Within the Institute, succubi wore low-powered noxite bracelets so they couldn't compel the guards. Out here, they had no such restrictions.

"It should be working on all *four* of you!" Naya yelled. "Turn back! You're not taking that monster from us."

Ava just laughed. "You have to be *powerful* to compel another supernatural. You can't brainwash all four of us at once."

"Do as she says," Mad Dog sneered, but nobody listened. He was only a vampire and didn't have the extra powers of an incubus or succubus. I'd learned from the other inmates that succubi like Naya were basically vampires on steroids. They were superior to vampires because of their power of compulsion.

But Naya's compulsion wasn't strong enough. It wasn't something the Institute taught or allowed her to practice.

I slapped Marcus a few times to get him to come back to us. After a third slap, he shook his head.

Mad Dog let out a heavy sigh, though there was satisfaction in his tone. "It looks like we're going to have to do this the hard way."

Kallie shrieked and jumped backward, almost toppling over Marcus and me. "He's got a knife!"

He must've found one at a checkpoint. Mad Dog moved at an inhuman speed, so fast that the air billowed behind him. He aimed for the girls first. I threw out my hands, and a gust of wind blasted him backward onto his ass. Satisfying as hell.

I stalked forward, planting myself in front of the girls so he couldn't get to them. "You really want to have this fight again?"

Mad Dog laughed as he got to his feet. "Gladly. Because this time, I'll win."

"Like hell!" I conjured up another blast of air, but Mad Dog moved so fast that it never reached him. He dodged around it and tackled me to the ground. The blade he held sliced through the air. I caught his wrist before the dagger could cut my face, though I felt the point of the knife against my cheek.

Hell, he was strong. I had to use my Air powers to press against him. Sweat broke out on my brow. Oberi whined, and I was sure Ava called out my name, but I couldn't make sense of the scuffle going on nearby. Naya was attacking my friends. I was sure of it. But all I could focus on was the blade hovering a mere inch from my nose.

"I won't get points for killing you," Mad Dog sneered. "But it will be worth it, you filthy Elementai."

"In your fucking dreams," I snapped. I gathered enough energy to create another blast of wind. Mad Dog went flying off of me, flipping several times as he flew through the air.

I scrambled to my feet just in time to hear the unfolding of wings. At first, I thought it was Kallie, but these wings weren't the small, delicate ones Kallie had. They were heavy and leathery, like a bat's.

The succubus. She had freaking *wings*!

Kallie laughed, and then came the buzz of her insect-like wings. "You think flying makes you stronger, Naya? I'll kick your ass in the air and be proud of it."

"Be my guest." Naya chuckled.

The two took off to the skies. I was ready to knock Naya out of the air with my magic, but Mad Dog was on the move again. Marcus screeched as he dove for him, and Ava conjured a fireball. It hit Mad Dog, but didn't slow him down. The buzz of a battle orb sounded as it erupted from Marcus' hands. Mad Dog tripped, but he was on his feet again in moments.

How the hell did you fight a vampire? We could match his strength and speed with our magic, but he was freaking immortal.

I wasn't here to kill the other teams, though. Our only goal was to kill that monster— and kill it first.

I conjured roots from the ground. If I couldn't kill Mad Dog, slowing him down was the next best thing. He tripped as my roots wrapped around his legs. His heavy body shook the earth as he landed, and the dagger skidded across the ground. Mad Dog let out a pained cry as the roots tugged on his legs.

"We have to get out of here!" I cried.

Ava already had another fireball blazing in her hand. "It's not going to do anything, pidge," I told her as I hoisted her onto Oberi's back. "Let's go!"

I reached up to knock Naya out of the sky with my Air, but Oberi grabbed my collar in her teeth and threw me onto her back. She took off running. I was only half on, and had to dig my fingers into her coat to keep from falling off.

"Oberi!" I yelled, heart pounding. We couldn't leave the others behind! The trees rustled around us as we raced through the woods. I couldn't tell how far we'd gone.

"*Oberi!*" I repeated.

Ava must've tugged on Oberi's mane, because the unicorn slowed to a trot. I groaned as I pulled myself onto her fully and sat behind Ava.

Ava's tone was hollow. "We lost Marcus and Kallie."

My head swiveled from side to side as I listened for his clumsy footsteps or the sound of Kallie's paws, but they never came. Even the sound of the drone was gone.

"They shouldn't be far behind," I said, more to myself than to Ava. I was sure Marcus and Kallie could handle the vampire and succubus themselves, but they shouldn't have to.

"We have to go back," I ordered Oberi.

Oberi spun, and she stomped in place.

"What is it, girl?" I demanded. "Let's go!"

Oberi didn't move.

"Shit, we're lost," I realized. "Why'd you take off, girl?"

"I think she got spooked," Ava said, stroking Oberi's fur softly. "We'll find them. Marcus and Kallie can handle those pricks."

"I know that," I stated, though my confidence wavered. Marcus had proven himself in the Games, and Kallie had long before that. But there were more to the Games than the other teams. They might not make it if they ran into the monster alone. We had to find them— and fast.

"Any idea where we came from?" I asked Ava. I hadn't been paying close enough attention.

"It all looks the same to me," she admitted.

"Oberi, come on," I pleaded. "Your sense of direction has been infallible until now."

Oberi nickered and shook her head, like she wasn't quite sure she deserved the compliment. She'd spun in so many circles, I couldn't find my bearings.

"Let's continue straight ahead," Ava suggested.

I'd been thinking the same thing, but it was unusual for Ava and I to have the same idea. Usually, we disagreed on everything. "Why that way?" I asked.

"I don't know..." she said slowly. "It just feels right."

I nodded. "That way it is, then."

I couldn't explain it, but something about it felt right to me, too.

Oberi didn't run this time. She took slow, deliberate steps. I listened carefully to the forest. Like earlier, the wildlife was quiet, but there was something that seemed to hum out in the distance. A waterfall, perhaps?

No, that wasn't right. This was less like a sound in my ears and more like an energy buzzing through me— like the high-pitched hum of a television.

Oberi walked farther, and the hum grew. Ava gasped. She reeled backward so fast I had to catch her to keep her from falling off Oberi's back.

"What is it?" I asked.

"I-I don't know how to explain it," Ava said breathlessly.

"Is it bad?" I questioned. Her tone was one of shock, but otherwise difficult to read.

"No," she replied. "It's... beautiful. There's a clearing ahead, but it's small enough that the canopy covers the whole thing— all except a small opening in the center. The sun is shining down onto this... Charlie, I can't explain it. Come see for yourself."

Oberi stopped, and Ava slid off her back. I was too curious to stay away. Whatever it was Ava saw, I *felt*. There was beauty and wonder here, permeating deep into my bones.

"Is this an illusion?" I asked. I couldn't imagine feeling this way on Darke Island. This wasn't the place for wonders. And yet it felt so real.

"This is real," Ava assured me.

She took my hand and led me forward. My Air magic met a block in the center of the forest, but I couldn't make sense of what it was. Ava guided my hand forward and placed it upon a rock. The rock was cool to the touch, but there was warmth to it, too— as if some sort of life force flowed straight through it. I was accustomed to the energy of the earth through my powers, but this was stronger. I didn't know what it meant.

I ran my hands over the rock. It was a wall, each stone placed expertly to fit together. As I began walking down the wall, it grew taller, until I couldn't reach the top. I moved my hands over the face of the wall, and the texture became smooth. It wasn't a rock at all. I would've guessed it was wood, but it seemed to emit a different energy signature than the trees.

"What is it?" I asked Ava.

"It's some sort of stone gate," Ava said in wonder. "There's a round wooden door right in the center. It's *sooo* pretty."

I could feel what she was talking about. As my hands moved over the door, I noticed it was intricately carved, obviously the work of a skilled craftsman. My fingers met cool metal, which outlined a hole in the door. I continued feeling and counted seven holes.

"What are these?" I asked. "Key holes?"

"That's what they look like," Ava said, leaning closer to the door.

"Why would a door need *seven* locks?" I wondered. "And in the middle of the forest, no less. What's on the other side?"

"Let's see..." Ava's footsteps shuffled through the underbrush as she rounded the stone gate. "There's nothing over here."

"So this door leads nowhere," I said.

"You're thinking with your human brain," Ava accused. "Think from a supernatural perspective."

"Oh," I realized. "You think it's a portal?"

"A door that leads to nowhere? You bet." Ava returned to my side and brushed her hands over the carvings. "What I want to know is what these runes mean."

"Runes?" I asked. "It's not just art?"

"No," Ava said. "They're letters of some sort, but I can't tell which language. It's old for sure. Maybe Arcanean, but something about this doesn't quite look fae."

Her voice mingled with surprise. "You know what? These are the same runes that we saw on the abandoned ships, and on the bow in the cave we found. I didn't realize this before, but I think these are Elvish."

My eyebrows shot up. "Elvish? I thought the Elves died out."

"Only a hundred years ago," Ava pointed out. "Who knows how long this door has been here?"

"So, what does this mean?" I asked. I sensed it had to be significant, but I didn't know how.

"I have no idea," Ava admitted. "I could be wrong about the portal. It could just be part of an old building that collapsed."

"Well, whatever it was, it seemed pretty important to need *seven* keys," I emphasized.

"You're right..." Ava said thoughtfully. "Too bad we don't have those keys."

Her curiosity was getting to her bad. I could hear it in her tone.

"We're not going to figure it out in the middle of the Games," I pointed out. "I'm sure it's nothing."

"I disagree. This is important." Ava stomped her foot and crossed her arms. She got so close to me, I could feel the heat of her skin. She thought she was exercising her dominance. *How cute.*

I frowned. "It doesn't matter right now, because we're supposed to be looking for Kallie and Marcus. We can investigate this weird ass door once we win the games."

Ava inched closer to me. "Who are you to say it doesn't matter?"

"I'm team Captain," I stated, closing the distance between us. I liked how close we were— like last night in the cabin. It made me want to reach out and grab her... make her mine.

I shouldn't have been thinking about that right now. I should've had my mind on one thing— finding my teammates. But Ava was right... there was something weird about this door. And finding it with her felt like we had one more secret to share. I *liked* sharing secrets with Ava.

"And I suppose the team *Captain* always gets his way," Ava challenged.

I smirked. "Now you understand."

Ancestors, this girl infuriated me sometimes. She drove me crazy when she'd gone against my orders and nearly gotten Kallie killed. She could be a real pain in the ass.

And yet... all I wanted was to save her. I was so torn. I barely understood what I was doing in the Games to begin with. Was it all for Ava? Or is that just what I'd told myself?

Ava must've been staring me down, because she didn't say anything for several long seconds. "So, what is the team Captain's plan?"

"I'm gonna kiss you." I heard the words come out of my mouth, but I hadn't planned on saying them. I wanted to take them back, but more than anything, I wanted to hear her response.

Ava's breath wavered. "Is that so?"

I nodded firmly. "It is."

"Then do it."

It was a challenge— that much was clear. Ava didn't think I would. *I* didn't think I would.

And yet my body betrayed me.

Before I could make sense of what was happening, I pressed my lips to hers. When her mouth touched mine, my whole world flipped on end. It was as if we weren't fighting in the Games anymore. There wasn't a deadly monster roaming the forest, nor a battle waiting for us as a ticket to our freedom. Right here beside Ava-Marie, I'd already found freedom a hundred times over. Air magic might as well have swept under my feet and carried me into the clouds, because I was flying. Beneath me, the earth was totally still and tranquil, like it'd been waiting a thousand years just for us to make this kiss.

Ava drew away far too soon, breathless. "I didn't expect you to—"

I couldn't think. I swooped down and kissed her again, cutting her off. All I wanted was to kiss her again, because when her lips were pressed against mine, all felt right in the world. Earth, Water, Fire and Air were all within balance and in perfect harmony.

Magic surged through me as my heart raced, and air swirled around us, rustling leaves all the way up into the canopy. The forest spun around me, and my knees grew weak. Oberi had to be watching nearby, but she totally fell from my mind, because nothing else existed but Ava.

Ava's lips were soft and sweet— intoxicating. I wrapped my arms around her body, pulling her small frame close to me. My pants tightened, and I was sure she could feel me against her. But I didn't care. She should know how I felt about her— like how she'd felt it last night.

All that mattered were her lips. She parted them, and my tongue slid into her mouth. The tip of my tongue rolled over something hard that tasted metallic.

A tongue ring.

I'd never given much thought to piercings, but on Ava, it was fucking hot. I couldn't control it when my hands went into her hair and cradled the back of her neck. She let out a breath, and her whole body sagged in my arms. Her hands moved over me, sending tingles over every inch of my body.

We pulled away only to catch our breath. It should've felt unnatural to kiss Ava, but it hadn't. It felt *right*.

And still, Ava stepped away from me, crushing my balls and my heart all in one swift move.

"We shouldn't have done that," Ava said quickly. "It's the excitement of the tournament... right?"

Ava was looking for my answer. She wanted me to say the same, that it was all in the heat of the moment. And I almost did, just to placate her.

But I couldn't lie.

"Pidge," I sighed. "If that's not what you wanted, I'm sorry. But I needed to know."

"Know what?" she asked hesitantly.

I stepped closer to her and reached out my fingers to run across her skin. "I needed to know if I was doing this for the right reasons."

She gulped. "Doing what? For what reasons?"

"Everything," I told her. "This tournament. Helping you with the prophecy once we win."

"And?" Ava asked, sounding hopeful.

"And I am," I said, though my voice wavered when I admitted it out loud. "I don't want to keep worrying about if I'm going to die young. If I do, it'll be worth it, because it will be for *you*."

Ava jerked away from me. She sounded horrified. "I don't want you dying for me! If you think you have to, I don't want your help with the prophecy!"

My stomach sank. "That's not what I meant, pidge. We're part of the same soul. I *have* to fight for you. And if we don't win the Games, so what? The fight was worth it."

"You *have* to?" she asked, sounding slightly offended.

Hell, what had I said?

"I'm not *obligated*," I quickly clarified. "I *choose* to. You're not just some fashion-centric Cali-girl like the persona you give off. You're so much more than that. You care about others, even when you act like you don't."

Ava opened her mouth to protest, but I cut her off.

"You can stop pretending around me," I told her. "I know you like to act like some badass chick who doesn't give a damn about the rules, but your heart is big, pidge. If you didn't care, would you have told me about Monica? Would you have fought so hard for my life— and Marcus and Kalina— while we were possessed by the lichen? Would you have entered this tournament at all? No, you wouldn't, because you're doing this for the prophecy. You're here to save the freaking *world*. I know what selfishness looks like, what it feels like to live day in and day out for only yourself. And you're not it, pidge. You're compassionate and adventurous and strong. You got all the good parts of our soul, and I'm *proud* to say I share a soul with you. And that's why I'm here, why I'm going to help you decode the prophecy. Because you care so much about everyone else. It's time that someone cares about you, too, Ava-Marie."

Ava had been silent the whole time I spoke. Though she stood right next to me, I couldn't read her at all. She'd gone as still as a statue.

It made me nervous. *I should take it all back.* But damn, it felt so good to say out loud. Ava had to know all this. She was worthy of knowing someone cared.

"Damn it, pidge, will you say something?" I demanded.

"You... you called me Ava-Marie," she said breathlessly.

"Yeah, that's your na—"

I was cut off by the warmth of her lips on mine once again, as she kissed me this time. I inhaled a deep breath, drinking in her sweet taste. Ancestors, I could kiss her forever and it wouldn't be enough. My lips parted—

Boom!

A huge explosion went off in the distance, and the earth trembled beneath us. Ava probably hadn't felt it, but my Earth magic buzzed. Ava and I jumped apart, the moment broken.

"Marcus and Kallie!" she cried breathlessly, as if she'd just remembered them.

My heart raced, and I spun around. "Where's Oberi?"

Oberi's hooves crunched sticks beneath her as she trotted over to us.

"Come on, girl. Time to go," Ava said as she swung herself onto Oberi's back. I jumped on behind her, and we took off through the forest in the direction of the explosion.

Voices came from up ahead, but they seemed closer than the explosion had been. Oberi slowed briefly as we passed by. The voices quieted.

"What's going on?" I asked lowly.

"It's one of the other teams," Ava said. "The gang who's in last place. They're just sitting in the middle of the forest, like they've given up."

"They have no chance of winning," I remarked. "It's better for them to keep their team alive. Let's keep moving."

Oberi sped up again, and we broke out of the trees and back onto the main road.

"How close are we to town?" I asked.

"Close," Ava replied. "I can see it from here."

"Any signs of the explosion?"

Ava was pressed so close to me I felt her moving her head around. "I don't see— ancestors!"

I heard the sounds of footsteps the same time Ava cursed. They were fast, like a few people were sprinting, along with a small animal. Ancestors, this better be my team.

Ava jumped off Oberi's back. "Marcus! Kallie! What happened?"

They slowed beside us, and Marcus heaved to catch his breath. "We knocked out Mad Dog and Naya. Our fight must've attracted the monster, because it came after us."

"And the explosion?" I questioned. "Did you kill it?"

Kallie laughed maniacally. "I tried. Biggest damn battle orb I ever conjured. But it didn't hardly touch it."

"What are we up against?" Ava asked in a rush.

"I'm not sure," Kallie admitted. "Nothing I've ever seen before. It's huge and ugly, like a troll, but it doesn't have any eyes. I think it hunts by smell and sound."

The ground began to shake, though the others didn't seem to notice. Each tremble came in even intervals... like footsteps.

"The monster's coming," I realized. I quickly jumped into Captain mode. "Kallie's battle orb didn't hurt it, which means we'll have to get creative. Blunt force isn't going to win us this fight. Kallie, can you create a trap with your illusion magic? Something to hold the monster down long enough for us to find its weakness and target it?"

"I can," she said confidently.

"And it'll be strong enough to become reality?"

Kallie cracked her fingers. "Now's not the time to underestimate me, Captain."

"Get to work, then," I ordered. "Anyone want to volunteer as bait?"

Marcus sighed. "That sounds like a job for a warlock."

I clapped him on the shoulder. "Don't worry. We'll be right here to back you up."

"Just don't let me get crushed by this thing," he said. "Or I'll haunt you from the afterlife."

I laughed, which felt a little unnatural in the middle of the Games, but it felt good, too. "If you don't haunt me, this was never a true friendship."

The ground trembled again, so hard this time that Ava stumbled into me. I grabbed her hand. "Let's go."

Ava and I ducked into the trees, along with Oberi and Rishi. Kallie was further down the road, creating an illusion to trap our troll friend. The ground shook, and a mighty roar erupted from the monster's mouth as he came around the bend in the road. As my Air magic reached out, I couldn't get a sense of what the creature looked like, only that it was huge— at least two stories tall.

"Hey, you ugly troll!" Marcus called. Rocks clinked against the monster's tough skin as Marcus threw them to get the monster's attention. "Over here!"

The creature grunted, and his heavy footsteps followed Marcus as he took off sprinting down the road.

"Ancestors," Ava breathed.

"What is it, pidge?"

"*Troll* was an apt description," she said. "But trolls aren't real. This is different. It's like a giant ogre, with skin that looks like rock. It doesn't have any eyes, just slits for its nose and ears. I swear I learned about them somewhere, but I can't remember. Come on, we're up."

Ava tugged on my arm, and we took off running. Marcus was already a ways down the road, still yelling at the monster and luring him toward Kallie's trap.

"Kallie's made a pit in the ground," Ava said as we ran. "Get ready with your magic. It's almost there."

I sensed the lightweight beat of Kallie's wings in the air as she swooped down to grab Marcus out of the way of the trap. "Now!" she screamed.

Ava and I reacted at once. I thrust out a blast of Air, and Ava shot a huge fireball at the monster. I felt the monster teeter beneath my magic, then came the sound of a loud *crash* as it fell into the pit.

"It's in!" Ava cried. "Kallie's creating ropes to hold it down."

Ava and I skidded to a halt near the edge of the pit. The sound of snapping ropes met my ears.

"That's not going to be enough!" I immediately used my Air to press the monster back into the pit, but he was strong and resisted me. I turned to Earth magic and made roots grow over top of the pit, but I couldn't create them fast enough. The monster snapped them as fast as I could create them.

"It's too strong for our magic," Ava breathed. "Oh, Great Spirit."

"What?" I demanded. The sheer horror in her tone was impossible to miss.

"Kallie's ropes are turning against her!" she screamed.

All the blood drained from my face. "How's that possible?"

"Fuck," Ava growled. "I remember where I learned about this monster. We used the hair of a deceptem demon in alchemy to brew illusion potions. It's more dangerous than we realized!"

"Kallie," I called to the other side of the pit. "Drop the illusion!"

"I can't!" she screamed, which quickly turned into sounds of pain. Marcus cried out from beside her, and I knew the ropes had them both. The monster had manipulated the illusion, so the magic worked for him instead.

"We have to give it all we've got!" I insisted.

"I thought you said brute force wouldn't work," Ava replied.

Hell, I didn't know what I was doing anymore. I didn't even know what a deceptem demon was. How the hell was I supposed to know how to fight it? "We have to try!"

Ava conjured fireballs, but they were cool in temperature beside me. Oberi shifted into husky form, and together we used our Earth magic to lift large boulders and throw them into the pit on top of the monster.

But neither of our magic was any use. The pavement cracked beneath our feet, and the deceptem groaned as it pulled itself out of the pit.

"How do you kill one of these things?" I asked, heart racing.

"I don't know!" Ava cried. "We didn't learn that."

I thrust another blast of Air at the creature, but the air swirled around it instead of impacting like I'd planned. The deceptem drew a heavy arm back, interrupting the air flow. I knew what was coming and didn't have time to get out of the way. I acted on instinct and shoved Ava to the ground. Instead of hitting her, the demon's arm swung out to meet my chest. I was thrown off my feet and soared through the air. I quickly gathered air around me to slow my fall, but I still landed on my ass with a hard *thud*. Fuck, that hurt.

The wind had been knocked out of me, but I knew I had to move. I scrambled to my feet, but before I could get upright, the most sickening sound met my ears. It was a rough, harsh *snap* that stopped the world from spinning—

And it'd come from right where Ava had been.

Something hit the ground... a sound I could only guess was a body.

I heard nothing. No screams. No cries of pain. Just my own pulse pumping in my ears.

"*Ava!*" I wailed. My voice echoed across the landscape.

Slowly, sound came back into focus. Marcus and Kallie screamed as the deceptem took heavy steps toward them. Magic whizzed through the air, but I couldn't focus enough to join in on the fight.

I raced over to where I thought Ava was. Oberi's hooves clicked on the pavement, and she blew a distressed breath. I knew she had to be standing over Ava.

I fell to my knees as my heart dropped out of my chest. Tremors went up my legs as I landed hard on the road. I barely felt them. All the pain was in my chest, tearing me apart from the inside out. I felt around, and my fingers met Ava's body. She was still, and her skin was cold to the touch.

"Pidge," I sobbed as tears began running down my face. I hoisted her into my lap, cradling her lifeless body. Her neck hung over my arm at an odd angle, and a warm, sticky liquid stuck to me all over.

Blood.

My whole body shook as I pushed the hair back from her face. I was acutely aware of each contour of her features. She was so beautiful. How had this happened so fast? Why hadn't I saved her?

I pulled her closer to my chest, trembling as I held my very soul in my arms. I wished that she would move... but she didn't. The troll had broken her neck... ended her life in one blow.

"I'm so sorry, pidge," I sobbed into her hair.

Oberi leaned down to nudge me. I expected her to show some goddamn emotion, but she bit my collar and tried to drag me upright. Rishi dug his claws into my leg.

I shrugged Oberi off. "Forget it. It's not worth it anymore. Not without my pidge."

Oberi stomped, pacing back and forth. She whinnied loudly, as if trying to get me to listen.

But I didn't care what she had to say. Ava-Marie was gone— her life force severed.

So why did it feel like she was waiting for something?

I felt it through the bond, frustration like I'd never felt from Ava before. Was it possible we were still connected, even if she was in the afterlife? And what was she so *mad* about?

Hold on. Ava and I shared a soul, along with Oberi. Which meant that if one of us died, we all did.

The tears halted in their tracks as realization hit. Slowly, I lifted my head. Ava had said they'd used deceptem hair for illusion potions, and the monster had managed to take control of Kallie's illusion. That's what Ava meant when she said it was more dangerous than we realized. This monster was fucking with our heads!

Oberi nudged me again and bit my ear.

"Ow! Fuck!" I cried, slapping a hand over my ear. After a moment for the shock to slip away, I turned to Oberi. "It's an illusion, isn't it? That's what you're trying to tell me?"

As soon as I said it, Ava's voice broke through. Her dead body was still wrapped in my arms, but her voice came from several paces away.

"No shit it's an illusion!" Ava-Marie snapped. "That's what makes deceptem demons dangerous! Now get up and help me! This deceptem is not going down easy."

My heart swelled, and the body vanished from my lap. I jumped to my feet and ran over to Ava— the *real* Ava. I threw my arms around her and drew her in close. "You're alive!"

Ava shrugged me off. "Of course I am. You don't think I'm going down without a fight, do you? What'd this bastard make you see?"

I swallowed the lump in my throat and answered quickly. "Nothing."

Ava threw another fireball. "Then help me!"

It took me a moment to take in the scene. The deceptem was smashing his heavy hands into the ground away from us— probably aimed at Kallie and Marcus. Its back was to us, so Ava and I had the advantage.

My nostrils flared. "Give it everything you've got."

"On it, Captain."

The air began to dry out around me as Ava drew water out of it. The water formed into a huge ball above our heads, sloshing like a swimming pool suspended in mid-air. I uprooted trees and used my Air magic to levitate them, shooting them at the monster at high speed. They cracked and splintered against his hard skin, but he roared like they hurt. Finally, I was getting somewhere.

"It's no use!" Marcus wailed. "Ava's gone. We're going to die, too!"

I realized they'd seen the same thing I had, and they hadn't broken through the illusion yet.

"Listen to me!" I yelled over the sound of magic whizzing through the air. Ancestors, I hoped they could hear me, because they were pretty far away. "Ava's not dead! It's an illusion demon!"

I could hear Kallie's sobs from here. My teammates kept fighting, but only to hang on to dear life. They sounded about ready to give up.

"Kallie!" I screamed. "It's not real!"

"Are you sure?" she cried.

"Yes, Ava's standing right next to me!" I told her. "We have a chance. We can still win this thing. But he's playing with our heads. We have to take away his greatest weapon. Can you do that?"

"I can try!" she responded, before yelping as another one of the monster's attacks came.

I threw another heavy tree branch at it, and this time, I felt it continue past his strong exterior, sinking into soft flesh. The creature roared.

"Right in the ear!" Ava said proudly.

The deceptem whirled on us.

"Get down!" Ava called.

I followed her instructions immediately and flattened myself to the ground. Oberi and Ava did the same on either side of me, and Rishi hissed. The demon's arm swept over top of us, and heavy winds billowed my hair.

"I've broken the illusion!" Kallie screamed at us. "Its mind games are over!"

That meant brute force was our last option. Maybe if I could get another branch in its ear, it'd do some real damage.

I didn't have time to come up with a plan. The ground shook as the deceptem took another step toward us.

"Charlie, what do we do!?" Ava screamed.

I ripped another tree from the ground, but it was bigger than the others. It took all I had to thrust it up into the air. But I had no point of reference for aiming. The log clunked off the top of the deceptem's head, and I knew that I'd missed.

"Run!" I didn't want to run from a fight, but staying here was a good way to get killed. We had to stay alive long enough to fight this thing.

Ava and I grabbed hands. We ducked into the trees, and she guided me as we started running toward Shade Hills. The monster followed, along with the sound of falling trees as he barreled his way through the forest. He was getting closer...

I was starting to formulate a plan, a way to lose the monster, but I never got the chance to share it with Ava. She yelped and was dragged upward, her hand slipping from mine. Oberi cried out in horror.

"*Charlie!*" Ava screamed, and I knew the deceptem had gotten her.

I whipped out blasts of air so narrow and fast it should've chopped the deceptem's arm off, but then held them back at the last second. I didn't want to hurt Ava. I had to keep on running, because the demon was still barreling toward me, and if I stopped I'd be crushed.

I sent another blast of air outward and thought I'd hit one of the deceptem's legs, then— *thwack!*

I hadn't been paying attention to where I was going. My whole body slammed into something hard, so much that I bounced backward and landed on my ass. My head spun, and I couldn't make sense of which way was up and which way was down. My ribs ached from whatever I'd run into, and my pulse thumped in my ears.

Oberi yanked me to my feet, but I was still coming to. As the world came back into focus, I realized something was off. I didn't know what it was at first.

Then I noticed the vibrations of the deceptem's footsteps were farther away, and getting even farther. It was leaving with Ava!

I stumbled forward and caught myself on a wall— the one I'd run into. It was a building, probably a house judging by the feel of the siding. We'd reached the outskirts of Shade Hills.

I gasped shallow breaths as I tried to find my bearings. *Ava's still alive*, I told myself. I could feel it in our bond.

Oberi made a loud noise in my ear, and I snapped back to attention. I quickly jumped onto her back and kicked her sides. "Follow that monster!"

Oberi found the main road quickly. I could hear Marcus and Kallie shouting in the distance, along with the hum of the drone overhead.

"Gods, Ava!" Kallie screamed as Oberi and I rushed to them. We came to a skidding halt beside Marcus and Kallie.

"What's happening!?" I demanded.

"Ava burned it to get away. The monster's chasing Ava up an apartment building. She's using the fire escape," Marcus said breathlessly. Rishi yowled loudly in worry.

Part of me feared for her. The other felt immensely proud. She'd escaped the demon's hold on her own. *That's my pidge.*

"How are we going to defeat it?" Marcus asked. "This monster is impenetrable."

"It has to have a weakness," Kallie insisted. "They always do."

"Its ears," I said. "One of my branches stuck in, but not far enough. If we can stab it with something else, there's no way it can survive."

"How do we get something in there?" Kallie asked.

I didn't have the luxury of thinking it through too long. "We need another trap— a bigger one this time," I decided. "Let's get to Ava first."

No sooner had we started forward did I hear the sound of crushing rock. Kallie screamed, and the first of the pebbles rained down on me. I threw my hands up on instinct and caught several large rocks with my Earth magic before they crushed us.

"What was that?" I asked in a clipped tone.

"Piece of building," Marcus answered. "The monster's trying to climb to get to Ava. Bricks are everywhere!"

My guts twisted. "And the people inside?"

"Looks like a new development," Kallie quickly explained. "It's not finished yet. I bet there's no one inside."

That was a relief, but it didn't do anything for rescuing Ava. Another crushing sound came, but this time, I couldn't control all the bricks coming at us. There were too many, and the bricks were too large.

"Ah!" Kallie screamed as one of the larger chunks smashed her into the ground. "My wings! Gods, my wings!"

Marcus rushed to her side and groaned as he tried moving the heavy piece of building. I jumped in with my Earth magic and moved it out of the way. It wasn't entirely made of earth, but there was enough rock inside the brick that I could control it.

"Goddess, Kallie," Marcus breathed as he knelt beside her.

Kallie whimpered in pain, and I hesitated. I didn't ask, but I knew Kallie's wings had to be crushed.

"I've got this," Marcus told me. "Make sure Ava's okay."

He didn't have to tell me twice. I whirled back around toward the building the demon was trying to scale. I could tell by the sound of crumbling brick that he was struggling to climb. I searched for Ava with my magic and found hot pockets of air. Those would be her fireballs.

"Ava!" I called up to her.

"I'm fine!" she called back— she had to be a hundred feet up. "Charlie, you have to level the building!"

"What!?" I screamed. "Not with you up there."

"You'll catch me with your Air," she insisted. Fireballs continued to whiz out of her hands.

I summoned an air stream to try knocking the monster off the side of the building, but he held on tight. I'd barely summoned half the power I'd intended. I swayed on my feet and grabbed Oberi to steady myself.

"I can't!" I yelled up at her. "My magic's wearing thin."

"You can do it, Charlie," she promised. "I *know* you can!"

Leveling the building was the smart thing to do. It would crush the demon and pin it down, if it didn't kill it. We could get our points and win this thing. We would be free of the Institute.

But I couldn't do it at the risk of Ava-Marie's life. I hadn't been able to fly anyone else around during practice. How could I catch her while she was falling through the sky?

"I trust you, Charlie!" Ava called down to me. "Hurry up and do it!"

The decision was impossible to make, until I realized that the only alternative was the monster catching her. It was obviously the kind to play with its prey, but Ava had already escaped its grasp once. It was done playing around. If it got Ava in its grasp again, she'd be dead— no illusion this time.

Fuck, what was I about to do?

I inhaled a deep breath and placed a hand on Oberi's back. "I'm going to need your help."

Oberi instantly shrank to the size of a husky and barked. I blew out the breath I'd been holding and shoved all doubt aside. I couldn't question my magic right now. I had to do this right.

"Here goes nothing..."

My heart hammered as I lifted my hands. At my command, the ground began to shake beneath our feet. It was nothing but tremors at first, but as Ava-Marie's screams grew from above me, power built inside my chest. The tremors grew to earthquake proportions. I forced a hole to open in the ground below the deceptem. It took everything I had, but I pushed myself even further, and my magic broke open the ground. The building began to creak and groan, and I could feel the structural integrity waning with each sway of the earth.

This was unlike any magic I'd ever done before. I'd never cast a spell on anything bigger than a tree. This was a fucking apartment complex. I wasn't sure I could do it.

And still, I pushed my magic as hard as I could, because it was my only choice. I had one chance to get Ava out of the deceptem's grasp. I had one chance to finish it off and win the Games. One chance...

Air began to swirl around the apartment complex, and the ground shook so much that it cracked nearby.

"Keep going, Charlie!" Marcus encouraged. "You're almost there!"

I would've told him to shut up and let me concentrate, but I couldn't focus on that right now. All I could do was hone in on my magic.

And I let it snap.

The Air spell I'd conjured blasted forward with tornado-grade speed. I commanded the earth to thrust upward on one end of the building, breaking all structural integrity left. The far wall crumbled, taking the others down like dominoes. The deceptem let out a deep roar as it realized it was going down. The sound of the falling building was deafening— but it wasn't the only one. All along the street, buildings groaned and fell over.

I let gravity do the rest of the work, because I had one goal, and one goal only. *Save pidge.*

Finding her was easy, as if she was tethered to me by a string. She'd jumped off the top of the building just as it began to crumble, and her legs flailed in the air.

Catching her? Not so easy.

I gritted my teeth and prayed to the ancestors that my power would be enough to hold her. Air swirled around her, but she was falling too fast. Fuck, no! I couldn't let this happen!

The urge to protect her swelled within me, and my Air magic burst. A strong gust of wind I didn't even realize I was capable of swept by, swooping my pidge out of the air as she fell.

I sighed in relief when she didn't smash into the ground. Instead, I manipulated the current to carry her toward me, setting her gently on her feet in front of me. All I could do was sweep her up into my arms and hold her tight. I buried my face into her hair, inhaling her sweet scent.

She hugged me back. "I told you that you could do it."

I chuckled in relief as I drew away from her, but all I wanted to do was weep. "You got lucky."

"You were good," she countered. "You trapped the deceptem."

Ava turned to admire my handiwork. The ground was still, and the town seemed eerily quiet.

"We won?" I asked breathlessly.

"Not yet," she replied solemnly. "The monster's under a pile of rubble, but he doesn't look dead yet."

I squared my shoulders. "Then let's kill it."

I walked forward toward the cavern I'd created. Oberi panted at my side, and the two of us worked together to uproot a large tree nearby. We twisted its branches until we formed a point— a massive weapon that would impale the monster straight through.

I lifted my hands—

Then came the sound of approaching footsteps. They were running, but they didn't seem like something to be afraid of. Rather, it sounded as if someone was rushing to our aid.

"Marcus! Kallie!" a girl with a high-pitched voice cried. "Are you okay?"

"We will be, cousin," Marcus replied. "Once we get to the infirmary. This thing is almost over."

Cousin? He could only be talking about one person— the last witch left in the Games.

Voices overlaid one another, and I counted two males and two females. I realized it was the last team. There was Alice, the witch who'd been falsely accused of crimes on her trip to Malovia; Despona, the vampire who'd killed a man trying to kidnap her; Carson, the merman who was framed for stealing an expensive car; and Wesley, the fae shifter who'd attempted to murder the vamp who touched his sister.

Ava grabbed my wrist before I could take the kill shot.

"What is it?" I asked.

"Just wait..." Ava trailed off thoughtfully.

"Pidge, I can't wait for the monster to come to. We have to finish it off and end this."

"I know, but..." Ava hesitated. "Alice's team saved us. They gave me the pot I needed to brew the potion against the lichen. Without them, we'd all be dead. They deserve to win."

I gaped. I'd known how much Ava wanted to win the Games— how much she wanted freedom. To hand the win over was awfully kind...

But it was also why I felt about her the way I did. She may have a criminal record, but she believed in doing the right thing.

And I believed in her.

"What about the prophecy?" I whispered.

"We'll find another way," Ava said. "If we win, I'm still staying here on Darke Island. It doesn't seem fair when the rest of them can get out of here. They *deserve* to go home, Charlie."

Everything I'd ever learned about survival told me to kill that demon and go free. We were so close.

But I hadn't entered the Games hoping to survive. I'd entered them for Ava, and if this was what she wanted, then I would back her up.

"As long as Marcus and Kallie agree," I said. "I won't give up their chance at freedom."

"All right," Ava agreed.

We walked to the other team, who were talking to Marcus and Kallie.

"Are your wings going to heal?" Despona asked, sounding worried.

"They damn well better," Kallie said. She was still on the ground, and Marcus was knelt beside her.

I turned to the other team. "Do you guys mind if we have a moment with our teammates?"

"Not at all," Carson said, and the four of them walked off.

"What's going on?" Kallie asked. "I thought you were going to take care of that thing!"

Ava was the one to answer. "I think we should give the win to the other team."

"What!?" Marcus and Kallie yelped at the same time.

"They're innocent," Ava reminded them.

Marcus sounded skeptical. "Didn't Despona kill a guy?"

"I heard Wesley tried, too," Kallie added.

"They were both in self-defense," Ava argued. "I know how hard we've fought for this, but we're all in the Institute for *real crimes*. We deserve to be here. The other team doesn't. If I took their ticket to freedom... well, I'm just not sure how I could live with that."

Marcus and Kallie were silent, as if contemplating it.

"They helped Ava with the potion that saved our asses," I added. At this point, I didn't even care about what was *fair*. This felt *right*. If Ava and I were going to decode a prophecy to save the world, it started here — with saving the ones we could. "These guys are the good guys. And let's be honest, guys— we're not."

Marcus made a sound of agreement. "Look, if it were any other team, I'd be killing that monster right now to win us points," Marcus said. "But Alice is my cousin— distant, but she's family. Our coven will be better off with her in it than me. I say we give it to them."

Kallie groaned. "You know I hate it when you're right. The Institute is probably the best place for me right now anyway, seeing as I was banished. I try to go back home now, I'll get my head cut off."

"So we're in agreement?" Ava asked.

"Yes," the three of us answered in unison.

Ava breathed a sigh. "Then let's tell them."

She took my hand and called the other team back over.

"What's up?" Despona asked.

"We want you to take the win," Ava told them.

"No way," Alice protested. "You guys found the monster first. This was your fight, and you're the ones who knocked it out. You deserve the points. It's your kill."

"I don't care about the points," Ava said. "This is about who gets to leave the Institute. You guys deserve that."

They stood there in shock, nobody saying anything.

Finally, Alice spoke. "Is your team sure about this?"

I squeezed Ava's hand. "We're sure. The monster has a weak spot near its ears. Pierce it there, and it should be enough to kill it."

Alice sniffled, like she was crying. "You guys have no idea what this means to us. Thank you so much. If there's anything we can do—"

"You can kill the monster before it wakes," Ava interrupted. "Go get those points. It's time for you to win the Games."

Alice squealed and threw her arms around Ava, nearly slapping me in the face as she did. Wesley and Carson both approached me in turn and shook my hand.

"How will we ever repay you?" Despona asked as she hugged Ava.

"Go live good lives once you're out of the Institute," Ava said. "That's all we can ask."

"Thank you," Alice repeated. "You truly don't know what you've done for us."

Ava turned, and we walked back toward Kallie and Marcus. We knelt beside Kallie and began helping her to her feet. I couldn't tell what the other team was doing to kill the monster. All I heard was a commotion that I couldn't make sense of. But it didn't really matter. I was done with the show. All I wanted was to go back home and sleep.

Home.

I chuckled lightly.

"What?" Ava asked.

"I just had the thought that I wanted to go home." I laughed as I draped Kallie's arm over my shoulder. "To the *Institute.*"

"It is our home now," Ava said softly.

"It's a shithole," Kallie teased, but she winced as she moved.

"Yeah," Marcus agreed from the other side of her. "But it's *our* shithole."

Ava snickered. "Our shithole for sure."

Marcus and I hoisted Kallie onto Oberi's back. Everyone stilled as the monster roared loudly from behind us, but the sound was quickly silenced as death overtook him. A single breath blew out of his monstrous nose, and then... nothing.

It didn't matter if I wanted to take back the offer. It was done. The other team had won.

The drone above us whirred as it flew down from the sky. I heard the gates of the Institute creak from beyond as they were opened, and the Warden's delighted voice rang out with the announcement. "Well done to all our teams. We have found our winners of this year's Darke Games. All other competitors must return to the Institute within the hour, or will be escorted back by guards. The winning team may remain in Shade Hills, where they will soon receive their just reward. Congratulations to all our participants, and remember— stay vigilant, stay alive."

As the broadcast ended, I thought the Warden's final farewell was odd. The Darke Games were over. What need was there to continue warning us about survival?

Whatever. It was probably some marketing thing for the Games. It wasn't worth my attention.

I should've been disappointed. We'd put all that effort into the Games, only to lose. But it didn't feel like we'd lost at all. I was walking home with all three of my teammates alive.

Even better... I had Ava.

I called that a win.

ava-marie

TWENTY-FOUR

"Do you think we fucked up, giving up our only shot at getting out?" Kallie asked.

"No. It was the right thing to do."

Kallie and I hurried to get ready for the Villain's Ball inside my dorm room. There was a heavy snowfall outside, coating the grounds and making everything seem magical.

Oberi sat on the bed and panted, wagging his tail as he watched me put the finishing touches on my hair. I set it in a low bun with curls framing my face.

"Since when have we ever been worried about doing the *right thing*?" Kallie sat beside Oberi as she glided on some red lipstick. She was wearing the very revealing dress she'd chosen, and I'd done a blowout on her hair earlier. She looked so hot. Marcus was going to flip.

"We're at the Institute for a reason," I said. "Maybe it's starting to change our bad behavior."

Kallie scoffed. "As if."

I pulled my mother's dress out of the closet. As I slipped it on, Kallie's face softened. "Oh, Ava, it suits you perfectly! Fire and ice."

"It turned out just like I planned it." I smoothed down the skirt and did a twirl. Over the blue dress I'd added layers of red and orange tulle that twisted around the skirt, as well as ruby rhinestones that mingled with the sapphire glitter. It gave the dress the appearance of a plume of fire wrapping around a column of ice, the different fabrics melding together as if I'd cast a spell over them. I really wanted something that symbolized both parts of my magic, and this dress pulled it off.

"No one else is going to have a dress like that at the party. Naya will be so jealous." Kallie snorted.

"She won't be looking at me when she's too busy worrying about you," I said. "You're hotter than she is for sure."

Kallie frowned. "At least all of Naya's parts work correctly. I can't say the same for my wings."

"Are your wings going to heal?" I asked.

"They're on the mend. Should be back to normal in a few weeks. I got very lucky," Kallie said. "But I already miss being able to fly."

"Don't bother with Naya. She's not our problem."

I finished my outfit by fastening the key Mama had given me around my neck. No matter what outfit I was wearing, the key always seemed to compliment it.

I put Oberi's veil on his head, over his ears. He jumped off the bed and threw back his head, parading around like he was a bride on the way to his reception.

"Oberi, you're so obnoxious." I laughed as he struck a pose, sticking out his butt.

There was a knock on the door, and Daddy poked his head inside. He and Mama were here to chaperone for the dance. His face softened when he saw me. "Oh, peanut, you look so beautiful."

"Don't get sentimental on me now," I teased. If Daddy teared up, so would I.

"Your mother and I want a quick word," he said. "It won't take long."

"I'm almost ready," Kallie said. "I'll meet you at the ball."

I nodded, then followed my dad out. Oberi pranced behind me, swinging his head to make the veil swish.

Mama was wearing a red gown that accentuated her figure. She looked so pretty. She never got dressed up anymore. It was nice they were going to the ball, even if they were only chaperoning. She beamed and took my hands as her eyes roamed the dress. "Ava, you are a *vision*. I knew that dress would suit you."

"It's so perfect. Thanks, Mama."

Mama's gaze shone with affection as she gave me a huge hug. "Honey, I'm *so* proud of you. You did the right thing during the Darke Games, giving your win to the other team."

"I figured they deserved it more than we did," I said. "And I think you were right all along. My place is here, at the Institute. Maybe if I stick around, I can get some answers from the school on what the prophecy means."

I stepped away from her. There was a curl dangling in my eyes, so I took my left hand to part it back. Daddy's eyes went upward, to my wrist.

Shit. I realized my mistake a second too late. I tried to hide it away, but Daddy grabbed my wrist and upturned it, exposing the sight of Charlie's name written all over my skin.

Daddy made a tiny noise of horror that would've been very funny in any other situation. Mama appeared smugger than I'd ever seen her.

"Ava, what did you do?" Daddy whimpered. His voice was high-pitched.

I went to unbury myself before this hole could get bigger. "Ancestors, it's no big deal. Charlie has my name on his wrist, too," I said.

"They're *matching*?" Daddy yelped. Mama covered her mouth, trying not to laugh.

"It's like, just a friend tattoo. It means nothing." I yanked my wrist away and hid it behind my skirt. Daddy went pale. Mama smiled.

"You're getting that removed as soon as possible," Daddy insisted.

My mouth dropped open. "Excuse me? No I'm not!"

"Don't backsass me! I'm not letting you walk around with a— a *tattoo* of a criminal's name on your wrist!"

"Oh my ancestors, you never let me do *anything* I want!" I whined.

Mama shook her head. "You two."

Daddy took a breath. "I suppose I can't force you to change your mind—"

"Yep."

Daddy's expression hardened, and I shut up. He went on to say, "But I do think we should have a quick talk."

"Oh, Liam, not this *again*," Mama complained.

Daddy's tone was impatient. "I just need a moment with my daughter, *please*."

Mama made an annoyed sound and walked off, like she'd been trying to talk Daddy out of this all night and was giving up.

Once Mama was out of sight, Daddy dug in his pocket. "Ava, sweetheart, I want you to have these."

"A present? Really?" My mood brightened. I thought he'd give me something sweet— you know, jewelry, or an equally cute father-daughter gift, to mark the night of my first-ever college dance.

My mouth fell open when I looked down at the packet he'd placed in my hands. "Are you kidding me? Fucking *condoms!*?"

"It's a college dance. Things happen," Daddy retorted.

"What the hell am I supposed to use these for?" I shouted.

"I... assume you know how to put them on. At least, I would hope."

Ancestors, save me. Apparently he thought now was a great time for the sex talk. I bet anything this was Uncle Jonah's doing. There was no other explanation. I could hear him right now. *Liam, I know you want to keep pretending Ava's your sweet little girl, but let's face the cold, hard facts. Remember what all of us were like as kids? Trust me, I teach college students, and they're feistier than rabbits.*

Oberi's tongue lolled, like he thought this was hilarious. I was still gaping. "What, do you think I'm gonna... go on some wild sexcapade or something?"

"I... don't know." Daddy's tone was firm. "But whatever you do, I want you to be safe."

"Ancestors!" I smacked my face. "Isn't this Mama's job?"

"Well, your mother insisted you didn't need them, but I thought it would be best if—"

"Mama was right! How do you expect me to use these? It's not like I'm dating anyone."

Daddy's face cleared. "You're... not?"

"Um, no." I scrunched up my nose. "Did you think I was with somebody?"

Daddy looked very confused. "I guess it doesn't matter."

"Yeah, it doesn't! And I'm not the type for one-night stands, just in case you're that paranoid."

"I don't need to know what you're up to," Daddy said quickly. "Trust me, that's none of my business."

"Apparently you're funding my supply!" I shouted, waving the foil packets in the air.

"I'm not saying I *approve*. I just know better," he grumbled. "I was your age once, you know."

I blew a curl out of my eyes. "Daddy, I know you're worried, but I promise I'm not going to have an accident like you and Mama."

Daddy's face contorted. "You were not an *accident*. You were one of the best things that's ever happened to me."

"Awesome, so are we done with this conversation?" I asked.

Daddy said, "Well—"

"Great, bye!"

I stomped away and shoved the condoms into my handbag before I hauled ass to the Room of Mirrors, where the dance was being held. It was the same room where we'd first met the Warden and heard his welcome speech.

Kallie was waiting for me outside the entrance. "Gods, you took long enough," she complained.

"Don't ask." I fixed my hair before we walked through the double doors.

I gasped in amazement as I took in the surrounding scene. From the ballroom's ceiling hung beautiful fabric canopies in black, purple, and green. The room was dark, only lit by the various pulsing lights around the room, which shone people's faces in emerald or amethyst. Tables swathed in black cloth were decorated with gold-colored plates, and a DJ at the front of the room played creepy, haunting music. Thunder clapped for ambiance, and lights flickered against the ceiling, giving the appearance lightning was flashing. Green fire crept up the walls and danced off the mirrors, an illusion sustained by one of the fae teachers, and black candles hovered over the dance floor. There was a table full of food, adorned with things like bubbling green punch, chocolate in the shape of bat wings, and apples that were dipped in purple caramel, giving the decorative appearance they were poisoned. There was a kissing booth in the corner that a few of the sirens were running, with a sign that said *Kisses of Death.* Professor Warbright used his necromancy magic to make a few skeletons dance. The skeletons twirled and turned with each other, dressed in elaborate ball gowns and suit tails as they waltzed around the room.

It definitely looked like a party for villains. I was loving this.

We waited in line to get in. Kallie and I stood by a twisted black arch, and Lupe took a few pictures of us with the school's professional camera. I was shocked it functioned at all, considering the finicky way electronics worked at the school. My eyes scanned the room, but I didn't see him... yet.

"You guys look amazing," Lupe said as she snapped the camera. "Hope you don't tear your gowns!"

"What do you mean?" I asked.

"There's always a huge brawl at the end, during the last dance. It's the best part. Everyone just goes at it before the guards can break it up," Lupe gushed.

"I get to punch people for fun and get away with it? That sounds *incredible,*" Kallie cried.

"And dangerous. Is it like a riot?" I asked.

"Nah. It's just for shits and giggles. Nobody gets hurt... bad." Lupe gave a sinister grin. "Anyway, enjoy the party!"

Kallie and I walked along the edge of the dance floor. Her face brightened as she waved. "Marcus! Hi!"

Marcus stood across from us, wearing a suit that was half open. His tie hung loose, and the top few buttons of his shirt were undone, exposing his chest.

Kallie was clearly enjoying the show. Her eyes roved Marcus' chest, but the warlock himself was speechless. His eyes nearly exploded out of his skull as he looked from Kallie's giant boobs to the slit in her dress revealing her thigh, and everything else.

Kallie batted her eyelashes. "So? How do I look?"

Marcus gulped. He was trying *so hard* not to rock a boner right now. Rishi was at his feet, meowing and wearing a tiny top hat.

My heart fell as I realized Marcus was alone. Charlie wasn't with him. Maybe he'd decided not to come.

But... he'd agreed to be my date to the ball, right? He wouldn't stand me up.

I hoped.

Marcus and Kallie moved to the food table and started taking appetizers. Kallie did most of the talking, while Marcus mostly tried not to gape. I wasn't very hungry. My gaze kept roaming the ball, and I didn't see a hint of Charlie anywhere. My parents had showed back up. They remained along the wall, supervising the dance with a few other guardians who'd volunteered. Daddy's expression was sullen. I was certain Mama was laughing at him.

As we sat down at a table, Kallie poked me. "So what did your dad want?"

"Huh?" I came out of my reverie. "Oh, um, it was stupid, really. He tried to give me the sex talk."

Not like I needed it. Charlie wasn't going to show, anyway.

"What?" Marcus broke his silence for the first time and laughed. "That's crazy."

"Isn't it? And he gave me these." I took the condoms out of my bag and threw them on the table. "I feel like I'm sixteen all over again."

"Um, I don't know who your dad thinks you're sleeping with, but these are extra-large," Kallie said, picking up a condom and waving it around.

"Oh my fucking—" I sighed and put my head in my hand. "We're a pretty open family, but this goes too far."

"Did he give you a play-by-play of where it's supposed to go? Because my dad would *not* shut up about it when he gave me the sex talk. I swear, I never needed to know that much about their wedding night," Marcus complained.

"He probably thought you'd put it in the wrong place," I suggested. Marcus sent me the finger.

"My parents *never* talk about their sex life in front of me, thank the gods," Kallie said. "I have no idea of how I came into this world, and I like it that way. I think they expected me to figure it out on my own."

"I was conceived out of wedlock!" I burst.

I was too loud. Daddy heard me from across the room and scowled. I quieted down.

Kallie dropped her voice and leaned in. "Speaking of... where's tall, dark and handsome? Isn't he supposed to be your date?"

"I'm not sure..." I mused. "Marcus, have you spoken to Charlie?"

Marcus shook his head as he bit into an apple. "Haven't seen him all day."

Dammit. He really had stood me up. Tears rose to my eyes, but I fought them back. No need to ruin good eyeliner.

"It's fine," I said. "I can have plenty of fun on my own."

"Miss Mitoh. May I interest you in a dance?"

A chilling voice made a crawling sensation creep up my spine. The Warden stood beside us, extending a hand. His large, feathery wings were out and draping on the floor. Every stitch of his designer suit was in place. It only made him that more intimidating.

Oberi gave a low growl, but I knew better than to refuse. "Certainly." I took the Warden's hand, and he led me to the dance floor.

The Warden put a hand on my waist and grabbed my hand just as the DJ put on a sharp and eerie tango. I felt like a rat trapped in a cage as he forced me to move with him. Ancestors, this was nearly as bad as being held down by John. The Warden's hollow stare penetrated right through me, making my knees quake and my stomach scramble.

I knew I was safe— relatively. Mama and Daddy were watching from afar, just in case they needed to step in, and Oberi would never let the Warden hurt me.

I wanted them to stay back. I knew they were powerful, but the Warden was dangerous, too. I didn't know what he might do.

As the tempo increased, the Warden said, "You and your team were very exceptional during the Darke Games. Color me impressed."

I swallowed down my nervousness. "Thank you, Doctor Taurus. It was a team effort."

"Please don't play coy with me, Miss Mitoh. The magic you and your friends performed during the Games is far beyond the power of any first-year college student, and even surpasses the abilities of the most talented supernaturals alive today. None of you should've been able to pull off the kind of power that you displayed in the Games. There is something very interesting about all of you."

I forced my voice to remain steady. "Perhaps you overestimate us. We didn't win."

"You didn't win because you chose to lose. You threw your chance at salvation away."

"I don't know what you're talking about. My team hesitated. The other team took advantage. It was a careless mistake."

"Clearly." The Warden smiled. His hand tightened on mine until I was in pain. I didn't wince, or give him the satisfaction of pulling away. I could take it.

The Warden drew away, then. My hand was white by the time he let go. "You are a curious thing, Miss Mitoh. I will be keeping an eye on you and those you associate with. Don't forget, you are living in *my* world. And in the world I have created, the lord sees all."

This guy had such a god complex. I didn't breathe until the Warden had turned his back and walked away. It was an effort not to shake in my heels.

Yes, the Warden scared me. And I wasn't afraid of much in this world. But he frightened me worse than any monster I'd fought in the Games. He wanted to use me.

For what, I wasn't sure.

I returned to Kallie and Marcus, who both wore knitted expressions. "You okay? The Warden looked intense," Marcus said.

"I just need some air." My eyes flickered to look for my parents. They were dealing with separating a couple who were shouting at each other near the food table.

Good. I couldn't take them suffocating me right now. I had to get some space. I picked up my skirts and ran out of the Room of Mirrors. Oberi followed me, nails clicking on the floor.

There was an abandoned cell block not too far away. People went there to smoke or get away from teachers. I just needed a second to stop my thoughts from racing.

My lungs stung when I finally stopped to get some air. I paused underneath a small barred window in a deserted hallway that was dark and damp.

I wasn't sure if I was strong enough to fight the Warden when he ordered me to do his bidding. I was just starting to get better. I couldn't become a pawn for someone else's evil plans. I wouldn't.

The snow smacked against the window outside. As I stared upward, the voices in my mind began to ramble and race.

You need to get out of here, Ava.

The Warden will kill you.

He'll use you to hurt the people you love.

Don't let him. Run.

Most of the guards were at the party, containing all the students within one place. I had a better chance. I could use my blue fire to melt the bars, break the window. Maybe get off the grounds before I was hunted down.

What if... what if I tried to break out, and never looked back? The Warden couldn't use me then. It seemed foolish, to try to run again when I'd thrown my only opportunity away during the Darke Games...

But I hadn't known the Warden's intentions then. I lit a blue fireball in my hand and drew back, taking aim.

"Trying to sneak out?"

A knot formed in my throat. I turned and saw two rivals— the gang leader that we'd defeated in the Games, and the merman Charlie had almost suffocated. There was malice in the leader's eyes... like he'd been looking for me. I bet he'd followed me out after he'd watched me leave the dance.

Stupid. I was unprotected.

The fireball in my hand grew larger. "You'll stay back if you know what's good for you."

"Deuce, maybe we should let her be," the merman said. His voice was raspy now. He'd probably lost most of it after Charlie had nearly killed him.

"Fuck that," Deuce spat. "Her and the dog are getting it."

Oberi's growls were so vicious and cruel. The gang member's friend appeared wary, but the leader himself didn't want to hold back.

"You took away our only chance of getting out of here," Deuce growled. "We're going to make you pay for it."

Deuce advanced, but before he could, a broad figure stepped in front of me. The merman paled and took a few steps back. The gang leader remained in place, but his confidence faltered as he faced off with none other than Charlie... who'd totally planted himself between them and me.

"Turn around if you don't want me to kill you," Charlie said coolly. "You know I won't hesitate."

Deuce's face flushed in rage. "I couldn't give a shit if she's your girl. She cost me my freedom. She's going to pay!"

I remained behind Charlie and berated myself for getting into another stupid situation. I was stuck here for good now, so I might as well get with the program. There were three rules to the Institute. One, don't try to break out, because they *will* catch you. Two, keep your head down and you just might stay alive.

And three: if you ever want to get out of here, don't fall for an inmate.

Those three rules? I just broke them all.

Charlie's knuckles cracked as he faced the thug. I could hear the deadly intent in his tone. "You dare to lay a hand on her, you won't be able to walk."

Was he serious? The Darke Games were over... and yet he was still being overprotective, defensive of me. Charlie, the guy I literally couldn't stand, the guy who swore up and down he wanted nothing to do with me just a few weeks ago, was defending me from a gang leader?

And I had completely fallen for him.

I was totally screwed.

"I'm outta here, man." The other guy scampered. He didn't want Charlie to suffocate him again.

The gang member looked between Charlie, Oberi and me. He knew he couldn't take us on alone. He spat at our feet. "Better watch your back. I don't forget."

Charlie didn't turn around until he no longer heard their footsteps. When he faced me, my heart stuttered. Now that we weren't in danger, I could appreciate what Charlie had to offer. He was wearing a tailored black suit that he must've gotten from the consignment shop, with a black shirt and matching tie. His hair was styled with gel and combed perfectly. He looked like some dark prince straight out of hell, and I was here for it.

"Are you all right?" Charlie asked. He grasped my elbows, and I drooled. What were my most secret fantasies? Sleeping with a mob boss? A gangster, maybe? Because he fit the description.

"Ava?" Charlie shook my arms.

Oberi barked, and I said, "Uh, sure. Just got cornered by those goons."

"What are you doing out here? I showed up at the ball just for Marcus to tell me you left a second before."

I couldn't lie to him. "I got scared," I confessed. "Before you arrived, the Warden spoke with me. It wasn't good... he knows we blew the Darke Games on purpose, and told me he's watching us. I have a bad feeling he wants to use me for something."

"So... you decide trying to run away again is a good idea?"

"It was a spur of the moment freak-out. I wasn't thinking."

"Ava, if the Warden wants you, you're safer here than anywhere else," Charlie insisted. "If you leave, he'll hunt you down. At least if you're in his grasp, it gives you a chance to outsmart him before he can make a move."

I relaxed then. "I know you're right."

Charlie's voice was scolding. "You shouldn't run off on your own. Why didn't you wait for me? It wasn't like I was going to stand you up."

The comment stung. "That's news to me. It sure felt like it when I showed up by myself," I bit back.

"If I tell you I'm going to show up, I'll be there. You should know better."

"Are you going to lecture me like a little girl?"

"So long as you keep acting like one."

My temper rose then, and I had to react. "I can't *stand* you." I shoved Charlie away from me, though once I touched him, heat spread throughout my body, making it tremble.

Oh, I had it bad. As much as I hated to admit it, something big was going on between us.

Charlie smirked. "The feeling's mutual, sweetheart."

I wasn't sure if he was pointing out how much he despised me... or the passion he'd shown in the dark moments we'd secretly had before, in front of the stone gate merely days ago.

I didn't care if the man made my panties melt off and run for cover. I had to stay away from him. For his own sake as much as mine. People couldn't know you were in love at the Institute. It made you a target— vulnerable and weak. "We can't do this again. We'll get caught."

Charlie leaned against the wall. "We've already been sent to a prison, princess. Might as well make it a life sentence."

He moved in front of me, so that both of his arms were on either side of my body. The action made my muscles turn to gelatin. When he boxed me in, it didn't feel like a prison, but a safe place. His broad shoulders left me nowhere to run but into him.

"I can't do this," I said.

"Can't, or don't want to?"

It wasn't the second one. "It doesn't matter what I want. Feeling this way... it's the worst thing I could do."

"Sometimes it's good to be bad," Charlie said. "If you need one more reason to sin, just use me."

"Kiss me, then," I told him. "And make sure it's worth the price I have to pay."

He did. And fuck, it felt *so good*. I'd kissed dozens of guys before, but Charlie made me forget about each of them in one fell swoop. Kissing him was like uniting two pieces of one soul. I was addicted to this madness he made me feel. I thought I'd been crazy before, but I hadn't been insane before this moment. Every movement of his mouth against my own made me grow weak. His tongue rolled against mine, and his heartbeats were pounding against my breasts. The effort made me so lightheaded I couldn't breathe.

I sagged toward the floor, and couldn't help it. Charlie's kisses made me go boneless. I'd thought I'd collapse with the bliss they made me experience, but Charlie didn't let me fall. He held me up and pressed closer against me, inviting me to lean into him so he could support us both.

I hadn't thought about our first kiss since we'd shared it. I'd forced myself not to, scared of what it might mean, but I had to confront it now.

Charlie scared me because his passion made me let go, and I came undone at what he did to me. I didn't like feeling out of control.

That's why this couldn't happen. He made me so fragile. In his arms, I forgot everything and became vulnerable. I was falling all over him like an obsessed schoolgirl.

It'd be embarrassing if my desire wasn't so bad. His masculine energy poured out of him and collided with my feminine nature, not overpowering it, but melding together in a seamless symphony.

I ran my hands through his hair and pulled as he kissed me, doing everything in my power to hold back the moans. He was practically making love to me with his mouth alone. Sex couldn't feel this good. The emotions I'd refused my body the pleasure of indulging in welled to the surface, and I realized that running away from Charlie was like running from myself. I could try to cover up all the bad parts, but it wouldn't do any good. I was constantly naked around him, and I knew that it showed.

I didn't want to keep hurting. I didn't want to keep closing the door on us over and over. I couldn't change for Charlie... but I didn't have to. He accepted the person I was, and no matter how little, or how much, he had to offer me, it was enough. All I wanted was him. Despite trying to conceal that from him, he saw straight through my walls, and was breaking them down brick by brick just to be able to touch me. We were two shattered people, but sometimes you could fit the broken pieces back together and make something new. His broken pieces fit with mine, and I swore now that the picture looked better than ever before.

If Charlie was my drug, this was one hell of a good high.

Charlie pressed me into the wall, and our bodies collided. I felt his hard dick press against my stomach, straining through his pants. I felt a roll of greed, a thirsting lust that craved and begged for his attention.

Oh, shit. Maybe I *did* need those condoms after all.

Charlie ended the kiss long before I was ready for it to be over. I was the one who had pulled back the first time, but now, that seemed like such a cruel gesture. Charlie ran his thumb over my warm cheeks. "You're blushing, pidge."

Yeah, something else is warm, too, I thought. I seriously needed to go to the bathroom and ditch the panties. Flash flood alert.

"I like your dress," Charlie said. He ran his hand over the fabric, then gently through a few of my curls. I didn't even care if he messed up my hair. I just wanted him to touch me again.

"You look amazing. The suit... defines you," I said as my fingers graced his sleeves.

"I prefer nicer things. Didn't always have access to them, but I enjoy looking good."

He was as vain as I was. He didn't have the money to buy designer labels, but I'm sure if he did, they'd be in his closet.

Charlie took a breath. "Pidge, I—"

"Don't ruin it." I put a finger to his mouth. "Give me this night. Just one night."

Charlie hesitated, but didn't press. It wasn't like I didn't want to tell him how I felt. I felt more for Charlie than I could ever imagine feeling for anyone else in this universe.

But if I said all that, I'd break down. And I wanted this to be a happy night. We deserved to celebrate, after everything we'd been through.

I dug in my handbag. "I have something for you."

"For me?"

"Yes. It's your birthday, isn't it? December twenty-first."

Charlie's face softened, like he was shocked I remembered. I slipped something soft over his right wrist.

"It's an armband," I explained as he ran his fingers over the threads curiously. "Every Hawkei child gets one. Someone close to them usually weaves it. Mine is red and green, for me and Monica. Your armband is red and purple... for us."

Charlie reached out and grasped my forearm. "Ava-Marie... I don't know what to say."

I loved it when he said my name. It felt like he truly knew me. "Don't say anything. Keep it perfect."

Oberi wound between us and wagged his tail. Charlie patted his head, while I stared at him. He was twenty-three years old today. And he'd been through more in two decades than most people suffered through in several lifetimes.

But he had me, and I wasn't going to let anyone make him suffer again. I was coming for all those who had hurt him. Everyone that had caused him pain, everyone that was the source of his sorrow. They'd touched his dreams and twisted them into dark realities he couldn't escape.

I remembered Charlie's ruthless actions during the Games, his desperate efforts to keep me alive. The greatest monsters we had to fight weren't out there; they were inside of us.

They turned Charlie into a monster. Now I was going to be their reckoning.

A guard peeked down the hall. "Hey, what are you kids doing down there?" he barked. "Get back to the dance immediately, before I escort you personally!"

Charlie ducked his head, and we ran off. When we came back to the dance, I saw Marcus had found a way to use the condoms. He blew them up and tied them off into balloon animals. Kallie used her magic to levitate them into the air. They flew over the crowd, and people bonked them back and forth, like volleyballs.

As he was making the balloon animals, a crowd had formed around him. Marcus was bragging loudly about his efforts during the Darke Games, which I found to be exaggerated.

"Yeah, all those monsters were totally running from me," he boasted. "Ripping up trees, using necromancy, casting battle magic, it was a total snoozefest. The Warden made it too easy. I think I'm gonna enter again next year, you know? I could win all by myself. My team just slowed me up."

He'd nearly pissed himself every moment of the Games, but I let him have his fun. Kallie sat up when she saw us approaching. "There you two are. I was beginning to think you'd left the Institute for the holidays."

"We can't leave," Charlie said. "We don't get to leave the Institute for summer break or holidays. We're stuck here until we graduate."

"*Most* people are. All the rich kids get to go home for Christmas. The ones that pay off the Warden, anyway," Marcus said.

"Yeah. They let a certain wealthy percentage of the prison population go home for the holidays. They don't have to call it a *real* prison if some kids can visit home during break." Kallie gave a skeptical sound.

"We figured you two must've been getting ready to leave with Ava's parents."

"Don't think so," Charlie said. "Ava's dad doesn't really like me."

But he leaned into me as a question, and I said, "Um... my dad bribed the Warden to get me home for a few weeks, but I have to check in with an Institute officer every day, so they're certain I don't go running off. I'm leaving tonight and won't be back until the first."

"Oh." Charlie's voice was disappointed. "I hoped you'd be spending Christmas here."

I kinda hoped so, too. I really missed my family, but... Charlie.

"Hey, at least you'll have us," Kallie subbed. "I'm not leaving."

"Me, neither," Marcus added.

Kallie jumped up. "Let's stop talking about sad shit. We're here tonight! We need to celebrate!"

Both she and I let out screams, and Rishi batted a balloon animal away. Oberi began chasing it around, and nearly yelped as a girl came out of Marcus' crowd and staggered up to us. I didn't know her, but she looked half-drunk. Someone had probably snuck some booze in. She completely fawned over us as she said, "Oh my gosh! You guys did *amazing* in the Games! I watched every second. I couldn't take my eyes away!"

"Thanks," I told her. "It was hard, but I'm sure all the teams did pretty good."

The girl shook her head. "No, you don't get it. Everyone has *massive* respect for you now, for the magic you pulled off. You guys are like, the prison's premier villain's club!"

The girl stumbled away, giggling. Marcus, Kallie and I looked between each other, while Charlie leaned in.

"The Villain's Club..." I mused. "That sounds like a pretty good gang name, right?"

"Only the best," Marcus said.

"People will know not to fuck with us," Kallie added.

"At the Institute, reputation is everything." Charlie put an arm around my shoulders. "I think it's time the Villain's Club earned a bad one for itself."

Kallie and Marcus both agreed at once, and excitement coursed through me. The Villain's Club was going down in infamy, and from this moment on, I knew whatever I was going through, I could depend on my fellow villains to be there.

Out of the corner of my eye, I saw someone prowling along the edge of the room. I recognized Coyote's heckling smile at an instant. He switched from his animal form to his human one, beckoning me to him with his playful eyes. Though he passed near students and teachers alike, none of them noticed him or looked his way. No one else could see him.

I touched Charlie's arm lightly. "I'll be right back. I need to talk to someone."

Oberi trotted after me. He looked up at Coyote and wagged his tail, like he was greeting an old friend. Not wanting to look crazy, I leaned against the wall near Coyote and stared out ahead. Though the music of the dance was loud, I still dropped my voice. "You're back."

"*I'll be around,*" Coyote said. "*You did well during the Games. The Great Spirit is pleased.*"

"Are you going to tell me what the gods want with me now?" I asked.

Coyote hissed with laughter. "*That would ruin the fun.*"

"I hope someone more helpful is being sent my way, or I'm doomed." Coyote wasn't very much help in terms of a guide.

Coyote played with the strands of my hair. I ignored him. He tugged on my curls as he said, "*Do you know about demigods?*"

He had my attention. "Not extensively," I admitted.

"*Your grandfather has studied them. They aren't children of the gods, but rather, supernaturals of astonishing power. Claims they no longer exist, but walked the earth in centuries before. They were harnessers of exceptional magic. Stronger than talented supernaturals, but not as great as the gods that came before them.*"

"What's that got to do with me?"

"*Have you ever considered you could be one of them?*"

"Me?"

"*You, and your friends.*"

My veins froze over as my heart skipped. The Warden's accusations that my team was too powerful came rushing back at me. The monsters had been difficult to beat, yes, but our abilities during the Darke Games had been unmatched. The fights themselves were difficult, but the magic? Easy. Me and my teammates were pulling off spells that would kill most other supernaturals our age, flinging them around like they were child's play.

And the scariest thing was, I knew I hadn't hit my limits yet. Not even close.

I swallowed. "What does this mean for the prophecy?"

"*What do you think it means?*"

"Dammit, can you just answer me plainly?" I snapped.

"Ava?" Charlie's voice broke our conversation. He stood beside me and took my hand. His mouth turned down as Coyote continued to snicker. "Are you okay? Is this guy bothering you?"

My eyes widened as I realized Charlie could hear him, too. And I was pretty sure if he had his eyesight, he'd be able to see Coyote just as well as I could.

"He's just a friend," I said. "Let's go, Charlie."

Coyote's laughter grew more intense as I took Charlie's arm and led him away. Oberi went on ahead, and I looked back. By the time I did, Coyote had vanished.

"Is that guy deranged?" Charlie asked me. "He seemed a little... off."

"More than you know," I said. I was still reeling with the fact Charlie could hear him. What did it all mean? I wanted to tell him about Coyote, but... I felt like now wasn't the time. I still needed to come up with an explanation of how and why this was all possible, and dropping a bombshell on Charlie like that would only be cruel on a night when we were supposed to be celebrating.

I was more confused than ever. I had no answers to the prophecy. If anything, I only had more questions.

But I was certain this changed everything. I was no longer a defense-less little girl. I was a full-on demigoddess. And I was going to imprison every single liar who'd dared to lay a finger on me. After that, I'd tear apart anyone else who tried again. There were too many innocent victims on this earth who went without justice. Too many evil-doers who walked free.

If I had the power to change that, I would. The magic I'd been given... it was a gift. I had people to fight for and friends who'd fight with me. If Coyote was right and I was a demigod, there were no boundaries to what my magic could do. I would reshape this world into a better one, and if it fought back, I'd force it to succumb to my will. I'd push myself every moment until this world bowed at my feet. If it refused to succumb, I'd level it to the ground.

The Warden, the gods... they could all come for me. Or at least, they could try.

I'd be waiting to save the world— if there was still a chance it could be saved. And if not, so be it.

At least I'd enjoy watching it burn.

charlie

TWENTY-FIVE

I twirled Ava-Marie around as we headed back to our table. Her dress flared, and the fabric brushed against my legs. Ava giggled as I caught her around the waist. I didn't know why I did it. It just felt right in the moment.

"Pidge, I've been meaning to ask you something," I admitted.

Ava stopped, and we stood near the edge of the dance floor to talk in low whispers. "Ask me what?"

I cocked my head toward Oberi, who I could feel through our bond. He radiated glee, and was obviously having the time of his life at the Villain's Ball. I could only guess how many cupcakes Marcus had slipped him already.

"I thought things would feel different with Oberi after the Games," I said. "I thought... maybe I'd be able to hear him talk to me now, but I haven't. It was only the one time when we bonded. What does it mean to secure your bond with your Familiar?"

Ava paused. "I don't know what it's supposed to feel like, to be honest," she said sheepishly. "It happens when you and your Familiar go through trauma together. The trauma brings you closer, and the stronger bond intensifies your magic."

"That's what I mean," I said. "I don't feel any closer to Oberi than I did before."

Ava drew a deep breath. Her tone was hollow. "I'm not sure we secured the bond, Charlie."

My stomach sank. "Oh. That's... um..."

"Unexpected? Not ideal?" Ava listed off options. "I agree. I thought for sure the Games would change us."

They did, I thought, but I didn't say it out loud.

Ava continued. "And maybe it would've worked, if Oberi wasn't bonded to us both. He was torn between us the whole time."

I remembered how Oberi had hesitated when Ava went running off to fight the malumuto. Somehow, the Games had brought Ava and I together, but it'd only driven a wedge between us and Oberi. It didn't feel right.

I fingered the beads around Ava's hips. "What if we *never* secure the bond, pidge? I don't want you going through any more trauma than you've been through."

Ava scoffed. "I'm part of a prophecy. There's plenty more to come."

"I wish you wouldn't think that way." Just the thought of Ava going through more pain felt like a knife to the gut.

"It's not about the trauma," Ava explained. "It's about what brings you and your Familiar together. We'll secure the bond, Charlie. I know it."

I relaxed a little and smirked. "And to think how powerful you were during the Games. You'll be *amazing* once the bond is secure."

Ava groaned. "Can we not talk about our powers, or the prophecy, or any of it right now? I just want to have fun at the dance."

"Okay, pidge." I took her hand. "Let's have fun."

Ava started dragging me back toward our table. I knew the dance was nothing more than an illusion— a way to keep the students in their place— but I didn't care about that right now. Ava's hand in mine was all that seemed to matter.

We returned to our table, where Marcus and Kallie were gossiping about the other students.

"Ew, look at Naya and Mad Dog," Kallie complained. "This isn't a fucking porno."

Marcus laughed. "The way she's grinding on him? It could be."

"Naya's giving Mad Dog a lap dance?" I balked as I sat.

"Believe me, you don't want to see it," Ava replied. "Mad Dog just reached up Naya's skirt, and I'm pretty sure I just saw vadge."

I almost gagged.

Ava went to grab the chair next to me, but I accidentally stepped on the hem of her dress. She tripped, and I caught her in my lap.

"Whoa," Ava laughed, before leaning in to whisper. "Is that some kind of a move or something?"

I smirked as my hands curled around her waist. "Do you want it to be?"

She hesitated a moment. "Charlie Wahkin, you are a mystery to me."

That was all she said before she turned and leaned forward to grab something off the table. She didn't get off my lap, and I wasn't sure what it meant. I didn't ask, though, because I didn't want her to leave.

"Here, try this," Ava said with a full mouth.

I didn't trust people with that kind of offer, but I trusted Ava. I opened my mouth, and she popped something sweet into it. I crunched into a hard outer shell, and sweet, fruity flavors burst inside my mouth.

"Mm..." I said. "Chocolate-covered strawberries."

"They're the best, aren't they?" Ava replied.

"Oh, get a room," Kallie said sarcastically.

Marcus whispered something to Kallie, and she burst out in laughter.

"Hey!" Ava scolded. "You better not be reading minds again."

"I didn't mean to!" Marcus defended.

I sank a little in my chair. What thoughts exactly had he heard? Mine, or Ava's? I couldn't deny there were some pretty dirty thoughts going through my head right now. Bro or not, Marcus did *not* need to know what I was thinking.

"I'm really trying to block it out," Marcus promised. "But it's like Junior prom in here. Everyone's hormones are all over the place. There aren't enough guards at the Institute to deal with all the fucking that's going to happen tonight."

I shivered at the thought of Ava and me running off together after the dance. But we wouldn't, because no matter how Ava kissed me, I didn't think she'd let me get that close.

I was okay with it. She could have all the time she needed. No matter what, I'd always be here.

"Rishi!" Marcus cried, the same time Ava yelled, "Oberi!"

"Bad kitty," Marcus scolded.

"What happened?" I questioned.

Ava blew a breath. "They're getting themselves into trouble. Oberi, stop drinking from the punch bowl!"

Ava jumped off my lap to deal with Oberi, and Marcus hurried after her.

"Gods," Kallie sighed.

"What?" I asked.

"Ava's straightening Oberi's veil. She's more worried about the veil getting in the punch bowl than about Oberi's slobber."

I crossed my arms as Ava returned. "Is that how we're going to deal with him?"

"What?" Ava asked innocently as she sat beside me. I was a little disappointed she hadn't taken my lap again, but I wasn't being exactly welcoming.

"You can't coddle him!" I cried. "He needs to learn how to behave himself."

"I was not coddling— how did you even know?" Ava gasped. "Kallie!"

"Hey," she replied. "I just say it like it is. I didn't interject any opinions."

Marcus returned, but Rishi was screeching. "Um... a little help?"

"Ancestors, did Rishi fall *in*?" Ava sighed.

"Only a little," Marcus said sheepishly. He set Rishi on the table, but the cat immediately took off running. He jumped onto my lap, before racing across the dance floor. I was soaked.

"Ew, Marcus," I complained. "That's what you call *a little*? Now I've got punch in places I don't care to admit."

"Here, let me help," Ava offered. Immediately, the punch began to draw out of my clothing as Ava used her Water magic to gather it up.

"Thanks," I said.

"Hey, can you do that on Rishi?" Marcus asked.

"If you can catch him," Ava replied.

Marcus sighed. "I'll try."

Kallie's chair squeaked as she stood. "Well, I'm going to gorge myself on fae cheesecake. All the flavor with none of the calories."

Kallie abandoned us, leaving Ava and I alone with Oberi. Silence stretched between us, and I waited for her to stay something. Oberi nudged my leg with his nose, and it clicked. Ava was waiting for me.

Ugh. I had to *ask her* to dance? It felt so awkward. Just the thought of it made my heart speed up. I didn't get the chance to ask, though. Ava caved first.

"Everyone's dancing." She made it sound like she was making small-talk, but I heard the suggestion in her tone.

"I'm no good at dancing," I told her.

"It's not that hard," she insisted.

"For a guy who's never been to a dance, it is."

"You've never been to a dance!?" Ava balked. She grabbed my hand before I could protest. "Now you *have* to dance."

I drew back as she yanked on my arm. "I don't know how."

"Then let me teach you. You can't spend your first dance sitting here the whole time."

"I won't be," I objected. "I'll visit the snack table eventually."

"Come on, Charlie," Ava begged. "*Please.* Just one dance."

Hell, when Ava said *please*, I couldn't resist. She might as well have been begging for all of me— and I would've given it to her, too.

I grumbled as Ava dragged me to my feet, because I couldn't let her know I was kind of eager to get on the dance floor. At least there, I could hold her in my arms.

"Oberi, stay," I commanded as I stood. Oberi whined, because he knew he was in trouble for drinking from the punch bowl.

We started toward the dance floor. I didn't miss the pad of Oberi's feet as he escaped.

"He's gone already, isn't he?" I asked.

Ava sighed. "I think he's off to find some of the fae cheesecake Kallie mentioned."

"As long as he doesn't get into the real stuff. He could get sick," I pointed out.

"He'll be fine," Ava promised. "He can eat anything."

The song changed to a slow melody I recognized— an old Motown song from the 1960s. Ava faced me. "Your hands go here," she told me as she planted them around her waist.

Holy shit, they were close to her ass. I wondered if she meant to do that.

Ava draped her arms around my shoulders and began gently swaying from side to side. The tempo was slow enough to sway in circles with her, but with an upbeat edge that had her moving her hips.

Ancestors, her hips must've been carved by the Great Spirit himself. She was so freaking hot. I began singing the words to the song under my breath.

"You like this song?" she asked.

I shrugged. "The classics are the best. I come from Detroit— it's practically gospel to know Motown music."

"Agreed," she said, before we both went silent again.

I didn't know how long we danced without saying anything. It could've been a lifetime, or only seconds. Time didn't seem to have any meaning when I held Ava. All I could do was drink in every second with her.

"See?" She finally broke the silence. "Dancing isn't hard at all."

I melted into her, daring to draw her closer to me until our bodies were pressed against each other. Based on the description I got from my friends earlier, I assumed this was one of the more chaste positions on the dance floor. Ava leaned her head against my shoulder, and all the tension in my body left me.

"Yeah." I sighed. "Not hard at all."

And it wasn't. When I held Ava in my arms, everything seemed easy. The Games were over, and I could breathe again. Even the prophecy seemed a distant worry. The Warden was nowhere nearby. There was nothing here that could touch us.

"Marcus!" Ava gasped.

"Hey, now," I teased. "I thought I was your date for the night."

"No, not that!" Ava drew away from me, and I heard a foot connect with someone's gut, followed by an *oof*. "Marcus, what the fuck are you doing under my dress?"

My hands curled into fists.

"Rishi slid under your skirt to hide!" Marcus defended. "I had to sneak up on him, or he'd run away."

"Ask next time, you douche!" Ava slapped Marcus' shoulder, but it didn't sound like it hurt.

The song changed to a more upbeat tempo. Kallie's heels clicked on the dance floor as she came running over to us. She slammed into Ava, body-checking her.

"Hey, bit—" Ava started, but Kallie quickly cut in.

"Partner change!" Kallie started dancing on me, grinding her ass against my dick. I wish I could say it turned me on, but she wasn't the girl I was interested in tonight. I had to assume this was some sort of move to make Marcus jealous.

"What the hell is this?" I asked.

"It's the Monster Mash!" Kallie cried. "A classic. I requested it. It seemed perfect for the Villain's Ball."

"Ancestors," Ava said. "I've never seen the Monster Mash like *this* before. Everyone is being so filthy."

"Exactly," Kallie laughed. "Except for you. Partner change!"

Kallie grabbed Ava and shoved her in my direction. I had to catch her so she wouldn't trip over her dress.

"Now that's what I'm talking about!" Marcus cried in glee. I could only assume that meant Kallie was grinding against him now. "Woohoo!"

Ava hesitated. "Well, everyone else is doing it."

My heart sped up. I couldn't *admit* I wanted her on me, but I'd be damned if I weren't thinking about it. "We can't disappoint Kallie."

I was glad to say I didn't have to do anything but stand there as Ava danced around me. She spun around me a few times, before ending in front, her ass pressed against me. Holy shit, Ava could twerk. I had to resist the urge to reach out and grab it while she shimmied.

"Hell, pidge," I teased. "Where'd you learn to do that?"

Ava laughed. "You wouldn't believe me if I told you."

"Well, I'm already thinking strip club."

"I learned from my Aunt Imogen," she admitted, before sheepishly adding, "who learned from my Uncle Jonah."

I grimaced. "I think I'm going to have to have a talk with your Uncle Jonah. He sounds like a creep."

"He's harmless!" Ava defended. "And the sweetest guy you'll ever meet."

"Partner change!" Kallie announced again. She shoved herself between Ava and me, then dragged Ava away.

"Ooh, work it, girl!" Ava yelled over the dance floor.

I felt someone come up to me, their ass shaking in my direction as awkward as could be. "What the hell, Marcus!?" I shoved him away.

"Kallie said partner change," he explained nonchalantly.

"It works for girls. Not so much for us bros."

"Don't be homophobic," Marcus insisted.

"I am not! I don't even want *Kallie* on me."

"Ooh," Marcus sang. "So you only have a boner for one lady."

"Shut up." I shoved him again. "It's not like you haven't already read my mind."

"Hey, I don't eavesdrop and tell." Marcus made a zipping noise, like he was locking his lips.

"Wait... you won't even tell me what you hear from Ava?" I asked. "I thought we were friends."

"Psychic confidentiality," he stated. "But let's just say whatever you're thinking, you can bet your ass Ava's version is ten times worse."

My jaw dropped, and Marcus made a whipping sound. I frowned at him. "Stop it. Ava is *not* into whips and chains."

Though as I said it, I realized it wouldn't surprise me. I'd bet anything if she managed to get cuffs off one of the guards, she'd sure as hell use them.

What was I thinking? Ava wasn't going to be using fucking *handcuffs* at the Institute! I mean, I knew people fooled around in here, but never in the dorms where the guards could catch them. We'd have to go—

Marcus started snickering, and I realized he was reading my thoughts.

"Would you stop!?" I snapped.

"I told you I don't mean it!" he defended. "There are just too many thoughts to block out. Though that time—"

I shoved my hand into his face. "Partner change."

"Hey," Kallie objected. "You're not the one who gets to announce partner change."

Ava whispered something to Kallie, but I couldn't hear it over the music. The two of them came over without a word and started grinding on me from both sides. A huge grin spread across my face.

"Hey, where's the love for your favorite warlock?" Marcus asked.

"I'll dance with you!" a girl nearby offered.

"Ooh, looking hot tonight, Lupe," Marcus said in a tease.

Kallie immediately jumped away from me. "Oh, *hell no.*"

Ava laughed loudly as Kallie rushed off to claim Marcus. "Well, that was— oh, no."

Ava's tone immediately shifted as the song changed.

I groaned. "Someone requested a heavy metal song?"

"I don't think this is a request," Ava pointed out. "I think it's the last song of the night, which means—"

"Mosh pit!" someone screamed.

I barely had a chance to process it before bodies were pressing in on me from all angles. Someone threw a punch, and my head snapped to the side at the impact.

For a moment, I was totally clueless. I thought it might be some sort of terrorist attack or something. Then I heard the sound of Ava's maniacal laughter.

"Come on, Charlie!" She dragged me deeper into the crowd of people. "It's the final send-off for the night. Enjoy the brawl!"

"Enjoy the—?"

Another fist cracked into my jaw, and I heard Oberi yowl from the edge of the dance floor. Ava whirled around, her dress billowing near my ankles. "Hey!" she screamed. "Don't fucking touch my date."

Ava's fist cracked into someone's face. I didn't know who it was, but all I heard in response was laughter.

"This is nuts!" I cried.

Ava laughed with glee. "It's *amazing*! Now punch someone before the guards can stop you!"

"Grr... gaaah!" Marcus made noises like he was the freaking Hulk. "I just knocked out a vampire!"

"I punched Naya in the back of the head!" Kallie cried happily. "She didn't even see me. It felt great!"

Oberi finally pushed his way through the crowd. He growled and snapped his jaws at anyone who dared come close to Ava and me. But Ava didn't give a shit about being protected. She dove into the crowd, stirring up trouble in her wake. And she sounded like she was having one hell of a great time doing it.

My hands curled into fists, and pent-up energy rocked my body. What the hell?

I spun around and flung my fists into any flesh I could find— first a face, then a gut. I knew I had one hell of a punch, but no one seemed to care how much it hurt. We just shoved and kicked and punched... and laughed. It was total insanity.

It was villainy.

By the time the guards broke up the brawl, I was sweating buckets. I'd stripped off my suit coat at one point and couldn't find it, but I didn't really care. It wasn't like I was going to be wearing a suit anytime soon again. I yanked off my bow tie and unbuttoned the first few buttons of my shirt, using my Air power to blow cool air across my skin.

Marcus nudged me as we headed out of the Room of Mirrors. "Ava's digging the look."

My heart fluttered, and my voice came out a pitch higher than normal. "Really?"

"Oh, yeah," Marcus sang. "Somebody's getting some tonight."

I elbowed him in the side. "Shut up. It's not like that between us."

Or was it?

I didn't know what we were. We'd never really talked about it. And I didn't want to ask either, because I was afraid it would only drive Ava away. The last thing I wanted to do was scare her off.

"*Sure* it isn't," Marcus said sarcastically. "Have fun with your hand tonight."

"I'm sure you and Kallie have all sorts of plans."

Marcus lowered his voice. "I don't kiss and tell."

"Liar," I accused. He hadn't made a move, and I knew it, because he'd tell me the second it happened. And if he didn't, Kallie would tell Ava, who would tell me.

"Shh..." Marcus hissed. "The girls are coming."

Ava and Kallie came over, giggling. Oberi nudged his wet nose into my hand, and I stroked his back.

"What's so funny?" I asked.

"Nothing." Kallie dragged out the word, and the girls laughed again. It had to be sexual.

"We should probably get back to our dorms before the guards catch us," I suggested.

"Charlie's right," Kallie agreed. "We'll see you two later."

Marcus and Kallie headed off toward their respective dorms, while Ava and I walked back to ours. Other students were shuffling back to their rooms, so we weren't totally alone.

Too bad. I really liked what happened when we were alone.

"I hope you enjoyed yourself," I told her.

"I had the *best* time," Ava said. "I wish the school held more dances."

"Same." I let the confession slip. Despite my protests against dancing, I really had enjoyed myself.

"Charlie Wahkin had a good time?" Ava gasped playfully. "Is the world on fire?"

I laughed. "No, I just... finally gave myself permission."

Ava stopped outside our dorm rooms and turned to me. "I'm glad. That makes this night totally worth it."

We stood there a few seconds, as if waiting for the other to say something. I didn't think we really knew how to say goodbye.

"I have to grab my stuff," Ava said. "My parents want to get back to the mainland tonight. They've been away from my siblings too long."

My shoulders fell. "Well, um... thanks again for the gift."

I was blabbing. This was new. What the hell was wrong with me?

"Don't mention it," Ava said.

Doors throughout the hall closed as students returned to their rooms. Ava and I were the last ones in the hall. Oberi came up behind me and shoved his head into my legs. I stumbled forward and caught myself on Ava.

She laughed. "I think Oberi might be trying to tell you something."

I couldn't help but smile. "Oberi gets what Oberi wants."

I leaned down until my lips were a mere inch from hers. My heart lifted in my chest, giving me a high that could rival any hard drug. Ava closed the distance between us, pressing her soft mouth against mine. I melted all over again, dragging her close. She inhaled a deep breath.

She drew away far too soon. "You make me..." she started breathlessly, before trailing off.

I pressed my forehead against hers. "I make you...?"

Ava drew a deep breath and whispered, "I hate the way you make me feel, Charlie Wahkin."

Her tone didn't reflect her words. She loved every second of it, though she wouldn't admit it.

"I hate you, too, pidge," I whispered.

Ava's hands roamed over my chest, before curling around my collar and dragging me closer. "You should hate me more."

She pressed her lips to mine again. I couldn't help it when my tongue slid inside her mouth.

"I hate you so much," I gasped. My hands dropped to grab her ass, and she bit my lower lip. I moaned as my dick jerked inside my pants.

Hell, where were those handcuffs right about now? Ava could chain me up and do whatever she wanted to me.

"I hate you more," Ava claimed, but the way she kissed me and the way her hands moved over my body said otherwise. Prison had taught her nothing— she was still a bad liar.

Passion surged between us as we made out, intensified by our bond. I feared my heart may beat straight out of my chest and I might come at the first stroke of my dick. Just the thought of her touching me there made me shiver.

A door opened, and Ava and I leapt apart. I heard heavy footsteps coming down the hall, and suddenly my heart was pounding for different reasons. Had we been caught?

"We should get going," Ava said quickly. "The guards are coming for bed check, and I'm supposed to be leaving already."

I squeezed her hand one final time. "Sweet dreams, pidge."

"You too, Charlie," she whispered, before turning to her door and slipping inside. Oberi licked my hand as a goodbye before following Ava into her room.

I was still riding the high of her kiss, and I stumbled into the wall when I turned. Hell, I was two feet off from my door! I grabbed the handle and hurried inside before the guards could catch me.

The moment I stepped inside, I knew I wasn't alone. I could feel a person's presence in the air, then came the squeak of the bed springs as someone stood.

"Charlie," a female voice said.

My palms shot upward instinctively, warning the intruder of my magic. "Who the hell are you?"

"Don't attack!" she exclaimed in a hushed whisper. "Please. I'm only here to help."

"Then answer the question," I demanded.

"My name is Maddie Mitoh," she introduced.

"Mitoh," I repeated flatly. "You're one of Ava's aunts— the one who wrote her prophecy."

"Yes," she answered. "I've come tonight because it was the only time I could get into the school unnoticed."

"You could've called, or wrote," I suggested, lowering my hands. "Ava's room is the next door down."

"You misunderstand, Charlie," she said in a low voice, as if she was afraid someone might overhear. "I didn't come to talk to Ava. I came to speak to *you*. What I have to say must be heard in person."

I furrowed my brow. I wasn't entirely sure if I could trust her— or if she was even who she said she was. "Talk fast, or I'm calling Ava in here."

"No, please," Maddie begged. "She can't know I've come. There are parts of the prophecy that I did not write down for her— pieces meant only for *you*."

I took a step back and caught myself on the door. "What do you mean?"

"You're a part of it, Charlie," she said ominously, sending a shiver down my spine. "You and Ava share a soul, which means you are just as involved in this prophecy as she is."

I held my chin up. "Whatever you have to say to me, you can say in front of Ava. I'll tell her myself either way."

"You *can't*," Maddie insisted. "Doing so could compromise the future of supernatural society as a whole. Ava's choices cannot be influenced by what I'm about to tell you. You must keep what I say a secret, even from her."

The air seemed as cold as ice— or maybe it was just that all the blood had drained to my toes. What could Maddie possibly have to say to me? And how could I keep it from Ava?

I didn't have answers, but I had to know what she came here to tell me. It could help Ava unravel the mysteries around the prophecy.

My breath wavered. "What is it?"

Maddie sounded worried, which chilled me to the bone. "There will come a time when you need to make a choice. There will be no other options. You will need to destroy Ava— or the world will be destroyed *by her.*"

I sagged against the wall. It was worse than I could possibly fear. Somehow, I managed to find my voice. "Hell no. I'm not killing Ava."

"You won't kill her," Maddie stated firmly. "You don't understand. What you will do... this is a fate far worse than death."

What could possibly be worse than dying? Nothing I wanted to do to Ava, I was certain.

My tongue turned to ash. "Then I won't do it," I snarled. "Nothing can make me harm her."

"You don't have any other option." Maddie's tone was firm and clear. "You have a choice, Charlie Wahkin. The decision is in your hands. If you want to save the world, you must bring Ava to her end— or doom us all. Which will you choose?"

END OF BOOK ONE

Continue on to read a special excerpt from book two: *The Criminal Lair*!

HIDDEN LEGENDS

Read more from the Hidden Legends universe! Each Hidden Legends series takes place within the same world, but in separate and unique societies. Every series stands on its own, and they can be read in any order.

ELEMENTALS, DRAGONS, & MORE

Academy of Magical Creatures by Megan Linski & Alicia Rades

SHIFTERS, FAE, & SORCERESSES

University of Sorcery by Megan Linski

WITCHES, DEMONS, & REAPERS

College of Witchcraft by Alicia Rades

Never miss a new release! Join our newsletter at
hiddenlegendsbooks.com/fanclub/

THE CRIMINAL LAIR
CHAPTER ONE

Charlie

I never knew what two weeks without a man's soul could do to him. It'd been tortuous to be away from Ava-Marie and Oberi for so long. I was literally trapped in a prison— the Darke Institute for Supernatural Offenders— and that didn't seem half as bad as the prison I'd built up in my mind. The distance was agonizing, every second waiting for the pieces of my soul to return to my side... waiting to be made whole again.

I knew the moment Ava left the mainland, because I felt a sense of excitement well within me. My pidge was coming home.

I paced the main entrance to the Institute for what felt like hours, awaiting Ava and Oberi's arrival. They were getting closer. I could feel it.

The doors to the Institute opened, creaking on the antique hinges. Cool air swept through the hall, and the sound of dozens of footsteps met my ears. Everyone who'd been allowed off campus during Christmas break had returned. There weren't many, as it required one hell of a donation from your parents to get permission to leave. But they had to let a few kids out every now and then, to keep up the appearance that they were in fact a school, and not a prison.

None of the inmates were buying that crap.

A dog barked, and I knelt with my arms spread wide. "Oberi!" I called.

He tore through the entryway, panting. Oberi slammed into me, nearly knocking me backward as he gleefully licked my face. I laughed and scratched behind his ears. It was the best I'd felt since the night of the Villain's Ball.

Heels clicked against the floor, and I swore my heart stopped. The scent of lilac and raspberries surrounded me, and my soul once again felt whole.

I stood and faced her. "Pidge," I said breathlessly. "You're back— *oof!*"

"Charlie!" Ava cried, throwing her arms around me. Her duffel bag hit me in the side. I went still in surprise, before relaxing into the embrace. I wrapped my arms around her and inhaled her scent.

She drew away far too soon, sounding amused. "You sound surprised I'm back. You think I could escape this place forever? I get into so much trouble, they'd send me back in a heartbeat."

"In true pidge fashion," I teased.

Ava shifted, hoisting her bag up on her shoulder.

"Do you want help with your bags?" I asked.

"I only have the one," she told me. "But you can walk me to my dorm to drop it off."

"Sure." There was literally nowhere else I'd rather be right now.

Ava and I fell into step side-by-side, and Oberi trotted along ahead of us, panting happily. He seemed to miss me, too, and was happy to be back. As if magnetized, mine and Ava's fingers intertwined, but only slightly— as if we were trying to hide what we were to the rest of the world.

We weren't really *anything*— not officially. Though we shared a soul, Ava wasn't exactly my *girlfriend*.

But I'd be damned if it didn't feel good to hold her hand like she was.

"How was your break?" Ava asked while we walked to the Elementai cellblock.

I shrugged. "I bummed around with Marcus and Kallie. We snuck into the chapel on Christmas for a gift exchange. Marcus gave me a used roll of toilet paper."

Ava laughed out loud. "That sounds like him. I'm sure he stole it from the men's room."

"Honestly, my break was pretty boring," I admitted. The truth was, I'd spent most of it just waiting for her to come back. "I hope your break was better."

"It was nice seeing my parents and my siblings again," Ava remarked. "I had to check in with an officer every day, so that sucked a pair of dragon balls. But otherwise my break was... productive."

"Oh? Productive how?"

Ava slowed outside her room and lowered her voice. "I can't tell you here."

My stomach sank. If Ava found something she couldn't talk about out in the open, it might have to do with the prophecy. The last thing I wanted was to play a part in this prophecy coming true.

The words her aunt Maddie had spoken to me echoed in my mind, like a voice recording on repeat. I didn't think I'd ever be able to get them out of my head.

A choice will be made by the twin of her soul
To save her and damn the realm
Or curse her, and save us all
A fate worse than death
Is the chosen one's destiny.

Maddie had visited me the night of the Villain's Ball and spoken the prophecy to me. She was a *naderei*, a Hawkei prophet, and I had to trust that what she said was true. She'd been very clear with me on what the prophecy meant. There'd come a day when I would have to make a choice— a choice between Ava and the rest of the world. For Ava, this would be *a fate far worse than death*, Maddie had said.

It was cruel to ask of me. Ava was part of my soul. I'd do anything for her—

Including hiding this from her.

Maddie had been adamant that Ava couldn't know, and that telling her would compromise the outcome of the prophecy. If Ava knew my part, it would only push her toward her own demise. I shuddered to think about it.

Ava dropped her bag off in her room, then took my hand. "Come on. I think I know a place where we can talk."

Ava led me through the halls of the Darke Institute, and Oberi followed at her side. The halls were lively with chatter, as this was our last day off before classes started up again, and no one liked being cooped up in their dorms. I paid careful attention to the twists and turns we took, and soon realized where we were headed.

"We're going to the balcony," I realized. It's where Ava and I had spoken of the prophecy before. The balcony was secluded and was difficult to get to, as its entrance was hidden down a maze of hallways. I didn't think I'd be able to find it again without Ava's guidance.

"It's the only place in the Institute where we can talk in private without being overheard or interrupted," she said.

We turned down a few more halls, and Ava opened a door. The air was chill but not totally unpleasant, as the Institute was located on a Pacific island. I was used to bitterly cold winters this time of year, so I didn't mind. With Ava here, my heart was warm.

Oberi pushed his way between us and barked happily as he ran out onto the balcony. Ava and I followed behind him, and I heard the door click shut.

We stopped at the end of the balcony, and I leaned my elbows on the banister. My heart hammered in anticipation of what she had to tell me.

"So, you made progress on the prophecy," I stated flatly.

"Yes," Ava said, sounding a hell of a lot more enthusiastic about it than I was. "Do you remember that door we found in the woods during the Darke Games?"

I nodded. It'd been strange, and obviously magical, though we hadn't had a chance to really explore or understand it, as there was a monster chasing us at the time. "I remember."

"Well, I don't believe in coincidences," Ava said. "Those runes we found on the door keep popping up— first on those ships we found in the alcove in Kinpago, then on that bow in the cave, and then on the door in the woods."

I didn't know as much about the supernatural world as Ava, but the way she spoke of these runes made it sound undeniable. They were too ancient and rare for it to be coincidence.

"What do you think it means?" I asked.

"They're elven runes," Ava replied. "And I think the door is crucial to the prophecy."

I tilted my head. "How so?"

Pages began to slide over one another, and I realized Ava was flipping through a book. It must've been that journal she kept that detailed the wording of her prophecy. She began reciting a line. "*A discovery of the ancient ones on the island of shadow will change the course of our universe.* I already know the *island of shadow* is Darke Island. It's why I came here in the first place. The *ancient ones* obviously refers to the Elves. They're the oldest known supernatural race, and they died out a century ago. So this *discovery...* it *has* to be the door, or something similar."

"What do you think is behind the door?"

"I don't know," she admitted, flipping through pages again. "Maybe a weapon that will win us the war. I went back to those ships while I was on break. I can't translate the runes yet, but I wrote them down, along with any of the symbols I remembered from the door."

My mouth went dry. If Ava managed to translate those runes and got answers about that door, it would push her further toward fulfilling the prophecy— push her toward me making that decision between her and the world.

The sound of pages flipping stopped instantly. "Are you okay?" she asked. "You look a little sick."

I cleared my throat and reached for her hand. "Are you *sure* you want to pursue this, pidge?"

She drew away from me. "I *have* to, Charlie. The fate of the world is at stake."

So is your life, I wanted to say, but I couldn't.

"I know this is going to be hard, but I'm prepared to face that," Ava said. "And I was hoping you were willing to face it with me, after everything we went through in the Darke Games. I *need* your help, Charlie. I can't do this without you."

Hell. How could I deny her when she begged me like that?

"What exactly do you need my help with?" I asked warily. I was already being asked to choose the world over her, and I wasn't sure it was a decision I could make.

"I need you to find out everything you can about the history of the Elves on Darke Island. If the door *does* have something to do with this, we need to learn what it is, and how to open it. I bet they left something behind before they went extinct— clues of some sort. We need to find out what else they left here besides that door, because it's going to give us answers."

A lump rose to my throat. "What about you? What's your plan?"

"I need to work on decoding these runes and learning what the rest of the prophecy means," Ava said. "There's still so much of this prophecy I don't understand. You'll help me, won't you?"

I hesitated, and I knew she sensed it. "I just... I don't want you to get hurt."

She'd never know how deeply I meant that.

Ava sighed. "I wish I could promise you I wouldn't, but I can't. I know the possibility is there, but either way, I have to do this. I really don't want to have to do it alone, though, Charlie."

Her voice was soft, almost broken, and it tore my heart to shreds. I opened my mouth, but couldn't answer.

Ava blew a breath. "Well, if you're not going to help me, I'll figure it out on my own."

Ava turned toward the door, but I grabbed her arm. I couldn't stand to let her hurt for even one second. I spun her around and caught her in my arms. I didn't say anything, because I didn't trust my words to do it justice.

I wrapped Ava in my arms and pressed my lips to hers. She stilled a moment, before relaxing into it. Passion surged between us, and I lifted my hand to cradle the back of her neck. Ava wrapped her arms under mine and clung to my shoulders, dragging me closer until our bodies were pressed against each other. Her fingers dug into my skin as her tongue moved in and out of my mouth. A euphoric high took over my entire body, and my dick hardened in my trousers. I couldn't help but press my hips into hers, to show her just how much I was head over heels for her.

The kiss ended far too soon, though we were both gasping as we drew away. I rested my forehead on hers to catch my breath.

"I will *never* let you go through anything alone," I promised.

But the promise didn't feel like the saving grace it should've been. It didn't warm my heart or inspire me. Instead, it felt like a rock had been dropped onto my stomach. I realized how horrible a promise it was the second I made it. If I helped her with this, I pushed her closer to the end of the prophecy, where I— the twin of her soul— would be the one to hurt her most.

"Thank you," Ava whispered as she drew away. "That means a lot to me. With your help, I think we really have a chance of solving this."

"Hey, pidge..." I dared to ask. "What are we to each other?"

Ava froze. "What do you mean?"

"Well... I've never really dated anyone before. Kinda just messed around." I shrugged. "I was thinking—"

"I get it," she responded, almost too quickly. "But... Charlie, I'm not ready for that right now. I don't know if I ever will be."

My voice sounded crushed. "So you don't want to be my girlfriend."

"It's not like that," she rushed to say. "I just need to focus on the prophecy first. You understand, don't you?"

I understood she was afraid. And I knew she was pushing me away because she was worried I'd get too close.

She didn't want to get her heart broken. I didn't, either.

"Pidge, I'm gonna be here no matter what. If you just want to be friends, fine," I said.

"I want to be *more* than friends," she insisted. "But I don't know if I can put labels on... *us*, you know? Whatever we are."

Hell if I knew. I had a policy of not fucking my friends, but Ava wasn't exactly just a friend. She was so much more.

"Can we just see where this leads?" she offered. "I don't want to force anything. Why can't we have fun with no strings attached?"

I knew that wasn't going to work. There were *always* strings attached. More so with Ava and I, because we were bonded. Whatever we did would just bring us closer.

But I wasn't going to push her. She had trauma in her past. I had to wait for her to be ready.

"If that's what you want, I'm fine with it," I said. "We can mess around without any promises."

That was a lie. I was imploding on the inside. But this is what Ava wanted, and my heart craved to satisfy hers.

"I'm sorry," she whispered. "I just haven't dated since John... well, you know. I couldn't trust him, but I trust *you*. I don't want to do anything to screw up what we have."

"I don't want to, either," I said. "I'll always be here for you. No matter what happens, we'll get through this together."

Ava placed her hand on the side of my face, then stood on her toes to kiss me. I melted into the kiss, nearly forgetting everything we'd come out here to talk about. Adrenaline coursed through my blood, and I felt the passion rise within Ava through our bond. I couldn't help it when my hands tangled in her hair, begging for more.

Ava inhaled a deep breath, then shoved me backward, until my back was pressed against the side of the building. I drank her in like nectar from the gods, clinging to her as if she were my very life force— and she was. My tongue slid into her mouth, rolling over her tongue ring. She pressed her breasts against me like she wanted me *so* fucking badly.

I bet I wanted her more. It was pretty obvious.

My hands moved over her, though I was careful to avoid any areas that might make her uncomfortable. Apparently, she didn't have the same reservations, because she grabbed my hands and placed them on her ass.

Dear ancestors.

I moaned as I squeezed her ass, and my head spun as if the balcony had dropped out from beneath our feet. When she kissed me like this, I didn't give a damn about the labels. Ava-Marie owned half of my soul, and though it wasn't a choice I had made, it was one I would choose a thousand times. Nothing would ever change that.

That was something I could always rely on.

I just wished she didn't rely on me. Deep down, I knew I was lying to her. I couldn't help her with this prophecy the way she wanted. If I did, it pushed her closer to the prophecy Maddie spoke of to me. Every answer got her closer to her fate.

I realized then that the only way to save her was to stall her. The world was in danger, but damn the world, because I had to keep my pidge safe. I'd prolong this as long as I possibly could— and sabotage her if need be.

Because there was no way in hell I was letting this prophecy come true.

Continue The Criminal Lair to unlock the mysteries of the prophecy!

BONUS OFFERS

Find coloring pages, games, quizzes, and bonus content at
hiddenlegendsbooks.com

Join *Orenda Academy of Magical Creatures* on Facebook for all things
Hidden Legends!

Check out the *Prison for Supernatural Offenders Official Playlist* on
Spotify!

Never miss a new release! Join our newsletter at
hiddenlegendsbooks.com/fanclub/

ABOUT THE AUTHORS

Megan Linski (left) and Alicia Rades (right) are best friends and the authors of the Hidden Legends universe. Both are USA Today best-selling authors of young adult and new adult fiction. Megan Linski is a coffee connoisseur who enjoys ice skating, horseback riding, and shopping. Her stories feature themes of community and friendship while advocating for the rights of the disabled. Alicia Rades is a mother who loves baking cookies, reading tarot, and binge-watching Netflix. She has a passion for personal development and strives to incorporate emotional-empowerment themes into her books. Both girls love nature, animals, sexy romances, and eating cheese.

www.ingramcontent.com/pod-product-compliance
Lightning Source LLC
Chambersburg PA
CBHW060938190726
48286CB00005B/1322